An Introduction to Language

11e

VICTORIA FROMKIN
Late, University of California, Los Angeles

ROBERT RODMAN
North Carolina State University, Raleigh

NINA HYAMS
University of California, Los Angeles

D0218058

CENGAGE

Australia • Brazil • Mexico • Singapore • United Kingdom • United States

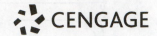

An Introduction to Language, Eleventh Edition
Victoria Fromkin, Robert Rodman, Nina Hyams

Product Team Manager: Laura Ross

Product Manager: Vanessa Coloura

Project Manager: Julia Giannotti

Content Developer: Melissa Sacco, Lumina Datamatics, Inc.

Product Assistant: Shelby Nathanson

Marketing Manager: Heather Thompson

Content Project Manager: Samantha Rundle

Manufacturing Planner: Marcia Locke

IP Analyst: Ann Hoffman

IP Project Manager: Betsy Hathaway

Production Service/Compositor: SPi Global

Art Director: Marissa Falco

Cover Designer: NYMDesign

Cover Image: Courtesy of Janet Echelman

For product information and technology assistance, contact us at **Cengage Customer & Sales Support, 1-800-354-9706.**

For permission to use material from this text or product, submit all requests online at **www.cengage.com/permissions.** Further permissions questions can be e-mailed to **permissionrequest@cengage.com.**

Library of Congress Control Number: 2017948368

ISBN-13: 978-1-337-55957-7
Loose-leaf Edition:
ISBN: 978-1-33755958-4

Cengage
20 Channel Center Street
Boston, MA 02210
USA

Cengage is a leading provider of customized learning solutions with employees residing in nearly 40 different countries and sales in more than 125 countries around the world. Find your local representative at: **www.cengage.com.**

Cengage products are represented in Canada by Nelson Education, Ltd.

To learn more about Cengage platforms and services, register or access your online learning solution, or purchase materials for your course, visit **www.cengage.com.**

Printed at CLDPC, USA, 08-18

Classification of American English Vowels

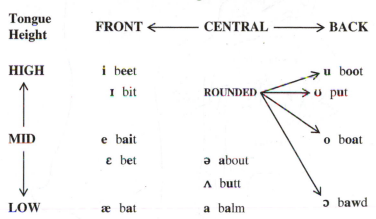

Part of the Tongue Involved

Tongue Height	FRONT ⟵ CENTRAL ⟶ BACK		
HIGH	i beet		u boot
	ɪ bit	ROUNDED	ʊ put
MID	e bait		o boat
	ɛ bet	ə about	
		ʌ butt	
LOW	æ bat	a balm	ɔ bawd

A Phonetic Alphabet for English Pronunciation

	Consonants						Vowels			
p	pill	t	till	k	kill	i	beet	ɪ	bit
b	bill	d	dill	g	gill	e	bait	ɛ	bet
m	mill	n	nil	ŋ	ring	u	boot	ʊ	foot
f	feel	s	seal	h	heal	o	boat	ɔ	bore
v	veal	z	zeal	l	leaf	æ	bat	a	pot/bar
θ	thigh	tʃ	chill	r	reef	ʌ	butt	ə	sofa
ð	thy	ʤ	gin	j	you	aɪ	bite	aʊ	bout
ʃ	shill	ʍ	which	w	witch	ɔɪ	boy		
ʒ	measure								

The Vocal Tract. Places of articulation: 1. bilabial; 2. labiodental; 3. interdental; 4. alveolar; 5. (alveo)palatal; 6. velar; 7. uvular; 8. glottal.

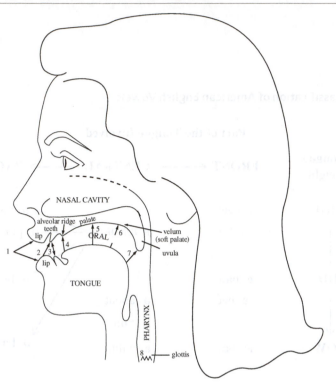

Some Phonetic Symbols for American English Consonants

	Bilabial	Labiodental	Interdental	Alveolar	Palatal	Velar	Glottal
Stop (oral)							
voiceless	p			t		k	ʔ
voiced	b			d		g	
Nasal (voiced)	m			n		ŋ	
Fricative							
voiceless		f	θ	s	ʃ		h
voiced		v	ð	z	ʒ		
Affricate							
voiceless					tʃ		
voiced					dʒ		
Glide							
voiceless	ʍ					ʍ	
voiced	w				j	w	
Liquid (voiced)							
(central)				r			
(lateral)				l			

In memory of Robert David Rodman and Joseph Hyams

Contents

CHAPTER 10

Language Processing and the Human Brain   430

Preface

> Well, this bit which I am writing, called Introduction, is really the er-h'r'm of the book, and I have put it in, partly so as not to take you by surprise, and partly because I can't do without it now. There are some very clever writers who say that it is quite easy not to have an er-h'r'm, but I don't agree with them. I think it is much easier not to have all the rest of the book.
>
> **A. A. MILNE,** *Now We Are Six,* 1927

> The last thing we find in making a book is to know what we must put first.
>
> **BLAISE PASCAL** (1623–1662)

Robert Rodman passed away on January 15, 2017, shortly after the completion of the eleventh edition of *An Introduction to Language*. His breadth of knowledge, charm, and wit touch every page of this new edition, and will be sorely missed in future editions. Robert and Vicki Fromkin published the first edition of *An Introduction to Language* in 1974. Their goal was to share with students their love of language and linguistics by presenting complex material in a light-hearted and personal way that included witty quotations (A. A. Milne was one of Vicki's favorites) and cartoons (Robert kept a huge file of them, which he regularly updated). This edition continues in the style and spirit of my friends, colleagues, and co-authors, Robert Rodman and Victoria Fromkin.

The first ten editions of *An Introduction to Language* succeeded, with the help of dedicated teachers, in introducing the nature of human language to hundreds of thousands of students. This is a book that students enjoy and understand and that professors find effective and thorough. Not only have majors in linguistics benefited from the book's easy-to-read yet comprehensive presentation, but also majors in fields as diverse as teaching English as a second language, foreign language studies, general education, the cognitive and neurosciences, psychology, sociology, and anthropology have enjoyed learning about language from this book.

Highlights of This Edition

This edition has been rewritten for improved clarity, conciseness, and currency. It includes **new developments in linguistics and related fields** that will strengthen its appeal to a wider audience. Much of this information will enable students to gain insight and understanding about linguistic issues and debates appearing in the national media and will help professors and students stay current with important linguistic research. We hope that it may also dispel certain common misconceptions that people have about language and language use.

The eleventh edition has been reduced to ten chapters from the original twelve of earlier editions. The chapters on Computer Processing of Human Language and Writing have been eliminated, with some of the material on the history of writing incorporated into Chapter 8 (Language Change). This more streamlined edition will enable teachers and students on a quarter system to more fully utilize the material, and for those on the semester system, it allows extra time for the more challenging chapters such as phonology and syntax.

Exercises (more than 200) continue to be abundant in this edition, and additional research-oriented exercises have been added for those instructors who wish their students to pursue certain topics more deeply. Some exercises continue to be marked as "challenge" questions: they go beyond the scope of what is ordinarily expected in a first course in language study. An **answer key** is available to instructors to assist them in areas outside of their expertise.

Chapter 1, "What Is Language?" continues as a concise introduction to the general study of language. It contains many "hooks" for engaging students, including "Language and Thought," which takes up the Sapir–Whorf hypothesis; the universal properties of languages including signed languages of the deaf; a consideration of animal "languages"; and the occasional silliness of self-appointed mavens of "good" grammar who beg us not to carelessly split infinitives and who find sentence-ending prepositions an abomination not to be put up with. New to this edition is a section on "Can computers learn human language."

Chapter 2, "Morphology: The Words of Language," launches the book into the study of grammar with morphology, the study of word formation, as that is the most familiar and intuitive aspect of grammar to most students. The subject is treated with clarity and an abundance of simple illustrations from non-English languages emphasize the universality of word structure, including the essentials of derivational versus inflectional morphology, free and bound morphemes, and the hierarchical structure of words. The section on compounds words has been expanded to include a detailed discussion of their internal structure.

Chapter 3, "Syntax: The Sentence Patterns of Language," is the most heavily revised chapter from the previous edition. The first half of the chapter introduces the universal and easily understood notions of constituency, syntactic categories (parts of speech), phrase structure trees and rules, structural ambiguity, and the infinite scope of language. Phrase structure trees are painstakingly built up, level by level, using traditional (pre-X-Bar) notation. The second half of the chapter delves into the internal structure of phrases, including the concepts of heads, complements, and selection. Current X-bar notation is introduced at this point, in a very restricted and clear way, to describe some of the deeper and more subtle syntactic structures of English and other languages. The chapter ends with a basic introduction to grammatical dependencies, including agreement rules and the transformational analysis of questions, carefully explained and illustrated. Formalisms are held to the bare minimum required to enhance clarity. Non-English examples abound in this chapter as in the rest of book, and the weighty elements of theory are lightened by the inclusion of insightful examples and explanations, supplemented as always by quotations, poetry, cartoons, and humor.

Chapter 4, "The Meaning of Language," on semantics, is finely structured so that the challenging topics of this complex subject can be digested in smaller pieces. The chapter first introduces students to truth-conditional semantics and the principle of compositionality. Following are discussions of what happens when compositionality fails, as with idioms, metaphors, and semantically anomalous sentences. Lexical semantics take up various approaches to word meaning, including the concepts of reference and sense, semantic features, argument structure, and thematic roles. The most heavily revised parts of this chapter are the sections on argument structure, thematic roles, and semantic features, the latter now containing a discussion of how these features affect the syntax. In the final section on pragmatics, we discuss and illustrate in depth the influence of situational versus linguistic context on the communicative content of utterances, the significance of implicature in comprehension, Grice's Maxims of Conversation, presuppositions, and J. L. Austin's speech acts.

Chapter 5, "Phonetics: The Sounds of Language," retains its former organization and continues to embrace IPA (International Phonetics Association) notation for English in keeping with current practices, with the sole exception of using /r/ in place of the technically correct /ɹ/ when illustrating English. We continue to mention alternative notations that students may encounter in other publications.

Chapter 6, "Phonology: The Sound Patterns of Language," continues to be presented with a greater emphasis on insights through linguistic data accompanied by small amounts of well-explicated formalisms, so that the student can appreciate the need for formal theories without experiencing the burdensome details. In this spirit, we have eliminated the section on Optimality Theory, which we now feel is beyond the scope of an introductory text. The chapter covers central concepts in segmental and prosodic phonology, and contains numerous exercises structured to guide students through the basics of phonological analysis.

Chapter 7, "Language in Society," retains its forward position in the book from earlier editions reflecting its growing importance as a major sub-field of linguistics. The chapter presents the established facts and principles of sociolinguistics while bringing up to date subjects such as banned languages (it's still happening); dead and dying languages (also still happening); gender differences; minority dialects such as Hispanic English ("Spanglish"), and African American English. Included in this edition a discussion of Black American Sign Language (BASL), a dialect of American Sign Language (ASL). In addition, included are sections on contact languages such as pidgins, creoles, and lingua francas that may be found in linguistically heterogeneous areas; the use of computers in sociolinguistic analysis; second language teaching; and bilingual education, among others.

Chapter 8, "Language Change: The Syllables of Time," has been updated with the latest research on language families, language relatedness, and language typology. In addition, in response to reviewers' requests, a detailed and more complex illustration of the application of the comparative method to two contemporary dialects to reconstruct their ancestor—often called "internal reconstruction"—is now part of this chapter. The thematically related section on the history of writing is also included, moved from its previous location in a separate chapter.

Chapter 9, "Language Acquisition," has been heavily revised for clarity and conciseness. It covers the basic stages and data from childhood language development including sections on bilingual language acquisition and child second language acquisition, all couched in the more general theoretical question of how children accomplish the complex task of learning a language. In addition, much of what has been learned about adult second language acquisition included in this chapter along with a section on "heritage languages," the learning of an intrafamily language after immigration to a country where that language is not spoken (e.g., Yiddish by Jews who emigrated from Russia).

Chapter 10, "Language Processing and the Human Brain," could well have been entitled "psycholinguistics and neurolinguistics" but that may have made the subject seem overly daunting. This chapter combines a straightforward discussion of many of the issues that regard the psychology of language—what the mind does—with the neurology of language—what the brain does—during language usage. Dramatic changes in the understanding of the brain's role in language processing are occurring virtually every day owing to the rapid enhancement of the ability of neurolinguists to measure brain activity to tiny degrees of sensitivity at extremely precise locations. This chapter reports on those techniques and some of the results regarding language and the brain that ensue.

As in the tenth edition, language and brain is discussed at the end of the book so that we may report on recent advances in neurolinguistic research of interest to beginning linguistics students, but which require an understanding of the different components of grammar, discussed in earlier chapters.

Terms that appear bold in the text are defined in the revised **glossary** at the end of the book. The glossary has been expanded and improved so that the Eleventh edition provides students with a linguistic lexicon of nearly 700 terms, making the book a worthy reference volume.

The **order of presentation of Chapters 2 through 6** was once thought to be nontraditional. Our experience, backed by previous editions of the book and the recommendations of colleagues throughout the world, has convinced us that it is easier for the novice to approach the structural aspects of language by first looking at morphology (the structure of the most familiar linguistic unit, the word). This is followed by syntax (the structure of sentences), which is also familiar to many students, as are numerous semantic concepts. We then proceed to the more novel (to students) phonetics and phonology, which students often find daunting. However, the book is written so that individual instructors can present material in the traditional order of phonetics, phonology, morphology, syntax, and semantics (Chapters 5, 6, 2, 3, and 4) without confusion, if they wish.

As in previous editions, the primary concern has been basic ideas rather than detailed expositions. This book assumes no previous knowledge on the part of the reader. An updated list of references at the end of each chapter is included to accommodate any reader who wishes to pursue a subject in more depth. Each chapter concludes with a summary and exercises to enhance the students' interest in and comprehension of the textual material.

Additional Resources

MindTap: Empower Your Students

MindTap is a platform that propels students from memorization to mastery. It gives you complete control of your course, so you can provide engaging content, challenge every learner, and build student confidence. Customize interactive syllabi to emphasize priority topics, then add your own material or notes to the eBook as desired. This outcomes-driven application gives you the tools needed to empower students and boost both understanding and performance.

Access Everything You Need in One Place

Cut down on prep with the preloaded and organized MindTap course materials. Teach more efficiently with interactive multimedia, assignments, quizzes, and more. Give your students the power to read, listen, and study on their phones, so they can learn on their terms.

Empower Students to Reach Their Potential

Twelve distinct metrics give you actionable insights into student engagement. Identify topics troubling your entire class and instantly communicate with those struggling. Students can track their scores to stay motivated toward their goals. Together, you can be unstoppable.

Control Your Course—and Your Content

Get the flexibility to reorder textbook chapters, add your own notes, and embed a variety of content including Open Educational Resources (OER). Personalize course content to your students' needs. They can even read your notes, add their own, and highlight key text to aid their learning.

Get a Dedicated Team, Whenever You Need Them

MindTap isn't just a tool, it's backed by a personalized team eager to support you. We can help set up your course and tailor it to your specific objectives, so you'll be ready to make an impact from day one. Know we'll be standing by to help you and your students until the final day of the term.

Answer Key

The Answer Key for *An Introduction to Language* contains answers to all of the exercises in the core text, and is available to instructors through the publisher.

Instructor Companion Web Site

This password-protected companion site contains useful resources for instructors—including chapter-level PowerPoint lecture slides, and a downloadable version of the Answer Key. Go to www.cengagebrain.com to access the site.

Acknowledgments

We would like to express our deep appreciation to UCLA Professors Susan Curtiss and Jesse Harris for helping us maintain the currency of Chapter 10, *Language Processing and the Human Brain*, two areas of rapid progress.

Brook Danielle Lillehaugen undertook the daunting task of writing the Answer Key to the ninth, tenth, and eleventh editions. Her thoroughness, accuracy, and insightfulness in construing solutions to problems and discussions of issues are appreciated by all who avail themselves of this useful document, including us, the authors.

We also express deep appreciation for the incisive comments of the reviewers of the tenth edition, whose frank assessment of the work, both critical and laudatory, heavily influenced this new edition:

Ellyn Arwood, University of Portland; Craig Barrette, Brescia University; Althea Bradford, Winston-Salem State University; Ulrike Christofori, San Joaquin Delta College; Liliana Cobas, Carlos Albizu University; Anthony DeFazio, New York University; Michael Duffett, San Joaquin Delta College; Laurie Durzo, Penn State University; Carmen Fought, Pitzer College; Brent Green, Salt Lake Community College; Alicia Holland, Capella University; Susan Inouye, Kapiolani Community College; John Jeep, Miami University; McLoddy Kadyamusuma, State University of New York at Fredonia; Patti Kurtz, Minot State University; Nancy Lee-Jones, Endicott College; Sally LeVan, Gannon University; Keming Liu, The City University of New York; Deanna Nisbet, Regent University; Silvia Peart, United States Naval Academy; Edward Rielly, Saint Joseph's College; Kelly Schroeder, Fresno Pacific University; Jefferey Taylor, Metropolitan State University of Denver; and Elizabeth Winkler, Western Kentucky University.

We continue to be deeply grateful to the individuals who have sent us suggestions, corrections, criticisms, cartoons, language data, and exercises over the course of many editions. Their influence is still strongly felt in this eleventh edition. The list is long and reflects the global, communal collaboration that a book about language—the most global of topics—merits. To each of you, our heartfelt thanks and appreciation. Know that in this eleventh edition lives your contribution:[1]

Natasha Abner, Montclair State University; Byron Ahn, Princeton University; Adam Albright, Massachusetts Institute of Technology; Otto Santa Ana, University of California, Los Angeles; Rebecca Barghorn, University of Oldenburg; Seyed Reza Basiroo, Islamic Azad University; Karol Boguszewski, Poland; Melanie Borchers, Universität Duisburg-Essen; Donna Brinton, Emeritus, University of California, Los Angeles; Daniel Bruhn, University of California, Berkeley; Lynn A. Burley, University of Central Arkansas; Ivano Caponigro, University of California, San Diego; Ralph S. Carlson, Azusa Pacific University; Robert Channon, Purdue University; Judy Cheatham, Greensboro College; Leonie Cornips, Meertens Institute; Antonio Damásio, University of Southern California; Hanna Damásio, University of Southern California; Julie Damron, Brigham Young University; Rosalia Dutra, University of North Texas; Christina Esposito, Macalester

[1]Some affiliations may have changed or are unknown to us at this time.

College; Fred Field, California State University, Northridge; Susan Fiksdal, Evergreen State College; Beverly Olson Flanigan and her teaching assistants, Ohio University; Jackson Gandour, Purdue University, West Lafayette; Jule Gomez de Garcia, California State University, San Marcos; Deborah Grant, Independent consultant; Loretta Gray, Central Washington University; Xiangdong Gu, Chongqing University; Helena Halmari, University of London; Karin Hedberg, Sam Houston State University; Sharon Hargus, University of Washington; Benjamin H. Hary, Emory University; Tometro Hopkins, Florida International University; Eric Hyman, University of North Carolina, Fayetteville; Dawn Ellen Jacobs, California Baptist University; Seyed Yasser Jebraily, University of Tehran; Kyle Johnson, University of Massachusetts, Amherst; Paul Justice, San Diego State University; Simin Karimi, University of Arizona; Edward Keenan, University of California, Los Angeles; Robert D. King, University of Texas; Sharon M. Klein, California State University, Northridge; Nathan Klinedinst, Institut Jean Nicod/CNRS, Paris; Otto Krauss Jr., late, unaffiliated; Elisabeth Kuhn, Virginia Commonwealth University; Peter Ladefoged, late, University of California, Los Angeles; Mary Ann Larsen-Pusey, Fresno Pacific University; Rabbi Robert Layman, Philadelphia; Byungmin Lee, Korea; Virginia "Ginny" Lewis, Northern State University; David Lightfoot, Georgetown University; Ingvar Lofstedt, University of California, Los Angeles; Giuseppe Longobardi, Università di Venezia; Harriet Luria, Hunter College, City University of New York; Jeff MacSwan, Arizona State University; Tracey McHenry, Eastern Washington University; Craig Melchert, University of California, Los Angeles; Pamela Munro, University of California, Los Angeles; Tom Nash, Southern Oregon University; Carol Neidle, Boston University; Don Nilsen, Arizona State University; Reiko Okabe, Nihon University, Tokyo; John Olsson, Forensic Linguistic Institute, Wales, UK; Robyn Orfitelli, Sheffield University; Anjali Pandey, Salisbury University; Barbara Hall Partee, University of Massachusetts, Amherst; Maria "Masha" Polinsky, University of Maryland; Fernanda Pratas, Universidade Nova de Lisboa; Vincent D. Puma, Flagler College; Mousa Qasem, Kuwait University; Ian Roberts, Cambridge University; Tugba Rona, Istanbul International Community School; Natalie Schilling-Estes, Georgetown University; Philippe Schlenker, Institut Jean-Nicod, Paris and New York University; Carson Schütze, University of California, Los Angeles; Bruce Sherwood, North Carolina State University; Koh Shimizu, Beijing; Dwan L. Shipley, Washington University; Muffy Siegel, Temple University; Andrew Simpson, University of Southern California; Neil Smith, University College London; Nancy Stenson, University of Minnesota, Twin Cities; Donca Steriade, Massachusetts Institute of Technology; Mel Storm, Emporia State University; Nawaf Sulami, University of Northern Iowa; Megha Sundara, University of California, Los Angeles; Erik Thomas, North Carolina State University; Robert (Bob) Trammell, Florida Atlantic University, Boca Raton; Dalys Vargas, College of Notre Dame; Willis Warren, Saint Edwards University; Donald K. Watkins, University of Kansas; Walt Wolfram, North Carolina State University; Maria Luisa Zubizarreta, University of Southern California; and Kie Zuraw, University of California, Los Angeles.

Please forgive us if we have inadvertently omitted any names, and if we have spelled every name correctly, then we shall believe in miracles.

Finally, we wish to thank our editorial and production teams. They have been superb and supportive in every way: Vanessa Coloura, product manager; Julia Giannotti, project manager; Melissa Sacco, content development project manager, Michael Lepera, content project manager. Our thanks also to Eleanor Glewwe, University of California, Los Angeles, for her editorial assistance and to Nicoletta Loccioni, for her meticulous work on the tree diagrams in Chapter 3.

Last but certainly not least, we acknowledge our debt to those we love and who love us and who inspire our work when nothing else will: Nina's son, Michael; Robert's children Zack and Emily together with a quartet of grandchildren: Cedar, Luke, Juniper, and Henry; our parents and siblings; and our dearly beloved and still deeply missed colleagues, Vicki Fromkin and Peter Ladefoged.

The responsibility for errors in fact or judgment is, of course, ours alone. We continue to be indebted to the instructors who have used the earlier editions and to their students, without whom there would be no eleventh edition.

Robert Rodman
Nina Hyams

About the Authors

VICTORIA FROMKIN received her bachelor's degree in economics from the University of California, Berkeley, in 1944 and her M.A. and Ph.D. in linguistics from the University of California, Los Angeles, in 1963 and 1965, respectively. She was a member of the faculty of the UCLA Department of Linguistics from 1966 until her death in 2000, and served as its chair from 1972 to 1976. From 1979 to 1989 she served as the UCLA Graduate Dean and Vice Chancellor of Graduate Programs. She was a visiting professor at the Universities of Stockholm, Cambridge, and Oxford. Vicki served as president of the Linguistics Society of America in 1985, president of the Association of Graduate Schools in 1988, and chair of the Board of Governors of the Academy of Aphasia. She received the UCLA Distinguished Teaching Award and the Professional Achievement Award, and served as the U.S. Delegate and a member of the Executive Committee of the International Permanent Committee of Linguistics (CIPL). She was an elected Fellow of the American Academy of Arts and Sciences, the American Association for the Advancement of Science, the New York Academy of Science, the American Psychological Society, and the Acoustical Society of America, and in 1996 was elected to membership in the National Academy of Sciences. She published more than one hundred books, monographs, and papers on topics concerned with phonetics, phonology, tone languages, African languages, speech errors, processing models, aphasia, and the brain/mind/language interface—all research areas in which she worked. Vicki Fromkin passed away on January 19, 2000, at the age of 76.

ROBERT RODMAN received his bachelor's degree in mathematics from the University of California, Los Angeles, in 1961, a master's degree in mathematics in 1965, a master's degree in linguistics in 1971, and his Ph.D. in linguistics in 1973. He was on the faculties of the University of California at Santa Cruz, the University of North Carolina at Chapel Hill, Kyoto Industrial College in Japan, and North Carolina State University. His research areas included forensic linguistics and computer speech processing. In 2009, he was elected into the American Academy of Social Sciences as an Associate Fellow for his achievements in computational forensic linguistics. Robert Rodman passed away on January 15, 2017, at the age of 76.

NINA HYAMS received her bachelor's degree in journalism from Boston University in 1973 and her M.A. and Ph.D. degrees in linguistics from the Graduate Center of the City University of New York in 1981 and 1983, respectively. She joined the faculty of the University of California, Los Angeles, in 1983, where she is currently a professor of linguistics. Her main areas of research are childhood language development and syntax. She is author of the book *Language Acquisition and the Theory of Parameters* (D. Reidel Publishers, 1986), a milestone in language acquisition research. She has also published numerous articles on the development of syntax, morphology, and semantics in children. She has been a visiting scholar at the University of Utrecht and the University of Leiden in the Netherlands and has given lectures throughout Europe and Japan. Nina lives in Los Angeles with her pal Spot, a rescued border collie mutt, and his olde English bulldogge companion, the ever soulful Nellie.

1

What Is Language?

When we study human language, we are approaching what some might call the "human essence," the distinctive qualities of mind that are, so far as we know, unique to man.

NOAM CHOMSKY, *Language and Mind*, 1968

Whatever else people do when they come together—whether they play, fight, make love, or make automobiles—they talk. We live in a world of language. We talk to friends, associates, wives and husbands, lovers, teachers, parents, rivals, and even enemies. We talk face-to-face and over all manner of electronic media, and everyone responds with more talk. Hardly a moment of our waking lives is free from words, and even our dreams are filled with talk. We also talk when there is no one to answer. Some of us talk aloud in our sleep. We talk to our pets and sometimes to ourselves.

The capacity for language, perhaps more than any other attribute, distinguishes humans from other animals. According to the philosophy expressed in many myths and religions, language is the source of human life and power. To some people of Africa, a newborn child is a *kintu*, a "thing," not yet a *muntu*, a "person." It is only by the act of learning language that the child becomes a human being. To understand our humanity, we must understand the nature of language that makes us human. That is the goal of this book. We begin with a simple question: What does it mean to "know" a language?

Linguistic Knowledge

Do we know only what we see, or do we see what we somehow already know?

CYNTHIA OZICK, "What Helen Keller Saw," *New Yorker*, June 16 & 23, 2003

When you know a language, you can speak and be understood by others who also know that language. This means you are able to produce strings of sounds that signify certain meanings and to understand or interpret the sounds produced by others. But language is much more than speech. Deaf people produce and understand sign languages just as hearing persons produce and understand spoken languages. The languages of the deaf communities throughout the world are equivalent to spoken languages, differing only in their modality of expression.

Most everyone knows at least one language. Five-year-old children are nearly as proficient at speaking and understanding as their parents. Yet, the ability to carry out the simplest conversation requires profound knowledge that most speakers are unaware of. This is true for speakers of all languages, from Albanian to Zulu. A speaker of English can produce a sentence having two relative clauses without knowing what a relative clause is. For example:

My goddaughter who was born in Sweden and who now lives in Iowa is named Disa, after a Viking queen.

In a parallel fashion, a child can walk without understanding or being able to explain the principles of balance and support or the neurophysiological control mechanisms that permit one to do so. The fact that we may know something unconsciously is not unique to language.

Knowledge of the Sound System

When I speak it is in order to be heard.

ROMAN JAKOBSON

Part of knowing a language means knowing what sounds (or signs[1]) are in that language and what sounds are not. One way this unconscious knowledge is revealed is by the way speakers of one language pronounce words from another language. If you speak only English, for example, you may substitute an English sound for a non-English sound when pronouncing "foreign" words such as French *ménage à trois*. If you pronounce it as the French do, you are using sounds outside the English sound system.

French people speaking English often pronounce words such as *this* and *that* as if they were spelled *zis* and *zat*. The English sound represented by the initial letters *th* in these words is not part of the French sound system, and the mispronunciation reveals the French speaker's unconscious knowledge of this fact.

---

[1]The sign languages of the deaf will be discussed throughout the book. A reference to "language," then, unless speech sounds or spoken languages are specifically mentioned, includes both spoken and signed languages.

Knowing the sound system of a language includes more than knowing the inventory of sounds. It means also knowing which sounds may start a word, end a word, and follow each other. The name of a former president of Ghana was *Nkrumah*, pronounced with an initial sound like the sound ending the English word *sink*. While this is an English sound, no word in English begins with the *nk* sound. Speakers of English who have occasion to pronounce this name often mispronounce it (by Ghanaian standards) by inserting a short vowel sound, like *Nekrumah* or *Enkrumah*, making the word correspond to the English system. Children develop the sound patterns of their language very rapidly. A one-year-old learning English already knows that *nk* cannot begin a word, just as a Ghanaian child of the same age knows that it can in his language. We will learn more about sounds and sound systems in Chapters 5 and 6.

Knowledge of Words

Sounds and sound patterns of our language constitute only one part of our linguistic knowledge. Beyond that we know that certain sequences of sounds signify certain concepts or **meanings**. Speakers of English understand what *boy* means, and that it means something different from *toy* or *girl* or *pterodactyl*. We also know that *toy* and *boy* are words, but *moy* is not. When you know a language, you know words in that language; that is, you know which sequences of sounds have specific meanings and which do not.

Arbitrary Relation of Form and Meaning

What's in a name? That which we call a rose

By any other name would smell as sweet;

WILLIAM SHAKESPEARE, *Romeo and Juliet*, Act II, Scene II

If you do not know a language, the words (and sentences) of that language will be mainly incomprehensible, because the relationship between speech sounds and the meanings they represent is, for the most part, an **arbitrary** one. When you are acquiring a language, you have to learn that the sounds represented by the letters *house* signify the concept ; if you know French, this same meaning is represented by *maison*; if you know Russian, by *dom*; if you know Spanish, by *casa*. Similarly, is represented by *hand* in English, *main* in French, *nsa* in Twi, and *ruka* in Russian. The same sequence of sounds can represent different meanings in different languages. The word *bolna* means "speak" in Hindi–Urdu and "aching" in Russian; *bis* means "devil" in Ukrainian and "twice" in Latin; a *pet* is a domestic animal in English and a fart in Catalan; and the sequence of sounds *taka* means "hawk" in Japanese, "fist" in Quechua, "a small bird" in Zulu, and "money" in Bengali.

These examples show that the words of a particular language have the meanings they do only by convention. Despite a penchant that biologists have for Greek roots, a pterodactyl could have been called *ron, blick,* or *kerplunkity*.

HERMAN®/LaughingStock Licensing Inc., Ottawa, Canada

This **conventional** and arbitrary relationship between the **form** (sounds) and **meaning** (concept) of a word is also true in sign languages. If you see someone using a sign language you do not know, it is doubtful that you will understand the message from the signs alone. A person who knows Chinese Sign Language (CSL) would find it difficult to understand American Sign Language (ASL), and vice versa.

Many signs were originally like miming, where the relationship between form and meaning is not arbitrary. Bringing the hand to the mouth to mean "eating," as in miming, would be nonarbitrary as a sign. Over time these signs may change, just as the pronunciation of words changes, and the miming effect is lost. These signs become conventional, so that the shape or movement of the hands alone does not reveal the meaning of the signs.

There is some **sound symbolism** in language—that is, words whose pronunciation suggests their meanings. Most languages contain **onomatopoeic** words like *buzz* or *murmur* that imitate the sounds associated with the objects or actions they refer to. But even here, the sounds differ from language to language and reflect the particular sound system of the language. In English *cock-a-doodle-doo* is an onomatopoeic word whose meaning is the crow of a rooster, whereas in Finnish the rooster's crow is *kukkokiekuu*. Forget *gobble gobble* when you're in Istanbul; a turkey in Turkey goes *glu-glu*.

Sometimes particular sound combinations seem to relate to a particular concept. Many English words beginning with *gl* relate to sight, such as *glare, glint, gleam, glitter, glossy, glaze, glance, glimmer, glimpse,* and *glisten.* However, *gl* words and their like are a very small part of any language, and *gl* may have nothing to do with "sight" in another language, or even in other words in English, such as *gladiator, glucose, glory, glutton,* and *globe.*

To know a language, we must know words of that language. But no speaker knows all the entries in an unabridged dictionary—and even if someone did, he would still not know that language. Imagine trying to learn a foreign language from an online dictionary. However, many words you learned, you would not be able to form nor understand very many phrases. And even if you could manage to get your message across using a few words from a traveler's dictionary, such as "car—gas—where?" the best you could hope for is to be pointed in the direction of a gas station. If you were answered with a sentence, it is doubtful that you would understand what was said or be able to look it up, because you would not know where one word ended and another began. Chapter 3 will discuss how words are put together to form phrases and sentences, and Chapter 4 will explore word and sentence meanings.

The Creativity of Linguistic Knowledge

All humans are artists, all of us . . . Our greatest masterpiece of art is the use of a language to create an entire virtual reality within our mind.

DON MIGUEL RUIZ, 2012

ALBERT: So are you saying that you were the best friend of the woman who was married to the man who represented your husband in divorce?

ANDRÈ: In the history of speech, that sentence has never been uttered before.

NEIL SIMON, *The Dinner Party*, 2000

Knowledge of a language enables you to combine sounds to form words, words to form phrases, and phrases to form sentences. No matter how smart your smartphone is, it cannot contain all the sentences of a language because the number is infinite. Knowing a language means being able to produce and understand new sentences never spoken before. This is the **creative aspect** of language. Not every speaker can create great literature, but everybody who knows a language can create and understand novel sentences.

That language is creative and sentences potentially infinite in length and number is shown by the fact that any sentence can be made indefinitely longer. In English, you can say:

This is the house.

or

This is the house that Jack built.

or

This is the malt that lay in the house that Jack built.

or

This is the dog that worried the cat that killed the rat that ate the malt that lay in the house that Jack built.

The longer these sentences become the less likely we are to hear or say them. A sentence such as "The old, old, old, old, old, old man fell" with half-dozen occurrences of *old* would be highly unusual in either speech or writing, even to describe Methuselah. But such a sentence is theoretically possible. If you know English, you have the knowledge to add any number of adjectives to a noun, and any number of clauses to a sentence, as in "the house that Jack built."

All human languages permit their speakers to increase the length and complexity of sentences in these ways; creativity is a universal property of human language.

Our creative ability is reflected not only in what we say, but also in our understanding of new or novel sentences. Consider the following sentence: "Daniel Boone decided to become a pioneer because he dreamed of pigeon-toed giraffes and cross-eyed elephants dancing in pink skirts and green berets on the wind-swept plains of the Midwest." You may not believe the sentence; you may question its logic; but you can understand it, although you probably never heard or read it before now.

In pointing out the creative aspect of language, Noam Chomsky, who many regard as the father of modern linguistics, argued persuasively against the view that language is a set of learned responses to stimuli. It's true that if someone steps on your toes, you may automatically respond with a scream or a grunt, but these sounds are not part of language. They are involuntary reactions to stimuli. After we reflexively cry out, we can then go on to say: "Thank you very much for stepping on my toe, because I was afraid I had elephantiasis and now that I can feel the pain I know I don't," or any one of an infinite number of sentences, because the particular sentences we produce are not controlled by any stimulus.

Even some involuntary cries such as "ouch" change according to the language we speak. Step on an Italian's toes and he will cry "ahi." French speakers often fill their pauses with the vowel sound that starts their word for "egg"—*oeu(f)*—a sound that does not occur in English. Even conversational fillers such as *er, uh,* and *you know* in English are constrained by the language in which they occur.

The fact of human linguistic creativity was well expressed more than 400 years ago by Huarte de San Juan (1530–1592): "Normal human minds are such that . . . without the help of anybody, they will produce 1,000 (sentences) they never heard spoke of . . . inventing and saying such things as they never heard from their masters, nor any mouth."

Knowledge of Sentences and Nonsentences

A person who knows a language has mastered a system of rules that assigns sound and meaning in a definite way for an infinite class of possible sentences.

NOAM CHOMSKY, *Language and Mind*, 1968

Our knowledge of language not only allows us to produce and understand an infinite number of well-formed (even if silly and illogical) sentences. It also permits us to distinguish well-formed (grammatical) from ill-formed (ungrammatical) sentences. This is further evidence of our linguistic creativity because ungrammatical sentences are typically novel, not sentences we have previously heard or produced, precisely because they are ungrammatical!

Consider the following sentences:

a. John kissed the little old lady who owned the shaggy dog.
b. Who owned the shaggy dog John kissed the little old lady.
c. John is difficult to love.
d. It is difficult to love John.
e. John is anxious to go.
f. It is anxious to go John.
g. John, who was a student, flunked his exams.
h. Exams his flunked student a was who John.

If you were asked to put an asterisk or star before the examples that seemed ill formed or ungrammatical or "not good" to you, which ones would you mark? Our intuitive knowledge about what is or is not an allowable sentence in English convinces us to star *b, f,* and *h.* Which ones did you star?

Would you agree with the following judgments?

a. What he did was climb a tree.
b. *What he thought was want a sports car.[2]
c. Drink your beer and go home!
d. *What are drinking and go home?
e. I expect them to arrive a week from next Thursday.
f. *I expect a week from next Thursday to arrive them.
g. Linus lost his security blanket.
h. *Lost Linus security blanket his.

If you find the starred sentences unacceptable, as we do, you see your linguistic creativity at work.

These sentences also illustrate that not every string of words constitutes a well-formed sentence in a language. Sentences are not formed simply by placing one word after another in any order, but by organizing the words according to the rules of sentence formation of the language. These rules are finite in length and finite in number so that they can be stored in our finite brains. Yet, they permit us to form and understand an infinite set of new sentences. They also enable us to judge whether a sequence of words is a well-formed sentence of our language or not. These rules are not determined by a judge or a legislature, or even taught in a grammar class. They are unconscious rules that we acquire as young children as we develop language and they are responsible for our linguistic creativity. Linguists refer to this set of rules as the **grammar** of the language.

---

[2]The asterisk is used before examples that speakers find ungrammatical. This notation will be used throughout the book.

Returning to the question we posed at the beginning of this chapter—what does it mean to know a language? It means knowing the sounds and meanings of many, if not all, of the words of the language, and the rules for their combination—the grammar, which accounts for infinitely many possible sentences. We will have more to say about these rules of grammar in later chapters.

Linguistic Knowledge and Performance

"What's one and one and one and one and one and one and one and one and one and one?" "I don't know," said Alice. "I lost count." "She can't do Addition," the Red Queen interrupted.

LEWIS CARROLL, *Through the Looking-Glass*, 1871

Speakers of all languages have the knowledge to understand or produce sentences of any length. Here is an example from the ruling of a federal judge:

We invalidate the challenged lifetime ban because we hold as a matter of federal constitutional law that a state initiative measure cannot impose a severe limitation on the people's fundamental rights when the issue of whether to impose such a limitation on these rights is put to the voters in a measure that is ambiguous on its face and that fails to mention in its text, the proponent's ballot argument, or the state's official description, the severe limitation to be imposed.

Theoretically, there is no limit to the length of a sentence, but in practice very long sentences are unlikely, the verbose federal judge's ruling notwithstanding. Evidently, there is a difference between having the knowledge required to produce or understand sentences of a language and applying this knowledge. It is a difference between our knowledge of words and grammar, which is our **linguistic competence**, and how we use this knowledge in actual speech production and comprehension, which is our **linguistic performance**.

Our linguistic knowledge permits us to form longer and longer sentences by joining sentences and phrases together or adding modifiers to a noun. However, there are physiological and psychological reasons that limit the number of adjectives, adverbs, clauses, and so on that we actually produce and understand. Speakers may run out of breath, lose track of what they have said, or die of old age before they are finished. Listeners may become tired, bored, disgusted, or confused, like poor Alice when being interrogated by the Red Queen.

When we speak we usually wish to convey some message. At some stage in the act of producing speech, we must organize our thoughts into strings of words. Sometimes the message is garbled. We may stammer, or pause, or produce **slips of the tongue** such as saying *preach seduction* when *speech production* is meant (discussed in Chapter 10).

What Is Grammar?

We use the term "grammar" with a systematic ambiguity. On the one hand, the term refers to the explicit theory constructed by the linguist and proposed as a description of the speaker's competence. On the other hand, it refers to this competence itself.

NOAM CHOMSKY AND MORRIS HALLE, *The Sound Pattern of English*, 1968

Descriptive Grammars

There are no primitive languages. The great and abstract ideas of Christianity can be discussed even by the wretched Greenlanders.

JOHANN PETER SUESSMILCH, In a paper delivered before the Prussian Academy, 1756

The way we are using the word *grammar* differs from most common usages. In our sense, the grammar is the knowledge speakers have about the units and rules of their language—rules for combining sounds into words (called *phonology*), rules of word formation (called *morphology*), rules for combining words into phrases and phrases into sentences (called *syntax*), as well as rules for assigning meaning (called *semantics*). The grammar, together with a mental dictionary (called a *lexicon*) that lists the words of the language, represents our linguistic competence. To understand the nature of language, we must understand the nature of grammar.

Every human being who speaks a language knows its grammar. When linguists wish to describe a language, they make explicit the rules of the grammar that exist in the minds of the speakers of the language. There will be some differences among speakers, but there must be shared knowledge too. The shared knowledge—the common parts of the grammar—makes it possible to communicate through language. To the extent that the linguist's description is a true model of a speaker's linguistic capacity, it is a successful description of the grammar and of the language itself. Such a model is called a **descriptive grammar**. It does not tell you how you *should* speak; it tells you how you *do* speak. It explains how it is possible for you to speak and understand and make judgments about well-formedness, and it describes what you know about the sounds, words, phrases, and sentences of your language.

When we say that a sentence is **grammatical**, we mean that it conforms to the rules of the mental grammar (as described by the linguist); when we say that it is **ungrammatical**, we mean it deviates from the rules in some way. If, however, we posit a rule for English that does not agree with your intuitions as a speaker, then the grammar we are describing differs in some way from the mental grammar that represents your linguistic competence; that is, your language is not the one described. That's okay. No language or variety of a language (called a *dialect*) is superior or inferior to any other in a linguistic sense. Every grammar is equally complex, logical, and capable of producing an infinite set of sentences to express any thought. (We will have more to say about dialects in Chapter 7.)

Prescriptive Grammars

It is certainly the business of a grammarian to find out, and not to make, the laws of a language.

JOHN FELL, *Essay towards an English Grammar*, 1784

Just read the sentence aloud, Amanda, and listen to how it sounds. If the sentence sounds OK, go with it. If not, rearrange the pieces. Then throw out the rule books and go to bed.

JAMES KILPATRICK, "Writer's Art" (syndicated newspaper column), 1998

Any fool can make a rule

And every fool will mind it

HENRY DAVID THOREAU, journal entry, 1860

Not all grammarians, past or present, share the view that all grammars are equal. Language "purists" of all ages believe that some versions of a language are better than others, that there are certain "correct" forms that all educated people should use in speaking and writing, and that language change is corruption. The Greek Alexandrians in the first century, the Arabic scholars at Basra in the eighth century, and numerous English grammarians of the eighteenth and nineteenth centuries held this view. They wished to *prescribe* rather than *describe* the rules of grammar, which gave rise to the writing of **prescriptive grammars**.

In the Renaissance, a new middle class emerged who wanted their children to speak the dialect of the "upper" classes. This desire led to the publication of many prescriptive grammars. In 1762, Bishop Robert Lowth wrote *A Short Introduction to English Grammar with Critical Notes*. Lowth prescribed a number of new rules for English, many of them influenced by his personal taste. Before the publication of his grammar, practically everyone—upper-class, middle-class, and lower-class—said *I don't have none* and *You was wrong about that*. Lowth, however, decided that "two negatives make a positive" and therefore one should say *I don't have any*; and that even when *you* is singular it should be followed by the plural *were*. Many of these prescriptive rules were based on Latin grammar and made little sense for English. Because Lowth was influential and because the rising new class wanted to speak "properly," many of these new rules were legislated into English grammar, at least for the **prestige dialect**—that variety of the language spoken by people in positions of power.

The view that using double negatives in a sentence is a sign of inferiority cannot be justified unless you want to lose an argument with your French or Italian teacher. In both of those languages double negatives are "good grammar":

French:	Je	ne	veux	parler	avec	personne.
	I	not	want	speak	with	no-one.

Italian:	Non	voglio	parlare	con	nessuno.
	not	I-want	speak	with	no-one.

English translation: "I don't want to speak with anyone."

Prescriptive grammars such as Lowth's are different from the descriptive grammars that linguists develop. Their goal is not to describe the rules people know, but to tell them what rules they should follow. The great British Prime Minister Winston Churchill is credited with this response to the "rule" against ending a sentence with a preposition: "This is the sort of nonsense up with which I will not put."

rhymeswithorange.com Distributed by King Features Syndicate

Even today language purists write books and blogs attempting to "save the English language." For example, they criticize the use of *enormity* to mean "enormous" instead of "monstrously evil", its original meaning. But languages change in the course of time and words change meaning. Language change is a natural process, as we discuss in Chapter 8. Over time *enormity* has been used increasingly used to mean "enormous," and now that former U.S. President Barack Obama has used it that way (in his victory speech of November 4, 2008), and that British author J. K. Rowling uses it similarly in the immensely popular *Harry Potter and the Deathly Hallows*, that usage will gain acceptance.

Still, the "saviors" of the English language will never disappear. They will continue to blame TV, the Internet, and especially texting for corrupting the English language, and are likely to continue to dis (oops, we mean disparage) anyone who suggests that African American English (AAE)[3] and other dialects are viable, complete languages.

All human languages and dialects are fully expressive, complete, and logical, as much as they were two hundred or two thousand years ago. Hopefully (another frowned-upon usage), this book will convince you that all languages and dialects are rule-governed, whether spoken by rich or poor, powerful or weak, learned or illiterate. Grammars and usages of particular groups in society may be dominant for social and political reasons, but from a linguistic (scientific) perspective they are neither superior nor inferior to the grammars and usages of less prestigious members of society.

---

[3]AAE is also called African American Vernacular English (AAVE), Ebonics, and Black English (BE). It is spoken by some (but by no means all) African Americans. It is discussed in Chapter 7.

Having said all this, it is undeniable that the **standard** dialect (defined in Chapter 7) may indeed be a better dialect for someone wishing to obtain a particular job or achieve a position of social prestige. In a society where "linguistic profiling" is used to discriminate against speakers of a minority dialect, it may behoove those speakers to learn the prestige dialect rather than wait for social change. But linguistically, prestige and standard dialects do not have superior grammars.

Finally, all of the preceding remarks apply to *spoken* language. Writing is another story. Writing follows certain prescriptive rules of grammar, usage, and style that the spoken language does not. Moreover, and importantly, writing must be taught and is not acquired naturally through simple exposure to the spoken language (see Chapter 9).

Teaching Grammars

I don't want to talk grammar. I want to talk like a lady.

G. B. SHAW, *Pygmalion*, 1912

The descriptive grammar of a language attempts to describe the rules internalized by a speaker of that language. It is different from a **teaching grammar**, which is used to learn another language or dialect. Teaching grammars can be helpful to people who do not speak the standard or prestige dialect, but find it would be advantageous socially and economically to do so. They are used in schools in foreign language classes. This kind of grammar gives the words and their pronunciations, and explicitly states the rules of the language, especially where they differ from the language of instruction.

It is often difficult for adults to learn a second language without formal instruction even when they have lived for an extended period in a country where the language is spoken. (Second language acquisition is discussed in more detail in Chapter 9.) Teaching grammars assume that the student already knows one language and compares the grammar of the target language with the grammar of the native language. The meaning of a word is provided by a **gloss**— the parallel word in the student's native language, such as *maison*, "house" in French. It is assumed that the student knows the meaning of the gloss "house" and so also the meaning of the word *maison*.

Sounds of the target language that do not occur in the native language are often described by reference to known sounds. Thus, the student might be aided in producing the French sound *u* in the word *tu* by instructions such as "Round your lips while producing the vowel sound in *tea*."

The rules about how to put words together to form grammatical sentences may also make reference to the learner's knowledge of his native language. For example, the teaching grammar *Learn Zulu* by Sibusiso Nyembezi states that "The difference between singular and plural is not at the end of the word but at the beginning of it," and warns that "Zulu does not have the indefinite and definite articles 'a' and 'the.'" Such statements assume students know the rules of their own grammar, in this case English. Although such grammars might be considered prescriptive in the sense that they attempt to teach the student what is or is not a grammatical construction in the new language, their aim is different from grammars that attempt to change the rules or usage of a language that is already known by the speaker.

This book is not primarily concerned with either prescriptive or teaching grammars. However, these kinds of grammars are considered in Chapter 7 in the discussion of standard and nonstandard dialects.

Universal Grammar

In a grammar there are parts that pertain to all languages; these components form what is called the general grammar. In addition to these general (universal) parts, there are those that belong only to one particular language; and these constitute the particular grammars of each language.

CÉSAR CHESNEAU DU MARSAIS, c. 1750

There are rules of particular languages such as English or Arabic or Zulu that form part of the individual grammars of these languages, and then there are rules that hold in all languages. The universal rules are of particular interest because they give us a window into the human "faculty of language," which enables us to learn and use any particular language.

Interest in language universals has a long history. Early scholars encouraged research into the nature of language in general and promoted the idea of *general grammar* as distinct from *special grammar*. General grammar was to reveal those features common to all languages.

Students trying to learn Latin, Greek, French, or Swahili as a second language are generally so focused on learning aspects of the new language that differ from their native language that they may overlook the universal laws of language. Yet, there is much that all language learners know unconsciously even before they begin to learn a new language. They know that a language has its own set of sounds, perhaps thought of as its alphabet, that combine according to certain patterns to form words, and that the words themselves recombine to form phrases and sentences. Learners will expect to find verbs and nouns—as these are universal grammatical categories; they will know that the language—like all languages—has a way of negating, forming questions, issuing commands, referring to past or future time, and more generally, has a system of rules that will allow them to produce and understand an infinite number of sentences.

The more linguists explore the intricacies of human language, the more evidence we find to support Chomsky's view that there is a **Universal Grammar (UG)** that is part of the biologically endowed human language faculty. We can think of UG as the blueprint that all languages follow that forms part of the child's innate capacity for language learning. It specifies the different components of the grammar and their relations, how the different rules of these components are constructed, how they interact, and so on. A major aim of **linguistic theory** is to discover the nature of UG.

The linguist's goal is to reveal the "laws of human language," as the physicist's goal is to reveal the "laws of the physical universe." The complexity of language undoubtedly means this goal will never be fully achieved. All scientific theories are incomplete, and new hypotheses must be proposed to account for new data. Theories are continually changing as new discoveries are made. Just as physics was enlarged by Einstein's theories of relativity, so grows the linguistic theory of UG as new discoveries shed new light on the nature of human language. The comparative study of many different languages is of central importance to this enterprise.

The Development of Grammar in the Child

> How comes it that human beings, whose contacts with the world are brief and personal and limited, are nevertheless able to know as much as they do know?
>
> BERTRAND RUSSELL, *Human Knowledge: Its Scope and Limits*, 1948

Linguistic theory is concerned not only with describing the knowledge that adult speakers have of their language, but also with explaining how this knowledge is acquired.

All typically developing children acquire (at least one) language in a relatively short period with apparent ease. They do this despite the fact that parents and other caregivers do not provide them with any specific language instruction. Indeed, it is often remarked that children seem to "pick up" language just from hearing it spoken around them. Children are language-learning virtuosos—whether a child is male or female, from a rich family or a disadvantaged one, grows up on a farm or in the city, attends day care or has home care, none of these factors fundamentally affects the way language develops. Children can acquire any language they are exposed to with comparable ease—English, Dutch, French, Swahili, Japanese—and even though each of these languages has its own peculiar characteristics, children learn them all in very much the same way. For example, all children go through a babbling stage; their babbles gradually give way to words, which then combine to form simple sentences, and then sentences of ever-increasing complexity. The same four-year-old child who may be unable to tie her shoes or even count to five has managed to master the complex grammatical structures of her language and acquire a substantial lexicon.

How children accomplish this remarkable cognitive feat is a topic of intense interest to linguists. The child's inexorable path to adult linguistic competence and the uniformity of the acquisition process point to a substantial innate component to language development, what we referred to earlier as Universal Grammar. Children acquire language as quickly and effortlessly as they do because they do not have to figure out all the grammatical rules, only those that are specific to their particular language. The universal properties—the laws of language—are part of their biological endowment. In Chapter 9, we will discuss language acquisition in more detail.

Sign Languages: Evidence for Language Universals

It is not the want of organs that [prevents animals from making] . . . known their thoughts . . . for it is evident that magpies and parrots are able to utter words just like ourselves, and yet they cannot speak as we do, that is, so as to give evidence that they think of what they say. On the other hand, men who, being born deaf and mute . . . are destitute of the organs which serve the others for talking, are in the habit of themselves inventing certain signs by which they make themselves understood.

RENÉ DESCARTES, *Discourse on Method*, 1637

The sign languages of deaf communities provide some of the best evidence to support the view that all languages are governed by the same universal principles. Current research on sign languages has been crucial to understanding the biological underpinnings of human language acquisition and use.

The major language of the deaf community in the United States is **American Sign Language (ASL)**. ASL is an outgrowth of the sign language used in France and brought to the United States in 1817 by the great educator Thomas Hopkins Gallaudet.

ASL and other sign languages do not use sounds to express meanings. Instead, they are visual-gestural systems that use hand, body, and facial gestures as the forms used to represent words and grammatical rules. Sign languages are fully developed languages, and signers create and comprehend unlimited numbers of new sentences, just as speakers of spoken languages do. Signed languages have their own grammatical rules and a mental lexicon of signs, all encoded through a system of gestures, and are otherwise equivalent to spoken languages. Signers are affected by performance factors just as speakers are; slips of the hand occur similar to slips of the tongue. Finger fumblers amuse signers just as tongue twisters amuse speakers. These and other language games play on properties of the "sound" systems of the spoken and signed languages.

Deaf children who are exposed to signed languages acquire them just as hearing children acquire spoken languages, going through the same linguistic stages, including the babbling stage. Deaf children babble with their hands, just as hearing children babble with their vocal tracts. Neurological studies show that signed languages are organized in the brain in the same way as spoken languages, despite their visual modality. We discuss the brain basis of language in Chapter 10.

In short, signed languages resemble spoken languages in all major aspects. This universality is expected because, regardless of the modality in which it is expressed, language is based in human biology. Our knowledge, use and acquisition of language are not dependent on the ability to produce and hear sounds, but on a far more abstract cognitive capacity.

What Is Not (Human) Language

It is a very remarkable fact that there are none so depraved and stupid, without even excepting idiots, that they cannot arrange different words together, forming of them a statement by which they make known their thoughts; while, on the other hand, there is no other animal, however perfect and fortunately circumstanced it may be, which can do the same.

RENÉ DESCARTES, *Discourse on Method and Meditation on First Philosophy*

MUTTS by Patrick McDonnell

Patrick McDonnell/King Features Syndicate

All languages share certain fundamental properties, and children naturally acquire these languages because human beings are designed for human language. But what of the "languages" of other species: Are they like human languages? Can other species be taught a human language?

The Birds and the Bees

Most animal species possess some kind of communication system. Humans also communicate through systems other than language such as head nodding or facial expressions. The question is whether the communication systems used by other species are at all like human language with its very specific properties, most notably its creative aspect.

Many species have a non vocal system of communication. Among certain species of spiders there is a complex system for courtship. Before approaching his ladylove, the male spider goes through an elaborate series of gestures to tell her that he is indeed a spider and a suitable mate, and not a crumb or a fly to be eaten. These gestures are invariant. One never finds a creative spider changing or adding to the courtship ritual of his species.

A similar kind of gestural language is found among the fiddler crabs. There are forty species, and each uses its own claw-waving movement to signal to another member of its "clan." The timing, movement, and posture of the body never change from one time to another or from one crab to another within the particular variety. Whatever the signal means, it is fixed. Only one meaning can be conveyed.

An essential property of human language not shared by the communication systems of spiders, crabs, and other animals is its **discreteness**. Human languages are not simply made up of a fixed set of invariant signs. They are composed of discrete units—sounds, words, phrases—that are combined according to the rules of the grammar of the language. The word *top* in English has a particular meaning, but it also has individual parts that can be rearranged to produce other meaningful sequences—*pot* or *opt*. Similarly, the phrase *the cat on the mat* means something different from *the mat on the cat*. We can arrange and rearrange the units of our language to form an infinite number of expressions. The creativity of human language depends on discreteness.

In contrast to crabs and spiders, birds communicate vocally and bird-songs have always captured the human imagination. Musicians and composers have been moved by these melodies, sometimes imitating them in their compositions, other times incorporating birdsongs directly into the music. Birdsongs have also inspired poets as in Percy Bysshe Shelley's *To a Skylark*:

> Teach me half the gladness
> That thy brain must know;
> Such harmonious madness
> From my lips would flow,
> The world should listen then, as I am listening now.

Birds do not sing for our pleasure, however. Their songs and calls communicate important information to other members of the species and sometimes to other animals. **Birdcalls** (consisting of one or more short notes) convey danger, feeding, nesting, flocking, and so on. **Bird songs** (more complex patterns of notes) are used to stake out territory and to attract mates. Like the messages of crabs and spiders, however, there is no evidence of any internal structure to these songs; they cannot be segmented into discrete meaningful parts and rearranged to encode different messages as can the words, phrases, and sentences of human language.

In his territorial song, the European robin alternates between high-pitched and low-pitched notes to indicate how strongly he feels about defending his territory. The different alternations indicate intensity and nothing more. The robin is creative in his ability to sing the same song in different ways, but not creative in his ability to use the same units of the system to express different messages with different meanings. Recently, scientists have observed that finches will react when the units of a familiar song are rearranged. It is unclear, however, whether the birds recognize a violation of the rules of the song or are just responding to a pattern change.

Though crucial to the birds' survival, the messages conveyed by these songs and calls are limited, relating only to a bird's immediate environment and needs. Human language is different of course. Our words and sentences are not simply responses to internal and external stimuli. If you're tired you may yawn, but you may also say "I'm tired," or "I'm going to bed," or "I'm going to Starbucks for a double espresso." Notably, you also have the right to remain silent, or talk about things completely unrelated to your physical state—the weather, Facebook, your plans for the weekend, or most interesting of all, your linguistics class.

Linguists call this property of human language **displacement**: the capacity to talk (or sign) messages that are unrelated to here and now. Displacement and discreteness are two fundamental properties that distinguish human language from the communication systems of birds and other animals.

One respect in which birdsongs do resemble human languages is in their development. In many bird species, the full adult version of the birdsong is acquired in several stages, as it is for children acquiring language. The young bird sings a simplified version of the song shortly after hatching and then learns the more detailed, complex version by hearing adults sing. However, he must hear the adult song during a specific fixed period after birth—the period differs from species to species; otherwise song acquisition does not occur. For example, the chaffinch is unable to learn the more detailed song elements after ten months of age. A baby nightingale in captivity may be trained to sing melodiously by another nightingale, a "teaching bird," but only before its tail feathers are grown. These birds show a **critical period** for acquiring their "language" similar to the critical period for human language acquisition, which we will discuss in Chapters 9 and 10. As with human language acquisition, the development of the birdsongs of these species involves an interaction of both learned and innate structure.

An interesting consequence of the fact that some birdsongs are partially learned means that variation can develop. There can be "regional dialects" within the same species, and as with humans, these dialects are transmitted from parents to offspring. Researchers have noted, in fact, that dialect differences may be better preserved in songbirds than in humans because there is no homogenization of regional accents due to radio or TV. We will discuss human language dialects in Chapter 7.

Honeybees have a particularly interesting signaling system. When a forager bee returns to the hive she communicates to other bees where a source of food is located by performing a dance on a wall of the hive that reveals the location and quality of the food source. For one species of Italian honeybee, the dancing may assume one of three possible patterns: *round* (which indicates locations near the hive, within 20 feet or so); *sickle* (which indicates locations at 20 to 60 feet from the hive); and *tail-wagging* (for distances that exceed 60 feet). The number of repetitions per minute of the basic pattern in the tail-wagging dance indicates the precise distance: the slower the repetition rate, the longer the distance. The number of repetitions and the intensity with which the bee dances the round dance indicates the richness of the food source: the more repetitions and the livelier the bee dance the more food to be gotten.

Bee dances are discrete in some sense, consisting of separate parts, and in principle they can communicate infinitely many different messages, like human language; but unlike human language the topic is always the same, namely food. They lack the displacement property. As experiments have shown, when a bee is forced to walk to a food source rather than fly, she will communicate a distance many times farther away than the food source actually is. The bee has no way of communicating the special circumstances of its trip. This absence of creativity makes the bee's dance qualitatively different from human language.

As we will discuss in Chapter 10, the human language ability is rooted in the human brain. Just like human language, the communication system of each species is determined by its biology. This raises the interesting question of whether it is possible for one species to acquire the language of another; more specifically, can animals learn human language?

Can Animals Learn Human Language?

It is a great baboon, but so much like man in most things . . . I do believe it already understands much English; and I am of the mind it might be taught to speak or make signs.

ENTRY IN SAMUEL PEPYS'S DIARY, 1661

The idea of talking animals is as old and as widespread among human societies as language itself. All cultures have legends in which some animal speaks. All over West Africa, children listen to folktales in which a "spider-man" is the hero. "Coyote" is a favorite figure in many Native American tales, and many an animal takes the stage in Aesop's famous fables. Bugs Bunny, Mickey Mouse, and Donald Duck are icons of American culture. The fictional Doctor Doolittle communicated with all manner of animals, from giant snails to tiny sparrows, as did Saint Francis of Assisi.

In reality, various species show abilities that seem to mimic aspects of human language. Talking birds such as parrots and mynahs can be taught to faithfully reproduce words and phrases, but this does not mean they have acquired a human language. As the poet William Cowper put it: "Words learned by rote a parrot may rehearse; but talking is not always to converse."

Talking birds do not decompose their imitations into discrete units. *Polly* and *Molly* do not rhyme for a parrot. They are as different as *hello* and *goodbye*. If Polly learns "Polly wants a cracker" and "Polly wants a doughnut" and also learns to say *whiskey* and *bagel*, she will not then spontaneously produce "Polly wants whiskey" or "Polly wants a bagel" or "Polly wants whiskey and a bagel." If she learns *cat* and *cats*, and *dog* and *dogs*, and then learns the word *parrot*, she will not be able to form the plural *parrots*, as children do. Unlike every developing child, a parrot cannot generalize from particular instances and so cannot produce utterances that have not been directly taught. A parrot—even a very chatty one—cannot produce an unlimited set of sentences from a finite set of units. The imitative utterances of talking birds mean nothing to the birds; these utterances have no communicative function. Simply knowing how to produce a sequence of speech sounds is not the same as knowing a language. But what about animals that appear to learn the meanings of words? Do they have human language?

Dogs can easily be taught to respond to commands such as *heel, sit,* and *fetch* and even seem to understand object words such as *ball* and *toy*. Indeed, in 2004 German psychologists reported on a Border Collie named Rico who had acquired a 200-word vocabulary (containing both German and English words). When asked to fetch a particular toy from a pile of many toys Rico was correct over 90 percent of the time. When told to fetch a toy whose name he had not been previously taught, Rico could match the novel name to a new toy among a pile of familiar toys about 70 percent of the time—a rate comparable to that of young children performing a similar novel name task.

More recently, a Border Collie named Chaser who lives in South Carolina is reported to understand the names of 1022 toys! Chaser was taught these names over a three-year period. And like Rico he is able to connect a novel name to a new toy placed in a huge pile of toys whose names he already knows.

Rico and Chaser are clearly very intelligent dogs and their name recognition skills are amazing. It is unlikely, however, that Rico or Chaser (or Spot or Rover) understand the *meanings* of words or have acquired a symbolic system in the way that children do. Rather, they learn to associate a particular sequence of sounds with an object or action. For Chaser and Rico the name "Sponge Bob," for example, might mean something like "fetch Sponge Bob"—what the dog has been taught to do. The young child who has learned the name "Sponge Bob" knows that it refers to a particular toy or TV character independent of any a particular game or context. The philosopher Bertrand Russell summed up the dog rather insightfully, noting that ". . . however eloquently he may bark, he cannot tell you that his parents were honest though poor."

In their natural habitat, chimpanzees, gorillas, and other nonhuman primates communicate with each other through visual, auditory, olfactory, and tactile signals. Many of these signals seem to have meanings associated with the animals' immediate environment or emotional state. They can signal danger and can communicate aggressiveness and subordination. However, the natural sounds and gestures produced by all nonhuman primates are highly stereotyped and limited in the number and kind of messages they convey. Their signals cannot be broken down into discrete units and rearranged to create new meanings. They also lack the property of displacement: Intelligent though they are, these animals have no way of expressing the anger they felt yesterday or the anticipation of tomorrow.

Even though primate communication systems are quite limited, many people have been interested in the question of whether they have the latent capacity to acquire complex linguistic systems similar to human language. Throughout the second half of the twentieth century, there were a number of studies designed to determine whether nonhuman primates could learn human language, including both words (or signs) and the grammatical rules for their combination.

In early experiments, researchers raised chimpanzees in their own homes alongside their children in order to recreate the natural environment in which human children acquire language. The chimps were unable to vocalize words despite the efforts of their caretakers, though they did achieve the ability to understand a number of individual words. Primate vocal tracts do not permit them to pronounce many different sounds, but because of their manual dexterity, sign language was an attractive alternative to test their cognitive linguistic ability.

Starting with a chimpanzee named Washoe, and continuing over the years with a gorilla named Koko and another chimp ironically named Nim Chimpsky (after Noam Chomsky), intense efforts were made to teach them American Sign Language. Though the primates achieved small successes such as the ability to string two signs together, and occasionally showed flashes of creativity, none remotely reached the qualitative linguistic ability of a human child.

Similar results were obtained in attempts to teach primates artificial languages designed to resemble human languages in some respects. Chimpanzees Sarah, Lana, Sherman, Austin, and a male bonobo (or pygmy chimpanzee) named Kanzi, were taught languages whose "words" were plastic chips, or keys on a keyboard, that could be arranged into "sentences." The researchers were particularly interested in the ability of primates to communicate using such abstract symbols.

But these experiments, like previous ones, were subject to scientific scrutiny. Questions arose over what kind of knowledge Sarah and Lana and Kanzi were showing with their symbol manipulations and to what extent their responses were being inadvertently cued by experimenters. Many scientists, including some who were directly involved with these projects, have concluded that the creative ability that is so much a part of human language is not evidenced by the chimps' use of the artificial languages. As often happens in science, the search for the answers to one kind of question leads to answers to other questions. The linguistic experiments with primates have led to many advances in our understanding of primate cognitive ability. Researchers have gone on to investigate other capacities of the chimp mind, such as causality. These studies also underscore how remarkable it is that all human children are able to create new and complex sentences never spoken or heard before within just a few short years, without the benefit of explicit guidance.

Can Computers Learn Human Language?

"Zits", 2001 Zits Partnership. Reprinted with permission of King Features Syndicate

Man is still the most extraordinary computer of all.

JOHN F. KENNEDY (1917–1963)

Computers are prolific. If you are reading this book, there is a high likelihood that you use a computer, be it as large as a desktop or as small as an Apple Watch. You may also be able to speak to your computer and it may speak back. Your computer may take dictation, translate between languages, read an electronic newspaper out loud and give you the definition of *eleemosynary*. These are the trappings of human language, but does your computer, or any computer, have human language competence?

We saw earlier that two key properties of human language are discreteness and displacement. Computer speech has both these properties. Spoken words are assembled from discrete, prestored units of sound; and sentences from a prestored lexicon of words. Moreover, computer speech may refer to the past, present, or future and to its current location or another place.

Unlike talking birds, computers have no trouble generalizing sentences such as "Polly wants a cracker" to "Polly wants some whiskey" or even to "Hedwig likes mice." Forming plurals or past tenses are also easily programmable. A computer could associate one million spoken names of objects to pictures of those objects, putting poor Chaser (and all of us) to shame. As to the lack of creativity among nonhuman primates, computers suffer from no such drawback. Computers have been programed to write poetry, learn new words, and even provide psychological counseling.

Even the best of language-using computers have distinctly nonhuman-language traits. While humans never pronounce the same word twice identically, computers always do. Humans suffer from slips of the tongue, fumbled pronunciations, and convoluted phrasing. Humans often speak in fits and starts, hemming and hawing, inserting filler sounds such as "um" and "you know." Humans repeat words in a sentence such as "I . . . I . . . I don't want to paint uh I mean stain . . . stain my floor, no, I mean the decking." Humans bollix their syntax and realize it after they may have said "The horses away ran from the barn jumped the fence over." Computers never do any of this unless they are purposefully programmed to do so, and even when they are, the "mistakes" sound disingenuous.

Nonetheless, it may be argued that these are issues of linguistic performance. The toughest test of linguistic competence is a version of one first suggested by Alan M. Turing (1912–1954), the British mathematician who is considered the founder of modern computer science. Behind two screens are placed a computer and a human. An interrogator engages both voices behind the screens in conversation. If based on language usage, the interrogator is unable to determine which is the human and which is the computer, then one might argue that the computer has attained human linguistic competence.

No computer has come close to passing this "Turing test," fictional computers and robots to the contrary notwithstanding. Indeed, the test has never been seriously administered. Moreover, if in an unforeseeable future a computer was programmed to pass this test, it would be the ingenuity and linguistic competence of the programmers on display, not the computer nor its software. Despite the intelligence of animals and machines, none has achieved the linguistic competence of any healthy human being.

Language and Thought

It was intended that when Newspeak had been adopted once and for all and Oldspeak forgotten, a heretical thought—that is, a thought diverging from the principles of IngSoc—should be literally unthinkable, at least so far as thought is dependent on words.

GEORGE ORWELL, appendix to *1984*, 1949

The limits of my language mean the limits of my world.

LUDWIG WITTGENSTEIN, *Tractatus Logico-Philosophicus*, 1922

Many people are fascinated by the question of how language relates to thought. It is natural to imagine that something as powerful and fundamental to human nature as language would influence how we think about or perceive the world around us. This is clearly reflected in the appendix of George Orwell's masterpiece *1984*, quoted above. Over the years, there have been many claims made regarding the relationship between language and thought. The claim that the structure of a language influences how its speakers perceive the world around them is most closely associated with the linguist Edward Sapir and his student Benjamin Whorf, and is therefore referred to as the **Sapir–Whorf hypothesis**. In 1929 Sapir wrote:

> Human beings do not live in the objective world alone, nor in the world of social activity as ordinarily understood, but are very much at the mercy of the particular language which has become the medium of expression for their society . . . we see and hear and otherwise experience very largely as we do because the language habits of our community predispose certain choices of interpretation.[4]

Whorf made even stronger claims:

> The background linguistic system (in other words, the grammar) of each language is not merely the reproducing instrument for voicing ideas but rather is itself the shaper of ideas, the program and guide for the individual's mental activity, for his analysis of impressions, for his synthesis of his mental stock in trade . . . We dissect nature along lines laid down by our native languages.[5]

The strongest form of the Sapir–Whorf hypothesis is called **linguistic determinism** because it holds that the language we speak *determines* how we perceive and think about the world. According to this view, language acts like a filter on reality. One of Whorf's best-known claims in support of linguistic determinism was that the Hopi Indians do not perceive time in the same way as speakers of European languages because the Hopi language does not make the grammatical distinctions of tense that, for example, English does with words and word endings such as *did, will, shall, -s, -ed,* and *-ing.*

A weaker form of the hypothesis is **linguistic relativism**, which says that languages differ in the categories they encode and therefore speakers of different languages think about the world in different ways. For example, languages break up the color spectrum at different points. In Navaho, blue and green are one word. Russian has different words for dark blue *(siniy)* and light blue

[4]Sapir, E. 1929. *Language.* New York: Harcourt, Brace & World, p. 207.

[5]Whorf, B. L., and J. B. Carroll. 1956. *Language, thought, and reality: Selected writings.* Cambridge, MA: MIT Press.

(goluboy), while in English we need to use the additional words *dark* and *light* to express the difference. The American Indian language Zuni does not distinguish between the colors yellow and orange.

Languages also differ in how they express locations. For example, in Italian, you ride "in" a bicycle and you go "in" a country while in English you ride "on" a bicycle and you go "to" a country. In English, we say that a ring is placed "on" a finger and a finger is placed "in" the ring. Korean, on the other hand, has one word for both situations, *kitta*, which expresses the idea of a tight-fitting relation between the two objects. Spanish has two different words for the inside of a corner *(rincón)* and the outside of a corner *(esquina)*.

That languages show linguistic distinctions in their lexicons and grammar is certain, and we will see many examples of this in later chapters. The question is to what extent—if at all—such distinctions determine or influence the thoughts and perceptions of speakers. The Sapir–Whorf hypothesis is controversial, but it is clear that the strong form of this hypothesis is false. Peoples' thoughts and perceptions are not determined by the words and structures of their language. We are not prisoners of our linguistic systems. If speakers were unable to think about something for which their language had no specific word, translations would be impossible, as would learning a second language. English may not have separate words for the inside of a corner and the outside of a corner, but we are perfectly able to express these concepts using more than one word. In fact, we just did. If humans could not think about something for which we don't have a word, how would infants ever learn their first words, much less languages?

Many of the specific claims of linguistic determinism have been shown to be wrong. For example, the Hopi language may not have words and word endings for specific tenses, but the language has other expressions for time, including words for the days of the week, parts of the day, yesterday and tomorrow, lunar phases, seasons, and so on. The Hopi people use various kinds of calendars and various devices for time-keeping based on the sundial. Clearly, they have a sophisticated concept of time despite the lack of a tense system in the language.

The Munduruku, an indigenous people of the Brazilian Amazon, have no words in their language for triangle, square, rectangle, or other geometric concepts, except circle. The only terms to indicate direction are words for upstream, downstream, sunrise, and sunset. Yet, Munduruku children understand many principles of geometry as well as American children, whose language is rich in geometric and spatial words.

Though languages differ in their color words, speakers can readily perceive colors that are not named in their language. Grand Valley Dani is a language spoken in New Guinea with only two color words, black and white (dark and light). In experimental studies, however, speakers of the language showed recognition of the color red, and they did better with fire-engine red than off-red. This would not be possible if their color perceptions were fixed by their language. Our perception of color is determined by the structure of the human eye, not by the structure of language. However, some experiments have shown that speakers are better at discriminating two colors when their language has different words for each, supporting a weaker version of the Whorfian hypothesis.

by Jim Toomey

SHERMAN'S LAGOON © 2011 JIM TOOMEY

One Whorfian claim that has taken on the cast of an urban legend is that the Inuit language, spoken in the Canadian Arctic, has many more words for snow than English, and that this affects the worldview of the Inuit people. However, anthropologists have shown that Inuit has no more words for snow than English does: around a dozen, including *sleet, blizzard, slush,* and *flurry*. But even if it did, this would not show that language conditions the Inuits' experience of the world. Rather, it suggests that experience with a particular world creates the need for certain words. In this respect, the Inuit speaker is no different from the computer programmer, who has a technical vocabulary for Internet protocols, or the linguist, who has many specialized words regarding language. In this book, we will introduce you to many new words and linguistic concepts, and surely you will learn them! This would be impossible if your thoughts about language were determined by the linguistic vocabulary you now have.

Politicians and marketers certainly believe that language can influence our thoughts and values. One political party may refer to "assisted suicide" while another "compassion and choices." In the abortion debate, some refer to the "right to choose" and others to the "right to life." The terminology reflects different ideologies, but the choice of expression is primarily intended to sway public opinion. Politically correct (PC) language also reflects the idea that language can influence thought. Many people believe that by changing the way we talk, we can change the way we think; that if we eliminate racist and sexist terms from our language, we will become a less racist and sexist society. As we will discuss in Chapter 7, language itself is not sexist or racist, but people can be, and because of this, particular words take on negative meanings.

In his book *The Language Instinct*, the psychologist Steven Pinker uses the expression *euphemism treadmill* to describe how the euphemistic terms that are created to replace negative words often take on the negative associations of the words they were coined to replace. For example, *handicapped* was once a euphemism for the offensive term *crippled*, and when *handicapped* became politically incorrect it was replaced by the euphemism *disabled*, which was then replaced by yet another euphemism, *challenged*, and most recently, *person with a disability*. Nonetheless, in all such cases, changing language has not resulted in a new worldview for the speakers. Rather, it is changing sensibilities that drive the changes in language.

Some language changes inspired by political correctness can be quite extreme. For example, a local council in Britain banned the term *brainstorming* and replaced it with *thought showers* because local lawmakers worried that the original term might offend people with epilepsy. Or the instruction to newly recruited holiday Santa Clauses in Sidney, Australia, to not say *Ho Ho Ho* deemed too close to the American slang for prostitute and therefore degrading to women.

Prescient as Orwell was with respect to how language could be used for social control, he was more circumspect with regard to the relation between language and thought. He was careful to qualify his notions with the phrase "at least so far as thought is dependent on words." Current research shows that language does not determine how we think about and perceive the world. Future research should show the extent to which language influences other aspects of cognition such as memory and categorization.

Summary

We are all intimately familiar with at least one language, our own. Yet, few of us ever stop to consider what we know when we know a language. No book contains, or could possibly contain, the English or Russian or Zulu language. The words of a language can be listed in a dictionary, but not all the sentences can be. Speakers use a finite set of rules to produce and understand an infinite set of possible sentences.

These rules are part of the **grammar** of a language, which develops when you acquire the language and includes the sound system (the **phonology**), the structure and properties of words (the **morphology** and **lexicon**), how words may be combined into phrases and sentences (the **syntax**), and the ways in which sounds and meanings are related (the **semantics**). The sounds and meanings of individual words are related in an **arbitrary** fashion. If you had never heard the word *syntax*, you would not know what it meant by its sounds. The gestures used by signers are also arbitrarily related to their meanings. Language, then, is a system that relates sounds (or hand and body gestures) with meanings. When you know a language, you know this system.

This knowledge **(linguistic competence)** is different from behavior **(linguistic performance)**. You have the competence to produce a million-word sentence but performance limitations such as memory and endurance keep this from occurring.

There are different kinds of "grammars." The **descriptive grammar** of a language represents the (often unconscious) linguistic knowledge of its speakers. Such a grammar is a model of the **mental grammar** every speaker of the language possesses. It does not teach the rules of the language; it describes the rules that are already there.

A grammar that attempts to legislate what your grammar should be is called a **prescriptive grammar**. It specifies a standard of usage. It does not describe, except incidentally. **Teaching grammars**, while prescriptive in nature, are written to help people learn a foreign language or a dialect of their own language.

The more linguists investigate the nearly 7,000 languages of the world and describe the ways in which they differ from one another, the more they discover that these differences are limited. There are linguistic universals that pertain to the components of the grammar, the ways in which these components are related, and the forms of rules that govern them. These principles compose **Universal Grammar (UG)**, which provides a blueprint for the grammars of all possible human languages. Universal Grammar constitutes the innate component of the human language faculty that makes language development in children possible.

Strong evidence for Universal Grammar is found in the way children acquire language. Children learn language by exposure. They need not be deliberately taught, though parents may enjoy "teaching" their children to speak or sign. Children will learn any human language to which they are exposed, and they learn it in definable stages, beginning at a very early age.

The fact that deaf children learn **sign language** shows that the ability to hear or produce sounds is not a prerequisite for language learning. All the sign languages in the world, which differ among themselves as much as spoken languages do, are visual-gestural systems that are as fully developed and as structurally complex as spoken languages. The major sign language used in the United States is **American Sign Language (ASL)**. The ability of human beings to acquire, know, and use language is a biologically based ability rooted in the structure of the human brain, and expressed in different modalities (spoken or signed).

If language is defined merely as a system of communication, or the ability to produce speech sounds, then language is not unique to humans. There are, however, certain characteristics of human language not found in the communication systems of any other species. A basic property of human language is its **creativity**—a speaker's ability to combine the basic linguistic units to form an infinite set of "well-formed" grammatical sentences, most of which are novel, never before produced or heard.

Human languages consist of discrete units that combine according to the rules of the grammar of the language. Human languages also allow us to talk about things that are removed in time and space from our immediate environment or mental or physical state. These are the properties of **discreteness** and **displacement** and they distinguish human language from the "languages" of other species.

For many years, researchers were interested in the question of whether language is a uniquely human ability. There have been many attempts to teach nonhuman primates to communicate using sign language or symbolic systems that resemble human language in certain respects. Overall, results have been disappointing. Some chimpanzees have been trained to use an impressive number of symbols or signs. But a careful examination of their multi-sign utterances reveals that unlike children, the chimps show little creativity or spontaneity. Their "utterances" are highly imitative (echoic), often unwittingly cued by trainers, and have little syntactic structure. Some highly intelligent dogs have also learned a significant number of words, but their learning is restricted to a specific context and it is likely that their "meanings" for these words are very different from the symbolic or referential meanings that would be learned by a human child.

Computer scientists have labored for decades to program computers with the linguistic competence of a human. While the results are impressive, and computers appear to be able to talk, listen, and understand, there is little evidence that human linguistic competence has been achieved.

The **Sapir–Whorf hypothesis** holds that the particular language we speak determines or influences our thoughts and perceptions of the world. Much of the early evidence in support of this hypothesis has not stood the test of time. More recent experimental studies suggest that the words and grammar of a language may affect certain aspects of cognition such as memory.

References for Further Reading

Bickerton, D. 1990. *Language and species*. Chicago: Chicago University Press.

Chomsky, N. 1986. *Knowledge of language: Its nature, origin, and use*. New York and London: Praeger.

Emmorey, K. 2002. *Language, cognition and the brain: Insights from sign language research*. London, UK: Routledge

Gentner, D., and S. Goldin-Meadow. 2003. *Language in mind*. Cambridge, MA: MIT Press.

Klima, E. S., and U. Bellugi. 1979. *The signs of language*. Cambridge, MA: Harvard University Press.

Pilley, J. W. 2013. Chaser: *Unlocking the genius of the dog who knows a thousand words*. Boston: Houghton Mifflin Harcourt.

Pinker, S. 1999. *Words and rules: The ingredients of language*. New York: HarperCollins.

___. 1994. *The language instinct*. New York: William Morrow.

Premack, A. J., and D. Premack. 1972. Teaching language to an ape. *Scientific American* (October): 92–99.

Terrace, H. S. 1979. *Nim: A chimpanzee who learned sign language*. New York: Knopf.

Exercises

1. An English speaker's knowledge includes the sound sequences of the language. When new products are put on the market, the manufacturers have to think up new names for them that conform to the allowable sound patterns. Suppose, you were hired by a manufacturer of soap products to name five new products. What names might you come up with? List them.

   We are interested in how the names are pronounced. Therefore, describe in any way you can how to say the words you list. Suppose, for example, you named one detergent *Blick*. You could describe the sounds in any of the following ways:

   bl as in *blood*, *i* as in *pit*, *ck* as in *stick*
   bli as in *bliss*, *ck* as in *tick*
   b as in *boy*, *lick* as in *lick*

2. Consider the following sentences. Put a star (*) after those that do not seem to conform to the rules of your grammar, that are ungrammatical for you. State, if you can, why you think the sentence is ungrammatical.
   a. Robin forced the sheriff go.
   b. Napoleon forced Josephine to go.
   c. The devil made Faust go.
   d. He passed by a large pile of money.

    e. He drove by my house.
    f. He drove my house by.
    g. Did in a corner little Jack Horner sit?
    h. Elizabeth is resembled by Charles.
    i. Nancy is eager to please.
    j. It is easy to frighten Emily.
    k. It is eager to love a kitten.
    l. That birds can fly flabbergasts.
    m. The fact that you are late to class is surprising.
    n. Has the nurse slept the baby yet?
    o. I was surprised for you to get married.
    p. I wonder who and Mary went swimming.
    q. Myself bit John.
    r. What did Alice eat the toadstool with?
    s. What did Alice eat the toadstool and?

3. It was pointed out in this chapter that a small set of words in languages may be onomatopoeic; that is, their sounds "imitate" what they refer to. *Ding-dong, tick-tock, bang, zing, swish*, and *plop* are such words in English. Construct a list of ten new onomatopoeic words. Test them on at least five friends to see whether they are truly nonarbitrary as to sound and meaning.

4. Although sounds and meanings of most words in all languages are arbitrarily related, there are some communication systems in which the "signs" unambiguously reveal their "meanings."
    a. Describe (or draw) five different signs that directly show what they mean. *Example*: a road sign indicating an S curve.
    b. Describe any other communication system that, like language, consists of arbitrary symbols. *Example*: traffic signals, in which red means stop and green means go.

5. Consider these two statements: I learned a new word today. I learned a new sentence today. Do you think the two statements are equally probable, and if not, why not?

6. An African grey parrot named Alex who was the subject of a 30-year experiment was reported to have learned the meanings of 150 words. There are many reports on the Internet about Alex's impressive abilities. In the light of evidence presented in this chapter, or based on your own Internet research, discuss whether Alex's communications were the results of classical operant conditioning, as many scientists believe, or whether he showed true linguistic creativity, as his trainers maintain.

7. A wolf is able to express subtle gradations of emotion by different positions of the ears, the lips, and the tail. There are eleven postures of the tail that express such emotions as self-confidence, confident threat, lack of tension, uncertain threat, depression, defensiveness, active submission, and complete submission. This system seems to be complex. Suppose that there were a thousand different emotions that the wolf could express in this way. Would you then say a wolf had a language similar to a human's? If not, why not?

8. Suppose you taught a dog to *heel, sit up, roll over, play dead, stay, jump,* and *bark* on command, using the italicized words as cues. Would you be teaching it language? Why or why not?

9. State some rule of grammar that you have learned is the correct way to say something, but that you do not generally use in speaking. For example, you may have heard that *It's me* is incorrect and that the correct form is *It's I*. Nevertheless, you always use *me* in such sentences; your friends do also, and in fact *It's I* sounds odd to you.

    Write a short essay presenting arguments against someone who tells you that you are wrong. Discuss how this disagreement demonstrates the difference between descriptive and prescriptive grammars.

10. Noam Chomsky has been quoted as saying:

    It's about as likely that an ape will prove to have a language ability as that there is an island somewhere with a species of flightless birds waiting for human beings to teach them to fly.

    In the light of evidence presented in this chapter, or based on your own Internet research, comment on Chomsky's remark. Do you agree or disagree, or do you think the evidence is inconclusive?

11. Think of song titles that are "bad" grammar, but that, if corrected, would lack effect. For example, the title of the 1929 "Fats" Waller classic "Ain't Misbehavin'" is clearly superior to the bland "I am not misbehaving." Try to come up with five or ten such titles.

12. Linguists who attempt to write a descriptive grammar of linguistic competence are faced with a difficult task. They must understand a deep and complex system based on a set of sparse and often inaccurate data. (Children learning language face the same difficulty.) Albert Einstein and Leopold Infeld captured the essence of the difficulty in their book *The Evolution of Physics*, written in 1938:

    In our endeavor to understand reality we are somewhat like a man trying to understand the mechanism of a closed watch. He sees the face and the moving hands, even hears its ticking, but he has no way of opening the case. If he is ingenious he may form some picture of a mechanism which could be responsible for all the things he observes, but he may never be quite sure his picture is the only one which could explain his observations. He will never be able to compare his picture with the real mechanism and he cannot even imagine the possibility of the meaning of such a comparison.

    Write a short essay that speculates on how a linguist might go about understanding the reality of a person's grammar (the closed watch) by observing what that person says and doesn't say (the face and moving hands). For example, a person might never say *the sixth sheik's sixth sheep is sick as a dog,* but the grammar should specify that it is a well-formed sentence, just as it should somehow indicate that *Came the messenger on time* is ill-formed.

13. View the motion picture *My Fair Lady* (drawn from the play *Pygmalion* by George Bernard Shaw). Write down every attempt to teach grammar (pronunciation, word choice, and syntax) to the character of Eliza Doolittle. This is an illustration of a "teaching grammar."

14. Many people are bilingual or multilingual, speaking two or more languages with very different structures.
    a. What implications does bilingualism have for the debate about language and thought?
    b. Many readers of this textbook have some knowledge of a second language. Think of a linguistic structure or word in one language that does not exist in the second language and discuss how this does or does not affect your thinking when you speak the two languages. (If you know only one language, ask this question to a bilingual person you know.)
    c. Can you find an example of an untranslatable word or structure in one of the languages you speak?

15. The South American indigenous language Piraha is said to lack numbers beyond two and distinct words for colors. Research this language using the Internet with regard to whether Piraha supports or fails to support linguistic determinism and/or linguistic relativism.

16. English (especially British English) has many words for woods and woodlands. Here are some:

    woodlot, carr, fen, firth, grove, heath, holt, lea, moor, shaw, weald, wold, coppice, scrub, spinney, copse, brush, bush, bosquet, bosky, stand, forest, timberland, thicket

    a. How many of these words do you recognize?
    b. Look up several of these words in the dictionary and discuss the differences in meaning. Many of these words are obsolete, so if your dictionary doesn't have them, try the Internet.
    c. Do you think that English speakers have a richer concept of woodlands than speakers whose language has fewer words? Why or why not?

17. English words containing *dge* in their spelling *(trudge, edgy)* are said mostly to have unfavorable or negative connotations. Research this notion by accumulating as many *dge* words as you can and classifying them as unfavorable *(sludge)* or neutral *(bridge)*. What do you do about *budget?* Unfavorable or not? Are there other questionable words?

18. With regard to the "euphemism treadmill": Identify three other situations in which a euphemism evolved to be as offensive as the word it replaced, requiring yet another euphemism. *Hint*: Sex, race, and bodily functions are good places to start.

19. **Research project**: Read the Cratylus Dialogue—it's online. In it is a discussion (or "dialogue") of whether names are "conventional" (i.e., what we have called *arbitrary*) or "natural." Do you find Socrates' point of view sufficiently well-argued to support the thesis in this chapter that the relationship between form and meaning is indeed arbitrary? Argue your case in either direction in a short (or long, if you wish) essay.

20. **Research project**: (Cf. exercise 15) It is claimed that Piraha—an indigenous language of Brazil—violates some of the universal principles hypothesized by linguists. Which principles are in question? Is the evidence persuasive? Conclusive? Speculative? (Hint: Use the journal *Current Anthropology*, Volume 46, Number 4, August–October 2005 and the journal *Language*, Volume 85, Number 2, June 2009.)

21. There are, very roughly, about half a million words in use in today's English language according to current unabridged dictionaries. However, if we reach back to the beginnings of the printing press and examine large amounts of published English we find an additional half a million words now no longer in use such as *slethem*, a musical instrument. Write a short essay arguing one way or the other that the lexicon of the English language ought to be counted as containing one million or so words. Feel free, as always, to poke around the Internet to inform yourself further. *Google Books Ngram Viewer* may prove useful as well.

22. In his book *1984*, George Orwell proposed that if a concept does not exist, it is nameless. In the passage quoted below, he suggests that if a crime were nameless, it would be unimaginable, hence impossible to commit:

    > A person growing up with Newspeak as his sole language would no more know that . . . *free* had once meant "intellectually free," than, for instance, a person who had never heard of chess would be aware of the secondary meanings attaching to *queen* and *rook* and *checkmate*. There would be many crimes and errors which it would be beyond his power to commit, simply because they were nameless and therefore unimaginable.

    Critique this notion.

23. In the sci-fi movie *Arrival* (based on Ted Chiang's novella *Story of Your Life*), linguist Louise Banks learns the language (Heptapod B) of aliens visiting the Earth and then realizes she can see the future. Watch the movie and explain how the Sapir–Whorf hypothesis shapes the story.

Morphology: The Words of Language

Every speaker of every language knows tens of thousands of words. Unabridged dictionaries of English contain nearly 500,000 entries, but most speakers don't know all of these words. It has been estimated that a child of six knows as many as 13,000 words and the average high school graduate about 60,000. A college graduate presumably knows many more than that, but whatever our level of education, we learn new words throughout our lives, such as the many words in this book that you will learn for the first time.

Words are an important part of linguistic knowledge and constitute a component of our mental grammars, but one can learn thousands of words in a language and still not know the language. Anyone who has tried to communicate in a foreign country by merely using a dictionary knows this is true. On the other hand, without words we would be unable to convey our thoughts through language or understand the thoughts of others.

Someone who doesn't know English would not know where one word begins or ends in an utterance like *Thecatsatonthemat*. We separate written words by spaces, but in the spoken language there are no pauses between most words. Without knowledge of the language, one can't tell how many words are in an utterance. Knowing a word means knowing that a particular sequence of sounds is associated with a particular meaning. A speaker of English has no difficulty in segmenting the stream of sounds into six individual words—*the, cat, sat, on, the,* and *mat*—because each of these words is listed in his or her mental dictionary, or lexicon (the Greek word for *dictionary*), that is part of a speaker's linguistic knowledge. Similarly, a speaker knows that *uncharacteristically,* which has more letters than *Thecatsatonthemat,* is nevertheless a single word.

The lack of pauses between words in speech has provided humorists with much material. The comical hosts of the show *Car Talk,* aired on National Public Radio (as reruns nowadays), close the show by reading a list of credits that includes the following cast of characters:

Copyeditor:	Adeline Moore (add a line more)
Accounts payable:	Ineeda Czech (I need a check)
Pollution control:	Maury Missions (more emissions)
Purchasing:	Lois Bidder (lowest bidder)
Statistician:	Marge Innovera (margin of error)
Russian chauffeur:	Picov Andropov (pick up and drop off)
Legal firm:	Dewey, Cheetham, and Howe (Do we cheat 'em? And how!)[1]

In all these instances, you would have to have knowledge of English words to make sense of and find humor in such plays on words.

The fact that the same sound sequences (Lois Bidder—lowest bidder) can be interpreted differently shows that the relation between sound and meaning is an arbitrary pairing, as discussed in Chapter 1. For example, *Un petit d'un petit* in French means "a little one of a little one," but to an English speaker the sounds resemble the name *Humpty Dumpty.*

When you know a word, you know its sound (pronunciation) and its meaning. Because the sound-meaning relation is arbitrary, it is possible to have words with the same sound and different meanings (*bear* and *bare*) and words with the same meaning and different sounds (*sofa* and *couch*).

Because each word is a sound-meaning unit, its pronunciation is stored in our mental lexicon alongside the corresponding meaning. For literate speakers, the spelling of most of the words is also included.

Each word in your mental lexicon includes other information as well, such as whether it is a noun, a pronoun, a verb, an adjective, an adverb, a preposition, or a conjunction. That is, the mental lexicon also specifies the **grammatical category** or **syntactic class** of the word. You may not consciously know that a form such as *love* is listed as both a verb and a noun, but as a speaker you have such knowledge, as shown by the phrases *I love you* and *You are the love of my life.* If such information were not in the mental lexicon, we would not know how to form grammatical sentences, nor would we be able to distinguish grammatical from ungrammatical sentences.

---

[1] Car Talk" credits from National Public Radio.™ Dewey, Cheetham & Howe, 2006, all rights reserved.

Content Words and Function Words

" . . . and even . . . the patriotic archbishop of Canterbury found it advisable—"

"Found what?" said the Duck.

"Found it," the Mouse replied rather crossly; "of course you know what 'it' means."

"I know what 'it' means well enough, when I find a thing," said the Duck; "it's generally a frog or a worm. The question is, what did the archbishop find?"

LEWIS CARROLL, *Alice's Adventures in Wonderland*, 1865

Languages make an important distinction between two kinds of words—content words and function words. Nouns, verbs, adjectives, and adverbs are the **content words**. These words denote concepts such as objects, actions, attributes, and ideas that we can think about like *children, build, beautiful,* and *seldom*. Content words are sometimes called the **open class** words because we can and regularly do add new words to these classes, such as *Facebook* (noun), *blog* (noun, verb), *frack* (verb), and *online* (adjective, adverb).

Other classes of words do not have clear lexical meanings or obvious concepts associated with them, including conjunctions such as *and, or,* and *but*; prepositions such as *in* and *of*; the articles *the* and *a/an*, and pronouns such as *it*. These kinds of words are called **function words** because they specify grammatical relations and have little or no semantic content. For example, the articles indicate whether a noun is definite or indefinite—*the* boy or *a* boy. The preposition *of* indicates possession, as in "the book of yours," but this word indicates many other kinds of relations too. The *it* in *it's raining* and *the archbishop of Canterbury found it advisable* are further examples of words whose function is purely grammatical—they are required by the rules of syntax and are indispensable to the grammar.

Function words are sometimes called **closed class** words. This is because it is difficult to think of any articles, conjunctions, prepositions, or pronouns that have recently entered the language. The small set of personal pronouns such as *I, me, mine, he,* and *she,* are part of this class. So are the complementizers *if, that,* and *whether* which we will discuss the next chapter.

The difference between content and function words is illustrated by the following test that has circulated over the Internet:

Count the number of Fs in the following text without reading further, then check the footnote:[2]

FINISHED FILES ARE THE
RESULT OF YEARS OF SCIENTIFIC
STUDY COMBINED WITH THE
EXPERIENCE OF YEARS.

---

[2]Most people come up with three. If you came up with fewer than six, count again, and this time, pay attention to the function word *of*.

This little test illustrates that the brain treats content and function words (such as *of*) differently. A great deal of psychological and neurological evidence supports this claim. As will be discussed in Chapter 10, in reading tasks people tend to skip over the function words. And some brain-damaged patients with language impairments are unable to read function words such as *in* or *which*, but can read the lexical content words *inn* and *witch*.

The two classes of words also seem to function differently in **slips of the tongue** produced by normal individuals. For example, a speaker may inadvertently switch words producing "the journal of the editor" instead of "the editor of the journal," but the switching or exchanging of function words has not been observed. There is also evidence for this distinction from language acquisition (discussed in Chapter 9). In the early stages of development, children often omit function words from their speech as in "doggie barking."

The linguistic evidence suggests that content words and function words play different roles in language. Content words bear the brunt of the meaning, whereas function words connect the content words to the larger grammatical context.

Morphemes: The Minimal Units of Meaning

"They gave it me," Humpty Dumpty continued, "for an un-birthday present."

"I beg your pardon?" Alice said with a puzzled air.

"I'm not offended," said Humpty Dumpty.

"I mean, what is an un-birthday present?"

"A present given when it isn't your birthday, of course."

LEWIS CARROLL, *Through the Looking-Glass*, 1871

Humpty Dumpty is well aware that the form *un-* means "not," as further shown in the following pairs of words:

A	B
desirable	undesirable
likely	unlikely
inspired	uninspired
happy	unhappy
developed	undeveloped
sophisticated	unsophisticated

Thousands of English adjectives begin with *un-*. If we assume that the most basic unit of meaning is the word, what do we say about parts of words, such as *un-*, which has a fixed meaning? In all the words in the B column, *un-* means the same thing—"not." *Undesirable* means "not desirable," *unlikely* means "not likely," and so on. All the words in column B consist of at least two meaningful units: *un + desirable, un + likely, un + inspired,* and so on.

Just as *un-* occurs with the same meaning in the previous list of words, so does *phon-* in the following words. (You may not know the meaning of some of them, but you will when you finish this book.)

phone	phonology	phoneme
phonetic	phonologist	phonemic
phonetics	phonological	allophone
phonetician	telephone	euphonious
phonic	telephonic	symphony

Phon- is a minimal form in that it can't be decomposed. *Ph* doesn't mean anything; *pho*, though it may be pronounced like *foe*, has no relation in meaning to it; and *on* is not the preposition spelled *o-n*. In all the words on the list, *phon* has the identical meaning "pertaining to sound."

These examples illustrate that many words are composed by rules and have internal structure. *Uneaten, undisputed,* and *ungrammatical* are words in English, but **eatenun, *disputedun,* and **grammaticalun* (to mean "not eaten," "not disputed," "not grammatical") are not words because we form a negative meaning of a word by adding *un-* to the beginning of a word not the end.

When Samuel Goldwyn, the pioneer moviemaker, announced, "In two words: impossible," he was reflecting the common view that words are the basic meaningful elements of a language. We have seen that this cannot be so, because some words contain several distinct units of meaning. The linguistic term for the most elemental unit of grammatical form is **morpheme**. The word is derived from the Greek word *morphe*, meaning "form." If Goldwyn had taken a linguistics course, he would have said, more correctly, "In two morphemes: im-possible."

The study of the internal structure of words, and of the rules by which words are formed, is **morphology**. This word itself consists of two morphemes, *morph + ology*. The morpheme *-ology* means "branch of knowledge," so the meaning of *morphology* is "the branch of knowledge concerning (word) forms." Morphology also refers to our internal grammatical knowledge concerning the words of our language, and like most linguistic knowledge we are not consciously aware of it.

A single word may be composed of one or more morphemes:

One morpheme	boy
	desire
	meditate
two morphemes	boy + ish
	desire + able
	meditate + tion
three morphemes	boy + ish + ness
	desire + able + ity
four morphemes	gentle + man + li + ness
	un + desire + able + ity
more than four	un + gentle + man + li + ness
	anti + dis + establish + ment + ari + an + ism

A morpheme may be represented by a single letter such as the morpheme *a-* meaning "without" as in *amoral* and *asexual*, or by a single syllable, such as *child* and *ish* in *child + ish*. A morpheme may also consist of more than one syllable: of two syllables, as in *camel, lady,* and *water*; of three syllables, as in *Hackensack* and *crocodile*; or of four or more syllables, as in *hallucinate, apothecary, helicopter,* and *accelerate.*

A morpheme—the minimal linguistic unit—is thus an arbitrary union of a sound and a meaning (or grammatical function) that cannot be further analyzed. So, solidly welded is this union in the mind that it is impossible for you to hear or read a word you know and not be aware of its meaning, even if you try! These two sides of the same coin are often called a **linguistic sign**, not to be confused with the *sign* of sign languages. Every word in every language is composed of one or more morphemes.

The Discreteness of Morphemes

9 CHICKWEED LANE © 2011 Brooke McEldowney. Reprinted by permission of Universal Uclick for UFS. All rights reserved.

Internet bloggers love to point out "inconsistencies" in the English language. They observe that while singers sing and flingers fling, it is not the case that fingers "fing." However, English speakers know that *finger* is a single morpheme, or a **monomorphemic word**. The final *-er* syllable in *finger* is not a separate morpheme because a finger is not "something that fings." Similarly, *butter* when not referring to goat-like behavior is monomorphemic food stuff, and *buttress*, to be sure, is neither a feminine form of *butt* nor has anything to do with locks of hair.

The meaning of a morpheme must be constant. The agentive morpheme *-er* means "one who does" in words such as *singer, painter, lover,* and *worker,* but the same sounds represent the comparative morpheme, meaning "more," in *nicer, prettier,* and *taller.* Thus, two different morphemes may be pronounced identically. The identical form represents two morphemes because of the different meanings. The same sounds may occur in another word and not represent a separate morpheme at all, as in *finger.*

Conversely, the two morphemes *-er* and *-ster* have the same meaning, but different forms. Both *singer* and *songster* mean "one who sings." And like *-er, -ster* is not a morpheme in *monster* because a monster is not something that "mons" or someone that "is mon" the way *youngster* is someone who is young. All of this follows from the concept of the morpheme as a *sound* plus a *meaning* unit.

The decomposition of words into morphemes illustrates one of the fundamental properties of human language—discreteness—a property that sets it apart from the animal communication systems, as discussed in Chapter 1. In all languages, sound units combine to form morphemes, morphemes combine to form words, and words combine to form larger units—phrases and sentences.

Discreteness is an important part of linguistic creativity. We can combine morphemes in novel ways to create new words whose meaning will be apparent to other speakers of the language. If you know that "to tweet" means to post an update to the social media site Twitter, you automatically understand that a *tweetable* message is one that is suitable for posting on Twitter; that a *tweeter* is someone who tweets, and that when a *tweet* is *retweeted* thousands of times, it has gone viral! You know the meanings of all these words by virtue of your knowledge of the discrete morphemes *tweet, re-, -able,* and *-er,* and the rules for their combination.

Bound and Free Morphemes

LUANN © (2005) GEC Inc. Reprinted by permission of Universal Uclick for UFS. All rights reserved.

Our morphological knowledge has two components: knowledge of the individual morphemes and knowledge of the rules that combine them. We will see a similar situation in the next chapter where our syntactic knowledge consists of knowledge of words and the rules for combining them, and we will see yet another example of the discreteness of human language in succeeding chapters where speakers have knowledge of the individual sounds of their language and the rules for combining them into morphemes and words.

One of the things we know about particular morphemes is whether they can stand alone or whether they must be attached to a base morpheme. Some morphemes such as *boy, desire, gentle,* and *man* may constitute words by themselves. These are **free morphemes**. Other morphemes such as *-ish, -ness, -ly, pre-, trans-,* and *un-* are never words by themselves but are always parts of words. These **affixes** are **bound morphemes** and they may attach at the beginning, the end, in the middle, or both at the beginning and end of a word. The humor in the cartoon is Brad's stumbling over the bound morpheme *un-* in a questionable attempt to free it.

Prefixes and Suffixes

We know whether an affix precedes or follows other morphemes, for example, *un-, pre- (premeditate, prejudge),* and *bi- (bipolar, bisexual)* are **prefixes**. They occur before other morphemes. Some morphemes occur only as **suffixes**, following other morphemes. English examples of suffix morphemes are *-ing (sleeping, eating, running, climbing), -er (singer, performer, reader), -ist (typist, pianist, novelist, linguist),* and *-ly (manly, sickly, friendly),* to mention only a few.

Many languages have prefixes and suffixes, but languages may differ in how they deploy these morphemes. A morpheme that is a prefix in one language may be a suffix in another and vice versa. In English, the plural morphemes *-s* and *-es* are suffixes (*boys, lasses*). In Isthmus Zapotec, spoken in Mexico, the plural morpheme *ka-* is a prefix:

zigi	"chin"	kazigi	"chins"
zike	"shoulder"	kazike	"shoulders"
diaga	"ear"	kadiaga	"ears"

Languages may also differ in what meanings they express through affixation. In English, we do not add an affix to derive a noun from a verb. We have the verb *dance* as in "I like to dance," and we have the noun *dance* as in "There's a dance or two in the old dame yet." The form is the same in both cases. In Turkish, you derive a noun from a verb with the suffix *-ak,* as in the following examples:

| dur | "to stop" | durak | "stopping place" |
| bat | "to sink" | batak | "sinking place" or "marsh/swamp" |

To express reciprocal action in English we use the phrase *each other,* as in *understand each other, love each other.* In Turkish, a morpheme is added to the verb:

| anla | "understand" | anla*sh* | "understand each other" |
| sev | "love" | sev*ish* | "love each other" |

The reciprocal suffix in these examples is pronounced *sh* after a vowel and *ish* after a consonant. This is similar to the process in English in which we use *a* as the indefinite article morpheme before a noun beginning with a consonant, as in *a dog,* and *an* before a noun beginning with a vowel, as in *an apple.* The same morpheme may have more than one slightly different form (see Exercise 6, for example). We will discuss the various pronunciations of morphemes in more detail in Chapter 6.

In Piro, an Arawakan language spoken in Peru, a single morpheme, *-kaka,* can be added to a verb to express the meaning "cause to":

| cokoruha | "to harpoon" | cokoruhakaka | "cause to harpoon" |
| salwa | "to visit" | salwakaka | "cause to visit" |

In Karuk, a Native American language spoken in the Pacific Northwest, adding *-ak* to a noun forms the locative adverbial meaning "in."

| ikrivaam | "house" | ikrivaamak | "in a house" |

It is accidental that both Turkish and Karuk have a suffix *-ak.* Despite the similarity in *form,* the two meanings are different. Similarly, the reciprocal suffix *-ish* in Turkish is similar in form to the English suffix *-ish* as in *boyish.*

Similarity in meaning may give rise to different forms. In Karuk, the suffix *-ara* has the same meaning as the English *-y*, that is, "characterized by" (*hairy* means "characterized by hair").

aptiik   "branch"   aptikara   "branchy"

These examples illustrate again the arbitrary nature of the linguistic sign, that is, of the sound-meaning relationship, as well as the distinction between bound and free morphemes.

Infixes

Some languages also have **infixes**, morphemes that are inserted into other morphemes. Bontoc, spoken in the Philippines, is such a language, as illustrated by the following:

Nouns/Adjectives		Verbs	
fikas	"strong"	fumikas	"to be strong"
kilad	"red"	kumilad	"to be red"
fusul	"enemy"	fumusul	"to be an enemy"

In this language, the infix *-um-* is inserted after the first consonant of the noun or adjective. Thus, a speaker of Bontoc who knows that *pusi* means "poor" would understand the meaning of *pumusi*, "to be poor," on hearing the word for the first time, just as an English speaker who learns the verb *sneet* would know that *sneeter* is "one who sneets." A Bontoc speaker who knows that *ngumitad* means "to be dark" would know that the adjective "dark" must be *ngitad*.

Oddly enough, the only infixes in English are full-word obscenities, usually inserted into adjectives or adverbs. The most common infix in America is the word *fuckin'* and all the euphemisms for it, such as *friggin, freakin, flippin,* and *fuggin,* as in *ri-fuckin-diculous* or *Kalama-flippin-zoo,* based on the city in Michigan. In Britain, a common infix is *bloody,* an obscene term in British English, and its euphemisms, such as *bloomin'.* In the movie and stage musical *My Fair Lady,* the word *abso-bloomin-lutely* occurs in one of the songs sung by Eliza Doolittle.

Circumfixes

Some languages have **circumfixes**, morphemes that are attached to a base morpheme both initially and finally. These are sometimes called **discontinuous morphemes**. In Chickasaw, a Muskogean language spoken in Oklahoma, the negative is formed by surrounding the affirmative form with both a preceding *ik-* and a following *-o* working together as a single negative morpheme. The final vowel of the affirmative is dropped before the negative part *-o* is added. Examples of this circumfixing are:

Affirmative		Negative	
chokma	"he is good"	ik + chokm + o	"he isn"t good"
lakna	"it is yellow"	ik + lakn + o	"it isn't yellow"
palli	"it is hot"	ik + pall + o	"it isn't hot"
tiwwi	"he opens (it)"	ik + tiww + o	"he doesn't open (it)"

An example of a more familiar circumfixing language is German. The past participle of regular verbs is formed by tacking on *ge-* to the beginning and *-t* to the end of the verb root. This circumfix added to the verb root *lieb* "love" produces *geliebt*, "loved" (or "beloved," when used as an adjective).

Roots and Stems

Morphologically complex words consist of a morpheme **root** and one or more affixes. Some examples of English roots are *paint* in *painter*, *read* in *reread*, *ceive* in *conceive*, and *ling* in *linguist*. A root may or may not stand alone as a word (*paint* and *read* do; *ceive* and *ling* don't). In languages that have circumfixes, the root is the form around which the circumfix attaches, for example, the Chickasaw root *chokm* in *ikchokmo* ("he isn't good"). In infixing languages, the root is the form into which the infix is inserted; for example, *fikas* in the Bontoc word *fumikas* ("to be strong").

Semitic languages such as Hebrew and Arabic have a unique morphological system. Nouns and verbs are built on a foundation of three consonants, and one derives related words by varying the pattern of vowels and syllables. For example, the root for "write" in Egyptian Arabic is *ktb*, from which the following words (among others) are formed by infixing vowels:

katab	"he wrote"
kaatib	"writer"
kitàab	"book"
kútub	"books"

When a root morpheme is combined with an affix, it forms a **stem**. Other affixes can be added to a stem to form a more complex stem, as shown in the following:

root	Chomsky	(proper) noun
stem	Chomsky + ite	noun + suffix
word	Chomsky + ite + s	noun + suffix + suffix
root	believe	verb
stem	believe + able	verb + suffix
word	un + believe + able	prefix + verb + suffix
root	system	noun
stem	system + atic	noun + suffix
stem	un + system + atic	prefix + noun + suffix
stem	un + system + atic + al	prefix + noun + suffix + suffix
word	un + system + atic + al + ly	prefix + noun + suffix + suffix + suffix

With the addition of each new affix, a new stem and a new word are formed. Linguists sometimes use the word **base** to mean any root or stem to which an affix is attached. In the preceding example, *system, systematic, unsystematic,* and *unsystematical* are bases.

Bound Roots

It had been a rough day, so when I walked into the party I was very chalant, despite my efforts to appear gruntled and consolate. I was furling my wieldy umbrella . . . when I saw her. . . . She was a descript person . . . Her hair was kempt, her clothing shevelled, and she moved in a gainly way.

JACK WINTER, "How I Met My Wife" by Jack Winter from *The New Yorker*, July 25, 1994. Reprinted by permission of the Estate of Jack Winter.

Bound roots do not occur in isolation and they acquire meaning only in combination with other morphemes. For example, words of Latin origin such as *receive, conceive, perceive,* and *deceive* share a common root, *-ceive;* and the words *remit, permit, commit, submit, transmit,* and *admit* share the root *-mit.* For the original Latin speakers, the morphemes corresponding to *ceive* and *mit* had clear meanings, but for modern English speakers, Latinate morphemes such as *ceive* and *mit* have no independent meaning. Their meaning depends on the entire word in which they occur.

A similar class of words is composed of a prefix affixed to a bound root morpheme. Examples are *ungainly,* but no **gainly; discern,* but no **cern; nonplussed,* but no **plussed; downhearted* but no **hearted,* and others to be seen in this section's epigraph.

The morpheme *huckle,* when joined with *berry,* has the meaning of a berry that is small, round, and purplish blue; *luke* when combined with *warm* has the meaning "somewhat." Both these morphemes and others like them (*cran, boysen*) are bound morphemes that convey meaning only in combination.

Rules of Word Formation

"I never heard of 'Uglification,'" Alice ventured to say. "What is it?" The Gryphon lifted up both its paws in surprise. "Never heard of uglifying!" it exclaimed. "You know what to beautify is, I suppose?" "Yes," said Alice doubtfully: "it means—to make—prettier." "Well, then," the Gryphon went on, "if you don't know what to uglify is, you are a simpleton."

LEWIS CARROLL, *Alice's Adventures in Wonderland,* 1865

When the Mock Turtle listed the branches of Arithmetic for Alice as "Ambition, Distraction, Uglification, and Derision," Alice was very confused. She wasn't really a simpleton, since *uglification* was not a common word in English until Lewis Carroll used it. Still, most English speakers would immediately know the meaning of *uglification* even if they had never heard or used the word before because they would know the meaning of its individual parts—the root *ugly* and the affixes *-ify* and *-cation.*

We said earlier that knowledge of morphology includes knowledge of individual morphemes, their pronunciation, their meaning, and knowledge of the rules for combining them into complex words. The Mock Turtle added *-ify* to the adjective *ugly* and formed a verb. Many verbs in English have been formed from adjectives in this way: *purify, amplify, simplify, falsify*; and from nouns, too: *objectify, glorify, personify*. Notice that the Mock Turtle went even further: he added the suffix *-cation* to *uglify* and formed a noun, *uglification*, as in *glorification, simplification, falsification,* and *purification*. By using the **morphological rules** of English, he created a new word. The rules that he used are as follows:

Adjective + ify	→	Verb	"to make Adjective"
Verb + cation	→	Noun	"the process of making Adjective"

Derivational Morphology

Macnelly/King Features Syndicate

Bound morphemes such as *-ify, - cation,* and *- arian* are called **derivational morphemes**. When they are added to a base, a new word with a new meaning is derived. The addition of *-ify* to *pure*—*purify*—means "to make pure," and the addition of *-cation*—*purification*—means "the process of making pure." If we invent an adjective, *pouzy*, to describe the effect of static electricity on hair, you will immediately understand the sentences "Walking on that carpet really pouzified my hair" and "The best method of pouzification is to rub a balloon on your head." This means that we must have a list of the derivational morphemes in our mental dictionaries as well as the rules that determine how they are added to a root or stem. The form that results from the addition of a derivational morpheme is called a **derived word**.

Derivational morphemes have clear semantic content. In this sense, they are like content words, except that they are not words. As we have seen, when a derivational morpheme is added to a base, it adds meaning. The derived word may also be of a different grammatical class than the original word, as shown by suffixes such as *-able* and *-en*. When a verb is suffixed with *-able*, the result is an adjective, as in *desire + able*. When the suffix *-en* is added to an adjective, a verb is derived, as in *dark + en*. One may form a noun from an adjective, as in *sweet + ie*. Other examples are:

Noun to Adjective	Verb to Noun	Adjective to Adverb
boy + -ish	acquitt + -al	exact + -ly
virtu + -ous	clear + -ance	**Noun to Adverb**
Elizabeth + -an	accus + -ation	
pictur + -esque	sing + -er	home + -ward
affection + -ate	conform + -ist	side + -ways
health + -ful	predict + -ion	length + -wise
alcohol + -ic		

Noun to Verb	Adjective to Noun	Verb to Adjective
moral + -ize	tall + -ness	read + -able
vaccin + -ate	specific + -ity	creat + -ive
hast + -en	feudal + -ism	migrat + -ory
im- + prison	free + -dom	run(n) + -y
be- + friend		
en- + joy		
in- + habit		

Adjective to Verb

en- + large
en- + dear
en- + rich

Some derivational affixes do not cause a change in grammatical class.

Noun to Noun	Verb to Verb	Adjective to Adjective
friend + -ship	un- + do	pink + -ish
human + -ity	re- + cover	red + -like
king + -dom	dis- + believe	a- + moral
New Jersey + -ite	auto- + destruct	il- + legal
vicar + -age		in- + accurate
Paul + -ine		un- + happy
America + -n		semi- + annual
libr(ary) + -arian		dis- + agreeable
mono- + theism		sub- + minimal
dis- + advantage		
ex- + wife		
auto- + biography		
un- + employment		

When a new word enters the lexicon by the application of morphological rules, other complex derivations may be **blocked**. For example, when *Commun + ist* entered the language, words such as *Commun + ite* (as in *Trotsky + ite*) or *Commun + ian* (as in *grammar + ian*) were not needed; their formation was blocked. Sometimes, however, alternative forms do coexist: for example, *Chomskyan* and *Chomskyist* and perhaps even *Chomskyite* (all meaning "follower of Chomsky's views of linguistics"). *Semanticist* and *semantician* are both used for linguists who study meaning in language, but the possible word *semantite* is not.

Finally, derivational affixes appear to come in two classes. In one class, the addition of a suffix triggers subtle changes in pronunciation. For example, when we affix *-ity* to *specific* (pronounced "specifik" with a *k* sound), we get specificity (pronounced "specifisity" with an *s* sound). When deriving *Elizabeth* + *-an* from *Elizabeth*, the fourth vowel sound changes from the vowel in *Beth* to the vowel in *Pete*. Other suffixes such as *-y, -ive,* and *-ize* may induce similar changes: *sane/sanity, deduce/deductive, critic/criticize.*

On the other hand, suffixes such as *-er, -ful, -ish, -less, -ly,* and *-ness* may be tacked onto a base word without affecting the pronunciation, as in *baker, wishful, boyish, needless, sanely,* and *fullness.* Moreover, affixes from the first class cannot be attached to a base containing an affix from the second class: **need + less + ity, *moral + ize + ive*; but affixes from the second class may attach to bases with either kind of affix: *moral + iz(e) + er, need + less + ness.*

Inflectional Morphology

Zits Partnership/King Features Syndicate

Function words such as *to, it,* and *be* are free morphemes. Many languages, including English, also have bound morphemes that have a strictly grammatical function. They mark properties such as tense, number, person, and so forth. Such bound morphemes are called **inflectional morphemes.** Unlike derivational morphemes, they never change the grammatical category of the stems to which they are attached. Consider the forms of the verb in the following sentences:

1. I sail the ocean blue.
2. He sails the ocean blue.
3. John sailed the ocean blue.
4. John has sailed the ocean blue.
5. John is sailing the ocean blue.

In sentence (2) the *-s* at the end of the verb is an agreement marker; it signifies that the subject of the verb is third-person and is singular, and that the verb is in the present tense. It doesn't add lexical meaning. The suffix *-ed* indicates past tense, and is also required by the syntactic rules of the language when verbs are used with auxiliary *have,* just as *-ing* is required when verbs are used with auxiliary *be.* (This will be discussed in Chapter 3.)

Inflectional morphemes represent relationships between different parts of a sentence. For example, *-s* expresses the relationship between the verb and the third-person singular subject; -*ed* expresses the relationship between the time the utterance is spoken (e.g., now) and the time of the event (past). If you say "John danced," the -*ed* affix places the activity before the utterance time. Inflectional morphology is closely connected to the syntax and semantics of the sentence.

English also has other inflectional endings, such as the plural suffix, which is attached to certain singular nouns, as in *boy/boys* and *cat/cats*. In contrast to Old and Middle English, which were more richly inflected languages, as we discuss in Chapter 8, Modern English has only eight bound inflectional affixes:

English	Inflectional Morphemes	Examples
-s	third-person singular present	She wait-s at home.
-ed	past tense	She wait-ed at home.
-ing	progressive	She is eat-ing the donut.
-en	past participle	Mary has eat-en the donuts.
-s	plural	She ate the donut-s.
-'s	possessive	Disa's hair is short.
-er	comparative	Disa has short-er hair than Karin.
-est	superlative	Disa has the short-est hair.

Inflectional morphemes in English follow the derivational morphemes in a word. Thus, to the derivationally complex word *commit* + *ment* one can add a plural ending to form *commit* + *ment* + *s*, but the order of affixes may not be reversed to derive the impossible *commit* + *s* + *ment* = **commitsment*.

Yet another distinction between inflectional and derivational morphemes is that all inflectional morphemes are **productive**: They apply freely to nearly every appropriate base (except "irregular" forms such as *feet*, not **foots*). Most nouns take an -*s* inflectional suffix to form a plural and most verbs take -*ed* to form a past tense, and any new verb added to the language will immediately take these inflections, witness *tweets, tweeting, tweeted*. Derivational morphemes vary a lot in their productivity; only some nouns take the derivational suffix -*ize* to form a verb: *idolize*, but not **picturize*, while -*er* can attach to almost any verb (even very new ones) to make an agent, *sing/singer, dance/dancer, blog/blogger, tweet/tweeter*.

Compared to many languages of the world, English has relatively little inflectional morphology. Some languages are highly inflected. In Swahili, which is widely spoken in eastern Africa, verbs can be inflected with multiple morphemes, as in *kimeanguka* (ki + me + anguka), meaning "it has fallen." Here the verb root *anguka* meaning "fall" has two inflectional prefixes: *ki-* meaning "it" and *me* meaning "completed action." (See Exercise 9.)

Even the more familiar European languages have many more inflectional endings than English. In the Romance languages (languages descended from Latin), the verb has different inflectional endings depending on the subject of the sentence. The verb is inflected to agree in person and number with the subject, as illustrated by the Italian verb *parlare* meaning "to speak":

Io parl**o**	"I speak"	Noi parl**iamo**	"We speak"
Tu parl**i**	"You (singular) speak"	Voi parl**ate**	"You (plural) speak"
Lui/Lei parl**a**	"He/she speaks"	Loro parl**ano**	"They speak"

Russian has a system of inflectional suffixes for nouns that indicates the nouns grammatical relation—whether a subject (nominative), direct object (accusative), indirect object (dative), possessor (genitive), and so on—something English usually does with word order or prepositions:

Russian	Case	Translation
Drug čitaet	nominative	"a friend is reading"
Ja vstretil drug**a**	accusative	"I met a friend"
Ja dala èto drug**u**	dative	"I gave it to a friend"
Bereg rek**i**	genitive	"the bank of the river"
Ja pišu karandaš**om**	instrumental	"I write with a pencil"
Cvety stojat na stol**e**	prepositional	"the flowers are on the table"

The grammatical relation of a noun in a sentence is called the **case** of the noun. When case is marked by inflectional morphemes (the boldfaced underline suffixes), the process is referred to as **case morphology**. Russian has a rich case morphology, whereas English case morphology is limited to the one possessive -'s and to its system of pronouns: *I-me-my-mine, you-you-your-yours, he-him-his-his, she-her-her-hers, they-them-their-theirs, we-us-our-ours*. Many of the grammatical relations that Russian expresses with its case morphology are expressed in English with prepositions, as the translations to English indicate.

Among the world's languages is a richness and variety of inflectional processes. Earlier we saw how German uses circumfixes to inflect a verb stem to produce a past particle: *lieb* to **geliebt**, similar to the -*ed* ending of English. Arabic infixes vowels for inflectional purposes: *kitàab* "book" but *kútub* "books." Samoan (see Exercise 10) uses a process of **reduplication**—inflecting a word through the repetition of part or all of the word: *savali* "he travels," but *savavali* "they travel." Malay does the same with whole words: *orang* "person," but *orang orang* "people." Languages such as Finnish have an extraordinarily complex case morphology, whereas Mandarin Chinese lacks case morphology entirely.

Inflection achieves a variety of purposes. In English, verbs are inflected with -*s* to show third-person singular agreement. Languages such as Finnish and Japanese have a dazzling array of inflectional processes for conveying everything from "temporary state of being" (Finnish nouns) to "strong negative intention" (Japanese verbs). English spoken 1,000 years ago had considerably more inflectional morphology than Modern English, as we shall discuss in Chapter 8.

The differences between inflectional and derivational morphemes in Modern English are summarized in the table below and in Figure 2.1 that follows it:

Inflectional	Derivational
Grammatical function	Lexical function
No word class change	May cause word class change
Small or no meaning change	Some meaning change
Often required by rules of grammar	Never required by rules of grammar
Follow derivational morphemes in a word	Precede inflectional morphemes in a word
Productive	Some productive, many nonproductive

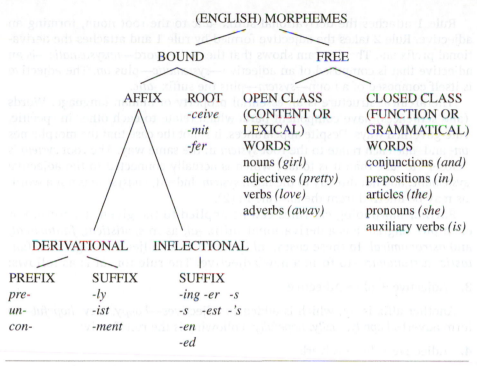

(ENGLISH) MORPHEMES

BOUND   FREE

AFFIX   ROOT   OPEN CLASS   CLOSED CLASS
        -ceive   (CONTENT OR   (FUNCTION OR
        -mit   LEXICAL)   GRAMMATICAL)
        -fer   WORDS   WORDS
                  nouns *(girl)*   conjunctions *(and)*
                  adjectives *(pretty)* prepositions *(in)*
                  verbs *(love)*   articles *(the)*
                  adverbs *(away)*   pronouns *(she)*
                                    auxiliary verbs *(is)*

DERIVATIONAL   INFLECTIONAL

PREFIX   SUFFIX   SUFFIX
pre-   *-ly*   *-ing -er -s*
un-   *-ist*   *-s -est -'s*
con-   *-ment*   *-en*
                   -ed

FIGURE 2.1 | Classification of English morphemes.

The Hierarchical Structure of Words

We saw earlier that morphemes are added in a fixed order. This order reflects the *hierarchical structure* of the word, entirely analogous to the hierarchical structure of sentences that we observed in the previous chapter. A word is not a simple sequence of morphemes just as a sentence is not a simple sequence of words. It has an internal structure. For example, the word *unsystematic* is composed of three morphemes: *un-*, *system,* and *-atic*. The root is *system,* a noun, to which we add the suffix *-atic,* resulting in an adjective, *systematic*. To this adjective, we add the prefix *un-,* forming a new adjective, *unsystematic*.

The hierarchical organization of words can be represented using tree diagrams, as illustrated for *unsystematic*:

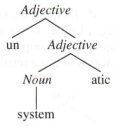

Adjective

un   *Adjective*

Noun   atic

system

This tree represents the application of two morphological rules:

1. Noun + atic → Adjective
2. un + Adjective → Adjective

Rule 1 attaches the derivational suffix *-atic* to the root noun, forming an adjective. Rule 2 takes the adjective formed by rule 1 and attaches the derivational prefix *un-*. The diagram shows that the entire word—*unsystematic*—is an adjective that is composed of an adjective—*systematic*—plus *un*. The adjective is itself composed of a noun—*system*—plus the suffix *-atic*.

Hierarchical structure is an essential property of human language. Words (and sentences) have component parts which relate to each other in specific, rule-governed ways. Despite appearances, it is not the case that the morphemes *un-* and *-atic* each relate to the root *system* in the same way. The root *system* is "closer" to *-atic* than it is to *un-,* which is actually connected to the adjective *systematic,* and not directly to the noun *system.* Indeed, **unsystem* is not a word, as may be inferred from the *un-* rule in (2).

Further morphological rules can be applied to the given structure. For example, English has a derivational suffix *-al,* as in *egotistical, fantastical,* and *astronomical.* In these cases, *-al* is added to an adjective—*egotistic, fantastic, astronomic*—to form a new adjective. The rule for *-al* is as follows:

3.   Adjective + al → Adjective

Another affix is *-ly,* which is added to adjectives—*happy, lazy, hopeful*—to form adverbs *happily, lazily, hopefully.* Following is the rule for *-ly:*

4.   Adjective + ly → Adverb

Applying these two rules to the derived form *unsystematic,* we get the following tree for *unsystematically:*

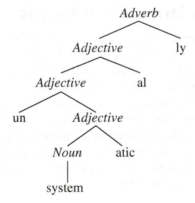

This is a rather complex word. Despite its complexity, it is well-formed because it follows the morphological rules of the language. On the other hand, a very simple word can be ungrammatical. Suppose in the above example we first added *un-* to the root *system.* That would have resulted in the nonword **unsystem.*

Unsystem is not a possible word because the rule of English that allows *un-* to be added to nouns is restricted to very few cases, and those are always nouns that already have a suffix such as *un + employment, un +cceptance* or *un + feasability*. The large soft-drink company whose ad campaign promoted the *Uncola* successfully flouted this linguistic rule to capture people's attention. Part of our linguistic competence includes the ability to recognize possible versus impossible words, such as **unsystem* and **Uncola*. Possible words are those that conform to the rules; impossible words are those that do not.

Tree diagrams make explicit the way speakers represent the internal structure of sentences as well as morphologically complex words. In speaking and writing, we appear to string morphemes together sequentially as in *un + system + atic*. However, our mental representation of words is hierarchical as well as linear, and this is shown by tree diagrams.

Inflectional morphemes are equally well represented. The following tree shows that the inflectional agreement morpheme *-s* follows the derivational morphemes *-ize* and *re-* in *refinalizes*:

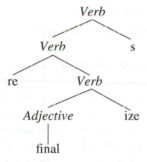

The tree also shows that *re-* applies to *finalize,* which is correct as **refinal* is not a word, and that the inflectional morpheme follows the derivational morpheme.

The hierarchical organization of words is even more clearly shown by structurally ambiguous words, words that have more than one meaning by virtue of having more than one structure. Consider the word *unlockable*. Imagine you are inside a room and you want some privacy. You would be unhappy to find the door is *unlockable*—"not able to be locked." Now imagine you are inside a locked room trying to get out. You would be very relieved to find that the door is *unlockable*—"able to be unlocked." These two meanings correspond to two different structures, as follows:

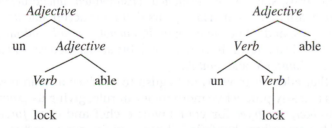

In the first structure, the verb *lock* combines with the suffix *-able* to form an adjective *lockable* ("able to be locked"). Then, the prefix *un-,* meaning "not," combines with the derived adjective to form a new adjective *unlockable*

("not able to be locked"). In the second case, the prefix *un-* combines with the verb *lock* to form a derived verb *unlock*. Then, the derived verb combines with the suffix *-able* to form *unlockable,* "able to be unlocked."

An entire class of words in English follows this pattern: *unbuttonable, unzippable,* and *unlatchable,* among others. The ambiguity arises because the prefix *un-* can combine with an adjective, as illustrated in rule 2, or it can combine with a verb, as in *undo, unstaple, unearth,* and *unloosen.*

If words were only strings of morphemes without any internal organization, we could not explain the ambiguity of words such as *unlockable.* These words also illustrate another key point, which is that structure is important to determining meaning. The same three morphemes occur in both versions of *unlockable,* yet there are two distinct meanings. The different meanings arise because of the different structures.

Rule Productivity

"Curiouser and curiouser!" cried Alice (she was so much surprised, that for the moment she quite forgot how to speak good English).

LEWIS CARROLL, *Alice's Adventures in Wonderland*, 1865

We have noted that some morphological processes, inflection in particular, are productive, meaning that they can be used freely to form new words from the list of free and bound morphemes. Among derivational morphemes, the suffix *-able* can be conjoined with any verb to derive an adjective with the meaning of the verb and the meaning of *-able,* which is something like "able to be" as in *accept + able, laugh + able, pass + able, change + able, breathe + able, adapt + able,* and so on. The productivity of this rule is illustrated by the fact that we find *-able* affixed to new verbs such as *tweetable,* meaning a message suitable for posting on Twitter (140 characters or fewer).

The prefix *un-* derives same-class words with an opposite meaning: *unafraid, unfit, un-American,* and so on. Additionally, *un-* can be added to derived adjectives that have been formed by morphological rules, resulting in perfectly acceptable words such as *un + believe + able* or *un + pick + up + able.*

Yet, *un-* is not fully productive. We find *happy* and *unhappy, cowardly* and *uncowardly,* but not *sad* and **unsad, brave* and **unbrave,* or *obvious* and **unobvious.* It appears that the "un-Rule" is most productive for adjectives that are derived from verbs, such as *unenlightened, unsimplified, uncharacterized, unauthorized,* and *undistinguished.* It also appears that most acceptable *un-*words have polysyllabic bases, and while we have *unfit, uncool, unread,* and *unclean,* many of the unacceptable *un-* forms have monosyllabic stems such as **unbig, *ungreat, *unred, *unsad, *unsmall,* and **untall.*

The rule that adds *-er* to verbs in English to produce a noun meaning "one who does" is a nearly productive morphological rule, giving us *examiner, exam-taker, sleepwalker, stir-fryer* for your favorite chef and even *force-feeder* for *thwarters* of *hunger-strikers,* but fails full productivity owing to "unwords" such as **chairer,* which is not "one who chairs."

The "other" *-er* suffix, the one that means "more" as in *greedier,* also fails to be entirely productive as Alice's **curiouser* points out. The more syllables a word has, the less likely *-er* will work and we will need the word *more,* as in *more beau-tiful* (but not **beautifuler*) compared with the well-formed *prettier* and *lovelier.*

Other derivational morphemes fall farther short of productivity. Consider:

sincerity	from	*sincere*
warmth	from	*warm*
moisten	from	*moist*

The suffix *-ity* is found in many other words in English, such as *chastity, scarcity,* and *curiosity;* and *-th* occurs in *health, wealth, depth, width,* and *growth.* We find *-en* in *sadden, ripen, redden, weaken,* and *deepen.* Still, the phrase "*The tragicity of Hamlet" sounds somewhat strange, as does "*I'm going to *heaten* the sauce." Someone may say *coolth,* but when "words" such as *tragicity, heaten,* and *coolth* are used, it is usually either a slip of the tongue or an attempt at humor. Most adjectives will not accept any of these derivational suffixes.

Even less productive to the point of rareness are such derivational mor-phemes as the diminutive suffixes in the words *pig* + *let* and *sap* + *ling.*

In the morphologically complex words that we have seen so far, we can generally predict the meaning based on the meanings of the morphemes that make up the word. *Unhappy* means "not happy" and *acceptable* means "fit to be accepted." However, one cannot always know the meaning of the words derived from free and derivational morphemes by knowing the morphemes themselves. The following *un-* forms have unpredictable meanings:

unloosen	"loosen, let loose"
unrip	"rip, undo by ripping"
undo	"reverse doing"
untread	"go back through in the same steps"
unearth	"dig up"
unfrock	"deprive (a cleric) of ecclesiastic rank"
unnerve	"fluster"

Morphologically complex words whose meanings are not predictable must be listed individually in our mental lexicons. However, the morphological rules must also be in the grammar, revealing the relation between words and provid-ing the means for forming new words.

Exceptions and Suppletions

The exception gives Authority to the Rule

GIOVANNI TORRIANO, *A Common Place of Italian Proverbs*, 1666

The morphological rule that forms plural nouns from singular nouns does not apply to words like *child, man, foot,* and *mouse.* These words are exceptions to the rule. Similarly, verbs such as *go, sing, bring, run,* and *know* are exceptions to the inflectional rule for producing past-tense verbs in English. These exceptional forms must be stored in the lexicon. There are therefore two mechanisms for forming complex words; regular forms such as *danced* and *books* are formed by applying morphological rules to the base morpheme, which is stored in the lexicon. Irregu-lar, also called **suppletive**, forms must be retrieved directly from the lexicon.

When children are learning English (or any other language), they first learn the regular rules, which they apply to all forms. Thus, we often hear them say *mans* and *goed*. Later in the acquisition process, they specifically learn irregular plurals such as *men* and *mice*, and irregular past tense forms such as *came* and *went*. These children's errors are actually evidence that the regular rules exist. It also suggests that the "rule route" for forming complex words is more accessible to the child than accessing irregular forms in the lexicon. Children's morphological learning is discussed more fully in Chapter 9.

When a new word enters the language, the regular inflectional rules generally apply. The plural of *geek*, when it was a new word in English, was *geeks*, not **geeken*, although we are advised that some geeks wanted the plural of *fax* to be **faxen*, like *oxen*, when *fax* entered the language as a shortened form of *facsimile*. Never fear: its plural is *faxes*. The exception to this may be a word "borrowed" from a foreign language. For example, the plural of Latin *datum* has always been *data*, never *datums*, though nowadays *data*, the one-time plural, is treated by many as a singular word like *information*.

The past tense of the verb *hit*, as in the sentence *Yesterday you hit the ball*, and the plural of the noun *sheep* as in *The sheep are in the meadow*, show that some morphemes have no phonological shape at all. We know that *hit* in the above sentence is *hit + past* because of the time adverb *yesterday*, and we know that *sheep* is the phonetic form of *sheep + plural* because of the plural verb form *are*.

When a verb is derived from a noun, even if it is pronounced the same as an irregular verb, the regular rules apply to it. Thus, *ring*, when used in the sense of encircle, is derived from the noun *ring*, and as a verb it is regular. We say *the police ringed the bank with armed men*, not **rang the bank with armed men*. In the jargon of baseball one says that *the hitter flied out* (hit a lofty ball that was caught), rather than **flew out*, because the verb came from the compound noun *fly ball*.

Lexical Gaps

The vast majority of letter (sound) sequences that could be words of English—*crint, spleek, feg*—are not. Similar comments apply to morphological derivations like *disobvious* or *inobvious*. "Words" that conform to the rules of word formation but are not truly part of the vocabulary are called **accidental gaps** or **lexical gaps**. Accidental gaps are well-formed but non-existing words.

The actual words in a language constitute a mere subset of the possible words. There are always gaps in the lexicon—words not present but that could be added. Some of the gaps are due to the fact that a permissible sound sequence has no meaning attached to it (such as *blick,* or *slarm,* or *krobe*). The sequence of sounds must be in keeping with the constraints of the language, however; **bnick* is not a "gap" because no word in English can begin with *bn*. We will discuss such constraints in chapter 6.

Other gaps result when possible combinations of morphemes never come into use. Speakers can distinguish between impossible words such as **unsystem* and **needlessity* and possible but nonexisting words such as *magnificenter* or *disobvious* (cf. *distrustful*). The latter are blocked, as noted earlier, owing to the presence of *more magnificent* and *nonobvious*. Psycholinguistic experiments show that listeners respond more slowly to "possible" nonwords such as *floop* and *plim* than to "impossible" nonwords such as *tlat* and *mrock* (see Chapter 10). The ability to make this distinction is further evidence that the morphological component of our mental grammar consists of not just a lexicon—a list of existing words—but also of rules that enable us to create and understand new words, and to recognize possible and impossible words.

Other Morphological Processes

The various kinds of affixation that we have discussed are by far the most common morphological processes among the world's languages. But, as we continue to emphasize in this book, the human language capacity is enormously creative, and that creativity extends to ways other than affixation in which words may be altered and created.

Back-Formations

> [A girl] was delighted by her discovery that *eats* and *cats* were really *eat* + *-s* and *cat* + *-s.* She used her new suffix snipper to derive *mik* (mix), *upstair, downstair, clo* (clothes), *len* (lens), *brefek* (from *brefeks,* her word for breakfast), *trappy* (trapeze), even *Santa Claw.*
>
> STEVEN PINKER, *Words and Rules: The Ingredients of Language,* 1999

Misconception can sometimes be creative, and nothing in this world both misconceives and creates like a child, as we shall see in Chapter 9. A new word may enter the language because of an incorrect morphological analysis. *Peddle* was derived from *peddler* on the mistaken assumption that the *-er* was the agentive suffix. Such words are called **back-formations**. The verbs *hawk, stoke, swindle, burgle,* and *edit* all came into the language as back-formations—of *hawker, stoker, swindler, burglar,* and *editor*. *Pea* was derived from a singular word, *pease,* by speakers who thought *pease* was a plural.

Some word creation comes from deliberately miscast back-formations. The word *bikini* comes from the Bikini atoll of the Marshall Islands. Because the first syllable *bi-* is a morpheme meaning "two" in words like *bicycle,* some clever person called a topless bathing suit a *monokini* and a tank top with a bikini bottom a *tankini.* Historically, a number of new words have entered the English lexicon in a similar way, some of the most recent being the *appletini, chocotini, mintini,* and *God-knows-what-else-tini* to be found as flavor additives to the traditional martini libation. Based on analogy with such pairs as *act/action, exempt/exemption,* and *revise/revision,* new words *resurrect, preempt,* and *televise* were formed from the existing words *resurrection, preemption,* and *television.*

Language purists sometimes rail against back-formations and cite *enthuse* and *liaise* (from *enthusiasm* and *liaison*) as examples of language corruption. However, language is not corrupt; it is adaptable and changeable. Don't be surprised to discover in your lifetime that *shevelled* and *chalant* have infiltrated the English language (from *disheveled* and *nonchalant*) to mean "tidy" and "concerned," and if it happens do not cry "havoc" and let slip the dogs of prescriptivism; all will be well.

Compounds

[T]he Houynhnms have no Word in their Language to express any thing that is evil, except what they borrow from the Deformities or ill Qualities of the Yahoos. Thus they denote the Folly of a Servant, an Omission of a Child, a Stone that cuts their feet, a Continuance of foul or unseasonable Weather, and the like, by adding to each the Epithet of Yahoo. For instance, Hnhm Yahoo, Whnaholm Yahoo, Ynlhmnawihlma Yahoo, and an ill contrived House, Ynholmhnmrohlnw Yahoo.

JONATHAN SWIFT, *Gulliver's Travels*, 1726

Two or more words may be joined to form new, compound words. English is very flexible in the kinds of combinations permitted, as the following table of compounds shows.

	Adjective	Noun	Verb
Adjective	bittersweet	smartwatch	whitewash
Noun	headstrong	homework	spoonfeed
Verb	feel-good	pickpocket	sleepwalk
Preposition	overeager	outpatient	undergo

Some compounds that have been recently introduced into English are *Facebook, LinkedIn, android apps, e-commerce, crowdfunding, cyber café, flash mob,* and *robocall.*

In English, the rightmost word in a compound is the **head** of the compound. The head is the part of a word or phrase that determines its broad meaning and grammatical category. The head of the compound *smartwatch* is *watch,* which determines the core meaning (*smartwatch* is a kind of watch), and syntactic category (*watch* is a noun so *smartwatch* is also a noun). The head of *sleepwalk* (a kind of walking) is *walk,* a verb, so *sleepwalk* is also a verb. If you go through the examples given above, you will see that they mostly conform to this "right-hand head rule." But there are exceptions. Compounds whose rightmost member is a preposition are not themselves prepositions. A *meet-up* is a kind of meeting, not a direction, *meltdown* and *knockout* are nouns, not prepositions. This is further evidence that prepositions form a closed-class category that does not readily admit new members, in contrast to nouns, verbs, and adjectives.

Some compounds are said to be "unheaded" because the rightmost member does not determine their core meaning. An example is *flatfoot*, which is not a kind of *foot*, but a slang term meaning policeman. *Policeman* is also a compound, but unlike *flatfoot*, it is headed by *man*. A policeman is a kind of man. The head of a compound transmits not only its meaning and syntactic category to the compound, but also whatever irregular morphological form it takes. The plural of *man* is the irregular form *men* and the plural of *policeman* is *policemen* (same for *policewomen*). But in the case of unheaded compounds such as *flatfoot*, irregular morphology is not inherited by the compound—just as the meaning is not inherited. A *flatfoot* is not a kind of foot, and its plural is not *flatfeet*, but rather *flatfoots*. It undergoes the regular rule. Absent a head the compound transmits neither its meaning nor its irregular morphology. Similar examples are given below:

walkman	*walkmen	walkmans	(device for playing music)
sabertooth	*saberteeth	sabertooths	(extinct species of tiger)
lowlife	*lowlives	lowlifes	(a disreputable person)

There are a few English compounds that appear to be left-headed. An *attorney-general* is not a general but an attorney, a *mother-in-law* is a kind of mother. A *passer-by* is a person who passes. In these and similar cases the, plural inflection occurs "inside" the compound, on the head, *attorneys-general*, *passers-by*, *sons-in-law*, *courts-martial*, *sergeants-major*. Many of these left-headed compounds are legal or military terms. They were borrowed into English from French—a language in which adjectives follow nouns—during the Norman occupation of England when French was used for legal, military, and other affairs of state (see Chapter 8). It is fair to say, however, that for many people outside the military and legal professions these compounds behave like regular plurals, *attorney generals*, *court-martials*, and so on.

Although two-word compounds are the most common in English, it would be difficult to state an upper limit: Consider *three-time loser, four-dimensional space-time, sergeant-at-arms, mother-of-pearl, master of ceremonies, daughter-in-law*, and the military slang *fire-in-the-hole* meaning "watch out!"

Spelling does not tell us what sequence of words constitutes a compound; whether a compound is spelled with a space between the two words, with a hyphen, or with no separation at all depends on the idiosyncrasies of the particular compound, as shown in *blackbird, six-pack*, and *smoke screen*.

Like derived words, compounds have internal structure. This is clear from the ambiguity of a compound such as *top + hat + rack*, which can mean "a rack for top hats" corresponding to the structure in tree diagram (1), or "the highest hat rack," corresponding to the structure in (2).

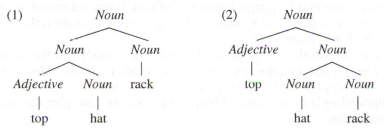

Meaning of Compounds

The head of compound carries its core or basic meaning. *Homework* is a kind of work done at home. But the meaning of a compound is not always simply the sum of the meanings of its parts; a *blackboard* may be green or white, an online newspaper is still a *newspaper* though no paper is involved, an albino *goldfish* would still be a goldfish, and a rattlesnake, though more stealthy, remains a *rattlesnake* even without its rattle.

Other compounds reveal other meaning relations between the parts, which are not entirely consistent because many compounds are idiomatic (idioms are discussed in Chapter 4). A *boathouse* is a house for boats, but a *cathouse* is not a house for cats. (It is slang for a house of prostitution or whorehouse.) A *jumping bean* is a bean that jumps, a *falling star* is a star that (appears to) fall, and a *magnifying glass* is a glass that magnifies; but a *looking glass* is not a glass that looks, nor is an *eating apple* an apple that eats, and *laughing gas* does not laugh. *Peanut oil* and *olive oil* are oils made from something, but what about *baby oil*? And is this a contradiction: "horse meat is dog meat"? Not at all, since the first is meat *from* horses and the other is meat *for* dogs.

In the examples so far, the meaning of each compound includes at least to some extent the meanings of the individual parts. However, many compounds nowadays do not seem to relate to the meanings of the individual parts at all. A *jack-in-a-box* is a tropical tree, and a *turncoat* is a traitor. A *highbrow* does not necessarily have a high brow, nor does a *bigwig* have a big wig, nor does an *egghead* have an egg-shaped head.

Like certain words with the prefix *un-*, the meaning of many compounds must be learned as if they were individual whole words. Some of the meanings may be figured out, but not all. If you had never heard the word *hunchback,* it might be possible to infer the meaning; but if you had never heard the word *flatfoot,* it is doubtful you would know it means "detective" or "policeman," even though the origin of the word, once you know the meaning, can be figured out.

The pronunciation of English compounds differs from the way we pronounce the sequence of two words that are not compounded. In an actual compound, the first word is usually stressed (pronounced somewhat louder and higher in pitch), and in a noncompound phrase the second word is stressed. Thus, we stress *hot* in *hotdog* the food, but *dog* in *hot dog* the canine. (Stress, pitch, and other similar features are discussed in Chapters 5 and 6.)

Universality of Compounding

Other languages have rules for conjoining words to form compounds, as seen by French *cure-dent,* "toothpick"; German *Panzerkraftwagen,* "armored car"; Russian *cetyrexetaznyi,* "four-storied"; and Spanish *tocadiscos,* "record player." In the Native American language Tohono O'odham, the word meaning "thing" is *haʔichu,* and it combines with *doakam,* "living creatures," to form the compound *haʔichu doakam,* "animal life."

In Thai, the word "cat" is *mɛɛw,* the word for "watch" (in the sense of "to watch over") is *fâw,* and the word for "house" is *bâan.* The word for "watch cat" (like a watchdog) is the compound *mɛɛwfâwbâan*—literally, "catwatchhouse."

Compounding is a common and frequent process for enlarging the vocabulary of all languages.

"Malapropisms"

A malapropism is the confusion of a word through misinterpretation of its morphemes, usually with a humorous effect. Such "mistakes" reveal much of the lexical knowledge of the speaker. Here are a few examples. Many more circulate on the Internet.

Word	Humorous Definition
abdicate	to give up all hope of ever having a flat stomach
adamant	pertaining to original sin
circumvent	opening in the front of boxer shorts worn by Jewish men
coffee	the person upon whom one coughs
deciduous	able to make up one's mind
flabbergasted	appalled over how much weight you have gained
frisbeetarianism	the belief that after death your soul flies up and gets stuck in a tree
gubernatorial	having to do with peanuts
gullible	to do with seabirds
longevity	being very tall
metronome	a city dwelling diminutive troll
oxymoron	a really stupid cow
polyglot	more than one glot

The poor English-class student who used the word *indefatigable* in the sentence

> She tried many reducing diets, but remained indefatigable.

clearly shows morphological knowledge: *in* meaning "not" as in *ineffective*; *de* meaning "off" as in *decapitate*; "fat" as in fat; *able* as in *able*; and combined meaning, "not able to take the fat off."

Sign Language Morphology

Sign languages are rich in morphology. They have root and affix morphemes, free and bound morphemes, lexical and grammatical morphemes, derivational and inflectional morphemes, and morphological rules for their combination to form morphologically complex signs. The affixation is accomplished by preceding or following a particular gesture with another "affixing" gesture.

The suffix meaning "negation," roughly analogous to *un-* or *non-* or *dis-*, is accomplished as a rapid turning over of the hand(s) following the end of the root sign that is being negated. For example, "want" is signed with open palms facing upward; "don't want" follows that gesture with a turning of the palms to face downward. This "reversal of orientation" suffix may be applied, with necessary adjustments, to many root signs.

In sign language, many morphological processes are not linear. Rather, the sign stem occurs nested within various movements and locations in signing space so that the gestures are simultaneous, an impossibility with spoken languages.

Inflection of sign roots also occurs in ASL and all other sign languages, which characteristically modify the movement of the hands and the spatial contours of the area near the body in which the signs are articulated. For example, movement away from the signer's body toward the "listener" might inflect a verb as in "I see you," whereas movement away from the listener and toward the body would inflect the verb as in "you see me."

Morphological Analysis: Identifying Morphemes

Case Study 1

As we have seen in this chapter, speakers of a language know the internal structure of words because they know the morphemes of their language and the rules for their combination. This is unconscious knowledge of course and it takes a trained linguist to make this knowledge explicit as part of a descriptive grammar of the language. The task is challenging enough when the language you are analyzing is your own, but linguists who speak one language may nevertheless analyze languages for which they are not native speakers.

Suppose you were a linguist from the planet Zorx who wanted to analyze English. How would you discover the morphemes of the language? How would you determine whether a word had one, two, or more morphemes, and what they were?

The first thing to do would be to ask native speakers how they say various words. (It would help to have a Zorxese–English interpreter along; otherwise, copious gesturing is in order.) Assume you are talented in miming and manage to collect the following forms:

Adjective	Meaning
ugly	"very unattractive"
uglier	"more ugly"
ugliest	"most ugly"
pretty	"nice looking"
prettier	"more nice looking"
prettiest	"most nice looking"
tall	"large in height"
taller	"more tall"
tallest	"most tall"

To determine what the morphemes are in such a list, the first thing a field linguist would do is to see whether some forms mean the same thing in different words, that is, to look for *recurring* forms. We find them: *ugly* occurs in *ugly, uglier,* and *ugliest,* all of which include the meaning "very unattractive." We also find that *-er* occurs in *prettier* and *taller,* adding the meaning "more" to the adjectives to which it is attached. Similarly, *-est* adds the meaning "most." Furthermore, by having our Zorxese–English interpreter pose additional questions to our native English-speaking consultant we find that *-er* and *-est* do not occur in isolation with the meanings of "more" and "most." We can therefore conclude that the following morphemes occur in English:

ugly	root morpheme
pretty	root morpheme
tall	root morpheme
-er	bound morpheme "comparative"
-est	bound morpheme "superlative"

As we proceed, we find other words that end with -er (e.g., *singer, lover, bomber, writer, teacher*) in which the -er ending does not mean "comparative" but, when attached to a verb, changes it to "a noun who 'verbs,'" (e.g., *sings, loves, bombs, writes, teaches*). So, we conclude that this is a different morpheme, even though it is pronounced the same as the comparative. We go on and find words such as *number, somber, butter,* and *member* in which the -er has no separate meaning at all—a *somber* is not "one who sombs" and a *member* does not *memb*—and therefore these words must be monomorphemic.

Case Study 2

Once you have practiced on the morphology of English, you might want to go on to describe another language. Paku was invented by the linguist Victoria Fromkin for a 1970s TV series called *Land of the Lost,* made into a major motion picture of the same name starring Will Farrell in 2009. This was the language used by the monkey people called Pakuni. Suppose you found yourself in this strange land and attempted to find out what the morphemes of Paku were. Again, you would collect your data from a native Paku speaker and proceed as the Zorxian did with English. Consider the following data from Paku:

me	"I"	meni	"we"
ye	"you (singular)"	yeni	"you (plural)"
we	"he"	weni	"they (masculine)"
wa	"she"	wani	"they (feminine)"
abuma	"girl"	abumani	"girls"
adusa	"boy"	adusani	"boys"
abu	"child"	abuni	"children"
Paku	"one Paku"	Pakuni	"more than one Paku"

By examining these words, you find that the plural forms end in -*ni* and the singular forms do not. You therefore conclude that -*ni* is a separate morpheme meaning "plural" that is attached as a suffix to a noun.

Case Study 3

Here is a more challenging example, but the principles are the same. Look for repetitions and near repetitions of the same word parts, taking your cues from the meanings given. These are words from Michoacan Aztec, an indigenous language of Mexico:

nokali	"my house"	mopelo	"your dog"
nokalimes	"my houses"	mopelomes	"your dogs"
mokali	"your house"	ikwahmili	"his cornfield"
ikali	"his house"	nokwahmili	"my cornfield"
nopelo	"my dog"	mokwahmili	"your cornfield"

We see there are three base meanings: *house, dog,* and *cornfield*. Starting with *house* we look for commonalities in all the forms that refer to "house." They all contain *kali* so that makes a good first guess. (We might, and you might, have reasonably guessed *kal,* but eventually we wouldn't know what to do with the *i* at the end of *nokali* and *mokali.*) With *kali* as "house" we may infer that *no* is a prefix meaning "my," and that is supported by *nopelo* meaning "my dog." This being the case, we guess that *pelo* is "dog," and see where that leads us. If *pelo* is "dog" and *mopelo* is "your dog," then *mo* is probably the prefix for "your." Now that we think that the possessive pronouns are prefixes, we can look at *ikali* and deduce that *i* means "his." If we're right about the prefixes, then we can separate out the word for "cornfield" as *kwahmili.* The only morpheme unaccounted for is "plural." We have two instances of plurality, *nokalimes,* and *mopelomes,* but since we know *no, kali, mo,* and *pelo,* it is straightforward to identify the plural morpheme as the suffix *mes.*

The end results of our analysis are:

kali	"house"
pelo	"dog"
kwahmili	"cornfield"
no-	"my"
mo-	"your"
i-	"his"
-mes	"plural"

Case Study 4

Here is a final example of morphological analysis complicated by some changes in spelling (pronunciation), a bit like the way we spell the indefinite article "a" as either *a* before a consonant or *an* before a vowel in English.

Often the data you are given (or record in the field) are a hodge-podge, such as these examples from a Slavic language:

gledati	"to watch"	nazivaju	"they call"
diram	"I touch"	sviranje	"playing (noun)"
nazivanje	"calling (noun)"	gladujem	"I starve"
dirati	"to touch"	kupuju	"they buy"
kupovanje	"buying (noun)"	stanovati	"to live"
sviraju	"they play"	kupujem	"I buy"
gledam	"I watch"	diranje	"touching (noun)"
stanovanje	"living (noun)"	stanujem	"I live"
diraju	"they touch"	gladovanje	"starving (noun)"
nazivati	"to call"	stanuju	"they live"
kupovati	"to buy"	gledaju	"they watch"
gladuju	"they starve"	svirati	"to play"
gladovati	"to starve"	sviram	"I play"
gledanje	"watching (noun)"	nazivam	"I call"

The first step is often merely to rearrange the data, grouping commonalities. Here, we see that after (possibly considerable) perusal, the data involve seven stems, which we group by meaning. We also note that there are exactly four forms for each stem (infinitive, I (first-person singular), they (third-person plural), and the noun form or gerund) and we fold that into the reorganization.

We even alphabetize to emphasize the orderliness. Thus, rearranged the data appear less daunting:

	touch	starve	watch	buy	call	live	play
Infinitive	dirati	gladovati	gledati	kupovati	nazivati	stanovati	svirati
1st, Sing.	diram	gladujem	gledam	kupujem	nazivam	stanujem	sviram
3rd, Plur.	diraju	gladuju	gledaju	kupuju	nazivaju	stanuju	sviraju
Noun	diranje	gladovanje	gledanje	kupovanje	nazivanje	stanovanje	sviranje

Now, the patterns become more evident. We hypothesize that in the first column *dir-* is a stem meaning "touch" and that the suffix *-ati* forms the infinitive; the suffix *-am* is the first-person singular; the suffix *-aju* is the third-person plural; and finally that the suffix *-anje* forms a noun, similar to the suffix *-ing* in English. We need to test our guess and the second column belies our hypothesis, but undaunted we push on and we see that the columns for "watch," "call," and "play" work exactly like the column for "touch," with stems *gled-, naziv-,* and *svir-.*

But columns "starve," "buy," and "live" are not cooperating. They follow the pattern for the infinitive (first row) and noun formation (fourth row), and give us stems *gladov-, kupov-,* and *stanov-* but something is awry in the second and third row for these three verbs. Instead of *-am* meaning "I" it appears to be *-em.* (Yes, it could be *-ujem* or even *-jem,* but we stay with the form that's nearest to *-am.*) So, the suffix meaning "I" has two forms, *am/em,* again analogous to the English *a/an* alternation.

But horrors, something is going haywire with the stems in just these three cases and now our effort to rearrange the data pays off. We see fairly quickly that the misbehaving cases are all verbs ending in *ov.* And if we stick with our decision that *-am/-em* means "I," then we can hypothesize that the stem alternates pronunciation in certain cases when it ends in ov, kind of like English *democrat/democracy.* If we accept this we are forced into the decision that the third-person plural morpheme also has an alternate form, namely *u,* so its two forms are *-aju/-u.*

We may sum up our analysis as follows:

Stems *dir-, gled-, naziv-, svir-* take suffixes *-ati, -am, -aju, -anje.* The verbs ending in *ov* have stems *gladov-, kupov-, stanov-* when expressed as infinitives with *-ati,* and noun-forms with *-anje;* and stems *gladuj-, kupuj-, stanuj-* when expressed as "I" with *-em* or as "they" with *-u.*

Finally, if we discover in our field work that *razarati* means "to destroy" then we immediately know that "I destroy" is *razaram,* "they destroy" is *razaraju,* and "destruction" is *razaranje.* Or, if we're told that *darujem* means "I gift" then we deduce that the noun "gift" is *darovanje,* the infinitive "to gift" is *darovati,* and "they gift" is *daruju.*

In Chapter 6, we'll see *why* the "same" morpheme may be spelled or pronounced differently in different contexts, and that the variation, like most grammatical processes, is rule-governed. By following the analytical principles discussed in the preceding four case studies you should be able to solve the morphological puzzles that appear in the exercises.

Summary

Knowing a language means knowing the **morphemes** of that language, which are the elemental units that constitute words. *Moralizers* is an English word composed of four morphemes: *moral* + *ize* + *er* + s. When you know a word or morpheme, you know both its **form** (sound or gesture) and its **meaning**; these are inseparable parts of the **linguistic sign**. The relationship between form and meaning is **arbitrary**. There is no inherent connection between them (i.e., the words and morphemes of any language must be learned).

Morphemes may be free or bound. **Free morphemes** stand alone such as *girl* or *the,* and they come in two types: **open class**, containing the content words of the language, and **closed class,** containing function words such as *the* or *of*. **Bound morphemes** may be **affixes** or bound roots such as *-ceive*. Affixes may be **prefixes, suffixes, circumfixes,** or **infixes**. Affixes may be derivational or inflectional. **Derivational affixes** derive new words; **inflectional affixes**, such as the plural affix *-s,* make grammatical changes to words. Complex words contain a **root** around which **stems** are built by affixation. Rules of morphology determine what kind of affixation produces actual words such as *un* + *system* + *atic,* and what kind produces nonwords such as **un* + *system*.

Words have hierarchical structure evidenced by ambiguous words such as *unlockable,* which may be *un* + *lockable* "unable to be locked" or *unlock* + *able* "able to be unlocked."

Some morphological rules are **productive**, meaning they apply freely to the appropriate stem; for example, *re-* applies freely to verbal stems to give words like *redo, rewash,* and *repaint*. Other rules are more constrained, forming words such as *young* + *ster* but not **smart* + *ster*. Inflectional morphology is extremely productive: the plural *-s* applies freely even to nonsense words. **Suppletive forms** escape inflectional morphology, so instead of **mans* we have *men;* instead of **bringed* we have *brought*.

There are many ways for new words to be created other than affixation. **Compounds** are formed by uniting two or more root words in a single word, such as *homework*. The **head** of the compound (the rightmost word) bears the basic meaning, so *homework* means a kind of work done at home, but often the meaning of compounds is not easily predictable and must be learned as individual lexical items, such as *laughing gas*. **Back-formations** are words created by misinterpreting an affix look-alike such as *-er* as an actual affix, so, for example, the verb *peddle* was formed under the mistaken assumption that peddler was *peddle* + *-er*.

The grammars of sign languages also include a morphological component consisting of a root, derivational and inflectional sign morphemes, and the rules for their combination.

Morphological analysis is the process of identifying form-meaning units in a language, taking into account small differences in pronunciation, so that prefixes *in-* and *im-* are seen to be variants of the "same" prefix in English (cf. *intolerable, impeccable*) just as *democrat* and *democrac* are stem variants of the same morpheme, which shows up in *democratic* with its "t" and in *democracy* with its "c."

References for Further Reading

Aronoff, M. and Fudeman, K. 2011. *What is morphology? 2nd ed.* Malden, MA: Wiley-Blackwell Publishing.

Bauer, L. 2003. *Introducing linguistic morphology, 2nd ed.* Washington, DC: Georgetown University Press.

Haspelmath, M. and Sims, A. 2010. *Understanding morphology, 2nd ed.* New York, NY: Routledge.

Katamba, F. and Stonham, J. 2006. *Morphology, 2nd ed.* New York, NY: Palgrave MacMillan.

Pinker, S. 1999. *Words and rules: the ingredients of language.* New York: Harper Collins.

Stockwell, R., and D. Minkova. 2009. *English words: History and structure, 2nd ed.* New York: Cambridge University Press.

Exercises

1. Here is how to estimate the number of words in your mental lexicon. Consult any standard dictionary. (Note that Internet dictionaries may not work for this exercise.)

   a. Count the number of entries on a typical page. They are usually boldfaced.

   b. Multiply the number of words per page by the number of pages in the dictionary.

   c. Pick four pages in the dictionary at random, say, pages 50, 75, 125, and 303. Count the number of words on these pages.

   d. How many of these words do you know?

   e. What percentage of the words on the four pages do you know?

   f. Multiply the words in the dictionary by the percentage you arrived at in (e). You know approximately that many English words.

2. Divide the following words by placing a + between their morphemes. (Some of the words may be monomorphemic and therefore indivisible.)

   Example: replaces = re + place + s

a. retroactive	**n.** airsickness
b. befriended	**o.** bureaucrat
c. televise	**p.** democrat
d. margin	**q.** aristocrat
e. endearment	**r.** plutocrat
f. psychology	**s.** democracy
g. unpalatable	**t.** democratic
h. holiday	**u.** democratically
i. grandmother	**v.** democratization
j. morphemic	**w.** democratize
k. mistreatment	**x.** democratizer
l. deactivation	**y.** democratizing
m. saltpeter	**z.** democratized

3. Match each expression under A with the one statement under B that characterizes it.

    A   **B**

    a. noisy crow   **(1)** compound noun
    b. scarecrow   **(2)** root morpheme plus derivational prefix
    c. the crow   **(3)** phrase consisting of adjective plus noun
    d. crowlike   **(4)** root morpheme plus inflectional affix
    e. crows   **(5)** root morpheme plus derivational suffix
                        (6) grammatical morpheme followed by lexical morpheme

4. Write the one proper description from the list under B for the italicized part of each word in A.

    A   **B**

    a. *terrorized*   **(1)** free root
    b. *uncivilized*   **(2)** bound root
    c. *terrorize*   **(3)** inflectional suffix
    d. *lukewarm*   **(4)** derivational suffix
    e. *impossible*   **(5)** inflectional prefix
                         (6) derivational prefix
                         (7) inflectional infix
                         (8) derivational infix

5. **Part One:**

    Consider the following nouns in Zulu and proceed to look for the recurring forms.

umfazi	"married woman"	abafazi	"married women"
umfani	"boy"	abafani	"boys"
umzali	"parent"	abazali	"parents"
umfundisi	"teacher"	abafundisi	"teachers"
umbazi	"carver"	ababazi	"carvers"
umlimi	"farmer"	abalimi	"farmers"
umdlali	"player"	abadlali	"players"
umfundi	"reader"	abafundi	"readers"

    a. What is the morpheme meaning "singular" in Zulu?
    b. What is the morpheme meaning "plural" in Zulu?
    c. List the Zulu stems to which the singular and plural morphemes are attached, and give their meanings.

    Part Two:

    The following Zulu verbs are derived from noun stems by adding a verbal suffix.

fundisa	"to teach"	funda	"to read"
lima	"to cultivate"	baza	"to carve"

    d. Compare these words to the words in section A that are related in meaning, for example, *umfundisi* "teacher," *abafundisi* "teachers," *fun-disa* "to teach." What is the derivational suffix that specifies the category verb?

e. What is the nominal suffix (i.e., the suffix that forms nouns)?

f. State the morphological noun formation rule in Zulu.

g. What is the stem morpheme meaning "read"?

h. What is the stem morpheme meaning "carve"?

6. Sweden has given the world the rock group ABBA, the automobile Volvo, and the great film director Ingmar Bergman. The Swedish language offers us a noun morphology that you can analyze with the knowledge gained reading this chapter. Consider these Swedish noun forms:

en lampa	"a lamp"	en bil	"a car"
en stol	"a chair"	en soffa	"a sofa"
en matta	"a carpet"	en tratt	"a funnel"
lampor	"lamps"	bilar	"cars"
stolar	"chairs"	soffor	"sofas"
mattor	"carpets"	trattar	"funnels"
lampan	"the lamp"	bilen	"the car"
stolen	"the chair"	soffan	"the sofa"
mattan	"the carpet"	tratten	"the funnel"
lamporna	"the lamps"	bilarna	"the cars"
stolarna	"the chairs"	sofforna	"the sofas"
mattorna	"the carpets"	trattarna	"the funnels"

a. What is the Swedish word for the indefinite article *a* (or *an*)?

b. What are the two forms of the plural morpheme in these data? How can you tell which plural form applies?

c. What are the two forms of the morpheme that make a singular word definite, that is, correspond to the English article *the?* How can you tell which form applies?

d. What is the morpheme that makes a plural word definite?

e. In what order do the various suffixes occur when there is more than one?

f. If *en flicka* is "a girl," what are the forms for "girls," "the girl," and "the girls"?

g. If *bussarna* is "the buses," what are the forms for "buses" and "the bus"?

7. Here are some nouns from the Philippine language Cebuano.

sibwano	"a Cebuano"
ilokano	"an Ilocano"
tagalog	"a Tagalog person"
inglis	"an Englishman"
bisaja	"a Visayan"
binisaja	"the Visayan language"
ininglis	"the English language"
tinagalog	"the Tagalog language"
inilokano	"the Ilocano language"
sinibwano	"the Cebuano language"

a. What is the exact rule for deriving language names from ethnic group names?

b. What type of affixation is represented here?

c. If *suwid* meant "a Swede" and *italo* meant "an Italian," what would be the words for the Swedish language and the Italian language?

d. If *finuranso* meant "the French language" and *inunagari* meant "the Hungarian language," what would be the words for a Frenchman and a Hungarian?

8. The following infinitive and past participle verb forms are found in Dutch.

Root	Infinitive	Past Participle	
wandel	wandelen	gewandeld	"walk"
duw	duwen	geduwd	"push"
stofzuig	stofzuigen	gestofzuigd	"vacuum-clean"

With reference to the morphological processes of prefixing, suffixing, infixing, and circumfixing discussed in this chapter and the specific morphemes involved:

a. State the morphological rule for forming an infinitive in Dutch.

b. State the morphological rule for forming the Dutch past participle form.

9. Below are some sentences in Swahili:

mtoto	amefika	"The child has arrived."
mtoto	anafika	"The child is arriving."
mtoto	atafika	"The child will arrive."
watoto	wamefika	"The children have arrived."
watoto	wanafika	"The children are arriving."
watoto	watafika	"The children will arrive."
mtu	amelala	"The person has slept."
mtu	analala	"The person is sleeping."
mtu	atalala	"The person will sleep."
watu	wamelala	"The persons have slept."
watu	wanalala	"The persons are sleeping."
watu	watalala	"The persons will sleep."
kisu	kimeanguka	"The knife has fallen."
kisu	kinaanguka	"The knife is falling."
kisu	kitaanguka	"The knife will fall."
visu	vimeanguka	"The knives have fallen."
visu	vinaanguka	"The knives are falling."
visu	vitaanguka	"The knives will fall."
kikapu	kimeanguka	"The basket has fallen."
kikapu	kinaanguka	"The basket is falling."
kikapu	kitaanguka	"The basket will fall."
vikapu	vimeanguka	"The baskets have fallen."
vikapu	vinaanguka	"The baskets are falling."
vikapu	vitaanguka	"The baskets will fall."

One of the characteristic features of Swahili (and Bantu languages in general) is the existence of noun classes. Specific singular and plural prefixes occur with the nouns in each class. These prefixes are also used for purposes of agreement between the subject noun and the verb. In the sentences given, two of these classes are included (there are many more in the language).

a. Identify all the morphemes you can detect, and give their meanings.

> *Example*: -toto "child"
>
> *m-* prefix attached to singular nouns of Class I
>
> *a-* prefix attached to verbs when the subject is a singular noun of Class I

Be sure to look for the other noun and verb markers, including tense markers.

b. How is the verb constructed? That is, what kinds of morphemes are strung together and in what order?

c. How would you say in Swahili:
  (1) "The child is falling."
  (2) "The baskets have arrived."
  (3) "The person will fall."

10. **Part One:**

We mentioned the morphological process of reduplication—the formation of new words through the repetition of part or all of a word—which occurs in many languages. The following examples from Samoan illustrate this kind of morphological rule.

manao	"he wishes"	mananao	"they wish"
matua	"he is old"	matutua	"they are old"
malosi	"he is strong"	malolosi	"they are strong"
punou	"he bends"	punonou	"they bend"
atamaki	"he is wise"	atamamaki	"they are wise"
savali	"he travels"	pepese	"they sing"
laga	"he weaves"		

a. What is the Samoan for:
  (1) "they weave"
  (2) "they travel"
  (3) "he sings"

b. Formulate a general statement (a morphological rule) that states how to form the plural verb form from the singular verb form.

Part Two:

Consider these data from M'nong (spoken in Vietnam) with some simplifications for this exercise: (The ? is a sound called a glottal stop.)

dang	"hard"	da dang	"a little hard"
kloh	"clean"	klo kloh	"a little clean"
ndreh	"green"	ndre ndreh	"light green"
guh	"red"	go? guh	"reddish"
duh	"hot"	do? duh	"luke warm"
kat	"cold"	ka kat	"chilly"

1. What kind of morphological process do you observe to achieve the semantic effect of weakening an adjective?
2. If *thong* meant "light," how would M'nong express "kind of light"?
3. If *khul* meant "evasive," how would M'nong express "a little shifty"?
4. If *lo? luq* meant "a little paunchy," how would M'nong express "fat"?
5. If *kho khot* meant "a little crazy," how would M'nong express "crazy"?
6. Formulate a general statement (a morphological rule) of how M'nong speakers weaken certain kinds of adjectives. To be completely accurate and account for the given data, you will have to take spelling (pronunciation) into account.

11. Following are a few more malapropisms:

Word	Definition
stalemate	"husband or wife no longer interested"
effusive	"able to be merged"
tenet	"a group of ten singers"
dermatology	"a study of derms"
ingenious	"not very smart"
finesse	"a female fish"
amphibious	"able to lie on both sea and land"
deceptionist	"secretary who covers up for his boss"
mathemagician	"an accountant who 'cooks the books'"
sexcedrin	"medicine for mate who says, 'sorry, I have a headache'"
testostoroni	"hormonal supplement administered as pasta"
aesthetominophen	"medicine to make you look beautiful"
histalavista	"say goodbye to those allergies"
aquapella	"singing in the shower"
melancholy	"dog that guards the cantaloupe patch"
plutocrat	"a dog that rules"

Give some possible reasons for the source of these silly "definitions." Illustrate your answers by reference to other words or morphemes. For example, *stalemate* comes from *stale* meaning "having lost freshness" and *mate* meaning "marriage partner." When mates appear to have lost their freshness, they are no longer as desirable as they once were.

12. **a.** Draw tree diagrams for the following words: *construal, disappearances, irreplaceability, misconceive, indecipherable, redarken.*

    b. Draw two tree diagrams for *undarkenable* to reveal its two meanings: "able to be less dark" and "unable to be made dark."

13. There are many asymmetries in English in which a root morpheme combined with a prefix constitutes a word, but without the prefix is a non-word. A number of these are given in this chapter.

    a. Following is a list of such nonword roots. Add a prefix to each root to form an existing English word.

Word	Nonwords
_____	descript
_____	cognito
_____	beknownst
_____	peccable
_____	promptu
_____	plussed
_____	domitable
_____	nomer
_____	crat

    b. There are many more such multimorphemic words for which the root morphemes do not constitute words by themselves. Can you list five more?

14. We have seen that the meaning of compounds is often not revealed by the meanings of their composite words. Crossword puzzles and riddles often make use of this by providing the meaning of two parts of a compound and asking for the resulting word. For example, infielder = diminutive/cease. Read this as asking for a word that means "infielder" by combining a word that means "diminutive" with a word that means "cease." The answer is *shortstop*. See if you can figure out the following:

    a. sci-fi TV series = headliner/journey
    b. campaign = farm building/tempest
    c. at-home wear = tub of water/court attire
    d. kind of pen = formal dance/sharp end
    e. conservative = correct/part of an airplane

15. Consider the following dialogue between parent and schoolchild:

PARENT: When will you be done with your eight-page book report, dear?
CHILD: I haven't started it yet.
PARENT: But it's due tomorrow, you should have begun weeks ago. Why do you always wait until the last minute?
CHILD: I have more confidence in myself than you do.
PARENT: Say what?
CHILD: I mean, how long could it possibly take to read an eight-page book?

The humor is based on the ambiguity of the compound *eight-page book report*. Draw two trees similar to those in the text for *top hat rack* to reveal the ambiguity.

16. One of the characteristics of Italian is that articles and adjectives have inflectional endings that mark agreement in gender (and number) with the nouns they modify. Based on this information, answer the questions that follow the list of Italian phrases.

un uomo	"a man"
un uomo robusto	"a robust man"
un uomo robustissimo	"a very robust man"
una donna robusta	"a robust woman"
un vino rosso	"a red wine"
una faccia	"a face"
un vento secco	"a dry wind"

    a. What is the root morpheme meaning "robust"?
    b. What is the morpheme meaning "very"?
    c. What is the Italian for:
        (1) "a robust wine"
        (2) "a very red face"
        (3) "a very dry wine"

17. Following is a list of words from Turkish. In Turkish, articles and morphemes indicating location are affixed to the noun.

deniz	"an ocean"	evden	"from a house"
denize	"to an ocean"	evimden	"from my house"
denizin	"of an ocean"	denizimde	"in my ocean"
eve	"to a house"	elde	"in a hand"

    a. What is the Turkish morpheme meaning "to"?
    b. What kind of affixes in Turkish correspond to English prepositions (e.g., prefixes, suffixes, infixes, free morphemes)?
    c. What would the Turkish word for "from an ocean" be?
    d. How many morphemes are there in the Turkish word *denizimde*?

18. The following are some verb forms in Chickasaw, a member of the Muskogean family of languages spoken in south-central Oklahoma.[3]

sachaaha	"I am tall"
chaaha	"he/she is tall"
chichaaha	"you are tall"
hoochaaha	"they are tall"
satikahbi	"I am tired"
chitikahbitok	"you were tired"
chichchokwa	"you are cold"
hopobatok	"he was hungry"
hoohopobatok	"they were hungry"
sahopoba	"I am hungry"

---

[3]The Chickasaw examples are provided by Pamela Munro.

    a. What is the root morpheme for the following verbs?
        (1) "to be tall"
        (2) "to be hungry"
    b. What is the morpheme meaning:
        (1) past tense
        (2) "I"
        (3) "you"
        (4) "he/she"
    e. If the Chickasaw root for "to be old" is *sipokni*, how would you say:
        (1) "You are old"
        (2) "He was old"
        (3) "They are old"[3]

19. The language Little-End Egglish, whose source is revealed in Exercise 14, Chapter 8, exhibits the following data:

kul	"omelet"	zkulego	"my omelet"	zkulivo	"your omelet"
vet	"yolk (of egg)"	zvetego	"my yolk"	zvetivo	"your yolk"
rok	"egg"	zrokego	"my egg"	zrokivo	"your egg"
ver	"egg shell"	zverego	"my egg shell"	zverivo	"your egg shell"
gup	"soufflé"	zgupego	"my soufflé"	zgupivo	"your soufflé"

    a. Isolate the morphemes that indicate possession, first-person singular, and second person (we don't know whether singular, plural, or both). Indicate whether the affixes are prefixes or suffixes.
    b. Given that *vel* means egg white, how would a Little-End Egglisher say "my egg white"?
    c. Given that *zpeivo* means "your hard-boiled egg," what is the word meaning "hard-boiled egg"?
    d. If you knew that *zvetgogo* meant "our egg yolk," what would be likely to be the morpheme meaning "our"?
    e. If you knew that *borokego* meant "for my egg," what would be likely to be the morpheme bearing the benefactive meaning "for"?

20. Here are some data from the indigenous language Zoque spoken in Mexico. (The ? is a glottal stop.) Hint: Rearrange the data as in the Slavic example at the end of the chapter.

sohsu	"he/it cooked"	cicpa	"he/it tears"
witpa	"he/it walks"	kenu	"he/it looked"
sikpa	"he/it laughs"	cihcu	"he/it tore"
ka?u	"he/it died"	sospa	"he/it cooks"
kenpa	"he/it looks"	wihtu	"he/it walked"
sihku	"he/it laughed"	ka?pa	"he/it dies"

    a. What is the past tense suffix?
    b. What is the present tense suffix?

       c. This language has some verb stems that assume two forms. For each verb (or stem pair), give its meaning and form(s).

       d. What morphological environment determines which of the two forms occurs, when there are two?

21. **Research project:** Consider what are called "interfixes" such as *-o-* in English *jack-o-lantern*. They are said to be meaningless morphemes attached to two morphemes at once. What can you learn about that notion? Where do you think the *-o-* comes from? Are there languages other than English that have interfixes?

3

Syntax: Infinite Use of Finite Means

> To grammar even kings bow.

J. B. MOLÈIRE, *Les Femmes Savantes, II*, 1672

It is a remarkable fact that any speaker of a human language can learn and store in his or her mental lexicon thousands of words, each of which is an arbitrary pairing of sound and meaning. Even more astonishing is our ability to combine these words to produce and understand an infinite number of novel sentences, as we showed with the following sentence:

> This is the dog that worried the cat that killed the rat that ate the malt that lay in the house that Jack built . . .

To further illustrate, consider the following:

> Snorlax is asleep.
> The monster is asleep.
> The friend of the monster is asleep.
> The rightmost person in the first row is asleep.
> The person immediately to the left of the rightmost person in the front row is asleep.
> The person behind the person immediately to the left of the rightmost person in the first row is asleep.
> Snorlax is asleep.
> Pikachu noticed that Snorlax is asleep.

> Nobody cares that Pikachu noticed that Snorlax is asleep.
> Squirtle knows that nobody cares that Pikachu noticed that Snorlax is asleep.

We can do this because we know (a finite number of) rules, which can be applied repeatedly. All spoken language is governed by rules—the set of rules is called a **grammar**. Every speaker has a mental grammar of the rules of his or her language that he or she follows in producing, understanding, and making judgments of well-formedness (grammaticality) about his or her language.

If we modify the order of words or omit some of the words, the sentences sound "weird" or "odd." (Recall that the asterisk or star preceding a sentence is the linguistic conventio or indicating that the sentence is ungrammatical or ill-formed according to the rules of the grammar.)

> *Asleep is Homer.
> *Professor the is asleep.
> *Rightmost person the in the first row is asleep.
> *Homer asleep.
> *Right most person front row is asleep.

The oddness of these sentences indicates that some rule of the language has been violated. The sentences are ungrammatical.

To further illustrate this idea let's look at a simple made-up rule of English that we'll call the "everybody knows" rule:

> Rule: If S is a sentence of English then *Everybody knows that S* is a sentence of English.

This rule can be iterated (repeated) any number of times to produce an arbitrary number of new sentences.

> Snorlax is asleep.
> Everybody knows that Snorlax is asleep.
> Everybody knows that everybody knows that Snorlax is asleep.
> Everybody knows that everybody knows that everybody knows that Snorlax is asleep.

This simple rule in the mind of a speaker enables him or her to produce and understand a potentially infinite number of sentences. The "everybody knows" rule describes (generates) an infinite set of sentences. Any sentence that conforms to the rule is judged well-formed and any sentence that does not conform to the rule is judged ungrammatical, such as the following:

> *Knows everybody that Snorlax is asleep.

Given any sentence a speaker could create another sentence by adding a (nother) prepositional phrase, relative clause, or by embedding one sentence inside another as in the "everybody knows" examples. Or simply by adding another adjective:

> The kindhearted boy had many girlfriends.
> The kindhearted, intelligent boy had many girlfriends.
> The kindhearted, intelligent, handsome boy had many girlfriends.

All languages have mechanisms of this sort that make the number of sentences limitless. Like words, discussed in the previous chapter, sentences are composed of finitely many discrete units that are combined by rules. Thus languages make infinite use of finite means. In this respect knowledge of language is like knowledge of integers. There is no limit to the number of even integers you could enumerate: 2, 4, 6, 8, 10, ... Clearly, you didn't memorize all of them. Rather, you know a rule that allows you to produce new integers from old ones.

Rule: If E is an integer, E+2 is an integer.

This ability to make infinite use of finite means shows the creative nature of human linguistic knowledge—not creative in the sense that we are all accomplished poets, but creative in that none of us is limited to a fixed repertoire of expressions. Rather, we can exploit the resources of our language and grammar to produce, understand and make judgments about a limitless number of sentences embodying a limitless range of ideas and emotions.

The part of grammar that represents a speaker's knowledge of sentences and their structures is called **syntax**. The aim of this chapter is to first show you what syntactic structures look like and then to familiarize you with some of the rules that determine them. Most of the examples will be from the syntax of English, but the principles that account for syntactic structures are universal.

What the Syntax Rules Do

"Then you should say what you mean," the March Hare went on.

"I do," Alice hastily replied, "at least—I mean what I say—that's the same thing, you know."

"Not the same thing a bit!" said the Hatter. "You might just as well say that 'I see what I eat' is the same thing as 'I eat what I see'!"

"You might just as well say," added the March Hare, "that 'I like what I get' is the same thing as 'I get what I like'!"

"You might just as well say," added the Dormouse . . . "that 'I breathe when I sleep' is the same thing as 'I sleep when I breathe'!"

"It is the same thing with you," said the Hatter.

LEWIS CARROLL, *Alice's Adventures in Wonderland*, 1865

The rules of syntax combine words into phrases and phrases into sentences. Among other things, the rules define the correct word order for a language. For example, English is a Subject–Verb–Object (SVO) language. The English sentence in (1) is grammatical because the words occur in the right order; the sentence in (2) is ungrammatical because the word order is incorrect for English.

1. The President nominated a new Supreme Court justice.
2. *President the Supreme new justice Court a nominated.

The rules of the syntax also specify the **grammatical relations** of a sentence, such as **subject** and **direct object**. In other words, they provide information about who is doing what to whom. This information is crucial to understanding the meaning of a sentence. For example, the grammatical relations in (3) and (4) are reversed, so the otherwise identical sentences have very different meanings.

3.   Your dog chased my cat.
4.   My cat chased your dog.

The word order of a sentence is crucial to its meaning. The sentences in (5) and (6) contain the same words, but the meanings are quite different, as the Mad Hatter points out.

5.   I mean what I say.
6.   I say what I mean.

Although the structure of a sentence contributes to its meaning, as illustrated in the examples 3–6, grammaticality and meaningfulness are not the same thing. Consider the following sentences:

> Colorless green ideas sleep furiously.
> A verb crumpled the milk.

Although these sentences do not make much sense, they are syntactically well–formed. They sound funny, but their funniness is different from what we find in the following strings of words, which are not syntactically well-formed:

> *Furiously sleep ideas green colorless.
> *Milk the crumpled verb a.

There are also sentences that we understand even though they are not well-formed according to the rules of the syntax. We can easily interpret Yoda's words to Luke Skywalker although the word order is incorrect for English.

> ". . . when gone I am . . . the last of the Jedi will you be"

To be a sentence, words must conform to specific patterns determined by the specific syntactic rules of the language.

Some sentences are grammatical even though they are difficult to interpret because they include nonsense words, that is, words with no agreed-on meaning. This is illustrated by the following lines from the poem "Jabberwocky" by Lewis Carroll:

> 'Twas brillig, and the slithy toves
> Did gyre and gimble in the wabe

These lines are grammatical in the linguistic sense that they obey the word order and other constraints of English. Such nonsense poetry is amusing precisely because the sentences comply with syntactic rules and sound like English. Ungrammatical strings of nonsense words are not entertaining:

> *Toves slithy the and brillig 'twas
> wabe the in gimble and gyre did

Grammaticality does not depend on the truth of sentences. If it did, lying would be easy to detect. Nor does it depend on whether real objects are being discussed or whether something is possible in the real world. Untrue sentences can be grammatical, sentences discussing unicorns can be grammatical, and sentences referring to pregnant fathers can be grammatical.

The ability to produce, understand, and judge the grammaticality of a sentence depends on whether it conforms to the unconscious rules of our mental grammar. This grammar is different from the prescriptive grammar rules that we are taught in school. We develop the mental rules of grammar long before we attend school, as we shall see in Chapter 9.

Sentence Structure

I really do not know that anything has ever been more exciting than diagramming sentences.

GERTRUDE STEIN, "Poetry and Grammar," 1935

The job of the linguist is to describe the structure of the sentences in a language in a way that matches the linguistic knowledge of its speakers. We can compare two competing hypotheses. The first says that a sentence consists simply of a string of words organized in a flat structure as in (1).

1.

The child found a puppy

We have already seen that word order is an important aspect of syntactic knowledge and this simple diagram correctly captures the SVO word order of English: The subject (S) *the child*, comes before the verb (V) *found*, which comes before the object (O) *a puppy*.

Let us contrast this kind of description with another, one that says that sentences have a tree-like structure in which words are grouped together into natural units nested within other natural units in a hierarchical arrangement, as in (2).

2.

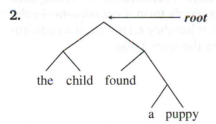

the child found

a puppy

The "tree" in (2) is upside down with its "root" encompassing the entire sentence, "The child found a puppy," and its "leaves" being the individual words *the, child, found, a,* and *puppy*. The **tree diagram** in (2), embodies the hypothesis that these words are organized into subunits (or subtrees) and that speakers mentally represent sentences not as flat strings of words, but as complex structures with an internal organization. The subunits (or subtrees) of the sentence are called **constituents**.

In the tree diagram in (2), the words *a* and *puppy* form a constituent, as indicated below:

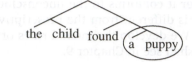

We can also represent constituents by using square brackets around the words [a puppy]. Constituents can be nested inside one another. So, [a puppy] occurs inside the constituent [found a puppy], as illustrated in the following tree.

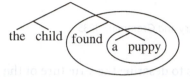

Using bracket notation, we would write this as [found [a puppy]].

There is one more constituent in the tree in (2). Do you know what it is? If you guessed [the child] you would be correct.

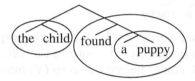

A constituent consists not just of the words, but of the subtree that branches into the words, and it ends at the **node** where the branches meet. A constituent corresponds to a node on the tree. And to be a constituent all the words under the node must be included. The words that form a constituent are contiguous (next to one another), but not all contiguous words form a constituent. In the following tree, the words *found a* are contiguous but they do not form a constituent. They are not contained exclusively under the same node.

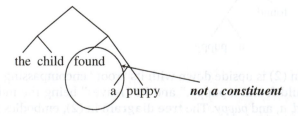

We began our discussion with a simple sentence "The child found a puppy," but this simple sentence belies a complex internal structure. The tree diagram in (2) groups the words of the sentence into the constituents *the child* and *found*

a puppy, corresponding to the subject and predicate of the sentence. A further division of the phrase *found a puppy* divides naturally into two branches, one for the verb *found* and the other for the direct object *a puppy*. This division conforms to our intuitions about the natural units of the sentence in a way that a different division, say, *found a* and *puppy*, would not.

Constituents and Constituency Tests

In addition to our intuitions of naturalness, various linguistic tests reveal the constituents of a sentence. The first test is the "stand alone" test. If a group of words can stand alone, for example, as an answer to a question, they form a constituent. So, in response to the question "What did the child find?" a speaker might answer *a puppy*, but not *found a. A puppy* can stand alone while *found a* cannot. We have a clear intuition that one of these is a meaningful unit and the other is just a list of words.

The second test is "replacement by a pronoun." Pronouns can substitute for natural groups. In answer to the question, "Where did the child find *a puppy*?" a speaker can say, "I found *him* in the park." Words such as *do* (which is not a pronoun per se) can also take the place of the entire predicate *found a puppy*, as in "The boy found a puppy and the girl *did* too." If a group of words can be replaced by a pronoun or a word like *do*, it forms a constituent.

A third test of constituency is the "move-as-a-unit" test. If a group of words can be moved together and remain grammatical, they form a constituent. For example, if we compare the following sentences to the sentence "The child found a puppy," we see that certain elements have moved:

It was *a puppy* that the child found.
A puppy was found by *the child*.

In the first example, the constituent *a puppy* has moved from its position following *found*; in the second example, the positions of *a puppy* and *the child* have been changed. In all such rearrangements, the constituents *a puppy* and *the child* remain intact. *Found a* does not remain intact, because it is not a constituent. Nor does *child found* for the same reason. Even though both these pairs of words occur next to each other in the original sentence *The child found a puppy*; they do not pass constituency tests, illustrating again that sentences are not simply string of words.

Some sentences have prepositional phrases in the predicate, for example:

The puppy played in the garden.

We can use our tests to show that *in the garden* is also a constituent, as follows:

Where did the puppy play? *In the garden* (stand alone)
The puppy played *there*. (replacement by a pronoun-like word)
In the garden the puppy played. (move as a unit)
It was *in the garden* that the puppy played. (move as a unit)

The prepositional phrase in this example passes all three constituent tests. But in general a constituent need not pass all three tests. It is sufficient to pass one.

As before, our knowledge of the **constituent structure** of a sentence may be graphically represented by a tree diagram. The tree diagram for the sentence "The puppy played in the garden" is as follows:

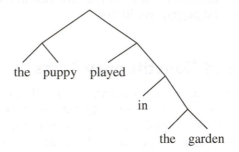

The move-as-a-unit test can also tell us when what appears to be a constituent, such as a prepositional phrase, is in fact something different. The two phrases *ran up the hill* and *ran up the bill* are superficially quite similar, but we see in (3) and (4) that they behave quite differently. Consider first the expression *ran up the hill*, as in (3a). The rules of the syntax allow the word orders in (3b, c) as variants, revealing that *up the hill* is a constituent. By contrast, the expression *run up the bill* in (4a) does not have these same options, as shown in (4b, c), which means that *up the bill* is neither a prepositional phrase nor a constituent.

3. **(a)** Jack ran up the hill.
   (b) Up the hill Jack ran.
   (c) Up the hill ran Jack.
4. **(a)** Jack ran up the bill.
   (b) *Up the bill Jack ran.
   (c) *Up the bill ran Jack.

Structural Ambiguity

Hilary B. Price/King Features Syndicate

Syntactic trees reflect our judgments about the internal organization of sentences; flat structures do not. They can also account for other linguistic judgments, such as when a sentence is **ambiguous**. A sentence is ambiguous if it has two or more meanings. Sometimes an ambiguity arises because a word has more than one meaning, as in the following sentence:

This will make you smart.

The two interpretations of this sentence are due to the two meanings of *smart*— "clever" and "burning sensation." This is referred to as a **lexical ambiguity** and will be discussed further in Chapter 4. Other times multiple meanings arise because a sentence has more than one tree structure associated with it, resulting in a **structural ambiguity**. Each tree will correspond to one of the possible meanings of the sentence. For example, the sentence:

Sue saw the man with the telescope.

has two different meanings:

Meaning 1: The seeing is done with the telescope.
Meaning 2: The man is holding the telescope.

Notice that none of the individual words is ambiguous. The ambiguity is structural: The sentence has two different trees. Meaning 1 corresponds to the tree in (1), what we might call the instrumental meaning in which Sue is using the telescope to see the man. In this tree, the *the man* and the prepositional phrase *with the telescope* do not form a constituent.

1.

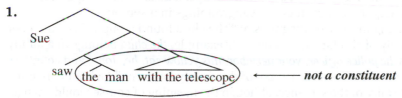

Meaning 2 corresponds to the tree in (2). In this case, the phrases *the man* and *with a telescope* do form a constituent, reflecting the meaning in which the man is holding the telescope.

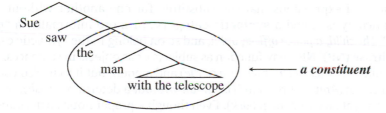

The availability of these two structures leads to a prediction: If we do a constituency test that forces *the man with the telescope* to be a constituent (e.g. move it as a unit), then meaning 1 (instrumental) should disappear and we should only have the meaning corresponding to the tree in (2). The following sentences confirm this prediction:

It was the man with the telescope that Mary saw.

The man with the telescope was seen by Mary.

What Mary saw was the man with the telescope.

None of these sentences has the interpretation in which the seeing is done with the telescope. In each, the only possible meaning is that the man is holding the telescope. This shows us that the structure of a sentence contributes importantly to its meaning, a point we will come back to in Chapter 4.

Structural ambiguities of the sort just discussed provide striking evidence in support of our hypothesis that sentences have a tree-like (hierarchical) structure, and against the idea that they are simply strings of words. The flat structure hypothesis could not explain how there can be two different meanings associated with *the same string of words*.

The cartoon at the head of this section illustrates both lexical and structural ambiguity. The lexical ambiguity is on the two meanings of *ring*; the structural ambiguity is whether *nose ring* is understood as a compound noun or a noun followed by a verb.

Syntactic Categories

There are ten parts of speech, and they are all troublesome.

MARK TWAIN, "The Awful German Language," in *A Tramp Abroad*, 1880

In the previous section, we illustrated how tree structures reflect our knowledge of the hierarchical organization of sentences. Speakers also have implicit knowledge of the categories of each of the subgroupings in a sentence.

Each grouping in the tree diagrams of "The child found a puppy" is a member of a large family of similar expressions. For example, *the child* belongs to a family that includes *the police officer, your neighbor, this yellow cat, he, John,* and countless others. We can substitute any member of this family for *the child* without affecting the grammaticality of the sentence, although the meaning of course would change.

A police officer found a puppy.
Your neighbor found a puppy.
This yellow cat found a puppy.

A family of expressions that can substitute for one another without loss of grammaticality is called a **syntactic category**, or more informally, a "part of speech." *The child, a police officer, John,* and so on belong to the syntactic category **noun phrase (NP)**. NPs may function as subjects or as objects in sentences. An NP often contains a *determiner* (such as *a* or *the*) and a noun, but it may also consist of a proper name (*Ann*), a pronoun (*I*), a noun without a determiner (*fish*), or even a clause or a sentence (*that dogs bark*). Even though a proper noun such as *John* and pronouns such as *he* and *him* are single words, they are technically NPs, because they pattern like NPs in being able to fill a subject, object or other NP slot.

John found the puppy.
He found the puppy.
Boys love puppies.
The puppy loved him.
The puppy loved John.

NPs can be quite complex, as illustrated by the sentence:

The girl that Professor Snape loved married the man of her dreams.

The NP subject of this sentence is *the girl that Professor Snape loved,* and the NP object is *the man of her dreams.* We know this because each of these lengthy expressions fills a slot otherwise occupied by a simpler NP as in *Mary loved John.*

Syntactic categories are part of a speaker's knowledge of syntax. That is, speakers of English know that only items (a), (b), (e), (f), and (g) in the following list are NPs even if they have never heard the term *noun phrase* before.

1. **(a)** a bird
    (b) the red banjo
    (c) have a nice day
    (d) with a balloon
    (e) the woman who was laughing
    (f) it
    (g) John
    (h) went

You can test this claim by inserting each expression into three contexts: *What/ who I heard was _____, Who found _____?* and _____ *was seen by everyone.* For example, **Who found with a balloon?* is ungrammatical, as is **Went was seen by everyone,* as opposed to *Who found it?* or *John was seen by everyone.* Only NPs fit into these contexts because only NPs can function as subjects and objects.

There are other syntactic categories. The expression *found a puppy* is a **verb phrase (VP)**. A verb phrase always contains a **verb (V)**, and it may contain other categories, such as a noun phrase or **prepositional phrase (PP)**, which is a preposition followed by an NP, such as *in the park, on the roof,* and *with a balloon.* In (2) the VPs are those phrases that can complete the sentence "The child _____."

2. **(a)** saw a clown
    (b) a bird
    (c) slept
    (d) smart
    (e) ate the cake
    (f) found the cake in the cupboard
    (g) realized that the Earth was round

Inserting (a), (c), (e), (f), and (g) will produce grammatical sentences, whereas the insertion of (b) or (d) would result in an ungrammatical sentence. Thus, (a), (c), (e), (f), and (g) are verb phrases.

Lexical and Functional Categories

"Very traditional. He's the noun. She's the adjective."

Syntactic categories include both phrasal categories such as NP, VP, AP (adjective phrase), PP (prepositional phrase), and AdvP (adverbial phrase), as well as lexical categories such as noun (N), verb (V), preposition (P), adjective (A), and adverb (Adv). Each lexical category has a corresponding phrasal category. Following is a list of phrasal categories and lexical categories with some examples of each type:

Phrasal categories

Noun Phrase (NP)	*men, the man, the man with a telescope sees, always*
Verb Phrase (VP)	*sees, rarely sees the man, often sees the man with a telescope*
Adjective Phrase (AP)	*happy, very happy, very happy about winning*
Prepositional Phrase (PP)	*over, nearly over, nearly over the hill*
Adverbial Phrase (AdvP)	*brightly, more brightly, more brightly than the Sun*

Lexical categories

Noun (N)	*puppy, boy, man, soup, happiness, fork, kiss, pillow*
Verb (V)	*find, run, sleep, throw, realize, see, try, want, believe*
Preposition (P)	*up, down, across, into, from, by, with, over*
Adjective (A)	*red, big, happy, candid, hopeless, fair, idiotic, lucky*
Adverb (Adv)	*again, always, brightly, often, never, very, fairly*

Many of these categories may already be familiar to you. Other categories may be less familiar such as the category **determiner (Det)**, which includes the articles *a* and *the*, as well as **demonstratives** such as *this, that, these,* and *those,* and "quantifiers" such as *each* and *every*. Another less familiar category is **T**(ense), which includes the **modal** auxiliaries *may, might, can, could, must, shall, should, will,* and *would,* and abstract tense elements that we discuss below. Lastly, there are **complementizers (Comp)** words such as *that, for,* and *if, whether* that occur in complex (multi-clause), sentences such as the following:

John thinks that Mary is pretty.
John wonders whether/if Mary will date him.

T, Det, and Comp are **functional categories**, so called because their members have grammatical functions rather than descriptive meanings. For example, determiners specify whether a noun is indefinite or definite (*a boy* versus *the boy*), or the proximity of the person or object to the context (*this boy* versus *that boy*). Tense provides the verb with a time frame, whether present *(John knows Mary),* or past *(John danced).* And complementizers introduce embedded clauses. In English, T is expressed as a (sometimes silent) morpheme on the verb, except in the future tense, which is expressed with the modal *will.* Modals also express notions such as possibility *(John may dance);* necessity *(John must dance);* and ability *(John can dance).* The modals belong to a larger class of verbal elements traditionally referred to as **auxiliaries** or helping verbs, which also include *have* and *be* in sentences such as *John is dancing* or *John has danced.*

Each lexical category typically has a particular kind of meaning associated with it. For example, verbs usually refer to actions, events, and states *(kick, marry, love);* adjectives to qualities or properties *(lucky, old);* common nouns to general entities *(dog, elephant, house);* and proper nouns to particular individuals *(Noam Chomsky)* or places *(Dodger Stadium)* or other things that people give names to, such as commercial products *(Coca-Cola, Viagra).*

But the relationship between grammatical categories and meaning is more complex than these few examples suggest. For example, some nouns refer to events *(marriage* and *destruction)* and others to states *(happiness, loneliness).* We can use abstract nouns such as *honor* and *beauty,* rather than adjectives, to refer to properties and qualities. In the sentence "Seeing is believing," *seeing* and *believing* are nouns, but they are not entities. Prepositions are generally used to express relationships between two entities involving a location (e.g., *the boy is in the room, the cat is under the bed*), but this is not always the case; the prepositions *of, by, about,* and *with* often have nonlocational meanings.

Because of the difficulties involved in specifying the precise meaning of lexical categories, we do not define grammatical categories in terms of their meanings, but rather on the basis of where they occur in a sentence, what categories co-occur with them, and what kind of inflections they can take. For example, we define a noun as a word that can occur with a determiner *(the boy)* and that can (ordinarily) take a plural marker *(boys);* a verb as a word that can occur with an adverb *(run fast)* or modal *(may go, will dance);* an adjective as a word that can occur with a degree word *(very hungry)* or a comparative or superlative marker *(hungrier, hungriest),* among other properties.

All languages have syntactic categories such as N, V, and NP. Speakers know the syntactic categories of their language even if they do not know the technical terms. Our knowledge of syntactic classes is revealed when we substitute equivalent phrases, as we just did in examples (1) and (2) above, and when we use the various syntactic tests that we have discussed.

Our knowledge of syntactic categories is also revealed through our intuitions about nonsensical sentences. Recall the sentences in (1) and (2) below. Although neither of these sentences makes sense, we have a clear intuition that (1) is grammatical in a way that (2) is not.

1. Colorless green ideas sleep furiously.
2. *Sleep colorless green furiously ideas.

This is because sentence (1) obeys the word order constraints of English while sentence (2) does not. In other words, we recognize the category of each of the words: *Colorless* is an adjective, *ideas* is a noun, *colorless green ideas* is a noun phrase, and *sleep furiously* is a verb phrase, and know that they fit properly together in (1) but not in (2). We are not taught these categories nor their word order. We know this implicitly before we go to school. They are part of our grammar that we develop as a child growing up (see Chapter 9).

In these sentences, we can identify when the order is correct and when it is not, even though the meanings of the different words and constituents do not jibe. An idea cannot be green or colorless, (except in a metaphorical sense), but even if ideas had color we would say *colorless green ideas* and not *ideas green colorless* or *green ideas colorless*.

Similarly, we may not be able to make sense of Lewis Carroll's Jabberwocky, but we can identify the words *brillig, slithy*, and *mimsy* as adjectives, *toves, wabe, borogoves, and momeraths* as nouns, and *outgrabe, gyre, and gimble* as verbs, all based on their position in the sentences.

'Twas brillig, and the slithy toves
Did gyre and gimble in the wabe:
All mimsy were the borogoves,
And the momeraths outgrabe.

Speakers know the syntactic category of the various constituents and how they are ordered with respect to one another. They also know how to group words into units—*constituents*. This knowledge is graphically represented in tree structures that reveal the grammatical organization of the words of a sentence. Tree structures also explain how the grouping of words in a sentence relates to its meaning, such as when a sentence or phrase is ambiguous. And even when the meaning is nonsensical the structure must obey the syntactic rules of the language. The rules of syntax also permit speakers to produce and understand a limitless number of sentences never produced or heard before—*the creative aspect of linguistic knowledge*, illustrated at the beginning of this chapter. A major goal of linguistics is to show clearly and explicitly how syntactic rules account for what speakers implicitly know about their language.

Phrase Structure Trees

Who climbs the Grammar-Tree distinctly knows

Where Noun and Verb and Participle grows.

JOHN DRYDEN, "The Sixth Satyr of Juvenal," 1693

Now that you know something about constituent structure and grammatical categories, you are ready to learn how the phrases and sentences of a language are constructed. We will begin by illustrating trees for simple phrases and then proceed to more complex structures. The trees that we will build here are more detailed than those we saw in the previous sections, because the branches of the tree will have category labels identifying each constituent. In this section, we will also introduce the kind of syntactic rules that **generate** (a technical term for describe or specify) the different structures.

The tree diagram in (1) provides labels for each of the constituents of the sentence "The child found a puppy." These labels show that the entire sentence belongs to the syntactic category of S (because the S-node encompasses all the words). It also reveals that *the child* and *a puppy* belong to the category NP, that is, they are noun phrases, and that *found a puppy* belongs to the category VP or is a verb phrase, consisting of a verb and an NP. It also shows the syntactic category of each of the words in the sentence.

1.

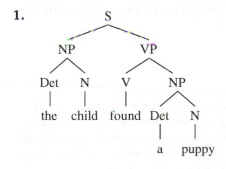

A tree diagram with syntactic category information is called a **phrase struc-ture tree** or a **constituent structure tree**. Phrase Structure trees (PS trees) represent three aspects of a speaker's syntactic knowledge:

1. The linear order of the words in the sentence
2. The identification of the syntactic categories of words and groups of words
3. The hierarchical structure of the syntactic categories (e.g., an S is com-posed of an NP followed by a VP, a VP is composed of a V that may be followed by an NP, and so on).

The syntactic category of each word is listed in our mental dictionaries, as we will discuss in more detail in Chapter 4. This lexical information guides the syntax of the language. Words appear in trees under labels that correspond to their syntac-tic category. Nouns are under *N*, determiners under *Det*, verbs under *V*, and so on.

The larger syntactic categories such as *VP* consist of all the syntactic catego-ries and words below that node in the tree. The *VP* in the PS tree above con-sists of syntactic category nodes *V* and *NP* and the words *found, a,* and *puppy*. Because *a puppy* can be traced up the tree to the node *NP*, this constituent is a noun phrase. Because *found* and *a puppy* can be traced up to the node *VP*, this constituent is a verb phrase. In discussing trees, every higher node is said to **dominate** all the categories beneath it. S dominates every node. A node is said to **immediately dominate** the categories one level below it. VP immediately dominates V and NP, the categories of which it is composed. Categories that are immediately dominated by the same node are **sisters**. V and NP are sisters in the phrase structure tree of "the child found a puppy."

PS trees are also useful for defining various grammatical relations in a precise way. For example, the subject of a sentence is the NP immediately dominated by S (*the child* in the tree in (1) and the direct object is the NP immediately dominated by VP (*the puppy* in the tree in (1).

Phrase Structure Rules

The information shown in a PS tree can also be represented by another formal device: phrase structure (PS) rules. PS rules capture the knowledge that speakers have about the possible structures of a language. Just as a speaker cannot have an infinite list of sentences in his or her head, so he or she cannot have an infinite set of PS trees in his or her head. Rather, a speaker's knowledge of the permissible and impermissible structures must exist as a finite set of rules that characterize a tree for any sentence in the language. To express the structure given above, we need the following PS rules:

1. S → NP VP
2. NP → Det N
3. VP → V NP

You can think of PS rules as templates that a tree must match to be grammatical. They express the regularities of the language and make explicit a speaker's knowledge of the order of words and the grouping of words into syntactic categories. For example in English an NP may contain a determiner followed by a noun. This is represented by rule 2. This rule conveys two facts:

A noun phrase may contain a determiner followed by a noun in that order.
A determiner followed by a noun is a noun phrase.

Phrase structure rules specify the well-formed structures of a language precisely and concisely. To the left of the arrow is the dominating category NP. The categories that it immediately dominates appear on the right side, in this case Det and N. The right side of the arrow also shows the linear order of these components. Thus, the subtree for the English NP looks like this:

Rule 1 says that a sentence (S) contains (immediately dominates) an NP and a VP in that order. Rule 3 says that a verb phrase consists of a verb (V) followed by an NP. These rules are general statements and do not refer to any specific VP, V, or NP. The subtrees represented by rules 1 and 3 are as follows:

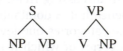

A VP need not contain an NP object, however. It may include a verb alone, as in the following sentences:

The woman laughed.
The man danced.
The horse galloped.

These sentences have the structure:

Thus, a tree may have a VP that immediately dominates only V, as specified by rule 4, which we include in our grammar:

4. VP → V

The following sentences contain prepositional phrases following the Verb:

The puppy played in the garden.
The boat sailed up the river.
A girl laughed at the monkey.
The sheepdog rolled in the mud.

The PS tree for such sentences is

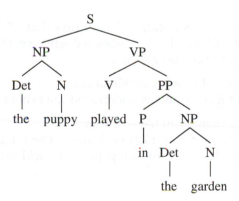

To generate structures of this type we need two additional PS rules as in 5 and 6.

5. VP → V PP
6. PP → P NP

Another option open to the VP is to contain or *embed* a sentence. For example, the sentence "The professor hoped that the students read the chapter" contains the sentence "the students read the chapter." Preceding the **embedded sentence** is the word *that*, which belongs to the category of complementizers

C(omp), a functional category like T(ense) and Det. Here is the structure of such sentence types:

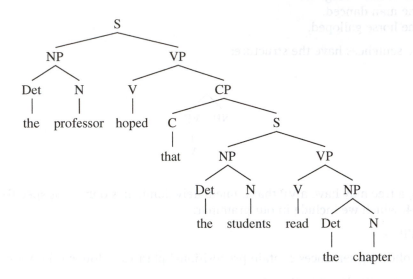

To allow such embedded sentences, we need to add these two new rules to our set of phrase structure rules.

7. VP → V CP
8. CP → C S

CP stands for complementizer phrase. Rule 8 says that CP contains a complementizer such as *that* followed by the embedded sentence. Other complementizers are *if* and *whether* in sentences such as

I don't know <u>whether</u> I should talk about this.
The teacher asked <u>if</u> the students understood the syntax lesson.

which have structures similar to the one above.

Here are the PS rules we have discussed so far. The rules have been slightly renumbered to keep all the VP rules together. We will introduce some other rules later.

1. S → NP VP
2. NP → Det N
3. VP → V NP
4. VP → V
5. VP → V PP
6. VP → V CP
7. PP → P NP
8. CP → C S

Building Phrase Structure Trees

Everyone who is master of the language he speaks . . . may form new . . . phrases, provided they coincide with the genius of the language.

JOHANN DAVID MICHAELIS, "Dissertation," 1739

The phrase structure rules can be used as a guide for building trees that follow the structural constraints of the language. In so doing, certain conventions are followed. The S occurs at the top or "root" of the tree (remember the tree is upside down). So, first find the rule with S on the left side of the arrow (rule 1) and put the categories on the right side below the S, as shown here

Continue by matching any syntactic category at the bottom of the partially constructed tree to a category on the left side of a rule, then expand the tree with the categories on the right side. For example, we may expand the tree by applying the NP rule to produce:

The categories at the bottom are Det, N, and VP, but only VP occurs to the left of an arrow in the set of rules and so needs to be expanded using one of the VP rules. Any one of the rules will work. The order in which the rules appear in the list of rules is irrelevant. (We could have begun by expanding the VP rather than the NP.) Suppose we use rule 4 next. Then, the tree has grown to look like this:

We continue in this way until all phrasal categories are expanded, that is, none of the categories at the bottom of the tree appears on the left side of any rule. The PP must expand into a P and an NP (rule 7), and the NP into a Det and an N. (Proper names and pronouns which are NPs and not nouns are an exception to the "full expansion convention.") We can use a rule as many times as it can apply. In this tree, we used the NP rule twice. After we have applied all the rules that can apply, the tree looks like this:

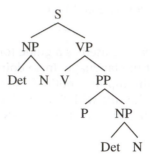

By following these conventions, we generate only trees specified by the PS rules, and hence only trees that conform to the syntax of the language. By implication, any tree not so specified will be ungrammatical, that is, not permitted by the syntax. At any point during the construction of a tree, any rule may be used as long as its left-side category occurs somewhere at the bottom of the tree. By choosing different VP rules, we could specify different structures corresponding to sentences such as:

The boys left. (VP → V)
The wind blew the kite. (VP → V NP)
The senator hopes that the bill passes. (VP → V CP)

Because the number of possible sentences in a language is infinite, there are also an infinite number of trees. However, all trees are built out of a finite set of phrase structure rules.

The Infinity of Language: Recursive Rules

Though incomplete, the set of PS rules we have introduced thus far is sufficient to illustrate the mechanisms by which languages generate a limitless number of sentences. Consider the following set of sentences, similar to those discussed at the beginning of this chapter.

1. Homer caught a pokémon.
2. Marge noticed that Homer caught a pokémon.
3. Bart wonders whether Marge noticed that Homer caught a pokémon.
4. Lisa knows that Bart wonders whether Marge noticed that Homer caught a pokémon.

We see that sentence 1 is embedded inside sentence 2, sentence 2 inside sentence 3, sentence 3 inside sentence 4. We could continue this process indefinitely. This is made possible by the fact that rule phrase structure rule 6 (VP → V CP) in combination with rules 8 (CP → C S) and 1 (S → NP VP) form a **recursive** set, in which the symbols S and VP occur on both the left and right side of the rules. Therefore, the rules allow S to contain VP, which in turn contains CP, which in turn contains S, which in turn again contains VP and so on, potentially without end. Recursive rules are of critical importance because they allow the grammar to generate an infinite set of sentences. The PS tree for sentence 4 illustrates the application of these rules (here we use triangles under the NPs to indicate that proper names are full NPs, not nouns):

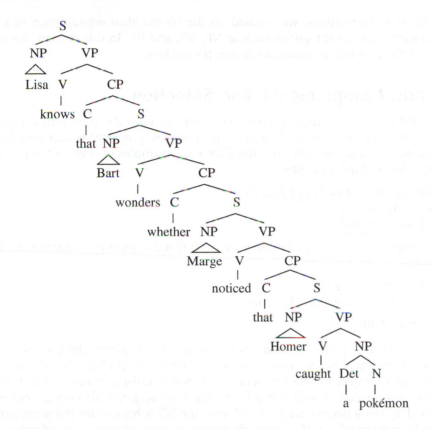

The property of recursion also illustrates the difference between competence and performance, discussed in Chapter 1. All speakers of English (and all other languages) have as part of their linguistic competence—their mental grammars—the ability to embed phrases within each other ad infinitum. However, as the structures grow longer, they become increasingly more difficult to produce and understand. This can be due to short-term memory limitations, muscular fatigue, breathlessness, boredom, or any number of performance factors. (We will discuss performance factors more fully in Chapter 10.) Nevertheless, these very long sentences would be well-formed according to the rules of the grammar.

Below, we will see other examples of recursive rule sets such as the one responsible for the potentially infinite number of prepositional phrases in sentences like:

The person behind the person immediately to the left of the rightmost person in the first row is asleep.

The Internal Structure of Phrases

I really do think that science has an internal structure, and it makes sense, and we can test it.

LISA RANDALL, Theoretical Physicist

In the previous sections, we focused on the hierarchical organization of sentences into phrasal categories such as NP, VP, and PP. In this section, we will look at the internal structure of phrases themselves.

Heads, Complements, and Selection

One of the striking things we observe when we consider the various phrase structure rules given above (and the subtrees they generate) is that they have a similar organization. Consider the following examples of each of the phrasal categories we have discussed:

NP: the *mother* of James Whistler
VP: *sing* an aria
PP: *over* the hill

For completeness, we add the category AP (adjective phrase), illustrated by the example

AP: *wary* of snakes
generated by the following rule:

9. AP → A PP

As we noted in our discussion of grammatical categories, the core of every phrase is a lexical category of its same syntactic type (italicized), which is its **head**; for example, the NP *the mother of James Whistler* is headed by the noun *mother;* the VP *sing an aria* is headed by the verb *sing;* the AP *wary of snakes* is headed by the adjective *wary;* the PP *over the hill* is headed by the preposition *over.* Loosely speaking, the entire phrase refers to whatever the head refers to. For example, the VP *sing an aria* refers to a "singing" event; the NP *the mother of James Whistler* to someone's mother.

In addition to the head, the phrasal categories may contain other categories such as NP, PP or CP. These sister categories are called **complements**. A complement is a phrasal category that occurs next to a head, and only there, and which elaborates on the meaning of the head. The complements are underlined: For example, the head N *mother* takes the PP complement of James Whistler; the head V *sing* takes the NP complement an aria; the head A(djective) *wary* takes the PP of snakes, and the P(reposition) *over* takes the NP the hill as complement.

Selection

Complements are not always present in the phrase structure. They are optional; only the head is obligatory. The choice of complement type for any particular phrase depends on the specific properties of the head of that phrase. For example, verbs select different kinds of complements: *find* is a transitive verb and requires an NP complement (direct object), as in *The boy found the ball*, but not **The boy found*, or **The boy found in the house*. Some verbs such as *eat* are optionally transitive. *John ate* and *John ate a sandwich* are both grammatical. *Sleep* is an **intransitive verb**; it cannot take an NP complement:

Michael slept.
*Michael slept the baby.

Some verbs, such as *think*, may select both a PP and a sentence complement (underlined):

Let's think about it.
I think a girl won the race.

Other verbs, such as *tell*, select an NP and a sentence:

I told the boy a girl won the race.

Yet other verbs such as *feel* select either an AP or a sentence complement:

Paul felt strong as an ox.
He feels he can win.

Categories besides verbs also select their complements. For example, the noun *belief* selects either a PP or a sentence, while the noun *sympathy* selects a PP, but not a sentence, as shown by the following examples:

the belief in freedom of speech
the belief that freedom of speech is a basic right
their sympathy for the victims
*their sympathy that the victims are so poor

Adjectives can also have complements. For example, the adjectives *tired* and *proud* select PPs:

tired of stale sandwiches
proud of her children

The information about the complement types selected by particular verbs and other lexical items is called **C-selection** or **subcategorization**, and is included in the lexical entries of the items in our mental lexicons. (C stands for "category.")

A verb also includes in its lexical entry a specification that imposes certain semantic requirements its subjects and complements, just as it selects for syntactic categories. This kind of selection is called **S-selection**. (S stands for "semantic.") For example, the verb *murder* requires its subject and object to be animate, while the verb *quaff* requires its subject to be animate and its object liquid. Verbs such as *like,* and *hate* select animate subjects. The following sentences violate S-selection and can only be used in a metaphorical sense. (We will use the symbol "!" to indicate a semantic anomaly.)

!Golf plays John.
!The beer drank the student.
!The tree liked the boy.

The famous sentence *Colorless green ideas sleep furiously* cited above is anomalous because (among other things) S-selection is violated (e.g., the verb *sleep* requires an animate subject). In Chapter 4, we will discuss the semantic relationships between a verb and its subject and objects in far more detail.

The well-formedness of a phrase depends, then, on at least two factors: whether the phrase conforms to the structural constraints of the language as expressed in the PS rules, and whether it obeys the selectional requirements of the head—both syntactic (C-selection) and semantic (S-selection).

The Three Levels of Phrases

In addition to the head and its complements, a phrase may have an element preceding the head. These elements are called **specifiers**. For example, in the NP *the mother of James Whistler,* the determiner *the* is the specifier of the NP. In English, possessives may also be specifiers of NP, as in *Nellie's ball*. The specifier position may also be empty, as in the NP *dogs with bones*. PPs, APs, and VPs also have specifiers, but for various reasons they are harder to see. They usually show up when the phrase is embedded in another sentence, as in

a. Betty made [Jane wary of snakes].
b. I heard [Pavarotti sing an aria].
c. I saw [everyone at the stadium].

In (a) *Jane* is the specifier of the AP *wary of snakes,* in (b) *Pavarotti* is the specifier of the VP *sing an aria,* and in (c) *everyone* is the specifier of the PP *at the stadium. Specifier* is a purely structural notion. In English, it is the first position in the phrase, if it is present at all, and a phrase may contain at most one specifier.

Unlike complements, specifiers are not sisters of the head, but rather sisters of the phrase formed by the head and the complement. These observations tell us that all of the phrasal categories, NP, VP, AP, and PP, have a similar three-tiered structure, as follows:

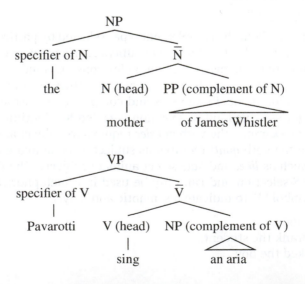

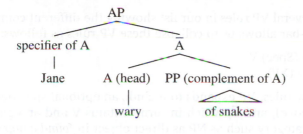

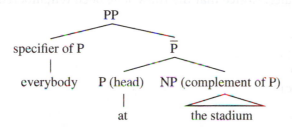

To capture the generalization that each phrasal category has the same internal structure, we substitute X in place of N, V, P, A and we get the following tree:

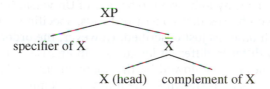

This three-tiered structure, referred to as **X-bar (X̄) schema**, is a template or blueprint that specifies how the phrases of a language are organized, or alternatively, how PS rules are formed. The X-bar schema "stands for" the various phrasal categories given above (and others we will see later) and applies to all syntactic phrases. The parentheses around the specifier and complement indicate that these expansions are optional and depend on the selectional properties of the head. The head is the only obligatory category of a phrase. The "bar" category is an intermediate level category necessary to account for certain syntactic phenomena that we'll see shortly.

Assuming X-bar schema we must modify our PS rules to incorporate the three tiers. Here are the revised rules for NP:

2a: NP → (Det) N̄
2b: N̄ → N (XP)

Under the new rules, NP expands as an optional Det and N̄ and N̄ expands as N and an optional complement of any category (XP). These rules will generate the PS tree for phrase *the mother of Whistler*, illustrated on the previous page, where XP stands for the PP *of Whistler* as complement to the head N *mother*.

We have several VP rules in our list showing the different complements to V (rules 3–6). X-bar allows us to collapse these VP rules as follows:

3a: VP → (Spec) $\overline{V}$
3b: $\overline{V}$ → V (XP)

Under the new rules, VP expands to include an optional specifier (*Pavarotti* in sentence b above), and $\overline{V}$, which in turn contains V and an optional complement of any category such as NP as direct object in *found a puppy*. Here is the revised set of rules. Notice that the rules have been renumbered and are more compact:

1. S → NP VP
2. NP → (Det) $\overline{N}$
3. $\overline{N}$ → N (XP)
4. VP → (Spec) $\overline{V}$
5. $\overline{V}$→V (XP)
6. PP → P NP
7. CP → C S
8. AP → A PP

Our PS rules for PP, and AP (rules 6 and 8) also adhere to X-bar (e.g., PP → (Spec) $\overline{P}$ etc.) but we omit the details. We will revisit the rules for S (rule 1) and CP (rule 7) below.

The X-bar schema is hypothesized to be part of Universal Grammar. As such, all languages have phrases that consist of heads, specifiers, and complements that relate to each other as just described. However, the order of the head and complement may differ in different languages. In English, for example, we see that the head comes first, followed by the complement. In Japanese, complements precede the head, as shown in the following examples:

Taro-ga	inu-o	mitsuketa	
Taro-subject marker	dog-object marker	found	"Taro found a dog"

Inu-ga	niwa-de	asonde	iru	
Dog-subject marker	garden-in	playing	is	"The dog is playing in the garden"

In the first sentence, the direct object complement *inu-o*, "dog," precedes the head verb *mitsuketa*, "found." In the second, the NP complement *niwa*, "garden," precedes the head preposition *de*, "in." English is a VO language, meaning that the verb ordinarily precedes its object. Japanese is an OV language, and this difference is reflected in the head/complement word order. For Japanese, the X-bar schema looks like this:

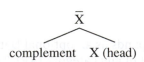

Compare this to the English schema:

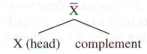

X-bar schema specifies a vast amount of syntactic knowledge in a concise way. If, as many linguistics believe, X-bar is universal (order aside) and hence part of children's innate endowment for language, it also helps explain how they so quickly learn the abstract hierarchical structures of phrases in their language (see Chapter 9). Upon hearing *Taro-ga inu-o mitsuketa* (Taro dog finds), the Japanese child automatically knows not only that NP complements precede the verb in his or her language, but also that all other complements do so as well. For example, NPs precede their prepositional heads, as in *niwa-de* (garden in). The English-speaking child will just as easily come to the opposite order based on sentences such as *John found the dog.*

What Heads the Sentence

Might, could, would—they are contemptible auxiliaries.

GEORGE ELIOT (MARY ANN EVANS), *Middlemarch*, 1872

We have suggested that the structure of all phrasal categories follows the X-bar schema. One category that we have not yet discussed in this regard is sentence (S). To preserve the powerful syntactic generalization that the X-bar schema offers, we want all the phrasal categories to have a three-tiered structure with specifiers, heads, and complements, but what would these be in the case of S? To answer this question, we first observe that sentences are always "tensed." Tense provides a time-frame for the event or state described by the verb. In English, present and past tenses are marked on the verb:

John danc**e**s. (present)
John danc**ed**. (past)

Future tense is expressed with the modal *will* (*John* will *dance*). Modals also express notions such as possibility (*John* may *dance*); necessity (*John* must *dance*); and ability (*John can dance*). A modal such as *may* says it is possible that the event will occur at some future time, *must* that it is necessary that the event occur at some future time, and so on. The English modals are inherently "tensed," as shown by their compatibility with various time expressions:

John may/must/can win the race today/tomorrow.
*John may/must/can win the race yesterday.
John could/would have tantrums when he was a child.
John could leave the country tomorrow.

Just as the VP is about the situation described by the verb—*eat ice cream* is about "eating"—so a sentence is about a situation or state of affairs that occurs at some point in time. Thus, the category Tense is a natural category to head S.

Using this insight, linguists refer to sentences as TPs (Tense Phrases) with the following structure conforming to the X-bar schema:

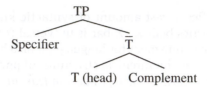

For sentences, or TPs, the specifier is the subject of the sentence and the complement of the T is a verb phrase. The head T contains the tense ($\pm$ pst) and modal verbs such as *can* or *would* and takes VP as its complement. The introduction of $\overline{\text{T}}$ gives the sentence its traditional subject–predicate form.

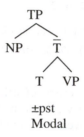

The NP left daughter of the TP functions as the subject of the sentence; the $\overline{\text{T}}$ right daughter is what is traditionally called the predicate. We are now able to represent the structures of such sentences as *The girl may cry* and *The child ate*:

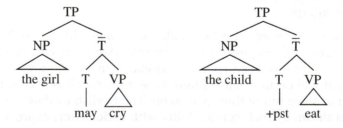

In these structures, the T containing +pst and *eat* is ultimately pronounced *ate*. When there is no modal under T, the present or past tense is realized on the verbal head of the VP.

Another way tense is expressed in English is by the tense-bearing word *do* that is inserted into negative sentences such as *John did not go* and questions such as *Where did John go?* In these sentences, *did* means "past tense." Later in this chapter, we will see how *do*-insertion works.

While many of the details of X-bar syntax are beyond the scope of an introductory text, we will briefly show how the inclusion of an intermediate $\overline{X}$ tier allows the grammar to generate a wide range of sentences that could not be otherwise produced, and also further explains the recursive property of human languages.

The Infinity of Language Revisited

So, naturalists observe, a flea

Hath smaller fleas that on him prey;

And these have smaller still to bite 'em,

And so proceed ad infinitum.

JONATHAN SWIFT, "On Poetry, a Rhapsody," 1733

We noted at the beginning of the chapter that languages have various means of creating longer and longer sentences. For example, an NP may contain any number of adjectives as in the *kind-hearted, intelligent, handsome boy*. One benefit of positing the abstract category $\overline{N}$ is that it allows us to account for the potentially limitless number of adjectives. Here we need a recursive rule—one that repeats itself—on $\overline{N}$:

9. $\overline{N} \rightarrow A\,\overline{N}$

This rule generates the NP structure in question:

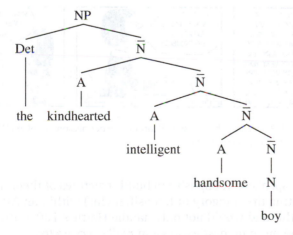

Without $\overline{N}$ we would be forced to have a recursive rule on NP such as NP → A NP. Such a rule would capture the recursion of the adjective, but it would also allow the Det to show up in an impossible place as in *kind-hearted, intelligent, the boy*:

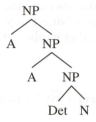

A similar kind of recursion occurs in this cartoon:

Another way speakers of English can build structures of theoretically limitless size is by repeating the category of Intensifier (Int) within an AP. The recursive rule looks like this and would not only handle Hattie's 100-word essay but also takes care of the more modest expression *really very pretty*:

10. $\overline{A} \rightarrow$ Int $\overline{A}$

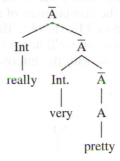

A slightly different form of recursion involves PP recursion, as illustrated by *she went over the hills through the woods to grandmother's house. . . .* Sentences of this sort requires recursion on $\overline{V}$.

11. $\overline{V} \rightarrow \overline{V}$ PP

giving rise to the following subtree

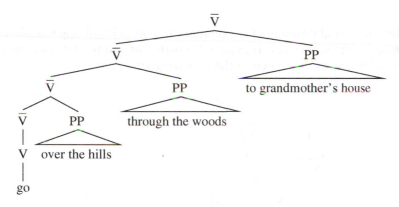

Note that the PP in (11), like the adjective in (9) and the intensifier in (10), are not complements, they are not sisters to the head of the phrase. Rather, they are sisters to $\overline{V}$, $\overline{N}$, and $\overline{A}$ respectively. A phrasal category that is sister to an $\overline{X}$ and daughter of a higher $\overline{X}$, as in the above structures, is called an **adjunct**. Like complements, adjuncts may be of any grammatical category.

Distinguishing between complements and adjuncts is not always straightforward. Structurally, the distinctions are unambiguous: complements are sisters to X; adjuncts are sisters to $\overline{X}$. But in analyzing sentences it is not always clear whether an addendum to a head is a complement or an adjunct. Here's one example illustrating the difference between a complement and an adjunct, an example that will bring us back to our discussion of the structural ambiguity of the sentence:

Sue saw the man with the telescope.

As discussed earlier, this sentence has more than one PS tree, each corresponding to a different meaning. Under the "instrumental" meaning (Sue used the telescope to see the man) the complement of *saw* is the simple NP *the man* and the PP is an *adjunct* introduced by rule 11. The sentence has the following constituent structure: (From now on we'll adopt the convention of using a triangle when we are not concerned with the internal structure of the category.)

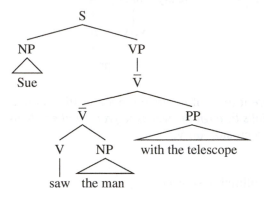

Under the second meaning of the sentence (the man is holding the telescope), *the man* and *with the telescope* form an NP constituent and the PP is a *complement* to the head noun, as illustrated in the following structure:

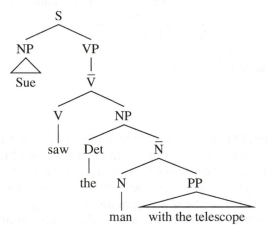

Thus, the different meanings arise from the fact that in the first case the PP *with the telescope* is sister to (hence modifies) the $\overline{\text{V}}$ *see the man*; but in the second case it is sister to (hence modifies) *man*. The two interpretations of this sentence are possible because the rules of syntax permit different structures for the same linear order of words.

Let us sum up our discussion thus far. We have seen that sentences have a tree-like organization. They are not simply "flat" strings of words, as shown by various constituency tests, as well as structural ambiguities. Phrase structure trees specify (i) the grammatical categories of words and groups of words in a sentence, for example, N, V, VP, and so on, (ii) the position of categories with respect to each other, that is, word order, and (iii) the internal organization of words into hierarchically arranged phrases. The PS rules for a language thus define the (infinite set) of well-formed (grammatical) structures in that language.

Grammatical Dependencies

> Method consists entirely in properly ordering and arranging the things to which we should pay attention.
>
> RENÉ DESCARTES, *Oeuvres*, vol. X, c. 1637

In addition to the properties discussed above, the syntactic component of the grammar must describe various relationships and dependencies that hold across and within sentences. It is clear that certain sentence types are related, for example, the declarative-question pair below:

Homer will sleep.
Will Homer sleep?

Our grammar must reflect the speaker's knowledge of relationships of this sort.

Similarly, within a sentence two elements can be related even when they are separated by an arbitrary number of words. These "dependencies at a distance" provide further evidence for the hierarchical organization of sentences provided by the PS rules. Two such rules are subject–verb agreement, and question formation.

Subject–Verb Agreement

In many languages, including English, the verb must agree with the subject. The verb (in English) is marked with an *-s* when the subject is third-person singular and otherwise unmarked.

1. This **guy seems** kind of cute.
2. These **guys seem** kind of cute.

A simple rule that expresses the agreement relationship in terms of the linear adjacency of the noun (*guy/guys*) and verb (*seem/seems*) would work for the sentences in 1 and 2:

Linear Agreement Rule

The verb agrees in person and number with the word to its left.

But what about the sentences in 3 and 4?

3. The **guy** we met at the party next door **seems** kind of cute.
4. The **guys** we met at the party next door **seem** kind of cute.

The verb *seem* must agree with the head of the subject NP, *guy* or *guys*, regardless of the number of words between the head noun and the verb. Moreover, there is no limit to how many words may intervene, or whether they are singular or plural, as the following sentence illustrates:

The **guy (guys)** we met at the party next door that lasted until 3 a.m. and was finally broken up by the cops who were called by the neighbors **seems (seem)** kind of cute.

The (much abbreviated) phrase structure tree below explains why this is so.

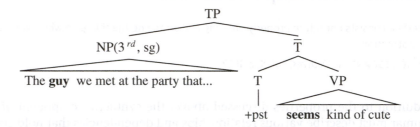

In the tree, the NP may in principle be indefinitely long and complex. However, speakers of English (and all other languages) know that agreement depends on sentence structure and not on the linear order of words: agreement is between the head of the subject NP and the main verb. As far as the rule of agreement is concerned, all other material can be ignored. (Although in actual performance, if the distance is too great, the speaker may forget what the subject was.) Thus, the rules of grammar that relate different elements in the sentence are **structure dependent** and therefore a more accurate agreement rule must be stated in terms of hierarchical structure:

Structure dependent agreement rule: The verb agrees in person and number with the *subject* of the sentence, where *subject* is defined as the NP immediately dominated by S (TP).

The fact that rules are structure dependent supports the tree-like arrangement of constituents in a sentence. If sentences were just flat strings of words, it would be impossible to state an agreement rule.

Structure dependency is a principle of Universal Grammar, and is thus found in all languages. In languages that have subject–verb agreement, the dependency is between the verb and the subject, and never some other NP such as the closest one, as shown in the following examples from Italian, German, Swahili, and English, respectively (the third-person singular agreement affix in the verb is in boldface and is governed by the boldfaced NP, not the underlined one, even though the latter is nearest the main verb):

La madre con tanti figli lavor**a** molto.
Die Mutter mit den vielen Kindern arbeit**et** viel.
Mama anao watoto wengi **anajitahidi.**
The mother with many children work**s** a lot.

Question Formation Rules

THE ARGYLE SWEATER © 2012 Scott Hilburn. Dist.
By ANDREWS MCMEEL SYNDICATION. Reprinted with
permission. All rights reserved.

Yes–no questions

I put the words down and push them a bit.

EVELYN WAUGH, quoted in *The New York Times*, April 11, 1966

Within any language certain sentence types relate systematically to other sentence types, such as the following pairs:

The boy will sleep.	Will the boy sleep?
The dog is barking.	Is the dog barking?
The man has eaten a fish.	Has the man eaten a fish?

Each pair of sentences is about the same situation. For example, the first sentence asserts that a "boy-sleeping" situation will happen. Such sentences are called **declarative** sentences. The corresponding question asks whether such a "boy-sleeping" situation will occur. Sentences of the second sort are called **yes–no questions**. The only actual difference in meaning between these sentences is that one asserts information while the other asks for confirmation of information. This meaning difference is indicated by the different word orders, illustrating that two sentences may have a structural difference that corresponds *in a systematic way* to a meaning difference. The grammar of the language must account for this fact.

The standard way of describing these relationships is to say that the related sentences come from a common underlying structure. Yes–no questions are a case in point. A yes–no question begins life as a declarative sentence, a TP in the X-bar schema, for example:

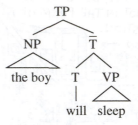

The head of the TP, namely T (the modal *will* in this example), is central to the formation of yes–no questions as well as certain other types of sentences in English. In yes–no questions, the modal or auxiliary verb *have* or *be* appears in a different position; it precedes the subject.

The relationship between a declarative sentence and a yes–no question can be described by a rule that moves the material in T before the subject NP. This rule applies to the tree structure.

For the sentence *The boy will sleep* shown on the previous page to derive the structure below:

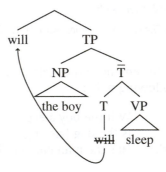

For descriptive purposes, we'll call this rule **Aux inversion**. Aux inversion is an example of what is traditionally referred to as a **transformational rule**. For now, we will leave unspecified the structural position that the auxiliary moves to in the tree above. We return to that below.

Thus, yes–no questions are thus generated in two steps:

1. PS-rules generate a basic structure.
2. Aux inversion applies to the basic structure to produce the derived structure.

By generating questions in two steps, we are claiming that a principled structural relationship exists between a question and its corresponding statement. Intuitively, we know that such sentences are related. The transformational rule is a formal way of representing this knowledge.

More generally, the basic structures of sentences are called **deep structures** or **d-structures**. Variants on the basic sentence structures are derived via transformational rules. The derived structures—the ones that follow the application of transformational rules—are called **surface structures** or **s-structures**. Loosely said, we *speak* and *hear* s-structures but mentally connect s-structures to d-structures. If no transformations apply, then d-structure and s-structure are the same. If transformations apply, then s-structure is the result after all transformations have taken effect.

In our discussion of the constituency test "move as a unit," we saw other rules that dislocate elements of a sentence, for example, the active-passive pair in 1 and PP-preposing in 2:

1. The child found a puppy → A puppy was found by the child.
2. The puppy played in the garden → In the garden the puppy played.

We saw earlier that the rule of subject–verb agreement is sensitive to structure and not to the linear position of elements in a sentence. We can now go further and state that all grammatical rules are structure dependent. For example, the PP-preposing rule in 2 cannot move just any string of words that begins with a preposition: It looks at the specific structure of the sentence containing the PP. This is made evident by the fact that *with a telescope, Sue saw the man* is not ambiguous. It has only the meaning "Sue used a telescope to see the man," corresponding to the first phrase structure on page 106 where the PP is immediately dominated by the $\overline{V}$. In the structure corresponding to the other meaning, "the boy saw a man who had a telescope," the PP is in the NP, as in the second tree on page 106. The PP-preposing transformation applies to the first structure but not the second.

Aux inversion provides yet another illustration of structure dependency.

1. The boy who **can** run fastest **will** win.
2. **Will** the boy who **can** run fastest win?
3. *****Can** the boy who run fastest **will** win?

The contrast in grammaticality of the sentences in 2 and 3 shows that to form a question Aux inversion applies to the modal within the $\overline{T}$ that is dominated by the root (highest) TP, and not simply to the *first* modal in the sentence, as illustrated in this highly abbreviated structure.

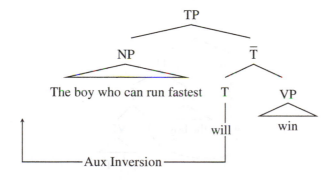

Let's now look at the structure of "Will the boy sleep?" in more detail. Thus far we have been assuming S (TP) is the root of the sentence. Strictly speaking, this is not correct. Remember our PS rule 7, repeated below.

7. CP → C S

From this rule, we see that CP (Complementizer Phrase) dominates S (TP). Though this rule was previously used only for embedded sentences such as *Marge noticed that Homer caught a pokémon*, yes–no questions (and many other structures) tell us that all sentences have CP as their root. Like all other categories, CP conforms to X-bar schema and hence we modify rule 7 accordingly:

7(a).:   CP → (Spec) $\overline{\text{C}}$
7(b).: $\overline{\text{C}}$ → C TP

The sentence root is CP and TP is the complement to the head C. C contains the abstract element $+Q$ for questions or $-Q$ for declaratives. Putting aside the specifier of CP for the moment, the X-bar analysis of CP has the advantage that C provides a home for T when Aux inversion relocates it. The d-structure for questions is:

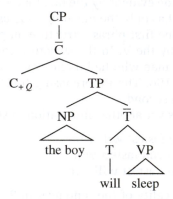

and the modal is moved to C:

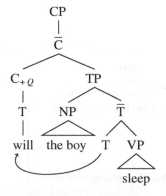

The auxiliaries *have* and *be* also undergo Aux inversion in yes–no question:

Spot has chased a squirrel.   Has Spot chased a squirrel?
Nellie is snoring.   Is Nellie snoring?

But the d-structure position of these auxiliaries is not under T. We know this because they can also occur with modals (which occupy the T position) as in:

Nellie may be snoring.
Spot must have found a squirrel.

Moreover, like other verbs in English (and unlike modals) *have* and *be* inflect for tense (and agreement): *am, is, are, was, were, have, has, had.* These observations lead us to conclude that *have/be* originate under V. When there is no modal in the sentence, *have* or *be* can undergo a movement that is not available to other verbs: they can "raise" from the position under V to T, and then undergo a second movement to C to form a question, as follows:

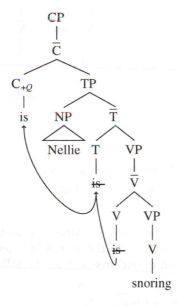

Additional PS rules would be needed to account for sentences with both *have* and *be* such as *Spot has been chasing squirrels* and even such unusual sentences as *The squirrels have been being chased by Spot.*

In addition to questions, the need for the complementizer phrase (CP) is provided by phrasal categories that take sentences (TPs) in their complements (underlined):

belief that iron floats (CP complement to head N)
wonders if iron floats (CP complement to head V)
happy that iron floats (CP complement to head A)
about whether iron will sink (CP complement to head P)

The words *that, if,* and *whether* are complementizers and the CP has a place for them under its head C, for example:

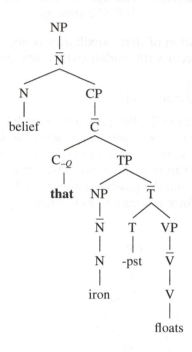

Wh Questions

Whom are you? said he, for he had been to night school.

GEORGE ADE, "The Steel Box," in *Bang! Bang!*, 1928

We have shown that syntactic rules are structure dependent and do not pay attention to the length or content of the words in a sentence. Nowhere is this better illustrated than in **wh questions** such as the following.

1. **(a)** What will Max chase _____?
   (b) Where should Pete put his dog bone _____?
   (c) Which toys does Pete like _____?

Wh questions contain *wh* phrases of various syntactic categories, for example, *what* is an NP, *which* is a determiner, and *where* is a PP. They are inserted into a PS tree under the appropriate category node, like all other words. In English and many other languages, *wh* phrase generally have to move from their d-structure position, indicated by the _____ in the sentences in (1), to the beginning of the sentence ("echo questions" like *you ate what!?* behave differently and we'll ignore them here).

Several clues tell us that the *wh* phrases in (1) have undergone movement. For example, the verb *chase* in sentence (a) is transitive, yet there is no direct object following it. There is a "gap" where the direct object should be. The verb *put* in sentence (b) is subcategorized for a direct object and a prepositional phrase, yet there is no PP following *his bone*. Finally, in sentence (c) *like* is followed by a gap and also has the third-person singular *-s* morpheme though it is preceded by a plural noun.

We can explain the grammaticality of the sentences in (1) despite these "abnormalities" by assuming that in each case the *wh* phrase originates in the position of the gap, as in (2), and is then moved to the beginning of the sentence by transformational rule.

2. **(a)** Max will chase *what?*
   (b) Pete should put his dog bone *where?*
   (c) Pete likes *which toys?*

The sentences in (1) are grammatical because the requirement that *chase* and *like* have a direct object is satisfied by the *what* and *which toys*, while the PP requirement of *put* is satisfied by *where*. The subcategorization requirements of the verbs are met prior to movement of the *wh* phrase. In any *wh* question, there is a dependency between the *wh* phrase at the beginning of the sentence and a gap somewhere else in the sentence.

Wh questions such as those in (1) are generated in several steps: phrase structure principles provide the basic declarative word orders in (2) (or more precisely the d-structure) with the *wh* expression in complement position, as required by the X-bar schema and the selectional properties of the verbs *chase*, *put* and *like*. Transformational operations then apply. Taking (2a) as illustrative, the rule *wh* movement relocates the *wh* expression from its d-structure position to a structural position at the beginning of the sentence, which we now identify as the Specifier of CP. Aux inversion moves the modal to the C, as in the derivation of yes–no questions. Following are the d-structure and s-structure trees for the sentence "What will Max chase?" is:

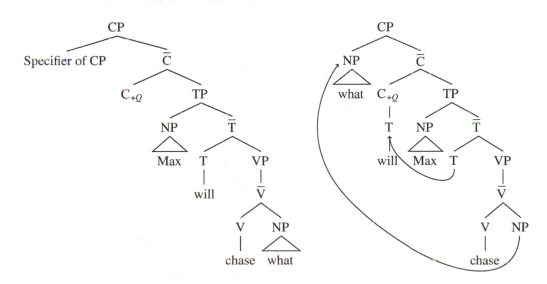

At this point, it is worth observing that like proper names and pronouns, *wh* expressions such as *what* and *who* are full NPs, not Ns. Unlike nouns, *who* and *what* cannot appear with a determiner, an adjective, or any other NP element.

*The what did you see?

*The fast who won the race?

However, *what* can be a determiner, like *which*. This is reflected in the structure for the sentence *Which toys does Pete like?* Following is the d-structure of this sentence:

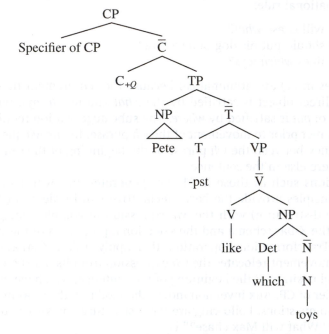

After *wh* movement and Aux Inversion have done their work we have this near s-structure:

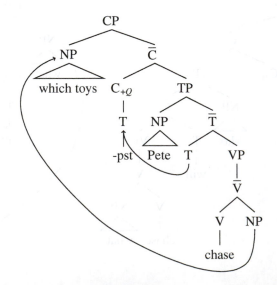

Additionally, when T lacks an actual word and carries only the present tense, as in this sentence, it still undergoes movement because Aux Inversion is *structure dependent* and doesn't pay attention to the particular words (or lack thereof) under a category. With T separated from the main verb by an NP, something is needed to carry the tense. That something is the "dummy" word *do*, and it is put in place by a transformational rule of *do-insertion*, yielding the final s-structure:

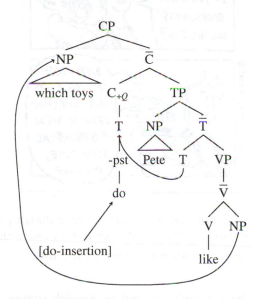

Do combines with [-pst] to yield the present tense *does*. Rules that convert inflectional features such as *past tense* or *third-person present tense* into their proper phonological forms are called **spell-out rules**. They apply to the syntactic output of s-structures.

A notable property of *wh* questions is that the *wh* phrase is relocated to a position outside its original d-structure clause. Indeed, there is no limit to the distance that a *wh* phrase can move, as illustrated by the following sentences. The dashes indicate the d-structure position from which the *wh* phrases has been moved.

Who did Helen say the senator wanted to hire _____?
Who did Helen say the senator wanted the congressional representative to try to hire _____?
Who did Helen say the senator wanted the congressional representative to try to convince the Speaker of the House to get the Vice President to hire _____?

"Long-distance" dependencies such as those created by *wh* movement are a fundamental part of human language. They provide still further evidence that sentences are not simply strings of words but are supported by a rich scaffolding of phrase structure trees. These trees express the underlying structure of a sentence as well as its relation to other sentences in the language, and as always reflect a person's knowledge of syntax.

UG Principles and Parameters

Savage Chickens   by Doug Savage

www.savagechickens.com

Whenever the literary German dives into a sentence, that is the last you are going to see of him till he emerges on the other side of the Atlantic with his Verb in his mouth.

MARK TWAIN, *A Connecticut Yankee in King Arthur's Court*, 1889

In this chapter, we have largely focused on English syntax, but many of the grammatical structures we have described for English also hold in other languages. This is because Universal Grammar (UG) provides the basic design for all human languages, and individual languages are simply variations on this basic blueprint. Imagine a new housing development. All of the houses have the same floor plan, but the occupants have some choices to make. They can have carpet or hardwood floors, curtains or blinds; they can choose their kitchen cabinets and the countertops, the bathroom tiles, and so on. This is more or less how the syntax operates. Languages conform to a basic design, and then there are choice points or points of variation.

All languages have structures that conform to the X-bar schema. Phrases consist of specifiers, heads, and complements; barred categories express recursive properties; sentences are headed by T, which is specified for information such as tense and modality; and so on.

However, languages may have different orders within the phrases and sentences. The word order differences between English and Japanese, discussed earlier, illustrate this interaction of general and language-specific properties. UG specifies the structure of a phrase. It must have a head and may take a complement of some type and have adjuncts. However, each language defines for itself the relative order of these constituents: English is head-initial, Japanese is head-final. We call the points of variation **parameters**.

All languages appear to have transformational rules for reordering elements to achieve certain purposes such as creating questions or emphasizing certain constituents. In Dutch, for example, in which the modal moves, if there is one, as in (1), and otherwise the main verb moves, as in (2):

1. Zal Femke fietsen? (from "Femke zal fietsen.")
    will Femke bicycle ride
    (Will Femke ride her bicycle?)
2. Leest Meindert veel boeken? (from "Meindert leest veel boeken.")
    reads Meindert many books
    (Does Meindert read many books?)

Main verbs in Standard American English do not move. Instead, *do* spells out the stranded tense and agreement features. All languages have expressions for requesting information about *who, when, where, what,* and *how.* Even if the question words in other languages do not necessarily begin with "wh," we will refer to such questions as *wh* questions. In some languages, such as Japanese and Swahili, the *wh* phrase does not move. It remains in its original d-structure position. In Japanese the sentence is marked with a question suffix *-no:*

Taro-ga	nani-o	mitsuketa-no?
Taro	what	found

Recall that Japanese word order is SOV, so the *wh* phrase *nani* ("what") is an object and occurs before the verb.

In Swahili, the *wh* phrase—*nani* by pure coincidence—also stays in its base position:

Ulipatia	nani	kitabu?
you gave	who	a book

However, in all languages with *wh* movement (i.e., movement of the question phrase), the question element moves to the same sentence-initial position. The "landing site" of the moved phrase is determined by UG. Among the *wh* movement languages, there is some variation. In the Romance languages, such as Italian, the *wh* phrase moves as in English, but when the *wh* phrase questions the object of a preposition, the preposition must move together with the *wh* phrase. In English the preposition can be "stranded" (i.e., left behind in its original position):

A chi hai dato il libro?
To whom (did) you give the book?
*Chi hai dato il libro a?
Who(m) did you give the book to?

In some dialects of German, long-distance *wh* movement leaves a trail of *wh* phrases:

Mit	Wem	glaubst	Du	Mit	wem	Hans	spricht?
With	whom	think	you	with	whom	Hans	talks

(Whom do you think Hans talks to?)

Wen	willst	Du	wen	Hans	anruft?
Whom	want	you	whom	Hans	call

(Whom do you want Hans to call?)

In Czech a quantity question phrase can be moved, leaving behind the NP it modifies:

Jak	velké	Václav	koupil	auto?
How	Big	Václav	bought	car

(How big a car did Vàclav buy?)

Despite these variations and despite the fact the wh phrase can move a very long distance, there are certain instances in which it cannot apply and these constraints are universal and structure dependent. For example, consider the following three "sentences:" (Remember that the position from which the *wh* phrase has moved is indicated with _____.)

1. **(a)** Spock asked Kirk if Scotty had fixed the warp drive?
   (b) Who did Spock ask _____ whether Scotty had fixed the warp drive?
   (c) *Who did Spock ask Kirk whether _____ had fixed the warp drive?

The only difference between the grammatical (1b) and the ungrammatical (1c) is that in (1b) the *wh* phrase originates in the higher clause, whereas in (1c) the *wh* phrase comes from inside the *whether* clause. This illustrates that the constraint against movement depends on structure and not on the length of the sentence. Some sentences can be very short and still not allow *wh* movement:

2. **(a)** George admired Martha's mother.
   (b) Who did George admire?
   (c) Whose mother did George admire?
   (d) *Whose did George admire mother?

The sentences in (2) show that a *wh* phrase cannot be extracted from inside a possessive NP. In (2b) it is okay to question the whole direct object. In (2c) it is even okay to question a piece of the possessive NP, providing the entire *wh* phrase is moved, but (2d) shows that moving the *wh* word alone out of the possessive NP is illicit.

The principle of structure dependency, the X-bar principles governing the organization of phrases, and the constraints on movement just illustrated, are part of UG. These aspects of grammar need not be learned. They are part of the innate blueprint for language that the child brings to the task of acquiring a language. What children must learn are the language-specific aspects of grammar. Where there are parameters of variation, children must determine the correct choices for their language. The Japanese child must determine that the verb comes after the object in the VP, and the English-speaking child that the verb comes before it. The Dutch-speaking child acquires a rule that moves the verb to make a question, while the English-speaking child has a more restrictive rule regarding such movement. Italian, English, and Czech children learn that to form a question the *wh* phrase moves, whereas Japanese and Swahili children determine that there is no movement. As far as we can tell, children fix these parameters very quickly. We will have more to say about how children set UG parameters in Chapter 9.

Sign Language Syntax

All languages have rules of syntax similar in kind, if not in detail, to those that we have seen for English, and sign languages are no exception. Signed languages have phrase structure (PS) rules that build hierarchical structures out of linguistic constituents and specify the word order of a given signed language. ASL is an SVO language. The signer of ASL knows that the first two sentences below are grammatical sentences of ASL, but the third is not. [The capitalized words represent signs.]

CAT CHASE DOG
"The cat chased the dog."
DOG CHASE CAT
"The dog chased the cat."
*CHASE CAT DOG

Unlike in English, however, adjectives can follow the head noun in ASL, as in Spanish, for example, and other spoken languages.

The PS rules also determine the grammatical functions of a sentence such as subject and object, so that a signer of ASL knows that while the first two sentences are both grammatical, they differ with respect to who is chasing whom. Finally, the PS rules of signed languages exhibit language-specific variation, just as those of spoken languages do. The grammatical sentences given above for ASL would not be grammatical for signers of Italian Sign Language (LIS or "Lingua dei Segni Italiana"), because LIS is an SOV language.

In ASL, as in English and other spoken languages, the basic word order can be modified by movement rules. For example, a direct object or other constituent such as a temporal adverb can be moved to the beginning of the sentence in a process called *topicalization*. This is done to bring attention to this constituent:

BOOK, JOHN READ YESTERDAY
YESTERDAY, JOHN READ BOOK

It is also possible for movement to apply iteratively, giving a double topicalization structure, as in:

YESTERDAY, BOOK, JOHN READ

Topicalization in ASL is accompanied by raising the eyebrows and tilting the head upward, marking the special word order, much as intonation does in English. The use of such non-manual markers is a salient feature of signed languages and something that distinguishes them from spoken languages. Spoken language may be accompanied by facial expressions and other non-manual gestures. But however expressive or informative such gestures are, they do not form part of the grammatical system of a spoken language as they do in signed languages.

Wh questions in ASL may also be formed via movement. In contrast to English, the movement is optional. In ASL, *wh* phrases may remain in the d-structure position as in Japanese and Swahili. The ASL equivalents of *Who did Bill see yesterday?* and *Bill saw who yesterday?* are both grammatical. As in English and other spoken languages, *wh* movement in signed languages is constrained in various ways (see Appendix D). For example, in ASL it is not possible to question one member of a coordinate structure:

> *WHO JOHN KISS MARY AND _____ YESTERDAY?
> *"Who did John kiss Mary and yesterday?"

Similar constraints operate in topicalization. For example, a constituent cannot be moved out of the clause beginning with another *wh* phrase:

> *MOTHER, I NOT-KNOW WHAT LIKE
> *"(As for) Mother, I don't know what _____ likes."

Wh questions in ASL are accompanied by an obligatory facial expression with a tilted head and furrowed brows. These nonmanual markers are analogous to the special intonation that indicates interrogatives in many spoken languages.

Signed languages also have complex structural means to express notions such as tense, modality, and negation. In ASL, as in English, there are several forms of negation, including NO, NOT, NONE, and NEVER, and they may follow different rules. The sign NOT, for example, can come at the end of an ASL sentence, quite unlike the behavior of the English word *not*. The structural rules for negation in ASL also require that the signer shake his or her head while producing a negative sentence, and even allow a signer to "shorten" or "reduce" the negation of a sentence to just a head shake, without producing the actual sign for NOT or NEVER. This is similar to how a speaker of English can shorten *not* to *n't*.

ASL and other sign languages show an interaction of universal and language-specific properties. The rules of sign languages are structure-dependent, and movement rules are constrained in various ways. Other properties such as the nonmanual markers and the use of space are an integral part of the grammar of sign languages but not of spoken languages. The fact that sign languages appear to be subject to the same principles and parameters of UG that spoken languages are subject to shows us that the human brain is designed to acquire and use language, not simply speech.

Summary

Speakers of a language recognize the grammatical sentences of their language and know how the words in a sentence must be ordered and grouped to convey a certain meaning. All speakers are capable of producing and understanding an unlimited number of new sentences that have never before been spoken or heard. They also recognize ambiguities, know when different sentences mean the same thing, and correctly interpret the grammatical relations in a sentence, such as **subject** and **direct object**. This kind of knowledge comes from their knowledge of the rules of syntax.

Sentences have structure that can be represented by **phrase structure trees** containing **syntactic categories**. Phrase structure trees reflect the speaker's mental representation of sentences. Ambiguous sentences may have more than one phrase structure tree.

Phrase structure trees reveal the linear order of words and the constituency of each syntactic category. There are different kinds of syntactic categories: **Phrasal categories**, such as NP and VP, are composed of other syntactic categories; **lexical categories**, such as Noun and Verb, and **functional categories**, such as Det and T, often correspond to individual words. The hierarchical structure of the phrasal categories is universal and is specified by *X-bar schema*. NPs, VPs, and so on are headed by nouns, verbs, and the like. The sentence (S or TP) is headed by T, which carries such information as tense and modality.

The particular order of elements within the phrase is subject to language-particular variation and can be expressed through the **phrase structure rules** of each language, which conform to the X-bar schema. Here is a composite of all the phrase structure rules given in this chapter renumbered to keep phrasal types together.

1. $S\ (=TP) \rightarrow NP\ \overline{T}$
2. $\overline{T} \rightarrow T\ VP$
3. $NP \rightarrow (Det)\ \overline{N}$
4. $\overline{N} \rightarrow N\ (XP)$
5. $\overline{N} \rightarrow A\ \overline{N}$
6. $VP \rightarrow (Spec)\ \overline{V}$
7. $\overline{V} \rightarrow V\ (XP)$
8. $\overline{V} \rightarrow \overline{V}\ PP$
9. $PP \rightarrow P\ NP$
10. $CP \rightarrow (Spec)\ \overline{C}$
11. $\overline{C} \rightarrow C\ TP\ (=S)$
12. $AP \rightarrow A\ PP$
13. $\overline{A} \rightarrow Int\ \overline{A}$

A grammar is a formally stated, explicit description of the mental grammar or the speaker's linguistic competence. The **lexicon** represents the knowledge that a speaker has about the vocabulary of his or her language. This knowledge includes the syntactic categories of words as well as the **subcategorization** or **C-selection** properties of particular lexical items that specify the complements they can take, for example, whether a verb is **transitive** or **intransitive**. The lexicon also contains semantic information, including the kinds of NPs that can function as semantically coherent subjects and objects: **S-selection**. Selectional restrictions must be satisfied in the **d-structure** representation of the sentence.

Transformational rules such as Aux Inversion, Wh Movement, and do-insertion account for relationships between sentences such as declarative and interrogative pairs, including *wh* questions. The output of the transformational rules is the **s-structure** of a sentence, the structure that most closely determines how the sentence is to be pronounced (or signed). Inflectional information, such as tense, may be represented as abstract features in the phrase structure tree. After the rules of the syntax have applied, these features are sometimes spelled out as affixes such as *-ed* or as function words such as *do*.

The basic design of language is universal. Universal Grammar specifies that syntactic rules are **structure-dependent** and that movement rules may not move phrases out of certain structures, among many other constraints, including a need to not violate the X-bar schema. These constraints exist in all languages—spoken and signed—and need not be learned. UG also contains parameters of variation, including the order of heads and complements, and the variations on movement rules. A child acquiring a language must fix the parameters of UG for that language.

References for Further Reading

Baker, M. C. 2001. *The atoms of language: The mind's hidden rules of grammar.* New York: Basic Books.

Carney, A. 2012. *Syntax: A generative introduction, 3rd ed.* Cambridge, MA: Blackwell.

Chomsky, N. 1995. *The minimalist program.* Cambridge, MA: MIT Press.

___. 1972. *Language and mind, rev. ed.* New York: Harcourt Brace Jovanovich.

___. 1965. *Aspects of the theory of syntax.* Cambridge, MA: MIT Press.

Jackendoff, R. S. 1994. *Patterns in the mind: Language and human nature.* New York: Basic Books.

Pinker, S. 1999. *Words and rules: The ingredients of language.* New York: HarperCollins.

Radford, A. 2009. *Analysing English sentences: A minimalist approach.* Cambridge, UK: Cambridge University Press.

___. 2004. *English syntax: An introduction.* Cambridge, UK: Cambridge University Press.

Exercises

1. Besides distinguishing grammatical from ungrammatical sentences, the rules of syntax account for other kinds of linguistic knowledge, such as:
   a. when a sentence is structurally ambiguous. (Cf. *The boy saw the man with a telescope.*)
   b. when two sentences with different structures mean the same thing. (Cf. *The father wept silently.* and *The father silently wept.*)
   c. systematic relationships of form and meaning between two sentences, like declarative sentences and their corresponding interrogative forms. (Cf. *The boy can sleep.* and *Can the boy sleep?*)

   Draw on your linguistic knowledge of English to come up with an example illustrating each of these cases. (Use examples that are different from the ones in the chapter.) Explain why your example illustrates the point. If you know a language other than English, provide examples in that language, if possible.

2. Consider the following sentences:

   a. I hate war.
   b. You know that I hate war.
   c. He knows that you know that I hate war.
       i. Write another sentence that includes sentence (c).
       ii. What does this set of sentences reveal about the nature of language?
       iii. How is this characteristic of human language related to the difference between linguistic competence and performance? (Hint: Review these concepts in Chapter 1.)

3. Paraphrase each of the following sentences in two ways to show that you understand the ambiguity involved:

   Example: Smoking grass can be nauseating.

       i. Putting grass in a pipe and smoking it can make you sick.
       ii. Fumes from smoldering grass can make you sick.

   a. Dick finally decided on the boat.
   b. The professors appointment was shocking.
   c. The design has big squares and circles.
   d. That sheepdog is too hairy to eat.
   e. Could this be the invisible mans hair tonic?
   f. The governor is a dirty street fighter.
   g. I cannot recommend him too highly.
   h. Terry loves his wife and so do I.
   i. They said she would go yesterday.
   j. No smoking section available.
   k. We will dry clean your clothes in 24 hours.
   l. I bought cologne for my boyfriend containing 25% alcohol.
   m. The new magazine has between one and two billion readers.

4. Here are two examples where structural ambiguities lead to humorous results.

   For sale: an antique desk suitable for lady with thick legs and large drawers.

   We will oil your sewing machine and adjust tension in your home for $10.00.

   Using square brackets to delineate constituents, explained the ambiguity and the resulting humor of these two sentences by doing a constituent analysis.

5. Following the X-bar schema, draw two phrase structure trees to represent the two meanings of the sentence *The magician touched the child with the wand.* Be sure you indicate which meaning goes with which tree. (Hint: this is similar to an example in the text)

6. Indicate the grammatical category of each of the words in the following sentences.

   a. The girls love sushi.
   b. That boy has won many races.
   c. Mary will finish her homework in the library.
   d. A strong wind uprooted the tall trees.
   e. My dog is exceptionally smart.

7. Consider the phrase structure rule NP → (Det) $\overline{\text{N}}$ as given in this chapter to account for NPs such as *dogs* in *dogs bark*. Why would this rule not work for expressions such as *who, he, Mary*.

8. Draw the NP subtrees for the italicized NPs in the following sentences:

   a. *Every mother* hopes for good health.
   b. *A big black dog is* barking.
   c. *Angry men in dark glasses* roamed the streets.
   d. Challenge exercise: *Melissa's garden* is beautiful.

9. In all languages, sentences can occur within sentences. For example, in Exercise 2, sentence (b) contains sentence (a), and sentence (c) contains sentence (b). Put another way, sentence (a) is embedded in sentence (b), and sentence (b) is embedded in sentence (c). Sometimes embedded sentences appear slightly changed from their normal forms, but you should be able to recognize and underline the embedded sentences in the following examples. Underline in the non-English sentences, when given, not in the translations (the first one is done as an example):

   a. Yesterday I noticed <u>my accountant repairing the toilet</u>.
   b. Becky said that Jake would play the piano.
   c. I deplore the fact that bats have wings.
   d. That Guinevere loves Lorian is known to all my friends.
   e. Who promised the teacher that Maxine wouldn't be absent?
   f. It's ridiculous that he washes his own Rolls-Royce.
   g. The woman likes for the waiter to bring water when she sits down.
   h. The person who answers this question will win $100.
   i. The idea of Romeo marrying a 13-year-old is upsetting.
   j. I gave my hat to the nurse who helped me cut my hair.
   k. For your children to spend all your royalty payments on recreational drugs is a shame.
   l. Give this fork to the person I'm getting the pie for.

   m. khâw   chyâ   waǎ   khruu   maa. (Thai)
      He   believe   that   teacher   come

      He believes that the teacher is coming.

   n. Je   me   demande   quand   il   partira. (French)
      I   me   ask   when   he   will leave

      I wonder when he'll leave.

   o. Jan zei   dat Piet dit   boek niet heeft gelezen. (Dutch)
      Jan said that Piet this book not has   read

      Jan said that Piet has not read this book.

10. Adhering to the X-bar schema, draw phrase structure trees for the following sentences.
    a. The puppy found the child.
    b. A surly passenger insulted the attendant.
    c. The house on the hill collapsed in the earthquake.
    d. The ice melted.
    e. The hot sun melted the ice.
    f. The old tree swayed in the wind.
    g. The wondrous, beautiful, blue guitar sold for a song.

11. Create three phrase structure trees of 6, 7, 8, 9, and 10 words. Use your mental lexicon to fill in the bottoms of the trees.

12. Using one or more of the constituency tests (i.e., stand alone, move as a unit, replacement by a pronoun) discussed in the chapter, determine which of the boldfaced portions in the sentences are constituents (and which are not). Provide the grammatical category of the constituents.
    a. Martha found **a lovely pillow** for the couch.
    b. The **light in this room** is terrible.
    c. I wonder **whether Bonnie has finished packing her books.**
    d. Melissa slept **in her class**.
    e. **Pete and Max** are fighting over the bone.
    f. I gave a bone to Pete **and to Max** yesterday.
    g. I gave a bone to **Pete and** to Max yesterday.

13. The two sentences below contain a **verbal particle** up:
    He *ran* up the bill.
    He *ran* the bill *up*.
    a. The verbal particle *up* and the verb *run* depend on each other for the unique idiosyncratic meaning of the phrasal verb *run up*. (*Running up a bill* involves neither running nor the location up.) Does *up the bill* form a constituent? Give at least one argument that favors your answer.
    b. List five other verb+ particle combinations in English.

14. In terms of C-selection restrictions, explain why the following are ungrammatical:
    a. *The man located.
    b. *Jesus wept the apostles.
    c. *Robert is hopeful of his children.
    d. *Robert is fond that his children love animals.
    e. *The children laughed the man.

15. The complement of V may be a single NP direct object as for *find*. English also has **ditransitive verbs**, ones whose complement may be two NPs, such as *give*:
    The emperor gave the vassal a castle.
    Think of three other ditransitive verbs in English and give example sentences.

16. Tamil is a language spoken in India by upward of 70 million people. Following are word-for-word translations of PPs from Tamil to English:

Tamil to English Meaning

the bed on   "on the bed"
the village from   "from the village"

a. Based on these data, is Tamil a head initial or a head final language?
b. What would the PS tree for a Tamil PP look like?

17. Here are three more word-for-word glosses in Tamil:

a story tell   "tell a story"
the boy a cow saw   "the boy saw a cow"
woman this slept   "this woman slept"

Do these additional data support or argue against your analysis in Exercise 16? What would the pertinent VP and NP trees look like in Tamil, based on these data?

18. Provide the d-structure for each of the following *wh* questions. Then state the grammatical function of the *wh* phrase (e.g., subject, object, etc.)

Example: Who did Mary see?
d-structure: Mary saw who
Who is the direct object

a. Who left the party early?
b. Where did Mary leave her wallet?
c. What did you eat for dinner last night?
d. Who did Mary write to?
e. Which book did Sue read?
f. Whose jacket are you wearing?
g. Who did Al forget that Betty invited to the party?
h. Which bear did Goldilocks say that Mama Bear gave porridge to?
i. What did Goldilocks say that Mama Bear gave to Baby Bear?

19. As illustrated in the last two examples of the previous question, a *wh* phrase can move a very long distance. But as we saw in the chapter, there are certain instances in which it cannot apply and these constraints are universal and structure dependent. Consider the following sentences and state (in your own words) the constraint that blocks *wh* movement in the ungrammatical examples.

a. Paul and John play beautiful music.
b. Who plays beautiful music?
c. Paul and who (else) play beautiful music?
d. *Who do Paul and play beautiful music.
e. The children love macaroni and cheese?
f. What do the children love?
g. What do the children love macaroni with?
h. *What do the children love macaroni and?

20. There are many systematic, structure-dependent relationships among sentences similar to the one discussed in the chapter between declarative and interrogative sentences. Here are some example sentences based on existential *there* sentences:

   a. (i) A boy is on the roof.
      (ii) There is a boy on the roof.
   b. (i) A boy danced on the roof.
      (ii) *There danced a boy on the roof.
   c. (i) A boy was dancing on the roof.
      (ii) There was a boy dancing on the roof.
   d. (i) A wallet was left in the restaurant.
      (ii) There was a wallet left in the restaurant.
   e. (i) The boy is on the roof.
      (ii) *There is the boy on the roof.
   f. (i) A man seems to be in the garden.
      (ii) There seems to be a man in the garden.

   Formulate in your own words a transformational rule relating the pairs in (i) and (ii). Be careful that your rule generates the grammatical pairs but not the ungrammatical ones.

Challenge exercise:
Now consider the following pair of sentences:

   g. (i) Students must be in the dorm by midnight.
      (ii) There must be students in the dorm by midnight.

Can you describe the difference in meaning between sentence (i) and (ii)?
   Does this meaning difference undermine the transformational analysis of *there* sentences?

21. State at least three differences between English and the following languages, using just the sentence(s) given. Ignore lexical differences (i.e., the different vocabulary). Here is an example:

Thai:	Dèg	khon	níi	kamlang	kin.
	boy	*classifier*	this	*progressive*	eat

   "This boy is eating."

Mǎa	tua	nán	kin	khâaw.
dog	classifier	that	eat	rice

   "That dog ate rice."

   Three differences are (1) Thai has "classifiers." They have no English equivalent. (2) The words (determiners, actually) *this* and *that* follow the noun in Thai, but precede the noun in English. (3) The "progressive" is expressed by a single separate word in Thai. The verb does not change form. In English, the progressive is indicated by the presence of the verb *to be* and the adding of *-ing* to the verb.

   a. French

Cet	homme	intelligent	comprendra	la question.
this	man	intelligent	will understand	the question

'This intelligent man will understand the question.'

Ces	hommes	intelligents	comprendront	les questions.
these	men	intelligent	will understand	the questions

"These intelligent men will understand the question."

b. Japanese

Watashi	ga	sakana	o	tabete	iru.
I	*subject marker*	fish	*object marker*	eat (ing)	am

"I am eating fish."

c. Swahili

Mtoto			alivunja			kikombe.	
m-	toto	a-		li-	vunja	ki-	kombe
class marker	child	he		*past*	break	*class marker*	cup

"The child broke the cup."

Watoto			wanavunja			vikombe.	
wa-	toto	wa-		na-	vunja	vi-	kombe
class marker	child	they		*present*	break	*class marker*	cup

"The children break the cups."

d. Korean

Kɨ	sonyɔn-iee			wɨyu-lɨl		masi-ass-ta.		
kɨ	sonyɔn-	iee		wɨyu-	lɨl	masi-	ass-	ta
the	boy	*subject marker*	milk	*object marker*	drink	*past*	*assertion*	

"The boy drank milk."

kɨ nɨn		muɔs-ɨl		mɔk-ass-nɨnya		
kɨ	nɨn	muɔs-	ɨl	mɔk-	ass-	nɨnya
he	*subject marker*	what	*object marker*	eat	*past*	*Question*

"What did he eat?"

e. Tagalog

Nakita	ni	Pedro-ng		puno	na	ang	bus.
nakita	ni	Pedro	-ng	puno	na	ang	bus
saw	*article*	Pedro	that	full	already	*topic marker*	bus

"Pedro saw that the bus was already full."

22. Transformations may delete elements, as in the following "elliptical" sentences:

(i.) Mary will study hard for the exam and John will too.

(ii.) John wrote a letter to someone, but I don't know who.

(iii.) John loves carrots and Mary broccoli.

a. Identify the omitted constituent in each of the examples above. (Hint: Do this by providing the d-structure for each sentence.)

b. Provide three more examples of each kind of "ellipsis" illustrated above.

Research question: Consult with a speaker of another language and determine whether this language has the same kinds of ellipsis as English does, or other kinds. (If you know another language you can use your own intuitions to answer this question.)

23. **Challenge exercise:** Compare the following French and English sentences:

French	English
Jean boit toujours du vin. Jean drinks always some wine (*Jean toujours boit du vin.)	John always drinks some wine. *John drinks always some wine.
Marie lit jamais le journal. Marie reads never the newspaper (*Marie jamais lit le journal.)	Mary never reads the newspaper. *Mary reads never the newspaper.
Pierre lave souvent ses chiens. Pierre washes often his dogs. (*Pierre souvent lave ses chiens.)	Peter often washes his dogs. *Peter washes often his dogs.

a. Based on the above data, what would you hypothesize concerning the relative positions of adverbs of frequency (e.g., *toujours, jamais, souvent, always, never, often*) and the verbs they modify in French and English?

b. Now suppose that UG specifies that in *all languages* the adverbs of frequency must precede $\overline{V}$ reflecting a phrase structure rule $\overline{V} \rightarrow$ Adv $\overline{V}$. Describe in words—don't worry about the details—a transformational rule needed to derive the correct surface word order for French? (Hint: review the discussion of the auxiliaries *have* and *be* raising and the phrase structure tree that illustrates that process.)

c. In terms of that transformational rule how do French and English differ?

24. Dutch and German are Germanic languages related to English, and as in English, *wh* questions are formed by moving a *wh* phrase to sentence-initial position.

In what way are the rules of question formation in Dutch and German different from those in English? Base your answer on the following data:

German				Dutch			
i. Was	hat	Karl	gekauft?	Wat	heeft	Wim	gekocht?
what	has	Karl	bought	what	has	Wim	bought
"What has Karl bought?"				"What has Wim bought?"			

German				Dutch			
ii. Was	kauft	Karl?		Wat	koopt	Wim?	
What	buys	Karl		what	buys	Wim	
"What does Karl buy?"				"What does Wim buy?"			

iii. Kauft	Karl	das	Buch?	Koopt	Wim	het	boek?
buys	Karl	the	book	buys	Wim	the	book
"Does Karl buy the book?"				"Does Wim buy the book?"			

25. **Challenge exercise:** We noted that it is often not straightforward to distinguish adjuncts from complements. "One-replacement" provides a test: only nouns with adjuncts can be substituted for by *one*, as in *a patient with a broken arm and* one *with a broken leg* (adjunct), but nouns with true complements do not allow one-replacement, so that **a patient of the doctor and one of the chiropractor* is not well-formed. Here are four examples of complements and four of adjuncts. Apply the *one*-replacement test to determine which is which:

    a. the man with the golden arm
    b. a voter for proposition eighteen
    c. my cousin's arrival at his home
    d. the construction of a retaining wall
    e. the boat in the river
    f. the ocean white with foam
    g. the desecration of the temple
    h. the betrayal of Julius Caesar

26. **Challenge research exercise:** X-bar theory demands binary branching and that a head may have one and only one complement. Ditransitive verbs such as *write* and *give.* (they are numerous) pose problems insofar as fitting into the strict (dare we say "Procrustean") requirements of X-bar. This research project asks you to examine the work that has been done to accommodate the facts of ditransitive verbs with X-bar theory.

4

The Meaning of Language

> Surely all this is not without meaning.

HERMAN MELVILLE, *Moby-Dick*, 1851

For thousands of years, philosophers have pondered the **meaning** of *meaning*, yet speakers of a language can easily understand what is said to them and can produce strings of words that are meaningful to other speakers. We use language to convey information to others *(My new bike is pink)*, ask questions *(Who left the party early?)*, give commands *(Stop lying!)*, and express wishes *(May there be peace on Earth)*.

What do you know about meaning when you know a language? You know when a "word" is meaningful *(flick)* or meaningless *(blick)*, and you know when a "sentence" is meaningful *(Jack swims)* or meaningless *(Colorless green ideas sleep furiously)*. You also know when a word has two meanings *(bear)* and when a sentence has two meanings *(Jack saw a man with a telescope)*. You know when two words have the same meaning *(sofa and couch)*, and when two sentences have the same meaning *(Jack put off the meeting, Jack put the meeting off)*. And you know when words or sentences have opposite meanings *(alive/dead; Jack swims/Jack doesn't swim)*.

You are generally familiar with the real-world objects that words refer to such as *the chair in the corner*; and even if the words do not refer to actual objects, such as *the unicorn behind the bush*, you still have a sense of what they mean.

Importantly, if you know the meaning of a (declarative) sentence, you know its **truth conditions**, or in other words, you know the circumstances under which the sentence is true or false. In some cases, it's obvious, or redundant *(all kings are male* [true], *all bachelors are married* [false]); in other cases, you need some further, nonlinguistic knowledge *(Molybdenum conducts electricity)*, but by knowing the meaning, you know the kind of world knowledge that is needed. Often, if you know that a sentence is true *(Nina bathed her dogs)*, you can infer that another

133

sentence must also be true *(Nina's dogs got wet)*: that is, the first sentence **entails** the second sentence.

Like our syntactic knowledge, knowledge about meaning extends to an unlimited set of sentences, and is part of the grammar of the language. The study of the linguistic meaning of morphemes, words, phrases, and sentences is called **semantics**. Subfields of semantics are **lexical semantics**, which is concerned with the meanings of words and the meaning relationships among words; and **compositional semantics**, which is concerned with how the meanings of words are combined to form the meanings of larger syntactic units such as phrases and sentences. The study of how context affects meaning—for example, how the sentence *It's cold in here* comes to be interpreted as "close the windows" in certain situations—is called **pragmatics**.

What Speakers Know about Sentence Meaning

Language without meaning is meaningless.

ROMAN JAKOBSON

For speakers to understand the meaning of (an infinite number of) sentences requires a system of semantic rules. These rules build the meaning of a sentence from the meanings of its words and its syntactic structure. They allow speakers to determine which conditions need to hold for a sentence to be true or false, when one sentence implies the truth or falseness of another, and whether a sentence has multiple meanings. This is called compositional semantics or **truth-conditional semantics** because it calculates the **truth conditions** of a sentence by composing, or putting together, the meanings of smaller units according to semantic rules. When you know the general truth conditions of a sentence, you can then apply them to any specific situation in which the sentence is used and determine the **truth value** of the sentence, that is, whether it is true or false in that situation.

We will limit our discussion to declarative sentences such as *Jack swims* and *Jack kissed Laura*, because we can specify precisely what the truth conditions are. For example, the sentence *Jack swims* is true if it's uttered in a situation in which the person named Jack can swim or is a habitual swimmer.

Truth

. . . Having Occasion to talk of Lying and false Representation, it was with much Difficulty that he comprehended what I meant . . . For he argued thus: That the Use of Speech was to make us understand one another and to receive Information of Facts; now if any one said the Thing which was not, these Ends were defeated; because I cannot properly be said to understand him . . . And these were all the Notions he had concerning that Faculty of Lying, so perfectly well understood, and so universally practiced among human Creatures.

JONATHAN SWIFT, *Gulliver's Travels*, 1726

Suppose you are at the poolside and Jack is swimming in the pool. If you hear the sentence *Jack swims*, and you know the meaning of that sentence, then you will judge the sentence to be true. On the other hand, if you are indoors and you happen to believe that Jack never learned to swim, then when you hear the very same sentence *Jack swims*, you will judge the sentence to be false and you will think the speaker is misinformed or lying. More generally, if you know the meaning of a sentence, then you can determine under what conditions it is true or false. Knowing the meaning tells you how to determine the truth value.

The converse is not true; you don't need to actually know whether a sentence is true or false to know its meaning. Rather, you just need to know (or be able to figure out) the conditions under which it is true or false. The sentence *copper conducts electricity* has meaning and is understood because we know how to determine whether it's true or false: for example, by use of a voltmeter. We could also comment sensibly on the sentence by noting the use of copper wire in lamps. On the other hand, we find the sentence *Crumple-horned snork-acks incarnadine nargles* is meaningless because we don't have the foggiest idea how to determine whether it is true or false.

For most sentences, it does not make sense to say that they are always true or always false. Rather, they are true or false in a given situation, as we previously saw with *Jack swims*. But a restricted number of sentences are indeed always true regardless of the circumstances. They are called **tautologies**. (The term **analytic** is also used for such sentences.) Examples of tautologies are sentences such as *Circles are round* and *A person who is single is not married*. Their truth is guaranteed solely by the meaning of their parts and the way they are put together. Similarly, some sentences are always false. These are called **contradictions**. Examples of contradictions are sentences such as *Circles are square* or *A bachelor is married*.

Entailment and Related Notions

You mentioned your name as if I should recognize it, but beyond the obvious facts that you are a bachelor, a solicitor, a Freemason, and an asthmatic, I know nothing whatever about you.

SIR ARTHUR CONAN DOYLE, "The Norwood Builder," in *The Memoirs of Sherlock Holmes*, 1894

Much of what we know is deduced from what people say alongside our observations of the world. Sherlock Holmes took deduction to the ultimate degree, as illustrated in the quotation. Often, deductions can be made based on language alone.

If you know that the sentence *Jack swims beautifully* is true, then you also know that the sentence *Jack swims* is true. This meaning relation is called **entailment**. We say that *Jack swims beautifully* entails *Jack swims*. More generally, one sentence entails another if whenever the first sentence is true the second one is also true in all conceivable circumstances.

Generally, entailment goes only in one direction. So, while the sentence *Jack swims beautifully* entails *Jack swims*, the reverse is not true. Knowing merely that

Jack swims is true does not necessitate the truth of *Jack swims beautifully.* Jack could be a poor swimmer. On the other hand, negating both sentences reverses the entailment. *Jack doesn't swim* entails *Jack doesn't swim beautifully.*

The notion of entailment can be used to reveal knowledge that we have about other meaning relations. For example, omitting tautologies and contradictions, two sentences are **synonymous** (or **paraphrases**) if they are both true or both false with respect to the same situation. Sentences such as *Jack put off the meeting* and *Jack postponed the meeting* are synonymous, because when one is true the other must be true; and when one is false the other must also be false. We can describe this pattern in a more concise way by using the notion of entailment:

Two sentences are synonymous if they entail each other.

Thus, if sentence A entails sentence B and vice versa, then whenever A is true B is true, and vice versa. Although entailment says nothing specifically about false sentences, it's clear that if sentence A entails sentence B, then whenever B is false, A must be false. (If A were true, B would have to be true.) And if B also entails A, then whenever A is false, B would have to be false. Thus, mutual entailment guarantees identical truth values in all situations; the sentences are synonymous. Two sentences are **contradictory** if, whenever one is true, the other is false or, equivalently, there is no situation in which they are both true or both false. For example, the sentences *Jack is alive* and *Jack is dead* are contradictory because if the sentence *Jack is alive* is true, then the sentence *Jack is dead* is false, and vice versa. In other words, *Jack is alive and Jack is dead* always have opposite truth values. Like synonymy, contradiction can be defined in terms of entailment.

Two sentences are *contradictory* if one entails the negation of the other. For instance, *Jack is alive* entails the negation of *Jack is dead*, namely *Jack is not dead.* Similarly, *Jack is dead* entails the negation of *Jack is alive*, namely *Jack is not alive.*

The notions of *contradiction* (always false) *and contradictory* (opposite in truth value) are related in that if two sentences are contradictory, their conjunction with *and* is a contradiction. Thus, *Jack is alive and Jack is dead* is a contradiction; it cannot be true under any circumstances.

Describing meaning in terms of truth conditions has proved to be very fruitful in understanding semantic properties of language such as entailment and synonymous or contradictory sentences.

Ambiguity and the Principle of Compositionality

Let's pass gas.

In Chapter 2, we saw that the sentence *The boy saw the man with a telescope* was an instance of structural ambiguity. It is ambiguous because it can mean that the boy saw the man by using a telescope or that the boy saw the man who was holding a telescope. The sentence is structurally ambiguous because it is associated with two different phrase structures, each corresponding to a different meaning. Here are the two structures:

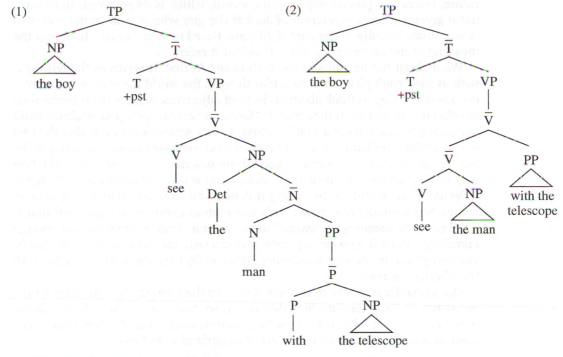

In (1) the PP *with the telescope* modifies *man*, so the interpretation is that the man has the telescope. In (2) the PP *with a telescope* modifies the action of seeing the man, so the interpretation is that the boy saw the man by using the telescope.

Lexical ambiguity arises when a word has more than one meaning. The sentence *This will make you smart* is ambiguous because of the two meanings of the word *smart*: "clever" and "feel a burning sensation."

Lexical and structural ambiguities clearly illustrate that the meaning of a linguistic expression is built both on the words it contains and on its syntactic structure. The notion that the meaning of an expression is composed of the meanings of its parts and how they are combined structurally is referred to as the **principle of compositionality**. In the next section, we discuss the rules by which the meaning of a phrase or sentence is determined based on its composition.

Compositional Semantics

To manage a system effectively, you might focus on the interactions of the parts rather than their behavior taken separately.

RUSSELL L. ACKOFF

To account for speakers' ability to determine the meaning of a limitless number of expressions, the mental grammar must contain semantic rules that combine the meanings of words into meaningful phrases and sentences.

Semantic Rules

In the sentence *Jack swims*, we know that the word *Jack*, which is a **proper name**, refers to a precise object in the world, which is its **referent**. In the scenario given earlier, the referent of *Jack* is the guy who is your friend and who is swimming happily in the pool right now. Based on this, we conclude that the meaning of the name *Jack* is the individual it refers to.

What about the meaning of the verb *swim*? At first, it seems as though verbs such as *swim* can't pick out a particular thing in the world the way proper names do. There is a way to think about verbs (and adjectives, and common nouns such as *cake*) in terms of what they refer to. Based in part on early philosophical work conducted by Gottlob Frege and Bertrand Russell, semanticists think that the best way to define **predicates** (verbs, adjectives, and common nouns) is in terms of the individuals that those predicates successfully describe. Under this view, the best way to characterize the meaning of *swim*—and a way in which that meaning is reflected in the world—is by having it denote the *set* of individuals (e.g. human beings and animals) that swim. This assumption captures the intuition that if you know the meaning of "swim," then, given a specific situation and enough knowledge about it, you can separate who is a swimmer from who is not, that is, you can group the swimmers together. You can do the same with any other verb (or adjective or nouns).

Our semantic rules are sensitive not only to the meaning of individual words but also to the structure in which they occur. So, taking as an example our simple sentence *Jack swims*, let us see how the semantic rules compute its meaning. The meanings of the individual words are summarized as follows:

Word	Meanings
Jack	refers to (or means) the individual Jack
swims	refers to (or means) the set of individuals that swim

The phrase structure tree for our sentence is as follows:

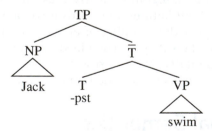

The tree tells us that syntactically the NP *Jack* and the T̄ *swims* combine to form a sentence (TP). We want to mirror that combination at the semantic level: In other words, we want to combine the meaning of the NP *Jack* (an individual) and the meaning of the VP *swims* (a set of individuals) to obtain the meaning of the sentence *Jack swims*. This is done by means of Semantic Rule I.

Semantic Rule I

The meaning of

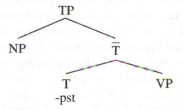

is the following truth condition:

If the meaning of NP (an individual) is a member of the meaning of VP (a set of individuals), then the sentence is *true*; otherwise it is *false*.

Rule I states that a sentence composed of a subject NP and a predicate VP is true if the subject NP refers to an individual who is among the members of the set that constitute the meaning of the VP. This rule is entirely general; it does not refer to any particular sentence, individual, or verb. It works equally well for sentences such as *Ellen sings* or *Max barks*. Thus, the meaning of *Max barks* is the truth condition (i.e., the "if-sentence") that states that the sentence is true if the individual denoted by *Max* is among the set of *barking* individuals.

Let us now try a slightly more complex case: the sentence *Jack kissed Laura*. The main syntactic difference between this example and the previous one is that we now have a transitive verb that requires an NP in object position; otherwise our semantic rules derive the meaning using the same mechanical procedure as in the first example. We again start with the word meaning and syntactic structure:

Word	Meanings
Jack	refers to (or means) the individual Jack
Laura	refers to (or means) the individual Laura
kissed	refers to (or means) the set of pairs of individuals X and Y such that X kissed Y.

Here is the phrase structure tree:

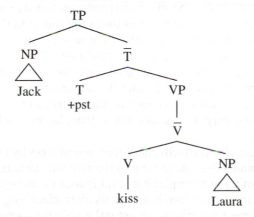

The meaning of the transitive verb *kiss* is still a set, but this time the set consists of *pairs* of individuals. The first individual of each pair is the kisser, while the second is the one kissed. This captures the intuition that if you know the meaning of *kiss*, then, given enough knowledge, you are able to established who kissed who in a given situation, that is, you are able to group people into pairs of kissers and kissees. If a set of pairs is the meaning of a transitive verb like *kiss*, what's the meaning of the VP resulting from combining a transitive verb with its object as in the VP *kissed Laura*? Like the simple VP *swim* we saw earlier, the meaning of the complex VP *kissed Laura* is a set of individuals—all and only those individuals that kissed Laura in a given situation.

This may be expressed formally in Semantic Rule II.

Semantic Rule II

The meaning of

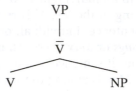

is the set of individuals X such that X is the first member of any pair in the meaning of V whose second member is the meaning of NP.

The meaning of the sentence is derived by first applying Semantic Rule II, which establishes the meaning of the VP as a certain set of individuals, namely those who kissed Laura. Now, Semantic Rule I applies and gives the meaning of the sentence to be true whenever the meaning of *Jack* is a member of the set that is the meaning of the VP *kissed Laura*. In other words, the sentence is true if Jack kissed Laura and false otherwise. These two semantic rules handle a limitless number of intransitive and transitive sentences.

One last example will illustrate how the semantic knowledge of entailment may be represented in the grammar. In the sentence, *Jack swims beautifully* the meaning of *beautifully* is an operation that reduces the size of the sets that are the meanings of verb phrases. It reduces the set of individuals who swim to the smaller set of those who swim beautifully. We won't express this rule formally, but it is now easy to see one source of entailment. The truth conditions that make *Jack swims beautifully* true are narrower than the truth conditions that make *Jack swims* true by virtue of the fact that among the individuals who swim, fewer of them swim beautifully. Therefore, any situation that makes *Jack swims beautifully* true necessarily makes *Jack swims* true; hence, *Jack swims beautifully* entails *Jack swims*.

Rules such as these give the truth conditions of sentences by taking the meanings of words and combining them according to the syntactic structure of the sentence. It is easy to see from these examples how ambiguous meanings arise. Because the meaning of a sentence is computed based on its hierarchical organization, different trees will have different meanings—structural ambiguity—even when the words are the same, as in the example *The boy saw the man with the telescope.*

When Compositionality Goes Awry

A loose sally of the mind; an irregular undigested piece; not a regular and orderly composition.

SAMUEL JOHNSON (1709–1784)

The meaning of an expression is not always obvious, even to a native speaker of the language. Meanings may be obscured in many ways, or at least may require some imagination or special knowledge to be apprehended. Poets, pundits, and yes, even professors can be difficult to understand.

In the previous sections, we saw that semantic rules compute sentence meaning compositionally based on the meanings of words and the syntactic structure that contains them. There are, however, interesting cases in which compositionality breaks down, either because there is a problem with words or with the semantic rules. If one or more words in a sentence do not have a meaning, then obviously we will not be able to compute a meaning for the entire sentence. Even when the individual words have meaning, if they cannot be combined together as required by the syntax and related semantic rules we will also not get to a meaning. Situations of this sort are referred to as semantic **anomaly**. Sometimes a lot of creativity and imagination are required to derive a meaning. This is what happens in **metaphors**. Finally, some expressions—called **idioms**—have a fixed meaning. Because the meaning of idioms is not given by the meaning of its parts applying compositional rules to them gives rise to funny or inappropriate meanings.

Anomaly

Don't tell me of a man's being able to talk sense; everyone can talk sense. Can he talk nonsense?

WILLIAM PITT

There is no greater mistake in the world than the looking upon every sort of nonsense as want of sense.

LEIGH HUNT, "On the Talking of Nonsense," 1820

The semantic properties of words determine what other words they can be combined with. A sentence widely used by linguists that we encountered in Chapter 2 illustrates this fact:

Colorless green ideas sleep furiously.

The sentence obeys all the syntactic rules of English. The subject is *colorless green ideas* and the predicate is *sleep furiously*. It has the same syntactic structure as the sentence

Dark green leaves rustle furiously.

but there is obviously something semantically wrong with the sentence. The meaning of *colorless* includes the semantic feature "without color," but it is combined with the adjective *green*, which has the feature "green in color." How can something be both "without color" and "green in color"? Other semantic violations occur in the sentence. Such sentences are semantically **anomalous**.

Other "sentences" make no sense at all because they include "words" that have no meaning; they are **uninterpretable**. They can be interpreted only if some meaning for each nonsense word can be dreamt up. Lewis Carroll's "Jabberwocky" is probably the most famous poem in which most of the content words have no meaning—they do not exist in the lexicon of the language. Still, all the sentences sound as if they should be or could be English sentences:

> 'Twas brillig, and the slithy toves
> Did gyre and gimble in the wabe;
> All mimsy were the borogoves,
> And the mome raths outgrabe.
>
> . . .
>
> He took his vorpal sword in hand:
> Long time the manxome foe he sought—
> So rested he by the Tumtum tree,
> And stood awhile in thought.

Without knowing what *vorpal* means, you nevertheless know that

> He took his vorpal sword in hand means

the same thing as

> He took his sword, which was vorpal, in hand

and

> It was in his hand that he took his vorpal sword.

Knowing the language, and assuming that *vorpal* means the same thing in the three sentences (because the same sounds are used), you can decide that the sense—the truth conditions—of the three sentences are identical. In other words, you are able to decide that two sentences mean the same thing even though you do not know what either one means. You decide by assuming that the semantic properties of *vorpal* are the same whenever it is used.

We now see why Alice commented, when she had read "Jabberwocky": "It seems very pretty, but it's *rather* hard to understand!" (You see she didn't like to confess, even to herself, that she couldn't make it out at all.) "Somehow it seems to fill my head with ideas—only I don't exactly know what they are! However, *somebody* killed *something*: that's clear, at any rate—"

Semantic violations in poetry may form strange but interesting esthetic images, as in Dylan Thomas's phrase *a grief ago*. *Ago* is ordinarily used with words specified by some temporal semantic feature:

a week ago		*a table ago
an hour ago	but not	*a dream ago
a month ago		*a mother ago
a century ago		

When Thomas used the word *grief* with *ago*, he added a durational feature to grief for poetic effect, so while the noun phrase is anomalous, it evokes certain emotions.

In the poetry of E. E. Cummings, there are phrases such as

the six subjunctive crumbs twitch
a man . . . wearing a round jeer for a hat
children building this rainman out of snow[1]

Though all of these phrases violate semantic rules, we can understand them; breaking the rules creates the desired imagery. That we are able to assign some meaning to such expressions, and at the same time recognize that they are anomalous, demonstrates our knowledge of the semantic system, just as the recognition of ungrammatical sentences shows our knowledge of the rules of syntax.

Metaphor

Our doubts are traitors.

WILLIAM SHAKESPEARE, *Measure for Measure*, c. 1603

Walls have ears.

MIGUEL DE CERVANTES, *Don Quixote*, 1605

The night has a thousand eyes and the day but one.

FRANCES WILLIAM BOURDILLON, "Light," 1873

When what appears to be an anomaly is nevertheless understood in terms of a meaningful concept, the expression becomes a metaphor. There is no strict line between anomalous and metaphorical expressions. Technically, metaphors are anomalous, but the nature of the anomaly creates the salient meanings that metaphors usually have. The anomalous *A grief ago* might come to be interpreted by speakers of English as "the unhappy time following a sad event" and therefore become a metaphor.

Metaphors may have a literal meaning as well as their metaphorical meaning, so in some sense they are ambiguous. However, when the semantic rules are applied to an expression such as *Walls have ears*, the literal meaning is so unlikely

[1]The line from "sonnet entitled how to run the world." Copyright 1935, © 1963, 1991 by the Trustees for the E. E. Cummings Trust. Copyright © 1978 by George James Firmage. The line from "A man who had fallen among thieves." Copyright 1926, 1954, © 1991 by the Trustees for the E. E. Cummings Trust. Copyright © 1985 by George James Firmage. The line from "here is little Effie's head." Copyright 1923, 1925, 1951, 1953, © 1991 by the Trustees for the E. E. Cummings Trust. Copyright © 1976 by George James Firmage. From Complete Poems: 1904–1962 by E. E. Cummings, edited by George J. Firmage. Used by permission of Liveright Publishing Corporation.

that listeners use their imagination for another interpretation. The principle of compositionality is very "elastic" and when it fails to produce an acceptable literal meaning, listeners try to accommodate and stretch the meaning. This accommodation is based on semantic properties that are inferred or that provide some kind of resemblance or comparison that can end up as a meaningful concept.

To interpret a metaphor, we need to understand the individual words, the literal meaning of the whole expression, and facts about the world. To understand the metaphor

Time is money

it is necessary to know that in our society we are often paid according to the number of hours or days worked. In fact, "time," which is an abstract concept, is the subject of multiple metaphors. We "save time," "waste time," "manage time," push things "back in time," live on "borrowed time," and suffer the "ravages of time" as the "sands of time" drift away. In effect, the metaphors take the abstract concept of time and treat it as a concrete object of value.

Metaphor has a strong cultural component. Shakespeare used metaphors that are lost on many of today's playgoers. "I am a man whom Fortune hath cruelly scratched," is most effective as a metaphor in a society like Shakespeare's that commonly depicts "Fortune" as a woman. On the other hand, *There's a bug in my program* would make little sense in a culture without computers, even if the idea of having bugs in something indicates a problem.

Many expressions now taken literally may have originated as metaphors, such as "the fall of the dollar," meaning its decline in value on the world market. Many people wouldn't bat an eyelash (another metaphor) at the literal interpretation of saving or wasting time. Metaphorical use of language is language creativity at its highest. Nevertheless, the basis of metaphorical use is very much the ordinary linguistic knowledge that all speakers possess about words, their semantic properties, and their combinatorial possibilities.

Idioms

...CAPITAL PUNISHMENT? MY THOUGHTS EXACTLY! AND I TOTALLY AGREE WITH YOUR VIEWS ON TEEN PREGNANCY... AND I JUST LOVED YOUR DEFICIT SOLUTIONS.

LYLE SOON REALIZED HE HAD MISTAKENLY BEEN GIVEN A SEEING-EYE-TO-EYE DOG.

THE ARGYLE SWEATER © 2010
Scott Hilburn. Dist. By ANDREWS
MCMEEL SYNDICATION. Reprinted
with permission. All rights reserved.

Because the words (or morphemes) of a language are arbitrary (not pre-dictable by rule), they must be listed in a mental lexicon. The lexicon is a repository of the words (or morphemes) of a language with their gram-matical properties and their meanings. On the other hand, the meanings of morphologically complex words, phrases, and sentences are compositional and are derived by rules. We noted in Chapter 2 that the meaning of some words (e.g., compounds) is not entirely predictable, so these must also be given in the lexicon. It turns out that languages also contain many phrases whose meanings are not predictable on the basis of the meanings of the individual words. These phrases typically start out as metaphors that "catch on" and are repeated so often that they become fixtures in the language. Such expressions are called *idioms*, or **idiomatic phrases**, as in these Eng-lish examples:

sell down the river
rake over the coals
drop the ball
let their hair down
put his foot in his mouth
throw her weight around
snap out of it
give a piece of your mind
bring a knife to a gunfight

The usual semantic rules for combining meanings do not apply in these cases. Idioms act very much like individual morphemes in that they are not decom-posable, but have a fixed meaning that must be learned. Idioms are similar in structure to ordinary phrases except that they tend to be frozen in form and hence do not readily undergo rules that change word order or substitution of their parts.

The sentence in (1) has the same structure as the sentence in (2).

1.   She put her foot in her mouth.
2.   She put her bracelet in her drawer.

But while (2) is clearly related to the sentences in (3) and (4),

3.   The drawer in which she put her bracelet was her own.
4.   Her bracelet was put in her drawer.

the idiomatic sense of sentence (1) is lost in sentence (5) and (6), except, per-haps, humorously.

5.   The mouth in which she put her foot was her own.
6.   Her foot was put in her mouth.

In addition, if we know the meaning of (2) and the meaning of the word *necklace* we will immediately understand (7).

7.   She put her necklace in the drawer.

But if we try substituting *hand* for *foot* in sentence (1), we lose the idiomatic meaning, and derive a literal compositional meaning.

There are exceptions: some idioms allow their parts to be moved without losing their idiomatic sense:

The FBI kept tabs on radicals.
Tabs were kept on radicals by the FBI.
Radicals were kept tabs on by the FBI.

Like metaphors, idioms can break the rules on combining semantic properties. The object of *eat* must usually be something with the semantic feature "edible," but in

He ate his hat.

and

Eat your heart out.

this restriction is violated.

Idioms often lead to humor:

What did the doctor tell the vegetarian about his surgically implanted
   heart valve from a pig?
That it was okay as long as he didn't "eat his heart out."

Idioms may even show disrespect for syntax, for example, the expression *deep six*, while containing parts that are never used as verbs, is itself a verb meaning "to put the kibosh on," yet another idiom.

With some imagination, idioms may also be used to create what appears to be a **paradox**, a situation to which it is impossible to ascribe a truth value. Consider the idiom "drop the ball" meaning to blunder. In many places such as Times Square in New York, a ball is dropped at midnight on New Year's Eve. Now, if the person in charge doesn't drop the ball, then he or she has "dropped the ball." And if that person does indeed drop the ball, then he or she has not "dropped the ball." Neither can be true nor false, right?

Because of their special semantic and syntactic properties idioms must be listed in the mental lexicon as single items with their meanings specified, and speakers must learn the special restrictions on their use.

Although all languages have idioms, they rarely if ever translate word for word from one language to another. Most speakers of American English understand the idiom *to kick the bucket* as meaning "to die." The same combination of words in Spanish (*patear el cubo*) has only the literal meaning of striking a specific bucket with a foot. On the other hand, *estirar la pata*, literally "to stretch the (animal) leg," has the idiomatic sense of "to die" in Spanish.

Lexical Semantics (Word Meanings)

"There's glory for you!"
"I don't know what you mean by 'glory,'" Alice said.
Humpty Dumpty smiled contemptuously.
"Of course you don't—till I tell you. I meant 'there's a nice knock-down argument for you!'"
"But 'glory' doesn't mean 'a nice knock-down argument,'" Alice objected.

"When I use a word," Humpty Dumpty said, in rather a scornful tone, "it means just what I choose it to mean—neither more nor less."

"The question is," said Alice, "whether you can make words mean so many different things."

LEWIS CARROLL, *Through the Looking-Glass*, 1871

As just discussed, the meaning of a phrase or sentence is partially a function of the meanings of the words it contains. Similarly, the meaning of a morphologically complex word is a function of its component morphemes, as we saw in Chapter 2. However, there is a fundamental difference between word meaning—or *lexical semantics*—and sentence meaning. The meaning of most sentences is constructed by the application of semantic rules. The meaning of words (morphemes and idioms), on the other hand, is conventional; that is, speakers of a language implicitly agree on their meaning, and children acquiring the language must simply learn those meanings outright.

Although the agreed-upon meaning of a word may shift over time within a language community, we are not free as individuals to change the meanings of words at will; if we did, we would be unable to communicate with each other. Humpty Dumpty seems unwilling to accept this convention, though fortunately for us there are few such bad eggs among speakers. All the speakers of a language share a basic vocabulary—the sounds and meanings of thousands of morphemes and words. This linguistic knowledge permits us to use words to express our thoughts and to understand the thoughts of others. These meanings are stored in our mental lexicons.

Theories of Word Meaning

It is natural . . . to think of there being connected with a sign . . . besides . . . the reference of the sign, also what I should like to call the sense of the sign . . . .

GOTTLOB FREGE, "On Sense and Reference," 1892

Dictionaries are filled with words and give their meanings using other words rather than in terms of some more basic units of meaning, whatever they might be. In this sense, a dictionary really provides *paraphrases* rather than meanings. It relies on our *knowledge* of the language to understand the definitions. The meanings associated with words in our mental lexicon are not like what we find in a conventional dictionary, although it is a challenge to linguists to specify precisely how word meanings are represented in the mind.

Reference

If the meaning of a word is not like a dictionary entry, what is it? This question has been debated by philosophers and linguists for centuries. One proposal is that the meaning of a word or expression is its **reference**, its association with the object it refers to. This real-world object is called the *referent*.

"There's nothing here under 'Superman'—is it possible you made the reservation under another name?"

We have already determined that the meaning of a proper name like *Jack* is its reference: the link between the word *Jack* and the person named Jack, which is its referent. Proper names are noun phrases (NPs); you can substitute a proper name in any NP position in a sentence and preserve grammaticality. There are other NPs that refer to individuals as well. For instance, NPs such as *the happy swimmer, my friend*, and *that guy* can all be used to refer to Jack in the situation in which you've observed Jack swimming. The same is true for pronouns such as *I, you*, and *him*, which also function as NPs. In all these cases, the reference of the NP—which singles out the individual referred to under the circumstances—is part of the meaning of the NP.

On the other hand, not every NP refers to an individual. For instance, the sentence *No baby swims* contains the NP *no baby*, but your linguistic knowledge tells you that this NP does not refer to any specific individual. If *no baby* has no reference, but is not meaningless, there must be more to the meaning of NPs than reference alone.

In the fictional world of *Superman* and *Clark Kent*, they have the same reference—they are one and the same person. But there is more meaning to their names than that. If we substitute *Clark Kent* for *Superman* in the sentence *Lois Lane is in love with Superman* we alter its truth value from true to false. Again, we see that there must be a dimension of meaning beyond mere reference.

Similarly, *Barack Obama* and *the President* have (at this writing) the same reference, but the meaning of the NP *the President* is additionally "the head of state of the United States of America," which is an element of meaning separate from reference and more enduring.

Sense

There must be something more to meaning than reference alone. This is also suggested by the fact that speakers know the meanings of many words that have no real-world referents (e.g., *hobbits, unicorns,* and *Harry Potter*). Similarly, what real-world entities would function words such as *of* and *by*, or modal verbs such as *will* or *may* refer to?

These additional elements of meaning are often termed **sense**. It is the extra something referred to earlier. *Unicorns, hobbits,* and *Harry Potter* have sense but no reference (with regard to objects in the real world). Conversely, proper names typically have only reference. A name such as *Clem Kadiddlehopper* may point out a certain person, its referent, but has little linguistic meaning beyond that.

Philosophers of language dating back to ancient Greece have suggested that part of the meaning of a word is the mental image it conjures up. This helps with the problem of unicorns, hobbits, and Harry Potter; we may have a clear image of these entities from books, movies, and so on, and that connection might serve as reference for those expressions. However, many meaningful expressions are not associated with any clear, unique image agreed on by most speakers of the language. For example, what image is evoked by the words *very, if,* and *every*? It's difficult to say, yet these expressions are certainly meaningful. What is the image of oxygen as distinct from nitrogen—both are colorless, odorless gases, yet they differ in meaning. What mental image would we have of *dog* that is general enough to include Yorkshire Terriers and Great Danes and yet excludes foxes and wolves? And the image of *no man* in *no man is an island* presents a riddle worthy of a Zen koan.

Although the idea that the meaning of a word corresponds to a mental image is intuitive (because many words do provoke imagery), it is clearly inadequate as a general explanation of what people know about word meanings.

Perhaps the best we can do is to note that the reference part of a word's meaning, if it has reference at all, is the association with its referent; and the sense part of a word's meaning contains the information needed to complete the association, and to suggest properties that the referent may have, whether it exists in the real world or in the world of imagination.

Lexical Relations

> Does he wear a turban, a fez or a hat?
> Does he sleep on a mattress, a bed or a mat, or a Cot,
> The Akond of Swat?
> Can he write a letter concisely clear,
> Without a speck or a smudge or smear or Blot,
> The Akond of Swat?
>
> EDWARD LEAR, "The Akond of Swat," in *Laughable Lyrics*, 1877

Although we do not have a complete theory of word meaning, we know that speakers have considerable knowledge about the meaning relationships among different words in their mental lexicons, and any theory must account for that knowledge. Words are semantically related to one another in a variety of ways. Words that describe these relations often contain the bound morpheme *-nym*. The best-known lexical relation is synonymy, illustrated in the poem by Edward Lear, and antonymy, or opposites. Synonyms are words or expressions that have the same meaning in some or all contexts. There are dictionaries of synonyms that contain many hundreds of entries, such as:

apathetic/phlegmatic/passive/sluggish/indifferent
pedigree/ancestry/genealogy/descent/lineage

A sign in the San Diego Zoo Wild Animal Park states:

Please do not annoy, torment, pester, plague, molest, worry, badger, harry, harass, heckle, persecute, irk, bullyrag, vex, disquiet, grate, beset, bother, tease, nettle, tantalize, or ruffle the animals.

It has been said that there are no perfect synonyms—that is, no two words ever have *exactly* the same meaning. Still, the following two sentences have very similar meanings:

He's sitting on the sofa./He's sitting on the couch.

During the French Norman occupation of England that began in 1066 CE, many French words of Latin origin were imported into English. For this reason, English contains many synonymous pairs consisting of a word with an English (or Germanic) root, and another with a Latin root, such as:

English	Latin
manly	virile
heal	recuperate
send	transmit
go down	descend

Words that are opposite in meaning are **antonyms**. There are several kinds of antonymy. There are **complementary pairs**:

alive/dead   present/absent   awake/asleep

They are complementary in that *alive = not dead* and *dead = not alive*, and so on. There are **gradable pairs** of antonyms:

big/small   hot/cold   fast/slow   happy/sad

The meaning of adjectives in gradable pairs is related to the objects they modify. The words do not provide an absolute scale. For example, we know that "a small elephant" is much bigger than "a large mouse." *Fast* is faster when applied to an airplane than to a car.

Another kind of opposition involves pairs such as

give/receive   buy/sell   teacher/pupil

They are called **relational opposites**, and they display symmetry in their meanings. If X *gives* Y to Z, then Z *receives* Y from X. If X is Y's *teacher*, then Y is X's *pupil*. Pairs of words ending in *-er* and *-ee* are usually relational opposites. If Mary is Bill's *employer*, then Bill is Mary's *employee*.

Other lexical relations include homonyms, polysemy, and hyponyms. Words like *bear* and *bare* are **homonyms** (also called **homophones**). Homonyms are words that are pronounced the same but have different meanings. Near nonsense sentences such as *Entre nous, the new gnu knew nu is a Greek letter* tease us with homonyms. Homonyms easily lead to ambiguity, as the confused goat in the cartoon confirms.

stephan Pastis (cartoonist)/Gocomics.com

When a word has multiple meanings that are related conceptually or historically, it is said to be **polysemous**. For example, the word *diamond* referring to a jewel and also to a baseball field is polysemous. Speakers of English know that the words *red*, *white*, and *blue* are color words. Similarly, *lion, tiger, leopard,* and *lynx* are all felines. *Hyponymy* is the relationship between the more general term such as *color* and the more specific instances of it, such as *red*. Thus, *red* is a hyponym of *color*, and *lion* is a hyponym of *feline*; or equivalently, *color* has the hyponym *red* and *feline* has the hyponym *lion*.

Semantic Features

If it is true that words have meanings, why don't we throw away words and keep just the meanings?

LUDWIG WITTGENSTEIN

In Chapter 2, we observed that many words can be decomposed into morphemes, the most basic units of meaning. But, it is possible to find a more basic set of **semantic features** or properties that comprise some of the meaning of a word or morpheme and that clarify how certain words relate to other words. For example, two words can be antonyms only if they share a principal semantic feature in which they differ. The antonyms *wet* and *dry* share, but differ in, the feature "liquid." Similarly, *buy/sell* are relational opposites because both contain a semantic feature such as "change in possession," and differ only in the direction of the change. On the other hand, *big* and *red* are not antonyms because the principal feature of one is "size" and of the other "color."

Semantic features are among the conceptual elements that contribute to the meanings of words and sentences. Consider the sentence:

The assassin killed Thwacklehurst.

If the word *assassin* is in your mental dictionary, you know that it was some *person* who murdered some *important person* named Thwacklehurst. Your knowledge of the meaning of *assassin* tells you that an animal did not do the killing, and that Thwacklehurst was not an average citizen. Knowledge of *assassin* includes knowing that the individual to whom that word refers is human, is a murderer, and is a killer of important people. These bits of information are among the semantic features of the word that speakers agree on. The meaning of all nouns, verbs, adjectives, and adverbs—the content words—and even of some of the function words, such as *with* and *over*, can at least partially be specified by such features.

Evidence for Semantic Features

Semantic features are not directly observable. Their existence must be inferred from linguistic evidence. Speech errors, or "slips of the tongue," provide one such source of evidence. The following are some unintentional word substitutions actually produced by speakers:

Intended Utterance	Actual Utterance (Error)
bridge of the nose	bridge of the neck
when my gums bled	when my tongues bled
he came too late	he came too early
Mary was young	Mary was early
the lady with the Dachshund	the lady with the Volkswagen
that's a horse of another color	that's a horse of another race
his ancestors were farmers	his descendants were farmers
he has to pay her alimony	he has to pay her rent

These errors, and thousands of others that have been collected and catalogued, reveal that the incorrectly substituted words are not random but share some semantic features with the intended words. *Nose, neck, gums,* and *tongues* are all "body parts" or "parts of the head." *Young, early,* and *late* are related to "time." *Dachshund* and *Volkswagen* are both "German" and "small." The shared semantic features of *color* and *race*, *ancestor* and *descendant*, and *alimony* and *rent* are apparent.

The semantic features that describe the linguistic meaning of a word should not be confused with other nonlinguistic properties, such as physical properties. Scientists know that water is composed of hydrogen and oxygen, but such knowledge is not part of a word's meaning. We know that water is an essential ingredient of lemonade and baths. However, we don't need to know any of these things to know what the word *water* means, and to be able to use and understand it in a sentence.

Semantic Features and Grammar

King Features Syndicate

Further evidence that words are composed of smaller bits of meaning is that semantic features interact with different aspects of the grammar such as morphology or syntax. These effects show up in both nouns and verbs.

Semantic Features of Nouns

Semantic features can be morphologically marked. In English, the feature "female" is sometimes indicated by the suffix *–ess*:

tigress	waitress	goddess
actress	princess	adulteress
poetess	hostess	baroness

In some languages, though not English, nouns occur with **classifiers**, grammatical morphemes that indicate the semantic class of the noun. In Swahili, a noun that has the semantic feature "human" is prefixed with *m-* if singular and *wa-* if plural, as in *mtoto* (child) and *watoto* (children). A noun that has the feature "human artifact," such as *bed*, *chair*, or *knife*, is prefixed with the classifiers *ki-* if singular as in *kiti* (chair) and *vi-* if plural as in *viti* (chairs).

Semantic features may have syntactic and semantic effects, too. In English and many (though not all) languages, the kinds of determiners that a noun may occur with are controlled by whether it is a "count" noun or a "mass" noun. Consider these data:

I have two dogs.	*I have two rice(s).
I have a dog.	*I have a rice.
*I have dog.	I have rice.
He has many dogs.	*He has many rice(s).
*He has much dogs.	He has much rice.

Count nouns can be enumerated and pluralized—*one potato, two potatoes*. They may be preceded by the indefinite determiner *a*, and by the quantifier *many* as in *many potatoes*, but not by *much*: **much potato*. They must also occur with a determiner of some kind. Nouns such as *rice, water*, and *milk*, which cannot be enumerated or pluralized, are **mass nouns**. They cannot be preceded by *a* or *many*, and they can occur with the quantifier *much* or without any determiner at all. The humor of the cartoon is based both on the ambiguity of *toast* and the fact that as a food *French toast* is a mass noun, but as an oration it is a count noun. The count/mass distinction captures the fact that speakers know the properties that govern which determiner types go with different nouns. Without it, we could not describe these differences.

Generally, the count/mass distinction corresponds to the difference between discrete objects and homogeneous substances. But it would be incorrect to say that this distinction is grounded in human perception because different languages may treat the same object differently. For example, in English, the words *hair, furniture,* and *spaghetti* are mass nouns. We say *Some hair is curly, Much furniture is poorly made, John loves spaghetti.* In Italian, however, these words are count nouns, as illustrated in the following sentences:

> Ivano ha mangiato molti spaghetti ieri sera.
> "Ivano ate many spaghettis last evening"
> Piero ha comprato un mobile nuovo.
> "Piero bought a new (piece of) furniture."
> Luisella ha pettinato i suoi capelli.
> "Luisella combed her hairs."

We would have to assume a radical form of linguistic determinism (remember the Sapir–Whorf hypothesis from Chapter 1) to say that Italian and English speakers have different perceptions of hair, furniture, and spaghetti. It is more reasonable to assume that languages can differ to some extent in the semantic or syntactic features they assign to words with the same referent, somewhat independently of the way their speakers conceptualize that referent. Even within a particular language, we can have different words—count and mass—to describe the same object or substance. For example, in English, we have *shoes* (count) and *footwear* (mass), *coins* (count), and *change* (mass).

Semantic Features of Verbs

Verbs also have semantic features as part of their meaning. For example, "cause" is a feature of verbs such as *darken, kill, and uglify*.

darken	cause to become dark
kill	cause to die
uglify	cause to become ugly

"Go" is a feature of verbs that mean a change in location or possession, such as *swim, crawl, throw, fly, give,* or *buy*:

> Jack swims.
> The baby crawled under the table.
> The boy threw the ball over the fence.
> John gave Mary a beautiful engagement ring.

Words such as *swim* have an additional feature such as "in liquid," while *crawl* has "close to a surface."

"Become" is a feature expressing the end state of the action of certain verbs. For example, the verb *break* can be broken down into the following components of meaning: "cause" to "become" broken.

Semantic features of verbs, like features of nouns, may have syntactic consequences. For example, verbs can either describe **events**, such as *John kissed Mary/John ate oysters,* or **states**, such as *John knows Mary/John likes oysters.* The eventive/ stative difference is mirrored in the syntax. Eventive sentences still sound natural when passivized, when expressed progressively, when used as imperatives, and with certain adverbs:

Eventives

Mary was kissed by John.	Oysters were eaten by John.
John is kissing Mary.	John is eating oysters.
Kiss Mary!	Eat oysters!
John deliberately kissed Mary.	John deliberately ate oysters.

But stative sentences seem peculiar, if not ungrammatical or anomalous, when cast in the same form. (The preceding "?" indicates the strangeness.)

Statives

?Mary is known by John.	?Oysters are liked by John.
?John is knowing Mary.	?John is liking oysters.
?Know Mary!	?Like oysters!
?John deliberately knows Mary.	?John deliberately likes oysters.

Negation is a particularly interesting component of the meaning of some verbs. Expressions such as *ever, anymore, have a red cent,* are ungrammatical in certain simple affirmative sentences, but grammatical in corresponding negative ones.

*Mary will ever smile. (Cf. Mary will not ever smile.)
*I can visit you anymore. (Cf. I cannot visit you anymore.)
*It's worth a red cent. (Cf. It's not worth a red cent.)

Such expressions are called **negative polarity items** because they require a negative element such as "not" elsewhere in the sentence. Consider these data:

*John thinks that he'll ever fly a plane again.
*John hopes to ever fly a plane again.
John doubts that he'll ever fly a plane again.
John refuses to ever fly a plane again.

This suggests that verbs such as *doubt* and *refuse*, but not *think* and *hope*, have "negative" as a component of their meaning. *Doubt* may be analyzed as "think that not," and *refuse* as "intend not to." The negative feature in the verb provides the required support for the negative polarity item *ever* even without the overt presence of *not*.

Even rather subtle differences in a verb's semantic features can affect the syntactic operations that apply to sentences. For example, the verbs in (1) can take two objects—they're **ditransitive verbs**. Moreover, the arguments can be rearranged as it (2).

1. John threw/tossed/kicked/flung the ball to the boy.
2. John threw/tossed/kicked/flung the boy the ball.
3. John pushed/pulled/lifted/hauled the ball to the boy.
4. *John pushed/pulled/lifted/hauled the boy the ball.

The verbs in (3) are also ditransitive. However, these verbs do not allow the rearrangement of their arguments, as indicated by the ungrammatical examples in (4). Though the verbs in (1) and (3) are all verbs of motion, they differ in how the force of the motion is applied: the verbs in (1) involve a single quick motion whereas those in (3) involve a prolonged use of force. This semantic difference gives rise to different word order possibilities.

Similarly, the verbs in (5) and (7) are verbs of communication, but their meanings differ in the way the message is communicated; those in (5) involve an external apparatus whereas those in (7) involve the type of voice used. The verbs in (5) allow their arguments to be rearranged, as in (6), while the verbs in (7) do not.

5. Mary faxed/radioed/e-mailed/phoned the news to Helen.
6. Mary faxed/radioed/e-mailed/phoned Helen the news.
7. Mary murmured/mumbled/muttered/shrieked the news to Helen.
8. *Mary murmured/mumbled/muttered/shrieked Helen the news.

The verbs in (1)–(8) all have the feature "transfer." The to-be-transferred argument is the direct object, while the recipient of the transfer is the indirect object. In (1) the ball is transferred to the boy. In (5) the news is transferred, or leastwise transmitted, to Helen. Even when the transference is not overt, it may be inferred. In *John baked Mary a cake,* there is an implied transfer of the cake from John to Mary. A subtle difference in the manner of transfer affect the syntax of these verbs, and indeed, this connection between form and meaning may help children acquire the syntactic and semantic rules of their language, as will be discussed in Chapter 9.

Argument Structure and Thematic roles

Verbs also differ in terms of the number and type of phrases they can take as complements. As we noted in Chapter 3, transitive verbs such as *find, hit,* and *chase* are subcategorized for (c-select) a direct object, whereas intransitive verbs such as *arrive* or *sleep* are not. Ditransitive verbs such as *give* or *throw* take two objects, as in *John threw Mary a ball.* In addition, most verbs take a subject.

The various NPs that occur with a verb are its **arguments**. Thus, intransitive verbs have one argument: the subject; transitive verbs have two arguments: the subject and direct object; ditransitive verbs have three arguments: the subject, direct object, and indirect object. The **argument structure** of a verb is part of its meaning and is included in its lexical entry.

The verb not only determines the number of arguments in a sentence, but it also determines the **thematic roles** of its arguments. Thematic roles express the kind of semantic relation that holds between the arguments of the verb and the type of situation that the verb describes. For example, in the following sentence the NP *the boy*

1. The boy rolled a red ball.

    agent   theme

is the "doer" of the rolling action, also called the **agent**. The NP *a red ball* is the **theme** or the "undergoer" of the rolling action. Relations such as agent and theme are thematic roles.

    A further example is the sentence:

2. The boy threw the red ball to the girl.

    agent   theme   goal

Here, *the girl* bears the thematic role of **goal**, that is, the endpoint of a change in location or possession. The verb phrase is interpreted to mean that the theme of *throw* ends up in the position of the *goal*.

    Other thematic roles are **source**, where the action originates; **instrument**, the means used to accomplish the action; and **experiencer**, one receiving sensory input:

3. Professor Snape awakened Harry Potter with his wand.

    source   experiencer   instrument

    The particular thematic roles assigned by a verb can be traced back to components of the verb's meaning. Verbs such as *throw, buy,* and *fly* contain a feature "go" expressing a change in location or possession. The feature "go" is thus linked to the presence of the thematic roles of theme, source, and goal. Verbs such as *awaken* or *frighten* have a feature "affects mental state" so that one of its arguments takes on the thematic role of experiencer.

    Thematic role assignment, or **theta assignment**, is also connected to syntactic structure. In the sentence in (2), the role of theme is assigned to the direct object *the red ball* and the role of goal to the indirect object *the girl*. Verb pairs such as *sell* and *buy* as in the sentences in (4) and (5) both involve the feature "go." They are therefore linked to a thematic role of theme, which is assigned to the direct object:

4. John sold the book to Mary.

    agent   theme   goal

5. Mary bought the book from John.

    agent   theme   source

In addition, *sell* is linked to the presence of a goal (the recipient or endpoint of the transfer), and *buy* to the presence of a source (the initiator of the transfer). Thus, *buy/sell* are relational opposites because both contain the semantic feature "go" (the transfer of goods or services) and they differ only in the direction of transfer, that is, whether the indirect object is a source or goal. Thematic roles are not assigned to arguments randomly. There is a connection between the meaning of a verb and the syntactic structure of sentences containing the verb.

Our knowledge of verbs includes their syntactic category, which arguments they select, and the thematic roles they assign to their arguments. The thematic roles assigned by a particular verb to its arguments are constant even though the arguments may show up in different s-structure positions:

6. The dog bit the stick./The stick was bitten by the dog.
7. The trainer gave the dog a treat./The trainer gave a treat to the dog.

In both sentences in (6), *the dog* is the agent and *the stick* is the theme. Similarly in (7), *the treat* is the theme and *the dog* is the goal. This is because thematic roles are always assigned to the same d-structure position: for example, theme is assigned to the object of *bit/bitten*. The arguments then carry their theta roles with them when they move to a different s-structure position owing to syntactic rules. Our linguistic intuition that the two sentences in (6) and the two sentences in (7) are related to each other is due to the fact that *the stick* in the passive sentence *the stick was bitten by the dog* originated in object position in d-structure and moved to subject position in s-structure by a syntactic rule:

8. ___ was bitten the stick by the dog → the stick was bitten ___ by the dog

      d-structure   s-structure

Thus, the sentence pairs in (6) and (7) express the same semantic relationships between the verb and its arguments.

Even in cases in which not all the arguments of a verb are expressed, the theta roles for the realized NPs are constant, as the following examples illustrate:

9. The boy opened the door with the key.
10. The key opened the door.
11. The door opened.

In all three of these sentences, *the door* is the theme, the object that is opened. Thus, *the door* in (11) originates as the object of *open* in d-structure and undergoes a movement rule, much like in the passive example above.

___ opened the door → The door opened ___

Although the sentences in (9)–(11) are not strict paraphrases of one another, they are structurally and semantically related in that they have similar d-structure configurations. Indeed, sentence (9) entails (10) and (11), and (10) entails (11).

In the sentences in (9) and (10), *the key*, despite its different s-structure positions, has the thematic role of instrument, suggesting that these sentences also have a similar d-structure configuration. The semantics of the three sentences is determined by the meaning of the verb *open* and the rules that determine how thematic roles are assigned to the verb's NP arguments.

Pragmatics

We interpret this sketch instantly and effortlessly as a gathering of people before a structure, probably a gateway; the people are listening to a single declaiming figure in the center . . . . But all this is a miracle, for there is little detailed information in the lines or shading (such as there is). Every line is a mere suggestion . . . . So here is the miracle: from a merest, sketchiest squiggle of lines, you and I converge to find adumbration of a coherent scene . . . . The problem of utterance interpretation is not dissimilar to this visual miracle.

An utterance is not, as it were, a veridical model or "snapshot" of the scene it describes . . . .

Rather, an utterance is just as sketchy as the Rembrandt drawing.

STEPHEN C. LEVINSON, *Presumptive Meanings: The Theory of Generalized Conversational Implicature*, 2000

We've just discussed lexical semantics (the literal meanings of words) and compositional semantics (the literal meaning of sentences). We described the latter in terms of truth conditions. The idea is that you know what a sentence means if you know what the world would have to look like in order for that sentence to be true.

Literal meaning isn't the only sort of meaning we use when we use language to communicate with others. Some meaning is **extra-truth-conditional**: It comes about as a result of how a speaker uses the literal meaning in conversation, or as a part of a **discourse**. The study of extra-truth-conditional meaning is pragmatics.

Just as artists depict scenes with representations that aren't 100 percent explicit, like the sketch on page 159, language users describe states of affairs with sentences that aren't 100 percent explicit. And just as there are a number of reasons an artist might choose a sketch or an abstract painting to depict a scene (instead of a photograph), there are a number of reasons a speaker might choose a particular sentence or discourse to describe a state of affairs. In what follows, we'll discuss different ways in which speakers can convey meaning without expressing it literally.

Pronouns and Other Deictic Words

CHICKEN (shouting to friend across the road): *Hey, how do I get to the other side?*

FRIEND: *You're on the other side!*

SOURCE OBSCURE

One way in which context can supplement a less-than-explicit sentence meaning is through words that receive part of their meaning via context and the orientation of the speaker. Such words are referred to as **deictic** and include pronouns (*she, it, I*), demonstratives (*this, that*), adverbs (*here, there, now, today*), prepositions (*behind, before*) and complex expressions involving such words (*those towers over there*).

Imagine the sets of sentences in (1) and (2) being spoken by Taylor Swift in Venice on September 16, 2016.

1. Taylor Swift really likes it in Venice, Italy. On September 16, 2016, there was a boat parade in the canals in Venice, Italy. On September 17, 2016, an art festival will be held. The art festival on September 17, 2016 will be extremely fun. Italy is a great country to visit.
2. I really like it in Venice. Today there was a boat parade in the canals here. Tomorrow an art festival will be held. It will be extremely fun. This is a great country to visit.

The difference between (1) and (2) is that (1) is extremely explicit, while (2) relies on deictic terms to determine part of the meaning of the sentences, and real-world knowledge that Venice is in Italy and not Illinois. Because our use of language is relatively inexplicit we're used to interpreting such terms so that (2) sounds perfectly natural, far more natural than (1), as we are entirely accustomed to using these shortcuts.

And this is despite the fact that we often have to look to context to determine the reference of a pronoun. While proper nouns such as *September 16, 2016,* and *Taylor Swift* have context-independent meanings, that is they'll always pick out the same referents regardless of the context, other words such as *here, tomorrow,* and *this* have context-dependent meanings; their reference is determined in part by the context in which they're uttered.

We say "in part" because the particular deictic word itself helps provide restrictions on its own referent. *Here* and *there* have locations as referents; *then* and *now* are temporal referents, *this* and *that* refer to things already mentioned or known, *he* and *she* have human referents, and *I* is extremely restrictive: it can only refer to the speaker.

Even though the referent of a pronoun is lexically restricted, we need to look to the context in which the pronoun is uttered to determine the referent. This process is called **reference resolution**. There are two types of context relevant for the resolution of a pronoun: **linguistic** and **situational**. Linguistic context is anything that has been uttered in the discourse prior to or along with the pronoun. Situational context is anything nonlinguistic such as knowing that Venice is in Italy.

Pronouns and Situational Context

Hank Ketcham/North America Syndicate/King Features Syndicate

Situational context often takes the form of a gesture, such as pointing or nodding, as in *He went that way!* or *Who IS that masked man?* Similarly, *next week* has a different reference when uttered today than a month from today. If you found an undated notice announcing a "BIG SALE NEXT WEEK," you would not know whether the sale had already taken place.

The "Dennis the Menace" cartoon illustrates the hilarity that may ensue if deictic words are misinterpreted.

Directional terms such as

before/behind   left/right   front/back

are deictic insofar as you need to know the orientation in space of the conversational participants to know their reference. In Japanese, the verb *kuru*, "come," can only be used for motion toward the speaker. A Japanese speaker cannot call up a friend and ask

May I *kuru* to your house?

as you might, in English, ask "May I come to your house?" The correct verb is *iku*, "go," which indicates motion away from the place of utterance. In Japanese, these verbs have a deictic aspect to their meaning. The verbs *come* and *go* have a similar effect in English. If someone says *A thief came into the house* versus *A thief went into the house*, you would assume the speaker to have been in the house in the first case, and not in the house in the second.

Pronouns and Linguistic Context

King Features Syndicate

There are two different ways in which the reference of a pronoun can be resolved by the linguistic context. The first is sentence-internal; the second is sentence-external. We'll illustrate the first way by discussing reflexive pronouns.

A **reflexive pronoun** is a sort of pronoun that needs to receive its reference via linguistic context, and more specifically by sentence-internal linguistic context. In other words, it requires that the sentence contain another NP—an **antecedent**–that it can **co-refer** with. In English, reflexive pronouns end with -*self* or -*selves*, such as *himself* or *themselves*. (1a) shows that a reflexive pronoun requires an antecedent in the sentence. (1b) shows that a reflexive pronoun must match the person, gender, and number of its antecedent.

1.   **(a)** I saw Mary. *Herself left.
     (b) *John wrote herself/themselves a letter.

Interestingly, the restriction on reflexive pronouns is even stronger than (1) suggests. It's not enough that they have a matching antecedent in the sentence, but that antecedent must be in the right position with respect to the co-referring reflexive pronoun. (2a) shows that the antecedent cannot follow the reflexive pronoun; (2b) shows that there can't be another NP in between a reflexive pronoun and its antecedent.

2.   **(a)** *Himself washed John.
     (b) *Jane said the boy bit herself.

Thus, one of the things that you know when you know English is that pronouns can receive their reference from their linguistic context. You also know that some pronouns—reflexive pronouns—are particularly picky. Their reference can only be resolved if they have an antecedent which is nearby in the right sort of way.

Nonreflexive pronouns (which we'll refer to simply as *pronouns*) such as *he, she, him, her,* and *it* also have their reference resolved via linguistic context. These pronouns can have their antecedent in another, preceding sentence. This is demonstrated in (3).

3. Sue likes pizza. She thinks it is the perfect food.

Moreover, the antecedent doesn't even have to be in a sentence spoken by the same speaker. In the discourse in (4), Mary uses a pronoun (*there*) whose antecedent is in Sue's utterance.

4. SUE: I just got back from Rome.
MARY: I've always wanted to go there!

Depending on the context and the discourse, an antecedent can even be several sentences away from its co-referring pronoun. Language users are adroit at processing sentences with several different pronouns and their different antecedents. Consider the discourse in (5):

5. JOHN: It seems that the man loves the woman.
BILL: Many people think he loves her.

A natural interpretation of Bill's utterance is one in which *he* co-refers with *the man* and *she* co-refers with *the woman*. This is a classic case of reference resolution via linguistic context.

But now read Bill's utterance (5) out loud, and put emphasis on her. When *her* is emphasized it seems more natural to fix its referent from the situational context. This utterance—with *her* emphasized—seems natural for a situation in which Bill is pointing at some other woman across the room.

Language users tend to use pronouns to refer to individuals in contexts—linguistic or situational—in which the referent of the pronoun is clear. The reference of the pronoun is constrained by a number of different factors, including the gender- and number-marking on the pronoun, whether or not the pronoun is reflexive, and what linguistic and situational contexts the pronoun is uttered in.

Implicature

What does "yet" mean, after all? "I haven't seen *Reservoir Dogs* yet." What does that mean? It means you're going to go, doesn't it?

NICK HORNBY, *High Fidelity*, 1995

Pronouns are an example of how the context in which a sentence is uttered can help determine the meaning of that sentence. There is another way in which context can play a role in meaning: It can supplement the meaning of a sentence. Just as you were able to fill in the gaps in the sketch at the beginning of this chapter with extra details, you as a language user are able to fill in gaps in meaning. And just as there is a right and a wrong way to fill in the gaps in the sketch—Rembrandt probably didn't intend it to depict a sandwich—there is a right and a wrong way to fill in gaps in meaning.

We'll start with an example:

GREAT MEAL, TJ

THANKS, MATE. NEXT YEAR – SHRIMP ON THE BARBIE!

LET'S HOPE QUILL'S HERE NEXT YEAR

YOU FOLKS GO SIT. I'LL CLEAN UP

ISN'T TONI GREAT?

VERY NICE GIRL. WHAT DO YOU THINK, HON?

THE TURKEY SURE WAS MOIST

6. DAD: Very nice girl. What do you think, Hon?
   MOM: The turkey sure was moist.

From a semantic standpoint, (6) is very straightforward. With the right semantic theory, we can articulate the literal meanings of the parents' utterances. This semantic theory would summarize (6) literally as: Dad asked Mom whether she thinks the girl is nice and Mom asserts that the turkey was moist.

Of course, this summary already includes some extra-truth-conditional meaning. It assumes that *girl* gets its reference from the previous remark about Toni, and that the use of the definite article in *the turkey* assures that a turkey is known to the conversational participants. But there is still more meaning to attribute to (6). In many contexts, Dad (and the boy) will infer from Mom's statement that she doesn't particularly like Toni.

If this is right, Mom's answer is more of a sketch than a photograph. The most literal way Mom could have answered the question is "I do not like Toni." But instead of asserting this, Mom chooses to implicate it. An **implicature** is a great example of extra-truth-conditional meaning. An implicature is an inference based not only on an utterance, but also on what the speaker is trying to convey. An implicature is to an assertion what a sketch is to a photograph.

Just as there are a number of reasons to sketch something instead of photographing it, there are a number of reasons to implicate something as opposed to asserting it. Perhaps Mom is an adherent of Miss Manners and, being a good hostess, knows she mustn't disparage a guest. If Dad knows this about Mom then he might infer from the utterance *The turkey sure was moist*—which doesn't seem relevant—that Mom doesn't like Toni but is too polite to say so. Here are a few other examples of conversational implicatures:

7. SUE: Does Mary have a boyfriend?
   BILL: She's been driving to Santa Barbara every weekend.
8. JOHN: Do you know how to change a tire?
   JANE: I know how to call a tow truck.
9. DANA: Do these slacks make my butt look big?
   JAMIE: You look great in chartreuse.

In (7), Bill asserts that Mary has been driving to Santa Barbara every weekend. But he *implicates* that Mary has a boyfriend (and that the boyfriend lives in Santa Barbara). In (8), Jane asserts that she knows how to call a tow truck. But she *implicates* that she doesn't know how to change a tire. In (9), well, you figure it out.

These discourses should seem fairly natural to you. And it's likely that you calculated the same implicatures we did. That's what's interesting to linguists. Just as morphology, syntax, and semantics is rule-governed, as we have emphasized throughout this book, so is pragmatics (and, by extension, implication).

Maxims of Discourse

POLONIUS: Though this be madness, yet there is method in't.

WILLIAM SHAKESPEARE, *Hamlet*, c. 1600

The most notable effort made to formulate pragmatic rules is found in the work of the British philosopher H. Paul Grice. He attempted to formalize how we perceive implicature in a conversation. He concluded that language users can calculate implicatures because they are all following some implicit principles (and each language user can therefore assume that others are following those principles). Grice called these principles **"maxims" of discourse**, and used them to serve as the foundation of pragmatics, the study of extra-truth-conditional meaning. We'll list them and then provide examples of each.

Maxim of Quality: Truth

- Do not say what you believe to be false.
- Do not say that for which you lack adequate evidence.

Maxim of Quantity: Information

- Make your contribution as informative as is required for the current purposes of the exchange.
- Do not make your contribution more or less informative than is required.

Maxim of Relation: Relevance

- Be relevant to the matter under discussion.

Maxim of Manner: Clarity

- Avoid obscurity of expression.
- Avoid ambiguity.
- Avoid unnecessary wordiness.
- Be orderly.

These are not prescriptive rules but rather part of a strategy used by the community of language users to enable the use of conversational implicature. They tend to be violated only by uncooperative people. (The Maxims are sometimes referred to en masse as Grice's **cooperative principle**.) So, if John stops Mary on the street and asks her for directions to the library, and she responds "Walk up three streets and take a left," it's a successful discourse only because Mary is being cooperative (and John assumes Mary is being cooperative). In particular, John assumes that Mary is following the maxim of quality.

On the other hand, the following discourse (*Hamlet*, Act II, Scene II), which gave rise to Polonius's famous remark, does not seem quite right—it is not coherent, for reasons that Grice's maxims can explain.

POLONIUS: What do you read, my lord?

HAMLET: Words, words, words.

POLONIUS: What is the matter, my lord?

HAMLET: Between who?

POLONIUS: I mean, the matter that you read, my lord.

HAMLET: Slanders, sir: for the satirical rogue says here that old men have gray beards, that their faces are wrinkled, their eyes purging thick amber and plum-tree gum, and that they have a plentiful lack of wit, together with most weak hams: all which, sir, though I most powerfully and potently believe, yet I hold it not honesty to have it thus set down; for yourself, sir, should grow old as I am, if like a crab you could go backward.

Hamlet, who is feigning insanity, refuses to answer Polonius's questions "in good faith." He has violated the maxim of quantity, which states that a speaker's contribution to the discourse should be as informative as is required—neither more nor less. Hamlet has violated this maxim in both directions. In answering "Words, words, words" to the question of what he is reading, he is providing too little information. His final remark goes to the other extreme in providing too much information (this could also be seen as a violation of the maxim of manner). Hamlet also violates the maxim of relation when he "misinterprets" the question about the reading matter as a matter between two individuals.

A maxim is violated when a speaker chooses to be uncooperative for whatever reason. A maxim is obeyed in a literal discourse devoid of implicature, as in (10).

10. DAD: Very nice girl. What do you think, Hon?

MOM: Not really.

Implicatures can arise when a maxim is flouted. To flout a maxim is to choose not to follow that maxim in order to implicate something. In the Hamlet discourse above, Hamlet is violating the maxims in order to sound insane. But we can easily imagine a slightly different context, one in which Polonius and Hamlet have more or less the same exchange, but one in which Hamlet is not trying to be insane.

POLONIUS: What do you read, my lord?

HAMLET: Words, words, words.

In this context, Hamlet is still not obeying the maxim of quantity—he's not saying enough to really answer Polonius' question—but he is instead flouting the maxim to implicate that he doesn't want Polonius to know what he's reading.

The discourse in (6), repeated below, is an example of the maxim of relevance being flouted.

11. DAD: Very nice girl. What do you think, Hon?
    MOM: The turkey sure was moist.

Because Mom knows that the quality of the turkey isn't relevant to being a "very nice girl"—and because Dad is assuming that Mom knows it, too—Dad can pick up on the fact that Mom is implicating that she doesn't like the girl.

Bereft of context, if one man says (truthfully) to another "I have never slept with your wife," that would be provocative because the very topic of conversation should be unnecessary, a violation of the maxims of quantity and relevance.

Asking an able-bodied person at the dinner table "Can you pass the salt?"—if answered literally—would force the responder into stating the obvious, also a violation of the maxim of quantity. To avoid this, the person asked seeks a reason for the question, and understands that the asker would like to have the salt shaker.

The maxim of relevance explains how saying "It's cold in here" to a person standing by an open window might be interpreted as a request to close it: or else why make the remark to that particular person in the first place?

Because implicatures may result from violations of one or more maxims, they can be easily cancelled by providing further, clarifying information. For example:

DAD: Very nice girl. What do you think, Hon?
MOM: The turkey sure was moist. *Toni basted it every ten minutes.*

The additional remark cancels, or at least weakens, the implicature that Mom dislikes Toni.

In this respect, implicatures are different from entailments and presuppositions. An entailment cannot be cancelled; it is logically necessary. The truth of *Jon killed Jim* entails that Jim is dead and nothing anyone can say will resurrect him. But further world knowledge or verbal clarification may cancel an implicature.

Presupposition

"Take some more tea," the March Hare said to Alice, very earnestly.

"I've had nothing yet," Alice replied in an offended tone, "so I can't take more."

"You mean you can't take less," said the Hatter: "It's very easy to take more than nothing."

LEWIS CARROLL, *Alice's Adventures in Wonderland*

Nearly all utterances occur in context, and the context often contributes to the way the utterance is understood, and whether the utterance is appropriate. For example, *The present King of France is bald* is perfectly grammatical and meaningful except that it is inappropriate because nowadays France has no king. Situations that must exist for utterances to be appropriate are called **presuppositions**. *The present King of France is bald* has the presupposition that there is presently a king of France.

Questions such as *Have you stopped hugging your border collie?* presuppose that you hugged your border collie, and statements such as *The river Avon runs through Stratford* presuppose the existence of the river and the town. Presuppositions prevent utterances from being incongruous and when they are ignored, we get the confusion that Alice felt at the tea party. Statements such as *Take some more tea* or *Have another beer* carry the presupposition that one has already had some. The March Hare is oblivious to this aspect of language, of which the exasperated Alice is keenly aware.

Presuppositions hold up under negation. *I am **not** sorry that the team lost* still has the presupposition that the team lost. If a mad Mad Hatter said *Do **not** take any more tea* the presupposition of previous tea consumption would still be present.

Presuppositions are different from implicatures. Continuing with—*oh, the team didn't lose after all*—retracts the previous assertion *I'm sorry that the team lost*. No such incongruity arises when implicatures are cancelled.

Presuppositions also differ from entailments in that they are taken for granted by speakers. Unlike entailments, they remain when the sentence is negated. On the other hand, while *Jon killed Jim* entails *Jim died*, no such entailment follows from *Jon did not kill Jim*.

Speech Acts

ZITS © 1998 ZITS PARTNERSHIP, KING FEATURES SYNDICATE

You can use language to do things. You can use language to make promises, lay bets, issue warnings, christen boats, place names in nomination, offer congratulations, or swear testimony. The theory of **speech acts** describes how this is done.

By saying *I warn you that there is a sheepdog in the closet*, you not only say something, you *warn* someone. Verbs such as *bet, promise, and warn* are **performative verbs**. Using them in a sentence (in the first person, present tense) adds something extra over and above the statement.

There are hundreds of performative verbs in every language. The following sentences illustrate their usage:

I *bet* you five dollars the Yankees win.
I *challenge* you to a match.
I *dare* you to step over this line.
I *fine* you $100 for possession of oregano.
I *move* that we adjourn.

I *nominate* Batman for mayor of Gotham City.
I *promise* to improve.
I *resign*!
I *pronounce* you husband and wife.

In all of these sentences, the speaker is the subject (i.e., the sentences are in first person), who by uttering the sentence is accomplishing some additional action, such as daring, nominating, or resigning. In addition, all of these sentences are affirmative, declarative, and in the present tense. They are typical **performative sentences**.

An informal test to see whether a sentence contains a performative verb is to begin it with the words *I hereby* …. Only performative sentences sound right when begun this way. Compare *I hereby apologize to you* with the somewhat strange *I hereby know you*. The first is generally taken as an act of apologizing. In all of the examples given, insertion of *hereby* would be acceptable.

In studying speech acts, the importance of context is evident. In some situations, *Band practice, my house, 6 to 8* is a reminder, but the same sentence may be a warning in a different context. We call this underlying purpose of the utterance—be it a reminder, a warning, a promise, a threat, or whatever—the **illocutionary force** of a speech act. Illocutionary force may accompany utterances without overt performative verbs, for example, *I've got five bucks that says you're wrong* has the illocutionary force of a bet under appropriate circumstances. Because the illocutionary force of a speech act depends on the context of the utterance, speech act theory is a part of pragmatics.

Summary

Knowing a language means knowing how to produce and understand the meaning of infinitely many sentences. The study of linguistic meaning is called **semantics. Lexical semantics** is concerned with the meanings of morphemes and words; **compositional** or **truth-conditional semantics** with phrases and sentences. The study of how context affects meaning is called **pragmatics**.

Compositional semantics is the building up of phrasal or sentence meaning from the meaning of smaller units using **semantic rules**. Speakers' knowledge of sentence meaning includes knowing the **truth conditions** of declarative sentences; knowing when one sentence **entails** another sentence; knowing when two sentences are **paraphrases** or **contradictory**; knowing when a sentence is a **tautology**, **contradiction**, or **paradox**; and knowing when sentences are ambiguous, among other things. There are cases when the meaning of larger units does not follow from the meaning of its parts. **Anomaly** is when the pieces do not fit sensibly together, as in *colorless green ideas sleep furiously*. **Metaphors** are sentences that appear to be anomalous, but to which a meaningful concept can be attached, such as *time is money*. **Idioms** are fixed expressions whose meaning is not compositional but rather must be learned as a whole unit, such as *kick the bucket* meaning "to die."

Part of the meaning of words may be the association with the objects the words refer to (if any), called **reference**, but often there is additional meaning beyond reference, which is called **sense**. The reference of *the President* is Barack Obama, and the sense of the expression is "highest executive office." Some expressions have reference but little sense, such as proper names, and some have sense but no reference, such as *the present King of France*.

Words are related in various ways. They may be **synonyms**, various kinds of **antonyms** such as **relational opposites**, or **homonyms**, words pronounced the same but with different meanings such as *bare* and *bear*.

Part of the meaning of words may be described by **semantic features** such as "female," "young," "cause," or "go." Nouns may have the feature "count," wherein they may be enumerated (one potato, two potatoes), or "mass," in which enumeration may require contextual interpretation (*one milk, *two milks, perhaps meaning "one glass or quart or portion of milk"). Some verbs have the feature "eventive" and others "stative." The semantic feature of negation is found in many words and is evidenced by the occurrence of *negative polarity* items (e.g., *John doubts that Mary gives a hoot*, but **John thinks that Mary gives a hoot*).

Verbs have various **argument structures**, which describe the NPs that may occur with particular verbs. For example, intransitive verbs take only an NP subject, whereas **ditransitive** verbs take an NP subject, an NP direct object, and an NP indirect object. **Thematic roles** describe the semantic relations between a verb and its NP arguments. Some thematic roles are: **agent**, the doer of an action; **theme**, the receiver of an action; **goal; source; instrument**; and **experiencer**. The assignment of thematic roles to the NP arguments of verbs occurs in d-structure. However, the positions of the NP arguments may differ in s-structure owing to the application of syntactic rules that move elements.

Some meaning is **extra-truth-conditional:** it comes about as a result of how a speaker uses the literal meaning in conversation, or as a part of a **discourse**. The study of extra-truth-conditional meaning is **pragmatics**.

Language users generally describe states of affairs with sentences that aren't 100 percent explicit. Context can be used to supplement linguistic meaning in various ways. Context may be *linguistic*—what was previously spoken or written—or *knowledge of the world*, including the speech situation: what we've called **situational context**.

Many pronouns rely on context for their reference to be resolved. Reflexive pronouns such as *himself* and *themselves* require a sentence-internal **antecedent**. Nonreflexive pronouns such as *he, she, him*, and *her* can have an antecedent in another sentence or earlier in the discourse or even determined by context. **Deictic** terms such as *you, there, now*, and *the other side* require knowledge of the situation (person spoken to, place, time, and spatial orientation) of the utterance to be interpreted referentially.

Speakers of all languages adhere to various **maxims of discourse**, which are instances of a general **cooperative principle** for communicating sincerely. Such maxims as "be relevant" or "say neither more nor less than the discourse requires" permit a person to interpret *It's cold in here* as "Shut the windows" or "Turn up the thermostat." **Implicatures** are the inferences that may be drawn from an utterance in context when one or another of the maxims is violated (either purposefully or naively). When Mary says *It's cold in here*, one of many possible implicatures may be "Mary wants the heat turned up." Implicatures are like entailments in that their truth follows from sentences of the discourse, but unlike entailments, which are necessarily true, implicatures may be cancelled by information added later. Mary might wave you away from the thermostat and ask you to hand her a sweater. **Presuppositions** are situations that must be true for utterances to be appropriate, so that *Take some more tea* has the presupposition "already had some tea."

The theory of **speech acts** tells us that people use language to do things such as lay bets, issue warnings, or nominate candidates. By using the words, "I nominate Bill Smith," you may accomplish an act of nomination that allows Bill Smith to run for office. Verbs that "do things" are called **performative verbs**. The speaker's intent in making an utterance is known as **illocutionary force**. In the case of performative verbs, the illocutionary force is mentioned overtly. In other cases, it must be determined from context.

References for Further Reading

Austin, J. L. 1962. *How to do things with words*. Cambridge, MA: Harvard University Press.

Davidson, D., and G. Harman, eds. 1972. *Semantics of natural languages*. Dordrecht, The Netherlands: Reidel.

Grice, H. P. 1989. Logic and conversation. Reprinted in *Studies in the way of words*. Cambridge, MA: Harvard University Press.

Jackendoff, R. 1990. *Semantic Structures*, Cambridge, MA: MIT Press,

Lakoff, G., and M. Johnson. 2003. *Metaphors we live by, 2nd ed.* Chicago: University of Chicago Press.

Levinson, S. C. 2000. *Presumptive meanings: The theory of generalized conversational implicature*. Cambridge, MA: The MIT Press.

Saeed, J. 2009. *Semantics, 3rd ed.* Oxford, UK: Wiley-Blackwell.

Searle, J. R. 1969. *Speech acts: An essay in the philosophy of language*. Cambridge, UK: Cambridge University Press.

Exercises

1. (This exercise requires knowledge of elementary set theory.)
    a. Suppose that the reference (meaning) of *swims* is the set of individuals consisting of Anna, Lu, Paul, and Benjamin. For which of the following sentences are the truth conditions produced by Semantic Rule I met?
        i.   Anna swims.
        ii. Jack swims.
        iii. Benjamin swims.
    b. Suppose the reference (meaning) of *loves* is the set consisting of the following pairs of individuals: <Anna, Paul>, <Paul, Benjamin>, <Benjamin, Benjamin>, <Paul, Anna>. According to Semantic Rule II, what is the meaning of the verb phrase?
        i.   loves Paul
        ii. loves Benjamin
        iii. loves Jack

    c. Given the information in (b), for which of the following sentences are the truth conditions produced by Semantic Rule I met?
       i. Paul loves Anna.
      ii. Benjamin loves Paul.
     iii. Benjamin loves himself.
     iv. Anna loves Jack.

    d. Challenge exercise: Use Semantic Rules I and II to derive the truth conditions for the sentence *Jack kissed Laura*. Then determine the whether these conditions are met in the following situations:
       i. Nobody kissed Laura.
      ii. Jack did not kiss Laura, although other men did.

2. The following sentences are either tautologies (analytic), contradictions, or situationally true or false. Write T by the tautologies, C by the contradictions, and S by the other sentences.

    a. Queens are monarchs.
    b. Kings are female.
    c. Kings are poor.
    d. Queens are ugly.
    e. Queens are mothers.
    f. Kings are mothers.
    g. Dogs are four-legged.
    h. Cats are felines.
    i. Cats are stupid.
    j. Dogs are carnivores.
    k. George Washington is George Washington.
    l. George Washington is the first president.
    m. George Washington is male.
    n. Uncles are male.
    o. My aunt is a man.
    p. Witches are wicked.
    q. My brother is a witch.
    r. My sister is an only child.
    s. The evening star isn't the evening star.
    t. The evening star isn't Venus.
    u. Babies are adults.
    v. Babies can lift one ton.
    w. Puppies are human.
    x. My bachelor friends are all married.
    y. My bachelor friends are all lonely.
    z. Colorless ideas are green.

3. Here is a passage from *Alice's Adventures in Wonderland*:

    "How is bread made?"
    "I know *that*!" Alice cried eagerly.
    "You take some flour—"
    "Where do you pick the flower?" the White Queen asked.

"In a garden, or in the hedges?"

"Well, it isn't *picked* at all," Alice explained; "it's ground—"

"How many acres of ground?" said the White Queen.

On what kinds of pairs of words is the humor of this passage based? Identify each pair.

4. Should the semantic component of the grammar account for whatever a speaker means when uttering any meaningful expression? Defend your viewpoint.

5. **Part One**

The following sentences may be lexically or structurally ambiguous, or both.

Provide paraphrases showing that you comprehend all the meanings.

Example: I saw him walking by the bank.

Meaning 1: I saw him and he was walking by the bank of the river.

Meaning 2: I saw him and he was walking by the financial institution.

Meaning 3: I was walking by the bank of the river when I saw him.

Meaning 4: I was walking by the financial institution when I saw him.

a. We laughed at the colorful ball.
b. He was knocked over by the punch.
c. The police were urged to stop drinking by the fifth.
d. I said I would file it on Thursday.
e. I cannot recommend visiting professors too highly.
f. The license fee for pets owned by senior citizens who have not been altered is $1.50. (Actual notice)
g. What looks better on a handsome man than a tux? Nothing! (Attributed to Mae West)
h. Wanted: Man to take care of cow that does not smoke or drink. (Actual notice)
i. For sale: Several old dresses from grandmother in beautiful condition. (Actual notice)
j. Time flies like an arrow. (*Hint*: There are at least four paraphrases, but some of them require imagination.)

Part Two

Do the same thing for the following newspaper headlines:

a. POLICE BEGIN CAMPAIGN TO RUN DOWN JAYWALKERS
b. DRUNK GETS NINE MONTHS IN VIOLIN CASE
c. FARMER BILL DIES IN HOUSE
d. STUD TIRES OUT
e. SQUAD HELPS DOG BITE VICTIM
f. LACK OF BRAINS HINDERS RESEARCH
g. MINERS REFUSE TO WORK AFTER DEATH
h. EYE DROPS OFF SHELF
i. JUVENILE COURT TO TRY SHOOTING DEFENDANT
j. QUEEN MARY HAVING BOTTOM SCRAPED

      k. VOLUNTEERS NEEDED TO HELP TORTURE SURVIVORS

      l. HOMICIDE VICTIMS RARELY TALK TO POLICE

6. Explain the semantic ambiguity of the following sentences by providing two or more sentences for each that paraphrase the multiple meanings. *Example*: "She can't bear children" can mean either "She can't give birth to children" or "She can't tolerate children."

    a. He waited by the bank.

    b. Is he really that kind?

    c. The proprietor of the fish store was the sole owner.

    d. The long drill was boring.

    e. When he got the clear title to the land, it was a good deed.

    f. It takes a good ruler to make a straight line.

    g. He saw that gasoline can explode.

    h. You should see her shop.

    i. Every man loves a woman.

    j. You get half off the cost of your hotel room if you make your own bed.

    k. "It's his job to lose" (said the coach about his new player).

    l. "We will change your oil in 10 minutes" (sign in front of a garage).

    m. Challenge exercise: Bill wants to marry a Norwegian woman.

7. Go on an idiom hunt. In the course of some hours in which you converse or overhear conversations, write down all the idioms that are used. If you prefer, watch some reality TV for an hour or two and write down the idioms. Show your parents (or whomever) this book when they find you watching TV and you can claim you're doing your homework.

8. Take a half dozen or so idioms from Exercise 7, or elsewhere, and try to find their sources; if you cannot, speculate imaginatively on the source. For example, *sell down the river* meaning "betray" arose from American slave traders selling slaves from more northern states along the Mississippi River to the harsher southern states. For *snap out of it*, meaning "pay attention" or "get in a better mood," we (truly) speculate that ill-behaving persons were once confined in straitjackets secured by snaps, and to snap out of it meant the person was behaving better.

9. For each group of words given as follows, state what semantic feature or features distinguish between the classes of (a) words and (b) words. If asked, also indicate a semantic property that the (a) words and the (b) words share.

    Example: (a) widow, mother, sister, aunt, maid

               (b) widower, father, brother, uncle, valet

    The (a) and (b) words are "human."

    The (a) words are "female" and the (b) words are "male."

    a. (a) bachelor, man, son, paperboy, pope, chief

         (b) bull, rooster, drake, ram

       The (a) and (b) words are:

The (a) words are:

The (b) words are:

b. (a) table, stone, pencil, cup, house, ship, car
(b) milk, alcohol, rice, soup, mud

The (a) words are:

The (b) words are:

c. (a) book, temple, mountain, road, tractor
(b) idea, love, charity, sincerity, bravery, fear

The (a) words are:

The (b) words are:

d. (a) pine, elm, ash, weeping willow, sycamore
(b) rose, dandelion, aster, tulip, daisy

The (a) and (b) words are:

The (a) words are:

The (b) words are:

e. (a) book, letter, encyclopedia, novel, notebook, dictionary
(b) typewriter, pencil, pen, crayon, quill, charcoal, chalk

The (a) words are:

The (b) words are:

f. (a) walk, run, skip, jump, hop, swim
(b) fly, skate, ski, ride, cycle, canoe, hang glide

The (a) and (b) words are:

The (a) words are:

The (b) words are:

g. (a) ask, tell, say, talk, converse
(b) shout, whisper, mutter, drawl, holler

The (a) and (b) words are:

The (a) words are:

The (b) words are:

h. (a) absent/present, alive/dead, asleep/awake, married/single
(b) big/small, cold/hot, sad/happy, slow/fast

The (a) and (b) word pairs are:

The (a) words are:

The (b) words are:

i. (a) alleged, counterfeit, false, putative, accused
(b) red, large, cheerful, pretty, stupid

(*Hint*: Is an alleged murderer always a murderer? Is a pretty girl always a girl?)

The (a) words are:

The (b) words are:

10. **Research project:** There are many *-nym/-onym* words that describe classes of words with particular semantic properties. We mentioned a few in this chapter such as synonyms, antonyms, homonyms, and hyponyms. What is the etymology of *-onym?* What common English word is it related to? How many more *-nym* words and their meanings can you come up with? Try for five or ten on your own. With help from the Internet, dozens are possible. (*Hint:* One such *-nym* word was the winning word in the 1997 Scripps National Spelling Bee.)

11. There are several kinds of antonymy. By writing a *c, g,* or *r* in column C, indicate whether the pairs in columns A and B are complementary, gradable, or relational opposites.

A	B	C
good	bad	___
expensive	cheap	___
parent	offspring	___
beautiful	ugly	___
false	true	___
lessor	lessee	___
pass	fail	___
hot	cold	___
legal	illegal	___
larger	smaller	___
poor	rich	___
fast	slow	___
asleep	awake	___
husband	wife	___
rude	polite	___

12. For each definition, write in the first blank the word that has that meaning and in the second (and third if present) a differently spelled homonym that has a different meaning. The first letter of each of the words is provided.

    Example: "a pair": t(*wo*) t(*oo*) t(*o*)

a. "naked":	b _____	b _____	
b. "base metal":	l _____	l _____	
c. "worships":	p _____	p _____	p _____
d. "eight bits":	b _____	b _____	b _____
e. "one of five senses":	s _____	s _____	c _____
f. "several couples":	p _____	p _____	p _____
g. "not pretty":	p _____	p _____	
h. "purity of gold unit":	k _____	c _____	
i. "a horse's coiffure":	m _____	m _____	m _____
j. "sets loose":	f _____	f _____	f _____

13. Here are some proper names of some food and drink establishments. Can you figure out the basis for each name? (This is for fun—don't let yourself be graded.)

   a. Mustard's Last Stand
   b. Aunt Chilada's
   c. Tony's Toe-Main Café (Hint: silent "p")
   d. Lion on the Beach
   e. Wiener Take All
   f. Pizza Paul and Mary
   g. Franks for the Memories
   h. Dressed to Grill
   i. Deli Beloved
   j. Gone with the Wings
   k. Aunt Chovy's Pizza
   l. Polly Esther's
   m. Crepevine
   n. Thai Me Up (truly—it's in Edinburgh)
   o. Romancing the Cone
   p. Brew HaHa
   q. C U Latte
   r. Fish-cotheque
   s. Franks a lot
   t. Nincomsoup
   u. Via Agra (Indian take-away restaurant in London)
   v. Wok this way (Chinese restaurant)
   w. Planet of the Grapes (a wine shop)
   x. Brewed awakening
   y. The Codfather
   z. Syriandipity

14. The following sentences consist of a verb, its noun phrase subject, and various noun phrases and prepositional phrases. Identify the thematic role of each NP by writing the letter *a, t, i, s, g,* or *e* above the noun, standing for *agent, theme, instrument, source, goal,* and *experiencer*.

   　　　　　　a　　　　　　t　　　　　　s　　　　　　i
   Example: The boy took the books from the cupboard with a handcart.

   a. Mary found a ball.
   b. The children ran from the playground to the wading pool.
   c. One of the men unlocked all the doors with a paper clip.
   d. John melted the ice with a blowtorch.
   e. Helen looked for a cockroach.
   f. Helen saw a cockroach.
   g. Helen screamed.

h. The ice melted.
i. With a telescope, the boy saw the man.
j. The farmer loaded hay onto the truck.
k. The farmer loaded the hay with a pitchfork.
l. The hay was loaded on the truck by the farmer.
m. Helen heard music coming out of the speaker.

15. Find a complete version of "The Jabberwocky" from *Through the Looking-Glass* by Lewis Carroll. There are some on the Internet. Look up all the nonsense words in a good dictionary (also to be found online) and see how many of them are lexical items in English. Note their meanings.

16. In sports and games, many expressions are "performative." By shouting *You're out*, the first-base umpire performs an act. Think up half a dozen or so similar examples and explain their use.

17. A criterion of a performative utterance is whether you can begin it with "I hereby." Notice that if you say sentence (i) aloud, it sounds like a genuine apology, but to say sentence (ii) aloud sounds funny because you cannot willfully perform an act of noticing:

 i. I hereby apologize to you.
 ii. ?I hereby notice you.

Determine which of the following are performative sentences by inserting "hereby" and seeing whether they sound right.

a. I testify that she met the agent.
b. I know that she met the agent.
c. I suppose the Yankees will win.
d. He bet her $2,500 that Trump would win.
e. I dismiss the class.
f. I teach the class.
g. We promise to leave early.
h. I owe the IRS $1 million.
i. I bequeath $1 million to the IRS.
j. I swore I didn't do it.
k. I swear I didn't do it.

18. a. Explain, in terms of Grice's Maxims, the humor or strangeness of the following exchange between mother and child. The child has just finished eating a cookie when the mother comes into the room.

 MOTHER: What are these cookie crumbs doing in your bed?

 CHILD: Nothing, they're just lying there.

b. Do the same for this "exchange" between an owner and her cat:

 OWNER: If cats ruled the world, everyone would sleep on a pile of fresh laundry.

 CAT: Cats *don't* rule the world??

19. **a.** Spend an hour or two observing conversations between people, including yourself if you wish. Record five (or more if you're having fun) utterances where the intended meaning is mediated by Grice's Maxims and cite the maxim or maxims involved. For example, someone says "I didn't quite catch that," with the possible meaning of "Please say it again," or "Please speak a little louder." In the above example, we would cite the maxims of relevance and quantity.

   b. Here is a dialog excerpt from the 1945 motion picture *The Thin Man Goes Home*. The scene is in a shop that sells paintings and Nick Charles is leaving the shop.

   NICK CHARLES: Well, thank you very much. Goodbye now.

   SHOPKEEPER: I beg your pardon?

   NICK CHARLES: I said, goodbye now.

   SHOPKEEPER: "Goodbye now?" There's no sense to that! Obviously it's now! I mean, you wouldn't say "goodbye tomorrow" or "goodbye two hours ago!"

   NICK CHARLES: You got hold of somethin' there, brother.

   SHOPKEEPER: I've got hold of some . . . I haven't got hold of anything . . . And I'm not your brother!

   Analyze this dialogue, intended to be humorous (one assumes), in light of Grice's maxims.

20. Consider the following "facts" and then answer the questions. Part A illustrates your ability to interpret meanings when syntactic rules have deleted parts of the sentence; Part B illustrates your knowledge of semantic features and entailment.

   a. Roses are red and bralkions are too.
      Booth shot Lincoln and Czolgosz, McKinley.

      Casca stabbed Caesar and so did Cinna.

      Frodo was exhausted, as was Sam.

      a. What color are bralkions?
      b. What did Czolgosz do to McKinley?
      c. What did Cinna do to Caesar?
      d. What did Sam feel?

   b. Now consider these facts and answer the questions:
      Black Beauty was a stallion.

      Mary is a widow.

      John pretended to send Martha a birthday card.

      Jane didn't remember to send Tom a birthday card.

      Tina taught her daughter to swim.

      My boss managed to give me a raise last year.

      Flipper is walking.

(T = true; F = false)

a. Black Beauty was male.	T _____	F _____
b. Mary was never married.	T _____	F _____
c. John sent Martha a card.	T _____	F _____
d. Jane sent Tom a card.	T _____	F _____
e. Tina's daughter can swim.	T _____	F _____
f. I didn't get a raise last year.	T _____	F _____
g. Flipper has legs.	T _____	F _____

21. The following sentences have certain presuppositions that ensure their appropriateness. What are they?

    Example: The minors promised the police to stop drinking.

    Presupposition: The minors were drinking.

    a. We went to the ballpark again.
    b. Valerie regretted not receiving a new T-bird for Labor Day.
    c. That her pet turtle ran away made Emily very sad.
    d. The administration forgot that the professors support the students.
    e. It is an atrocity that the World Trade Center was attacked on September 11, 2001.
    f. It isn't tolerable that the World Trade Center was attacked on September 11, 2001.
    g. Disa wants more popcorn.
    h. Mary drank one more beer before leaving.
    i. Jack knows who discovered Pluto in 1930.
    j. Mary was horrified to find a cockroach in her bed.

22. Pronouns are so-called because they are nouns; they refer to individuals, just as nouns do. The word "proform" describes words such as "she" in a way that isn't category-specific. There are words that function as proverbs, pro-adjectives, and pro-adverbs, too. Can you come up with an example of each in English (or another language)?

23. Imagine that Alex and Bruce have a plan to throw Colleen a surprise party at work. It is Alex's job meet her for lunch at a local restaurant to get her out of the office, and Bruce's job to decorate as soon as she leaves. Alex phones Bruce and says, "The eagle has landed." What maxim is Alex flouting? What does his utterance implicate?

24. Each of the following single statements has at least one implicature in the situation described. What is it?

    a. Statement: You make a better door than a window.
    Situation: Someone is blocking your view.
    b. Statement: It's getting late.
    Situation: You're at a party and it's 4 a.m.
    c. Statement: The restaurants are open until midnight.
    Situation: It's 10 o'clock and you haven't eaten dinner.
    d. Statement: If you'd diet, this wouldn't hurt so badly.
    Situation: Someone is standing on your toe.

   e. Statement: I thought I saw a fan in the closet.
      Situation: It's sweltering in the room.

   f. Statement: Mr. Smith dresses neatly, is well groomed, and is always on time to class.
      Situation: The summary statement in a letter of recommendation to graduate school.

   g. Statement: Most of the food is gone.
      Situation: You arrived late at a cocktail party.

   h. Statement: John or Mary made a mistake.
      Situation: You're looking over some work done by John and Mary.

25. In each of the following dialogues between Jack and Laura, there is a conversational implicature. What is it?

   a. Jack: Did you make a doctor's appointment?
      Laura: Their line was busy.

   b. Jack: Do you have the play tickets?
      Laura: Didn't I give them to you?

   c. Jack: Does your grandmother have a live-in boyfriend?
      Laura: She's very traditional.

   d. Jack: How did you like the string quartet?
      Laura: I thought the violist was swell.

   e. Laura: What are Boston's chances of winning the World Series?
      Jack: Do bowling balls float?

   f. Laura: Do you own a cat?
      Jack: I'm allergic to everything.

   g. Laura: Did you mow the grass and wash the car like I told you to?
      Jack: I mowed the grass.

   h. Laura: Do you want dessert?
      Jack: Is the Pope Catholic?

26. **a.** Think of ten negative polarity items such as *give a hoot* or *have a red cent*.

   b. Challenge exercise: Can you think of other contexts without overt negation that "license" their use? *(Hint:* One answer is discussed in the text, but there are others.)

27. **Challenge exercise:** Suppose that, contrary to what was argued in the text, the noun phrase *no baby* does refer to some individual just like *the baby* does. It needn't be an actual baby but some abstract "empty" object that we'll call Ø. Show that this approach to the semantics of *no baby*, when applying Semantic Rule I and taking the restricting nature of adverbs into account (everyone who swims beautifully also swims), predicts that *No baby sleeps soundly* entails *No baby sleeps*, and explain why this is wrong.

28. Consider: "The meaning of words lies not in the words themselves, but in our attitude toward them," by Antoine de Saint-Exupéry (the author of *The Little Prince*). Do you think this is true, partially true, or false? Defend your point of view, providing examples if needed.

29. The Second Amendment of the Constitution of the United States explains: *A well-regulated Militia, being necessary to the security of a free State, the right of the people to keep and bear Arms, shall not be infringed.* It has long been argued that the citizens of the United States have an absolute right to own guns, based on this amendment. Apply Grice's Maxims to the Second Amendment and agree or disagree.

30. **Challenge exercise: Research Project.** We observed that ordinarily the antecedent of a reflexive pronoun may not have an intervening NP. Our example was the ungrammatical *Jane said the boy bit herself.* But there appear to be "funny" exceptions and many speakers of English find the following sentences acceptable: *?Yvette said Marcel really loved that sketch of herself that Renoir drew,* or *?Clyde realized that Bonnie had seen a photo of himself on the wall in the post office.* Investigate what's going on here.

31. In English, there are several ways to form antonyms using derivational morphemes. One example is the prefix *un,* as in *likely/unlikely, able/unable, fortunate/unfortunate,* and so on.

    a. List two other English prefixes that create antonyms? Give pairs of words to illustrate, as in the examples above.
    b. Can you think of word pairs that are exceptions to the rules, in other words, cases where the addition of the antonym-forming morpheme does not in fact change the meaning of the word?
    c. What are auto-antonyms? (You may have to look this up. That's okay, we think you will find them interesting.)

5

Phonetics: The Sounds of Language

> I gradually came to see that Phonetics had an important bearing on human relations—that when people of different nations pronounce each other's languages really well (even if vocabulary & grammar not perfect), it has an astonishing effect of bringing them together, it puts people on terms of equality, a good understanding between them immediately springs up.

FROM THE JOURNAL OF DANIEL JONES

When you know a language you know the *sounds* of that language, and you know how to combine those sounds into words. When you know English you know the sounds represented by the letters *b*, *s*, and *u*, and you are able to combine them to form the words *bus* and *sub*.

Although languages may contain different sounds, the sounds of all the languages of the world together constitute a class of sounds that the human vocal tract is designed to make. This chapter will discuss these speech sounds, how they are produced, and how they may be classified.

Sound Segments

HERMAN®   by Jim Unger

12-7   © Jim Unger/dist. by United Media, 1999

"Keep out! Keep out! K-E-E-P O-U-T."

Laughingstock Licensing/Ottawa, Canada

The study of speech sounds is called **phonetics**. To describe speech sounds, it is necessary to know what an individual sound is, and how each sound differs from all others. This is not as easy as it may seem, for when we speak, the sounds seem to run together and it isn't at all obvious where one sound ends and the next begins. But when we know the language being spoken, we hear the individual sounds in our "mind's ear" and are able to make sense of them, unlike the sign painter in the cartoon.

A speaker of English knows that there are three sounds in the word *bus*, yet physically the word is just one continuous sound. You can **segment** that continuous sound into individual pieces because you know English. And you recognize those pieces when they occur elsewhere, as *b* does in *bet* or *rob*, as *u* does in *up*, and as *s* does in *sister*.

It is not possible to segment the sound of someone clearing their throat, not because throat-clearing is one continuous sound, but because such sounds are not speech and may not be decomposed into the sounds of speech.

Speakers of English can separate *keepout* into the two words *keep* and *out* because they know the language. We do not generally pause between words (except to take a breath), even though we may think we do. Children learning a language reveal this fact. A two-year-old child going down stairs heard his mother say, "hold on." He replied, "I'm holing don, I'm holing don," not knowing where the break between words occurred. In fact, word boundary misperceptions have changed the forms of words historically. At an earlier stage of English, the word *apron* was *napron*. However, the phrase *a napron* was so often misperceived as *an apron* that the word lost its initial *n*.

Some phrases and sentences that are clearly distinct when printed may be ambiguous when spoken. Read the following pairs aloud and see why we might misinterpret what we hear:

grade A	gray day
I scream	ice cream
the sun's rays meet	the sons raise meat

The lack of breaks between spoken words and individual sounds often makes us think that speakers of foreign languages run their words together, unaware that we do too. X-ray motion pictures of someone speaking make the absence of breaks very clear. One can see the tongue, jaw, and lips in continuous motion as the individual sounds are produced.

Yet, if you know a language, you have no difficulty segmenting the continuous sounds of speech. It doesn't matter whether there is an alphabet for the language or whether the listener can read and write. Everyone who knows a language knows how to segment sentences into words, and words into sounds. It is not a question of literacy; it is part of being human.

Speech Sounds, Like Snowflakes

By infinitesimal movements of the tongue countless different vowels can be produced, all of them in use among speakers of English who utter the same vowels no oftener than they make the same fingerprints.

GEORGE BERNARD SHAW, 1950

It is truly amazing, given the continuity of the speech signal, that we are able to understand the individual words in an utterance. This ability is more surprising because no two speakers ever say the same word identically. The speech signal produced when one speaker says *cat* is not absolutely the same as that of another speaker's *cat* due to differences in people's size, age, and gender, among other things. Even two utterances of *cat* by the same speaker will differ to some degree.

Our knowledge of a language determines when we judge physically different sounds to be the same. We know which aspects of pronunciation are linguistically important and which are not. If someone coughs in the middle of saying "How (cough) are you?" a listener will ignore the cough and interpret this simply as "How are you?" People speak at different pitch levels, at different rates of speed, and even with their head encased in a helmet, such as Darth Vader. However, such personal differences are not linguistically significant.

Our linguistic knowledge makes it possible to ignore nonlinguistic differences in speech. Furthermore, we are capable of making sounds that we know are not speech sounds in our language. Many English speakers can make a clicking sound of disapproval that writers sometimes represent as *tsk*. This sound never occurs as part of an English word. It is even difficult for many English speakers to combine this clicking sound with other sounds. Yet, clicks are speech sounds in Xhosa, Zulu, Sesotho, and Khoikhoi—languages spoken in southern Africa— just like the *k* and *t* in English. Speakers of those languages have no difficulty producing them as parts of words. Thus, *tsk* is a speech sound in Xhosa but not in English. The sound represented by the letters *th* in the word *think* is a speech sound in English but not in French. Languages differ to a greater or lesser degree in the inventory of speech sounds that words are built from.

The science of phonetics attempts to describe all of the sounds used in all languages of the world. **Acoustic phonetics** focuses on the physical properties of sounds; **auditory phonetics** is concerned with how listeners perceive these sounds; and **articulatory phonetics**—the primary concern of this chapter—is the study of how the vocal tract produces the sounds of language.

The Phonetic Alphabet

The English have no respect for their language, and will not teach their children to speak it. They cannot spell it because they have nothing to spell it with but an old foreign alphabet of which only the consonants—and not all of them—have any agreed speech value.

GEORGE BERNARD SHAW, Preface to *Pygmalion*, 1912

Orthography, or "spelling," does not necessarily represent the sounds of a language in a consistent way. To be scientific—and phonetics *is* a science—we must devise a way for the same sound to be spelled with the same letter every time, and for the same letter to stand for the same sound every time.

To see that ordinary spelling with our Roman alphabet is woefully inadequate for the task, consider sentences such as:

Did **he** bel**ie**ve that C**ae**sar could s**ee** the p**eo**ple s**ei**ze the s**ea**s?
The sill**y** am**oe**ba stole the k**ey** to the machine.

The same sound is represented variously by **e, ie, ae, ee, eo, ei, ea, y, oe, ey**, and **i**. On the other hand, consider:

My f**a**ther w**a**nted m**a**ny **a** vill**a**ge d**a**me b**a**dly.

Here, the letter **a** represents the various sounds in *father, wanted, many*, and so on.

Making the spelling waters yet muddier, we find that a combination of letters may represent a single sound:

shoot	**ch**aracter	**Th**omas	**ph**ysics
ei**th**er	deal	rou**gh**	na**ti**on
coa**t**	gla**ci**al	**th**eater	plain

Or, conversely, the single letter **x,** when not pronounced as **z,** usually stands for the *two* sounds **ks** as in sex (you may have to speak aloud to hear that *sex* is pronounced seks).

And some letters have no sound at all in certain words (so-called *silent* letters):

mnemonic	autumn	asthma	corps
honest	chthonic	hole	Christmas
psychology	sword	debt	gnaw
bough	phthalate	island	knot

English scholars of the past have advocated spelling reform. George Bernard Shaw complained that spelling was so inconsistent that *fish* could be spelled *ghoti*: *gh* as in *tough*, *o* as in *women*, and *ti* as in *nation*. Nonetheless, spelling reformers failed to significantly change our spelling habits. It took phoneticians to invent a **phonetic alphabet** that absolutely guaranteed a one-sound-to-one-symbol correspondence. There could be no other way to study the sounds of all human languages scientifically.

The **International Phonetic Alphabet (IPA)** uses both ordinary letters and invented symbols to represent all of the sounds across all of the world's languages. If you know this alphabet, you know how to pronounce a word written in it, and upon hearing a word pronounced, you would know how to write it using the alphabetic symbols.

Table 5.1 is a list of the IPA symbols that we will use to represent English speech sounds. The symbols do not tell us everything about the sounds, which may vary from person to person and which may depend on their position in a word. They are not all of the phonetic symbols needed for English, but they will suffice for our purposes. When we discuss the sounds in more detail later in the chapter, we will add appropriate symbols. From now on, we will enclose phonetic symbols in square brackets [ ] to distinguish them from ordinary letters.

TABLE 5.1 | A Phonetic Alphabet for English Pronunciation

	Consonants						Vowels		
p	pill	t	till	k	kill	i	beet	ɪ	bit
b	bill	d	dill	g	gill	e	bait	ɛ	bet
m	mill	n	nil	ŋ	ring	u	boot	ʊ	foot
f	feel	s	seal	h	heal	o	boat	ɔ	bore
v	veal	z	zeal	l	leaf	æ	bat	a	pot/bar
θ	thigh	tʃ	chill	r	reef	ʌ	butt	ə	sofa
ð	thy	ʤ	gin	j	you	aɪ	bite	aʊ	bout
ʃ	shill	ʍ	which	w	witch	ɔɪ	boy		
ʒ	measure								

The symbol [ə] in *sofa* toward the bottom right of the chart is called a *schwa*. We use it to represent vowels in syllables that are not emphasized in speaking and whose duration is very short, such as *gen<u>e</u>ral, <u>a</u>bout,* and *read<u>e</u>r*. All other vowel symbols in the chart occur in syllables that receive at least some emphasis.

Some speakers of English pronounce *witch* and *which* with the same initial consonant, symbolized as [w] in the chart. Others pronounce them differently where the initial *w* in *which* has a little puff of air and is symbolized as [ʍ]. We have therefore listed both words in the chart of symbols.

It is difficult to include all the phonetic symbols needed to represent all differences in English. There may be sounds in your speech that are not represented, and vice versa, but that's okay. There are many varieties of English. The versions spoken in the United States, Canada, England, Australia, Ireland, India, and so on, and even within those countries, differ in their pronunciations.

The symbols in Table 5.1 are IPA symbols, with one small exception. The IPA uses an upside-down *r* ([ɹ]) for the English sound r. We, and many writers, prefer the right-side-up symbol [r] for clarity when writing for an English-reading audience. Using the IPA symbols, we can now unambiguously represent the pronunciation of words. For example, in the six words below, *ou* represents six distinct vowel sounds; the *gh* is silent in all but *rough*, where it is pronounced [f]; the *th* represents a single sound, either [θ] or [ð], and the *l* in *would* is silent. However, the phonetic transcription gives us the actual pronunciations.

Spelling	Pronunciation
though	[ðo]
thought	[θɔt]
rough	[rʌf]
bough	[baʊ]
through	[θru]
would	[wʊd]

Articulatory Phonetics

The voice is articulated by the lips and the tongue. . . . Man speaks by means of the air which he inhales into his entire body and particularly into the body cavities. When the air is expelled through the empty space it produces a sound, because of the resonances in the skull. The tongue articulates by its strokes; it gathers the air in the throat and pushes it against the palate and the teeth, thereby giving the sound a definite shape. If the tongue would not articulate each time, by means of its strokes, man would not speak clearly and would only be able to produce a few simple sounds.

HIPPOCRATES (460–377 BCE)

The production of any sound involves the movement of air. Most speech sounds are produced by pushing lung air through the *vocal cords*, up the throat, into the mouth or nose, and finally out of the body.

A brief anatomy lesson is in order. The *opening* between the vocal cords is the **glottis** and is located in the voice box or **larynx**, pronounced "lair rinks." The tubular part of the throat above the larynx is the **pharynx** (rhymes with *larynx*). What sensible people call "the mouth," linguists call the **oral cavity** to distinguish it from the **nasal cavity**, which is the nose and the plumbing that connects it to the throat. Finally, we have the tongue and the lips, both of which are capable of rapid movement and shape changing. All of these together make up the **vocal tract**. By moving the different parts of the vocal tract, we change its shape, which results in the different sounds of language. Figure 5.1 should make these descriptions clearer. (The vocal cords and larynx are not specifically labeled in the figure.)

Consonants

The sounds of all languages fall into two classes: consonants and vowels. Consonants are produced with some restriction or closure in the vocal tract that impedes the flow of air from the lungs. In phonetics, the terms *consonant* and *vowel* refer to types of *sounds*, not to the letters that represent them. In speaking of the alphabet, we may call *a* a vowel and *c* a consonant, but that means only that we use the letter *a* to represent vowel sounds and the letter *c* to represent consonant sounds.

Place of Articulation

Lolita, light of my life, fire of my loins. My sin, my soul. Lo-lee-ta: the tip of the tongue taking a trip of three steps down the palate to tap, at three, on the teeth. Lo. Lee. Ta.

VLADIMIR NABOKOV, *Lolita*, 1955

We classify consonants according to where in the vocal tract the airflow restriction occurs, called the **place of articulation**. Movement of the tongue and lips creates the constriction, reshaping the oral cavity in various ways to produce the various sounds. We are about to discuss the major places of articulation. As you read the description of each sound class, refer to Table 5.1, which provides key words containing the sounds. As you pronounce these words, try to feel which articulators are moving. (Watching yourself in a mirror helps, too.) Look at Figure 5.1 for help with the terminology.

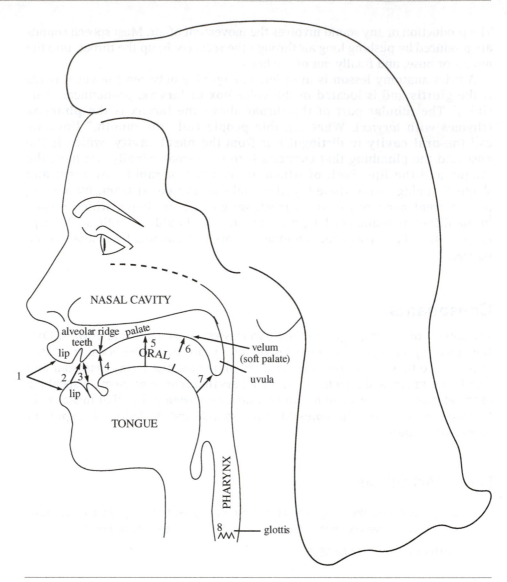

FIGURE 5.1 | The vocal tract. Places of articulation: 1. bilabial; 2. labiodental; 3. interdental; 4. alveolar; 5. (alveo)palatal; 6. velar; 7. uvular; and 8. glottal.

Bilabials [p] [b] [m] When we produce a [p], [b], or [m], we bring both lips together.

Labiodentals [f] [v] We also use our lips to form [f] and [v]. We make these sounds by touching the bottom lip to the upper teeth.

Interdentals [θ] [ð] These sounds, both spelled *th*, are pronounced by inserting the tip of the tongue between the teeth. However, for some speakers the tongue merely touches behind the teeth, making a sound more correctly called

dental. Watch yourself in a mirror and say *think* or *these* and see where your tongue tip goes.

Alveolars [t] [d] [n] [s] [z] [l] [r]   All seven of these sounds are pronounced with the tongue raised in various ways to the **alveolar ridge**.

- For [t], [d], and [n], the tongue tip is raised and touches the ridge, or slightly in front of it.
- For [s] and [z], the sides of the front of the tongue are raised, but the tip is lowered so that air escapes over it.
- For [l], the tongue tip is raised while the rest of the tongue remains down, permitting air to escape over its *sides*. Hence, [l] is called a **lateral** (meaning sideways) sound. You can feel this in the l's of *Lolita*.
- For [r] (IPA [ɹ]), the top of the tongue is curled back behind the alveolar ridge. As opposed to [l], when [r] is pronounced, air escapes through the central part of the mouth.

Palatals [ʃ] [ʒ] [tʃ] [dʒ] [j]   For these sounds, which occur in *mission* [mɪʃən], *measure* [mɛʒər], *cheap* [tʃip], *judge* [dʒʌdʒ], and *yoyo* [jojo], the constriction occurs by raising the front part of the tongue to the palate.

Velars [k] [g] [ŋ]   Another class of sounds is produced by raising the back of the tongue to the soft palate or **velum**. The initial and final sounds of the words *kick* [kɪk] and *gig* [gɪg], and the final sounds of the words *back* [bæk], *bag* [bæg], and *bang* [bæŋ], are all velar sounds.

Uvulars [ʀ] [q] [ɢ]   **Uvular** sounds are produced by raising the back of the tongue to the **uvula**, the fleshy protuberance that hangs down in the back of our throats. The *r* in French is often a uvular **trill** symbolized by [ʀ]. The uvular sounds [q] and [ɢ] occur in Arabic. These sounds do not ordinarily occur in English.

Glottals [h] [ʔ]   The sound of [h] is from the flow of air through the open **glottis** and past the tongue and lips as they prepare to pronounce a vowel sound, which always follows [h].

If the air is stopped completely at the glottis by tightly closed vocal cords, the sound upon release of the cords is a **glottal stop [ʔ]**. The interjection *uh-oh*, which you hope never to hear your dentist utter, has two glottal stops and is spelled phonetically [ʔʌʔo]. The late singer Michael Jackson made free use of glottal stops in many of his most well-known songs.

Table 5.2 summarizes the classification of these English consonants by their place of articulation.

Manner of Articulation

We have described several classes of consonants according to their places of articulation, yet we are still unable to distinguish the sounds within each class from one another. What distinguishes [p] from [b] or [b] from [m]? All are bilabial sounds. What is the difference between [t], [d], and [n], which are all alveolar sounds?

TABLE 5.2 | Places of Articulation of English Consonants

Bilabial	p	b	m			
Labiodental	f	v				
Interdental	θ	ð				
Alveolar	t	d	n	s	z	l r
Palatal	ʃ	ʒ	tʃ	ʤ	j	
Velar	k	g	ŋ			
Glottal	h	ʔ				

Speech sounds also vary in the way the airstream is affected as it flows from the lungs up and out of the mouth and nose. It may be blocked or partially blocked; the vocal cords may vibrate or not vibrate. We refer to this as the **manner of articulation**.

Voiced and Voiceless Sounds

Sounds are **voiceless** when the vocal cords are apart so that air flows freely through the glottis into the oral cavity. [s] and [p] in *super* [supər] are two of the several voiceless sounds of English.

If the vocal cords are together, the airstream forces its way through and causes them to vibrate. Such sounds are **voiced**. [b] and [z] in *buzz* [bʌz] are two of the many voiced sounds of English. To get a sense of voicing, try putting a finger in each ear and say the voiced "z-z-z-z-z." You can feel the vibrations of the vocal cords. If you now say the voiceless "s-s-s-s-s," you will not sense these vibrations (although you might hear a hissing sound). When you whisper, you are making all the speech sounds voiceless. Try it! Whisper "Sue" and "zoo." No difference, right?

The voiced/voiceless distinction is very important in English. This phonetic property distinguishes the words in pairs like the following:

rope/robe	fate/fade	rack/rag	wreath/wreathe
[rop]/[rob]	[fet]/[fed]	[ræk]/[ræg]	[riθ]/[rið]

The first word of each pair ends with a voiceless sound and the second word with a voiced sound. All other aspects of the sounds in each word pair are identical; the position of the lips and tongue is the same.

The voiced/voiceless distinction also occurs in the following pairs, where in each case the first word begins with a voiceless sound and the second with a voiced sound:

fine/vine	seal/zeal	choke/joke
[faɪn]/[vaɪn]	[sil/zil]	[tʃok]/[ʤok]
peat/beat	tote/dote	kale/gale
[pit]/[bit]	[tot]/[dot]	[kel]/[gel]

Though it is difficult to hear—for reasons explained in the next chapter—the initial sound in the word *pit* differs phonetically from the second sound in the word *spit*. During the production of the voiceless [p] (and [t] and [k]), the glottis is open and the air flows freely between the vocal cords. However, when a voiceless sound is followed by a voiced sound such as a vowel, the vocal cords must slam shut so they can vibrate.

Voiceless sounds fall into two classes depending on the timing of the vocal cord closure. When we say *pit*, the vocal cords remain open for a very short time after the lips come apart to release the *p*. We call this *p* **aspirated** because a brief puff of air escapes before the glottis closes.

When we pronounce the *p* in *spit*, however, the vocal cords start vibrating as soon as the lips open. That *p* is **unaspirated**. Hold your palm about two inches in front of your lips and say *pit*. You will feel a puff of air, which you will not feel when you say *spit*. The *t* in *tick* and the *k* in *kin* are also aspirated voiceless stops, while the *t* in *stick* and the *k* in *skin* are unaspirated.

Finally, in the production of the voiced [b] (and [d] and [g]), the vocal cords are vibrating throughout the closure of the lips, and continue to vibrate during the vowel sound that follows after the lips part.

We indicate aspirated sounds by writing the phonetic symbol with a raised h, as in the following examples:

pool	[pʰul]	spool	[spul]
tale	[tʰel]	stale	[stel]
kale	[kʰel]	scale	[skel]

Figure 5.2 shows in diagrammatic form the timing of lip closure in relation to the state of the vocal cords.

Nasal and Oral Sounds

The voiced/voiceless distinction differentiates the bilabials [b] and [p]. The sound [m] is also a bilabial, and it is voiced. What distinguishes it from [b]?

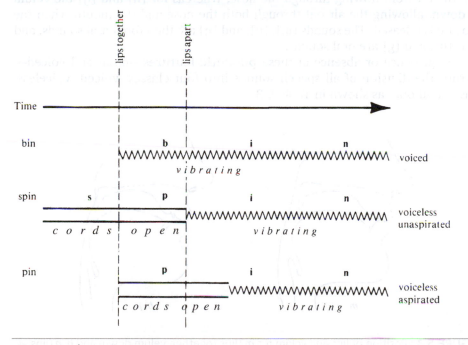

FIGURE 5.2 | Timing of lip closure and vocal-cord vibrations for voiced, voiceless unaspirated, and voiceless aspirated bilabial stops [b], [p] and [pʰ].

Figure 5.1 shows the roof of the mouth divided into the (hard) palate and the soft palate (or velum). The palate is a hard, bony structure at the front of the mouth. You can feel it with your thumb. First, wash your hands. Now, slide your thumb (nail down) along the hard palate back toward the throat; you will feel the velum, which is where the flesh becomes soft and pliable. Try not to throw up!

The velum terminates in the uvula, which you can see in a mirror if you open your mouth wide and say "aaah." The velum is movable, and when it is raised all the way to touch the back of the throat, the passage through the nose is cut off and air can escape only through the mouth.

Sounds produced with the velum up, blocking the air from escaping through the nose, are **oral sounds**, because the air can escape only through the oral cavity. Most sounds in all languages are oral sounds. When the velum is lowered, air escapes through both the nose and the mouth. Sounds produced this way are **nasal sounds**. The sound [m] is a nasal consonant. Thus, [m] is distinguished from [b] because it is a nasal sound whereas [b] is an oral sound.

The diagrams in Figure 5.3 show the position of the lips and the velum when [m], [b], and [p] are articulated. The sounds [p], [b], and [m] are produced by stopping the airflow at the lips; [m] and [b] differ from [p] by being voiced; [m] differs from [b] by being nasal. (If you ever wondered why people sound "nasally" when they have a cold, it's because excessive mucus prevents the velum from closing properly during speech.)

The same oral/nasal difference occurs in *raid* [red] and *rain* [ren], *rug* [rʌg] and *rung* [rʌŋ]. The velum is raised in the production of [d] and [g], preventing the air from flowing through the nose, whereas for [n] and [ŋ] the velum is down, allowing the air out through both the nose and the mouth when the closure is released. The sounds [m], [n], and [ŋ] are therefore nasal sounds, and [b], [d], and [g] are oral sounds.

The presence or absence of these **phonetic features**—nasal and voiced—permit the division of all speech sounds into four classes: voiced, voiceless, nasal, and oral, as shown in Table 5.3.

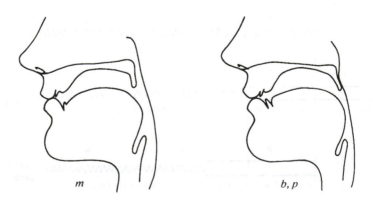

m   *b, p*

FIGURE 5.3 | Position of lips and velum for *m* (lips together, velum down) and *b, p* (lips together, velum up).

TABLE 5.3 | Four Classes of Speech Sounds

	Oral	Nasal
Voiced	b d g	m n ŋ
Voiceless	p t k	*

*Nasal consonants in English are usually voiced. Both voiced and voiceless nasal sounds occur in other languages.

We now have three ways of classifying consonants: by voicing, by place of articulation, and by nasalization. For example, [p] is a voiceless, bilabial, oral sound; [n] is a voiced, alveolar, nasal sound, and so on.

Stops [p] [b] [m] [t] [d] [n] [k] [g] [ŋ] [tʃ] [dʒ] [ʔ] We are seeing finer and finer distinctions of speech sounds. However, both [t] and [s] are voiceless, alveolar, and oral sounds. What distinguishes them? After all, *tack* and *sack* are different words.

Stops are consonants in which the airstream is completely blocked in the *oral* cavity for a short period (tens of milliseconds). All other sounds are **continuants**. The sound [t] is a stop, but the sound [s] is not, and that is what makes them different speech sounds.

- [p], [b], and [m] are *bilabial stops*, with the airstream stopped at the mouth by the complete closure of the lips.
- [t], [d], and [n] are *alveolar stops*; the airstream is stopped by the tongue, making a complete closure at or slightly behind the alveolar ridge.
- [k], [g], and [ŋ] are *velar stops*, with the complete closure at the velum.
- [tʃ] and [dʒ] are *palatal affricates* with complete stop closures. They will be further classified later.
- [ʔ] is a *glottal stop*; the air is completely stopped at the glottis.

We have been discussing the sounds that occur in English. A variety of stop consonants occur in other languages but not in English. For example, in Quechua, spoken in Bolivia and Peru, uvular stops occur, where the back of the tongue is raised and moved rearward to form a complete closure with the uvula. The phonetic symbol [q] denotes the voiceless version of this stop, which is the initial sound in the name of the language, *Quechua*. The voiced uvular stop [G] also occurs in Quechua.

Fricatives [f] [v] [θ] [ð] [s] [z] [ʃ] [ʒ] [x] [ɣ] [h] In the production of some continuants, the airflow is so severely obstructed that it causes friction, and the sounds are therefore called **fricatives**. The first of each of the following pairs of fricatives is voiceless; the second voiced.

- [f] and [v] are *labiodental fricatives;* the friction is created at the lips and teeth, where a narrow passage permits the air to escape.
- [θ] and [ð] are *interdental fricatives*, represented by *th* in *thin* and *then*. The friction occurs at the opening between the tongue and teeth.
- [s] and [z] are *alveolar fricatives,* with the friction created at the alveolar ridge.

- [ʃ] and [ʒ] are *palatal fricatives*, and contrast in such pairs as *mission* [mɪʃən] and *measure* [mɛʒər]. They are produced with friction created as the air passes between the tongue and the part of the palate behind the alveolar ridge. In English, the voiced palatal fricative never begins words except for foreign words such as *genre*. The voiceless palatal fricative begins the words *shoe* [ʃu] and *sure* [ʃur] and ends the words *rush* [rʌʃ] and *push* [puʃ].
- [x] and [ɣ] denote *velar fricatives*. They are produced by raising the back of the tongue toward, but not quite touching the velum. The friction is created as air passes through that narrow passage, and the sound is not unlike clearing your throat. These sounds do not commonly occur in English, though in some forms of Scottish English the final sound of *loch* meaning "lake" is [x]. In rapid speech, the *g* in *wagon* may be pronounced [ɣ]. The final sound of the composer J. S. Bach's name is also pronounced [x], which is a common sound in German.
- [h] is a glottal fricative. Its relatively weak sound comes from air passing through the open glottis and pharynx.

All fricatives are continuants. Although the airstream is obstructed as it passes through the oral cavity, it is not completely stopped.

Affricates [t͡ʃ] [d͡ʒ]   These sounds are produced by a stop closure followed immediately by a gradual release of the closure that produces an effect characteristic of a fricative. The palatal sounds that begin and end the words *church* and *judge* are voiceless and voiced affricates, respectively. Affricates are not continuants because of the initial stop closure.

Liquids [l] [r]   In the production of the sounds [l] and [r], there is some obstruction of the airstream in the mouth, but not enough to cause any real constriction or friction. These sounds are **liquids**. They are articulated differently, as described in the earlier alveolar section, but are grouped as a class because they are acoustically similar. Due to that similarity, foreign speakers of English may confuse the two sounds and substitute one for the other.

Glides [j] [w]   The sounds [j] and [w], the initial sounds of *you* [ju] and *we* [wi], are produced with little obstruction of the airstream. They are always followed directly by a vowel and do not occur at the ends of words (don't be fooled by spelling; words ending in *y* or *w* like *say* and *saw* end in a vowel sound). After articulating [j] or [w] the tongue glides quickly into place for pronouncing the next vowel, hence the term **glide**.

The glide [j] is a palatal sound; the blade of the tongue (the front part minus the tip) is raised toward the hard palate in a position almost identical to that in producing the vowel sound in the word *beat*. The glide [w] is produced by both rounding the lips and simultaneously raising the back of the tongue toward the velum. It is thus a **labiovelar** glide. Where speakers of English have different pronunciations for the words *which* and *witch*, the labiovelar glide in the first word is voiceless, symbolized as [ʍ] (an upside-down w). The position of the tongue and the lips for [w] is similar to that for producing the vowel sound in *flute*.

Approximants The sounds [w], [j], [r], and [l] may also be called approximants because the articulators approximate a frictional closeness, but no actual friction occurs. The first three are central approximants, whereas [l] is a lateral approximant.

Although in this chapter we focus on the sounds of English, the IPA has symbols and classifications for all the sounds of the world's languages. For example, many languages have sounds that are referred to as trills, and others have clicks. These are described in the following sections.

Trills and flaps The r-sound of many languages may be different from the English [r]. A trilled *r* is produced by rapid vibrations of an articulator. An alveolar **trill**, as in the Spanish word for "dog," *perro*, is produced by vibrating the tongue tip against the alveolar ridge. Its IPA symbol is [r], strictly speaking, though we have co-opted [r] for the English r. Many French speakers articulate the initial sound of *rouge* as a uvular trill, produced by vibrating the uvula. Its IPA symbol is [ʀ].

Another *r*-sound is called a **flap** and is produced by a flick of the tongue against the alveolar ridge. It sounds like a very fast *d*. It occurs in Spanish in words such as *pero* meaning "but." It may also occur in British English in words such as *very*. Its IPA symbol is [ɾ]. Most American speakers produce a flap instead of a [t] or [d] in words like *writer* and *rider*, which then sound identical and are spelled phonetically as [ɾaɪɾər].

Clicks These "exotic" sounds are made by moving air in the mouth between various articulators. The sound of disapproval often spelled *tsk* is an alveolar **click** that occurs in several languages of southern Africa such as Zulu. A lateral click, which is like the sound one makes to encourage a horse, occurs in Xhosa. In fact, the *X* in *Xhosa* stands for that particular speech sound.

Phonetic Symbols for American English Consonants

We are now capable of distinguishing all of the consonant sounds of English via the properties of voicing, nasality, and place and manner of articulation. For example, [f] is a voiceless, (oral), labiodental fricative; [n] is a (voiced), nasal, alveolar stop. The parenthesized features are usually not mentioned because they are redundant; all sounds are oral unless nasal is specifically mentioned, and all nasals are voiced in English.

Table 5.4 lists the consonants by their phonetic features. The rows stand for manner of articulation and the columns for place of articulation.

Examples of words in which these sounds occur are given in Table 5.5.

TABLE 5.4 | Some Phonetic Symbols for American English Consonants

	Bilabial	Labiodental	Interdental	Alveolar	Palatal	Velar	Glottal
Stop (oral)							
voiceless	p			t		k	ʔ
voiced	b			d		g	
Nasal (voiced)	m			n		ŋ	
Fricative							
voiceless		f	θ	s	ʃ		h
voiced		v	ð	z	ʒ		
Affricate							
voiceless					tʃ		
voiced					dʒ		
Glide							
voiceless	ʍ					ʍ	
voiced	w				j	w	
Liquid (voiced)							
(central)				r			
(lateral)				l			

TABLE 5.5 | Examples of Consonants in English Words

	Bilabial	Labiodental	Interdental	Alveolar	Palatal	Velar	Glottal
Stop (oral)							
voiceless	pie			tie		kite	(ʔ)uh-(ʔ)oh
voiced	buy			die		guy	
Nasal (voiced)	my			night		sing	
Fricative							
voiceless		fine	thigh	sue	shoe		high
voiced		vine	thy	zoo	measure		
Affricate							
voiceless					cheese		
voiced					jump		
Glide							
voiceless	which					which	
voiced	wipe				you	wipe	
Liquid (voiced)							
(central)				rye			
(lateral)				lye			

Vowels

HIGGINS: Tired of listening to sounds?

PICKERING: Yes. It's a fearful strain. I rather fancied myself because I can pronounce twenty-four distinct vowel sounds, but your hundred and thirty beat me. I can't hear a bit of difference between most of them.

HIGGINS: Oh, that comes with practice. You hear no difference at first, but you keep on listening and presently you find they're all as different as A from B.

GEORGE BERNARD SHAW, *Pygmalion*, 1912

Vowels are produced with little restriction of the airflow from the lungs out through the mouth and/or the nose. The quality of a vowel depends on the shape of the vocal tract as the air passes through. Different parts of the tongue may be high or low in the mouth; the lips may be spread or pursed; the velum may be raised or lowered.

Vowel sounds carry pitch and loudness; you can sing vowels or shout vowels. They may be longer or shorter in duration. Vowels can stand alone—they can be produced without consonants before or after them. You can say the vowels of *beat* [bit], *bit* [bɪt], and *boot* [but] without the initial [b] or the final [t], but you cannot say a [b] or a [t] alone without at least a little bit of vowel sound.

We describe vowels by their articulatory features as we did with consonants. Just as we say a [d] is pronounced by raising the tongue tip to the alveolar ridge, we say an [i] is pronounced by raising the body of the tongue toward the palate. With a [b] the lips come together; for an [æ] (the vowel in *cat*) the tongue is low in the mouth with the tongue tip forward, behind the front teeth.

If you watch a side view of an X-ray (that's *-ray*, not *-rated*!) video of someone's tongue moving during speech, you will see various parts of the tongue rise up high and fall down low; at the same time you will see it move forward and backward in the mouth. These are the dimensions over which vowels are produced. We classify vowels according to three questions:

1. How high or low in the mouth is the tongue?
2. How forward or backward in the mouth is the tongue?
3. Are the lips rounded (pursed) or spread?

Tongue Position

(In this section, we refer to the vowel symbols of Table 5.1 on page 187.) The upper two diagrams in Figure 5.4 show that the tongue is high in the mouth in the production of the vowels [i] and [u] in the words *he* [hi] and *who* [hu]. In *he* the front part (but not the tip) of the tongue is raised; in *who* it is the back of the tongue. (Prolong the vowels of these words and try to feel the raised part of your tongue.) These are both *high* vowels, and the [i] is a *high front* vowel while the [u] is a *high back* vowel.

To produce the vowel sound [a] of *hah* [ha], the tongue is low in the mouth, as the third diagram in Figure 5.4 shows. (The reason a doctor examining your throat may ask you to say *aah* is that the tongue is low and easy to see over.)

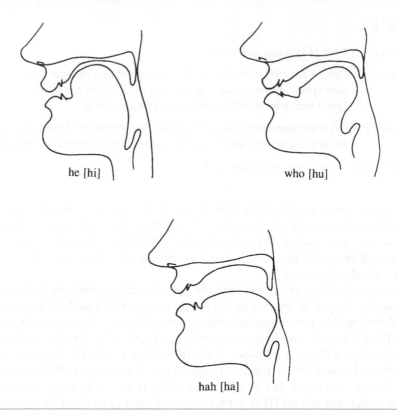

FIGURE 5.4 | Position of the tongue in producing the vowels in *he*, *who*, and *hah*.

The vowels [ɪ] and [ʊ] in the words *hit* [hɪt] and *put* [pʰʊt] are similar to those in *heat* [hit] and *hoot* [hut] but with slightly lowered tongue positions.

The vowels [e] and [o] in *bait* [bet] and *boat* [bot] are *midvowels*—they are neither high nor low. [ɛ] in *bet* [bɛt] is also a midvowel, produced with a slightly lower tongue position than [e]. As well, [e] and [ɛ] are *front* vowels and [o] is a *back* vowel.

The vowel [æ] in *hack* [hæk] or *cat* [kʰæt] is produced with the front part of the tongue low in the mouth. Thus, [æ] is a *low front* vowel. The [ɔ] in *saw* [sɔ] is also a low vowel, but with the tongue back toward the throat. It is therefore a *low back* vowel.

The vowel [ʌ] in the word *luck* [lʌk] is a central vowel pronounced with the tongue low in the mouth though not as low as with [a]. Finally, the schwa [ə], which occurs as the first sound in *about* [əbaʊt], or the final sound of *sofa* [sofə], is articulated with the tongue in a neutral position between the extremes of high/low, front/back. The schwa is used mostly to represent unstressed vowels. (Figure 5.5 makes this vowel "geography" more apparent.)

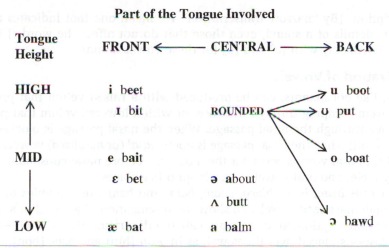

Part of the Tongue Involved

Tongue Height	FRONT ←	— CENTRAL →	BACK
HIGH	i beet		u boot
	ɪ bit	ROUNDED	ʊ put
MID	e bait		o boat
	ɛ bet	ə about	
		ʌ butt	
LOW	æ bat	a balm	ɔ hawd

FIGURE 5.5 | Classification of American English vowels.

Lip Rounding

Vowels also differ as to whether the lips are rounded or spread. The back vowels [u], [ʊ], [o], and [ɔ] in *boot, put, boat,* and *bawd* are the only **rounded vowels** in (American) English. They are produced with pursed or rounded lips. You can get a feel for the rounding by prolonging the word *who,* as if you were an owl: *whooooooooooo.* Now pose for the camera and say *cheese,* only say it with a prolonged vowel: *cheeeeeeeeeeese.* The high front [i] in *cheese* is unrounded, with the lips in the shape of a smile, and you can feel it or see it in a mirror.

Other languages may differ in whether or not they have rounded vowels. French and Swedish, for example, have *front* rounded vowels, which English lacks. English also lacks a high back *unrounded* vowel, but this sound occurs in Mandarin Chinese, Japanese, and the Cameroonian language Feʔfeʔ, among others. The IPA symbol for this vowel is [ɯ]. The rounding distinction is important, as in Mandarin Chinese the unrounded [sɯ] means "four" but the round [su] (like *sue*) means "speed."

Diphthongs

A **diphthong** is a sequence of two vowel sounds bonded together. Diphthongs occur in the phonetic inventory of many languages including English. The vowels we have studied so far are simple vowels, called **monophthongs.** The vowel sound in the word *bite* [baɪt], however, is the [a] of *father* joined to the [ɪ] of *fit,* resulting in the diphthong [aɪ]. Similarly, the vowel in *bout* [baʊt] is [a] joined to the [ʊ] of *put,* resulting in [aʊ]. Another diphthong that occurs in English is the vowel sound in *boy* [bɔɪ], which is the [ɔ] of *bore* joined to [ɪ], resulting in [ɔɪ]. The pronunciation of any of these diphthongs may vary from our description because of the diversity of English speakers.

To some extent, the midvowels [e] and [o] may be diphthongized, especially in American English, though not in other varieties such as Irish English. Many linguists therefore denote these sounds as [eɪ] and [oʊ] in a narrower transcription. [By "narrow transcription" we mean one that indicates all the phonetic details of a sound, even those that do not affect the words.] In this book, we will stay with [e] and [o] for these vowel sounds.

Nasalization of Vowels

Vowels, like consonants, can be produced with a raised velum that prevents the air from escaping through the nose, or with a lowered velum that permits air to pass through the nasal passage. When the nasal passage is blocked, *oral* vowels result; when the nasal passage is open, *nasal* (or *nasalized*) vowels result. In English, nasal vowels occur for the most part before nasal consonants in the same syllable, and oral vowels occur in all other places.

The words *bean, bone, bingo, boom, bam,* and *bang* are examples of words that contain nasalized vowels. To show the nasalization of a vowel in a narrow phonetic transcription, an extra mark called a **diacritic**—the symbol ~ (tilde) in this case—is placed over the vowel, as in *bean* [bĩn] and *bone* [bõn].

In languages such as French, Polish, and Portuguese nasalized vowels occur without nasal consonants. The French word for "good" is *bon* [bõ]. The *n* in the spelling is not pronounced but indicates that the vowel is nasal.

Tense and Lax Vowels

Figure 5.5 shows that the vowel [i] has a slightly higher tongue position than [ɪ]. This is also true for [e] and [ɛ]; and [u] and [ʊ]. The first vowel in each pair is generally produced with greater tension of the tongue muscles than its counterpart, and it is often a little longer in duration. These vowels are distinguished by the features **tense** and **lax** along with others:

Tense		Lax	
i	beat	ɪ	bit
e	bait	ɛ	bet
u	boot	ʊ	put
o	boat	ʌ	hut
ɔ	saw	æ	hat
a	pa	ə	about
aɪ	high		
aʊ	how		
ɔɪ	boy		

Tense vowels may occur at the ends of words: [si], [se], [su], [so], [pa], [saɪ], [haʊ], and [sɔɪ] represent the English words *see, say, sue, sew, pa, sigh, how,* and *soy.* Lax vowels do not ordinarily occur at the ends of words: [sɪ], [sɛ], [sʊ], [sʌ], [sæ], and [sə] are not possible words in English.

Major Phonetic Classes

Biologists divide life forms into larger and smaller classes. They may distinguish between animals and plants; within animals, between vertebrates and invertebrates; and within vertebrates, between mammals and reptiles; and so on.

Linguists describe speech sounds similarly. All sounds are consonant sounds or vowel sounds, though some play dual roles. Within consonants, all are voiced or unvoiced, and so on. All the classes of sounds described so far in this chapter combine to form larger, more general classes that are important in the patterning of sounds in the world's languages.

Noncontinuants and Continuants

Stops and affricates belong to the class of **noncontinuants**. There is a total obstruction of the airstream in the *oral cavity*. Nasal stops are included, although air does flow continuously out the nose. All other consonants, and all vowels, are continuants, in which the stream of air flows continuously out of the mouth.

Obstruents and Sonorants

The non nasal stops, the fricatives, and the affricates form a major class of sounds called **obstruents**. The airstream may be fully obstructed, as in nonnasal stops and affricates, or nearly fully obstructed, as in the production of fricatives.

Sounds that are not obstruents are **sonorants**. Vowels, nasal stops [m], [n], and [ŋ], liquids [l] and [r], and glides [j] and [w] are all sonorants. They are produced with much less obstruction to the flow of air than the obstruents, which permits the air to resonate. Nasal stops are sonorants because, although the air is blocked in the mouth, it continues to resonate in the nasal cavity.

Consonantal Sounds

Obstruents, nasal stops, liquids, and glides are all consonants. There is some degree of restriction to the airflow in articulating these sounds. With glides ([j], [w]), however, the restriction is minimal, and they are the most vowel-like, and the least consonant-like, of the consonants. Glides may even be referred to as "semivowels" or "semi-consonants." In recognition of this fact, linguists place the obstruents, nasal stops, and liquids in a subclass of consonants called **consonantal**, from which the glides are excluded.

Here are some other terms used to form subclasses of consonantal sounds. These are not exhaustive, nor are they mutually exclusive (e.g., the interdentals belong to two subclasses). A full course in phonetics would note further classes that we omit.

Labials [p] [b] [m] [f] [v] [w] [ʍ] Labial sounds are those articulated with the involvement of the lips. They include the class of *bilabial* sounds [p], [b], and [m], the *labiodentals* [f] and [v], and the *labiovelars* [w] and [ʍ].

Coronals [θ] [ð] [t] [d] [n] [s] [z] [ʃ] [ʒ] [tʃ] [dʒ] [l] [r] Coronal sounds are articulated by raising the tongue blade. Coronals include the *interdentals* [θ] and [ð], the *alveolars* [t], [d], [n], [s], and [z], the *palatals* [ʃ] and [ʒ], the *affricates* [tʃ] and [dʒ], and the *liquids* [l] and [r].

Anteriors [p] [b] [m] [f] [v] [θ] [ð] [t] [d] [n] [s] [z] Anterior sounds are consonants produced in the front part of the mouth, that is, from the alveolar area forward. They include the labials, the interdentals, and the alveolars.

Sibilants [s] [z] [ʃ] [ʒ] [tʃ] [dʒ] This class of consonantal sounds is characterized by an acoustic rather than an articulatory property of its members. The friction created by sibilants produces a hissing sound, which is a mixture of high-frequency sounds.

Syllabic Sounds

Sounds that may function as the core of a syllable possess the feature **syllabic**. Clearly vowels are syllabic, but they are not the only sound class that anchors syllables.

Liquids and nasals may also be syllabic, as shown by the words *dazzle* [dæzl̩], *faker* [fekr̩], *rhythm* [rɪðm̩], and *wagon* [wægn̩]. (The diacritic mark under the [l̩], [r̩], [m̩], and [n̩] is the notation for syllabic.) Placing a schwa [ə] before the syllabic liquid or nasal also shows that these are separate syllables. The four words could be written as [dæzəl], [fekər], [rɪðəm], and [wægən]. We will use this transcription. Similarly, the vowel sound in words such as *bird* and *verb* are sometimes written as a syllabic *r*: [br̩d] and [vr̩b]. For consistency, we shall transcribe these words using the schwa—[bərd] and [vərb]—the only instances where a schwa represents a stressed vowel.

Obstruents and glides are never syllabic sounds because an obstruent or glide is always accompanied by a vowel that functions as the syllabic core.

Prosodic Features

Length, pitch, and *stress* (or "accent") are **prosodic** or **suprasegmental** features. They are features *over and above* the segmental values such as place or manner of articulation, thus the *supra-* in *suprasegmental*. The term *prosodic* comes from poetry, where it refers to the metrical structure of verse. One of the essential characteristics of poetry is the placement of stress on particular syllables, which defines the versification of the poem.

Speech sounds that are identical in their place or manner features may differ in length (duration). Tense vowels are slightly longer than lax vowels, but only by a few milliseconds. However, in some languages when a vowel is prolonged to around twice its normal length, it can make a difference between words. In Japanese, the word *biru* [biru] with a regular *i* means "building," but with the *i* doubled in length as in *biiru*, spelled phonetically as [biːru], the meaning is "beer." (The colon-like ː is the IPA symbol for segment length or doubling.) In Japanese, vowel length can make the difference between two words.

Japanese, and many other languages such as Finnish and Italian, have long consonants that may contrast words. When a consonant is long, or doubled, either the closure or obstruction is prolonged. Pronounced with a short k, the word *saki* [saki] means "ahead" in Japanese; pronounced with a long *k*—prolonging the velar closure—the word *sakki* [sakːi] means "before." In effect, the extended silence of the prolonged closure is meaningful in these languages.

English is not a language in which vowel or consonant length can change a word. You might say "puleeeeeze" to emphasize your request, but the word is still *please*. You may also say in English "Whatttttt a dump!" to express your dismay at a hotel room, prolonging the t-closure, but the word *what* is not changed.

When we speak we also change the **pitch** of our voice. The pitch depends on how fast the vocal cords vibrate: the faster they vibrate, the higher the pitch. If the larynx is small, as in children, the shorter vocal cords vibrate faster and the pitch is higher, all other things being equal. If the larynx is larger, as in adults, the longer vocal cords vibrate more slowly and the pitch is lower. That is why men (being generally larger), women, and children have (to a greater or lesser degree) lower-, medium-, and higher-pitched voices.

In many languages including English, certain syllables in a word are louder, slightly higher in pitch, and somewhat longer in duration than other syllables in the word. They are **stressed** syllables. For example, in the adjective *PERfect* the first syllable is stressed, whereas in the verb *perFECT* the second syllable receives greater stress. Stress can be marked in several ways, as we did using capital letters or by using an accent mark as in *pérfect* versus *perféct*.

English is a "stress-timed" language, meaning that some syllables will be longer and some shorter and the intervals between stressed syllables are roughly equal in length. French, on the other hand, is a "syllable-timed" language, meaning that each syllable is more or less of equal length and equal (lack of) stress. When English speakers attempt to speak French, they cannot help but stress syllables, so their French is heard with "an English accent." When French speakers speak English, they often fail to stress syllables, and that contributes to what English speakers call "a French accent."

Tone and Intonation

We have already seen how length and stress can make sounds perceptually different despite having the same segmental properties. In some languages, these differences make different words, such as the two *perfects* in English. The pitch with which a word or syllable is spoken can also make a difference in certain languages.

Speakers of all languages vary the pitch of their voice when they speak. The effect of pitch on a syllable differs from language to language. In English, it doesn't matter whether you say *cat* with a high pitch or a low pitch; it will still mean "cat." But, if you say [ba] with a relatively high pitch in Nupe (a language spoken in Nigeria), it will mean "to be sour," whereas if you say it with a relatively low pitch, it will mean "to count." Languages that use the pitch of individual vowels or syllables to contrast meanings of words are called **tone languages**. Rather than *pitch* we use the term *tone*.

Over half the world's languages are tone languages. There are more than one thousand tone languages spoken in Africa alone. Many languages of Asia, such as Mandarin Chinese, Burmese, and Thai, are tone languages. In Thai, for example, the same string of segmental sounds represented by [na:] will mean different things if one says the sounds with a low tone, a mid-tone, a high tone, a falling tone from high to low, or a rising tone from low to high. Thai therefore has five linguistic tones, illustrated as follows:

(Diacritics are used to represent distinctive tones in the phonetic transcriptions.)

[`]	L	low tone	[nà:]	"a nickname"
[‾]	M	mid tone	[nā:]	"rice paddy"
[´]	H	high tone	[ná:]	"young maternal uncle or aunt"
[^]	HL	falling tone	[nâ:]	"face"
[ˇ]	LH	rising tone	[nǎ:]	"thick"

There are two kinds of tones. If the pitch is level across the syllable, we have a **register tone**. If the pitch changes across the syllable, whether from high to low or vice versa, we have a **contour tone**. Thai has three level and two contour tones. Commonly, tone languages will have two or three register tones and possibly several contour tones.

In a tone language, it is not the absolute pitch that counts, but the relative pitch of adjacent syllables. Thus men, women and children with differently pitched voices communicate perfectly well.

Intonation is variation of pitch that does not distinguish words. Languages that are not tone languages, such as English or French, are called intonation languages. The **pitch contour** of an utterance may affect the meaning of the whole sentence, so that *The President is here* spoken with falling pitch is interpreted as a statement, but with rising pitch, as a question. We'll have more to say about intonation in the next chapter.

Phonetic Symbols and Spelling Correspondences

I never had any large respect for good spelling.

MARK TWAIN, *Autobiography*

Table 5.6 shows some but not all sound/spelling correspondences for American English. We have included the symbols for the voiceless aspirated stops to illustrate that what is spelled with one letter—for example *p*—may occur phonetically as two sounds: [p], [pʰ].

Some of these pronunciations may differ from your own. For example, you may (or may not) pronounce the words *cot* and *caught* identically. In the form of English described here, *cot* and *caught* are pronounced differently, *cot* with the vowel [a] as in *car*, and *caught* with the vowel [ɔ] as in *core*.

There will be other differences, too, because English is a worldwide language and is spoken in many forms in many countries. The English examples used in

TABLE 5.6 | Phonetic Symbol/English Spelling Correspondences

	Consonants
Symbol	**Examples**
p	spit, tip, Lapp
pʰ	pit, prick, plaque, appear
b	bit, tab, brat, bubble
m	mitt, tam, smack, Emmy, comb, Autumn
t	stick, pit, kissed, write
tʰ	tick, intend, pterodactyl, attack
d	Dick, cad, drip, loved, ride
n	nick, kin, snow, mnemonic, gnome, pneumatic, know
k	skin, stick, scat, critique, elk
kʰ	curl, kin, charisma, critic, mechanic, close
g	girl, burg, longer, Pittsburgh
ŋ	sing, think, finger
f	fat, philosophy, flat, phlogiston, coffee, reef, cough
v	vat, dove, gravel
s	sip, skip, psychology, pass, pats, democracy, scissors, fasten, deceive, descent
z	zip, jazz, razor, pads, kisses, Xerox, design, lazy, scissors, maize
θ	thigh, through, wrath, ether, Matthew
ð	thy, their, weather, lathe, either
ʃ	shoe, mush, mission, nation, fish, glacial, sure
ʒ	measure, vision, azure, casual, genre, rouge
tʃ	match, rich, righteous
tʃʰ	choke, Tchaikovsky, discharge
dʒ	judge, midget, George, magistrate, residual
l	leaf, feel, call, single
r	reef, fear, Paris, singer
j	you, yes, feud, use
w	witch, swim, queen
ʍ	which, where, whale (for speakers who pronounce *which* differently from *witch*)
h	hat, who, whole, rehash
ʔ	bottle, button, glottal (for some speakers), (ʔ)uh-(ʔ)oh
ɾ	writer, rider, latter, ladder

	Vowels
i	beet, beat, be, receive, key, believe, amoeba, people, Caesar, Vaseline, serene, Raleigh
ɪ	bit, consist, injury, bin, women, build
e	gate, bait, ray, great, eight, gauge, greyhound, rein, feign
ɛ	bet, serenity, says, guest, dead, said
æ	pan, act, laugh, comrade
u	boot, lute, who, sewer, through, to, too, two, move, Lou, true, suit
ʊ	put, foot, butcher, could
ʌ	cut, tough, among, oven, does, cover, flood
o	coat, go, beau, grow, though, toe, own, sew
ɔ	caught, stalk, core, saw, ball, awe, auto
a	cot, father, palm, sergeant, honor, hospital, melodic
ə	sofa, alone, symphony, suppose, melody, bird, verb, the
aɪ	bite, sight, by, buy, die, dye, aisle, choir, guide, island, height, sign
aʊ	about, brown, doubt, coward, sauerkraut
ɔɪ	boy, oil, Reuters

this book are most closely related to American English. However, our aim is to teach phonetics in general, and to show you how phonetics might describe the speech sounds of any of the world's languages. We merely use American English for illustration.

The "Phonetics" of Signed Languages

Earlier we noted that signed languages, like all human languages, are governed by a grammatical system that includes syntactic and morphological rules. As well, just as spoken languages distinguish sounds according to place and manner of articulation, so signed languages distinguish signs according to the place and manner in which the signs are articulated with the hands. The signs of American Sign Language (ASL), for example, are formed by three major features:

1. The *configuration* of the hand (handshape)
2. The *movement* of the hand and arms in signing space
3. The *location* of the hands in signing space

"Signing space" is the area of space extending approximately forearm-distance from the signer's body, and from waist to forehead.

To illustrate how these features define a sign, the ASL sign meaning "mother" is produced by tapping your chin with the thumb of your hand with all of the fingers extended in a spread five-finger handshape (5-handshape). It has three features: the *5-handshape* configuration, the *tapping* movement, the *chin* location.

ASL has over 30 handshapes. But not all signed languages have the same hand-shapes, just as not all spoken languages share the same details of articulation. For example, Chinese Sign Language has a handshape formed with an open hand with all fingers extended except the ring finger. ASL lacks this handshape.

Movement and location vary as well, just as the manner and place of articulation vary in spoken languages. For example, movement can be either straight or in an arc; location may be on or near or away from a particular part of the body.

We saw that a difference in voicing or tone results in a different word in a spoken language. Similarly, a change in handshape, movement or location results in a different sign with a different meaning. The sign meaning "father" differs from the sign meaning "fine" only in location. Both signs are formed with the 5-handshape, but the thumb moves to the signer's forehead in "father" but to the chest in "fine."

The parallels that exist in the organization of sounds and signs are not surprising when we consider that similar cognitive systems underlie both spoken and signed languages.

Summary

The science of speech sounds is called **phonetics**. It aims to provide the set of properties necessary to describe and distinguish all the sounds in human languages throughout the world.

When we speak we produce continuous stretches of sound, which are the physical manifestations of strings of discrete linguistic **segments**. Knowledge of a language permits one to separate continuous speech into individual sounds and words.

The discrepancy between spelling and sounds motivated the development of phonetic alphabets in which one letter corresponds to one sound. The major **phonetic alphabet** in use is the **International Phonetic Alphabet (IPA)**, by means of which the sounds of all human languages can be represented. To distinguish between **orthography** (spelling) and **phonetic transcriptions**, we write the latter between square brackets, as in [fənɛɹɪk] for *phonetic*.

All English speech sounds come from the movement of lung air through the vocal tract. The air moves through the **glottis** (i.e., between the vocal cords), up the pharynx, through the oral (and possibly the nasal) cavity, and out the mouth or nose.

Human speech sounds fall into classes according to their phonetic properties. All speech sounds are either **consonants** or **vowels,** and all consonants are either **obstruents** or **sonorants.** Consonants have some obstruction of the airstream in the vocal tract, and the location of the obstruction defines their **place of articulation,** some of which are: **bilabial, labiodental, alveolar, palatal, velar, uvular,** and **glottal.**

Consonants are further classified according to their **manner of articulation.** They may be **voiced** or **voiceless, oral** or **nasal**, and long or short. They may be **stops, fricatives, affricates, liquids,** or **glides.** During the production of voiced sounds, the vocal cords are together and vibrating, whereas in voiceless sounds they are apart and not vibrating. Consonants may also be grouped according to certain features to form larger classes such as **labial, coronal, anterior,** and **sibilant.**

Vowels form the nucleus of syllables. They differ according to the position of the tongue and lips: high, mid, or low tongue; front, central, or back of the tongue; rounded or unrounded lips. The vowels in English may be **tense** or **lax.** Tense vowels are slightly longer in duration and slightly higher than lax vowels. Vowels may also be **stressed** (longer, higher in pitch, and louder) or **unstressed.** Vowels, like consonants, may be nasal or oral, although most vowels in all languages are oral.

Length, pitch, loudness, and stress are **prosodic,** or **suprasegmental,** features. They are imposed over and above the segmental values of the sounds in a syllable. In many languages, the pitch or **tone** of the syllable is linguistically significant. For example, two words with identical segments may contrast in meaning if one has a high tone and the other a low tone. Such languages are **tone languages.** There are also **intonation** languages in which the rise and fall of pitch over an entire phrase may affect meaning.

English and other languages use stress to distinguish different words, such as *cóntent* and *contént*. In some languages, long vowels and long consonants contrast with their shorter counterparts. Thus, *biru* [biru] and *biiru* [biːru], *saki* [saki] and *sakki* [sakːi] are different words in Japanese.

Diacritics to specify such properties as nasalization, length, stress, and tone may be combined with the phonetic symbols for more detailed (narrow) phonetic transcriptions. A phonetic transcription of *man* would use a tilde diacritic to indicate the nasalization of the vowel: [mæ̃n].

In sign languages, there are "phonetic" features analogous to those of spoken languages. In ASL these are handshape, movement, and location. As in spoken languages, changes along one of these parameters can result in a new word. In the following chapter, we discuss this meaning-changing property of features in much greater detail.

References for Further Reading

Grayson, G. 2003. *Talking with your hands, listening with your eyes: A complete photographic guide to American sign language.* Garden City Park, New York: Square One Publishers.

International Phonetic Association. 1999. *Handbook of the International Phonetic Association.* Cambridge, UK: Cambridge University Press.

Ladefoged, P. 2005. *Vowels and consonants, 2nd ed.* Oxford, UK: Blackwell Publishers.

Ladefoged, P., and Johnson, K. 2011. *A course in phonetics, 6th ed.* Boston, MA: Wadsworth, Cengage Learning.

Ladefoged, P., and I. Maddieson. 1995. *The sounds of the world's languages.* Oxford, UK: Blackwell Publishers.

Ogden, R. 2010. *An introduction to English phonetics.* Edinburgh, UK: Edinburgh University Press.

Pullum, G.K., and W. A. Ladusaw. 2013. *Phonetic symbol guide, 2nd ed.* Chicago: University of Chicago Press.

Exercises

1. Write the phonetic symbol for the first sound in each of the following words according to the way you pronounce it.

   Example: ooze   [u]   psycho   [s]

   a. judge   [   ]   **f.** thought   [   ]
   b. Thomas   [   ]   **g.** contact   [   ]
   c. though   [   ]   **h.** phone   [   ]
   d. easy   [   ]   **i.** civic   [   ]
   e. pneumonia   [   ]   **j.** usual   [   ]

2. Write the phonetic symbol for the *last* sound in each of the following words.

   Example: boy [ɔɪ] (Diphthongs should be treated as one sound.)

   a. fleece   [   ]   **f.** cow   [   ]
   b. neigh   [   ]   **g.** rough   [   ]
   c. long   [   ]   **h.** cheese   [   ]
   d. health   [   ]   **i.** bleached   [   ]
   e. watch   [   ]   **j.** rags   [   ]

3. Write the following words in phonetic transcription, according to your pronunciation.

   Examples: knot [nat]; *delightful* [dilaɪtfəl] or [dəlaɪtfəl]. Some of you may pronounce some of these words the same.

a. physics	**h.** Fromkin	**o.** touch
b. merry	**i.** tease	**p.** cough
c. marry	**j.** weather	**q.** larynx
d. Mary	**k.** coat	**r.** through
e. yellow	**l.** Rodman	**s.** beautiful
f. sticky	**m.** heath	**t.** honest
g. transcription	**n.** "your name"	**u.** president

4. Following is a **narrow** phonetic transcription of a verse in the poem "The Walrus and the Carpenter" by Lewis Carroll. There is *one major error* in each line that is a mispronunciation or incorrect phonetic symbol. Write the word in which the error occurs in the correct phonetic transcription.

	Corrected Word
a. ðə tʰāɪm hæz cʌ̃m	[kʰʌ̃m]
b. ðə wɔlrəs sed	
c. tʰu tʰɔlk əv mẽni θĩŋz	
d. əv ʃuz ãnd ʃɪps	
e. ænd silĩŋ wæx	
f. əv kʰæbəgəz ænd kʰĩŋz	
g. ænd waɪ ðə si ɪs bɔɪlĩŋ hat	
h. ænd wɛθər pʰɪgz hæv wĩŋz	

5. The following are all English words written in a broad phonetic transcription (omitting details such as nasalization and aspiration). Write the words using ordinary spelling.

   a. [hit]
   b. [strok]
   c. [fez]
   d. [ton]
   e. [boni]
   f. [skrim]
   g. [frut]
   h. [pritʃər]
   i. [krak]
   j. [baks]
   k. [θæŋks]
   l. [wɛnzde]
   m. [krɔld]
   n. [kantʃiɛntʃəs]
   o. [parləmɛntæriən]
   p. [kwəbɛk]
   q. [pitsə]
   r. [bərak obamə]
   s. [mɪt ramni]
   t. [tu θaʊzənd ænd twɛlv]

6. Write the symbol that corresponds to each of the following phonetic descriptions, then give an English word that contains this sound.

   Example: voiced alveolar stop   [d] *dough*

   a. voiceless bilabial unaspirated stop   [p]
   b. low front vowel   [h]
   c. lateral liquid   [l]
   d. velar nasal   [ŋ]
   e. voiced interdental fricative   [x]
   f. voiceless affricate   [t]
   g. palatal glide   [n]
   h. mid lax front vowel   [ı]
   i. high back tense vowel   [   ]
   j. voiceless aspirated alveolar stop   [   ]

7. In each of the following pairs of words, the **boldfaced** sounds differ by one or more phonetic properties (features). Give the IPA symbol for each of the boldfaced sounds, state their differences and, in addition, state what properties they have in common.

   Example: clean—clea**ns**e [i]-[ɛ]

   The *ea* in **cl**ean is high and tense.

   The *ea* in **cl**eanse is mid and lax.

   Both are front vowels.

   a. ba**th**—ba**th**e
   b. re**d**uce—re**d**uction
   c. co**o**l—c**o**ld
   d. wi**f**e—wi**v**es
   e. cat**s**—dog**s**
   f. i**m**polite—i**n**decent

8. Write a phonetic transcription for each of the words in the following sets. Note that the words in each set are <u>written</u> with the same vowel.

a	ea
swam	hear
swan	heart
	heard

o	ou
bone	shout
done	should
gone	shoulder
one	trouble
both	you
bother	
brother	

9. For each group of sounds listed, state the phonetic feature(s) they all share.

   Example: [p] [b] [m] Features: bilabial, stop, consonant

   a. [g] [p] [t] [d] [k] [b]
   b. [u] [ʊ] [o] [ɔ]
   c. [i] [ɪ] [e] [ɛ] [æ]
   d. [t] [s] [ʃ] [p] [k] [tʃ] [f] [h]
   e. [v] [z] [ʒ] [ʤ] [n] [g] [d] [b] [l] [r] [w] [j]
   f. [t] [d] [s] [ʃ] [n] [tʃ] [ʤ]

10. Write the following broad phonetic transcriptions in regular English spelling.

    a. nom tʃamski ɪz e lɪŋgwɪst hu titʃəz æt ɛm aɪ ti
    b. fənɛtɪks ɪz ðə stʌdi əv spitʃ saundz
    c. ɔl spokən læŋgwɪʤəz juz saundz prədust baɪ ðə ʌpər rɛspərətɔri sɪstəm
    d. ɪn wʌn daɪəlɛkt əv ɪŋglɪʃ kat ðə naun ænd kɔt ðə vərb ar prənaunst ðə sem
    e. sʌm pipəl θɪŋk fənɛtɪks ɪz vɛri ɪntərɛstɪŋ
    f. vɪktɔrijə framkən rabərt radmən ænd ninə haɪəmz ar ðə ɔθərz əv ðɪs bʊk

11. What phonetic property or feature distinguishes the sets of sounds in column A from those in column B?

A	**B**
a. [i] [ɪ]	[u] [ʊ]
b. [p] [t] [k] [s] [f]	[b] [d] [g] [z] [v]
c. [p] [b] [m]	[t] [d] [n] [k] [g] [ŋ]
d. [i] [ɪ] [u] [ʊ]	[e] [ɛ] [o] [ɔ] [æ] [a]
e. [f] [v] [s] [z] [ʃ] [ʒ]	[tʃ] [ʤ]
f. [i] [ɪ] [e] [ə] [ɛ] [æ]	[u] [ʊ] [o] [ɔ]

12. Which of the following sound pairs have the same manner of articulation, and what is that manner of articulation?

    a. [h] [ʔ]   **f.** [f] [ʃ]
    b. [r] [w]   **g.** [k] [θ]
    c. [m] [ŋ]   **h.** [s] [g]
    d. [ð] [v]   **i.** [j] [w]
    e. [r] [t]   **j.** [j] [ʤ]

13. **Part One**

    Which of the following vowels are lax and which are tense?

    a. [i]
    b. [ɪ]
    c. [u]
    d. [ʌ]
    e. [ʊ]
    f. [e]
    g. [ɛ]
    h. [o]
    i. [ɔ]

j. [æ]
k. [a]
l. [ə]
m. [aɪ]
n. [aʊ]
o. [ɔɪ]

Part Two
Think of ordinary, nonexclamatory one-syllable English words that end in [ʃ] preceded directly by each of the vowels in Part One. Which are possible (or actual) words? Are any such words impossible in English?

Example: push [pʊʃ] is an actual word; *nish* [nɪʃ] is a possible word; but words ending in [-aɪʃ] are not possible in English.

Part Three
In terms of tense/lax, which vowel type is found in most such words?

14. Write a made-up sentence in narrow phonetic transcription that contains at least six different vowels and two different diphthongs.

15. The front vowels of English, [i], [ɪ], [e], [ɛ], and [æ], are all unrounded. However, many languages have rounded front vowels, such as French. Here are three words in French with rounded front vowels. Transcribe them phonetically by finding out the correct IPA symbols for front rounded vowels: (Hint: Try one of the books given in the references, or Google around.)

    a. *tu*, "you," has a high front rounded vowel and is transcribed phonetically as [ ]
    b. *bleu*, "blue," has a midfront rounded vowel and is transcribed phonetically as [ ]
    c. *heure*, "hour," has a low midfront rounded vowel and is transcribed phonetically as [ ]

16. **Challenge exercise:**

    a. Take all of the vowels from Exercise 13, Part One, except the schwa and for each find a monosyllabic word containing that vowel followed directly by [t], and give both the spelling and the phonetic transcription.

    Example: beat [bit], *foot* [fʊt]

    b. Now do the same thing for monosyllabic words ending in [r]. Indicate when such a word appears not to occur in the way you speak English.
    c. And do the same thing for monosyllabic words ending in [g].
    d. Is there a quantitative difference in the number of examples found as you went from Part One to Part Three in Exercise 13?
    e. Are most vowels that "work" in B tense or lax? How about in C?
    f. Write a brief summary of the difficulties you encountered in trying to do this exercise.

17. In the first column are the last names of well-known authors. In the second column are their best-known works (one for each). Match each work to its author and write the author's name and work in conventional spelling.

Example: **a. 1.**

| *Example:* | **a.** [dɪkə̃nz] | **1.** [ɔləvər tʰwɪst] |
| *Answer:* | a—1 (Dickens, Oliver Twist) | |

b.	[sɛrvãntɛs]	**2.**	[ə fɛrwɛl tʰu armz]
c.	[dãnte]	**3.**	[æ̃nə̃məl farm]
d.	[dɪkə̃nz]	**4.**	[dõn kihote]
e.	[ɛliət]	**5.**	[greps ʌv ræθ]
f.	[hɛ̃mĩŋwe]	**6.**	[grɛt ɛkspɛktʰeʃə̃nz]
g.	[hõmər]	**7.**	[gʌləvərz tʰrævəlz]
h.	[mɛlvɪl]	**8.**	[hæ̃mlət]
i.	[ɔrwɛl]	**9.**	[mobi-dɪk]
j.	[ʃekspir]	**10.**	[saɪləs marnər]
k.	[staɪnbɛk]	**11.**	[ðə dɪvaɪn kʰãmədi]
l.	[swɪft]	**12.**	[ðə ɪliəd]
m.	[tʰɔlstɔɪ]	**13.**	[tʰãm sɔɪjər]
n.	[tʰwẽn]	**14.**	[wɔr ænd pʰis]

6

Phonology: The Sound Patterns of Language

Be a craftsman in speech that thou mayest be strong, for the strength of one is the tongue.

PTAHHOTEP, CA 2400 BCE

Phonology is the study of telephone etiquette.

A HIGH SCHOOL STUDENT

What do you think is greater: the number of languages in the world, or the number of speech sounds in all those languages? Well, there are thousands of languages, but only hundreds of speech sounds, some of which we examined in the previous chapter. Even more remarkable, only a few dozen features, such as *voicing* and *bilabial*, are needed to describe every speech sound that occurs in every human language.

That being the case, why, you may ask, do languages sound so different? One reason is that the sounds form different patterns in different languages. English has nasalized vowels, but only in syllables with nasal consonants. Portuguese puts nasal vowels anywhere it pleases, with or without nasal consonants. The speech sound that ends the word *song*—the velar nasal [ŋ]—cannot begin a word in English, but it can in Vietnamese. The common Vietnamese name spelled *Nguyen* begins with this sound, and the reason few of us can pronounce this name correctly is that it doesn't follow the English pattern. The ability to pronounce particular sounds depends on the speaker's knowledge of the sound patterns of his or her own language or languages.

The study of how speech sounds form patterns is **phonology**. These patterns may be as simple as the fact that the velar nasal cannot begin a syllable in English, or as complex as why *g* is silent in *sign* but is pronounced in the related word *signal*. To see that this is a pattern and not a one-time exception, just consider the slippery *n* in *autumn* and *autumnal,* or the illusive *b* in *bomb* and *bombard.*

The word *phonology* refers both to the linguistic knowledge that speakers have about the sound patterns of their language and to the description of that knowledge that linguists try to produce. It's like the way we defined *grammar:* your mental knowledge of your language, or a linguist's description of that knowledge.

Phonology tells you what sounds are in your language and which ones are foreign; it tells you what combinations of sounds comprise a possible word in your language, whether it is an actual word like *black,* or a nonword (in English) like *blick*; and it tells you what combination of sounds is not a possible word in your language like *mbick. It also explains why certain phonetic features are important to identifying a word, for example, voicing in English, as in *pat* versus *bat,* while other features such as vowel nasality in English are not crucial to identifying a word—though it is in Portuguese where the word *pão* with a nasalized vowel means "bread" and *pao* without the nasalization means "stick." Finally, it allows us to adjust our pronunciation of morphemes, for example, the past and plural morphemes, to suit the different phonological contexts in which they occur.

The Pronunciation of Morphemes

The *t* is silent, as in Harlow.

MARGOT ASQUITH, referring to her name being mispronounced by the actress Jean Harlow

Knowledge of phonology determines how we pronounce words and the parts of words or morphemes (Chapter 2). Often, certain morphemes are pronounced differently depending on their contexts, and we will introduce a way of describing this variation with (usually unconscious) phonological rules. We begin with some examples from English, and then move on to examples from other languages.

The Pronunciation of Plurals

Nearly all English nouns have a plural form: *cat/cats, dog/dogs, fox/foxes.* But have you ever paid attention to how plural forms are *pronounced?* Listen to a native speaker of English (or yourself if you are one) pronounce the plurals of the following nouns.

A	B	C	D
cab	cap	bus	child
cad	cat	bush	ox
bag	back	buzz	mouse
love	cuff	garage	criterion
lathe	faith	match	sheep
cam		badge	
can			
call			
bar			
spa			
boy			

The final sound of the plural nouns from Column A is a [z]—a *voiced* alveolar fricative. For column B the plural ending is an [s]—a *voiceless* alveolar fricative. And for Column C it's [əz]. Here is our first example of a morpheme with different pronunciations. Note also that there is a regularity in columns A, B, and C that does not exist in D. The plural forms in D—*children, oxen, mice, criteria,* and *sheep*—are a hodge-podge of special cases that are memorized individually when you acquire English, whether natively or as a second language. This is because there is no way to predict the plural forms of these words.

How do we know how to pronounce this plural morpheme? The spelling, which adds *s* or *es*, is misleading—not a *z* in sight—yet if you know English, you pronounce it as we indicated. When faced with this type of question, it's useful to make a chart that records the phonological environments in which each variant of the morpheme is known to occur. (The more technical term for a variant of a morpheme is **allomorph**.) Writing the words from the first three columns in broad phonetic transcription, we have our first chart for the plural morpheme. (And our first example of "phonological analysis.")

Allomorph	Environment
[z]	After [kæb], [kæd], [bæg], [lʌv], [leð], [kæm], [kæn], [bæŋ], [kɔl], [bar], [spa], [bɔɪ], e.g., [kæbz], [kædz] . . . [bɔɪz]
[s]	After [kæp], [kæt], [bæk], [kʌf], [feθ], e.g., [kæps], [kæts] . . . [feθs]
[əz]	After [bʌs], [bʊʃ], [bʌz], [gəraʒ], [mætʃ], [bædʒ], e.g., [bʌsəz], [bʊʃəz] . . . [bædʒəz]

To discover the pattern behind the way plurals are pronounced, we look for some property of the environment associated with each group of allomorphs. For example, what is it about [kæb] or [lʌv] that determines that the plural morpheme will take the form [z] rather than [s] or [əz]?

To guide our search, we look for **minimal pairs** in our list of words. A minimal pair is two words with different meanings that are identical except for one sound segment that occurs in the same place in each word. For example, *cab* [kæb] and *cad* [kæd] are a minimal pair that differ only in their final segments, whereas *cat* [kæt] and *mat* [mæt] are a minimal pair that differ only in their initial segments. Other minimal pairs in our list include *cap/cab, bag/back,* and *bag/badge.*

Minimal pairs whose members take different allomorphs are particularly useful for our search. For example, consider *cab* [kæb] and *cap* [kæp], which respectively take the allomorphs [z] and [s] to form the plural. Clearly, the final segment is responsible, because that is where the two words differ. The same for *bag* [bæg] and *badge* [bædʒ]: their final segments determine the different plural allomorphs [z] and [əz].

Apparently, the distribution of plural allomorphs in English is conditioned by the final segment of the singular form. We can make our chart more concise by considering just the final segment. (We treat diphthongs such as [ɔɪ] as single segments.)

Allomorph	Environment
[z]	After [b], [d], [g], [v], [ð], [m], [n], [ŋ], [l], [r], [a], [ɔɪ]
[s]	After [p], [t], [k], [f], [θ]
[əz]	After [s], [ʃ], [z], [ʒ], [tʃ], [dʒ]

We now want to understand *why* the English plural follows this pattern. We *always* answer questions of this type by inspecting the *phonetic properties* of the conditioning segments. Such an inspection reveals that the segments that trigger the [əz] plural have in common the property of being *sibilants*. Of the nonsibilants, the *voiceless* segments take the [s] plural, and the *voiced* segments take the [z] plural. Now the rules can be stated in more general terms:

Allomorph	Environment
[z]	After voiced nonsibilant segments
[s]	After voiceless nonsibilant segments
[əz]	After sibilant segments

An even more concise way to express these rules is to assume that the basic or underlying form of the plural morpheme is /z/, with the meaning "plural." This is the "default" pronunciation. The rules tell us when the default does *not* apply:

1. Insert a [ə] before the plural morpheme /z/ when a regular noun ends in a sibilant, giving [əz].
2. Change the plural morpheme /z/ to a voiceless [s] when preceded by a voiceless sound. (It's crucial that this rule apply after rule 1, as we'll see.)

These rules will derive the phonetic forms—that is, the pronunciations—of plurals for all regular nouns. Because the basic form of the plural is /z/, if no rule applies, then the plural morpheme will be realized as [z]. The following chart shows how the plurals of *bus, butt,* and *bug* are formed. At the top are the basic forms. The two rules apply or not as appropriate as one moves downward. The output of rule 1 becomes the input of rule 2. At the bottom are the phonetic realizations—the way the words are pronounced.

	bus + pl.	*butt* + pl.	*bug* + pl.
Basic representation	/bʌs + z/	/bʌt + z/	/bʌg + z/
Apply rule (1)	ə	NA*	NA
Apply rule (2)	NA	s	NA
Phonetic representation	[bʌsəz]	[bʌts]	[bʌgz]

*NA means "not applicable."

As we have formulated these rules, (1) must apply before (2). (See Exercise 6 at the end of the chapter.) If we applied the rules in reverse order, we would derive an incorrect phonetic form for the plural of *bus*, as a diagram similar to the previous one illustrates:

Basic representation	/bʌs + z/
Apply rule (2)	s
Apply rule (1)	ə
Phonetic representation	*[bʌsəs]

The particular phonological rules that determine the phonetic form of the plural morpheme and other morphemes of the language are **morphophonemic rules**. Such rules concern the pronunciation of specific morphemes. The pronunciation of a word like *horse* /hɔrs/ is with a final [s] because there is no morpheme boundary between the /s/ and the voiced /r/ that precedes it.

Additional Examples of Allomorphs

The formation of the regular past tense of English verbs parallels the formation of regular plurals. Like plurals, some irregular past tenses conform to no particular rule and must be learned individually, such as *go/went, sing/sang,* and *hit/hit.* And like plurals, there are three *phonetic* past-tense morphemes for regular verbs: [d], [t], and [əd]. Study example sets A, B, and C and try to see the regularity before reading further:

Set A: *gloat* [glot], *gloated* [glotəd]; *raid* [red], *raided* [redəd]

Set B: *grab* [græb], *grabbed* [grabd]; *hug* [hʌg], *hugged* [hʌgd]; *faze* [fez], *fazed* [fezd]; *plan* [plæn], *planned* [plænd]

Set C: *reap* [rip], *reaped* [ript]; *poke* [pok], *poked* [pokt]; *kiss* [kɪs], *kissed* [kɪst]; *fish* [fɪʃ], *fished* [fɪʃt]; *patch* [pætʃ], *patched* [pætʃt]

Set A suggests that if the verb ends in a [t] or a [d] (i.e., non-nasal alveolar stops), [əd] is added to form the past tense, similar to the insertion of [əz] to form the plural of nouns that end in sibilants. Set B suggests that if the verb ends in a voiced segment other than [d], you add a voiced [d]. Set C shows us that if the verb ends in a voiceless segment other than [t], you add a voiceless [t].

Just as /z/ was the basic form of the plural morpheme, /d/ is the basic form of the past-tense morpheme, and the rules for past-tense formation of regular verbs are much like the rules for the plural formation of regular nouns. These are also *morphophonemic* rules as they apply specifically to the past-tense morpheme /d/. As with the plural rules, the output of rule 1, if any, provides the input to rule 2, and the rules must be applied in order.

1.   Insert a [ə] before the past-tense morpheme when a regular verb ends in a non-nasal alveolar stop, giving [əd].
2.   Change the past-tense morpheme to a voiceless [t] when a voiceless sound precedes it.

Two further allomorphs in English are the possessive morpheme and the third-person singular morpheme, spelled *s* or *es*. These morphemes take on the same phonetic form as the plural morpheme *according to the same rules*! Add [s] to *ship* to get *ship's*; add [z] to *woman* to get *woman's*; and add [əz] to *judge* to get *judge's*. Similarly, for the verbs *eat, need,* and *rush,* the third-person singular forms are *eats* with a final [s], *needs* with a final [z], and *rushes* with a final [əz].

That the rules of phonology are based on properties of segments rather than on individual words is one of the factors that make it possible for young children to learn their native language in a relatively short period. The young child doesn't need to learn each plural, each past tense, each possessive form, and each verb ending, on a noun-by-noun or verb-by-verb basis. Once the rule is learned, thousands of word forms are automatically known. As we will see when we discuss language acquisition in Chapter 9, children give clear evidence of learning morphophonemic rules such as the plural rules by applying the rule too broadly and producing forms such as *mouses and mans*, which are ungrammatical in the adult language.

English is not the only language with morphemes that are pronounced differently in different phonological environments. Many languages have morpheme variation that can be described by rules similar to the ones we have written for English. For example, the negative morpheme in the West African language Akan has three nasal allomorphs: [m] before p, [n] before t, and [ŋ] before k, as the following examples show ([mɪ] means "I"):

mɪ pɛ	"I like"	mɪ **m**pɛ	"I don't like"
mɪ tɪ	"I speak"	mɪ **n**tɪ	"I don't speak"
mɪ kɔ	"I go"	mɪ **ŋ**kɔ	"I don't go"

The rule that describes the distribution of allomorphs is:

Change the place of articulation of the nasal negative morpheme to agree with the place of articulation of a following consonant.

The rule that changes the pronunciation of nasal consonants as just illustrated is called the **homorganic nasal rule**, or *same-place-of-articulation* rule, and is found in many of the world's languages.

Phonemes: The Phonological Units of Language

In the physical world the naive speaker and hearer actualize and are sensitive to sounds, but what they feel themselves to be pronouncing and hearing are "phonemes."

EDWARD SAPIR, "The Psychological Reality of Phonemes," 1933

The phonological rules discussed in the preceding section apply only to particular morphemes. However, other phonological rules apply to sounds as they occur in any morpheme in the language. These rules express our knowledge about the sound patterns of the entire language.

This section introduces the notions of **phoneme** and **allophone**. Phonemes are the abstract basic form of a sound as sensed mentally rather than spoken or heard. Phonemes distinguish one word or morpheme from another in our mental lexicon. Each phoneme is manifested physically by one or more actual sounds, called allophones, which are the perceptible sounds corresponding to the phoneme in various environments. For example, the phoneme /p/ is pronounced with the aspirated allophone [pʰ] in *pit* but without aspiration [p] in *spit*. Phonological rules operate on phonemes to make explicit which allophones are pronounced in which environments.

Illustration of Allophones

English contains a general phonological rule that determines the contexts in which vowels are nasalized. In Chapter 5, we noted that both oral and nasal vowels occur *phonetically* in English. The following examples show this:

bean	[bĩn]	bead	[bid]
roam	[rõm]	robe	[rob]

Taking oral vowels as the "default", we have a phonological rule that states:

Vowels are nasalized before a nasal consonant within the same syllable.

This rule expresses your knowledge of English pronunciation: nasalized vowels occur only before nasal consonants and never elsewhere. The effect of this rule is seen in Table 6.1.

As the table shows, oral vowels in English occur in final position and before non-nasal consonants; nasalized vowels occur only before nasal consonants. The nonwords (starred) show us that nasalized vowels do not occur finally or before non-nasal consonants, nor do oral vowels occur before nasal consonants.

You may be unaware of this variation in your vowel production, but this is to be expected because whether or not the vowel in *bean* is nasalized the meaning of the word is the same. Without nasalization, it might sound a bit

TABLE 6.1 | Nasal and Oral Vowels: Words and Nonwords

Words						Nonwords		
be	[bi]	bead	[bid]	bean	[bĩn]	*[bĩ]	*[bĩd]	*[bin]
lay	[le]	lace	[les]	lame	[lẽm]	*[lẽ]	*[lẽs]	*[lem]

strange, as if you had a foreign accent, but *bean* pronounced [bĩn] and *bean* pronounced [bin] would convey the same word. Likewise, if you pronounced *bead* as [bĩd], with a nasalized vowel, someone might suspect you had a cold, or that you spoke nasally, but the word would remain *bead*. Because nasalization is an *inessential difference* insofar as what the vowel actually is, we tend to be unaware of it.

Contrast this situation with a change in vowel height. If you intend to say *bead* but say *bed* instead, that makes a difference. The [i] in *bead* and the [ɛ] in *bed* are sounds from *different* phonemes. Substitute one for another and you get a different word (or no word). The [i] in *bead* and the [ĩ] in the nasalized *bead* do not make a difference in meaning. These two sounds, then, belong to the same phoneme, an abstract high front vowel that we denote between slashes as /i/.

Similarly, English also contains a phonological rule that determines the context in which voiceless stops—/p/, /t/, and /k/—are aspirated:

Voiceless stops are aspirated when they occur initially in a stressed syllable.

Table 6.2 illustrates the distribution of aspirated stops versus unaspirated stops.

Where the unaspirated stops occur, the aspirated ones do not, and vice versa. You could pronounce *spit* with an aspirated [pʰ], as [spʰɪt], and it would be understood as *spit*, even though listeners would probably think you were spitting out your words. Because aspiration is an *inessential difference* in English, we do not notice it (unless we're linguists or students of linguistics). Thus, there is one phoneme /p/—an abstract voiceless bilabial stop—which may be pronounced [pʰ] or [p] depending on the phonetic context.

TABLE 6.2 | Distribution of Aspirated Voiceless Stops

Syllable-Initial before a Stressed Vowel			After a Syllable Initial /s/			Nonword*		
[pʰ]	[tʰ]	[kʰ]	[p]	[t]	[k]			
pill	*till*	*kill*	*spill*	*still*	*skill*	[pɪl]*	[tɪl]*	[kɪl]*
[pʰɪl]	[tʰɪl]	[kʰɪl]	[spɪl]	[stɪl]	[skɪl]	[spʰɪl]*	[stʰɪl]*	[skʰɪl]*
par	*tar*	*car*	*spar*	*star*	*scar*	[par]*	[tar]*	[kar]*
[pʰar]	[tʰar]	[kʰar]	[spar]	[star]	[skar]	[spʰar]*	[stʰar]*	[skʰar]*

As a third illustration of allophones, consider the voiceless alveolar stop /t/ along with the following examples:

Spelling	Phonemic representation	Phonetic representation
tick	/tɪk/	[tʰɪk]
stick	/stɪk/	[stɪk]
blitz	/blɪts/	[blɪts]
bitter	/bɪtər/	[bɪɾər]

In *tick* we normally find an aspirated [tʰ], whereas in *stick* and *blitz* we find an unaspirated [t], and in *bitter* we find the flap [ɾ]. Swapping these sounds around will not change word meaning. If we pronounce *bitter* with a [tʰ], it will not change the word; it will simply sound unnatural (to most Americans).

We account for this knowledge of how *t* is pronounced by positing a phoneme /t/ with three allophones [tʰ], [t], and [ɾ]. We also note phonological rules that specify that the aspirated voiceless stop [tʰ] occurs initially in a stressed syllable, the unaspirated [t] occurs directly before or after /s/, and the flap [ɾ] occurs between a stressed vowel and an unstressed vowel.

Phonemes and How to Find Them

Phonemes are the dark matter of phonology; they are not physical sounds or directly observable. They are abstract mental representations of the phonological units of a language, the units used to represent words in our mental lexicon. The phonological rules of the language apply to phonemes to determine the actual pronunciation of words.

The process of substituting one sound for another in a word to see if it makes a difference is a good way to identify the phonemes of a language. Here are twelve words differing only in their vowels:

beat	[bit]	[i]	*boot*	[but]	[u]
bit	[bɪt]	[ɪ]	*but*	[bʌt]	[ʌ]
bait	[bet]	[e]	*boat*	[bot]	[o]
bet	[bɛt]	[ɛ]	*bought*	[bɔt]	[ɔ]
bat	[bæt]	[æ]	*bout*	[baʊt]	[aʊ]
bite	[baɪt]	[aɪ]	*bot*	[bat]	[a]

Any two of these words form a *minimal pair*: two *different* words that differ in one sound in the same position. The two sounds that cause the word difference belong to different phonemes.

From the minimal set of [b_t] words, we can infer that English has at least twelve vowel phonemes. (We consider diphthongs to function as single vowel sounds.) To that total we can add a phoneme corresponding to [ʊ] resulting from minimal pairs such as *book* [bʊk] and *beak* [bik]; and we can add one for [ɔɪ] resulting from minimal pairs such as *boy* [bɔɪ] and *buy* [baɪ].

Our minimal pair analysis has revealed eleven monophthongal and three diphthongal vowel phonemes, namely, /i/, /ɪ/, /e/, /ɛ/, /æ/, /u/, /ʊ/, /o/, /ɔ/, /a/,

/ʌ/, and /aɪ/, /aʊ/, and /ɔɪ/. (This set may differ somewhat in other variants of English.) Importantly, each of these vowel phonemes has (at least) two allophones (i.e., two ways of being pronounced): orally as [e] or [o] or [a], etc., and nasally as [ẽ] or [õ] or [ã], etc., when they occur in the context of a nasal consonant.

A particular realization (pronunciation) of a phoneme is called a **phone**. The aggregate of phones that are the realizations of the same phoneme are called the *allophones* of that phoneme. In English, each vowel phoneme has both an oral and a nasalized allophone. The choice of the allophone is not random or haphazard; it is *rule-governed.*

To distinguish graphically between a phoneme and its allophones, we use slashes / / to enclose phonemes and continue to use square brackets [ ] for allophones or phones. For example, [o] and [õ] are allophones of the phoneme /o/; thus, we will represent *bode* and *bone* phonemically as /bod/ and /bon/. We refer to these as *phonemic* transcriptions. The rule for the distribution of oral and nasal vowels in English shows that phonetically these words will be pronounced as [bod] and [bõn].

Complementary Distribution

Minimal pairs illustrate that some speech sounds in a language are contrastive and can be used to make different words such as *big* and *dig*. These contrastive sounds constitute the phonemes of that language. Some sounds are noncontrastive and cannot be used to make different words. The sounds [tʰ] and [ɾ] were cited as examples that do not contrast in English, so [raɪtʰər] and [raɪɾər] are not a minimal pair, but rather alternate ways in which *writer* may be pronounced.

Oral and nasal vowels in English are also noncontrastive sounds. Because their distribution is rule-governed, the oral and nasal allophones of each vowel phoneme never occur in the same phonological context, as Table 6.3 illustrates.

Where oral vowels occur, nasal vowels do not occur, and vice versa. In this sense, the phones are said to complement each other or to be in **complementary distribution**. Table 6.2 also shows that aspirated and unaspirated voiceless stop consonants are in complementary distribution. In general, then, the allophones of a phoneme are in complementary distribution—never occurring in identical environments. We can understand why this is so when we consider that the choice of one or another allophone is determined by its phonetic environment. Vowels are nasalized when they occur before nasal consonants, and otherwise they are not nasalized. Phonological rules of this sort give rise to the complementary distribution of allophones.

Complementary distribution is a fundamental concept of phonology, and interestingly enough, it shows up in everyday life. Here are a couple of examples that draw on the common experience of reading and writing English.

TABLE 6.3 | Distribution of Oral and Nasal Vowels in English Syllables

	In Final Position	Before Nasal Consonants	Before Oral Consonants
Oral vowels	Yes	No	Yes
Nasal vowels	No	Yes	No

The first example focuses on *printed* letters such as those that appear on the pages of this book. Each printed letter of English has two main variants: lowercase and uppercase (or capital). If we restrict our attention to words that are not proper names or acronyms (such as Ron or UNICEF), we can formulate a simple rule that does a fair job of determining how letters will be printed:

> A letter is printed in uppercase if it is the first letter of a sentence; otherwise, it is printed in lowercase.

Even ignoring names and acronyms, this rule is only approximately right, but let's go with it anyway. It helps to explain why written sentences such as the following appear so strange:

> phonology is the study of the sound patterns of human languageS.
> pHONOLOGY iS tHE sTUDY oF tHE sOUND pATTERNS oF hUMAN lANGUAGES.

These "sentences" violate the rule in funny ways. Despite that, they are comprehensible, just as the pronunciation of *cold* with a nasal [õ] as [cõld] would sound, well, like you had a cold but it would be understood.

To the extent that the rule is correct, the lowercase and uppercase variants of an English letter *are in complementary distribution*. The uppercase variant occurs in one particular context (namely, at the beginning of the sentence), and the lowercase variant occurs in every other context (or elsewhere). Therefore, just as every English vowel phoneme has an oral and a nasalized allophone that occur in different spoken contexts, every letter of the English alphabet has two variants, or allographs, that occur in different written contexts.

Our next example turns to *cursive* handwriting, which you are likely to have learned in elementary school. Writing in cursive is more similar to the act of speaking than printing because in cursive writing each letter of a word (usually) connects to the following letter—just as adjacent sounds connect during speech. The following figure illustrates that the connections between the letters of a word in cursive writing create different variants of a letter in different environments:

Compare how the letter *l* appears after a *g* (as in *glue*) and after a *b* (as in *blue*). In the first case, the *l* begins near the bottom of the line, but in the second case, the *l* begins near the middle of the line (which is indicated by the dashes). In other words, the same letter *l* has two variants. Meaning is unaffected by the position of *l*: wherever the *l* begins, it's still an *l*. Likewise, whether a vowel in English is nasalized or not does not affect meaning, it's still that same vowel. Which *l* variant occurs in a particular word is determined by the immediately preceding letter. The variant that begins near the bottom of the line appears after letters like *g* that end near the bottom of the line. The variant that begins near the middle of the line appears after letters like *b* that end near the middle of the line. The two variants of *l* are therefore in complementary distribution.

This pattern of complementary distribution is not specific to *l* but occurs for other cursive letters in English. By examining the pairs *sat* and *vat, mill* and *will*, and *rack* and *rock*, you can see the complementary distribution of the variants of *a, i,* and *c*, respectively. In each case, the immediately preceding letter determines which variant occurs, with the consequence that the variants of a given letter are in complementary distribution.

Finally, Superman and Clark Kent, Batman and Bruce Wayne, and Dr. Jekyll and Mr. Hyde—for those of you familiar with these fictional characters—are in complementary distribution *with respect to time*. At a given moment in time, the individual is either one or another of his alter egos.

The Need for Similarity

When sounds are in complementary distribution, they do not contrast with each other. The replacement of one sound for the other will not change the meaning of a word, although it might not sound like typical English pronunciation. Given these facts about the patterning of sounds in a language, a phoneme can be viewed as a set of phonetically similar sounds that are in complementary distribution. The phonetic environment determines which sound is chosen for pronunciation. A set may consist of as few as a single sound so that all occurrences of the phoneme are pronounced the same. In such a case, the phoneme has one allophone.

Complementary distribution alone is not sufficient to determine the allophones of a phoneme. The phones must also be *phonetically similar,* that is, share most phonetic features. In English, the velar nasal [ŋ] and the glottal fricative [h] are in complementary distribution; [ŋ] does not occur word-initially and [h] does not occur word-finally. But they share very few phonetic features; [ŋ] is a voiced velar nasal stop; [h] is a voiceless glottal fricative. Therefore, they are not allophones of the same phoneme; [ŋ] and [h] are allophones of different phonemes.

Speakers of a language generally perceive the different allophones of a single phoneme as the same sound or phone. For example, most speakers of English are unaware that the vowels in *bead* and *bean* are different phones because mentally, speakers produce and hear phonemes, not phones.

Distinctive Features of Phonemes

We are generally not aware of the phonetic properties or features that distinguish the phonemes of our language. *Phonetics* provides the means to describe the phones (sounds) of language, showing how they are produced and how they vary. *Phonology* tells us how various sounds form patterns to create phonemes and their allophones.

The minimal pairs *seal* [sil] and *zeal* [zil] show that [s] and [z] represent two contrasting phonemes in English. They cannot be allophones of one phoneme because one cannot replace the [s] with the [z] without changing the meaning of the word. The fact that you can find a minimal pair also means they are not in complementary distribution as both occur word initially before the vowel [i]. They are therefore allophones of the two different phonemes /s/ and /z/. From the discussion of phonetics in Chapter 5, we know that [s] and [z] differ in voicing: [s] is voiceless and [z] is voiced. The phonetic feature of voicing therefore distinguishes the two words. Voicing also distinguishes *feel* and *veal* [f]/[v] and *cap* and *cab* [p]/[b]. When a feature distinguishes one phoneme from another, hence one word from another, it is a **distinctive feature** or, equivalently, a **phonemic feature**.

Feature Values

One can think of voicing and voicelessness as the presence or absence of a single feature, *voiced*. This single feature may have two values: plus (+), which signifies its presence, and minus (–), which signifies its absence. For example, [b] is [+voiced] and [p] is [–voiced].

The presence or absence of nasality can similarly be designated as [+nasal] or [–nasal], with [m] being [+nasal] and [b] and [p] being [-nasal]. A [–nasal] sound is an *oral* sound.

We consider the phonetic and phonemic symbols to be *cover symbols* for sets of distinctive features. They are a shorthand method of specifying the phonetic properties of segments. Phones and phonemes are not indissoluble units; they are composed of phonetic features, similar to the way that molecules are composed of atoms. A more explicit description of the phonemes /p/, /b/, and /m/ may thus be given in a feature matrix of the following sort.

	p	b	m
Labial	+	+	+
Voiced	–	+	+
Nasal	–	–	+

Aspiration is not listed as a phonemic feature in the specification of these units for English (but is for Thai, say, as we shall see), because [p] and [pʰ] do not represent different phonemes in English. In a *phonetic* transcription, however, the aspiration feature would be specified where it occurs.

A phonetic feature is distinctive when the + and – values of that feature in certain words result in words with different meanings, for example [+voiced] on [z] in [zɪp] and [–voiced] on [s] in [sɪp].

At least one feature value difference must distinguish each phoneme from all the other phonemes in a language. Because the phonemes /b/, /d/, and /g/ contrast in English by virtue of the place of articulation features—*labial, alveolar,* and *velar*—these place features are also distinctive in English. The distinctive features of the voiced stops in English are shown in the following:

	b	**m**	**d**	**n**	**g**	**ŋ**
Voiced	+	+	+	+	+	+
Labial	+	+	−	−	−	−
Alveolar	−	−	+	+	−	−
Velar	−	−	−	−	+	+
Nasal	−	+	−	+	−	+

Each phoneme in this chart differs from all the other phonemes by at least one distinctive feature.

Vowels, too, have distinctive features. For example, the feature [±back] distinguishes the vowel in *look* [lʊk] ([+back]) from the vowel in *lick* [lɪk] ([−back]) and is therefore distinctive in English. Similarly, [±tense] distinguishes [i] from [ɪ] (*beat* versus *bit*) and is also a distinctive feature of the English vowel system.

Nondistinctive Features

As we saw, aspiration is not a distinctive feature of English consonants. It is a **nondistinctive** or **redundant** or **predictable feature** (all equivalent terms). "Predictable" means predictable by rule. Some features may be distinctive for one class of sounds but predictable for another. For example, nasality is a distinctive feature of English consonants but not for English vowels. There is no way to predict when an /m/ or an /n/ will occur in an English word. You learn this when you learn the word. On the other hand, the nasality feature value of the vowels in *bean, mean, comb,* and *sing* is predictable because the nasalized vowels occur before nasal consonants. Thus, the feature nasal is **nondistinctive** *for vowels*.

This is not the case in all languages. As we noted above, nasality on vowels is phonemic in Portuguese. Nasalization is also a distinctive feature for vowels in Akan (spoken in Ghana), as the following examples illustrate:

[ka]	"bite"	[kã]	"speak"
[fi]	"come from"	[fĩ]	"dirty"
[tu]	"pull"	[tũ]	"den"
[nsa]	"hand"	[nsã]	"liquor"
[tʃi]	"hate"	[tʃĩ]	"squeeze"
[pam]	"sew"	[pãm]	"confederate"

Nasalization is not predictable in Akan, as it is in English. There is no nasalization rule in Akan, as shown by the minimal pair [pam] and [pãm], or in Portuguese, as shown by the minimal pair [pão], "bread," and [pao], "stick." If you substitute an oral vowel for a nasal vowel, or vice versa, you will change the word.

Two languages may have the same phonetic segments (phones) but have two different phonemic systems. Phonetically, both oral and nasalized vowels exist in English, Portuguese, and Akan. However, English does not have nasalized vowel phonemes, but Akan and Portuguese do. The same phonetic segments function differently in English and the other two languages. Nasalization of vowels in English is redundant and nondistinctive; nasalization of vowels in Akan and Portuguese is nonredundant and distinctive.

Another nondistinctive feature in English is aspiration for voiceless stops. The voiceless aspirated stops [pʰ], [tʰ], and [kʰ] and the voiceless unaspirated stops [p], [t], and [k] are in complementary distribution. The presence of this feature is predicted by rule and therefore does not have to be learned by speakers when acquiring words.

Phonemic Patterns May Vary across Languages

The tongue of man is a twisty thing, there are plenty of words there of every kind, the range of words is wide, and their variance.

HOMER, *The Iliad*, c. 900 BCE

Aspiration is a phonetic feature in Thai just as in English, but it functions differently in the two languages. In English it is predictable; in Thai it is not, as the following examples show:

Voiceless Unaspirated		Voiceless Aspirated	
[paa]	*forest*	[pʰaa]	*to split*
[tam]	*to pound*	[tʰam]	*to do*
[kat]	*to bite*	[kʰat]	*to interrupt*

The voiceless unaspirated and the voiceless aspirated stops in Thai occur in minimal pairs; they contrast and are therefore phonemes. In both English and Thai, the phones [p], [t], [k], [pʰ], [tʰ], and [kʰ] occur. In English they are allophones of the phonemes /p/, /t/, and /k/; in Thai they represent the distinct phonemes /p/, /t/, /k/, /pʰ/, /tʰ/, and /kʰ/. Therefore, aspiration is a distinctive feature in Thai; it is a nondistinctive redundant feature in English.

The phonetic facts alone do not reveal what is distinctive or phonemic:

The *phonetic representation* of utterances shows what speakers know about the pronunciation of sounds.
The *phonemic representation* of utterances shows what speakers know about the patterning of sounds.

In English, vowel length and consonant length are nonphonemic. Prolonging a sound in English will not produce a different word. In other languages, long and short vowels that are identical except for length are phonemic. In such languages, length is a nonpredictable distinctive feature. For example, vowel length is phonemic in some dialects of Korean, as shown by the following minimal pairs (recall that the colon-like symbol : indicates length):

il	"day"	i:l	"work"
seda	"to count"	se:da	"strong"
kul	"oyster"	ku:l	"tunnel"

In Italian, the word for "grandfather" is *nonno* /nonːo/, which contrasts with the word for "ninth," which is *nono* /nono/, so consonant length is phonemic in Italian. In Luganda, an African language, consonant length is also phonemic: /kula/ with a short /k/ means "grow up," whereas /kːula/ with a long /kː/ means "treasure." Thus, consonant length is unpredictable in Luganda, just as whether a word begins with a /b/ or a /p/ is unpredictable in English.

In ASL phonology, signs can be broken down into smaller units that are in many ways analogous to the phonemes and distinctive features in spoken languages. Signs can be decomposed into handshape, movement, and location, as discussed in Chapter 5. There are minimal pairs that are distinguished by a change in one or another of these features. For example, the signs meaning "candy," "apple," and "jealous" are articulated at the same location on the face and involve the same movement, but contrast minimally in hand configuration. "Summer," "ugly," and "dry" are a minimal set contrasting only in place of articulation, and "tape," "chair," and "train" contrast only in movement. Like sounds, signs can be decomposed into smaller minimal units that contrast meaning. Some features are non-distinctive. Whether a sign is articulated on the right or left hand does not affect its meaning.

Natural Classes of Speech Sounds

It's as large as life, and twice as natural!

LEWIS CARROLL, *Through the Looking-Glass*, 1871

We show what speakers know about the predictable aspects of speech through phonological rules. In English, these rules determine the environments in which vowels are nasalized or voiceless stops aspirated. These rules apply to *all* the words in the language, and even apply to made-up words such as *sint, peeg*, and *sparg*, which would be /sɪnt/, /pig/, and /sparg/ phonemically and [sĩnt], [pʰig], and [sparg] phonetically.

As linguists examine more and more of the world's languages, they see similar rules affecting the same classes of sounds such as nasals and voiceless stops. For example, many languages besides English have a rule that nasalizes vowels before nasal consonants:

Nasalize a vowel when it precedes a nasal consonant in the same syllable.

The rule will apply to all vowel phonemes when they occur in a context preceding any segment marked [+nasal] in the same syllable, and will add the feature [+nasal] to the feature matrix of the vowel. Our description of vowel nasalization in English needs only this rule. It need not include a list of the individual vowels to which the rule applies or a list of the sounds that result from its application.

Many languages have rules that refer to [+voiced] and [−voiced] sounds. For example, the aspiration rule in English applies to the class of [−voiced] noncontinuant sounds in word-initial position. As in the vowel nasality rule, we do not need to consider individual segments. The rule automatically applies to initial /p/, /t/, /k/, and /tʃ/.

Phonological rules often apply to **natural classes** of sounds. A natural class is a group of sounds described by a small number of distinctive features such as [–voiced], [–continuant], which describe /p/, /t/, /k/, and /tʃ/. Any individual member of a natural class would require more features in its description than the class itself, so /p/ is not only [–voiced], [–continuant], but also [+labial].

The relationships among phonological rules and natural classes illustrate why segments are to be regarded as bundles of features. If segments were not specified as feature matrices, the similarities among /p/, /t/, and /k/ or /m/, /n/, and /ŋ/ would be lost. It would be just as likely for a language to have a rule such as

1. Nasalize vowels before *p*, *i*, or *z*.

as to have a rule such as

2. Nasalize vowels before *m*, *n*, or *ŋ*.

Rule 1 has no phonetic explanation, whereas rule 2 does: the lowering of the velum in anticipation of a following nasal consonant causes the vowel to be nasalized. In rule 1, the environment is a motley collection of unrelated sounds that cannot be described with a few features. Rule 2 applies to the natural class of nasal consonants, namely sounds that are [+nasal], [+consonantal].

The various classes of sounds discussed in Chapter 5 also define natural classes to which the phonological rules of all languages may refer. They also can be specified by + and − feature values. Table 6.4 illustrates how these feature values combine to define some major classes of phonemes. The presence of +/− indicates that the sound may or may not possess a feature depending on its context. For example, word-initial nasals are [–syllabic] but some word-final nasals can be [+syllabic], as in *wagon* [wægn̩], where the diacritic ˌ below the [n̩] indicates its syllabicity.

Feature Specifications for American English Consonants and Vowels

Here are feature matrices for vowels and consonants in English. By selecting all segments marked the same for one or more features, you can identify natural classes. For example, the natural class of high vowels /i/, /ɪ/, /u/, /ʊ/ is marked

TABLE 6.4 | Feature Specification of Major Natural Classes of Sounds

Features	Obstruents	Nasals	Liquids	Glides	Vowels
Consonantal	+	+	+	−	−
Sonorant	−	+	+	+	+
Syllabic	−	+/−	+/−	−	+
Nasal	−	+	−	−	+/−

TABLE 6.5 | Features of Some American English Vowels

Features	i	ɪ	e	ɛ	æ	u	ʊ	o	ɔ	a	ʌ	ə
High	+	+	−	−	−	+	+	−	−	−	−	−
Low	−	−	−	−	+	−	−	−	+	+	+	−
Back	−	−	−	−	−	+	+	+	+	−	−	−
Central	−	−	−	−	−	−	−	−	−	+	+	+
Round	−	−	−	−	−	+	+	+	+	−	−	−
Tense	+	−	+	−	−	+	−	+	+	+	−	−

[+high] in the vowel feature chart of Table 6.5; the natural class of voiced stops /b, m, d, n, g, ŋ, ʤ/ are the ones marked [+voice] [−continuant] in the consonant chart of Table 6.6.

The Rules of Phonology

But that to come

Shall all be done by the rule.

WILLIAM SHAKESPEARE, *Antony and Cleopatra*, 1623

Throughout this chapter, we have emphasized that the relationship between the *phonemic* representation of a word and its *phonetic* representation, or how it is pronounced, is *rule-governed*. Phonological rules are part of a speaker's knowledge of the language.

The phonemic representations are *minimally specified* because some features or feature values are predictable. For example, in English all nasal consonants are voiced, so we don't need to specify voicing in the phonemic feature matrix for nasals. Similarly, we don't need to specify the feature *round* for back vowels. If Table 6.6 was strictly phonemic, then instead of a + in the *voice* row for *m, n,* and *ŋ*, the cells would be left blank, as would the cells in the *round* row of Table 6.5 for *u, ʊ, o,* and *ɔ*. Such underspecification reflects the redundancy in the phonology, which is also part of a speaker's knowledge of the sound system. The phonemic representation should include only the nonpredictable, distinctive features of the phonemes in a word. The phonetic representation, derived by applying the phonological rules, includes all of the linguistically relevant phonetic aspects of the sounds. It does not include all of the physical properties of the sounds of an utterance, however, because the physical signal may vary in many ways that have little to do with the phonological system.

The absolute pitch of the sound, the rate of speech, or its loudness is not linguistically significant. The phonetic transcription is therefore also an abstraction

TABLE 6.6 | Features of Some American English Consonants

Features	p	b	m	t	d	n	k	g	ŋ	f	v	θ	ð	s	z	ʃ	ʒ	tʃ	dʒ	l	r	j	w	h
Consonantal	+	+	+	+	+	+	+	+	+	+	+	+	+	+	+	+	+	+	+	+	+	−	−	−
Sonorant	−	−	+	−	−	+	−	−	+	−	−	−	−	−	−	−	−	−	−	+	+	+	+	−
Syllabic	−	−	−/+	−	−	−/+	−	−	−/+	−	−	−	−	−	−	−	−	−	−	−/+	−/+	−	−	−
Nasal	−	−	+	−	−	+	−	−	+	−	−	−	−	−	−	−	−	−	−	−	−	−	−	−
Voiced	−	+	+	−	+	+	−	+	+	−	+	−	+	−	+	−	+	−	+	+	+	+	+	−
Continuant	−	−	−	−	−	−	−	−	−	+	+	+	+	+	+	+	+	−	−	+	+	+	+	+
Labial	+	+	+	−	−	−	−	−	−	+	+	−	−	−	−	−	−	−	−	−	−	−	+	−
Alveolar	−	−	−	+	+	+	−	−	−	−	−	−	−	+	+	−	−	−	−	+	+	−	−	−
Palatal	−	−	−	−	−	−	−	−	−	−	−	−	−	−	−	+	+	+	+	−	−	+	−	−
Anterior	+	+	+	+	+	+	−	−	−	+	+	+	+	+	+	−	−	−	−	+	−	−	−	−
Velar	−	−	−	−	−	−	+	+	+	−	−	−	−	−	−	−	−	−	−	−	−	−	+	−
Coronal	−	−	−	+	+	+	−	−	−	−	−	+	+	+	+	+	+	+	+	+	+	+	−	−
Sibilant	−	−	−	−	−	−	−	−	−	−	−	−	−	+	+	+	+	+	+	−	−	−	−	−

Note: The phonemes /r/ and /l/ are distinguished by the feature [lateral], not shown here. /l/ is the only phoneme that would be [+lateral].

from the physical signal; it includes the nonvariant phonetic aspects of the utterances, those features that remain relatively constant from speaker to speaker and from one time to another.

Although the specific rules of phonology differ from language to language, the kinds of rules, what they do, and the natural classes they refer to are universal.

Feature-Changing Rules

Many rules change features from one value to its opposite or even add features not present in the phonemic representation. In English, the /z/ plural morpheme has its voicing value changed from plus to minus when it follows a voiceless sound. Similarly, the /n/ in the phonemic negative prefix morpheme /ɪn/ undergoes a change in its place of articulation feature when preceding bilabials or velars.

The rule in English that aspirates voiceless stops at the beginning of a syllable simply adds a nondistinctive feature. Generally, aspiration occurs only if the following vowel is stressed. The /p/ in *pit* and *repeat* is an aspirated [pʰ], but the /p/ in *inspect* or *compass* is an unaspirated [p]. We also note that even with an intervening consonant, the aspiration takes place so that words such as *crib, clip,* and *quip* ([kʰrɪb], [kʰlɪp], and [kʰwɪp]) all begin with an aspirated [kʰ]. And finally, the affricate /tʃ/ is subject to the rule, so *chip* is phonetically [tʃʰɪp]. We can now state the rule:

> A voiceless noncontinuant has [+aspirated] added to its feature matrix at the beginning of a syllable when followed by a stressed vowel with an optional intervening consonant.

Aspiration is not specified in any phonemic feature matrix of English, as Table 6.6 shows. The aspiration rule adds this feature for reasons having to do with the timing of the closure release.

Assimilation Rules

A particular kind of feature-changing rule is assimilation. We have seen that nasalization of vowels in English is nonphonemic because it is predictable by rule. The vowel nasalization rule is an *assimilation rule* that makes neighboring segments more similar by adding the feature [+nasal] to the vowel.

For the most part, assimilation rules stem from articulatory processes. There is a tendency when we speak to make articulation easier. It is easier to lower the velum while a vowel is being pronounced before a nasal stop than to wait for the completion of the vowel and then require the velum to move suddenly.

We now wish to look more closely at the phonological rules we have been discussing. Previously, we stated the vowel nasalization rule:

> *Vowels are nasalized before a nasal consonant within the same syllable.*

This rule specifies the <u>class of sounds</u> affected by the rule:

Vowels

It states what <u>phonetic change</u> will occur by applying the rule:

Change phonemic oral vowels to phonetic nasal vowels.

And it specifies the context or <u>phonological environment</u>.

Before a nasal consonant within the same syllable.

A shorthand notation to write rules, similar to the way scientists and mathematicians use symbols, makes the rule statements more concise. Every physicist knows that $E = mc^2$ means "Energy equals mass times the square of the speed of light." We can use similar notations to state the nasalization rule as:

V → [+nasal] / _ [+nasal] $

Let's look at the rule piece by piece.

V	→	[+nasal]	/	_	[+nasal]	$
Vowels	become	nasalized	in the environment	before	nasal segments	within a syllable

To the left of the arrow is the <u>class of sounds</u> that is affected. To the right of the arrow is the <u>phonetic change</u> that occurs. <u>The phonological environment</u> follows the slash. The underscore _ is the relative position of the sound to be changed within the environment, in this case *before* a nasal segment. The dollar sign denotes a syllable boundary and guarantees that the environment does not cross over to the next syllable.

This rule tells us that the vowels in such words as *den* /dɛn/ will become nasalized to [dɛ̃n], but *deck* /dɛk/ will not be affected and is pronounced [dɛk] because /k/ is not a nasal consonant. As well, a word such as *dental* /dɛn$təl/ will be pronounced [dɛ̃n$təl]: we have showed the syllable boundary explicitly. However, the first vowel in *denote*, /di$not/, will not be nasalized, because the nasal segment does not precede the syllable boundary, so the "within a syllable" condition is not met.

Any rule written in formal notation can be stated in words. The use of formal notation is a shorthand way of presenting the information, and also a way of eliminating ambiguity and making sure the intended meaning of the rule is completely clear. Notation also reveals the *function* of the rule more explicitly than words. It is easy to see in the formal statement of the rule that this is an assimilation rule because the change to [+nasal] occurs before [+nasal] segments. Assimilation rules in languages reflect **coarticulation**—the spreading of phonetic features either in the anticipation or in the perseveration (the "hanging on") of articulatory processes. The auditory effect is that words sound smoother.

The following example illustrates how the English vowel nasalization rule applies. It also shows the assimilatory nature of the rule, that is, the change to [+nasal] before a [+nasal] segment:

	"bob"			"boom"		
Phonemic representation	/b	a	b/	/b	u	m/
Nasality: phonemic feature value	–	0*	–	–	0*	+
Apply nasal rule		NA			↓	
Nasality: phonetic feature value	–	–	–	–	+	+
Phonetic representation	[b	a	b]	[b	ū	m]

*The ⬤ means not present on the phonemic level.

There are many assimilation rules in English and other languages. Recall that the voiced /z/ of the English regular plural suffix is changed to [s] after a voiceless sound, and that similarly the voiced /d/ of the English regular past tense suffix is changed to [t] after a voiceless sound. These are instances of voicing assimilation. In these cases, the value of the voicing feature goes from [+voice] to [–voice] because of assimilation to the [–voice] feature of the final consonant of the stem, as in the derivation of *cats*:

/kæt + z/ → [kæts]

We saw a different kind of assimilation rule in Akan, where we observed that the nasal negative morpheme was expressed as [m] before /p/, [n] before /t/, and [ŋ] before /k/. (This is the homorganic nasal rule.) In this case, the place of articulation—bilabial, alveolar, velar—of the nasal assimilates to the place of articulation of the following consonant. The same process occurs in English: the negative morpheme prefix spelled *in-* or *im-* agrees in place of articulation with the word to which it is prefixed, so we have *impossible* [ĭmpʰasəbəl], *intolerant* [ĭntʰalərə̃nt], and *incongruous* [ĭŋkʰã̃ŋgruəs]. In effect, the rule makes two consonants that appear next to each other more similar.

ASL and other signed languages also have assimilation rules. One example is handshape assimilation, which takes place in compounds such as the sign for "blood." This ASL sign is a compound of the signs for "red" and "flow." The handshape for "red" alone is formed at the chin by a closed hand with the index finger pointed up. In the compound "blood" this handshape is replaced by that of the following word "flow," which is an open handshape (all fingers extended). In other words, the handshape for "red" has undergone assimilation. The location of the sign (at the chin) remains the same. Examples such as this tell us that while the features of signed languages are different from those of spoken languages, their phonologies are organized according to principles like those of spoken languages.

Dissimilation Rules

It is understandable that so many languages have assimilation rules; they permit greater ease of articulation. It might seem strange, then, to learn that languages also have feature-changing rules called **dissimilation rules**, in which certain segments becomes less similar to other segments. Ironically, such rules have the same explanation: it is sometimes easier to articulate dissimilar sounds. The difficulty of tongue twisters like "the sixth sheik's sixth sheep is sick" is based on the repeated similarity of sounds. If one were to make some sounds

Dennis the Menace, Hank Ketcham. Reprinted with permission of North America Syndicate.

less similar, as in "the second sheik's tenth sheep is sick," it would be easier to say. The cartoon makes the same point, with *toy boat* being more difficult to articulate repeatedly than *sail boat*, because the [ɔɪ] of *toy* is more similar to the [o] of *boat* than to the [e] of *sail*.

An example of easing pronunciation through dissimilation is found in some varieties of English, in which there is a fricative dissimilation rule. This rule applies to sequences /fθ/ and /sθ/, changing them to [ft] and [st]. Here the fricative /θ/ becomes dissimilar to the preceding fricative by becoming a stop. For example, the words *fifth* and *sixth* come to be pronounced as if they were spelled *fift* and *sikst.*

A classic example of the same kind of dissimilation occurred in Latin, and the results of this process show up in the derivational morpheme /-ar/ in English. In Latin, a derivational suffix *-alis* was added to nouns to form adjectives. When the suffix was added to a noun that contained the liquid /l/, the suffix was changed to *-aris;* that is, the liquid /l/ was changed to the dissimilar liquid /r/. These words came into English either as adjectives ending in *-al* or in its dissimilated form *–ar.* In the following examples, all of the *-ar* adjectives contain /l/ in the root, and as *columnar* illustrates, the /l/ need not be the consonant directly preceding the dissimilated segment.

-al	-ar
anecdot-al	angul-ar
annu-al	annul-ar
ment-al	column-ar
pen-al	perpendicul-ar
spiritu-al	simil-ar
ven-al	vel-ar

Assimilation rules, dissimilation rules, and other kinds of feature-changing rules are part of Universal Grammar (UG) and are found throughout the world's languages.

Segment Insertion and Deletion Rules

Phonological rules may add or delete entire segments. These are different from the feature-changing rules we have seen so far, which affect only parts of segments. The process of inserting a consonant or vowel is called **epenthesis**.

The rules for forming regular plurals, possessive forms, and third-person singular verb agreement in English all require an epenthesis rule. Here is the first part of that rule that we gave earlier for plural formation:

Insert a [ə] before the plural morpheme /z/ when a regular noun ends in a sibilant, giving [əz].

Letting the symbol Ø stand for "null," we can write this *morphophonemic* epenthesis rule more formally as "null becomes schwa between two sibilants," or like this:

Ø → ə / [+sibilant] ___ [+sibilant]

There is a plausible explanation for insertion of a [ə]. If we merely added a [z] to *squeeze* to form its plural, we would get [skwiz:], which would be hard for English speakers to distinguish from [skwiz] because in English we do not contrast long and short consonants. This and other examples suggest that the morphological patterns in a language are closely related to other generalizations about the phonology of that language.

Segment deletion rules are commonly found in many languages and are far more common than segment insertion rules. One such rule in English occurs in casual or rapid speech. We often delete the unstressed vowels in words such as the following:

mystery   general   memory   funeral   vigorous   Barbara

These words in casual speech can sound as if they were written:

mystry   genral   memry   funral   vigrous   Barbra

The silent *g* that torments spellers in such words as *sign* and *design* is actually the result of a segment deletion rule. Consider the following examples:

A		B	
sign	[sãɪn]	signature	[sɪgnətʃər]
design	[dəzãɪn]	designation	[dɛzɪgneʃən]
paradigm	[pʰærədãɪm]	paradigmatic	[pʰærədɪgmærək]

None of the words in column A have a phonetic [g], but a [g] occurs in each corresponding word in column B. Our knowledge of English phonology accounts for these phonetic differences. The "[g]—no [g]" alternation is regular and is also seen in pairs such as *gnostic* [nastɪk] and *agnostic* [ægnastɪk], and by the silent g's in the cartoon:

Tumbleweeds

"Tumbleweeds." Tom K. Ryan. Reprinted with permission of North America Syndicate.

This rule may be stated as:

Delete a /g/ word-initially before a nasal consonant or before a syllable-final nasal consonant.

Given this rule, the phonemic representations of the stems in *sign/signature, design/designation, malign/malignant, phlegm/phlegmatic, paradigm/paradigmatic, gnostic/agnostic,* and so on will include a /g/ that will be deleted by the regular rule if a prefix or suffix is not added. By stating the class of sounds that follow the /g/ (nasal consonants) rather than any specific nasal consonant, the rule deletes the /g/ before both /m/ and /n/.

From One to Many and from Many to One

As we've seen, phonological rules that relate phonemic to phonetic representations have several functions, among which are the following:

Function	Example
1. Change feature values	Nasal consonant assimilation rules in Akan and English
2. Add new features	Aspiration in English
3. Delete segments	g-deletion before nasals in English
4. Add segments	Schwa insertion in English plural and past tense

The relationship between the phonemes and phones of a language is complex and varied. Rarely is a phoneme realized as one and only one phone. We often find a phoneme realized as several phones, as in the case with English voiceless stops that may be realized as aspirated or unaspirated, among other possibilities. And we find the same phone may be the realization of several different phonemes. Here is a dramatic example of that many-to-one relationship.

Consider the vowels in the following pairs of words:

	A			B	
/i/	compete	[i]	competition	[ə]
/ɪ/	medicinal	[ɪ]	medicine	[ə]
/e/	maintain	[e]	maintenance	[ə]
/ɛ/	telegraph	[ɛ]	telegraphy	[ə]
/æ/	analysis	[æ]	analytic	[ə]
/a/	solid	[a]	solidity	[ə]
/o/	phone	[o]	phonetic	[ə]

In column A, all the various stressed vowels are boldfaced; in column B the corresponding boldfaced vowels are without stress, or **reduced**, and are pronounced as schwa [ə]. In these cases, the stress pattern of the word varies because of the different suffixes. The vowel that is stressed in one form becomes unstressed in a different form and is therefore pronounced as [ə]. In their phonemic representations all of the root morphemes contain a stressed vowel such as /i/ or /e/ that becomes phonetically [ə] when it is destressed. We can conclude, then, that [ə] is an allophone of all English vowel phonemes. The rule to derive the schwa is simple to state:

Change a vowel to a [ə] when the vowel is unstressed.

In the phonological description of a language, it is not always straightforward to determine phonemic representations from phonetic transcriptions. How would we deduce the /o/ in *phonetic* from its pronunciation as [fənɛrɪk] without a complete phonological analysis? However, given a phonemic representation and the phonological rules, we can always derive the correct phonetic representation. Because words in the mental lexicon occur in their phonemic forms and speakers know the rules of their language they have no trouble deriving the correct phonetic representations.

Similar rules exist in other languages that show that there is no one-to-one relationship between phonemes and phones. For example, in German both voiced and voiceless obstruents occur as phonemes, as is shown by the following minimal pair:

Tier [tiːr] "animal"   *dir* [diːr] "to you"

However, when voiced obstruents occur at the end of a word or syllable, they become voiceless. The words meaning "bundle," *Bund* /bʊnd/, and "colorful," *bunt* /bʊnt/, are phonetically identical and pronounced [bʊ̃nt] with a final [t]. Obstruent voicing is noncontrastive in syllable-final position.

The German devoicing rule changes feature specifications. The phonemic representation of the final stop in *Bund* is the [+voiced] /d/; it is changed by rule to [−voiced] to derive the phonetic [t] in word-final position. German presents us with this picture:

German Phonemes   /d/   /t/

German Phones   [d]   [t]

The devoicing rule in German provides a further illustration that we cannot discern the phonemic representation of a word given only the phonetic form: [bʊ̃nt] can be derived from either /bʊnd/ or /bʊnt/. The phonemic representations and the phonological rules together determine the phonetic forms.

The Function of Phonological Rules

The function of the phonological rules (P-rules) in a grammar is to provide the phonetic information necessary for the pronunciation of utterances. We may illustrate this point in the following way:

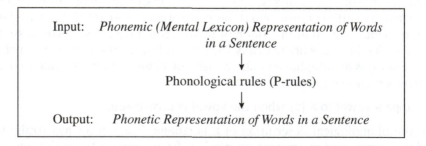

Input: *Phonemic (Mental Lexicon) Representation of Words in a Sentence*

Phonological rules (P-rules)

Output: *Phonetic Representation of Words in a Sentence*

The input to the P-rules is the phonemic representation. The P-rules apply to the phonemic strings and produce as output the phonetic representation.

The application of rules in this way is called a **derivation**. We have given examples of derivations that show how plurals are derived, how phonemically oral vowels become nasalized, and how /t/ and /d/ become flaps in certain environments. A derivation is an explicit way of showing both the effects and the function of phonological rules in a grammar.

All the examples of derivations we have so far considered show the application of just one phonological rule, except the plural and past-tense rules, which are actually one rule with two parts. In any event, it is common for more than one rule to apply to a word. For example, the word *tempest* is phonemically /tɛmpɛst/ (as shown by the pronunciation of *tempestuous* [tʰɛ̃mpʰɛstʃuəs]) but phonetically [tʰɛ̃mpəst]. Three rules apply to it: the aspiration rule, the vowel nasalization rule, and the schwa rule. We can derive the phonetic form from the phonemic representation as follows:

Underlying phonemic representation	/	t	ɛ	m	p	ɛ	s	t	/
Aspiration rule		tʰ						
Nasalization rule			ɛ̃					
Schwa rule						ə		
Surface phonetic representation	[	tʰ	ɛ̃	m	p	ə	s	t	]

Prosodic Phonology

Syllable Structure

Baby Blues. Baby Blues Partnership. King Features Syndic

Words are composed of one or more syllables. A **syllable** is a phonological unit composed of one or more phonemes. Every syllable has a **nucleus**, which is usually a vowel (but can be a syllabic liquid or nasal). The nucleus may be preceded and/or followed by one or more phonemes called the syllable **onset** and **coda**. In rhyming words, the nucleus and the coda of the final syllable of both words are identical, as in the following jingle:

Jack and **Jill**
Went up the **hill**
To fetch a pail of water.
Jack fell **down**
And broke his **crown**
And Jill came tumbling after.

For this reason, the nucleus + coda constitute the subsyllabic unit called a **rime** (note the spelling).

A syllable thus has a hierarchical structure. Using the IPA symbol σ (lower-case Greek letter "sigma") for the phonological syllable, the hierarchical structure of the monosyllabic word *splints* can be shown:

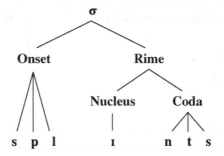

Word Stress

In many languages, including English, one or more of the syllables in every content word are stressed. A stressed syllable, which can be marked by an acute accent (´), is perceived as more prominent than an unstressed syllable, as shown in the following examples:

pérvert	(noun)	as in	"My neighbor is a pervert."
pervért	(verb)	as in	"Don't pervert the idea."
súbject	(noun)	as in	"Let's change the subject."
subjéct	(verb)	as in	"He'll subject us to criticism."

These pairs show that stress can be contrastive in English. In these cases, it distinguishes between nouns and verbs. It may also distinguish between words of other categories, such as the adjective inválid (not valid) and the noun ínvalid (a sickly person).

Some words may contain more than one stressed vowel, but exactly one of the stressed vowels is more prominent than the others. The vowel that receives primary stress is marked by an acute accent (´). The other stressed vowels are indicated by grave accents (`) over the vowels (these vowels receive secondary stress).

rèsignátion	lìnguístics	sỳstemátic
fùndaméntal	ìntrodúctory	rèvolútion

Generally, speakers of a stress-timed language like English (as opposed to French, say) know which syllable receives primary stress, which ones receive secondary stress, and which ones are unstressed. It is part of their implicit knowledge of the language. It's usually easy to distinguish between stressed and unstressed syllables because the vowels in unstressed syllables are pronounced as schwa [ə] in English except at the ends of certain words such as *confetti, laboratory,* and *motto.* It may be harder to distinguish between primary and secondary stress. If you are unsure of where the primary stress is in a word (and you are a native or near-native speaker of English), try shouting the word as if talking to a person across a busy street. Often, the difference in stress becomes more apparent.

The stress pattern of a word may differ among English-speaking people. For example, in most varieties of American English the word *láboratòry* [lǽbərəthɔ̀ri] has two stressed syllables, but in most varieties of British English it receives only one stress [ləbɔ́rətri]. Because English vowels generally reduce to schwa or delete when they are not stressed, the British and American vowels differ in this word. In fact, in the British version the fourth vowel is deleted because it is not stressed.

Stress is a property of the syllable rather than a segment; it is a **prosodic** or **suprasegmental feature**. To produce a stressed syllable, one can change the pitch (usually by raising it), make the syllable louder, or make it longer. We often use all three of these phonetic means to stress a syllable.

Sentence and Phrase Stress

"What can *I* do, Tertius?" said Rosamond, turning her eyes on him again. That little speech of four words, like so many others in all languages, is capable by varied vocal inflexions of expressing all states of mind from helpless dimness to exhaustive argumentative perception, from the completest self-devoting fellowship to the most neutral aloofness.

GEORGE ELIOT, *Middlemarch,* 1872

When words are combined into phrases and sentences, one syllable receives greater stress than all others. Just as there is only one primary stress in a word spoken in isolation, only one of the vowels in a phrase (or sentence) receives primary stress or accent. All of the other stressed vowels are demoted to secondary stress. As noted in Chapter 3, in English we place primary stress on the adjectival part of a compound noun (which may be written as one word, two words separated by a hyphen, or two separate words), but we place the stress on the noun when the words are a noun phrase consisting of an adjective followed by a noun. The differences between the following pairs are therefore predictable:

Compound Noun	Adjective + Noun
tíghtròpe ("a rope for acrobatics")	tìght rópe ("a rope drawn taut")
Rédcòat ("a British soldier")	rèd cóat ("a coat that is red")
hótdòg ("a frankfurter")	hòt dóg ("an overheated dog")
Whíte Hòuse ("the President's house")	whìte hóuse ("a house painted white")

Say these examples out loud, speaking naturally, and at the same time listen or feel the stress pattern. If English is not your native language, listen to a native speaker say them.

These pairs show that stress may be predictable from the morphology and syntax. The phonology interacts with the other components of the grammar. The stress differences between the noun and verb pairs discussed in the previous section (*subject* as noun or verb) are also predictable from the syntactic word category.

Intonation

Depending on inflection, *ah bon* [in French] can express shock, disbelief, indifference, irritation, or joy.

PETER MAYLE, *Toujours Provence*, 1991

In Chapter 5, we discussed pitch as a phonetic feature in reference to tone languages and intonation languages and noted its role in determining meaning. We can now see that pitch is also a *phonemic* feature in tone languages such as Chinese, Thai, and Akan. We refer to these relative pitches as **contrasting tones**. In non-tone languages, such as English, pitch still plays an important role, but only in the form of the **pitch contour** or **intonation** of the phrase or sentence.

In English, intonation may reflect syntactic or semantic differences. If we ask, "What is your middle name, David?" with falling pitch at the end it is a request to someone named David to reveal his middle name. With rising pitch at the end, it is a query as to whether the addressee's middle name is David.

A sentence that is ambiguous in writing may be unambiguous when spoken because of differences in the pitch contour. Written, the following sentence is unclear as to whether Tristram intended for Isolde to read and follow directions, or merely to follow him:

Tristram left directions for Isolde to follow.

Spoken, if Tristram wanted Isolde to follow him, the sentence would be pronounced with a rise in pitch on the first syllable of *follow*, followed by a fall in pitch:

Tristram left directions for Isolde to |follow.⏜

In this pronunciation of the sentence, the primary stress is on the word *follow*.

If the meaning is to read and follow a set of directions, the highest pitch comes on the second syllable of *directions*:

Tristram left di|rections| for Isolde to follow.

The primary stress in this pronunciation is on the word *directions*.

Pitch plays an important role in both tone and non-tone languages, but in different ways depending on the phonological systems of the respective languages.

Sequential Constraints of Phonemes

> If you were to receive the following telegram, you would have no difficulty in correcting the "obvious" mistakes:
>
> BEST WISHES FOR VERY HAPPP BIRTFDAY
>
> because sequences such as BIRTFDAY do not occur in the language.
>
> COLIN CHERRY, *On Human Communication*, 1957

Suppose you were given the following four phonemes and asked to arrange them to form all possible English words:

/b/   /ɪ/   /k/   /l/

You would most likely produce the following:

/blɪk/

/klɪb/

/bɪlk/

/kɪlb/

These are the only permissible arrangements of these phonemes in English. */lbkɪ/, */ɪlbk/, */bkɪl/, and */ɪlkb/ are not possible English words. Although /blɪk/ and /klɪb/ are not now existing words, if you heard someone say:

"I just bought a beautiful new blick."

you might ask: "What's a blick?"

If, on the other hand, you heard someone say:

"I just bought a beautiful new lbɪk."

you might reply, "You just bought a new *what*?"

Your knowledge of English phonology includes information about what sequences of phonemes are permissible, and what sequences are not. After a consonant such as /b/, /g/, /k/, or /p/, another stop consonant in the same syllable is not permitted by the phonology. If a word begins with an /l/ or an /r/, the next segment must be a vowel. That is why */lbɪk/ does not sound like an English word. It violates the restrictions on the sequencing of phonemes. People who like to work crossword puzzles are often more aware of these constraints than the ordinary speaker, whose knowledge, as we have emphasized, may not be conscious.

Other such constraints exist in English. If the initial sounds of *chill* or *Jill* begin a word, the next sound must be a vowel. The words /tʃʌt/ and /tʃon/ and /tʃæk/ are possible in English (*chut, chone, chack*), as are /dʒæl/ and /dʒil/ and /dʒalɪk/ (*jal, jeel, jolick*), but */tʃlɔt/ and */dʒpurz/ are not. No more than three sequential consonants can occur at the beginning of a word, and these three are restricted:

/spl/	*splay*	/spr/	*spruce*	*spw	—	/spj/	*spew*
/skl/	*sclerosis*	/skr/	*screen*	/skw/	*squat*	/skj/	*skew*
*stl	—	/str/	*streak*	*stw	—	*stj	—

Other languages have different sequential restrictions. In Polish, *zl* and *kt* are permissible syllable-initial combinations, as in /zlev/, "a sink," and /kto/, "who." Croatian permits words such as the name *Mladen*. Japanese has severe constraints on what may begin a syllable; most combinations of consonants (e.g., /br/, /sp/) are impermissible. In Twi, a word may end only in a vowel or a nasal consonant. The sequence /pik/ is not a possible Twi word because it breaks the sequencing rules of the language, whereas /mba/ is not a possible word in English, although it is a word in Twi.

The limitations on sequences of segments are called **phonotactic constraints**. Phonotactic constraints have as their basis the syllable, rather than the word. That is, only the clusters that can begin a syllable can begin a word, and only a cluster that can end a syllable can end a word.

In multisyllabic words, clusters that seem illegal may occur, for example, the /kspl/ in *explicit* /ɛksplɪsɪt/. However, there is a syllable boundary between the /k/ and /spl/, which we can make explicit using $: /ɛk $ splɪs $ it/. Thus, we have a permitted syllable coda /k/ that ends a syllable adjoined to a permitted onset /spl/ that begins a syllable. On the other hand, English speakers know that "condstluct" is not a possible word because the second syllable would have to start with an impermissible onset, either /stl/ or /tl/.

All languages have constraints on the permitted sequences of phonemes, although different languages have different constraints. Just as spoken language has sequences of sounds that are not permitted in the language, so sign languages have forbidden combinations of features. For example, in the ASL compound for "blood" (red flow) discussed earlier, the total handshape must be assimilated, including the shape of the hand and the orientation of the fingers. Assimilation of just the handshape but not the finger orientation is impossible in ASL. The constraints may differ from one sign language to another, just as the constraints on sounds and sound sequences differ from one spoken language to another. A permissible sign in a Chinese sign language may not be a permissible sign in ASL, and vice versa. Children learn these constraints when they acquire the spoken or signed language, just as they learn what the phonemes are and how they are related to phonetic segments.

Lexical Gaps

The Mungle pilgriffs far awoy

Religeorge too thee worled.

Sam fells on the waysock-side

And somforbe on a gurled,

With all her faulty bagnose!

JOHN LENNON

The words *bot* [bat] and *crake* [kʰrek] are not known to all speakers of English, but they are words. On the other hand [bʊt] (rhymes with *put*), *creck* [kʰrɛk], *cruke* [kʰruk], *cruk* [kʰrʌk], and *crike* [kʰraɪk] are not words in English now, although they are possible words.

Advertising professionals often use possible but nonoccurring words for the names of new products. Although we would hardly expect a new product or company to come on the market with the name *Zhleet* [ʒlit]—an impossible word in English—we do not bat an eye at *Bic, Xerox* /zɪraks/, *Kodak, Glaxo,* or *Spam* (a meat product, not junk mail), because those once nonoccurring words obey the phonotactic constraints of English.

A *possible word* contains phonemes in sequences that obey the phonotactic constraints of the language. An actual, occurring word is the union of a possible word with a meaning. Possible words without meaning are sometimes called nonsense words and are also referred to as **accidental gaps** in the lexicon, or **lexical gaps**. Thus, "words" such as *creck* and *cruck* are nonsense words and represent accidental gaps in the lexicon of English.

Why Do Phonological Rules Exist?

No rule is so general, which admits not some exception.

ROBERT BURTON, *The Anatomy of Melancholy*, 1621

A very important question that we have not addressed thus far is: Why do grammars have phonological rules at all? In other words, why don't underlying or phonemic forms surface intact rather than undergoing various changes?

In the previous section, we discussed *phonotactic constraints*, which are part of our knowledge of phonology. As we saw, phonotactic constraints specify which sound sequences are permissible in a particular language, so that in English *blick* is a possible word but **lbick* isn't. Many linguists believe that phonological rules exist to ensure that the surface or phonetic forms of words do not violate phonotactic constraints. If underlying forms remained unmodified, they would often violate the phonotactics of the language.

Consider, for example, the English past-tense rule and recall that it has two subrules. The first inserts a schwa when a regular verb ends in an alveolar stop (/t/ or /d/), as in *mated* [metəd]. The second devoices the past-tense morpheme /d/ when it occurs after a voiceless sound, as in *reaped* [ript] or *peaked* [pʰikt]. Notice that the part of the rule that devoices /d/ reflects the constraint that English words may not end in a sequence consisting of a voiceless stop -*d*. Words such as [lɪpd] and [mɪkd] do not exist, nor could they exist. They are impossible words of English, just as [bkɪl] is.

More generally, there are no words that end in a sequence of obstruents whose voicing features do not match. Thus, words such as [kasb], where the final two obstruents are [–voice] [+voice] are not possible, nor are words such as [kabs], whose final two obstruents are [+voice] [–voice]. On the other hand, [kasp] and [kɛbz] are judged to be possible words because the final two segments agree in voicing. Thus, there appears to be a phonotactic constraint in English, stated as follows:

(A) Obstruent sequences may not differ with respect to their voice feature at the end of a syllable.

We can see then that the devoicing part of the past-tense rule changes the underlying form of the past-tense morpheme to create a surface form that conforms to this general constraint.

Similarly, the schwa insertion part of the past-tense rule creates possible sound sequences from impossible ones. English does not generally permit sequences of sounds within a single syllable that are very similar to each other, such as [kk], [kg], [gk], [gg], [pp], [sz], and [zs]. (The words spelled *egg* and *puppy* are phonetically [ɛg] and [pʌpi].) Thus, the schwa insertion rule separates sequences of sounds that are otherwise not permitted in the language because they are too similar to each other: for example, the sequence of /d/ and /d/ in /mɛnd + d/, which becomes [mɛndəd] *mended*, and /t/ and /d/ in /vɛnt + d/, which becomes [vɛntəd] *vented*. The relevant constraint is stated as follows:

(B) Sequences of obstruents that are alike with the possible exception of voicing are not permitted within a syllable.

Constraints such as (A) and (B) are far more general than any particular rule like the past-tense rule. For example, constraint B might also explain why an adjective such as *smooth* turns into the abstract noun *smoothness*, rather than taking the affix *-th* [θ], as in *wide/width, broad/breadth,* and *deep/depth*. Suffixing *smooth* with *-th* would result in a sequence of too-similar obstruents, smoo[ðθ], which differ only in their voicing feature. This suggests that languages may satisfy constraints in various grammatical situations.

Thus, phonological rules exist because languages have general principles that constrain possible sequences of sounds. The rules specify minimal modifications of the underlying forms that bring them in line with the surface constraints. Therefore, we find different variants of a particular underlying form depending on the phonological context.

Phonological Analysis

Everything it is possible to analyze depends on a clear method of distinguishing the similar from the dissimilar.

CARL LINNAEUS

Children recognize phonemes at an early age without being taught, as we shall see in Chapter 9. Before reading this book, or learning anything about phonology, you knew a *p* sound was a phoneme in English because it contrasts words like *pat* and *cat, pat* and *sat, pat* and *mat*. But you probably did not know that the *p* in *pat* and the *p* in *spit* are different sounds. There is only one /p/ phoneme in English, but that phoneme has more than one allophone (pronunciation), including an aspirated one and an unaspirated one.

If a non-English-speaking linguist analyzed English, how could this fact about the sound *p* be discovered? More generally, how do linguists discover the phonological system of a language?

To do a phonological analysis, the words to be analyzed must be transcribed in great phonetic detail because we do not know in advance which phonetic features are distinctive and which are not.

Consider the following Finnish words:

1.	[kudot]	"failures"		5.	[madon]	"of a worm"
2.	[kate]	"cover"		6.	[maton]	"of a rug"
3.	[katot]	"roofs"		7.	[ratas]	"wheel"
4.	[kade]	"envious"		8.	[radon]	"of a track"

Given these words, do the voiceless/voiced alveolar stops [t] and [d] represent different phonemes, or are they allophones of the same phone?

Here are a few hints as to how a phonologist might proceed:

1. Check to see whether there are any minimal pairs.
2. Items (2) and (4) are minimal pairs: [kate] "cover" and [kade] "envious." Items (5) and (6) are minimal pairs: [madon] "of a worm" and [maton] "of a rug."
3. Conclude that [t] and [d] in Finnish represent the distinct phonemes /t/ and /d/.

That was an easy problem. Now consider the following data from English, again focusing on [t] and [d] together with the alveolar flap [ɾ] and primary stress′:

[ráɪt]	"write"		[ráɪɾər]	"writer"
[déɾə]	"data"		[dét]	"date"
[mǽd]	"mad"		[mǽt]	"mat"
[bətróð]	"betroth"		[lǽɾər]	"ladder"
[lǽɾər]	"latter"		[dístə̃ns]	"distance"
[ráɪɾər]	"rider"		[ráɪd]	"ride"
[déɾĩŋ]	"dating"		[bédsaɪd]	"bedside"
[mʌ́ɾər]	"mutter"		[túɾər]	"tutor"
[mǽɾər]	"madder"		[mǽdnɪs]	"madness"

A broad examination of the data reveals minimal pairs involving [t] and [d], so clearly /t/ and /d/ are phonemes. We also see some interesting homophones, such as *ladder* and *latter*, and *writer* and *rider*. And the flap [ɾ]? Is it a phoneme? Or is it predictable somehow? At this point, the linguist undertakes the tedious task of identifying *all* of the immediate environments for [t], [d], and [ɾ], using # for a word boundary:

[t]: áɪ_#, é_#, ǽ_#, ə_r, s_ə, #_ú
[d]: #_é (3 times), ǽ_#, #_í, áɪ_#, ɛ́_s, ǽ_n
[ɾ]: áɪ_ə (2 times), é_ə, ǽ_ə (3 times), é_ɪ, ú_ə, ʌ́_ə

It does not appear at this point that anything systematic is going on with vowel or consonant quality, so we abstract the data a little, using v for an unstressed vowel, v́ for a stressed vowel, C for a consonant, and # for a word boundary:

[t]: v́_#, #_v́, C_v, v_C
[d]: #_v́, v́_#, v́_C
[ɾ]: v́_v

Now we see clearly that [ɾ] is in complementary distribution with both [t] and [d]. It occurs only when preceded by a stressed vowel and followed by an unstressed vowel, and neither [t] nor [d] ever do. We may conclude, based on these data, that [ɾ] is an allophone of both /t/ and /d/. We tentatively propose the "alveolar flap rule":

> An alveolar stop becomes a flap in the environment between a stressed and unstressed vowel.

The phonemic forms lack a flap, so that *writer* is phonemically /raɪtər/ and *rider* is /raɪdər/, based on [raɪt] and [raɪd]. Similarly, we can propose /mædər/ for *madder* based on [mæd] and [mædnɪs], and /detɪŋ/ for *dating* based on [det]. But we don't have enough information to determine phonemic forms of *data*, *latter*, and *tutor*. This is typically the case in actual analyses. Rarely is there sufficient evidence to provide all the answers.

Finally, consider these data from Greek, focusing on the following sounds:

[x]   voiceless velar fricative
[k]   voiceless velar stop
[c]   voiceless palatal stop
[ç]   voiceless palatal fricative

1.	[kano]	"do"		9.	[çeri]	"hand"
2.	[xano]	"lose"		10.	[kori]	"daughter"
3.	[çino]	"pour"		11.	[xori]	"dances"
4.	[cino]	"move"		12.	[xrima]	"money"
5.	[kali]	"charms"		13.	[krima]	"shame"
6.	[xali]	"plight"		14.	[xufta]	"handful"
7.	[çeli]	"eel"		15.	[kufeta]	"bonbons"
8.	[ceri]	"candle"		16.	[oçi]	"no"

To determine the status of [x], [k], [c], and [ç], you should answer the following questions.

1. Are there are any minimal pairs in which these sounds contrast?
2. Are any noncontrastive sounds in complementary distribution?
3. If noncontrasting phones are found, what are the phonemes and their allophones?
4. What are the phonological rules by which the allophones can be derived?

1. By analyzing the data, we find that [k] and [x] contrast in a number of minimal pairs, for example, in [kano] and [xano]. [k] and [x] are therefore distinctive. [c] and [ç] also contrast in [cino] and [çino] and are therefore distinctive. But what about the velar fricative [x] and the palatal fricative [ç]? And the velar stop [k] and the palatal stop [c]? We can find no minimal pairs that would conclusively show that these represent separate phonemes.

2. We now proceed to answer the second question: Are these noncontrasting phones, namely [x]/[ç] and [k]/[c], in complementary distribution? One way to see whether sounds are in complementary distribution is to list each phone with the environment in which it is found, as follows:

Phone	Environment
[k]	before [a], [o], [u], [r]
[x]	before [a], [o], [u], [r]
[c]	before [i], [e]
[ç]	before [i], [e]

We see that [k] and [x] are not in complementary distribution; they both occur before non-front vowels. Nor are [c] and [ç] in complementary distribution. They both occur before front vowels. But the stops [k] and [c] are in complementary distribution; [k] occurs before non-front vowels and [r], and never occurs before front vowels. Similarly, [c] occurs only before front vowels and never before non-front vowels or [r]. Finally, [x] and [ç] are in complementary distribution for the same reason. We therefore conclude that [k] and [c] are allophones of one phoneme, and the fricatives [x] and [ç] are also allophones of one phoneme. The pairs of allophones also fulfill the criterion of phonetic similarity. The first two are [–anterior] stops; the second are [–anterior] fricatives. (This similarity discourages us from pairing [k] with [ç], and [c] with [x], which are less similar to each other.)

3. Which of the phone pairs are more basic, and hence the ones whose features would define the phoneme? When two allophones can be derived from one phoneme, one selects as the underlying segment the allophone that makes the rules and the phonemic feature matrix as simple as possible, as we illustrated with the English unaspirated and aspirated voiceless stops.

In the case of the velar and palatal stops and fricatives in Greek, the rules appear to be equally simple. However, in addition to the simplicity criterion, we wish to state rules that have natural phonetic explanations. Often these turn out to be the simplest solutions. In many languages, velar sounds become palatal before front vowels. This is an assimilation rule; palatal sounds are produced toward the front of the mouth, as are front vowels. Thus, we select /k/ as a phoneme with the allophones [k] and [c], and /x/ as a phoneme with the allophones [x] and [ç].

4. We can now state the rule by which the palatals can be derived from the velars.

Palatalize velar consonants before front vowels.

Using feature notation we can state the rule as:

[+velar] → [+palatal] /_____[–back]

Because only consonants are marked for the feature [velar], and only vowels for the feature [back], it is not necessary to include the features [consonantal] or [syllabic] in the rule. We also do not need to include any other features that are redundant in defining the segments to which the rule applies or the environment in which the rule applies. Thus, [+palatal] in the change part of the rule is sufficient, and the feature [–back] also suffices to specify the front vowels. The simplicity criterion constrains us to state the rule as simply as we can. Finally, it is important to note that this analysis describes the data at hand, and further data may oblige us to re-analyze the situation. In "real life" this is more often the case than not.

Summary

Part of our knowledge of a language is knowledge of the **phonology** or sound system of that language. It includes the inventory of **phones**—which are the phonetic sounds that occur in the language—and the ways in which they pattern. This patterning determines the inventory of **phonemes**—the abstract basic units that differentiate words.

When similar phones occur in **complementary distribution**, they are **allophones**—predictable phonetic variants—of one phoneme. Thus, the aspirated [pʰ] and the unaspirated [p] are allophones of the phoneme /p/ because they occur in different phonetic environments.

Some phones may be allophones of more than one phoneme. There is no one-to-one correspondence between the phonemes of a language and their allophones. In English, for example, stressed vowels become unstressed according to regular rules, and ultimately reduce to schwa [ə], which is an allophone of each English vowel.

Phonological segments—phonemes and phones—are composed of **phonetic features** such as *voiced, nasal, labial,* and *continuant,* whose presence or absence is indicated by + or − signs. The set of features is universal but languages can differ with respect to which of the features are distinctive (or phonemic) and which are non-distinctive (redundant, predictable). *Voiced, continuant,* and many others are **distinctive features** in English—they can contrast phonemes. Other features like *aspiration* are **nondistinctive** in English and are predictable from phonetic context. Some features like *nasal* may be distinctive for one class of sounds (e.g., English consonants) but nondistinctive for a different class of sounds (e.g., English vowels). Phonetic features that are nondistinctive in one language may be distinctive in another. Aspiration is distinctive in Thai and nondistinctive in English.

When two distinct words are distinguished by a single phone occurring in the same position, they constitute a **minimal pair** (e.g., *fine* /faɪn/ and *vine* /vaɪn/). Minimal pairs also occur in sign languages. Signs may contrast by handshape, location, and movement.

Words in some languages may also be phonemically distinguished by **prosodic** or **suprasegmental** features, such as pitch, stress, and segment length. Languages in which syllables or words are contrasted by pitch are called **tone languages**. Non-tone languages may still use pitch variations to distinguish meanings of phrases and sentences.

The relationship between phonemic representation and phonetic representation (pronunciation) is determined by phonological rules. Phonological rules apply to phonemic strings and alter them in various ways to derive their phonetic pronunciation, or in the case of signed languages, their hand configuration. They may be **assimilation rules, dissimilation rules,** rules that *add* **nondistinctive features, epenthetic** rules that *insert* segments, and **deletion** rules that *delete* segments.

Phonological rules generally refer to entire classes of sound. These are **natural classes,** characterized by a small set of phonetic features shared by all the members of the class, for example, [−continuant], [−voiced], to designate the natural class of voiceless stops.

Linguists may use a mathematical-like formulation to express phonological rules in a concise way. For example, the rule that nasalizes vowels when they occur before a nasal consonant within the same syllable may be written as: V → [+nasal] / __ [+nasal]$

Morphophonemic rules apply to specific morphemes such as the past tense morpheme /d/, which is phonetically [d], [t], or [əd] depending on the final phoneme of the verb to which it is attached.

The phonology of a language also includes sequential constraints **(phonotactics)** that determine which sounds may be adjacent within the syllable. These determine what words are possible in a language, and what phonetic strings are impermissible. Possible but nonoccurring words constitute **accidental gaps** and are **nonsense words,** for example, *blick* [blɪk]. Phonological rules exist in part to enforce phonotactic constraints.

To discover the phonemes of a language, linguists (or students of linguistics) can use a methodology such as looking for minimal pairs of words, or for sounds that are in complementary distribution.

The phonological rules in a language show that the phonemic shape of words is not identical with their phonetic form. The phonemes are not the actual phonetic sounds, but are abstract mental constructs that are realized as sounds by the operation of rules such as those described in this chapter. No one is taught these rules, yet everyone knows them subconsciously.

References for Further Reading

Gussenhoven, C., and Jacobs, H. 2014. *Understanding phonology, 3rd ed.* New York: Routledge.

Hayes, B. 2009. *Introductory phonology.* Oxford, UK: Wiley-Blackwell.

Odden, D. 2013. *Introducing phonology, 2nd ed.* New York: Cambridge University Press.

Exercises

Data in languages other than English are given in phonetic transcription without square brackets unless otherwise stated. The phonetic transcriptions of English words are given within square brackets.

1. The following sets of minimal pairs show that English /p/ and /b/ contrast in initial, medial, and final positions.

Initial	Medial	Final
pit/bit	rapid/rabid	cap/cab

Find similar sets of minimal pairs for each pair of consonants given:

   a. /k/—/g/
   b. /m/—/n/
   c. /l/—/r/
   d. /b/—/v/
   e. /b/—/m/
   f. /p/—/f/

  g. /s/—/ʃ/
  h. /tʃ/—/dʒ/
  i. /s/—/z/

2. A young patient at the Radcliffe Infirmary in Oxford, England, following a head injury, appears to have lost the spelling-to-pronunciation and pronunciation-to-spelling rules that most of us can use to read and write new words or nonsense strings. He is also unable to get to the phonemic representation of words in his lexicon. Consider the following examples of his reading pronunciation and his writing from dictation:

Stimulus	Reading Pronunciation	Writing from Dictation
fame	/fæmi/	FAM
café	/sæfi/	KAFA
time	/taɪmi/	TIM
note	/noti/ or /nɔti/	NOT
praise	/pra-aɪ-si/	PRAZ
treat	/tri-æt/	TRET
goes	/go-ɛs/	GOZ
float	/flɔ-æt/	FLOT

   What rules or patterns relate his reading pronunciation to the written stimulus? What rules or patterns relate his spelling to the dictated stimulus? For example, in reading, *a* corresponds to /a/ or /æ/; in writing from dictation /e/ and /æ/ correspond to written A.

3. Read "A Case of Identity," the third story in *The Adventures of Sherlock Holmes* by Sir Arthur Conan Doyle (and no fair reading summaries, synopses, or anything other than the original—it's online). Now all you have to do is explain what *complementary distribution* has to do with this mystery.

4. **Part One**

   Consider the distribution of [r] and [l] in Korean in the following words. (Some simplifying changes have been made in these transcriptions, which have no bearing on the problem.)

rubi	"ruby"	mul	"water"
kir-i	"road (nom.)"	pal	"arm"
saram	"person"	səul	"Seoul"
irum-i	"name (nom.)"	ilgop	"seven"
ratio	"radio"	ibalsa	"barber"

   a. Are [r] and [l] allophones of one or two phonemes?
   b. Do they occur in any minimal pairs?
   c. Are they in complementary distribution?
   d. In what environments does each occur?

e. If you conclude that they are allophones of one phoneme, state the rule that can derive the phonetic allophonic forms.

Part Two

Here are some additional data from Korean:

son	"hand"	ʃihap	"game"
som	"cotton"	ʃilsu	"mistake"
sosəl	"novel"	ʃipsam	"thirteen"
sɛk	"color"	ʃinho	"signal"
isa	"moving"	maʃita	"is delicious"
sal	"flesh"	oʃip	"fifty"
kasu	"singer"	miʃin	"superstition"
miso	"grin"	kaʃi	"thorn"

a. Are [s] and [ʃ] allophones of the same phoneme, or is each an allophone of a separate phoneme? Give your reasons.

b. If you conclude that they are allophones of one phoneme, state the rule that can derive the phonetic allophones.

5. Consider these data from a common German dialect ([x] is a velar fricative; [ç] is a palatal fricative; : indicates a long vowel).

nıçt	"not"	baːx	"Bach"
reːçə̃n	"rake"	laːxə̃n	"to laugh"
ʃlɛçt	"bad"	kɔxt	"cooks"
riːçə̃n	"to smell"	fɛrsuːxə̃n	"to try"
hãımlıç	"sly"	hoːx	"high"
rɛçts	"rightward"	ʃluxt	"canyon"
kriːçə̃n	"to crawl"	fɛrfluxt	"accursed"

a. Are [x] and [ç] allophones of the same phoneme, or is each an allophone of a separate phoneme? Give your reasons.

b. If you conclude that they are allophones of one phoneme, state the rule that can derive the phonetic allophones.

6. Reconsider the two rules for the plural morpheme /z/:

a. Insert a [ə] before the plural morpheme /z/ when a regular noun ends in a sibilant, giving [əz].

b. Change the plural morpheme /z/ to a voiceless [s] when preceded by a voiceless sound.

Reformulate these two rules so that their order of application doesn't matter. (This shows that the necessity for rule ordering depends on how the rules are formulated, but that if we make the rules very specific to avoid rule ordering, we may sacrifice a degree of simplicity.) How is your reformulation somehow less simple than the one that requires rule ordering?

7. In Southern Kongo, a Bantu language spoken in Angola, the nonpalatal segments [t], [s], and [z] are in complementary distribution with their palatal counterparts [tʃ], [ʃ], and [ʒ], as shown in the following words:

tobola	"to bore a hole"	tʃina	"to cut"
tanu	"five"	tʃiba	"banana"
kesoka	"to be cut"	ŋkoʃi	"lion"
kasu	"emaciation"	nselele	"termite"
kunezulu	"heaven"	aʒimola	"alms"
nzwetu	"our"	lolonʒi	"to wash house"
zevo	"then"	zeŋga	"to cut"
ʒima	"to stretch"	tenisu	"tennis"

   a. State the distribution of each pair of segments.
      Example: [t]—[tʃ]: [t] occurs before [o], [a], [e], and [u]; [tʃ] occurs before [i].
               [s]—[ʃ]:
               [z]—[ʒ]:

   b. Using considerations of simplicity, which phone should be used as the underlying phoneme for each pair of nonpalatal and palatal segments in Southern Kongo?

   c. State in your own words the *one* phonological rule that will derive all the phonetic segments from the phonemes. Do not state a separate rule for each phoneme; a general rule can be stated that will apply to all three phonemes you listed in (b). Try to give a formal statement of your rule.

   d. Which of the following are possible words in Southern Kongo, and which are not?

      i. tenesi   ii. lotʃunuta   iii. zevoʒiʒi   iv. ʃiʃi   v. ŋkasa
      vi. iʒiloʒa

8. In some dialects of English, the following words have different vowels, as is shown by the phonetic transcriptions:

A		B		C	
bite	[bʌɪt]	bide	[baɪd]	die	[daɪ]
rice	[rʌɪs]	rise	[raɪz]	by	[baɪ]
ripe	[rʌɪp]	bribe	[braɪb]	sigh	[saɪ]
wife	[wʌɪf]	wives	[waɪvz]	rye	[raɪ]
dike	[dʌɪk]	dime	[dãɪm]	guy	[gaɪ]
		nine	[nãɪn]		
		rile	[raɪl]		
		dire	[daɪr]		
		writhe	[raɪð]		

   a. How may the classes of sounds that end the words in columns A and B be characterized? That is, what feature specifies all the final segments in A and all the final segments in B?

b. How do the words in column C differ from those in columns A and B?

c. Are [ʌɪ] and [aɪ] in complementary distribution? Give your reasons.

d. If [ʌɪ] and [aɪ] are allophones of one phoneme, should they be derived from /ʌɪ/ or /aɪ/? Why?

e. Give the phonetic representations of the following words as they would be spoken in the dialect described here:

life _____   lives _____   lie _____

file _____   bike _____   lice _____

f. Formulate a rule that will relate the phonemic representations to the phonetic representations of the words given above.

9. Pairs such as *top* and *chop, dunk* and *junk, so* and *show,* and *Caesar* and *seizure* reveal that /t/ and /tʃ/, /d/ and /dʒ/, /s/ and /ʃ/, and /z/ and /ʒ/ are distinct phonemes in English. Consider these same pairs of nonpalatalized and palatalized consonants in the following data. (The palatal forms are optional forms that often occur in casual speech.)

Nonpalatalized

[hɪt mi]   "hit me"
[lid hĩm]   "lead him"
[pʰæs ʌs]   "pass us"
[luz ðem]   "lose them"

Palatalized

[hɪtʃ ju]   "hit you"
[lidʒ ju]   "lead you"
[pʰæʃ ju]   "pass you"
[luʒ ju]   "lose you"

Formulate the rule that specifies when /t/, /d/, /s/, and /z/ become palatalized as [tʃ], [dʒ], [ʃ], and [ʒ]. Restate the rule using feature notations. Does the formal statement reveal the generalizations?

10. Here are some Japanese words in broad phonetic transcription. Note that [ts] is an alveolar affricate (cf. the palatal affricate [tʃ]) and should be taken as a *single* symbol. It is pronounced as the initial sound in *tsunami.* Japanese words (except certain loan words) never contain the phonetic sequences *[ti] or *[tu].

tatami	"mat"	tomodatʃi	"friend"	utʃi	"house"
tegami	"letter"	totemo	"very"	otoko	"male"
tʃitʃi	"father"	tsukue	"desk"	tetsudau	"help"
ʃita	"under"	ato	"later"	matsu	"wait"
natsu	"summer"	tsutsumu	"wrap"	tʃizu	"map"
kata	"person"	tatemono	"building"	te	"hand"

a. Based on these data, are [t], [tʃ], and [ts] in complementary distribution?

b. State the distribution—first in words, then using features—of these phones.

c. Give a phonemic analysis of these data insofar as [t], [tʃ], and [ts] are concerned. That is, identify the phonemes and the allophones.

d. Give the *phonemic* representation of the phonetically transcribed Japanese words shown as follows. Assume phonemic and phonetic representations are the same except for [t], [tʃ], and [ts].

tatami	tsukue	tsutsumu
tomodatʃi	tetsudau	tʃizu
utʃi	ʃita	kata
tegami	ato	koto
totemo	matsu	tatemono
otoko	degutʃi	te
tʃitʃi	natsu	tsuri

11. The following words are Paku, a language created by V. Fromkin and spoken by the Pakuni in the cult classic *Land of the Lost,* originally an NBC television series and once a major motion picture. The acute accent indicates a stressed vowel.

a.	ótu	"evil" (N)	**h.**	mpósa	"hairless"
b.	túsa	"evil" (Adj)	**i.**	ámpo	"hairless one"
c.	etógo	"cactus" (sg)	**j.**	ãmpőni	"hairless ones"
d.	etógni	"cactus" (pl)	**k.**	ámi	"mother"
e.	páku	"Paku" (sg)	**l.**	ãmíni	"mothers"
f.	pakűni	"Paku" (pl)	**m.**	áda	"father"
g.	épo	"hair"	**n.**	adãni	"fathers"

   i. Is stress predictable? If so, what is the rule?

   ii. Is nasalization a distinctive feature for vowels? Give the reasons for your answer.

   iii. How are plurals formed in Paku?

12. Consider the following English verbs. Those in column A have stress on the penultimate (next-to-last) syllable, whereas the verbs in column B and C have their last syllables stressed.

A	B	C
astónish	collápse	amáze
éxit	exíst	impróve
imágine	resént	surpríse
cáncel	revólt	combíne
elícit	adópt	belíeve
práctice	insíst	atóne

   a. Transcribe the words under columns A, B, and C phonemically. (Use a schwa for the unstressed vowels even if they can be derived from different phonemic vowels. This should make it easier for you.)

   Examples: *astonish* /əstɑnɪʃ/, *collapse* /kəlæps/, *amaze* /əmez/

   b. Consider the phonemic structure of the stressed syllables in these verbs. What is the difference between the final syllables of the verbs in columns A and B? Formulate a rule that predicts where stress occurs in the verbs in columns A and B.

   c. In the verbs in column C, stress also occurs on the final syllable. What must you add to the rule to account for this fact? (Hint: for the forms in columns A and B, the final consonants had to be considered; for the forms in column C, consider the vowels.)

13. Following are listed the phonetic transcriptions of ten "words." Some are English words, some are not words now but are possible or nonsense words, and others are not possible because they violate English sequential constraints.

Write the English words in regular spelling. Mark the other words as *possible* or *not possible*. For each word that you mark as "not possible," state your reason.

Word	Possible	Not Possible	Reason
Example:			
[θrot] throat			
[slig]	X		
[lsig]		X	No English word can begin with a liquid followed by an obstruent.

	Word	Possible	Not Possible	Reason
a.	[pʰril]			
b.	[skritʃ]			
c.	[kʰno]			
d.	[maɪ]			
e.	[gnostɪk]			
f.	[jŭnəkʰɔrn]			
g.	[fruit]			
h.	[blaft]			
i.	[ŋar]			
j.	[æpəpʰlɛksi]			

14. Consider these phonetic forms of Hebrew words:

[v]—[b]		**[f]—[p]**	
bika	"lamented"	litef	"stroked"
mugbal	"limited"	sefer	"book"
ʃavar	"broke" (masc.)	sataf	"washed"
ʃavra	"broke" (fem.)	para	"cow"
ʔikev	"delayed"	mitpaxat	"handkerchief"
bara	"created"	haʔalpim	"the Alps"

Assume that these words and their phonetic sequences are representative of what may occur in Hebrew. In your answers, consider classes of sounds rather than individual sounds.

a. Are [b] and [v] allophones of one phoneme? Are they in complementary distribution? In what phonetic environments do they occur? Can you formulate a phonological rule stating their distribution?
b. Does the same rule, or lack of a rule, that describes the distribution of [b] and [v] apply to [p] and [f]? If not, why not?
c. Here is a word with one phone missing. An empty slot appears in place of the missing sound: hid_ik.

Check the one correct statement.

    i.   [b] but not [v] could occur in the empty slot.
   ii. [v] but not [b] could occur in the empty slot.
  iii. Either [b] or [v] could occur in the empty slot.
  iv. Neither [b] nor [v] could occur in the empty slot.

d. Which of the following statements is correct about the incomplete word__ana?

    i. [f] but not [p] could occur in the empty slot.
   ii. [p] but not [f] could occur in the empty slot.
  iii. Either [p] or [f] could fill the empty slot.
  iv. Neither [p] nor [f] could fill the empty slot.

e. Now consider the following possible words (in phonetic transcription):

    laval   surva   labal   palar   falu   razif

If these words actually occurred in Hebrew, would they:

    i. Force you to revise the conclusions about the distribution of labial stops and fricatives that you reached on the basis of the first group of words given above?
   ii. Support your original conclusions?
  iii. Neither support nor disprove your original conclusions?

15. Consider these data from the African language Maninka.

bugo	"hit"	bugoli	"hitting"
dila	"repair"	dilali	"repairing"
don	"come in"	donni	"coming in"
dumu	"eat"	dumuni	"eating"
gwen	"chase"	gwenni	"chasing"

a. What are the two forms of the morpheme meaning -*ing*?
b. Can you predict which phonetic form will occur? If so, state the rule.
c. What are the "-ing" forms for the following verbs?

    da   "lie down"
    men   "hear"
    famu "understand"

d. What does the rule that *you* formulated predict for the "-ing" form of *sunogo* "sleep"?
e. If your rule predicts *sunogoli*, modify it to predict *sunogoni* without affecting the other occurrences of -*li*. Conversely, if your rule predicts *sunogoni*, modify it to predict *sunogoli* without affecting the other occurrences of -*ni*.

16. Consider the following phonetic data from the Bantu language Luganda. (The data have been somewhat altered to make the problem easier.) In each line except the last, the same *root* occurs in both columns A and B, but it has one prefix in column A, meaning "a" or "an," and another prefix in column B, meaning "little."

A		B	
ẽnato	"a canoe"	aka:to	"little canoe"
ẽnapo	"a house"	aka:po	"little house"
ẽnobi	"an animal"	akaobi	"little animal"
ẽmpipi	"a kidney"	akapipi	"little kidney"
ẽŋko:sa	"a feather"	akako:sa	"little feather"
ẽm:ã:m:o	"a peg"	akabã:m:o	"little peg"
ẽŋ:õ:m:e	"a horn"	akagõ:m:e	"little horn"
ẽn:ĩmiro	"a garden"	akadĩmiro	"little garden"
ẽnugẽni	"a stranger"	akatabi	"little branch"

Base your answers to the following questions on only these forms. Assume that all the words in the language follow the regularities shown here. (*Hint:* You may write long segments such as /m:/ (: means long) as /mm/ to help you visualize more clearly the phonological processes taking place.)

a. Are nasal vowels in Luganda phonemic? Are they predictable?
b. Is the phonemic representation of the morpheme meaning "garden," /dimiro/?
c. What is the phonemic representation of the morpheme meaning "canoe"?
d. Are [p] and [b] allophones of one phoneme?
e. If /am/ represents a bound prefix morpheme in Luganda, can you conclude that [ãmdãno] is a possible phonetic form for a word in this language starting with this prefix?
f. Is there a homorganic nasal rule in Luganda?
g. If the phonetic representation of the word meaning "little boy" is [akapo:be], give the phonemic and phonetic representations for "a boy."

   Phonemic_____ Phonetic_____

h. Which of the following forms is the phonemic representation for the prefix meaning "a" or "an"?

   i. /en/   ii. /ẽn/   iii. /ẽm/   iv. /em/   v. /e:/

i. What is the *phonetic* representation of the word meaning "a branch"?
j. What is the *phonemic* representation of the word meaning "little stranger"?
k. State the three phonological rules revealed by the Luganda data.

17. Here are some Japanese verb forms given in broad phonetic transcription. They represent two styles (informal and formal) of present-tense verbs. Morphemes are separated by +.

Gloss	Informal	Formal
call	yob + u	yob + imasu
write	kak + u	kak + imasu
eat	tabe + ru	tabe + masu
see	mi + ru	mi + masu
leave	de + ru	de + masu

Gloss	Informal	Formal
go out	dekake + ru	dekake + masu
die	ʃin + u	ʃin + imasu
close	ʃime + ru	ʃime + masu
swindle	katar + u	katar + imasu
wear	ki + ru	ki + masu
read	yom + u	yom + imasu
lend	kas + u	kaʃ + imasu
wait	mats + u	matʃ + imasu
press	os + u	oʃ + imasu
apply	ate + ru	ate + masu
drop	otos + u	otoʃ + imasu
have	mots + u	motʃ + imasu
win	kats + u	katʃ + imasu
steal a lover	netor + u	netor + imasu

a. List each of the Japanese verb roots in its phonemic representation.

b. Formulate the rule that accounts for the different phonetic forms of these verb roots.

c. There is more than one allomorph for the suffix designating formality and more than one for the suffix designating informality. List the allomorphs of each. Formulate the rule or rules for their distribution.

18. Consider these data from the Native American language Ojibwa.[1] (The data have been somewhat altered for the sake of simplicity; /c/ is a palatal stop.)

anokːi	"she works"	nitanokːi	"I work"
aːkːosi	"she is sick"	nitaːkːosi	"I am sick"
ayeːkːosi	"she is tired"	kiʃayeːkːosi	"you are tired"
ineːntam	"she thinks"	kiʃineːntam	"you think"
maːca	"she leaves"	nimaːca	"I leave"
takoʃːin	"she arrives"	nitakoʃːin	"I arrive"
pakiso	"she swims"	kipakiso	"you swim"
wiːsini	"she eats"	kiwiːsini	"you eat"

a. What forms do the morphemes meaning "I" and "you" take; that is, what are the allomorphs?

b. Are the allomorphs for "I" in complementary distribution? How about for "you"?

c. Assuming that we want one phonemic form to underlie each allomorph, what should it be?

d. State a rule that derives the phonetic forms of the allomorphs. Make it as general as possible; that is, refer to a broad natural class in the

---

[1]From Baker, C. L. & John McCarthy, *The Logical Problem of Language Acquisition*, Table: Example of Ojibwa Allomorphy. © 1981 Massachusetts Institute of Technology, by permission of The MIT Press.

environment of the rule. You may state the rule formally, in words, or partially in words with some formal abbreviations.

e. Is the rule a morphophonemic rule? That is, does it (most likely) apply to specific morphemes but not in general? What evidence do you see in the data to suggest your answer?

19. Consider these data from Burmese, spoken in Myanmar. The small ring under the nasal consonants indicates a voiceless nasal. Tones have been omitted, as they play no role in this problem.

ma	"health"	n̥eɪ	"unhurried"
na	"pain"	m̥i	"flame"
mji?	"river"	m̥on	"flour"
nwe	"to flex"	m̥a	"order"
nwa	"cow"	n̥weɪ	"heat" (verb)
mi	"flame"	n̥a	"nostril"

Are [m] and [m̥], and [n] and [n̥], allophones or phonemic? Present evidence to support your conclusion.

What do the words mi and m̥i, both meaning "flame" show? Do they contradict your conclusion? (Hint: Think of the two American English pronunciations of "economics," namely [ɛkənamɪks] and [ikənamɪks], which are the same word although [ɛ] and [i] are different phonemes. This phenomenon is sometimes called free variation.)

20. Here are some short sentences in a made-up language called Wakanti. (Long consonants are written as doubled letters to make the analysis easier.)

aba	"I eat"	amma	"I don't eat"
ideɪ	"You sleep"	inneɪ	"You don't sleep"
aguʊ	"I go"	aŋŋuʊ	"I don't go"
upi	"We come"	umpi	"We don't come"
atu	"I walk"	antu	"I don't walk"
ika	"You see"	iŋka	"You don't see"
ijama	"You found out"	injama	"You didn't find out"
aweli	"I climbed up"	amweli	"I didn't climb up"
ioa	"You fell"	inoa	"You didn't fall"
aie	"I hunt"	anie	"I don't hunt"
ulamaba	"We put on top"	unlamaba	"We don't put on top"

a. What is the phonemic form of the negative morpheme based on these data?

b. What are its allomorphs?

c. State a rule that derives the phonetic forms of the allomorphs from the underlying, phonemic form.

d. Another phonological rule applies to these data. State explicitly what the rule does and to what natural class of consonants it applies.

e. Give the phonemic forms for all the negative sentences.

21. Here are some data from French:

Phonetic	Gloss
pəti tablo	"small picture"
no tablo	"our pictures"
pəti livr	"small book"
no livr	"our books"
pəti navɛ	"small turnip"
no navɛ	"our turnips"
pətit ami	"small friend"
noz ami	"our friends"
pətit wazo	"small bird"
noz wazo	"our birds"

 a. What are the two forms for the words "small" and "our"?
 b. What are the phonetic environments that determine the occurrence of each form?
 c. Can you express the environments by referring to word boundaries and using exactly one phonetic feature, which will refer to a certain natural class? (Hint: A more detailed phonetic transcription would show the word boundaries (#), e.g., [#no##livr#].)
 d. What are the basic or phonemic forms?
 e. State a rule in words that derives the nonbasic forms from the basic ones.
 f. **Challenge exercise:** State the rule formally, using Ø to represent "null" and # to represent a word boundary.

22. Consider these pairs of semantically related phonetic forms and meanings (+ indicates a morpheme boundary):

Phonetic	Gloss	Phonetic	Gloss
[bãm]	explosive device	[bãmb+ard]	to attack with explosive devices
[kʰrʌ̃m]	a morsel or bit	[kʰrʌ̃mb+əl]	to break into bits
[aɪæ̃m]	a metrical foot	[aɪæ̃mb+ɪk]	consisting of metrical feet
[θʌ̃m]	an opposable digit	[θʌ̃mb+əlĩnə]	a tiny woman of fairy tales
[rãm]	a rhombus	[rãmb+ɔɪd]	shaped like a rhombus
[tũm]	a burial chamber	[tũmb+əl]	like a burial chamber

 a. What are the two allomorphs of the root morpheme in each line of data?
 b. What is the phonemic form of the underlying root morpheme? (Hint: Consider pairs such as *atom/atomic* and *form/formal* before you decide.)
 c. State a rule that derives the allomorphs.
 d. Spell these words using the English alphabet.

23. Consider these data from Hebrew. (Note: *ts* is an alveolar affricate and is a single [+sibilant] sound. The word *lehit* is a reflexive pronoun.)

Nonsibilant-Initial Verbs		Sibilant-Initial Verbs	
kabel	"to accept"	*tsadek*	"to justify"
lehit-kabel	"to be accepted"	*lehits-tadek*	"to apologize"
		(not *lehit-tsadek*)	
pater	"to fire"	*shamesh*	"to use for"
lehit-pater	"to resign"	*lehish-tamesh*	"to use"
		(not *lehit-shamesh*)	
bayesh	"to shame"	*sader*	"to arrange"
lehit-bayesh	"to be ashamed"	*lehis-tader*	"to arrange
		(not *lehit-sader*)	oneself"

  a. Describe the phonological change taking place in the second column of Hebrew data.
  b. Describe in words as specifically as possible a phonological rule that accounts for the change. Make sure your rule doesn't affect the data in the first column of Hebrew.

24. Here are some Japanese data, many of them from Exercise 10, in a fine enough phonetic transcription to show voiceless vowels (the ones with the little rings under them).

Word	Gloss	Word	Gloss	Word	Gloss
tatami	mat	tomodatʃi	friend	utʃi	house
tegami	letter	totemo	very	otoko	male
sukiyaki	sukiyaki	kisetsu	a season	busata	silence
tʃitʃi	father	tsukue	desk	tetsudau	help
ʃita	under	kita	north	matsu	wait
degutʃi	exit	tsuri	fishing	kisetsu	existing
natsu	summer	tsutsumu	wrap	tʃizu	map
kata	person	futon	futon	fugi	discuss
matsuʃita	(a proper name)	etsuko	(a girl's name)	fukuan	a plan

  a. Which vowels may occur voiceless?
  b. Are they in complementary distribution with their voiced counterparts? If so, state the distribution.
  c. Are the voiced/voiceless pairs allophones of the same phonemes?
  d. State in words, or write in formal notation if you can, the rule for determining the allophones of those vowels that have voiceless allophones.

25. With regard to English plural and past-tense rules, we observed that the two parts of the rules must be carried out in the proper order. If we reverse the order, we would get *[bʌsəs] instead of [bʌsəz] for the plural of *bus* (as illustrated in the text), and *[stetət] instead of [stetəd] for the past tense of *state*. Although constraints A and B (given below) are the motivation for the plural and past-tense rules, both the correct

and incorrect plural and past-tense forms are consistent with those constraints. What additional constraint is needed to prevent [bʌsəs] and [stetət] from being generated?

  a. Obstruent sequences may not differ with respect to their voice features at the end of a syllable.
  b. Sequences of obstruents that are alike with the possible exception of voicing are not permitted within a syllable.

26. In German, the third-person singular suffix is -*t.* Following are three German verb stems (underlying forms) and the third-person forms of these verbs:

Stem	Third person	
/loːb/	[loːpt]	he praises
/zag/	[zakt]	he says
/raɪz/	[raɪst]	he travels

The final consonant of the verb *stem* undergoes devoicing in the third-person form, even though it is not at the end of the word. What rule is operating to devoice the final stem consonant? How is this similar to or different from the constraint that operates in the English plural and past tense?

27. Slips of the tongue, or **speech errors,** in which we deviate in some way from an intended utterance, show phonological rules in action. We all make speech errors, and they tell us interesting things about language and its use. Consider the following speech errors:

Intended Utterance	Actual Utterance
1. gone to seed	god to seen
[gãn tə sid]	[gad tə sĩn]
2. stick in the mud	smuck in the tid
[stɪk ĩn ðə mʌd]	[smʌk ĩn ðə tʰɪd]
3. speech production	preach seduction
[spitʃ pʰrədʌkʃən]	[pʰritʃ sədʌkʃən]

In each example, explain the phonetic form of the slip in terms of segment swapping and the phonological rules of nasalization and aspiration.

7

Language in Society

> Language is a city to the building of which every human being brought a stone.

RALPH WALDO EMERSON, *Letters and Social Aims*, 1876

Dialects

> A language is a dialect that has an army and a navy.

MAX WEINREICH (1894–1969)

All speakers of English can talk to each other and pretty much understand each other. Yet, no two of us speak exactly alike. Some differences are the result of age, sex, social situation, and where and when the language was learned. These differences are reflected in word choices, the pronunciation of words, and grammatical rules. The language of an individual speaker with its unique characteristics is referred to as the speaker's **idiolect**. English may then be said to consist of anywhere from 450 million to upwards of two billion idiolects (or speakers) according to the most generous estimates.

Differences may also exist among different groups of people who speak the same language. Bostonians, New Yorkers, Texans, blacks in Chicago, whites in Denver, and Hispanics in Albuquerque all show variation in the way they speak English. When there are systematic differences in the way groups speak a language, we say that each group speaks a **dialect** of that language. Dialects are *mutually intelligible* forms of a language that *differ in systematic ways*. *Every* speaker, whether rich or poor, regardless of region or racial origin, speaks at least one dialect, just as each individual speaks an idiolect. A dialect is *not* an inferior or degraded form of a language, and logically could not be so because all dialects are rule-governed and have limitless expressive power.

It is not always easy to decide whether the differences between two speech communities reflect two dialects or two languages. Sometimes this rule-of-thumb definition is used: When dialects become mutually unintelligible—when the speakers of one dialect group can no longer understand the speakers of another dialect group—these dialects become different languages.

However, this rule of thumb does not always jibe with how languages are officially recognized, which is determined by political and social considerations. For example, despite regular differences in their grammars, Danish speakers, Norwegian speakers, and Swedish speakers can converse with each other. Nevertheless, Danish, Norwegian, and Swedish are considered separate languages because they are spoken in separate countries. Hindi and Urdu, spoken in India and Pakistan, are considered different "languages" even though they are as mutually intelligible as American and Australian English. The fact that the two countries have contentious cultural and religious issues and use different writing systems contributes to the impression that they are different languages.

On the other hand, linguistically distinct languages in China, such as Mandarin and Cantonese, which are not mutually intelligible when spoken, are nevertheless referred to as dialects of Chinese in the media and elsewhere because they have a common writing system that can be read by all speakers (because it's ideographic—see Chapter 8), and because they are spoken in a single country.

It is also not easy to draw a distinction between dialects and languages on strictly linguistic grounds. Dialects and languages reflect the underlying grammars and lexicons of their speakers. It would be completely arbitrary to say, for example, that grammars that differ from one another by, say, twenty rules represent different languages whereas grammars that differ by fewer than twenty rules are dialects. Why not ten rules or thirty rules? In reality, there is no sudden major break between dialects. Rather, dialects merge into each other, forming a **dialect continuum**.

Imagine a traveler journeying from Vienna to Amsterdam by bicycle. She would notice small changes in the German spoken as she bicycled from village to village, and the people in adjacent villages would have no trouble communicating with one another. Yet, by the time our traveler reached Dutch-speaking Amsterdam, she would realize that the accumulated differences made the German of Vienna and the Dutch of Amsterdam nearly mutually unintelligible.

Because neither mutual intelligibility, nor degree of grammatical difference, nor the existence of political or social boundaries is decisive, it is not possible to precisely define the difference between a language and a dialect. We shall, however, use the rule-of-thumb definition and refer to dialects of one language as mutually intelligible linguistic systems, with systematic differences among them.

As we will discuss in the next chapter, languages change continually but these changes occur gradually. They may originate in one geographic region or in one social group and spread slowly to others, and often over several generations of speakers. Dialect diversity develops when the changes that occur in one region or group do not spread. When speakers are in regular contact with one another, linguistic properties spread and are acquired by children. However, when some communication barrier separates groups of speakers—be it a physical barrier such as an ocean or a mountain range, or social barriers of a political, racial, class, educational, or religious kind—linguistic changes do not spread so readily, and the differences between groups are reinforced and grow in number.

Dialect leveling is movement toward greater uniformity and less variation among dialects. Though one might expect dialect leveling to occur as a result of the ease of travel and mass media, this is not generally the case. Dialect variation in the United Kingdom is maintained although only a few major dialects are spoken on national radio and television. There may actually be greater dialect variation in urban areas, where different groups attempt to maintain their distinctness and group identity.

Regional Dialects

Phonetics . . . the science of speech. That's my profession . . . (I) can spot an Irishman or a Yorkshireman by his brogue. I can place any man within six miles. I can place him within two miles in London. Sometimes within two streets.

GEORGE BERNARD SHAW, *Pygmalion*, 1912

The educated Southerner has no use for an r except at the beginning of a word.

MARK TWAIN, *Life on the Mississippi*, 1883

When various linguistic differences accumulate in a geographic region (e.g., the city of Boston or the southern United States), the language spoken has its own character. Each version of the language is referred to as a **regional dialect**. The hypothetical journey from Vienna to Amsterdam discussed previously crossed regional dialects. In the United States, dialectal differences are based primarily though not entirely on geographic region.

The origins of many regional dialects of American English can be traced to the people who settled in North America in the seventeenth and eighteenth centuries. Because they came from different parts of England, these early settlers already spoke different dialects of English, and these differences were carried to the original thirteen American colonies. By the time of the American Revolution, there were three major dialect regions in the British colonies: the Northern dialect spoken in New England and around the Hudson River, the Midland dialect spoken in Pennsylvania, and the Southern dialect. (There were, of course, a number of minor dialect areas as well.) These dialects differed from one another and from the English spoken in England in systematic ways. Some of the changes that occurred in British English spread to the colonies; others did not.

How dialects develop is illustrated by the pronunciation of words with an *r* in different parts of United States. As early as the eighteenth century, the British in southern England were dropping their *r*'s before consonants and at the ends of words. Words such as *farm, farther,* and *father* were pronounced as [faːm], [faːðə] and [faːðə] and as the cartoon suggests, *card* and *cod* are homophones in the Bostonian version of that dialect, namely [kad].

© 2015 Grimmy, Inc. Distributed by King Features Syndicate, Inc.

By the end of the eighteenth century, *r*-drop was a general rule among many of the early settlers in New England and the southern Atlantic seaboard. Close commercial ties were maintained between the New England colonies and London, and Southerners sent their children to England to be educated, which reinforced the *r*-drop rule. The *r*-less dialect is still spoken today in Boston, New York, and Savannah, Georgia. Later settlers, however, came from northern England, where the *r* had been retained; as the frontier moved westward, so did the *r*. Pioneers from all three dialect areas spread westward. The mingling of their dialects leveled many of their dialect differences, which is why the English used in large sections of the Midwest and the West is similar.

Regional phonological or phonetic distinctions are often referred to as different **accents**. We typically use the term *accent* to refer to characteristics of speech that convey information about what country or in what part of the country the speaker grew up, or to which sociolinguistic group the speaker belongs. A person is said to have a Boston or Brooklyn or Midwestern accent, a Southern drawl, an Irish brogue, and so on. Thus, people in the United States often refer to someone as having a British accent or an Australian accent; in Britain they refer to an American accent.

The term *accent* is also used to refer to the speech of non-native speakers, who have learned a language as a second language. For example, a native French speaker's English is described as having a French accent and vice versa. In this sense, *accent* refers to phonological differences caused by one's native language. Unlike regional accents, such foreign accents do not reflect differences in the speech of the community where the language was learned.

Regional dialects may differ not only in their pronunciation but also in their lexical choices and grammatical rules. A comedian once remarked that "the Mason–Dixon line is the dividing line between *you-all* and *youse-guys*." In the following sections, we discuss the different linguistic levels at which dialects may vary.

Phonological Differences

> I have noticed in traveling about the country a good many differences in the pronunciation of common words. . . . Now what I want to know is whether there is any right or wrong about this matter. . . . If one way is right, why don't we all pronounce that way and compel the other fellow to do the same? If there isn't any right or wrong, why do some persons make so much fuss about it?
>
> LETTER QUOTED IN "THE STANDARD AMERICAN," in J. V. Williamson and V. M. Burke, eds., *A Various Language*, 1971

Most dialect differences in American English involve differences in pronunciation (phonology). These variations created difficulties for us in writing Chapter 5 (phonetics), where we wished to illustrate the different sounds of English by using key words in which the sounds occur. As mentioned, some people pronounce *caught* [kɔt] with the vowel [ɔ] and *cot* [kat] with [a], whereas others pronounce them both [kat]. Some pronounce *Mary, merry,* and *marry* the same; others pronounce the three words differently as [meri], [mɛri], and [mæri]; and still others pronounce just two of them the same. In the south and northeast *pajamas* is pronounced [pədʒãməz] with tense [a] but as [pədʒæ̃məz] with a lax [æ] in the Midlands. Many speakers of American English pronounce *pin* and *pen* identically, whereas others pronounce the first [pĩn] and the second [pẽn].

The pronunciation of British English (or many dialects of it) differs in systematic ways from many dialects of American English. In a survey of hundreds of American and British speakers conducted via the Internet, 48 percent of the Americans pronounced the mid consonants in *luxury* as voiceless [lʌkʃəri], whereas 96 percent of the British pronounced them as voiced [lʌgʒəri]. Sixty-four percent of the Americans pronounced the first vowel in *data* as [e] and 35 percent as [æ], as opposed to 92 percent of the British pronouncing it with an [e] and only 2 percent with [æ]. The most consistent difference occurred in the placement of primary stress, with most Americans putting stress on the first syllable and most British on the second or third in polysyllabic words such as *cigarette, applicable, formidable,* and *laboratory.*

The United Kingdom also has many regional dialects. The British vowels described in the phonetics chapter are used by speakers of the dialect called RP for "received pronunciation" because it is "received" (accepted) in the court of the monarch. In this dialect, *h* is pronounced at the beginning of both *head* and *herb*, whereas in most American English dialects *h* is not pronounced in *herb.* In some British English dialects, the *h* is regularly dropped from most words in which it is pronounced in American, such as *house*, pronounced [aʊs], and *hero*, pronounced [iro].

As is true of the origin of certain American dialects, many of the regional dialects of British English, such as the West Country dialect, the East Anglia dialect, and the Yorkshire dialect, are not deviations from the "standard" dialect spoken in London, but are direct descendants of earlier varieties that existed alongside London English as far back as the eleventh century. (Watch old Harry Potter movies to hear some of what we've been discussing vis-à-vis British English.)

English is the most widely spoken language in the world (as a first or second language). It is the national language of several countries, including the United

States, large parts of Canada, the British Isles, Australia, and New Zealand. For many years, it was the official language in countries that were once colonies of Britain, including India, Nigeria, Ghana, Kenya, and the other "anglophone" countries of Africa. There are many other phonological differences in the various dialects of English used around the globe.

Lexical Differences

Mort Walker (11/27/12). Copyright 2012 by King Features Syndicate

Regional dialects may differ in the words people use for the same object, as well as in phonology. Hans Kurath, an eminent dialectologist, in his paper "What Do You Call It?" asked:

> Do you call it a *pail* or a *bucket*? Do you draw water from a *faucet* or from a *spigot*? Do you pull down the *blinds*, the *shades*, or the *curtains* when it gets dark? Do you *wheel* the baby, or do you *ride* it or *roll* it? In a *baby carriage*, a *buggy*, a *coach*, or a *cab*?

People take a *lift* to the *first floor* (our *second floor*) in England, but an *elevator* in the United States; English drivers needn't mind pedestrians on the *pavement* (our *sidewalks*) and they fill up with *petrol* (not *gas*) in London; in Britain a *public school* is "private" (you have to pay), and if a student showed up there wearing *pants* ("underpants") instead of *trousers* ("pants"), he would be sent home to get dressed.

If you ask for a *tonic* in Boston, you will get a drink called *soda* or *soda-pop* in Los Angeles; ice cream cones can be covered in *jimmies* in Boston and *sprinkles* in New York; and a *freeway* in Los Angeles is a *thruway* in New York, a *parkway* in New Jersey, a *motorway* in England, and an *expressway* or *turnpike* in other dialect areas.

Syntactic Differences

Dialects can also be distinguished by systematic syntactic differences. In most American dialects, sentences may be conjoined as follows:

1. John will eat and Mary will eat. → John and Mary will eat.

In the Ozark dialect of southern Missouri, the following conjunction is also possible:

2. John will eat and Mary will eat. → John will eat and Mary.

In (1) the VP *will eat* in the first conjunct is deleted, while in (2) the VP in the second conjunct is deleted. Most dialects of English allow deletion of only the first conjunct and in those dialects *John will eat and Mary* is ungrammatical. The Ozark dialect differs in allowing the second VP to delete.

Speakers of some American dialects say *Have them come early!* where others would say *Have them **to** come early!* Many speakers of the latter dialect also exhibit double modal auxiliary verbs, so that expressions such as *He **might could** do it* or *You **might should** go home* are grammatical. Most dialects of English allow only one modal.

Some of the dialects that permit double modals (e.g., Appalachian English) also allow expressions such as *I caught me a fish*; and *a*-prefixing with progressives such as *He came a-runnin'*. In some American English dialects, the pronoun *I* occurs when *me* would be used in other dialects. This difference is a syntactically conditioned morphological difference.

Dialect 1	**Dialect 2**
between you and I	between you and me
Won't he let you and I swim?	Won't he let you and me swim?
*Won't he let I swim?	

The use of *I* in these structures is only permitted in a conjoined NP, as the starred (ungrammatical) sentence shows. *Won't he let me swim?*, however, is grammatical in both dialects. Dialect 1 is growing, and these forms are becoming Standard English, spoken by TV announcers, political leaders, and university professors, although language purists still frown on this usage.

In British English, the pronoun *it* in the sentence *I could have done it* can be deleted. British speakers say *I could have done*, which is not in accordance with the syntactic rules of American English. American English, however, permits the deletion of *done it*, and Americans say *I could have*, which does not accord with the British syntactic rules.

Despite such differences, we are still able to understand speakers of other English dialects. Although regional dialects differ in pronunciation, vocabulary, and syntactic rules, the differences are minor when compared with the totality of the grammar. Dialects typically share most rules and vocabulary, which explains why the dialects of a language are mutually intelligible.

If you speak American English and you would like fairly good guess at the actual dialect you speak, we encourage you to take the New York Times on-line interactive dialect quiz: http://www.nytimes.com/interactive/2013/12/20/sunday-review/dialect-quiz-map.html?_r=0

Dialect Atlases

Linguist Hans Kurath published **dialect maps** and **dialect atlases** of a region on which dialect differences are geographically plotted (see Figure 7.1). The dialectologists who created the map noted the places where speakers use one word or another word for the same item. For example, the area where the term *Dutch cheese* is used is not contiguous; there is a small pocket mostly in West Virginia where speakers use that term for what other speakers call *smearcase*.

In similar maps, areas were differentiated based on the variation in pronunciation of the same word, such as [krik] and [krɪk] for *creek*. The concentrations

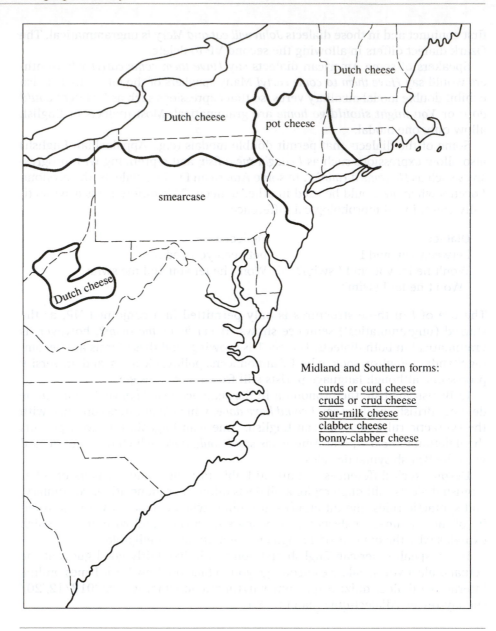

FIGURE 7.1 | A dialect map showing the isoglosses separating the use of different words that refer to the same cheese.

Kurath, Hans. "A Word Geography of the Eastern United States." Ann Arbor, MI: University of Michigan Press, copyright © 1949. Reprinted with permission of University of Michigan Press.

defined by different word usages and varying pronunciations, among other linguistic differences, form **dialect areas**.

A line drawn on the map to separate the areas is called an **isogloss**. When you cross an isogloss, you are passing from one dialect area to another. Sometimes several isoglosses coincide, often at a political boundary or at a natural barrier such as a river or mountain range. Sociolinguists call these groupings a *bundle* of isoglosses. Such a bundle can define a regional dialect.

DARE, the acronym for the *Dictionary of American Regional* English, consists of five volumes that embody decades of research and scholarship by American dialectologists. It is a major resource for those interested in American English dialects and its purpose has been described as follows:

> The *Dictionary of American Regional English (DARE)* is a reference tool unlike any other. Its aim is not to prescribe how Americans should speak, or even to describe the language we use generally, the "standard" language. Instead, it seeks to document the varieties of English that are **not** found everywhere in the United States—those words, pronunciations, and phrases that vary from one region to another, that we learn at home rather than at school, or that are part of our oral rather than our written culture. Although American English is remarkably homogeneous considering the tremendous size of the country, there are still many thousands of differences that characterize the various dialect regions of the United States. It is these differences that *DARE* records.

Social Dialects

> Why do these people speak in such a high pitch? Why do their jaws barely open when they talk? Why do the ends of their sentences go up as if they're asking a question? Odd vowels, clipped words, and always a hiss on the letter s . . . no wonder it's impossible not to mimic them.
>
> SUZANNE COLLINS, *The Hunger Games*, 2008

Social boundaries and class differences can be as confining as the physical barriers that often define regional dialects. It is therefore not surprising that different dialects of a language evolve within social groups.

The social boundaries that give rise to dialect variation are numerous. They may be based on socioeconomic status, religious, ethnic, and racial differences, country of origin, and even gender. Middle-class American and British speakers are often distinguishable from working-class speakers; in Baghdad the Christian, Muslim, and Jewish groups all speak different varieties of Arabic; in India people often use different dialects of a standard regional language such as Hindi, Gujarati, or Bengali depending on the social *caste* they belong to; in America, many speakers of African descent speak a different dialect than those of European, Asian, or Hispanic descent; and, as we shall see, women and men each have their own distinguishing speech characteristics.

Dialect differences that seem to come about because of social factors are called **social dialects**, as opposed to *regional dialects*, which are due to geographical factors. However, there are regional aspects to social dialects and, clearly, social aspects to regional dialects, so the distinction is not entirely cut and dried.

The "Standard"

We don't talk fancy grammar and eat anchovy toast. But to live under the kitchen doesn't say we aren't educated.

MARY NORTON, *The Borrowers*, 1952

Every language is a composite of dialects. But it is a widespread misconception that a language is a well-defined fixed system with various dialects diverging from this norm. One "language pundit" accused the editors of *Webster's Third New International Dictionary*, published in 1961, of confusing "to the point of obliteration the older distinction between standard, substandard, colloquial, vulgar, and slang," attributing to them the view that "good and bad, right and wrong, correct and incorrect no longer exist." In the next section, we argue that such criticisms are ill-founded.

Language Purists

A woman who utters such depressing and disgusting sounds has no right to be anywhere— no right to live. Remember that you are a human being with a soul and the divine gift of articulate speech: that your native language is the language of Shakespeare and Milton and the Bible; and don't sit there crooning like a bilious pigeon.

GEORGE BERNARD SHAW, *Pygmalion*, 1912

Prescriptive grammarians, or language purists, usually consider the dialect used by political leaders and national newscasters as the correct form of the language. (See Chapter 1 for a discussion of prescriptive grammars.) This is the dialect taught in "English" or "grammar" classes in school, and it is closer to the written form of the language than many other dialects, which also lends it an air of superiority.

Otto Jespersen, the great Danish linguist, ridiculed the view that a particular dialect is better than any other when he wrote: "We set up as the best language that which is found in the best writers, and count as the best writers those that best write the language. We are therefore no further advanced than before."

The dominant, or **prestige**, dialect is often called the standard dialect. **Standard American English (SAE)** is a dialect of English that many Americans *nearly* speak; divergences from this "norm" are labeled "Philadelphia dialect," "Chicago dialect," "African American English," and so on.

SAE is an idealization. Nobody speaks this dialect; and if somebody did, we would not know it, because SAE is not defined precisely (like most dialects, none of which are easy to clarify). Teachers and linguists held a conference in the 1990s that attempted to come up with a precise definition of SAE. This meeting did not succeed in satisfying everyone's view of SAE. SAE was once represented by the language used by national news broadcasters, but today many of them speak a regional dialect or a style of English that is not universally accepted as "standard." For example, the British Broadcasting Corporation (BBC) once used mostly speakers of RP English, but today speakers of Irish, Welsh, Scottish, and other regional dialects of English are commonly heard on BBC programs. The BBC describes its English as "the speech of educated professionals."

A standard dialect (or prestige dialect) of a particular language may have social functions. Its use in a group may bind people together or provide a common written form for multidialectal speakers. If it is the dialect of the wealthy, influential, and powerful members of society, this may have important implications for the entire society. All speakers who aspire to become successful may be required to speak that dialect even if it isn't their own.

Or they may desire it. For example, in 1954 the British scholar Alan Ross published *Linguistic Class-Indicators in Present-Day English* in which he compared the language of the English upper class, whom he labeled "U," with the speech habits of "non-U" speakers. Ross concluded that although the upper class has words and pronunciations peculiar to it, the main characteristic of U speech is the avoidance of non-U speech; and the main characteristic of non-U speech is, ironically, the effort to sound U. "They've a lovely home," for example, is pure non-U, because it is an attempt to be refined. Non-U speakers say "wealthy" and "ever so"; U speakers say "rich" and "very." Non-U speakers "recall"; U-speakers simply "remember."

Non-U language often includes **hypercorrections**, deviations from the norm *thought* to be "proper English," such as pronouncing *often* with a [t], or saying *between you and I*, while U speakers, who are generally more secure about their dialect, say [ɔfən] and *between you and me*. Ironically, in some cases non-U speech is so pervasive it eventually becomes part of the prestige dialect, as we are seeing today with *often* and *between you and I/me*.

No dialect, however, is more expressive, less corrupt, more logical, more complex, or more regular than any other dialect or language. They are simply different. More precisely, dialects reflect a different set of rules or lexical items represented in the minds of their speakers. Any judgments, therefore, as to the superiority or inferiority of a particular dialect or language are social judgments, which have no linguistic or scientific basis.

To illustrate the arbitrariness of "standard usage," consider the English *r*-drop rule discussed earlier. Britain's prestigious RP accent omits the *r* in words such as *car, far,* and *barn.* Thus, an *r*-less pronunciation is more prestigious than dialects that maintain the *r*. So much for England. In America, however, *r*-drop is generally considered substandard versus dialects that preserve the *r*. This shows that there is nothing inherently better or worse about one pronunciation over another, but simply that one variant is perceived as better or worse depending on a variety of social factors.

Banned Languages

A Wisconsin seventh-grader was suspended from a school's basketball team for speaking a Native American language. [The school] is 60 percent Native American, yet when a teacher heard [a female student], 12, telling a friend how to say "I love you" in the Menominee tongue, the teacher angrily objected, saying, "how do I know you're not saying something bad?"

THE WEEK, 2/24/12, P. 6

Language purists wish to prevent language or dialect differentiation because of their false belief that some languages are better than others, or that change leads to corruption. Languages and dialects have also been banned as a means of political control. Russian was the only legal language permitted by the Russian tsars, who banned the use of Ukrainian, Lithuanian, Georgian, Armenian, Azeri, and all the other languages spoken by national groups under the rule of Russia.

Cajun English and French were once banned in southern Louisiana by practice if not by law. Even as recently as August 8, 2006, Mary Tutwiler writes in a blog entitled "The French Connection," "Many local French speakers were so traumatized by the experience of being punished for speaking their mother tongue in school that they suppress their linguistic knowledge in public."

For many years, American Indian languages were banned in federal and state schools on reservations. Speaking Faroese was formerly forbidden in the Faroe Islands. A proscription against speaking Korean was imposed by the Japanese during their occupation of Korea between 1910 and 1945. Throughout history many languages and dialects have been banned to various degrees.

In France, a notion of the "standard" (the dialect spoken in Paris) as the only correct form of the language is promoted by the French Academy, an official panel of "scholars" who determine what usage constitutes the "official French language." Some years ago, the Academy enacted a law forbidding the use of "Franglais," which are words of English origin such as *le parking, le weekend,* and *le hotdog.* The French, of course, continue to use them, and because such words are notorious, they are widely used in advertising, where being noticed is more important than being correct. Only in government documents can these proscriptions be enforced.

In the past (and to some extent in the present), a French citizen from the provinces who wished to succeed in French society nearly always had to learn the prestigious Parisian French dialect. Then, several decades ago, members of regional autonomy movements demanded the right to use their own languages in their schools and for official business. In the section of France known as l'Occitanie, the popular singers sing in Langue d'oc, a Romance language of the region, both as a protest against the official language policy and as part of the cultural revival movement.

In many places in the world (including the United States), the use of sign languages of the deaf was once banned. Children in schools for the deaf were often punished if they used any gestures at all. The aim of these schools was to teach deaf children to read lips and to communicate exclusively through sound. Unfortunately, this policy prevented early exposure to language which is necessary for normal language and brain development. It was mistakenly thought that if children were exposed to sign they would not learn to read lips or produce sounds. Individuals who become deaf after learning a spoken language are often able to use their knowledge to learn to read lips and continue to speak. However, this is very difficult for someone who has never heard speech sounds. And even the best lip readers can comprehend only about one-third of the sounds of spoken language. Imagine trying to decide whether *lid* or *led* was said by reading the speaker's lips. Mute the sound on a TV set and see what percentage of a news broadcast you can understand, even if recorded and played back in slow motion, and even if you know the subject matter.

In 1981, an attempt to amend the U.S. Constitution to establish English as the national language arose but quickly became moribund. Nevertheless, an "Official English" initiative was passed by the electorate in California in 1986; in Colorado, Florida, and Arizona in 1988; and in Alabama in 1990. Today twenty-seven states have active Official English laws.

This kind of linguistic chauvinism is opposed on the grounds that such a measure could be used to prevent large numbers of non-English-speaking citizens from participating in civil activities such as voting, receiving a public education, and other rights of citizenship. Although the English-only movement has lost momentum, as recently as 2015 one presidential candidate castigated another for making a political statement in Spanish instead of English, although the audience was primarily Spanish speaking.

African American English

The language, only the language . . . It is the thing that black people love so much—the saying of words, holding them on the tongue, experimenting with them, playing with them. It's a love, a passion. Its function is like a preacher's: to make you stand up out of your seat, make you lose yourself and hear yourself. The worst of all possible things that could happen would be to lose that language.

TONI MORRISON, interviewed in *The New Republic*, March 21, 1981

Most regional dialects of the United States are largely free from stigma. Some regional dialects, like the *r*-less New Yorkese, are the victims of so-called humor, and speakers of one dialect may ridicule the "drawl" (vowel diphthongization) of southerners or the "twang" (excessive nasality) of Texans, even though not all speakers of southern dialects drawl, nor do all Texans twang.

There is, however, a *social* dialect of North American English that has been a victim of prejudicial ignorance. This dialect, **African American English (AAE),**[1] is spoken by a large population of Americans of African descent. The distinguishing features of this English dialect persist for social, educational, and economic reasons. The historical discrimination against African Americans has created the social boundaries that permit this dialect to thrive. In addition, particularly in recent years, many blacks have embraced their dialect as a means of positive group identification. AAE is generally used in casual and informal situations, and is much more common among working-class people. African Americans from middle- or upper-class backgrounds and with higher levels of education are now more likely to be speakers of SAE. Former U.S. President Barack Obama and First Lady Michelle Obama are cases in point.

Since the onset of the civil rights movement in the 1960s AAE has been the focus of national attention. Some critics claim that AAE is a "deficient, illogical, and incomplete" language. Such descriptions cannot be applied to any language, and they are as unscientific in reference to AAE as to Russian, Chinese, or Standard American English.

[1]AAE is actually a group of closely related dialects also variously called African American Vernacular English (AAVE), Black English (BE), Inner City English (ICE), and Ebonics.

Some people, white and black, think they can identify the race of a person by speech alone, believing that different races inherently speak differently. This belief is patently false. A black child raised in Britain will speak the British dialect of the household. A white child raised in an environment where AAE is spoken will speak AAE. Children learn the language they hear around them.

AAE is an especially interesting American dialect because it has a range of morphological and syntactic regularities that differ systematically from the so-called standard dialects. A vast body of research shows that linguistic differences between AAE and SAE are similar to those that occur between many of the world's major dialects.

Phonological Differences between African American English and SAE

Because AAE is not a single, monolithic dialect, but rather refers to a collection of tightly related dialects, not everything discussed in this section applies to all speakers of AAE.

r-Deletion

Similar to several dialects of both British and American English, some speakers of AAE have a rule of *r-deletion* that deletes /r/ everywhere except before a vowel. Pairs of words like *guard* and *god, nor* and *gnaw, sore* and *saw, poor* and *Poe, fort* and *fought,* and *court* and *caught* may be pronounced identically by those speakers of AAE because of this phonological rule. There is also an *l-deletion* rule for some speakers of AAE, creating identically pronounced pairs like *toll* and *toe, all* and *awe.*

A *consonant cluster reduction* rule in AAE simplifies consonant clusters, particularly at the ends of words and when one of the two consonants is an alveolar (/t/, /d/, /s/, or /z/). The application of this rule may delete the past-tense morpheme so that *meant* and *mend* are both pronounced as *men,* and *past* and *passed (pass + ed)* may both be pronounced like *pass.* When speakers of this dialect say *I pass the test yesterday,* they are not showing an ignorance of past and present-tense forms of the verb, but are pronouncing the past tense according to this phonological rule in their grammar.

The deletion rule is optional; it does not always apply, and studies have shown that it is more likely to apply in nouns like *paste* [pest], where the final [t] does not represent the past-tense morpheme, than in verbs like *chased* [tʃest] where it does. This has also been observed with final [s] and [z], which are more likely to be omitted by speakers of AAE in words like *Keats* /kits/ to yield a surface form /kit/, than in words where /s/ represents a plural morpheme, as in *seats* /sit + s/.

Consonant cluster reduction is not unique to AAE. It exists optionally for speakers of many other dialects including SAE. For example, in SAE the medial [d] in *didn't* is often deleted, producing [dĩnt]. Furthermore, nasals are commonly deleted before final voiceless stops, to result in [hĩt] versus [hĩnt]. The *r*-deletion rule mentioned above is also a feature of some dialects spoken in New York City.

Neutralization of [ɪ] and [ɛ] before Nasal Consonants

AAE shares with many regional dialects a lack of distinction between /ɪ/ and /ɛ/ before nasal consonants, producing identical pronunciations of *pin* and *pen*, *bin* and *Ben*, *tin* and *ten*, *him* and *hem*, and so on. The vowel sound in these words is roughly between the [ɪ] of *pit* and the [ɛ] of *pet*.

Diphthong Reduction

AAE has a rule that reduces the diphthong /ɔɪ/ to the simple vowel [ɔ] without the glide, so that *boil* and *boy* are pronounced [bɔ].

$$/ɔɪ/ → [ɔ]$$

This rule is common throughout the regional dialects of the South irrespective of race and social class.

Loss of Interdental Fricatives

A regular feature is the change of /θ/ to /f/ and /ð/ to /v/ at the ends of syllables so that *Ruth* is pronounced [ruf] and *brother* is pronounced [brʌvər]. This [θ]–[f] correspondence also holds in some dialects of British English, in which /θ/ is not even a phoneme. *Think* is regularly [fɪŋk] in Cockney English.

Initial /ð/ in such words as *this, that, these,* and *those* are pronounced as [d]. This is again not unique to AAE, but a common characteristic of certain regional, nonethnic dialects of English, many of which are found in the state of New Jersey as well as in New York City and Boston.

Another regular feature found in many varieties of AAE (and non-AAE) is the substitution of a glottal stop for /d/ at the end of non-word-final syllables; thus the name *Rodman* is pronounced [raʔmə̃n], but the word *rod* is pronounced [rad]. In fact, we observed in Chapter 5 on phonetics that the glottal stop [ʔ] is a common allophone of /t/ in many dialects of English.

All of these differences are rule-governed and similar to the kinds of phonological variation that is found in languages all over the world, including Standard American English.

Syntactic Differences between AAE and SAE

And of his port as meeke as is a mayde
He nevere yet no vileynye ne sayde

GEOFFREY CHAUCER, Prologue to *The Canterbury Tales*, 14th century

Syntactic differences also exist between dialects. They have often been used to illustrate that AAE is illogical, and yet these differences are evidence that AAE is as syntactically complex and as logical as any language.

Multiple Negatives

Constructions with multiple negatives akin to AAE *He don't know nothing* are commonly found in languages of the world, including French, Italian, and the English of Chaucer, as illustrated in the epigraph from *The Canterbury Tales*. The multiple negatives of AAE are governed by rules of syntax and are not illogical.

Deletion of the Verb Be

In most cases, if in Standard American English the verb can be contracted, in African American English sentences it is deleted; where it can't be contracted in SAE, it can't be deleted in AAE, as shown in the following sentences:

SAE	AAE
He is nice/He's nice.	He nice.
They are mine/They're mine.	They mine.
She is going to do it/She's gonna do it.	She gonna do it.
He is/he's as nice as he says he is.	He as nice as he say he is.
*He's as nice as he says he's.	*He as nice as he say he.
How beautiful you are.	How beautiful you are.
*How beautiful you're.	*How beautiful you.
Here I am.	Here I am.
*Here I'm.	*Here I.

These examples show that syntactic reduction rules operate in both dialects although they show small systematic differences.

Habitual Be

In SAE, the sentence *John is happy* can be interpreted to mean *John is happy now* or *John is generally happy*. One can make the distinction clear in SAE only by lexical means, that is, the addition of words. One would have to say *John is generally happy* or *John is a happy person* to disambiguate the meaning from *John is presently happy*.

In AAE, this distinction is made syntactically; an uninflected form of *be* is used if the speaker is referring to *habitual* state.

John be happy.	"John is usually happy."
John happy.	"John is happy now."
*John be happy at the moment.	
He be late.	"He is habitually late."
He late.	"He is late this time."
*He be late this time.	
Do you be tired?	"Are you generally tired?"
You tired?	"Are you tired now?"
*Do you be tired today?	

The ungrammatical sentences are caused by a conflict between the habitual meaning of *be* with the momentary meaning conveyed by *at the moment, this time*, and *today*. The syntactic distinction between habitual and nonhabitual aspect also occurs in SAE, but with verbs other than *be*. In SAE eventive verbs (see Chapter 4) such as *walk*, when marked with the present tense *-s* morpheme, have only a habitual meaning and cannot refer to an ongoing situation: *Susan walks to school* is habitual, and *Susan walks to school now* is ungrammatical if the intended meaning is *Susan is walking to school* as a description of a presently observed event. On the other hand, with a stative verb such as *love, John loves Mary* refers to an ongoing or habitual situation and *John is loving Mary* is ungrammatical with that meaning though it may be interpretable as something like "John is presently *making* love to Mary."

There Replacement

Some AAE dialects replace SAE *there* with *it's* in positive sentences, and *don't* or *ain't* in negative sentences.

It's a fly messing with me.	"There's a fly messing with me."
Ain't no one going to help you.	
Don't no one going to help you.	"There's no one going to help you."

Combined with multiple negatives, consonant cluster simplification, and complement deletion, speakers produce highly condemned, but clear, logically sound, even colorful sentences like *Ain't no hard worker never get no good payin' job*: "There isn't a hard worker who never gets a good paying job."

Several researchers at Gallaudet University in Washington, D.C., have been involved in a project to identify the linguistic features of a dialect of American Sign Language that they call Black ASL (BASL). BASL is used mainly by the Black Deaf in the United States and developed during the period in which schools in the United States (including schools for the deaf) were racially segregated, particularly in the southern states. It is still used by signers in southern states even though schools are legally desegregated.

BASL differs from other varieties of ASL in several respects. It has a larger signing space, different lexical items (some possibly based on AAE), and BASL signers use two-handed signs more frequently than signers of ASL, in particular when the following sign is also two-handed and when the sign makes contact with the face or body.

Latino (Hispanic) English

A major group of American English dialects is spoken by native Spanish speakers or their descendants. Among these groups are native speakers of Spanish who have learned or are learning English as a second language. There are also those born in Spanish-speaking homes whose native language is English, some of whom are monolingual, and others who speak Spanish as a second language.

One cannot speak of a homogeneous Latino dialect. In addition to the differences between bilingual and monolingual speakers, the dialects spoken by Puerto Rican, Cuban, Guatemalan, and El Salvadoran immigrants or their children are somewhat different from one another and also from those spoken by many Mexican Americans in the Southwest and California, called **Chicano English (ChE)**. Although ChE is not homogeneous, we can still recognize it as a distinct dialect of American English with systematic differences from other dialects of English.

Chicano English

Chicano English (ChE) is acquired as a first language by many children, making it the native language of hundreds of thousands, if not millions, of Americans. It is not English with a Spanish accent but, like African American English, a mutually intelligible dialect that differs systematically from SAE. Many of the differences, however, depend on the social context of the speaker. (This is also true of AAE and most "minority" dialects.) Linguistic differences of this sort that vary with the social situation of the speaker are termed **sociolinguistic variables**. For example, the use of nonstandard forms like double negation is often associated with pride of ethnicity, which is part of the social context. Many Chicano speakers (and speakers of AAE) are **bidialectal**; they can use either ChE (or AAE) or SAE, depending on the social situation.

Phonological Variables of ChE

Phonological differences between ChE and SAE reveal the influence of Spanish on ChE. For example, as discussed in Chapters 5 and 6, English has eleven vowel phonemes (not counting the diphthongs):/ i, ɪ, e, ɛ, æ, u, ʊ, o, ɔ, a, ʌ/. Spanish, however, has only five: /i, e, u, o, a/. Chicano speakers whose native language is Spanish may substitute the Spanish vowel system for the English. When this is done, several homonyms result that have distinct pronunciations in SAE. Thus, *ship* and *sheep* are both pronounced like *sheep*; *rid* is pronounced like *read*, and so on. Chicano speakers whose native language is English may choose to speak the ChE dialect despite having knowledge of the full set of American English vowels.

Other differences involve consonants. The affricate /tʃ/ and the fricative /ʃ/ are interchanged, so that *shook* is pronounced as if spelled with a *ch* and *check* as if spelled with an *sh*. In addition, some consonants are devoiced; for example, /z/ is pronounced [s] in words like *easy* [isi] and *guys* [gaɪs]. Another difference is the substitution of /t/ for /θ/, and /d/ for /ð/word initially, so *thin* is pronounced like *tin* or *teen* and *they* is pronounced *day*.

ChE has word-final consonant cluster reduction. *War* and *ward* are both pronounced like *war*; *star* and *start* like *star*. This process may also delete past-tense suffixes (*poked* is pronounced like *poke*) and third-person singular agreement suffixes (*He loves her* becomes *he love her*). Word-final alveolar-cluster reduction (e.g., pronouncing *fast* as if it were spelled *fass*) has become widespread among all dialects of English, including SAE. Although this process is often singled out for speakers of ChE and AAE, it is actually no longer dialect-specific.

Prosodic aspects of speech in ChE such as vowel length and intonation patterns may also differ from SAE and give ChE a distinctive flavor. The Spanish sequential constraint, which does not permit a word to begin with an /s/ cluster, is sometimes carried over to ChE in speakers who acquire English after early childhood. Thus, *scare* may be pronounced as if it were spelled *escare*, and *school* as if it were spelled *eschool*.

Syntactic Variables in ChE

There are also regular syntactic differences between ChE and SAE. In Spanish, a negative sentence uses a negative morpheme before the verb even if another negative appears; this "negative concord" (the multiple negatives mentioned earlier) is a regular rule of ChE syntax:

SAE	ChE
I don't have any money.	I don have no money.
I don't want anything.	I no want nothin.

Lexical differences also occur, such as the use of *borrow* in ChE for *lend* in SAE (*Borrow me a pencil*), or *barely* in ChE for *just* in SAE (*The new Prius had barely come out when I bought one*), as well as many other often subtle differences.

Genderlects

2006 Berkeley Breathed/Washington Post Writer's Group/Cartoonist Group

Dialects are defined in terms of groups of speakers, and speakers are most readily grouped by geography. Thus, regional dialects are the most apparent and generally are what people mean when they use the word *dialect*. Social groups are more amorphous, and social dialects correspondingly less well delineated and, until recently, less well studied. Surprisingly, the most obvious division of humankind into groups—women and men—has not engendered (if you'll pardon the expression) as much dialectal attention as regional and social divisions.

In the earliest work on women and language a number of features were identified that occurred more frequently in women's speech than in men's. For example, women "hedge" their speech more often than men do, with expressions such as *I suppose, I would imagine, This is probably wrong, sort of, and but. . . .* Women also use tag questions more frequently to qualify their statements *(He's not a very good actor, is he?),* as well as words of politeness (e.g., *please, thank you*) and intensifying adjectives such as *really* and *so (It's a really good film, It's so nice of you).* It was claimed that the use of these devices was due to uncertainty and a lack of confidence on the part of women.

Since this early work, an increasing number of scholars have been conducting research on language, gender, and sexism, investigating the differences between male and female speech and their underlying causes. Many sociolinguists studying gender differences in speech now believe that women use hedges and other, similar devices not because they lack confidence but in order to express friendliness and solidarity, a sharing of attitudes and values, with their listeners.

There is a widespread belief that when men and women converse, women talk more and that they tend to interrupt more than men in conversation. This is a frequent theme in sitcoms and the subject of jokes and sayings in various cultures, such as the Irish proverb: "Where there are women there is talk, and where there are geese there is cackling," or the Native American "A squaw's tongue runs faster than the wind's legs." However, serious studies of mixed-sex conversations show that in a number of different contexts men dominate the talking, particularly in non-private conversation such as television interviews, business meetings, and conference discussions where talking can increase one's status.

This dominance of males in mixed speech situations seems to develop at an early age. It occurs in classroom situations in which boys dominate talk time with the teachers. One study found that boys were eight times more likely to call out answers than girls. There is also evidence that teachers encourage this dominant behavior, reprimanding girls more often than boys when they call out.

It has also been observed that women typically have a more standard speech style. For example, they are less likely to use vernacular forms such as the reduction of -ing to -in' or him to 'im as in *I was walkin' down the street when I saw 'im*. Some dialects of British English drop word-initial [h] in casual speech as in *'arf an hour* (half an hour), *'enry* (Henry), *'appy* (happy). This *h*-less pronunciation happens more frequently in the speech of men than women. The tendency for women to speak more "properly" than men has been confirmed in many studies and appears to develop at an early age. Children as young as six show this pattern, with girls avoiding the vernacular forms used more commonly by boys from the same background.

The general view among sociolinguists is that women speak more "proper" English than men because of an insecurity caused by sexism in society. Among the more specific reasons that have been suggested are that women use more standard language to gain access to senior-level jobs that are often less available to them, that society tends to expect "better" behavior in general from women than men, that people who find themselves in subordinate roles (as women do in many societies) must be more polite, and that men prefer to use more vernacular forms because it helps to identify them as tough and strong. It has also been suggested that most sociolinguistic experiments are conducted by middle-class, well-educated academics and it is possible that the women who are interviewed "accommodate" to the interviewer, changing their speech to be more like the interviewer's or simply in response to the more formal nature of the interview situation. Men, on the other hand, may be less responsive to these perceived pressures.

The different variants of English used by men and women are sometimes called "genderlects" (a blend of *gender* and *dialect*). Variations in the language of men and women occur in many, if not all, languages. In Japanese, women may choose to speak a distinct female dialect, although they know the standard dialect used by both men and women. The Japanese language has many *honorific* words—words intended to convey politeness, respect, humility, and lesser social status in addition to their regular meaning. As noted earlier, women tend to use polite forms more often than men. Japanese has formal and informal verbal inflections (see exercise 17, Chapter 6), and again, women use the formal forms more frequently. There are also different words in Japanese used in male and female speech: For example,

	Women's Word	Men's Word
stomach	onaka	hara
delicious	oishii	umai
I/me	watashi	boku

and phrases such as:

eat a meal	gohan-o taberu	meshi-o kuu
be hungry	onaka-ga suita	hara-ga hetta
	"stomach become empty"	"stomach decrease"

One effect of the different genderlects of Japanese shows up in the training of guide and helper dogs. The animals learn their commands in English because the sex of the owner is not known in advance, and it is easier for an impaired person to use English commands than it is for trainers to train the dog in both language styles.

The differences discussed thus far have more to do with language use—lexical choices and conversational style—than with grammatical rules. There are, however, cases in which the language spoken by men and women differs in its grammar. In the Muskogean language Koasati, spoken in Louisiana, words that end in /s/ when spoken by men end in /l/ or /n/ when used by women; for example, the word meaning "lift it" is *lakawhol* for women and *lakawhos* for men. Similarly, in Bengali women often use [l] at the beginning of words where men use [n]. In Yana, women's words are sometimes shorter than men's because of a suffix that men use. For example, the women's form for "deer" is *ba,* the men's *ba-na;* for "person" we find *yaa* versus *yaa-na;* and so on. Early explorers reported that the men and women of the Carib Indians used different dialects. The putative historical reason for this is that long ago a group of Carib-speaking men invaded an area inhabited by Arawak-speaking people and killed all the men. The women who remained then continued to use Arawak while their new husbands spoke Carib.

In Chiquitano, a Bolivian language, the grammar of male language includes a noun-class gender distinction, with names for males and supernatural beings morphologically marked in one way, and nouns referring to females marked in another. In Thai, utterances may end with "politeness particles," $k^h rap$ for men and $k^h a$ for women (tones omitted). Thai also has different pronouns and fixed expressions like *please* and *thank you* that give each genderlect a distinctive character.

One obvious phonetic characteristic of female speech is its relatively higher pitch, caused mainly by shorter vocal tracts. Nevertheless, studies have shown that the difference in pitch between male and female voices is generally greater than could be accounted for by physiology alone, suggesting that some social factors may be at work, possibly beginning during language acquisition.

Margaret Thatcher, a former prime minister of England, is a well-known example of a woman altering her vocal pitch, in this case for political reasons. Thatcher's regular speaking voice was quite high and a little shrill. She was counseled by her advisors to lower her voice and to speak more slowly and monotonously in order to sound more like an authoritative man. This artificial speaking style became a strong characteristic of her public addresses.

Sociolinguistic Analysis

Speakers from different socioeconomic classes often display systematic speech differences, even when region and ethnicity are not factors. These social-class dialects differ from other dialects in that their sociolinguistic variables are often statistical in nature. With regional and social dialects, a differing factor is either present or absent (for the most part), so regional groups who say *frying pan* say it pretty much all the time, as do the regional groups who say *skillet*. Speakers of AAE dialects will say *she pretty* meaning "she is pretty" with great regularity, other factors being equal. But social-class dialects differentiate themselves in a more quantitative way; for example, one class of speakers may apply a certain rule 80 percent of the time to distinguish it from another that applies the same rule 40 percent of the time.

The linguist William Labov carried out a sociolinguistic analysis in New York City that focused on the rule of *r*-dropping that we discussed earlier, and its use by upper-, middle-, and lower-class speakers. In this classic study, a model for subsequent sociolinguistic analyses, Labov first identified three department stores that catered primarily to the three classes: Saks Fifth Avenue, Macy's, and S. Klein—upper, middle, and lower, respectively. To elicit data, he would go to the three stores and ask questions that he knew would evoke the words *fourth* and *floor*. People who applied the *r*-dropping rule would pronounce these words [fɔθ] and [flɔ], whereas ones who did not apply the rule would say [fɔrθ] and [flɔr].

The methodology behind much of this research is important to note. Labov interacted with all manner of people in their own environment where they were comfortable, although he took care when analyzing the data to take into account ethnic and gender differences. In gathering data he was careful to elicit naturally spoken language through his casual, unassuming manner. Finally, he would evoke the same answer twice by pretending not to hear or understand, and in that way was able to collect both informal, casual utterances, and utterances spoken (the second time) with more care.

In Saks, the high-end department store, 62 percent of respondents pronounced the *r* at least some of the time; in Macy's, the less expensive store, it was 52 percent, and in Klein's, the lower-end retailer, a mere 21 percent. The *r*-dropping rule, then, is socially "stratified," to use Labov's terminology, with the lower socio-class dialects applying the rule most often. What makes Labov's work so distinctive is his methodology and his discovery that the differences among dialects can be usefully defined on a quantitative basis of rule applications rather than as the strict presence or absence of a rule. He also showed that social context and the sociolinguistic variables that it governs play an important role in language change (discussed in the following chapter).

Languages in Contact

> Even a dog we do know is better company than a man whose language we know not.
>
> ST. AUGUSTINE, *City of God*, 5th century

Human beings are great travelers and traders and colonizers. The mythical tales of nearly all cultures tell of the trials and tribulations of travel and exploration, such as those of Odysseus (Ulysses) in Homer's *Odyssey*. Surely one of the tribulations of ranging outward from your home is that sooner or later you will encounter people who do not speak your language, nor you theirs. In some parts of the world, for example, in bilingual communities, you may not have to travel very far at all to find the language disconnect, and in other parts you may have to cross an ocean. Because this situation is so common in human history and society, several solutions for bridging this communication gap have arisen.

Lingua Francas

> Language is a steed that carries one into a far country.
>
> ARAB PROVERB

Many areas of the world are populated by people who speak diverse languages. In such areas, where groups desire social or commercial communication, one language is often used by common agreement. Such a language is called a **lingua franca**.

In medieval times, a trade language based largely on the languages that became modern Italian and Provençal came into use in the Mediterranean ports. That language was called Lingua Franca, "Frankish language." The term *lingua franca* was generalized to other languages similarly used. Thus, any language can be a lingua franca.

English has been called "the lingua franca of the whole world" and is standardly used at international business meetings and academic conferences. French, at one time, was "the lingua franca of diplomacy." Russian serves as the lingua franca in the countries of the former Soviet Union, where many different local languages are spoken. Latin was a lingua franca of the Roman Empire and of western Christendom for a millennium, just as Greek served eastern Christendom as its lingua franca. Yiddish has long served as a lingua franca among Jewish people, permitting Jews of different nationalities to communicate with one another.

More frequently, lingua francas serve as trade languages. East Africa is populated by hundreds of villages, each speaking its own language, but most Africans of this area learn at least some Swahili as a second language, and this lingua franca is used and understood in nearly every marketplace. A similar situation exists in Nigeria, where Hausa is the lingua franca.

Hindi and Urdu are the lingua francas of India and Pakistan. The linguistic situation of this area of the world is so complex that there are often regional lingua francas—usually local languages surrounding commercial centers. The Dravidian language Kannada is a lingua franca for the area surrounding the southwestern Indian city of Mysore. A similar situation existed in Imperial China.

In modern China, 94 percent of the people speak Han languages, which can be divided into eight major language groups that for the most part are mutually unintelligible. Within each language group there are hundreds of dialects. In addition to the Han languages, there are more than fifty "national minority" languages, including the five principal ones: Mongolian, Uighur, Tibetan, Zhuang, and Korean.

The situation is complex, and therefore the government inaugurated an extensive language reform policy to establish as a lingua franca the Beijing dialect of Mandarin, with elements of grammar from northern Chinese dialects, and enriched with the vocabulary of modern colloquial Chinese. They called this dialect *Putonghua*, meaning "common speech." The native languages and dialects are not considered inferior. Rather, the approach is to spread the "common speech" so that all may communicate with one another in this lingua franca.

Certain lingua francas arise naturally; others are instituted by government policy and intervention. In many parts of the world, however, people still cannot speak with their neighbors only a few miles away.

Contact Languages: Pidgins and Creoles

The charmer's name was Gaff. I'd seen him around. Bryant must have upped him to the Blade Runner unit. That gibberish he talked was city speak—gutter talk—a mishmash of Japanese, Spanish, German, what have you. I didn't really need a translator. I knew the lingo. Every good cop did. But I wasn't gonna make it easier for him.

DECKARD, from the motion picture *Bladerunner*, 1981

A lingua franca is typically a language with a broad base of native speakers, likely to be used and learned by persons with different native languages (usually in the same language family). Often in history, however, speakers of mutually unintelligible languages have been brought into contact under specific socioeconomic and political conditions and have developed a language to communicate with one another that is not native to anyone. Such a language is called a **pidgin**.

Many pidgins developed during the seventeenth, eighteenth, and nineteenth centuries, in trade colonies along the coasts of China, Africa, and the New World. These pidgins arose through contact between speakers of colonial European languages such as English, French, Portuguese, and Dutch, and the indigenous, non-European languages. Some pidgins arose among extended groups of slaves and slave owners in the United States and the Caribbean in the nineteenth century. Other cases include Hawaiian Pidgin English, which was established on the pineapple plantations of Hawaii among immigrant workers from Japan, China, Portugal, and the Philippines; Chinook Jargon, which evolved among the Indian tribes of the Pacific Northwest as a lingua franca among the tribes themselves as well as between the tribes and European traders; and various pidgins that arose during the Korean and Vietnam Wars for use between foreign soldiers and local civilians.

In all these cases, the contact is too specialized and the cultures too widely separated for the native language of any one group to function effectively as a lingua franca. Instead, the two or more groups use their native languages as a basis for developing a rudimentary lingua franca with reduced grammatical structures and small lexicons. Also in these situations, it is generally the case that one linguistic group is in a more powerful position, economically or otherwise, such as the relationship of plantation owner to worker or slave owner to slave. Most of the lexical items of the pidgin come from the language of the dominant group. This language is called the **superstrate** or **lexifier language**. For example, English (the language of the plantation owners) is the superstrate language for Hawaiian Pidgin English, Swahili for the various forms of Pidgin Swahili spoken in East and Central Africa, and Bazaar Malay for pidgins spoken in Malaysia, Singapore, and Indonesia. The other language or languages also contribute to the lexicon and grammar, but in a less obvious way. These are called **substrate languages**. Japanese, Chinese, Tagalog, and Portuguese were the substrate languages of Hawaiian Pidgin English and all contributed to its grammar. Chinook Jargon had features both from indigenous languages of the area such as Chinook and Nootka and from French and English.

Many linguists believe that pidgins form part of a linguistic "life cycle." In the very early stage of development the pidgin has no native speakers and is strictly a contact language. Its use is reserved for specialized functions, such as trading or work-oriented tasks, and its speakers speak their (respective) native languages in all other social contexts. In this early stage the pidgin has little in the way of clear grammatical rules and few (usually specialized) words. Later, however, if the language continues to exist and be necessary, a much more regular and complex form of pidgin evolves—what is sometimes called a "stabilized pidgin"—and this allows it to be used more effectively in a variety of situations. Further development leads to the creation of a **creole**, which most linguists believe has all the grammatical complexity of an ordinary language. **Pidginization** (the creation of a pidgin) thus involves a *simplification* of languages and a reduction in the number of domains of use. **Creolization**, in contrast, involves the linguistic *expansion* in the lexicon and grammar of existing pidgins, and an increase in the contexts of use. We discuss creoles and creolization further in the next section.

Although pidgins are in some sense rudimentary, they are not devoid of rules. The phonology is rule-governed, as in any human language. The inventory of phonemes is generally small. English dialects, for example, have forty-four phonemes more or less whereas pidgins commonly have half that number, and each phoneme may have an uncommon number of allophonic pronunciations. In one English-based pidgin, for example, [s], [ʃ] and [tʃ] are all possible pronunciations of the phoneme /s/; [masin], [maʃin], and [matʃin] all mean "machine." Sounds that occur in both the superstrate and substrate languages will generally be maintained, but if a sound occurs in the superstrate but not in the substrates, it will tend to be eliminated. For example, the English sounds [ð] and [θ] as in *this* and *thing* are usually converted to [d] and [t] so that "this thing" is pronounced *dis ting*.

Typically, pidgins have fewer grammatical words such as auxiliary verbs, prepositions, and articles, and inflectional morphology, including tense and case endings, as in:

He bad man.   "He is a bad man."
I no go bazaar.   "I'm not going to the market."

Bound morphology is largely absent. For example, some English pidgins have the word *sus* from the English *shoes*, but *sus* does not include a plural morpheme as it is used to refer to both a single shoe and multiple shoes. Note that this has happened in the development of English, too. Originally, the ending *-a* was a plural marker for Latinate words such as *agenda* but has come to have a singular meaning and the plural of agenda is now *agendas*.

Verbs and nouns usually have a single shape and are not altered to mark tense, number, gender, or case. The set of pronouns is often simpler in pidgins. In Kamtok, an English-based pidgin spoken in Cameroon, the pronoun system does not show gender or all the case differences that exist in Standard English (SE).

Kamtok			**SE**		
a	mi	ma	I	me	my
yu	yu	yu	you	you	your
i	i/am	i	he	him	his
i	i/am	i	she	her	her
wi	wi	wi	we	us	our
wuna	wuna	wuna	you	you	your
dem	dem/am	dem	they	them	their

Pidgins also may have fewer prepositions than the languages on which they are based. In Kamtok, for example, *fɔ* means "to," "at," "in," "for," and "from," as shown in the following examples:

Gif di buk fɔ mi.	"Give the book to me."
I dei fɔ fam.	"She is at the farm."
Dɛm dei fɔ chɔs.	"They are in the church."
Du dis wan fɔ mi, a bɛg.	"Do this for me, please."
Di mɔni dei fɔ tebul.	"The money is on the table."
You fit muf tɛn frank fɔ ma kwa.	"You can take ten francs from my bag."

Other morphological processes are more productive in pidgins. Reduplication is common, often to indicate emphasis. For example, in Kamtok, *big* means "big" and *big-big* means "enormous"; *luk* means "look" and *luk-luk* means "stare at." Compounding is also productive and serves to increase the otherwise small lexicons.

big ai	greedy
drai ai	brave
gras bilong fes	beard
gras antap long ai	eyebrow
gras bilong head	hair
han bilong pisin	wing (of a bird)
fella bilong Mrs. Queen	husband of the queen

Most words in pidgin languages also function as if they belong to several syntactic categories. For example, the Kamtok word *bad* can function as an adjective, noun, or adverb:

Adjective	tu bad pikin	two bad children
Noun	We no laik dis kain bad.	We don't like this kind of badness.
Adverb	A liakam bad.	I liked it very much.

In terms of syntax, early pidgins have a simple clausal structure, lacking embedded sentences and other complex complements. And word order may be variable so that speakers from different linguistic backgrounds can adopt the word order of their native language and still be understood. For example, Japanese is an SOV (verb final) language, and a Japanese speaker of an English-based pidgin may put the verb last, as in *The poor people all potato eat*. On the other hand, a Filipino speaker of Tagalog, a VSO language, may put the verb first, as in *Work hard these people*. Word order eventually becomes more established in pidgins and creoles, which over time become more like other languages with respect to the range of clause types.

Pidgin has come to have negative connotations, perhaps because many pidgins were associated with European colonial empires. The *Encyclopedia Britannica* once described a pidgin as "an unruly bastard jargon, filled with nursery imbecilities, vulgarisms and corruptions." It no longer uses such a definition. In recent times, there is greater recognition that pidgins reflect human creative linguistic ability and show many of the defining characteristics of language in general.

Pidgins also serve a useful function. For example, it is possible to learn an English-based pidgin well enough in six months to begin many kinds of semi-professional training. Learning English for the same purpose might take ten times as long. In areas with many mutually unintelligible languages, a pidgin can play a vital role in unifying people of different cultures and ethnicities.

In general, pidgins are short-lived, perhaps spanning several human generations, though a few have lasted much longer. Pidgins may die out because the speakers all come to share a common language. This was the fate of Chinook Jargon, whose speakers all learned English. In addition, because pidgins are often disdained, there is social pressure for speakers to learn a "standard" language, usually the one on which the pidgin is based. For example, through massive education, English replaced a pidgin spoken on New Zealand by the Maoris. Though it failed to succumb to years of government interdiction, Chinese Pidgin English could not resist the onslaught of English that fueled its demise by the close of the nineteenth century. Finally, and ironically, the death of a pidgin language may come about because of its success in uniting diverse communities; the pidgin proves so useful and becomes so widespread that successive generations in the communities in which it is spoken adopt it as their native tongue, elaborating its lexicon and grammar to become a creole.

Creoles and Creolization

Padi dɛm; kɔntri; una ɔl we de na Rom.
Mɛk una ɔl kak una yes. A kam bɛr Siza,
a nɔ kam prez am.

WILLIAM SHAKESPEARE, *Julius Caesar*, translated to Krio by Thomas Decker

A creole is defined as a language that has evolved in a contact situation to become the native language of a generation of speakers. The traditional view is that creoles are the creation of children who, exposed to an impoverished and unstable pidgin, develop a far richer and more complex language that shares the fundamental characteristics of a "regular" human language and allows speakers to use the language in all domains of daily life.

In contrast to pidgins, creoles may have inflectional morphology for tense, plurality, and so on. For example, in creoles spoken in the South Pacific the affix -im is added to transitive verbs, but when the verb has no object the -im ending does not occur:

> man i pairi**pim** masket.
> man be fired-him musket
> "The man fired the musket."
>
> masket i pairip.
> musket be fired
> "The gun was fired."

The same affix -im is used derivationally to convert adjectives into verbs like English -en in redden:

bik	big	bikim	to enlarge; to make something bigger
daun	down	daunim	to lower; to make something go down
nogut	no good	nogutim	to spoil, damage; to make something no good

Creoles typically develop more complex pronoun systems. For example, in the creoles of the South Pacific there are two forms of the pronoun we: inclusive we referring to speaker and listener, and exclusive we referring to the speaker and other people but not the listener. The Portuguese-based Cape Verdean Creole has three classes of pronouns: strong, weak, and clitic (meaning affixed to another word, like the possessive 's of English), as illustrated in Table 7.1.

The compounds of pidgins often reduce in creoles: for example, wara bilong skin (water belong skin) meaning "sweat" becomes skinwara. The compound baimbai (by and by), used to indicate future time, becomes a tense inflection ba

TABLE 7.1 | Cape Verdean Creole Pronouns

	Emphatic (Strong) Forms	Free (Weak) Forms	Subject Clitics	Object Clitics
1sg	ami	mi	N-	-m
2sg (informal)	abo	bo	bu-	-bu/-u
2sg (formal, masc.)	anho	nho	nhu-	
2sg (formal, fem.)	anha	nha		
3sg	ael	el	e-	-l
1pl	anos	nos	nu-	-nu
2pl	anhos	nhos		
3pl	aes	es		-s

in the creole. Thus, the sentence *baimbai yu go* ("you will go") becomes *yu bago*. The phrasal structure of creoles is also vastly enriched, including embedded and relative clauses, among many other features of "regular" languages.

How are children able to construct a creole based on the rudimentary input of the pidgin? One answer is that they use their innate linguistic capacities to rapidly transform the pidgin into a full-fledged language. This would account for the many grammatical properties that creoles have in common: for example, SVO word order and tense and aspect distinctions.

It should be noted that defining pidgins and creoles in terms of whether they are native (creoles) versus non-native second languages (pidgins) is not without problems. There are languages such as Tok Pisin, widely spoken in New Guinea, which are first languages to many speakers, but also used as second contact languages by other speakers. Some linguists have also rejected the idea that creoles derive from pidgins, claiming that the geographic areas and social conditions under which they develop are different.

Moreover, the view that children are the creators of creoles is not universally accepted. Various linguists believe that creoles are the result of imperfect second language learning of the lexifier or dominant language by adults and the "transfer" of grammatical properties from their native non-European languages. This hypothesis would account for some of the characteristics that creoles share with L2 "interlanguages" (see Chapter 9 on language acquisition): for example, invariant verb forms, lack of determiners, and the use of adverbs rather than verbs and auxiliaries to express tense and modality.

Although some linguists believe that creoles are simpler systems than "regular" languages, most researchers who have closely examined the grammatical properties of various creoles argue that they are not structurally different from non-creole languages and that the only exceptional property of creoles is the sociohistorical conditions under which they evolve.

Creoles often arose on slave plantations where Africans of many different tribes spoke mutually incomprehensible African languages. Haitian Creole, based on French, developed in this way, as did the "English" spoken in parts of Jamaica. Gullah is an English-based creole spoken by the descendants of African slaves on islands off the coast of Georgia and South Carolina. Louisiana Creole, related to Haitian Creole, is spoken by large numbers of blacks and whites in Louisiana. Krio, the language spoken by as many as a million Sierra Leoneans, and illustrated in the epigraph to this section, developed at least in part from an English-based pidgin.

One of the theories concerning the origins of African American English is that it derives from an earlier English-based creole that developed when Africans slaves had no common language other than the English spoken by their colonial masters. Proponents of this hypothesis point out that at least some of the unique features of AAE are traceable to influences of the West African languages once spoken by the slaves, or their parents/grandparents in any case. In addition, several of the features of AAE, such as aspect marking (distinct from that which occurs in Standard English), are typical of creole languages.

The alternative view is that AAE formed directly from English without any pidgin/creole stage. It is apparent that AAE is closer to Southern dialects of American English than to other dialects. It is possible that the African slaves learned the English of white Southerners as a second language. It is also possible that many of the distinguishing features of Southern dialects were acquired from AAE during the many decades in which a large number of Southern white children were raised by black women and played with black children.

Tok Pisin, originally a pidgin, was gradually creolized throughout the twentieth century. It evolved from Melanesian Pidgin English, once a widely-spoken lingua franca of Papua New Guinea used by English-speaking traders and the native population. Because New Guinea is so linguistically diverse—more than eight hundred different languages were once spoken on the island—the pidgin came to be used as a lingua franca among the indigenous population as well.

Tok Pisin has its own writing system, its own literature, and its own newspapers and radio programs; it has even been used to address a United Nations meeting. Papers in (not on!) Tok Pisin have been presented at linguistics conferences in Papua New Guinea, and it is commonly used for debates in the parliament of the country. Today, Tok Pisin is one of the three recognized national languages of The Independent State of Papua New Guinea, alongside English and Kiri Motu, another creole.

Sign languages may also be pidgins. In Nicaragua in the 1980s, adult deaf people came together and constructed a crude system of "home" signs and gestures in order to communicate. It had the characteristics of a pidgin in that different people used it differently and the grammatical rules were few and varied. However, when young deaf children joined the community, the impoverished sign language of the adults was tremendously enhanced by the children learning it, especially through the addition of agreement and other inflectional morphology. Today the language is a rich and complex sign language called Idioma de Signos Nicaraguense (ISN), or Nicaraguan Sign Language. ISN provides an impressive recent demonstration of the development of a grammatically complex language from impoverished input and the power of human linguistic creativity.

The study of pidgins and creoles has contributed a great deal to our understanding of the nature of human language and the processes involved in language creation and language change, and of the sociohistorical conditions under which these instances of language contact occurred.

Bilingualism

> He who has two languages has two souls.
>
> ANONYMOUS

The term **bilingualism** refers to the ability to speak two (or more) languages, either by an individual speaker, **individual bilingualism**, or within a society, **societal bilingualism**. In Chapter 9 on language acquisition, we will discuss how bilingual children may simultaneously acquire their two languages, and how second languages are acquired by children and adults. There are various degrees of individual bilingualism. Some people have native-like control of two languages, whereas others make regular use of two languages with a high degree of proficiency but lack the linguistic competence of a native or near-native speaker in one or the other language. In addition, some bilinguals may have oral competence but cannot read or write one or more of their languages.

The situations under which people become bilingual may vary. Some people grow up in a household in which more than one language is spoken; others move to a new country where they acquire the local language, usually from people outside the home. Still others learn second languages in school. In communities with rich linguistic diversity, contact between speakers of different languages may also lead to bilingualism.

Bilingualism (or multilingualism) also refers to the situation in which two (or more) languages are spoken and recognized as official or national languages of a particular nation. Societal bilingualism exists in many countries, including Canada, where English and French are both official languages, and Switzerland, where French, German, Italian, and Romansch all have official status.

Interestingly, research shows that there are fewer bilingual individuals in bilingual countries than in so-called "unilingual" countries. This makes sense when you consider that in unilingual countries such as the United States, Italy, and France, people who do not speak the dominant language must learn some amount of it to function. In addition, the main concern of multilingual states has been the maintenance and use of two or more languages, rather than the promotion of individual bilingualism among its citizens.

The United States is broadly perceived as a monolingual English-speaking society even though there is no reference to a national language in the Constitution. However, there are numerous bilingual communities with long histories throughout the country. English-Spanish bilinguals are measurably more numerous than any other combination according to the 2010 census, but the variety of languages found among bilingual and multilingual people living in the United States is far too numerous to mention and perhaps not even known to its fullest extent.

Recent studies reveal that a shift to monolingual English is growing rapidly and that knowledge of Spanish and other common bilingual partners of English (e.g., Tagalog, Vietnamese, and various languages of China) is being lost faster in the twenty-first century than at any other period of history.

Codeswitching

When they first met, she'd never seemed to stop talking, bubbling over, switching from German to English as if one language couldn't contain it, everything she had to say.

JOSEPH KANON, *Istanbul Passage*, 2012

Codeswitching is a speech style unique to bilinguals in which fluent speakers switch languages between or within sentences, as illustrated by the following sentence:

Sometimes I'll start a sentence in English and termino en español.
Sometimes I'll start a sentence in English and finish it in Spanish.

Codeswitching is a universal language-contact phenomenon that reflects the grammars of both languages working simultaneously. Bilingual Spanish-English speakers may switch between English and Spanish as in the above example, whereas Quebecois in Canada switch between French and English:

I mean, c'est un idiot, ce mec-là.
I mean, he's an idiot, that guy.

The following examples are from German-English, Korean-English, and Mandarin-English bilinguals:

Johan hat mir gesagt that you were going to leave.
Johan told me you were going to leave.

Chigum ton-uls ops-nunde, I can't buy it.
As I don't have money now, I can't buy it.

Women zuotian qu kan de movie was really amazing.
The movie we went to see yesterday was really amazing.

Codeswitching occurs wherever groups of bilinguals speak the same two languages. Furthermore, codeswitching occurs in specific social situations, enriching the repertoire of the speakers.

A common misconception is that codeswitching is indicative of a language disability of some kind, for example, that bilinguals use codeswitching as a coping strategy for incomplete mastery of both languages, or that they are speaking "broken" English. These characterizations are completely inaccurate. Recent studies of the social and linguistic properties of codeswitching indicate that it is a marker of bilingual identity, and has its own internal grammatical structure. For example, bilinguals will commonly codeswitch between a subject and a verb, as in:

Mis amigos finished first.   My friends finished first.

but would judge ungrammatical a switch between a subject pronoun and a verb as in:

*Ellos finished first.   They finished first.

Codeswitchers also follow the word order rules of the languages. For example, in a Spanish noun phrase, the adjective usually follows the noun, as opposed to the English NP in which it precedes, as shown by the following:

English: My mom fixes **green tamales**.   (Adj N)
Spanish: Mi mamà hace **tamales verdes**.   (N Adj)

A speaker might codeswitch as follows:

     My mom fixes **tamales verdes**.
or   Mi mamà hace **green tamales**.

but would not accept or produce such utterances as

    *My mom fixes **verdes tamales**.
or   *Mi mamà hace **tamales green**.

because the word order within the NPs violates the rules of the language.

301
Language and Education

Codeswitching is to be distinguished from (bilingual) **borrowing**, which occurs when a word or short expression from one language occurs embedded among the words of a second language and adapts to the regular phonology, morphology, and syntax of the second language. In codeswitching, in contrast, the two languages that are interwoven preserve their own phonological and other grammatical properties. Borrowing can be easily distinguished from codeswitching by the pronunciation of an element. Sentence (1) involves borrowing, and (2) codeswitching.

(1) I love biscottis [bɪskaɾiz] with my coffee.
(2) I love biscotti [biskɔt:i] with my coffee.

In sentence (1) *biscotti* takes on an (American) English pronunciation and plural -*s* morphology, while in (2) it preserves the Italian pronunciation and plural morpheme -*i* (plural for *biscotto*, "cookie").

What needs to be emphasized is that people who codeswitch have knowledge not of one but of two (or more) languages and that codeswitching, like linguistic knowledge in general, is highly structured and rule-governed.

Language and Education

Outside of a dog, a book is a man's best friend; inside of a dog, it's too dark to read.

GROUCHO MARX (1890–1977)

The study of language has important implications in various educational arenas. An understanding of the structure, acquisition, and use of language is essential to the teaching of foreign and second languages, as well as to reading instruction. It can also promote a fuller understanding of language variation and use in the classroom and inform the often heated debates surrounding issues such as how to teach reading to children, bilingual education, and the use of minority dialects.

Second-Language Teaching Methods

He can learn a language in a fortnight. Knows dozens of them: the sure mark of a fool.

HENRY HIGGINS, From the script of the motion picture *Pygmalion*, 1938.

We may disagree with Professor Higgins on two counts: First, despite claims on the Internet to the contrary, one cannot learn a language in two weeks, certainly not with a useful degree of fluency. And secondly, a person who *does* know "dozens of them" is surely not a fool.

Many approaches to second or foreign language teaching have been developed over the years. Though these methods can differ significantly from one another, many experts believe that there is no single best method for teaching a second language. All methods have something to offer, and virtually any method can succeed with a gifted teacher who is a native or near-native speaker, motivated students, and appropriate teaching materials. All methods are most effective when they fit a given educational setting and when they are understood and embraced by the teacher.

Second-language teaching methods fall into two broad categories: the *synthetic approach* and the *analytic approach*. As the name implies, the synthetic approach stresses the teaching of the grammatical, lexical, phonological, and functional units of the language step by step. This is a bottom-up method. The task of the learner is to put together—or synthesize—the discrete elements that make up the language. The more traditional language teaching methods, which stress grammar instruction, fall into this category.

An extreme example of the synthetic approach is the **grammar translation** method favored up until the mid-1960s, in which students learned lists of vocabulary, verb paradigms, and grammatical rules. Learners translated passages from the target language into their native language. The teacher typically conducted class in the students' native language, focusing on the grammatical parsing of texts, and there was little or no contextualization of the language being taught. Reading passages were carefully constructed to contain only vocabulary and structures to which learners had already been exposed, and errors in translation were corrected on the spot. Learners were tested on their mastery of rules, verb paradigms, and vocabulary. The students did not use the target language very much except in reading translated passages aloud.

Analytic approaches are more top-down. The goal is not to explicitly teach the component parts or rules of the target language. Rather, the instructor selects topics, texts, or tasks that are relevant to the needs and interests of the learner, whose job then is to discover the constituent parts of the language. This approach assumes that adults can extract the rules of the language from unstructured input, more or less like a child does when acquiring his first language.

Currently, one of the most widely practiced analytic approaches is *content-based instruction*, in which the focus is on making the language meaningful and on getting the student to communicate in the target language. Learners are encouraged to discuss issues and express opinions on various topics of interest to them in the target language. Topics for discussion might include "online dating" or "taking responsibility for our environment." Grammar rules are taught on an as-needed basis, and fluency takes precedence over grammatical accuracy. Classroom texts (both written and aural) are generally taken from sources that were not created specifically for language learners, on the assumption that these will be more interesting and relevant to the student. Assessment is based on the learner's comprehension of the target language.

Not all second-language teaching methods fall clearly into one or the other category. The synthetic and analytic approaches should be viewed as the opposite ends of a continuum along which various second-language methods may fall. In addition, teachers practicing a given method may not strictly follow all the principles of the method. Actual classroom practices tend to be more eclectic, with teachers using techniques that work well for them and to which they are accustomed—even if these techniques are not in complete accordance with the method they are practicing.

Teaching Reading

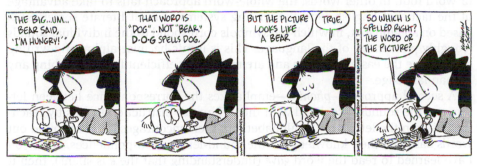

"Baby Blues", Baby Blues Partnership. Reprinted with permission of King Features Syndicate

As we shall discuss in Chapter 9, language development (whether of a spoken or sign language) is a biologically driven process with a substantial innate component. Parents do not teach their children the grammatical rules of their language. Indeed, they are typically not even aware of the rules themselves. Rather, the young child is naturally predisposed to uncover these rules from the language he hears around him. The way we learn to read and write, however, is quite different from the way we acquire the spoken/signed language.

First, and most obviously, children learn to talk (or sign) at a very young age, while reading typically begins when the child is school-age (around five or six years old in most cases, although some children are not reading-ready until even later). A second important difference is that across cultures and languages, given appropriate language input from the environment all children acquire a spoken/signed language while many children never learn to read or write. This may be because they are born into cultures for which there is no written form of the language. It is also unfortunately the case that even some children born into literate societies do not learn to read, either because they suffer from a specific reading disability, **dyslexia**; because of other yet-to-be-diagnosed learning disabilities; or simply because they have not been properly taught. It is important to recognize, however, that even an illiterate child or adult has a mental grammar of his or her language and is able to speak/sign and understand perfectly well.

The most important respect in which spoken/signed language development differs from learning to read is that reading typically requires specific instruction and conscious effort, whereas under normal circumstances language acquisition does not. Which kind of instruction works best for teaching reading has been a topic of considerable debate for many decades. Three main approaches have been tried.

The first—the *whole-word approach*—teaches children to recognize a vocabulary of some fifty to one hundred words by rote learning, often by seeing the words used repeatedly in a story: for example, *Run, Spot, Run* from the Dick and Jane series well-known to people who learned to read in the 1950s. Other words are acquired gradually. This approach does not teach children to "sound out" words according to the individual sounds that make up the words. Rather, it treats the written language as though it were a logographic system, like that of Chinese, in which a single written character corresponds to a whole word or word root. In other words, the whole-word approach fails to take advantage of the fact that English (and the writing systems of most literate societies) is based on an alphabet, in which the symbols correspond to the individual sounds (roughly phonemes) of the language. This is ironic because alphabetic writing systems are the easiest to learn and are maximally efficient for transcribing any human language.

A second approach—*phonics*—emphasizes the correspondence between letters and the sounds associated with them. Phonics instruction begins by teaching children the letters of the alphabet and then encourages them to sound out words based on their knowledge of the sound-letter correspondences. So, if you have learned to read the word *gave* (understanding that the *e* is silent), then it is easy to read *save* and *pave*.

However, English and many other languages do not show a perfect correspondence between sounds and letters. For example, the rule for *gave, save,* and *pave* does not extend to *have*. The existence of many such exceptions has encouraged some schools to adopt a third approach to reading, the *whole-language approach* (also called "literature-based" or "guided reading"), which was most popular in the 1990s. The key principle is that phonics should not be taught directly. Rather, the child is supposed to make the connections between sounds and letters herself based on exposure to text. For example, she would be encouraged to figure out an unfamiliar word based on the context of the sentence or by looking for clues in the story line or the pictures rather than by sounding it out, as illustrated in the cartoon.

The philosophy behind the whole-language approach is that learning to read, like learning to speak, is a natural act that children can basically do on their own—an assumption that, as we noted earlier, is questionable at best. With the whole-language approach, the main job of the teacher is to make the reading experience an enjoyable one. To this end, children are presented with engaging books and are encouraged to write stories of their own as a way of instilling a love of reading and words.

Despite the intuitive appeal of the whole-language approach—after all, who would deny the educational value of good literature and creative expression in learning?—research has clearly shown that under most circumstances understanding the relationship between letters and sounds is critically important in reading. One of the assumptions of the whole-language approach is that skilled adult readers do not sound out words when reading, so proponents question the value of focusing on sounding out in reading instruction. However, research shows that the opposite is true: skilled adult readers *do* sound out words mentally, and they do so very rapidly. In other research, investigators compared groups of college students who were taught to read unfamiliar symbols such as Arabic letters, one group was taught by a phonics approach and the other with a whole-word approach. Those trained with phonics could read many more new words. Similar results have been obtained through computer modeling of how children learn to read. Classroom studies have also compared phonics with whole-word or whole-language approaches and have shown that phonics instruction produces better results for beginning readers.

At this point, the consensus among psychologists and linguists who do research on reading—and a view shared by many teachers—is that reading instruction must be grounded in a firm understanding of the connections between letters and sounds, and that whole-language activities that make reading fun and meaningful for children should be used to supplement phonics instruction. Based on such research, the federal government now promotes the inclusion of phonics in reading programs across the United States.

Literacy in the Deaf Community

Hearing children use their knowledge of the sound-letter correspondences to learn to read, but deaf children do not have access to this phonological base. Learning to read poses a particular challenge for deaf children and literacy rates in the deaf community are very low. On average, deaf high school graduates in the Unites States read at a fourth-grade level, barely enough to read the newspaper. However, some deaf students learn to read very well, at levels equal to hearing students. How do they do this without being able to rely on a phonological code?

Prior to 1960, deaf children in the United States were educated exclusively through oral instruction, using lip reading and amplification via hearing aids to increase awareness of sound. Nowadays, a widespread method of reading instruction is to first teach deaf children one of a number of signing systems referred to as Manually Coded English (MCE), essentially English on the hands. Unlike ASL, MCE systems are synthesized, consisting essentially in the replacement of each spoken English word (and grammatical elements such as the -s ending for plurals and the -ed ending for past tense) by a sign. So, the syntax and morphology of MCE is approximately the same as those of spoken English. As a communication system MCE is unnatural—similar to trying to speak French by translating every English word or ending into its French counterpart. Difficulties also arise because there are not always corresponding forms in the two languages. The problem is amplified with sign languages because they use multidimensional space while spoken languages are sequential. Consequently, deaf children frequently modify aspects of MCE so that it more closely resembles a natural sign language, for example by making creative use of signing space. However, many teachers of the deaf believe that learning *to sign* English can facilitate learning *to read* English.

Surprisingly perhaps, the most successful deaf readers are not those with the most intensive oral training in English. Rather, various studies show that deaf children born to deaf parents—children who are fluent, early learners of ASL—tend to be better readers than deaf children born to hearing parents who are generally not exposed to ASL, or exposed later in life. Many researchers therefore believe that the most important factor contributing to reading success in deaf children is deep knowledge of a language. ASL and other signed languages are the most accessible to deaf people and therefore facilitate reading, despite the fact that ASL and English are structured quite differently. Additionally, some deaf children of hearing parents who receive sustained MCE input from parents and who are fluent users of MCE also achieve reading levels comparable to deaf children of deaf parents. According to Rachel Mayberry, a leading researcher of sign language and deaf education, this "confirms the suspicion that robust language is the key to learning to read."

In line with many bilingual educators, as discussed in the next section, the most current thinking in deaf education (though not the most widespread at this point) is that knowing one language (ASL) makes it easier to learn another language (English). Under this view, the goal of the deaf school should be to provide deaf bilingual education, promoting, or when necessary teaching ASL as a first language, and then English as a second language, through the use of print, sound, or sign.

Bilingual Education

The United States of America has more monolingual experts on bilingual education than any other country in the world.

ROBERTO BAHRUTH, Perspective on Teaching English Language Learners, 2004

As discussed earlier, there are many bilingual communities in the United States and members of these communities typically have varying levels of English proficiency. People who have recently arrived in the United States may have virtually no knowledge of English, other individuals may have only limited knowledge, and others may be fully bilingual. Native language development is untutored and happens before children begin school, but many children find themselves in classroom situations in which their native language is not the language of instruction. There has been a great deal of debate among researchers, teachers, parents, and the general public over the best methods for teaching English to school-age children as well as over the value of maintaining and promoting their native language abilities.

There are several kinds of bilingual programs in American schools for immigrant children. In **Transitional Bilingual Education (TBE)** programs, students receive instruction in both English and their native language, and the native language support is gradually phased out over two or three years. In **Bilingual Maintenance (BM)** programs, students remain in bilingual classes for their entire educational experience. Another program, **Dual Language Immersion**, enrolls English-speaking children and students who are native in another language in roughly equal numbers. The goal here is for all the students to become bilingual. This kind of program serves as a BM program for non-English speakers and a foreign language immersion program for the English-speaking children.

Many studies have shown that immigrant children benefit from instruction in their native language. Bilingual classes allow the children to first acquire in their native language school-related vocabulary, speech styles, and other aspects of language that are specific to a school environment while they are learning English. It also allows them to learn content material and keep up with other children during the time it takes them to master English. Recent studies that compared the effectiveness of different types of programs have found that children enrolled in bilingual programs outperformed children in English-only programs, and that children enrolled in BM programs did better than TBE students.

Despite the benefits that a bilingual education affords immigrant students, these programs have been under increasing attack since the 1970s. In the past few years measures against bilingual education have been passed in several states, including California, Arizona, and Massachusetts. These measures mandate that immigrant students "be taught English by being taught in English" in an English-only approach known as Sheltered English Immersion (SEI). Proponents claim that one year of SEI is sufficient for children, especially young children, to learn English well enough to be transferred to a mainstream classroom. Research does not bear out these claims, however. Studies show that only a small minority of children, around 3 percent to 4 percent of children in SEI programs and 13 percent to 14 percent in bilingual programs, acquire English within a year. A considerable body of research shows that for the vast majority of children it takes from two to five years to develop oral proficiency in English and four to seven years to develop proficiency in academic English.

There are several possible causes for the chasm between research results and public policy regarding bilingual education. Bilingual programs can be poorly implemented and so not achieve the desired results. There may also be a public perception that it is too costly to implement bilingual programs. It is likely that some of the backlash against bilingual education is due to anti-immigrant sentiment, but there are also many well-intentioned people who mistakenly believe that bilingualism is a handicap and that children will be more successful academically and socially if they are quickly and totally immersed in the more prestigious majority language.

Minority Dialects

Children who speak a dialect of English that differs from the language of instruction—usually close to Standard English—may also be disadvantaged in a school setting. Literacy instruction is generally based on SAE. It has been argued that the phonological and grammatical differences between African American English (AAE) and SAE make it harder for AAE-speaking children to learn to read and write.

One approach to this problem has been to discourage children from speaking AAE and to correct each departure from SAE that the children produce. SAE is presented as the "correct" way to speak and AAE as substandard or incorrect. This approach has been criticized as being psychologically damaging to the child as well as impractical. Attempts to consciously correct children's nonstandard dialect speech are routinely met with failure. Moreover, one's language/ dialect expresses group identity and solidarity with friends and family. A child may take a rejection of his language as a rejection of him and his culture. A more positive approach to teaching literacy to speakers of nonstandard dialects is to encourage **bidialectalism**. This approach teaches children to take pride in their language, encouraging them to use it in informal circumstances, with family and friends, while also teaching them a second dialect—SAE—that is necessary for reading, writing, and classroom discussion. As a point of comparison, in many countries, including Switzerland, Germany, and Italy, children grow up speaking a nonstandard dialect at home but learn the standard language once they enter school, illustrating that bidialectalism that combines a home dialect and a school/national language is entirely feasible. Educational programs that respect the home language may better facilitate the acquisition of a standard dialect. Ideally, the bidialectal method would also include class discussion of the phonological and grammatical differences between the two dialects, which would require that teachers understand the linguistic properties of AAE, or whatever the minority dialect happens to be, as well as some linguistics in general. One of the themes of this book is that you have a lot of linguistic knowledge that you may not be aware of, but that can be made explicit through the rules of phonology, morphology, syntax, and semantics. You also have a deep social knowledge of your language. You know the appropriate way to talk to your parents, your friends, your clergy, and your teachers. You know about "politically correct" (PC) language: to say "mail *carrier*," "fire*fighter*," and "police *officer*," and not to say the "n-word" or drop an "f-bomb". In short, you know how to *use* your language appropriately, even if you sometimes choose not to. This section discusses some of the many ways in which the use of language varies in society.

Language in Use

Language is not an abstract construction of the learned, or of dictionary-makers, but is something arising out of the work, needs, ties, joys, affections, tastes, of long generations of humanity, and has its bases broad and low, close to the ground.

WALT WHITMAN, "Slang in America," 1885

Styles

Most speakers of a language speak one way with friends, another on a job interview or presenting a report in class, another talking to small children, another with their parents, and so on. These "situation dialects" are called **styles**, or **registers**.

Nearly everybody has at least an informal and a formal style. In an informal style, the rules of contraction are used more often, the syntactic rules of negation and agreement may be altered, and many words are used that do not occur in the formal style.

Informal styles, although permitting certain abbreviations and deletions not permitted in formal speech, are also rule-governed. For example, questions are often shortened with the subject *you* and the auxiliary verb deleted. You can ask *Running the marathon?* or *You running the marathon?* instead of the more formal *Are you running the marathon?* but you cannot shorten the question to **Are running the marathon?* Informal talk is not anarchy. It is rule-governed, but the rules of deletion, contraction, and word choice are different from those of the formal language.

It is common for speakers to have competence in several styles, ranging between the two extremes of formal and informal. The use of styles is often a means of identification with a particular group (e.g., family, gang, church, and team), or a means of excluding groups believed to be hostile or undesirable (cops, teachers, parents).

Many cultures have rules of social behavior that govern style. Some Indo-European languages distinguish between *you* (familiar) and *you* (polite). German *du* and French *tu* are to be used only with "intimates"; *Sie* and *vous* are more formal and used with nonintimates. Thai has three words meaning "eat" depending on the social status of who is speaking with whom.

Social situations affect the details of language usage, but the core grammar remains intact, with a few superficial variations that lend a particular flavor to the speech.

Slang

Slang is a language that rolls up its sleeves, spits on its hands, and goes to work.

CARL SANDBURG, quoted in "Minstrel of America: Carl Sandburg," *New York Times*, February 13, 1959

One mark of an informal style is the frequent occurrence of **slang**. Slang is something that nearly everyone uses and recognizes, but nobody can define precisely. It is more metaphorical, playful, elliptical, vivid, and shorter-lived than ordinary language.

The use of slang has introduced many new words into the language by re-combining old words into new meanings. *Spaced out, right on, hang-up, drill down,* and *rip-off* have all gained a degree of acceptance. Slang also introduces entirely new words such as *barf, flub, hoodie,* and *dis.* Finally, slang often consists of ascribing entirely new meanings to old words. *Rave* has broadened its meaning to "an all-night dance party," where people take *ecstasy* (slang for a kind of drug) to get *high; crib* refers to one's home and *posse* to one's cohorts. *Weed* and *pot* widened their meaning to "marijuana"; *pig* and *fuzz* are derogatory terms for "police officer"; *rap, cool, dig, stoned, split,* and *suck* have all extended their semantic domains.

The words we have cited may sound slangy because they have not gained total acceptability. Words such as *dwindle, freshman, glib,* and *mob* are former slang words that in time overcame their "unsavory" origin. It is not always easy to know where to draw the line between slang words and regular words. The borderland between slang and formal language is ill-defined and is more of a continuum than a strict boundary.

There are scads (another slang word) of sources of slang. It comes from the underworld: *crack, payola,* to *hang paper.* It comes from college campuses: *crash, wicked, peace.* It even comes from the White House: *pencil* (writer), *still* (photographer), and *football* (black box of security secrets).

Slang is universal. It is found in all languages and all time periods. It varies from region to region, and from past to present. Slang meets a variety of social needs and rather than a corruption of the language, it is yet further evidence of the creativity of the human language user. If you are a lover of "crazy" words, you need to know about the online Urban Dictionary at http://www.urbandictionary.com/

Jargon and Argot

Practically every conceivable science, profession, trade, and occupation uses specific slang terms called **jargon**, or **argot**. Linguistic jargon, some of which is used in this book, consists of terms such as *phoneme, morpheme, case, lexicon, phrase structure rule,* and *X-bar schema.* Part of the reason for specialized terminology is for clarity of communication, but part is also for speakers to identify themselves with persons with whom they share interests.

Because the jargon used by different professional and social groups is so extensive (and so obscure in meaning), court reporters in the Los Angeles Criminal Courts Building have a library that includes books on medical terms, guns, trade names, and computer jargon, as well as street slang.

The computer age not only ushered in a technological revolution, it also introduced a slew of jargon, called slangily, *computerese*, used by computer "hackers" and others. So vast is this specialized vocabulary that *Webster's New World Computer Dictionary* has four hundred pages and contains thousands of computer terms as entries. A few such words that are familiar to most people are *modem* (from **modulator-dem**odulator*), bit* (from **binary digit**), and *byte* ("eight *bits"*). Acronyms and alphabetic abbreviations abound in computer jargon. *ROM* ("read-only memory"), *RAM* ("random-access memory"), *CPU* ("central processing unit"), and *DVD* ("digital video disk") are a small fraction of what's out there.

Some jargon may over time pass into the standard language. Jargon, like all types of slang, spreads from a narrow group that originally embraced it until it is used and understood by a large segment of the population.

Taboo or Not Taboo?

Sex is a four-letter word.

BUMPER STICKER SLOGAN

An item in a newspaper once included the following paragraph:

> "This is not a Sunday school, but it is a school of law," the judge said in warning the defendants he would not tolerate the "use of expletives during jury selection." "I'm not going to have my fellow citizens and prospective jurors subjected to filthy language," the judge added.

How can language be filthy? In fact, how can it be clean? The filth or beauty of language must be in the ear of the listener, or in the collective ear of society. The writer Paul Theroux points this out:

> A foreign swear-word is practically inoffensive except to the person who has learned it early in life and knows its social limits.

Nothing about a particular string of sounds makes it intrinsically clean or dirty, ugly or beautiful. If you say that you *pricked* your finger when sewing, no one would raise an eyebrow, but if you refer to your professor as a *prick*, the judge quoted previously would undoubtedly censure this "dirty" word.

You know the obscene words of your language, and you know the social situations in which they are desirable, acceptable, forbidden, and downright dangerous to utter. This is true of all speakers of all languages. All societies have their taboo words. (*Taboo* is a Tongan word meaning "forbidden.") People everywhere seem to have a need for undeleted expletives to express their emotions or attitudes.

Forbidden acts or words reflect the particular customs and views of the society. Among the Zuni Indians, it is improper to use the word *takka*, meaning "frogs," during a religious ceremony. In the world of Harry Potter, the evil Voldemort is not to be named but is referred to as "You-Know-Who." In some religions, believers are forbidden to "take the Lord's name in vain," and this prohibition often extends to other religious jargon. Thus, the taboo words *hell* and *damn* are changed to *heck* and *darn*, though the results are sometimes not euphonious. Imagine the last two lines of Act II, Scene 1, of *Macbeth* if they were "cleaned up":

Hear it not, Duncan; for it is a knell
That summons thee to heaven, or to *heck*

Words relating to sex, sex organs, and natural bodily functions make up a large part of the set of taboo words of many cultures. Often, two or more words or expressions can have the same linguistic meaning, with one acceptable and the other taboo. In English, words borrowed from Latin sound "scientific" and therefore appear to be technical and "clean," whereas native Anglo-Saxon counterparts are taboo. Such pairs of words are illustrated as follows:

Anglo-Saxon Taboo Words	Latinate Acceptable Words
cunt	vagina
cock	penis
prick	penis
tits	mammaries
shit	feces, defecate

There is no grammatical reason why the word *vagina* is "clean" whereas *cunt* is "dirty," or why *balls* is taboo but *testicles* acceptable. Although there is no grammatical basis for such preferences, there certainly are sociolinguistic reasons to embrace or eschew such usages, just as there are sociolinguistic reasons for speaking formally, respectfully, disrespectfully, informally, in jargon, and so on.

Euphemisms

Banish the use of the four-letter words
Whose meaning is never obscure.
The Anglos, the Saxons, those bawdy old birds
Were vulgar, obscene, and impure.
But cherish the use of the weaseling phrase
That never quite says what it means;
You'd better be known for your hypocrite ways
Than vulgar, impure, and obscene.

FOLK SONG ATTRIBUTED TO WARTIME ROYAL AIR FORCE OF GREAT BRITAIN

As we noted in Chapter 1, the existence of taboo words and ideas motivates the creation of **euphemisms**. A euphemism is a word or phrase that replaces a taboo word or serves to avoid frightening or unpleasant subjects. In many societies, because death is feared, there are many euphemisms related to this subject. People are less apt to *die* and more apt to *pass on* or *pass away*. Those who take care of your loved ones who have passed away are more likely to be *funeral directors* than *morticians* or *undertakers*. And then there's *feminine protection* . . .

The use of euphemisms is not new. It is reported that the Greek historian Plutarch in the first century CE wrote that "the ancient Athenians . . . used to cover up the ugliness of things with auspicious and kindly terms, giving them polite and endearing names. Thus, they called harlots *companions,* taxes *contributions,* and prison a *chamber.*"

Just as surely as all languages and societies have taboo words, they have euphemisms. The aforementioned taboo word *takka,* meaning "frogs," is replaced during a Zuni religious ceremony by a complex compound word that literally translates as "several-are-sitting-in-a-shallow-basin-where-they-are-in-liquid." The euphemisms for bodily excretions and sexual activity are legion, and lists of them may be found in online dictionaries of slang. There you will find such gems for urination as *siphon the python* and *point Percy at the porcelain,* and for intercourse *shag, hide the ferret (salami, sausage),* and *stuffin' the muffin,* among a gazillion others.

These euphemisms, as well as the difference between the accepted Latinate "genteel" terms and the "dirty" Anglo-Saxon terms, show that a word or phrase has not only a linguistic **denotative meaning** but also a **connotative meaning** that reflects attitudes, emotions, value judgments, and so on. In learning a language, children learn which words are taboo, and these taboo words differ from one child to another, depending on the value system accepted in the family or group in which the child grows up.

Racial and National Epithets

The use of epithets for people of different religions, nationalities, or races tells us something about the speakers. Words such as *kike* (for Jew), *wop* (for Italian), *nigger* or *coon* (for African American), *slant* (for Asian), and *towelhead* (for Middle Eastern Arab) reflect racist and chauvinist views of society.

Even words that sound like epithets are perhaps to be avoided (see Exercise 13). An administrator in Washington, D.C., described a fund he administers as "niggardly," meaning stingy. He resigned his position under fire for using a word "so close to a degrading word."

Language, however, is creative, malleable, and ever-changing. The epithets used by a majority to demean a minority may be reclaimed as terms of bonding and friendship among members of the minority. Thus, for *some*—we emphasize *some*—African Americans, the word *nigger* is used to show affection. Similarly, the ordinarily degrading word *queer* is used among *some* gay people as a term of endearment, as is *cripple* or *crip* among *some* individuals who share a disability.

Language and Sexism

doctor, n . . . a man of great learning.

THE AMERICAN COLLEGE DICTIONARY, 1947

A businessman is aggressive; a businesswoman is pushy. A businessman is good on details; she's picky . . . He follows through; she doesn't know when to quit. He stands firm; she's hard . . . He isn't afraid to say what is on his mind; she's mouthy. He exercises authority diligently; she's power mad. He's closemouthed; she's secretive. He climbed the ladder of success; she slept her way to the top.

FROM "HOW TO TELL A BUSINESSMAN FROM A BUSINESSWOMAN," *The Balloon*, Graduate School of Management, UCLA, 1976

The discussion of obscenities, blasphemies, taboo words, and euphemisms showed that words of a language are not intrinsically good or bad but reflect individual or societal values. This is also seen in references to a woman as a *castrating female, ballsy women's libber,* or *courageous feminist advocate,* depending on who is talking.

Early dictionaries often gave clues to the social attitudes of that time. In some twentieth-century dictionaries, examples used to illustrate the meaning of words include "manly courage" and "masculine charm," as opposed to "womanish tears" and "feminine wiles." Contemporary dictionaries are far more enlightened and try to be scrupulous in avoiding sexist language.

Until recently, most people who heard "My cousin is a professor (or a doctor, or the chancellor of the university, or a steelworker)" would assume that the cousin is a man; if they heard "My cousin is a nurse (or elementary school teacher, or clerk-typist, or house worker)," they would conclude that the cousin is a woman. This is changing because society is changing and increasingly, both women and men hold jobs once held primarily by one sex.

Despite flashes of enlightenment, words for women with abusive or sexual overtones abound: *dish, piece, piece of ass, piece of tail, bunny, chick, pussy, bitch, doll, slut, cow, cougar*—to name just a few. Far fewer such sexual terms exist for men, and those that do, such as *boy toy, stud muffin, hunk, and jock,* are not pejorative in the same way.

It's clear that language reflects sexism. It reflects any societal attitude, positive or negative. Languages are infinitely flexible and expressive, but is language itself amoral and neutral? Or is there something about language, or a particular language, that abets sexism? Before we attempt to answer that question, let's look more deeply into the subject, using English as the illustrative language.

Marked and Unmarked Forms

If the English language had been properly organized . . . then there would be a word which meant both "he" and "she," and I could write, "If John or Mary comes, heesh will want to play tennis," which would save a lot of trouble.

A. A. MILNE, *The Christopher Robin Birthday Book*, 1930

There is an asymmetry between male and female terms in which there are male/female pairs of words. The male form is *unmarked*, and is the more generally used term, whereas the female term is *marked* and often created by adding a bound morpheme or making a compound. We have many such examples in English:

Male	Female
heir	heir**ess**
major	major**ette**
hero	hero**ine**
Robert	Robert**a**
equestrian	equestri**enne**
aviator	avia**trix**
wolf	**she**wolf
scout	**Girl** Scout
cop	**lady** cop

When referring in general to the profession of acting, or flying, or riding horseback, the unmarked terms *actor, aviator,* and *equestrian* are used. The marked terms are used to emphasize the female gender. (Rare exceptions to this is the unmarked word *widow* for a woman with a deceased husband but *widow**er*** for a man with a deceased wife; and *escort* meaning a female prostitute but ***male** escort* for its gender opposite.)

The unmarked third person pronoun in English is male *(he, him, his)*. *Everybody had better pay **his** fee next time* allows for the clients to be male or female, but *Everybody had better pay **her** fee next time* presupposes a female client. Attempts to find a suitable genderless third person pronoun have included forms such as *e, hesh, po, tey, co, jhe, ve, xe, he'er, thon,* and *na,* none of which speakers have the least inclination to adopt. The use of the gender neutral pronoun *they,* as in *Every teenager loves their first car,* is close to becoming standard usage (except perhaps in your English class where you should probably stick to *he* and *she*).

With women occupying more and varied roles in society (from combat military to "Wichita Linemen"), many of the marked female forms have been replaced by the male forms, which are used to refer to either sex. Thus women, as well as men, are authors, actors, poets, heroes, heirs, postal carriers, firefighters, and police officers. Women, however, remain countesses, duchesses, and princesses, if they are among this small group of female aristocrats.

The Sapir–Whorf hypothesis, discussed in Chapter 1, proposes that the way a language encodes—puts into words—different categories like male and female subtly affects the way speakers of the language think about those categories. Thus, it may be argued that because English speakers are often taught to choose *he* as the unmarked pronoun *(Everyone should respect **himself**),* and to choose *she* only when the referent is specifically female, they tend to think of the male sex as predominant. Likewise, the fact that nouns require special affixes to make them feminine forces people to think in terms of male and female, with the female somehow more derivative because of affixing or compounding. The different titles, Mr., Mrs., Miss, and Ms., also emphasize the male/female distinction. Finally, the preponderance of words denigrating females in English and in many other languages may promote a climate that is more tolerant of sexist behavior.

Secret Languages and Language Games

Throughout the world and throughout history, people have invented secret languages and language games. They have used these special languages as a means of identifying with their group and/or to prevent outsiders from knowing what is being said. One such case is *Nushu,* the women's secret writing of Chinese, which originated in the third century as a means for women to communicate with one another in the sexually repressive societies of imperial China (see exercise 17, Chapter 12). American slaves developed an elaborate code that could not be understood by the slave owners. References to "the promised land" or the "flight of the Israelites from Egypt" sung in spirituals were codes for the North and the Underground Railroad.

Language games such as Pig Latin[2] and Ubbi Dubbi (see exercise 7) are used for amusement by children and adults. They exist in all the world's languages and take a wide variety of forms. In some, a suffix is added to each word; in others a syllable is inserted after each vowel. There are rhyming games and games in which phonemes are reversed. A game in Brazil substitutes an /i/ for all the vowels.

The Walbiri, natives of central Australia, play a language game in which the meanings of words are distorted. In this play language, all nouns, verbs, pronouns, and adjectives are replaced by semantically contrastive words. Thus, the sentence *Those men are small* means *This woman is big.*

These language games provide evidence for the phonemes, words, morphemes, semantic features, and so on that are posited by linguists for descriptive grammars. They also illustrate the boundless creativity of human language and human speakers.

Summary

Every person has a unique way of speaking, called an **idiolect**. The language used by a group of speakers is a **dialect**. The dialects of a language are the mutually intelligible forms of that language that differ in systematic ways from each other. Dialects develop because languages change, and the changes that occur in one group or area may differ from those that occur in another. **Regional dialects** and **social dialects** develop for this reason. Some differences in U.S. regional dialects may be traced to the dialects spoken by colonial settlers from England. Those from southern England spoke one dialect and those from the north spoke another. In addition, the colonists who maintained close contact with England reflected the changes occurring in British English, while earlier forms were preserved among Americans who spread westward and broke communication with the Atlantic coast. The study of regional dialects has produced **dialect atlases**, with **dialect maps** showing the areas where specific dialect characteristics occur in the speech of the region. A boundary line called an **isogloss** delineates each area.

Social dialects arise when groups are isolated socially, such as Americans of African descent in the United States, many of whom speak dialects collectively called African American (Vernacular) English, which are distinct from the dialects spoken by non-Africans.

Dialect differences include phonological or pronunciation differences (often called **accents**), vocabulary distinctions, and syntactic rule differences.

---

[2]Dog is pronounced *og-day,* parrot as *arrot-pay,* and elephant as *elephant-may,* etc., but see exercise 6.

The grammar differences among dialects are not as great as the similarities, thus permitting speakers of different dialects to communicate.

In many countries, one dialect or dialect group is viewed as the **standard**, such as **Standard American English (SAE)**. Although this particular dialect is not linguistically superior, some language purists consider it the only correct form of the language. Such a view has led to the idea that some non-standard dialects are deficient. Studies of minority dialects show them to be as logical, complete, rule-governed, and expressive as any other dialect. This is true of **African American English (AAE)** as well as the dialects spoken by Latino Americans whose native language or those of their parents is Spanish. There are bilingual and monolingual Latino speakers of English. One Latino dialect spoken in the Southwest, referred to as **Chicano English (ChE),** shows systematic phonological and syntactic differences from SAE that stem from the influence of Spanish. **Codeswitching** is shifting between languages within a single sentence or discourse by a bilingual speaker. It reflects both grammars working simultaneously and does not represent a form of "broken" English or Spanish or whatever language.

Attempts to legislate the use of a particular dialect or language have been made throughout history and exist today, even extending to banning the use of languages other than the preferred one.

In areas where many languages are spoken, one language may become a **lingua franca** to ease communication among people. In other cases, where traders, missionaries, or travelers need to communicate with people who speak a language unknown to them, a **pidgin** may develop. A pidgin is a simplified system with properties of both the **superstrate (lexifier)** and **substrate** languages. When a pidgin is widely used, and constitutes the primary linguistic input to children, it is *creolized*. The grammars of **creole** languages are similar to those of other languages, and languages of creole origin now exist in many parts of the world and include sign languages of the deaf.

The study of language has important implications for education especially as regards reading instruction and the teaching of second language learners, language-minority students, and speakers of nonstandard dialects. Several second-language teaching methods have been proposed for adult second language learners. Some of them focus more on the grammatical aspects of the target language, and others focus more on getting students to communicate in the target language, with less regard for grammatical accuracy.

Writing and reading, unlike speaking and understanding, must be taught. Three methods of teaching reading have been used in the United States: *whole-word, whole-language,* and *phonics*. In the whole-word and whole-language approaches, children are taught to recognize entire words without regard to individual letters and sounds. The phonics approach emphasizes the spelling-sound correspondences of the language, and thus draws on the child's phonological knowledge.

Immigrant children must acquire English (or whatever the majority language is in a particular country). Younger students must at the same time acquire literacy skills (reading and writing), and students of all ages must learn content material such as math and science. This is a formidable task. **Bilingual education** programs are designed to help achieve these multiple aims by teaching children literacy and content material in their native language while they are acquiring English. Research has shown that immigrant children benefit from instruction in their native language, but many people oppose these programs.

Children who speak a nonstandard dialect of English that differs from the language of instruction may also be at a disadvantage in a school setting, especially in learning reading and writing. There have been contentious debates over the use of AAE in the classroom as a method for helping speakers of that dialect learn Standard English.

Besides regional and social dialects, speakers may use different **styles**, or **registers**, depending on the context. **Slang** is not often used in formal situations or writing but is widely used in speech; **argot** and **jargon** refer to the unique vocabularies used by particular groups of people to facilitate communication, provide a means of bonding, and exclude outsiders.

In all societies, certain acts or behaviors are frowned on, forbidden, or considered **taboo**. The words or expressions referring to these taboo acts are then also avoided or considered "dirty." Language cannot be obscene or clean; attitudes toward specific words or linguistic expressions reflect the views of a culture or society toward the behaviors and actions of the language users. At times, slang words may be taboo while scientific or standard terms with the same meaning are acceptable in "polite society." Taboo words and acts give rise to **euphemisms**, which are words or phrases that replace the expressions to be avoided. Thus, *powder room* is a euphemism for *toilet*, which started as a euphemism for *lavatory*, which is now more acceptable than its replacement.

Just as the use of some words may indicate society's views toward sex, natural bodily functions, or religious beliefs, some words may also indicate racist, chauvinist, or sexist attitudes. Language is not intrinsically racist or sexist but reflects the views of various sectors of a society. However, the availability of offensive terms, and particular grammatical peculiarities such as the lack of a genderless third-person singular pronoun, may perpetuate and reinforce biased views and be demeaning and insulting to those addressed. Thus, culture influences language, and, arguably, language may have an influence on the culture in which it is spoken.

The invention or construction of secret languages and language games like Pig Latin attest to human creativity with language and the unconscious knowledge that speakers have of the phonological, morphological, and semantic rules of their language.

References for Further Reading

Carver, C. M. 1987. *American regional dialects: A word geography*. Ann Arbor, MI: University of Michigan Press.

Cassidy, F. G. (chief ed.). 1985, 1991, 1996, 2002, 2012. *Dictionary of American regional English*, Volumes 1, 2, 3, 4, 5. Cambridge, MA: Harvard University Press.

Chambers, J., and P. Trudgill. 1998. *Dialectology, 2nd ed*. Cambridge, UK: Cambridge University Press.

Holm, J. 2000. *An introduction to pidgins and creoles*.Cambridge, UK: Cambridge University Press.

Labov, W. 1972. *Sociolinguistic patterns*. Philadelphia: University of Pennsylvania Press.

_____. 1969. The logic of nonstandard English. *Georgetown University 20th Annual Round Table, Monograph Series on Languages and Linguistics,* No. 22.

_____. 1966. The social stratification of English in New York City. Washington, DC: Center for Applied Linguistics.

Lakoff, R. 1990. *Talking power: The politics of language.* New York: Basic Books.

Tannen, D. 1994. *Gender and discourse.* New York: Oxford University Press.

_____. 1990. *You just don't understand: Women and men in conversation.* New York: Ballantine.

Velupillai V. 2015. *Pidgins, Creoles and Mixed Languages: An Introduction.* Amsterdam, The Netherlands: John Benjamins Publishing Company

Wardhaugh, R. 2015. *An introduction to sociolinguistics, 7th ed.* London: Wiley-Blackwell Publishers.

Wolfram, W., and N. Schilling-Estes. 2006. *American English dialects and variation, 2nd ed.* London: Wiley-Blackwell Publishers.

Exercises

1. Each pair of words is pronounced as shown phonetically in at least one American English dialect. Write in phonetic transcription your pronunciation of each word that you pronounce differently.

   a. horse   [hɔrs]   hoarse   [hors]
   b. morning   [mɔrnĩŋ]   mourning   [mornĩŋ]
   c. for   [fɔr]   four   [for]
   d. ice   [ʌɪs]   eyes   [aɪz]
   e. knife   [nʌɪf]   knives   [naɪvz]
   f. mute   [mjut]   nude   [njud]
   g. din   [dĩn]   den   [dẽn]
   h. hog   [hɔg]   hot   [hat]
   i. marry   [mæri]   Mary   [meri]
   j. merry   [mɛri]   marry   [mæri]
   k. rot   [rat]   wrought   [rɔt]
   l. lease   [lis]   grease (v.)   [griz]
   m. what   [ʌat]   watt   [wat]
   n. ant   [æ̃nt]   aunt   [ãnt]
   o. creek   [kʰrɪk]   creak   [kʰrik]

2. **a.** Below is a passage from the Gospel according to St. Mark in Cameroon English Pidgin. See how much you can understand before consulting the English translation given below. State some of the similarities and differences between CEP and SAE.

   i. Di fos tok fo di gud nuus fo Jesus Christ God yi Pikin.
   ii. I bi sem as i di tok fo di buk fo Isaiah, God yi nchinda (Prophet), "Lukam, mi a di sen man nchinda fo bifo yoa fes weh yi go fix yoa rud fan."
   iii. Di vos fo som man di krai fo bush: "Fix di ples weh Papa God di go, mek yi rud tret."

Translation:

i. The beginning of the gospel of Jesus Christ, the Son of God.
ii. As it is written in the book of Isaiah the prophet, "Behold, I send my messenger before thy face, which shall prepare thy way before thee."
iii. The voice of one crying in the wilderness, "Prepare ye the way of the Lord, make his paths straight."

b. Here are some words from Tok Pisin. What are the English words from which they are derived? The answer is shown for the first entry.

Tok Pisin	Gloss	Answer
taim bilong kol	winter	time belong cold
pinga bilong fut	toe	
hamas krismas yu gat?	how old are you?	
kukim long paia	barbecue	
sapos	if	
haus moni	bank	
kamup	arrive	
tasol	only	
olgeta	all	
solwara	sea	
haus sik	hospital	
handet yia	century	

3. In the period from 1890 to 1904, *Slang and Its Analogues*, by J. S. Farmer and W. E. Henley, was published in seven volumes. The following entries are included in this dictionary. For each item (1) state whether the word or phrase still exists; (2) if not, state what the modern slang term would be; and (3) if the word remains but its meaning has changed, provide the modern meaning.

all out: completely, as in "All out the best" (The expression goes back to as early as 1300.)
to have apartments to let: be an idiot; one who is empty-headed
been there: in "Oh, yes, I've been there." (Applied to a man who is shrewd and who has had many experiences.)
belly-button: the navel
berkeleys: a woman's breasts
bitch: most offensive appellation that can be given to a woman, even more provoking than *whore*
once in a blue moon: seldom
boss: master; one who directs
bread: employment. (1785—"out of bread" = "out of work")
claim: to steal
cut dirt: to escape
dog cheap: of little worth (Used in 1616 by Dekker: "Three things there are dog-cheap, learning, poorman's sweat, and oathes.")

funeral: as in "It's not my funeral." "It's no business of mine."
to get over: to seduce, to fascinate
groovy: settled in habit; limited in mind
grub: food
head: toilet (nautical use only)
hook: to marry
hump: to spoil
hush money: money paid for silence; blackmail
itch: to be sexually excited
jam: a sweetheart or a mistress
leg bags: stockings
to lie low: to keep quiet; to bide one's time
to lift a leg on: to have sexual intercourse
looby: a fool
malady of France: syphilis (Used by Shakespeare in 1599.)
nix: nothing
noddle: the head
old: money (1900—"Perhaps it's somebody you owe a bit of the old to, Jack.")
to pill: talk platitudes
pipe layer: a political intriguer; a schemer
poky: cramped, stuffy, stupid
pot: a quart; a large sum; a prize; a urinal; to excel
puny: a freshman
puss-gentleman: an effeminate

4. Suppose someone asked you to help compile items for a new dictionary of slang. List ten slang words, and provide a short definition for each.

5. Below are some words used in British English for which different words are usually used in American English. See whether you can match the British and American equivalents.

British	American
a. clothes peg	candy
b. braces	truck
c. lift	line
d. pram	main street
e. waistcoat	crackers
f. shop assistant	suspenders
g. sweets	wrench
h. boot (of car)	flashlight
i. bobby	potato chips
j. spanner	vacation
k. biscuits	baby buggy
l. queue	elevator
m. torch	can
n. underground	cop
o. high street	wake up

	British	American
p.	crisps	trunk
q.	lorry	vest
r.	holiday	subway
s.	tin	clothes pin
t.	knock up	clerk

6. Pig Latin is a common language game of English; but even Pig Latin has dialects, forms of the "language game" with different rules.

   a. Consider the following data from three dialects of Pig Latin, each with its own rule applied to words beginning with vowels:

	Dialect 1	**Dialect 2**	**Dialect 3**
"eat"	[itme]	[ithe]	[itɛ]
"arc"	[arkme]	[arkhe]	[arke]
"expose"	[ɛkspozme]	[ɛkspozhe]	[ɛkspoze]

   i. State the rule that accounts for the Pig Latin forms in each dialect.

   ii. How would you say *honest, admire,* and *illegal* in each dialect? Give the phonetic transcription of the Pig Latin forms.

   b. In one dialect of Pig Latin, the word *strike* is pronounced [aɪkstre], and in another dialect it is pronounced [traɪkse]. In the first dialect *slot* is pronounced [atsle] and in the second dialect, it is pronounced [latse].

   i. State the rules for each of these dialects that account for these different Pig Latin forms of the same words.

   ii. Give the phonetic transcriptions for *spot, crisis,* and *scratch* in both dialects.

7. Below are some sentences representing different English language-games. Write each sentence in its undistorted form; state the language-game rule.

   a. /aɪ-o tʊk-o maɪ-o dag-o aʊt-o saɪd-o/

   b. /hirli ɪzli əli mɔrli kamlɪplɪlikelitədli gemli/

   c. Mary-shmary can-shman talk-shmalk in-shmin rhyme-shmyme.

   d. Betpeterer latepate thanpan nevpeverer.

   e. thop-e fop-oot bop-all stop-a dop-i op-um blop-ew dop-own/ðapə fapʊt bapɔl stape dapi apəm blapu dapaʊn/

   f. /kʌˈbæn jʌˈbu spʌˈbik ðʌˈbɪs kʌˈbaɪnd ʌˈbəv ʌˈbɪŋglʌˈbɪʃ/ (This sentence is in "Ubby Dubby" from a children's television program popular in the 1970s.)

8. Below are sentences that might be spoken between two friends chatting informally. For each, state what the nonabbreviated full sentence in SAE would be. In addition, state in your own words (or formally if you wish) the rule or rules that derived the informal sentences from the formal ones.

   a. Where've ya been today?

   b. Watcha gonna do for fun?

    c. Him go to church?

    d. There's four books there.

    e. Who ya wanna go with?

9. Compile a list of argot (or jargon) terms from some profession or trade (e.g., lawyer, musician, doctor, and longshoreman). Give a definition for each term in nonjargon terms.

10. "Translate" the first paragraph of any well-known document or speech— such as the Declaration of Independence, the Gettysburg Address, or the Preamble to the U.S. Constitution—into informal, colloquial language.

11. Cockney rhyming slang, which arose in the East End of London in the nineteenth century, is a language game played by creating a rhyme as a substitute for a specific word. Thus, for *table* the rhymed slang may be *Cain and Abel; missus* is *cows and kisses; stairs* are *apples and pears; head* is *loaf of bread,* and so on. Column A contains some Cockney rhyming slang expressions. Match these to the items in Column B to which they refer.

A	B
a. drip dry	balls (testicles)
b. in the mood	bread
c. insects and ants	ale
d. orchestra stalls	cry
e. Oxford scholar	food
f. strike me dead	dollar
g. ship in full sail	pants

    Now construct your own version of Cockney rhyming slang for the following words:

    h. chair

    i. house

    j. coat

    k. eggs

    l. pencil

12. Column A lists euphemisms for words in Column B. Match each item in A with its appropriate B word.

A	B
a. Montezuma's revenge	condom
b. joy stick	genocide
c. friggin'	fire
d. ethnic cleansing	diarrhea
e. French letter (old)	masturbate
f. diddle oneself	kill
g. holy of holies	urinate
h. spend a penny (British)	penis
i. ladies' cloak room	die
j. knock off (from 1919)	waging war

k. vertically challenged	vagina
l. hand in one's dinner pail	women's toilet
m. sanitation engineer	short
n. downsize	fuckin'
o. peace keeping	garbage collector

13. Defend or criticize the following statement in a short essay:

    A person who uses the word *niggardly* in a public hearing should be censured for being insensitive and using a word that resembles a degrading, racist word.

14. The words *waitron* and *waitperson* are currently fighting it out to see which, if either, will replace *waitress* as a gender-neutral term. Using dictionaries, the Internet, and whatever other resources you can think of, predict the winner or the failure of both candidates. Give reasons for your answers. If you count hits on Google, analyze the sources to support your conclusions. You may find Google Books Ngram Viewer useful as well.

15. Search for Tok Pisin on the Internet. You will quickly find Web sites where it is possible to hear Tok Pisin spoken. Listen to a passage several times. How much of it can you understand without looking at the text or the translation? Then follow along with the text (generally provided) until you can hear the individual words. Now try a new passage. Does your comprehension improve? How much practice do you think you would need before you could understand roughly half of what is being said the first time you heard it?

16. A popular language game is to take a word or (well-known) expression and alter it by adding, subtracting, or changing one letter, and supplying a new (clever) definition. Read the following examples, try to figure out the expressions from which they are derived, and then try to produce ten on your own. (Hint: Lots of Latin.)

Cogito eggo sum	I think, therefore I am a waffle.
Foreploy	A misrepresentation about yourself for the purpose of getting laid
Veni, vipi, vici	I came, I am important, I conquered.
Giraffiti	Dirty words sprayed very, very high
Ignoranus	A person who is both stupid and an asshole
Rigor Morris	The cat is dead (maybe for older students)
Felix navidad	Our cat has a boat.
Veni, vidi, vice	I came, I saw, I sold my sister.
Glibido	All talk, no action
Haste cuisine	Fast French food
L'état, c'est moo	I'm bossy around here.
Intaxication	The euphoria that accompanies a tax refund
Ex post fucto	Lost in the mail
Aporcalypse	A disastrous shortage of bacon

17. In his original, highly influential novel *1984*, George Orwell introduces Newspeak, a government-enforced language designed to keep the masses subjugated. He writes:

> Its vocabulary was so constructed as to give exact and often very subtle expression to every meaning that a Party member could properly wish to express, while excluding all other meanings and also the possibility of arriving at them by indirect methods. This was done partly by the invention of new words, but chiefly by eliminating undesirable words and by stripping such words as remained of unorthodox meanings, and so far as possible of all secondary meanings whatever. To give a single example, the word *free* still existed in Newspeak, but it could only be used in such statements as "This dog is free from lice" or "This field is free from weeds." It could not be used in its old sense of "politically free" or "intellectually free," since political and intellectual freedom no longer existed even as concepts, and were therefore of necessity nameless

Critique Newspeak. Will it achieve its goal? Why or why not? (Hint: You may want to review concepts such as language creativity and arbitrariness as discussed in the first few pages of Chapter 1.)

18. Write a thoughtful essay that grapples with one or more the following questions (review the discussion of the Sapir–Whorf hypothesis in Chapter 1):

Although people can undoubtedly be sexist, and even cultures can be sexist, can language be sexist?
Can language mold us into being something that we do not want to be?
Can language magnify any natural inclinations that we may have?
Can language be free of societal values?

19. One aspect of different English genderlects is lexical choice. For example, women say *darling* and *lovely* more frequently than men; men use sports metaphors such as *homerun* and *slam dunk* more than women. Think of other lexical usages that appear to be asymmetric between the sexes.

20. **Research project:** Throughout history many regimes have banned languages. Write a report in which you mention several such regimes, the languages they banned, and possible reasons for banning them (e.g., you might have discovered that the Basque language was banned in Spain under the regime of Francisco Franco (1936–1975) owing in part to the separatist desires of the Basque people and because the Basques opposed his dictatorship).

21. Abbreviated English (AE) is a register of written English used in newspaper headlines and elsewhere. Some examples follow:

CLINTON IN BULGARIA THIS WEEK
OLD MAN FINDS RARE COIN
BUSH HIRES WIFE AS SECRETARY
POPE DIES IN VATICAN

AE does not involve an arbitrary omission of parts of the sentence but is regulated by grammatical rules.

a. Translate each of these headlines into Standard American English (SAE).

b. What features or rules distinguish AE from SAE?

c. Are there other contexts (besides headlines) in which we find AE? If so, provide examples.

d. **Challenge exercise:** What is the time reference of the above headlines (e.g., present, recent past, remote past, and future)?

e. **Challenge exercise:** Is there a difference in possible tense interpretations when the predicate is eventive (e.g., *dies*) and when it is stative (e.g., *in Bulgaria*)? (You may have to review these terms in Chapter 4.)

22. Watch several hours of reality TV on television. Write down any euphemisms you think you hear and the taboo subjects they conceal. And yes, if anybody rags on you for wasting your life on reality shows, tell them it's part of a school assignment.

23. You overhear somebody say, "That's not a language, it's a dialect." Compose a brief retort.

24. Recommend three ways in which society can act to preserve linguistic diversity. Be realistic and concrete.

25. Research the history and controversy surrounding the use of "Ebonics" (African American English) in the classroom. The Internet is a good place to start. Consider both sides of the argument and discuss whether you think this is a good idea and why or why not.

26. The Karen-speaking people of Myanmar claim that their languages (dialects?)—thought to be a Tibeto-Burman group of the Sino-Tibetan family of languages—are banned by the government of Myanmar (as of the year 2012). Research the assertion of this ethnic minority that their language is outlawed and offer evidence regarding the validity of this claim or its falsehood.

27. Quoting again from the script of the movie *Pygmalion*, critique the following lines spoken by Professor Henry Higgins:

> "The English do not know how to speak their own language. Only foreigners who have been taught to speak it speak it well."

8

Language Change: The Syllables of Time

> No language as depending on arbitrary use and custom can ever be permanently the same, but will always be in a mutable and fluctuating state; and what is deem'd polite and elegant in one age, may be accounted uncouth and barbarous in another.

BENJAMIN MARTIN (1704–1782)

All living languages change with time. It is fortunate that they do so rather slowly compared to the human life span. It would be inconvenient to have to relearn our native language every twenty years. As years pass, we hardly notice any change. Yet, if we were to turn on a radio and miraculously receive a broadcast in our "native language" from the year 1000, we would probably think we had tuned into a foreign language station.

Bereft of spoken recordings, we must consult written records to achieve a sense of language change. We know a great deal of the history of English because it has been a written language for more than one thousand three-hundred years. Old English, spoken in England during the first millennium, is scarcely recognizable as English. (Of course, our linguistic ancestors did not call their language Old English!) A speaker of Modern English would find the language unintelligible. There are college courses in which Old English is studied as a foreign language.

A line from *Beowulf* illustrates why Old English must be translated:[1]

Wolde guman findan þone þe him on sweofote sare geteode.
"He wanted to find the man who harmed him while he slept."

---

[1]The letter þ is called *thorn* and is pronounced [θ] in this example.

Approximately five hundred years after *Beowulf*, Chaucer wrote *The Canterbury Tales* in what is now called Middle English, spoken from around 1100 to 1500. It is more easily understood by present-day readers, as seen by reading the opening of the *Tales*:

Whan that Aprille with his shoures soote
The droght of March hath perced to the roote . . .
"When April with its sweet showers
The drought of March has pierced to the root . . ."

Two hundred years after Chaucer, in a language that is considered an early form of Modern English, Shakespeare's Hamlet says:

A man may fish with the worm that hath eat of a king, and eat of the fish that hath fed of that worm.

The stages of English are Old English (449–1100 CE), Middle English (1100–1500), and Modern English (1500–present). This division is somewhat arbitrary, being marked by important dates in English history, such as the Norman Conquest of 1066, the results of which profoundly influenced the English language.

The branch of linguistics that deals with how languages change, what kinds of changes occur, and why they occurred is called **historical and comparative linguistics**. It is "historical" because it deals with the history of particular languages; it is "comparative" because it deals with relations among languages.

Changes in a language are changes in the grammar and lexicon of speakers and are carried forward as new generations of children acquire the altered grammars. All components of the grammar are subject to change over the course of time. Although most of the examples in this chapter are from English, all languages change over time. This is true of sign languages, too, which change in ways similar to spoken languages.

The Regularity of Sound Change

That's not a regular rule: you invented it just now.

LEWIS CARROLL, *Alice's Adventures in Wonderland*, 1865

The southern United States represents a major dialect area of American English. For example, words pronounced with the diphthong [aɪ] in non-Southern English will usually be pronounced with the monophthong [aː] in the South. Local radio and TV announcers at the 1996 Olympics in Atlanta called athletes to the [haː] "high" jump, and local natives invited visitors to try Georgia's famous pecan [paː] "pie." The [aɪ]-[aː] correspondence of these two dialects is an example of a **regular sound correspondence**. When [aɪ] occurs in a word in non-Southern dialects, [aː] occurs in the Southern dialect, and *this is true for all such words*.

The different pronunciations of *I, my, high, pie,* and so on did not always exist in English. In this chapter, we will discuss how such dialect differences arose and why the sound differences are usually regular and not confined to just a few words. We will also consider changes that occur in other parts of the grammar and in the lexicon.

Sound Correspondences

In Middle English a *mouse* [maʊs] was called a *mūs* [mu:s], and this *mūs* may have lived in someone's *hūs* [hu:s], as *house* was pronounced at that time. In general, Middle English speakers pronounced [u:] where we now pronounce [aʊ]. This is a regular correspondence like the one between [aɪ] and [a:]. Thus *out* [aʊt] was pronounced [u:t], *south* [saʊθ] was pronounced [su:θ], and so on. Many such regular correspondences show the relation of older and newer forms of English, just as they show the relation of different regional pronunciations of current forms of English.

The regular sound correspondences we observe are the result of phonological changes that affect certain sounds, or classes of sounds, rather than individual words. Centuries ago English underwent a phonological change called a **sound shift** in which [u:] became [aʊ].

Phonological changes can also account for dialect or regional differences. At an earlier stage of American English a sound shift of [aɪ] to [a:] took place among certain speakers in the southern region of the United States. The change did not spread beyond the South because the region was somewhat isolated. Many pronunciation differences among dialects result from sound shifts whose spread is limited.

Regional dialect differences may also arise when innovative changes occur everywhere but in a particular region. One regional dialect may be conservative relative to others. The pronunciation of *it* as *hit*, found in the Appalachian region of the United States, was standard in older forms of English. The dropping of the [h] was the innovation that affected many other dialects.

Ancestral Protolanguages

The living languages, as they were called by the Harvard fellows, were little more than cheap imitations, low distortions. Italian, like Spanish and German, particularly represented the loose political passions, bodily appetites, and absent morals of decadent Europe.

MATTHEW PEARL, *The Dante Club*, 2003

Many modern languages developed from regional dialects that became widely spoken and highly differentiated, finally becoming separate languages. The Romance languages—French, Spanish, Italian, and so on—were once dialects of Latin spoken in the Roman Empire. There is nothing degenerate about regional pronunciations. They are the result of natural sound changes that occur wherever human language is spoken.

In a sense, the Romance languages are the offspring of Latin, their metaphorical parent. Because of their common ancestry, the Romance languages are **genetically related**. Early forms of English and German, too, were once dialects of a common ancestor called **Proto-Germanic**. A **protolanguage** is the ancestral language from which related languages have developed. Both Latin and Proto-Germanic were descendants of an older language called **Indo-European** or **Proto-Indo-European**.

Protolanguages are not actually attested languages, but are hypothesized by linguists to explain the relationships between existing languages. Thus, Germanic languages such as English and German are genetically related to the Romance languages such as French and Spanish. All these national languages were once regional dialects. Proto-Indo-European explains these genetic relationships.

How do we know that the Germanic and Romance languages have a common ancestor? One clue is the large number of sound correspondences. If you have studied a Romance language such as French or Spanish, you may have noticed that where an English word begins with *f*, the corresponding word in a Romance language often begins with *p*, as shown in the following examples:

English /f/	French /p/	Spanish /p/	Italian /p/
father	père	padre	padre
fish	poisson	pescado	pesce

This /f/-/p/ correspondence is just one example of many such regular sound correspondences between the Germanic and Romance languages, and their prevalence cannot be explained by chance. What then accounts for them? A reasonable guess is that a common ancestor language used a *p* in words for *fish, father,* and so on. We posit a /p/ rather than an /f/ because more languages show a /p/ in these words.

At some point speakers of this language separated into two groups that lost contact with each other. In one of the groups a sound change of *p* → *f* took place. The language spoken by this group eventually became the ancestor of the Germanic languages. This ancient sound change left its trace in the *f-p* sound correspondence that we observe today, as illustrated in the diagram.

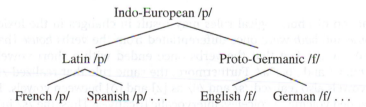

Phonological Change

Etymologists . . . for whom vowels did not matter and who cared not a jot for consonants.

VOLTAIRE (1694–1778)

Regular sound correspondences illustrate changes in the phonological system of a language. In earlier chapters, we discussed speakers' knowledge of phonology, including knowledge of the phonemes and phonological rules of the language. Both aspects of the phonology are subject to change.

The velar fricative /x/ is no longer part of the phonemic inventory of most Modern English dialects. *Night* used to be pronounced [nɪxt] and *drought* was pronounced [druxt]. This phonological change—the loss of /x/—took place between the times of Chaucer and Shakespeare. All words that were once pronounced with an /x/ no longer include this sound. In some cases, it disappeared altogether, as in *night* and *light*. In other cases, the /x/ became a /k/, as in *elk* (Old English *eolh* [ɛɔlx]). In yet other cases, it disappeared to be replaced by a vowel, as in *hollow* (Old English *holh* [hɔlx]). Dialects of Modern English spoken in Scotland have retained the /x/ sound in some words, such as *loch* [lɔx] meaning "lake."

These examples show that languages can lose phonemes over time. They can also add phonemes. Old English did not have the phoneme /ʒ/ of *leisure* [liʒər]. Through a process of palatalization—a change in place of articulation to the palatal region—certain occurrences of /z/ were pronounced [ʒ]. Eventually the [ʒ] sound became a phoneme in its own right. Similarly, occurrences of /f/ between vowels were once pronounced [v], which eventually became the additional phoneme /v/.

Similar changes occur in the history of all languages. Neither /tʃ/ nor /ʃ/ were phonemes of Latin, but /tʃ/ is a phoneme of modern Italian and /ʃ/ a phoneme of modern French, both of which descended from Latin. In American Sign Language, many signs that were originally formed at the waist or chest level are now produced at a higher level near the neck or upper chest, a reflection of changes in the "phonology."

Phonological Rules

It's a good idea to obey all the rules when you're young just so you'll have the strength to break them when you're old.

MARK TWAIN (1835–1910)

An interaction of phonological rules may result in changes in the lexicon. The nouns *house* and *bath* were once differentiated from the verbs *house* [haʊz] and *bathe* [beð] by the fact that the verbs once ended with a short vowel sound, namely /hu:sə/ and /ba:θə/. Furthermore, the same rule that realized /f/ as [v] between vowels also realized /s/ and /θ/ as [z] and [ð] between vowels. This general rule added voicing to voiceless intervocalic fricatives. Thus, the /s/ in the verb /hu:sə/ was pronounced [z], and the /θ/ in the verb /ba:θə/ was pronounced [ð].

Later, a rule was added to the grammar of English deleting unstressed short vowels at the end of words (even though the final vowel still appears in the written words). A contrast between the voiced and voiceless fricatives resulted, and new phonemes /z/ and /ð/ were added to the phonemic inventory. The verbs *house* [haʊz] and *bathe* [beð] were now represented in the mental lexicon with final voiced consonants.

Eventually, both the unstressed vowel deletion rule and the intervocalic-voicing rule were lost from the grammar of English. The set of phonological rules can change both by addition and by loss of rules.

Changes in phonological rules can, and often do, result in dialect differences. In the previous chapter, we discussed the addition of an *r*-dropping rule in

English (/r/ is not pronounced unless followed by a vowel) that did not spread throughout the language. Today, we see the effect of that rule in the *r*-less pronunciation of British English, and of American English dialects spoken in the northeastern and the southern United States.

From the standpoint of the language as a whole, phonological changes occur gradually over the course of many generations of speakers, although any given speaker's grammar may or may not reflect the change. The changes are not planned any more than we are presently planning what changes will take place in English by the year 2300. In a single generation, changes are evident only through dialect differences.

The Great Vowel Shift

Between 1400 and 1600 a major change took place in English that resulted in new phonemic representations of words and morphemes. This phonological restructuring is known as the **Great Vowel Shift**. The seven long, or tense, vowels of Middle English underwent the following change:

Shift		Example		
Middle English	**Modern English**	**Middle English**	**Modern English**	
[iː] →	[aɪ]	[miːs] →	[maɪs]	mice
[uː] →	[aʊ]	[muːs] →	[maʊs]	mouse
[eː] →	[iː]	[geːs] →	[giːs]	geese
[oː] →	[uː]	[goːs] →	[guːs]	goose
[ɛː] →	[eː]	[brɛːken] →	[breːk]	break
[ɔː] →	[oː]	[brɔːken] →	[broːk]	broke
[aː] →	[eː]	[naːmə] →	[neːm]	name

By diagramming the Great Vowel Shift on a vowel chart (Figure 8.1), we can see that the high vowels [iː] and [uː] became the diphthongs [aɪ] and [aʊ], while the long vowels underwent an increase in tongue height, as if to fill in the space vacated by the high vowels. In addition, [aː] was fronted to become [eː].

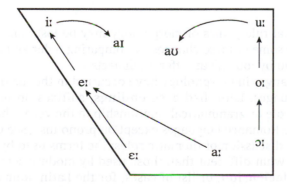

FIGURE 8.1 | The Great Vowel Shift.

TABLE 8.1 | Effect of Vowel Shift on Modern English

Middle English Vowel	Shifted Vowel	Short Vowel	Word with Shifted Vowel	Word with Short Vowel
ī	aɪ	ɪ	divine	divinity
ū	aʊ	ʌ	abound	abundant
ē	i	ɛ	serene	serenity
ō	u	a	fool	folly
ā	e	æ	sane	sanity

These changes are among the most dramatic examples of regular sound shift. The phonemic representation of many thousands of words changed. Today, some reflection of this vowel shift is seen in the alternating forms of morphemes in English: *please—pleasant, serene—serenity; sane—sanity; crime—criminal; sign—signal;* and so on. Before the Great Vowel Shift, the vowels in each pair were pronounced the same. Then the vowels in the second word of each pair were shortened by the **Early Middle English Vowel Shortening** rule. As a result, the Great Vowel Shift, which occurred later and applied only to long vowels, affected only the first word in each pair. This is why the vowels in the morphologically related words are pronounced differently today, as shown in Table 8.1.

Many spelling inconsistencies of English are due to the Great Vowel Shift because our spelling system still reflects the way words were pronounced before it occurred. In general, the written language changes more slowly than the spoken language.

Morphological Change

And is he well content his son should find

No nourishment to feed his growing mind,

But conjugated verbs and nouns declin'd?

WILLIAM COWPER "Tirocinium," 1785

Like phonological rules, rules of morphology may be lost, added, or changed. We can observe some of these changes by comparing older and newer forms of the language and by looking at different dialects.

Extensive changes in morphology have occurred in the history of the Indo-European languages. Latin had **case endings**, suffixes on nouns based on their thematic role or grammatical relationship to the verb. These are no longer found in the Romance languages except on pronouns. (See Chapter 4 for a more extensive discussion of thematic roles; the terms used by historical linguists are somewhat different than those used by modern semanticists.) The following is a **declension**, or list of cases, for the Latin noun *lupus,* "wolf":

Noun	Noun Stem		Case Ending	Case	Example
lupus	lup	+	us	nominative	The *wolf* runs.
lupī	lup	+	ī	genitive	A sheep in *wolf's* clothing.
lupō	lup	+	ō	dative	Give food *to the wolf*.
lupum	lup	+	um	accusative	I love *the wolf*.
lupō	lup	+	ō	ablative	She walked *with the wolf*.
lupe	lup	+	e	vocative	*Wolf,* come here!

In *Alice's Adventures in Wonderland,* Lewis Carroll has Alice give us a brief lesson in grammatical case. Alice has become very small and is swimming around in a pool of her own tears with a mouse that she wishes to befriend:

> "Would it be of any use, now," thought Alice, "to speak to this mouse? Everything is so out-of-the-way down here, that I should think very likely it can talk: at any rate, there's no harm in trying." So she began: "O Mouse, do you know the way out of this pool? I am very tired of swimming about here, O Mouse!" (Alice thought this must be the right way of speaking to a mouse: she had never done such a thing before, but she remembered having seen in her brother's Latin Grammar, "A mouse-of a mouse-to a mouse-a mouse-O mouse!")

Alice's examples are the English equivalents of the nominative, genitive, dative, accusative, and vocative cases, which existed in Latin and in Old English but not in Modern English, where word order and prepositions convey the same information.

Ancient Greek and Sanskrit also had extensive case systems expressed through noun suffixing, as did Old English, as illustrated by the following noun forms:

Case	OE Singular		OE Plural	
nominative	stān	"stone"	stānas	"stones"
genitive	stānes	"stone's"	stāna	"stones'"
dative	stāne	"stone"	stānum	"stones"
accusative	stān	"stone"	stānas	"stones"

Lithuanian and Russian retain much of the early Indo-European case system, but it is nearly obliterated in most modern Indo-European languages.

English retains traces of the genitive case, which is written with an apostrophe *s*, as in *Robert's dog,* but nothing more remains as far as possessives are concerned. Pronouns retain a few more case distinctions: *he/she* are nominative, *him/her* accusative and dative, and *his/hers* genitive. And of course English (barely) retains the *who/whom* distinction, much beloved by English teachers, reflecting nominative and non-nominative cases. English has replaced its depleted case system with an equally expressive system of prepositions, as shown in Alice's examples. For example, the dative case is often indicated by the preposition *to,* the genitive case by the preposition *of,* and the accusative case by the word order verb-noun phrase (V NP) with no intervening preposition.

Syntactic Change

Understanding changes in grammar is a key component in understanding changes in language.

DAVID LIGHTFOOT, *The Development of Language*, 1999

When we see a word-for-word translation of older forms of English, we are most struck by the differences in word order. Consider again the opening lines of *The Canterbury Tales*, this time translated word-for-word:

Whan that Aprille with his shoures soote
"When that April with its showers sweet"
The droght of March hath perced to the roote . . .
"The drought of March has pierced to the root . . ."

In Modern English, adjectives generally precede the nouns they modify. Thus, we would say *sweet showers* in place of *showers sweet*. Moreover, a direct object now generally follows its verb, so *has pierced the drought of March to the root* would be a modern rendering of the second line. Thus, the rules of syntax that govern these word orders, even taking "poetic license" into account, appear to have changed. It is safe to say that syntactic change in English and other languages is most evident in the changes of permitted word orders.

Syntactic change in English is a good illustration of the interrelationship of the various parts of the grammar. Changes in syntax were often influenced by changes in morphology, and these in turn by changes in the phonology of the language. And conversely, there is evidence that changes in syntax may very well have precipitated changes in the other two systems. These interrelations between the different components of grammar are complex. It is not always easy for historical linguists to determine which part of the grammar affected which other part and when. As in nearly all subfields of linguistics, much more research is needed to solve the many outstanding questions.

When the rich system of case endings of Old English became simplified, due in part to phonological changes and in part to syntactic changes that were underway, speakers of English were forced to rely more heavily on word order to convey the function of noun phrases. A sentence such as

sē	man	þone	kyning	sloh
"the (nominative)	man	the (accusative)	king	slew"

was understood to mean "the man slew the king." Because of the case of the noun phrases, there would have been no confusion as to who did what to whom.

In addition, in earlier stages of English the verb had a richer system of subject–verb agreement. For example, the verb *to sing* had the following forms: *singe* (I sing), *singest* (you sing), *singeth* (he sings), and *singen* (we, plural you, they sing). It was therefore possible to identify the subject on the basis of verb inflection even if it was not apparent from word order, which was already evolving from the subject–object–verb (SOV) word order of the example to the now more usual subject–verb–object (SVO).

In Modern English, *the man the king slew* is only grammatical as a relative clause meaning "the man that the king slew," with the subject and object of *slew* reversed. To convey the meaning "the man slew the king," Modern English speakers *must* rely on word order—subject–verb–object—or other syntactic devices such as the ones that generate sentences like *It was the king that the man slew*.

The change in English word order reflects a change in grammatical structure. In Old English, the verb came last in the basic verb phrase as it does today in Dutch and German. But English alone underwent a change that made the verb come first in the verb phrase. As a result, Modern English has a basic SVO word order whereas Old English (and modern Dutch and German) have a basic SOV word order.

However, Modern English still has remnants of the original SOV word order in "old-fashioned" kinds of expressions such as *I thee wed*. Word order and morphological distinctions, dancing as partners through time, affected each other: word order became more rigid at the same time that morphological distinctions were vanishing.

As discussed in Chapter 3, in Modern English we form questions by moving an auxiliary verb, if there is one, before the NP subject:

Can the girl kiss the boy?
Will the girl kiss the boy?
Has the girl kissed the boy yet?
Was the girl kissing the boy when you arrived?

However, if an auxiliary verb is absent, Modern English requires the word *do* to spell out the tense of the sentence:

Does the girl kiss the boy often?
*Kisses the girl the boy often?

Older forms of English had a more general rule that moved the first verbal element, which meant that if no auxiliary occurred in the sentence, then the main verb moved. The question

Kisses the girl the boy often?

was grammatical in English through the time of Shakespeare (e.g., *Goes Fleance with you?*, Macbeth, III, 1). This more general verb movement rule still exists in languages such as Dutch and German. In English, however, the rule of question formation changed, as indicated above: now only auxiliary verbs move and if no auxiliary verb is present, a *do* fills its role. This rule change interacted with the English case system. In Old English, *the girl* and *the boy* would have been marked for case, so there was no confusion over who was kissing whom. In effect, the sentence would be:

Kisses the (nominative) girl the (accusative) boy often?

Old English provides another example of how syntax influences morphology with its case endings on nouns that follow prepositions. In Old English, certain prepositions "governed" certain cases:

Old English	Modern English
in þæt hūs (accusative, singular)	"into that house"
fram þæm hūse (dative, singular)	"from that house"
til þæs hūses (genitive, singular)	"up to/as far as that house"

Since the meaning was already conveyed by the preposition, the case endings on *that* and *house* became redundant and therefore, over generations, no longer were pronounced.

Another syntactic change in English affected the rules of comparative and superlative constructions. Today we form the comparative by adding *-er* to the adjective or by inserting *more* before it; the superlative is formed by adding *-est* or by inserting *most*. In Malory's *Tales of King Arthur,* written in 1470, double comparatives and double superlatives occur, which today are ungrammatical: *more gladder, more lower, moost royallest,* and *moost shamefullest.*

Here is another interesting little change in syntactic rules. Both Old English and Middle English permitted split genitives, that is, possessive constructs in which the words that describe the possessor occur on both sides of the head noun:

Inwæres   broþur   ond   Healfdenes (Old English)
"Inwær's   brother   and   Healfden's"
"Inwær's and Healfden's brother"

The Wife's tale of Bath (Middle English)
"The Wife of Bath's tale"

Modern English does not allow such structures, but English does permit rather complex genitive expressions to precede the head noun:

The man with the two small children's hat
The girl whose sister I'm dating's roommate
When does you guys's party begin? (Cf. When does your (pl.) party begin?)

Because they do not occur in written records, we can infer that expressions like *the Queen of England's crown* were ungrammatical in earlier periods of English. The title *The Wife's Tale of Bath* (rather than *The Wife of Bath's Tale*) in *The Canterbury Tales* supports this inference.

Modern Brazilian Portuguese (BP) may illustrate a syntactic change in progress. Until the middle of the nineteenth century, speakers of BP didn't need to explicitly mention a subject pronoun because that information came from the person and number agreement on the verb, as illustrated for the verb *cozinhar* meaning 'to cook."

cozinho	"I cook"	cozinhamos	"we cook"
cozinhas	"you cook"		
cozinha	"he/she cooks"	cozinham	"they/you (pl.) cook"

At that time speakers dropped subjects in about 80 percent of their sentences, as in the second sentence of the following example:

A	Clara	sabe	fazer	tudo	muito	bem.
the	Clara	knows how	to do	everything	very	well

Cozinha	que	é	uma	maravilha.
cooks (3rd per.)	that	is	a	marvel

"Clara knows how to do everything well. She cooks wonderfully."

By the end of the twentieth century, subject-drop was reduced to 20 percent and the agreement endings were also reduced. In certain dialects only a two-way distinction is maintained: first-person singular is marked with -o, as in *cozinho*, and all other grammatical persons are marked with -*a*. While sentences without subjects are still grammatical in European Portuguese (spoken in Portugal), they are ungrammatical for most speakers of Modern BP, which requires the expression of an overt subject, for example *ela*, "she," as follows:

A Clara sabe fazer tudo muito bem. Ela cozinha que é uma maravilha.

Lexical Change

appletini – chocotini – crantini – flirtini – frostini – mintatini – mochatini – peachatini

A SELECTION OF MARTINI VARIANTS FROM THE MENU OF A "MARTINI BAR"

Changes in the lexicon also occur, among which are changes in the syntactic categories of words (i.e., their "parts of speech"), addition of new words, the "borrowing" of words from other languages, the loss of words, the shift in the meanings of words over time, and even the faux back formations (see Chapter 2) that create new bound morphemes such as –*tini* noted above (and, by the way, if you are a teetotaler you can always order a virgintini).

Change in Category

The words *food* and *verb* are ordinarily used as nouns, but Bucky the cat refuses to be so restricted and "wordifies" them into verbs. If we speakers of English adopt Bucky's usage, then *food* and *verb* will become verbs in addition to nouns.

Recently, a radio announcer said that Congress was *to-ing and fro-ing* on a certain issue, to mean "wavering." This strange compound verb is derived from the adverb *to and fro*. Now when we search on the Internet, we *google*, a verb derived from the company name *Google*. American police *Mirandize* arrested persons, meaning "read them their rights according to the Miranda rule." The judicial ruling was made in 1966, so we have a complete history of how a proper name became a verb. More recently the noun *text* has been "verbed" and means "to communicate by text message," and even more recent is the hijacking of the verb *twitter* and "Proper Noun-ing" it as the name of a social networking and micro-blogging service.

Addition of New Words

And to bring in a new word by the head and shoulders, they leave out the old one.

MONTAIGNE (1533–1592)

One of the most obvious ways a language changes is through the addition of new words. Unlike grammatical change, which may take generations to notice, new words are readily apparent. Societies often require new words to describe changes in technology, sports, entertainment, and so on. Languages are accommodating and inventive in meeting these needs.

In Chapter 2, we discussed some ways in which new words are born, such as through derivational processes, back-formations, and compounding. There are other ways that words may enter the vocabulary of a language. These include out-and-out word coinage, deriving words from names, blending words to form new words, shortening old words to form new ones, creating acronyms and borrowing words from other languages.

Word Coinage

Words may be created outright to fit some purpose. The advertising industry has added many words to English, such as *Kodak, nylon, Orlon*, and *Dacron*. Specific brand names such as *Xerox, Band-Aid, Kleenex, Jell-O, Brillo*, and *Vaseline* are now sometimes used as the generic names for different brands of these types of products. Some of these words were actually created from existing words (e.g., *Kleenex* from the word *clean* and *Jell-O* from *gel*).

The sciences have given us a raft of newly coined words over the ages. Words such as *asteroid, neutron, genome, krypton, pterodactyl*, and *vaccine* were created to describe the objects or processes arising from scientific investigation.

A word so (relatively) new that its spelling is still in doubt is *dot-com*, also seen in magazines as *.com, dot.com*, and even *dot com* without the hyphen. It means "a company whose primary business centers on the Internet."

Greek roots borrowed into English have also provided a means for coining new words. *Thermos*, "hot," plus *metron*, "measure," gave us *thermometer*. If you have an intense and all-consuming horror of cats you have *ailurophobia* from *aílouros* "cat" and *phóbos* "fear."

Latin, like Greek, has also provided prefixes and suffixes that are used productively with both native and nonnative roots. The prefix *ex-* comes from Latin:

ex-husband   ex-wife   ex-sister-in-law   ex-teacher

The suffix *-able/-ible* is also Latin and can be attached to almost any English verb:

writable   readable   answerable   movable   learnable

Even new bound morphemes may enter the language. The prefix *e-*, as in *e-commerce*, *e-mail*, and *e-trade*, meaning "electronic," is barely two decades old, and most interestingly has given rise to the prefix *s-* as in *s-mail* to contrast with *e-mail*. The suffix *-gate*, meaning "scandal," which was derived from the Watergate scandal of the 1970s, may now be suffixed to a word to convey that meaning. Thus, *Dianagate*, a British usage, refers to a scandal involving wire-tapped conversations of the then Princess of Wales, and *Qatar-gate*, a reference to unethical practices in the awarding of the soccer (football) world cup locale in 2022.

Finally, there are occasions when signers need to represent a word or concept for which there is no sign. For such cases, ASL may conceive a series of new hand shapes and movements, but absent this possibility, letters of the English alphabet may be expressed through *finger spelling* to convey any meaning that might be written.

Words from Names

Eponyms are words that are coined from proper names and are another way that the vocabulary of a language expands. For example, our favorite lunch food was named for the fourth Earl of *Sandwich*, who put his food between two slices of bread so that he could eat while he gambled. And the favorite material of our work clothes is *denim*, named for a kind of cloth originally imported *de Nîmes* ("from Nîmes") a city in France. If you like olives, be sure and get the *jumbo* size, the name of an elephant brought to the United States for a circus. ("Jumbo olives" need not be as big as an elephant, however.)

Blends

Blends are similar to compounds in that they are produced by combining two words, but in blends parts of the words that are combined are deleted. *Smog*, from *smoke* + *fog*; *brunch*, from *breakfast* and *lunch*; *motel*, from *motor* + *hotel*; *infomercial*, from *info* + *commercial*; and *urinalysis*, from *urine* + *analysis* are examples of blends that have attained full lexical status in English. *Podcast* (*podcasting, podcaster*) is a relatively new word meaning "Internet audio broadcast" and recently joined the English language as a blend of *iPod* and *broadcast*. Some more recent blends that are younger than most of our readers include *bromance* (a blend of "brother" and "romance" meaning a nonsexual relationship between two men), *locavore* (someone who eats locally sourced foods), *frenemy* (an enemy who pretends to be a friend), *staycation* (a vacation at home), *chillax* (be calm and relaxed), and *sexting* (sending text messages with sexual content).

Lewis Carroll's *chortle,* from *chuckle* + *snort,* has achieved limited acceptance in English. Carroll is famous for both coining and blending words. In *Through the Looking-Glass,* he describes the "meanings" of the made-up words in "Jabberwocky" as follows:

> "Brillig" means four o'clock in the afternoon—the time when you begin broiling things for dinner . . . "Slithy" means "lithe and slimy" . . . You see it's like a portmanteau—there are two meanings packed up into one word. . . . "Toves" are something like badgers—they're something like lizards—and they're something like corkscrews . . . also they make their nests under sun-dials—also they live on cheese. . . . To "gyre" is to go round and round like a gyroscope. To "gimble" is to make holes like a gimlet. And "the wabe" is the grass-plot round a sun-dial . . . It's called "wabe" . . . because it goes a long way before it and a long way behind it. . . . "Mimsy" is "flimsy and miserable" (there's another portmanteau . . . for you).

Carroll's "portmanteaus" are what we have called blends, and such words can become part of the regular lexicon.

Reduced Words

> This perpetual Disposition to shorten our Words, by retrenching the Vowels, is nothing else but a tendency to lapse into the Barbarity of those Northern Nations from whom we are descended, and whose Languages labour all under the same Defect.
>
> JONATHAN SWIFT, *A Proposal for Correcting, Improving and Ascertaining the English Tongue,* 1712

Speakers tend to abbreviate words in various ways to shorten the messages they convey. Texting has turned this skill into a national pastime. However, we will concern ourselves with *spoken* language and observe three reduction phenomena: *clipping, acronyms,* and *alphabetic abbreviations.*

Clipping is the abbreviation of longer words into shorter ones by leaving out one or more syllables such as *fax* for *facsimile,* the British word *telly* for *television, flu* for *influenza, porn* for *pornography,* and *droid* for *android.* Once marginalized as slang, and despite Jonathan Swift's contempt, many of these words have over time become lexicalized, that is, bona fide members of the English vocabulary. Clippings may clip the beginning of a word (*phone* for *telephone*), the end of a word (*auto* for *automobile*), or both ends (*fridge* for *refrigerator*).

There are two possible semantic outcomes of clipping. The most common by far is that the clipped word has the same meaning as its source. All of the examples in the previous paragraph are of that ilk. In a minority of instances, the clipped word takes on a different meaning. *Fan, van,* and *rad* are clipped from *fanatic, caravan,* and *radical,* but fans are not (generally) fanatics except at English football matches. Van is a single vehicle not a cavalcade, and something that is rad is marvelous though not necessarily radical. The use of *droid* to mean a certain kind of smartphone (itself a recent word) has a different meaning than *android,* though the use of the word is intended to convey robotic intelligence.

Clippings continue to come into existence. *Dis,* once rapper slang for *disrespect,* is gaining acceptance with the meaning "show contempt for." *Blog* (from *weblog*, another new word!) is perhaps the most successful clip of the current millennium, being today both a noun and a verb with all the related morphology (*blogs, blogging, blogged, blogger*, etc.; see Exercise 4f.)

Acronyms are words derived from the initials of several words. Such words are pronounced as the spelling indicates: *Radar* from *radio detecting and ranging, laser* from *light amplification* by *stimulated emission of radiation, scuba* from *self*-contained underwater breathing *apparatus* and *AIDS* from *acquired immunity deficiency syndrome* are beacons to the creative aspect of language.

When the string of letters is not easily pronounced as a word, the "acronym" becomes an **alphabetic abbreviation**, produced by sounding out each letter, as in *NFL* for *National Football League, UCLA* for *University of California at Los Angeles*, and *MRI* for *magnetic resonance imaging* and let us not forget *OMG* (Oh my God).

Unbelievable though it may seem, acronyms in use somewhere in the English-speaking world number more than one million according to the online Acronym Finder, about the same number as English words if we look back four centuries, a dramatic nod to the creativity and changeability of human language.

Borrowings or Loan Words

Neither a borrower, nor a lender be.

WILLIAM SHAKESPEARE, *Hamlet*, c. 1600

Languages pay little attention to Polonius's admonition quoted above, and many are avid borrowers and lenders, and poor ones at that, for the borrowers rarely return the borrowed items, and the lenders nearly never demand the return of the loans.

Borrowing words from other languages is an important source of new words, which are called **loan words**. Borrowing occurs when one language adds a word or morpheme from another language to its own lexicon. This often happens in situations of language contact, when speakers of different languages regularly interact with one another, and especially where there are many bilingual or multilingual speakers.

The pronunciation of loan words is often (but not always) altered to fit the phonological rules of the borrowing language. For example, English borrowed *ensemble* [ãsãblə] from French but pronounce it [ãnsãmbəl], with [n] and [m] inserted, because English doesn't ordinarily have syllables centered on nasal vowels alone. Other borrowed words such as the composer's name *Bach* will often be pronounced as the original German [bax], with a final velar fricative, even though such a pronunciation does not conform to the rules of English.

Larger units than words may be borrowed. French provides us with *ménage à trois* [menaʒ a tʀa], where [ʀ] is a uvular trill, meaning a "three-way romance," and which is pronounced in the French way by those who know French, but is also anglicized in various ways such as [mẽnaʤ a twa].

When an expression is borrowed and then translated into the borrowing language it is called a **loan translation**. *It goes without saying* from French *il va sans dire* is a loan translation from French. On the other hand, Spanish speakers eat *perros calientes*, a loan translation of *hot dogs* with an adjustment reversing the order of the adjective and noun as required by the rules of Spanish syntax.

The lexicons of most languages can be divided into native words and loan words. A native word is one whose history or **etymology** can be traced back to the earliest known stages of the language.

A language may borrow a word directly or indirectly. A direct borrowing means that the borrowed item is a native word in the language from which it is borrowed. For example, *feast* was borrowed directly from French, along with a host of terms, as a result of the Norman Conquest. By contrast, the word *algebra* was borrowed from Spanish, which in turn had borrowed it from Arabic. Thus, *algebra* was indirectly borrowed from Arabic, with Spanish as an intermediary. Some languages are heavy borrowers. Albanian has borrowed so heavily that few native words are retained. On the other hand, most Native American languages borrowed little from their neighbors.

English has borrowed extensively. Of the 20,000 or so words in common use, about three-fifths are borrowed. But of the 500 most frequently used words, only two-sevenths are borrowed, and because these words are used repeatedly in sentences—they are mostly function words—the actual frequency of appearance of native words is about 80 percent. The frequently used function words *and, be, have, it, of, the, to, will, you, on, that*, and *is* are all native to English.

Languages may borrow not only words and phrases but other linguistic units as well. The bound morpheme suffixes *ible/able* were borrowed from French, arriving in English by hitchhiking on French words such as *incredible* but soon attaching themselves to native words such as *drinkable*.

History through Loan Words

A morsel of genuine history is a thing so rare as to be always valuable.

THOMAS JEFFERSON, in a letter to John Adams, 1817

We may trace the history of the English-speaking peoples by studying the kinds of loan words in their language and when they were borrowed. Until the Norman Conquest in 1066, the Angles, the Saxons, and the Jutes inhabited England. They were of Germanic origin and they spoke Germanic dialects from which Old English developed. These dialects contained some Latin borrowings but few foreign elements beyond that. These Germanic tribes had displaced the earlier Celtic-speaking inhabitants, whose influence on Old English was confined mostly to a few Celtic place names. (The modern languages Welsh, Irish, and Scots Gaelic are descended from the Celtic dialects.)

The conquering Normans spoke French and French was used for all affairs of state and for most commercial, social, and cultural matters. Nevertheless, regional varieties of English continued to be used in homes, churches and the marketplace. This was a situation of language contact between French, the culturally dominant language, and English, the "language of the people." For three centuries vast numbers of French words entered English, of which the following are representative:

government	crown	prince	estate	parliament
nation	jury	judge	crime	sue
attorney	saint	miracle	charity	court
lechery	virgin	value	pray	mercy
religion	chapel	royal	money	society

Until the Normans came, when an Englishman slaughtered an ox for food, he ate *ox*. If it was a pig, he ate *pig*. If it was a sheep, he ate *sheep*. However, "*ox*" served at the Norman tables was *beef (boeuf)*, "pig" was *pork (porc),* and "sheep" was *mutton (mouton)*. These words were borrowed from French into English, as were the food-preparation words *boil, fry, stew,* and *roast*. Over the years, French foods have given English a flood of borrowed words for menu preparers:

aspic	bisque	bouillon	brie	brioche
canapé	caviar	consommé	coq au vin	coupe
crêpe	croissant	croquette	crouton	escargot
fondue	mousse	pâté	quiche	ragout

English borrowed many "learned" words from foreign sources during the Renaissance. In 1475, William Caxton introduced the printing press in England. By 1640, 55,000 books had been printed in English. The authors of these books used many Greek and Latin words, which consequently entered the language.

From Greek came *drama, comedy, tragedy, scene, botany, physics, zoology,* and *atomic*. Latin loan words in English are numerous. They include:

| bonus | scientific | exit | alumnus | quorum | describe |

Bin, flannel, clan, slogan, and *whisky* are all words of Celtic origin, borrowed at various times from Welsh, Scots Gaelic, or Irish. Dutch was a source of borrowed words, too, many of which are related to shipping: *buoy, freight, leak, pump, yacht*. From German came *quartz, cobalt,* and—as we might guess—*sauerkraut*. From Italian, many musical terms, including words describing opera houses, have been borrowed: *opera, piano, virtuoso, balcony,* and *mezzanine*. Italian also gave us *influenza*, which was derived from the Italian word for "influence" because the Italians were convinced that the disease was *influenced* by the stars. And more recently, courtesy of Starbucks, *barista*, referring to preparers of espresso (another Italian loan) drinks, from the Italian word for "bartender."

Many scientific words were borrowed indirectly from Arabic, because early Arab scholarship in these fields was quite advanced. *Alcohol, algebra, cipher,* and *zero* are a small sample. Spanish has loaned us (directly) *barbecue, cockroach,* and *ranch*, as well as *California*, literally "hot furnace." In America, the English-speaking colonists borrowed from Native American languages, another situation of language contact, but in which English is the culturally dominant language. Native American languages provided us with *hickory, chipmunk, opossum,* and *squash,* to mention only a few. Nearly half the names of U.S. states are borrowed from one American Indian language or another.

English has borrowed from Yiddish. Many non-Jews as well as non-Yiddish-speaking Jews use Yiddish words. There was once even a bumper sticker proclaiming: "Marcel Proust is a yenta." *Yenta* is a Yiddish word meaning "gossipy woman." *Lox,* meaning "smoked salmon," and *bagel,* "a doughnut dipped in cement," now belong to English, as well as Yiddish expressions such as *chutzpah, schmaltz, schlemiel, schmuck, schmo, schlep,* and *kibitz.*

English is a lender of many words to other languages, especially in the areas of technology, sports, and entertainment. Words and expressions such as *jazz, whisky, blue jeans, rock music, supermarket, baseball, picnic,* and *computer* have been borrowed from English into languages as diverse as Twi, Hungarian, Russian, and Japanese.

Loss of Words

Languages may be said to lose words in the sense that the frequency of usage falls below a certain threshold. Such words may still be counted when tallying up the size of the lexicon, but they are lost to the general population. The departure of an old word is never as striking as the arrival of a new one. When a new word comes into vogue, its unusual presence draws attention, but a word is lost through inattention—nobody thinks of it, nobody uses it, and its usage fades away to nothing.

A reading of Shakespeare's works shows that English has lost many words, such as these taken from *Romeo and Juliet: beseem,* "to be suitable," *mammet,* "a doll or puppet," *wot,* "to know," *gyve,* "a fetter," *fain,* "gladly," and *wherefore,* "why," as in Juliet's plaintive cry: "O Romeo, Romeo! wherefore art thou Romeo," in which she is questioning why he is so named, not his current whereabouts.

More recently, there are expressions used by your grandparents that have already been lost. *Two bits,* meaning "twenty-five cents," is rarely used nowadays and the same for *lickety-split* and *pell-mell,* meaning "very fast" and "recklessly hurried." Even words used by your parents (and us) sound dated, like *groovy* ("excellent"), *davenport* ("sofa"), and *grass* and *pot,* now called *weed,* referring to "marijuana." The word *stile,* meaning "steps crossing a fence or gate," is no longer widely understood. Other similar words for describing rural objects are fading out of the language as a result of urbanization. *Pease,* from which *pea* is a back-formation, is rare, and *porridge,* meaning "boiled cereal grain," is falling out of usage, although it is sustained by a discussion of its ideal serving temperature in the children's story *Goldilocks and the Three Bears* and its appearance on Harry Potter's breakfast table.

Technological change may also be the cause for the loss of words. *Acutiator* once meant "sharpener of weapons," and *tormentum* once meant "siege engine." Advances in warfare have put these terms out of business but given us *cruise missile* and an extension of the word *drone*, a pilotless aircraft. *Whiteboard* is in and *blackboard* is out insofar as classroom teaching is concerned. Although one still finds the words *buckboard, buggy, dogcart, hansom, surrey*, and *tumbrel* in the dictionary—all of them referring to subtly different kinds of horse-drawn carriages—progress in transportation is likely to render these terms obsolete and eventually they will be lost.

Semantic Change

The language of this country being always upon the flux, the Struldbruggs of one age do not understand those of another, neither are they able after two hundred years to hold any conversation (farther than by a few general words) with their neighbors the mortals, and thus they lie under the disadvantage of living like foreigners in their own country.

JONATHAN SWIFT, *Gulliver's Travels*, 1726

We have seen that a language may gain or lose lexical items. Additionally, the meaning or semantic representation of words may change, by becoming broader or narrower, or by shifting.

Broadening

When the meaning of a word becomes broader, it means everything it used to mean and more. The Middle English word *dogge* referred to a specific breed of dog, but was eventually **broadened** to encompass all members of the species *canis familiaris*. The word *holiday* originally meant a day of religious significance, from "holy day." Today the word refers to any day that we do not have to work. *Quarantine* once meant "forty days' isolation," but has broadened to mean any period of isolation. More recent broadenings, spurred by the computer age, are *mouse, cookie, cache, virus, worm,* and *hacker*. *Footage* used to refer to a certain length of film or videotape, but nowadays it means any excerpt from the electronic video media irrespective of whether its length can be measured in feet. *Twitter* and *tweet* were once words about birds—need we say more.

Narrowing

In the King James Version of the Bible (1611 CE), God says of the herbs and trees, "to you they shall be for meat" (Genesis 1:29). To a speaker of seventeenth-century English, *meat* meant "food," and *flesh* meant "meat." Since that time, semantic change has narrowed the meaning of *meat* to what it is in Modern English. The word *deer* once meant "beast" or "animal," as its German cognate *Tier* still does. The meaning of *deer* has been narrowed to a particular kind of animal. Similarly, the word *hound* used to be the general term for "dog," like German *Hund*. Today *hound* refers to a certain class of hunting dogs. *Skyline* once meant "horizon" but has been narrowed to mean "the outline of a city at the horizon."

Meaning Shifts

The third kind of semantic change that a lexical item may undergo is a shift in meaning. The word *knight* once meant "youth" but shifted to "mounted man-at-arms." *Lust* used to mean simply "pleasure," with no negative or sexual overtones. *Lewd* was merely "ignorant," and *immoral* meant "not customary." *Silly* used to mean "happy" in Old English. By the Middle English period, it had come to mean "naive," and only in Modern English does it mean "foolish." The overworked Modern English word *nice* meant "ignorant" a thousand years ago. When Juliet tells Romeo, "I am too *fond*," she is not claiming she likes Romeo too much. She means "I am too *foolish*." And if a drone has you in its sights, look forward to something rather worse than a bee sting.

Reconstructing "Dead" Languages

None of your living languages for Miss Blimber. They must be dead—stone dead—and then Miss Blimber dug them up like a Ghoul.

CHARLES DICKENS, *Dombey and Son*, 1848

"Shoe," 1989, Macnelly/King Features Syndicate

Despite the disdain for the modern languages expressed by Miss Blimber, and the lament of Skyler, the hapless Latin pupil, it is through the comparative study of the living languages that linguists are able to learn about older languages and the changes that occurred over time.

The Nineteenth-Century Comparativists

When agreement is found in words in two languages, and so frequently that rules may be drawn up for the shift in letters from one to the other, then there is a fundamental relationship between the two languages.

RASMUS RASK (1787–1832)

The chief goal of the nineteenth-century historical and comparative linguists was to develop and elucidate the genetic relationships that exist among the world's languages. They aimed to establish the major language families of the world and to define principles for the classification of languages. They based their theories on observations of regular sound correspondences among certain languages. They proposed that languages displaying systematic similarities and differences must have descended from a common source language—that is, were genetically related.

As a child, Sir William Jones had an astounding propensity for learning languages, including so-called dead ones such as Ancient Greek and Latin. While residing in India he added Sanskrit to his studies and observed that Sanskrit bore to Greek and Latin "a stronger affinity . . . than could possibly have been produced by accident." Jones suggested that these three languages had "sprung from a common source" and that probably Germanic and Celtic had the same origin.

Following up on Jones's research, the German linguist Franz Bopp pointed out relationships among Sanskrit, Latin, Greek, Persian, and Germanic. At the same time, a young Danish scholar named Rasmus Rask corroborated these results, and brought Lithuanian and Armenian into the relationship as well. Rask was the first scholar to formally describe the regularity of certain phonological differences between related languages.

Rask's work inspired the German linguist Jakob Grimm (of fairy-tale fame), who published a four-volume treatise (1819–1822) that specified the regular sound correspondences among Sanskrit, Greek, Latin, and the Germanic languages. Not only did the *similarities* intrigue Grimm, but so did the *systematic nature of the differences*. Where Latin has a [p], English often has an [f]; where Latin has a [t], English often has a [θ]; where Latin has a [k], English often has an [h].

Grimm posited a far earlier language (which we now refer to as Indo-European) from which all these languages evolved. He explained the sound correspondences by means of rules of phonological change (which historical linguists called **sound shift**, or **sound change**). Grimm's major discovery was that certain rules of sound change that applied to the Germanic family of languages, including the ancestors of English, did not apply to Sanskrit, Greek, and Latin. This accounted very nicely for many of the regular differences between the Germanic languages and the others. Because the sound changes discovered by Grimm were so strikingly regular, they became known as **Grimm's Law**, illustrated in Figure 8.2.

Earlier stage:[a]	bh	dh	gh	b	d	g	p	t	k
	↓	↓	↓	↓	↓	↓	↓	↓	↓
Later stage:	b	d	g	p	t	k	f	θ	x (or h)

FIGURE 8.2 | Grimm's Law, an early Germanic sound shift. Grimm's Law can be expressed in terms of natural classes of speech sounds: Voiced aspirates become unaspirated; voiced stops become voiceless; voiceless stops become fricatives.

[a]This "earlier stage" is Indo-European. The symbols bh, dh, and gh are breathy voiced stop consonants. These phonemes are often called "voiced aspirates."

Cognates

The Family Circus

"Shouldn't a unicorn be called a uniHORN?"

"Family Circus", Bil Keane Inc. Reprinted with the permission of King Features Syndicate

Cognates are words in related languages that developed from the same ancestral root, such as English *horn* and Latin *cornu*. Cognates often, but not always, have the same meaning in the different languages. From cognates, we can observe sound correspondences and from them deduce sound changes. In Figure 8.3, the regular correspondence *p-p-f* of cognates from Sanskrit, Latin, and Germanic (represented by English) indicates that the languages are genetically related. Indo-European **p* is posited as the origin of the *p-p-f* correspondence.[2]

Figure 8.4 is a more detailed chart of correspondences, showing an example of each regular correspondence. For each line in the chart linguists can identify many further correspondences such as Sanskrit *pād-*, Latin *ped-*, and English *foot* for *p-p-f*, thereby showing the consistent and systematic relationships that lead to the reconstruction of the Indo-European sound shown in the first column.

Sanskrit underwent the fewest consonant changes (has more sounds in common with Indo-European), Latin somewhat more, and Germanic (under Grimm's Law) underwent nearly a complete restructuring. The changes we observe are changes to the phonemes and phonological rules, and all words with those phonemes will reflect those changes (but see the "caveat" in the following paragraph).

If we imagine that the changes happened independently to individual words, rather than individual sounds, we could not explain why so many words beginning with /p/ in Sanskrit and Latin just happen to begin with /f/ in Germanic, and so on. It would far exceed the possibilities of coincidence. It is the fact

---

[2]The asterisk before a letter indicates a reconstructed sound, not an unacceptable form. This use of the asterisk occurs only in this chapter.

Indo-European	Sanskrit	Latin	English
*p	p	p	f
	pitar-	pater	father
	pad-	ped-	foot
	No cognate	piscis	fish
	paśu[a]	pecu	fee

FIGURE 8.3 | Cognates of Indo-European *p.

[a] ś is a sibilant pronounced differently from s.

that the changes are in the phonology of the languages that has resulted in the remarkably regular, pervasive correspondences that allow us to reconstruct much of the Indo-European sound system.

Grimm noted that there were exceptions to the regular correspondences he observed. He stated: "The sound shift is a general tendency; it is not followed in every case." Several decades later, in 1875, Karl Verner explained some of the exceptions to Grimm's Law. He formulated **Verner's Law** to show why Indo-European p, t, and k failed to correspond to f, θ, and x in certain cases:

Verner's Law: When the preceding vowel was unstressed f, θ, and x underwent a further change to b, d, and g.

Indo-European	Sanskrit		Latin		English	
*p	p	pitar-	p	pater	f	father
*t	t	trayas	t	trēs	θ	three
*k	ś	śun	k	canis	h	hound
*b	b	No cognate	b	labium	p	lip
*d	d	dva-	d	duo	t	two
*g	j	ajras	g	ager	k	acre
*bh	bh	bhrātar-	f	frāter	b	brother
*dh	dh	dhā	f	fē-ci	d	do
*gh	h	vah-	h	veh-ō	g	wagon

FIGURE 8.4 | Some Indo-European sound correspondences.

Encouraged by the regularity of sound change, a group of young nineteenth-century linguists proposed the **Neo-Grammarian hypothesis**, which says that sound shifts are not merely tendencies (as Grimm claimed), but apply in *all* words that meet their environment. If exceptions were nevertheless observed, it was trusted that further laws would be discovered to explain them, just as Verner's Law explained the exceptions to Grimm's Law. The **Neogrammarians** viewed linguistics as a natural science and therefore believed that laws of sound change were exceptionless. The "laws" they put forth often did have exceptions, however, which could not always be explained as dramatically as Verner's Law explained the exceptions to Grimm's Law. Still, the work of these linguists provides important data and insights into language change and why such changes occur.

The linguistic work that we have been discussing had some influence on Charles Darwin, and in turn, Darwin's theory of evolution had a profound influence on linguistics and on all science. Some linguists thought that languages had a "life cycle" and developed according to evolutionary laws. In addition, it was believed that every language could be traced to a common ancestor. This theory of biological naturalism has an element of truth to it, but it is an oversimplification of how languages change and evolve into other languages.

Comparative Reconstruction

... Philologists who chase

A panting syllable through time and space

Start it at home, and hunt it in the dark,

To Gaul, to Greece, and into Noah's Ark.

WILLIAM COWPER, "Retirement," 1782

When languages resemble one another in ways not attributable to chance or borrowing, or to general principles of Universal Grammar, we may conclude they are descended from a common source. That is, they evolved via linguistic change from an ancestral protolanguage.

The similarity of the basic vocabulary of languages such as English, German, Danish, Dutch, Norwegian, and Swedish is too pervasive for chance or borrowing. We therefore conclude that these languages have a common parent, Proto-Germanic. There are no written records of Proto-Germanic and certainly no native speakers alive today. Proto-Germanic is a partially reconstructed language whose properties have been deduced based on its descendants. In addition to related vocabulary, the Germanic languages share grammatical properties such as similar sets of irregular verbs, particularly the verb *to be*, and syntactic rules such as the verb (or auxiliary) movement rule discussed earlier in this chapter, further supporting their relatedness.

Once we know or suspect that several languages are related, their protolanguage may be partially determined by **comparative reconstruction**. This is done by applying the **comparative method**, which we illustrate with the following brief example.

Restricting ourselves to English, German, and Swedish, we find the word for "man" is *man* /mæn/, *Mann* /man/, and *man* /man/, respectively. This is one of many word sets in which we can observe the regular sound correspondence m-m-m and n-n-n in the three languages. Based on this evidence, the comparative method has us reconstruct **mVn* as the word for "man" in Proto-Germanic. The *V* indicates a vowel whose quality we are unsure of because, despite the similar spelling, the vowel is phonetically different in the various Germanic languages, and it is unclear how to reconstruct it without further evidence.

Although we are confident that we can reconstruct much of Proto-Germanic with relative accuracy, our reconstructions are hypotheses that we can never be sure about, and many details remain obscure. To build confidence in the comparative method, we can apply it to Romance languages such as French, Italian, Spanish, and Portuguese. Their parent language is the well-known Latin, so we can verify the method by testing it against written records of Latin. Consider the following data, focusing on the initial consonant of each word. In these data, *ch* in French is [ʃ], and *c* in the other languages is [k].

French	Italian	Spanish	Portuguese	English
cher	caro	caro	caro	"dear"
champ	campo	campo	campo	"field"
chandelle	candela	candela	candeia	"candle"

The French [ʃ] corresponds to [k] in the three other languages. This regular sound correspondence, [ʃ]-[k]-[k]-[k], supports the view that French, Italian, Spanish, and Portuguese descended from a common language. The comparative method leads to the reconstruction of [k] in "dear," "field," and "candle" of the parent language, and shows that [k] underwent a change to [ʃ] in French, but not in Italian, Spanish, or Portuguese, which retained the original [k] of the parent language, Latin.

To use the comparative method, linguists identify regular sound correspondences in the cognates of potentially related languages. For each correspondence, they deduce the most likely sound in the parent language. In this way, much of the sound system of the parent may be reconstructed. The various phonological changes in the development of each daughter language as it descended and changed from the parent are then identified. Sometimes the sound that analysts choose in their reconstruction of the parent language is the one that appears most frequently in the correspondence. This is the "majority rule" principle, which we illustrated with the four Romance languages.

Other considerations may outweigh the majority rule principle. The likelihood of certain phonological changes may persuade the linguist to reconstruct a less frequently occurring sound, or even a sound that does not occur in the correspondence. Consider the data in these four hypothetical languages:

Language A	Language B	Language C	Language D
hono	hono	fono	vono
hari	hari	fari	veli
rahima	rahima	rafima	levima
hor	hor	for	vol

Wherever Languages A and B have an *h*, Language C has an *f* and Language D has a *v*. Therefore, we have the sound correspondence *h-h-f-v*. Using the majority rule principle, we might first consider reconstructing the sound *h* in the parent language, but from other data on historical change, and from phonetic research, we know that *h* seldom becomes *v*. The reverse, /f/ and /v/ becoming [h], occurs both historically and as a phonological rule and has an acoustic explanation. Therefore, linguists reconstruct an **f* in the parent, and posit the sound change "*f* becomes *h*" in Languages A and B, and "*f* becomes *v*" in Language D. This is the "naturalness principle" and one obviously needs experience and knowledge to apply it.

The other correspondences are not problematic as far as these data are concerned:

o-o-o-o   n-n-n-n   a-a-a-e   r-r-r-l   m-m-m-m

They lead to the reconstructed forms **o, *n, *a, *r,* and **m* for the parent language, and the sound changes "*a* becomes *e*" and "*r* becomes *l*" in Language D. These are natural sound changes found in many of the world's languages.

It is now possible to reconstruct the words of the protolanguage. They are **fono, *fari, *rafima,* and **for.* In this example, Language D is the most innovative of the three languages, because it has undergone three sound changes.

Language C is the most conservative in that it is identical to the protolanguage insofar as these data are concerned.

The sound changes seen in the previous illustrations are examples of **unconditioned sound change**. The changes occurred irrespective of phonetic context. Following is an example of **conditioned sound change**, taken from three dialects of Italian:

Standard	Northern	Lombard	
fis:o	fiso	fis	"fixed"
kas:a	kasa	kasə	"cabinet"

The correspondence sets are:

f-f-f   i-i-i   s:-s-s   o-o-< >[3]   k-k-k   a-a-a   a-a-ə

It is straightforward to reconstruct **f, *i,* and **k.* Knowing that a long consonant like *s:* commonly becomes shortened to *s,* we reconstruct **s:* for the *s:-s-s* correspondence. A shortening change took place in the Northern and Lombard dialects.

There is evidence in these (very limited) data for a weakening of word-final vowels, again a change we discussed earlier for English. We reconstruct **o* for o-o-< > and **a* for a-a-ə. In Lombard, a conditioned sound change took place. The sound *o* was deleted in word-final position, but remained *o* elsewhere. The sound *a* became ə in word-final position and remained *a* elsewhere. As far as we can tell from the data presented, the conditioning factor is word-final position. Vowels in other positions do not undergo change.

---

[3]The empty angled brackets indicate a loss of the sound.

We reconstruct the parent dialect as having had the words *fisːo* meaning "fixed" and *kasːa* meaning "cabinet."

As our last example consider these data from an earlier and later form of a Slavic language. The question is, which came first? (When the comparative method is applied to earlier and later forms of a language the process is called **internal reconstruction**.)

L1	L2	
lovuka	lofkə	"clever"
gladuka	glatkə	"smooth"
ʒeʒika	ʒeʃkə	"burning hot"
kratuka	kratkə	"short"
blizuka	bliskə	"near"

The sound correspondences reading down through the data are: l-l, o-o, v-f, u-< >, k-k, a-ə, g-g, a-a, d-t, ʒ-ʒ, e-e, ʒ-ʃ, i-< >, r-r, t-t, b-b, i-i, z-s. These we reorganize into *nonproblematic*, where no change took place between older and newer forms, and *problematic*, where some kind of changes must have occurred:

Nonproblematic: l-l, o-o, k-k, g-g, e-e, r-r, b-b
Problematic: v-f, u-< >, a-ə, a-a, d-t, ʒ-ʒ, ʒ-ʃ, i-< >, t-t, i-i, z-s

To further understand the problematic correspondences we further reorganize by grouping vowels and consonants:

Vowel correspondences: a-a, a-ə; i-i, i-< >; u-< >
Consonant correspondences: d-t, t-t; v-f; ʒ-ʒ, ʒ-ʃ; z-s

We now see that as far as vowels are concerned, L1 is an earlier form because there is evidence of a vowel weakening change, with vowels either deleted or reduced to schwa. The opposite change, of vowel insertion or strengthening, is unlikely. This is clearly a conditioned change because it doesn't occur in all phonetic contexts. There appear to be two such changes:

Change A: *a* becomes schwa in word-final position
Change: B: *i* and *u* are deleted in penultimate syllables

This is the best we can do with the data at hand. Further research may reveal that Change A applies to all vowels in word-final position, and that Change B applies to high vowels only, or perhaps to all vowels. We can't say anything more about the vowel *o*, either, given this restricted data. The matter is under-determined.

As for consonants, there is a change in voicing, and while changes go both ways historically, from voiced to unvoiced or vice-versa, once persuaded by the vowel changes that L1 is earlier, a devoicing rule is seen as plausible. The t-t and d-t correspondence suggests a conditioned change, and a closer look at the data suggests a voicing assimilation rule.

Change C: Obstruents are devoiced when followed by a voiceless obstruent.

This is a commonly observed change and it supports the hypothesis that L1 is the earlier form.

There is one catch, however. In order for Change C to take place, Change B must have taken place first to bring the obstruents together. This, then, is an instance of historical rule ordering, not unlike the ordering of phonological rules that we observed in Chapter 6.

It is by means of the comparative method that nineteenth-century linguists were able to initiate the reconstruction of Indo-European, the long-lost ancestral language so aptly conceived by Jones, Bopp, Rask, and Grimm: a language that flourished about six thousand years ago.

Historical Evidence

You know my method. It is founded upon the observance of trifles.

SIR ARTHUR CONAN DOYLE, "The Boscombe Valley Mystery," in *The Adventures of Sherlock Holmes*, 1891

The comparative method is not the only way to explore the history of a language or language family, and it may prove unable to answer certain questions because data are lacking or because reconstructions are untenable. For example, how do we know positively how Shakespeare or Chaucer or the author of *Beowulf* pronounced their versions of English? The comparative method leaves many details in doubt, and we have no recordings that give us direct knowledge.

Various documents from the past can be examined for evidence. Private letters are an excellent source of data. Linguists prefer letters written by naive spellers, who misspell words according to the way they pronounce them. For instance, at one point in English history, all words spelled with *er* in their stems were pronounced as if they were spelled with *ar*, just as in modern British English *clerk* and *derby* are pronounced "clark" and "darby." Some poor speller kept writing *parfet* for *perfect*, which helped linguists discover the older pronunciation.

Clues are also provided by the writings of the prescriptive grammarians of the period. Between 1550 and 1750, scholars known as orthoepists attempted to preserve the "purity" of English. In prescribing how people should speak, they told us how people actually spoke. An orthoepist alive in the United States today might write in a manual: "It is incorrect to pronounce *Cuba* with a final r." Future scholars would know that some speakers of English pronounced it that way.

Some of the best clues to earlier pronunciation are provided by puns and rhymes in literature. Two words rhyme if the vowels and final consonants are the same. When a poet rhymes the verb *found* with the noun *wound*, as in Shakespeare's *Romeo and Juliet*, it strongly suggests that the vowels of these two words were identical:

BENVOLIO: . . . 'tis in vain to seek him here that means not to be found.
ROMEO: He jests at scars that never felt a wound.

Shakespeare's rhymes are helpful in reconstructing the sound system of Elizabethan English. The rhyming of *convert* with *depart* in Sonnet XI strengthens the conclusion that *er* was pronounced as *ar*.

For many languages, written records go back more than a thousand years. With the invention of the printing press in the fifteenth century, written matter became increasingly prolific. Today an effort is underway to digitize everything ever printed so as to make it computer analyzable. As this is being accomplished, it enables linguists to study these records to find out how languages were once pronounced. The spelling in early manuscripts tells us a great deal about the sound systems of older forms of modern languages. Two words spelled differently were probably pronounced differently. Once several orthographic contrasts are identified, good guesses can be made as to actual pronunciation. For example, because we spell *Mary, merry,* and *marry* differently, we may conclude that at one time most speakers pronounced them differently, probably [meri], [mɛri], and [mæri]. For at least one modern American dialect, only /ɛ/ can occur before /r/, so the three words are all pronounced [mɛri]. That is the result of a sound shift in which both /e/ and /æ/ shifted to /ɛ/ when followed immediately by /r/. This is another instance of a conditioned sound change.

Computer analysis of vast amounts of printed data may not only reveal subtle changes that have taken place historically–for example, the change in usage of irregular past tense forms (*swept* versus *sweeped*)–but also the rate of change as well. Taking the observed rate of change as a measuring rod, historical linguists may be able to determine the span of time between earlier forms and their later counterparts.

The historical comparativists working on languages with written records have a challenging job, but not nearly as challenging as that of linguists attempting to discover genetic relationships among languages with no written history. They must first transcribe large amounts of *spoken* language data from all the languages thought to be related, while seeking to establish a basis for relatedness such as similarities in vocabulary and regular sound correspondences. Only then can the comparative method be applied to reconstruct some extinct protolanguage.

Proceeding in this manner, linguists have discovered many relationships among Native American languages and have successfully reconstructed Amerindian protolanguages. Similar achievements have been made with the numerous languages spoken in Africa, which have been grouped into four overarching families: Afro-Asiatic, Nilo-Saharan, Niger-Congo, and Khoisan, spanning the continent more or less from the north to the south. For example, Somali is in the Afroasiatic family; Zulu is in the Niger-Congo family; and Khoekhoe (once derogatorily called Hottentot) is in the Khoisan family. These familial divisions are subject to revision if new discoveries or analyses deem it necessary.

Extinct and Endangered Languages

I am always sorry when any language is lost, because languages are the pedigree of nations.

SAMUEL JOHNSON (1709–1784)

A language dies and becomes extinct when no children learn it. Linguists have identified several ways in which a language might cease to exist, at least in its spoken form.

A language may die out more or less suddenly when all of the speakers of the language themselves die or are killed. Such was the case with Tasmanian languages, once spoken on the island of Tasmania, and Nicoleño, a Native American language once spoken in California.

Similarly, a language may cease to exist relatively abruptly when its speakers all stop speaking the language. This may happen under the threat of political repression or even genocide. Indigenous languages embedded in other cultures suffer death this way. In order to avoid being identified as "natives," speakers simply stop speaking their native language. Children are unable to learn a language that is not spoken to them, so when the last speaker dies, the language dies.

Most commonly, languages that become extinct do so gradually, often over several generations. This happens to minority languages that are in contact with a dominant language, much as American Indian languages are in contact with English. In each generation, fewer and fewer children learn the language until there are no new learners. The language is said to be dead when the last generation of speakers dies out. Cornish suffered this fate in Britain in the eighteenth century as have many Native American languages in both North and South America.

Uncommonly, some languages suffer "partial death" in that they survive only in specific contexts, such as a liturgical language. Latin and (at one time) Biblical Hebrew are such languages. Latin evolved into the Romance languages and by the ninth century there were few if any people speaking Latin itself in daily situations. Today its use is confined to scholarly and religious contexts.

Hebrew, on the other hand, has been revived and revised for use as the national language of Israel. The Academy of the Hebrew Language succeeded in awakening an ancient written language to serve the daily colloquial needs of the people. Many Native American languages are experiencing a reduction in the number of native speakers over time. Only 20 percent of the remaining indigenous languages in the United States are being acquired by children. Hundreds have already ceased to be written or spoken. In the 1500s, at the time of the first European contact, there were over 1,000 indigenous languages spoken throughout the Americas. Once widely spoken American Indian languages such as Comanche, Apache, and Cherokee have fewer native speakers every generation.

Doomed languages have existed throughout time. The Indo-European languages Hittite and Tocharian no longer exist. Hittite disappeared 3,200 years ago, and both dialects of Tocharian gave up the ghost around 1000 CE.

Dialects, too, may become extinct. Here is an excerpt from the first paragraph of an AP press release, 10/4/2012:

LONDON—In a remote fishing town on the tip of Scotland's Black Isle, the last native speaker of the Cromarty dialect has passed away, taking with him a little fragment of the English linguistic mosaic.

Many dialects spoken in the United States are considered endangered by linguists. For example, the sociolinguist Walt Wolfram is studying the dialect spoken on Ocracoke Island off the coast of North Carolina. One reason for the study is to preserve the dialect, which is in danger of extinction because so many young Ocracokers leave the island and raise their children elsewhere, a case of *gradual dialect death.* Vacationers and retirees are diluting the dialect-speaking population, because they are attracted to the island by its unique character, including, ironically, the quaint speech of the islanders.

Linguists have placed many languages on an endangered list. They attempt to preserve these languages by studying and documenting their grammars—the phonetics, phonology, and so on—and by recording for posterity the speech of the last few speakers. Through its grammar each language provides new evidence on the nature of the human language faculty. In its literature, poetry, ritual speech, and word structure, each language stores the collective intellectual achievements of a culture, offering unique perspectives on the human condition. The disappearance of a language is tragic; not only are these insights lost, but also the major medium through which a culture maintains and renews itself is gone as well.

Linguists are not alone in their preservation efforts. Under the sponsorship of language clubs, and occasionally even governments, adults and children learn an endangered language as a symbol of the culture. Gael Linn is a private organization in Ireland that runs language classes in Irish (Gaelic) for adults. Hundreds of public schools in Ireland and Northern Ireland are conducted entirely in Gaelic. In the U.S. state of Hawaii, a movement is under way to preserve and teach Hawaiian, the native language of the islands.

The United Nations, too, is concerned about endangered languages. In 1991, the United Nations Educational, Scientific, and Cultural Organization (UNESCO) passed a resolution that states:

> As the disappearance of any one language constitutes an irretrievable loss to mankind, it is for UNESCO a task of great urgency to respond to this situation by promoting . . . the description—in the form of grammars, dictionaries, and texts—of endangered and dying languages.

The documentation and preservation of dying languages is not only important for social and cultural reasons. There is also a scientific reason for studying these languages. Through examining a wide array of different types of languages, linguists can develop a comprehensive theory of language that accounts for both its universal and language-specific properties.

The Genetic Classification of Languages

> The Sanskrit language, whatever be its antiquity, is of a wonderful structure, more perfect than the Greek, more copious than the Latin, and more exquisitely refined than either, yet bearing to both of them a stronger affinity, both in the roots of verbs and in the forms of grammar, than could possibly have been produced by accident; so strong, indeed, that no philologer could examine all three, without believing that they have sprung from some common source, which, perhaps, no longer exists. . . .
>
> SIR WILLIAM JONES (1746–1794)

We have discussed how different languages evolve from one language and how historical and comparative linguists classify languages into families such as Germanic or Romance and reconstruct earlier forms of the ancestral language.

When we examine the languages of the world, we perceive similarities and differences among them that provide evidence for degrees of relatedness or for nonrelatedness.

Counting to five in English, German, and Vietnamese shows similarities between English and German not shared by Vietnamese (shown with tones omitted):

English	German	Vietnamese
one	eins	mot
two	zwei	hai
three	drei	ba
four	vier	bon
five	funf	nam

The similarity between English and German is pervasive. Sometimes it is extremely obvious *(man/Mann)*, but at other times a little less obvious *(child/Kind)*. No regular similarities or differences apart from those resulting from chance are found between them and Vietnamese.

Pursuing the metaphor of human genealogy, we say that English, German, Norwegian, Danish, Swedish, Icelandic, and so on are sister languages in that they descended from one parent and are more closely related to one another than any of them are to non-Germanic languages such as French or Russian.

The Romance languages are also sister languages whose parent is Latin. If we carry the family metaphor to an extreme, we might describe the Germanic languages and the Romance languages as cousins, because their respective parents, Proto-Germanic and early forms of Latin, were siblings.

As anyone from a large family knows, there are cousins, and then there are distant cousins, encompassing nearly anyone with a claim to family bloodlines. This is true of the Indo-European family of languages. If the Germanic and Romance languages are truly cousins, then languages such as Greek, Armenian, Albanian, and even the extinct Hittite and Tocharian are distant cousins. So are Irish, Scots Gaelic, Welsh, and Breton, whose protolanguage, Celtic, was once spoken widely throughout Europe and the British Isles. Breton is spoken in Brittany in the northwest coastal regions of France. It was brought there by Celts fleeing from Britain in the seventh century.

Russian is also a distant cousin, as are its sisters, Bulgarian, Serbo-Croatian, Polish, Czech, and Slovak. The Baltic language Lithuanian is related to English, as is its sister language, Latvian.

Sanskrit, although geographically far from Europe, is nonetheless a relative, as pointed out by Sir William Jones. Its offspring, Hindi and Bengali, spoken primarily in South Asia, are distantly related to English. Persian (called Farsi in Iran, Dari in Afghanistan) is a distant cousin of English, as is Kurdish, which is spoken in Iran, Iraq, and Turkey, and Pashto, which is spoken in Afghanistan and Pakistan. All these languages are related because they all descended from Indo-European.

Figure 8.5 on page 360 is an abbreviated family tree of the Indo-European languages that gives a genealogical and historical classification of the languages shown. This diagram is somewhat simplified. For example, it appears that all the

Slavic languages are sisters. In fact, the nine languages shown can be organized hierarchically, showing some more closely related than others. In other words, the various separations that resulted in the nine Slavic languages we see today occurred several times over a long stretch of time. Similar remarks apply to the other families, including Indo-European.

Another simplification is that the "dead ends"—languages that evolved and died leaving no offspring—are not included. We have already mentioned Hittite and Tocharian as two such Indo-European languages. The family tree also fails to show several intermediate stages that must have existed in the evolution of modern languages. Languages do not evolve abruptly, which is why comparisons with the genealogical trees of biology have limited usefulness. Finally, the diagram fails to show some Indo-European languages because of lack of space.

Languages of the World

And the whole earth was of one language, and of one speech.

GENESIS 11:1, *The Bible*, King James Version

Let us go down, and there confound their language, that they may not understand one another's speech.

GENESIS 11:7, *The Bible*, King James Version

Most of the world's languages do not belong to the Indo-European family. Linguists have also attempted to classify the non-Indo-European languages according to their genetic relationships. The task is to identify the languages that constitute a family and the relationships that exist among them.

The two most common questions asked of linguists are: "How many languages do you speak?" and "How many languages are there in the world?" Both questions are difficult to answer precisely. Most linguists have varying degrees of familiarity with several languages, and many are **polyglots**, persons who speak and understand several languages. Charles V, the Holy Roman Emperor from 1519 to 1558, was a polyglot, for he proclaimed: "I speak Spanish to God, Italian to women, French to men, and German to my horse."

As to the second question, it's difficult to ascertain the precise number of languages in the world because there are no clear criteria to decide what's a language and what's a dialect, as discussed in the previous chapter.

With this caveat in mind, the number of spoken languages in the world today (2016) is estimated at about 7,000 including sign languages. In the city of Los Angeles alone, more than 80 languages are spoken. Students at Hollywood High School go home to hear their parents speak Amharic, Armenian, Arabic, Marshallese, Urdu, Sinhalese, Igbo, Gujarati, Hmong, Afrikaans, Khmer, Ukrainian, Cambodian, Spanish, Tagalog, and Russian, among others.

It is often surprising to discover which languages are genetically related and which ones are not. Nepali, the language of remote Nepal, is an Indo-European

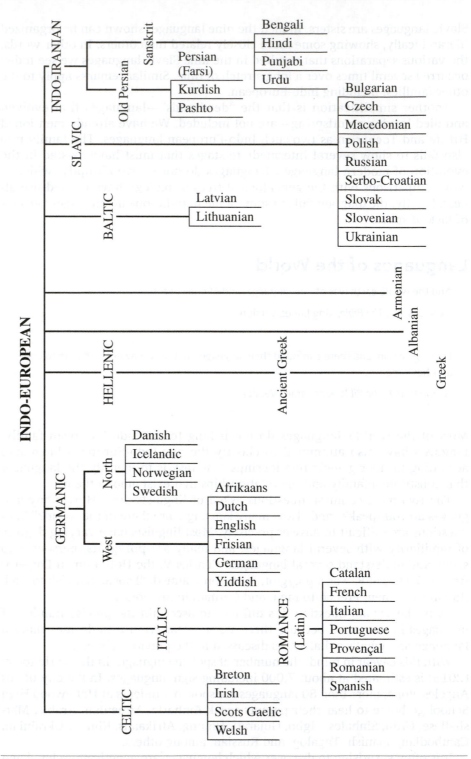

FIGURE 8.5 | The Indo-European family of languages.

language, whereas Hungarian, surrounded on all sides by Indo-European languages, is not.

Some languages have no demonstrable genealogical relationship with other living languages. They are called **language isolates**. Zuni, spoken in the southwestern United States, and Basque, spoken mainly in the Pyrenees mountains between Spain and France, are among the 75 or so isolates that have been identified.

It is not possible in an introductory text to give an exhaustive table of families, subfamilies, and individual languages, although this information is readily available online at *http://www.ethnologue.com*. We simply mention several language families in the following paragraphs with a few of their members. These language families do not appear to be related to one another or to Indo-European. This, however, may be an artifact of being unable to delve far enough into the past to see common features that time has erased. Indeed, we cannot eliminate the possibility that the entire world's languages spring ultimately from a single source, an "ur-language" that some have termed **Nostratic**, obscured by the past.

Uralic is the other major family of languages apart from Indo-European that is spoken on the European continent. Hungarian, Finnish, and Estonian are the major representatives of this group.

Afro-Asiatic is a large family of languages spoken in northern Africa and the Middle East. It includes the modern *Semitic* languages of Hebrew and Arabic, as well as languages spoken in biblical times such as Aramaic, Babylonian, Canaanite, and Moabite.

The *Sino-Tibetan* family includes Mandarin, the most populous language in the world, spoken by more than one billion Chinese. This family also includes all of the other Chinese languages, as well as Burmese and Tibetan.

Most of the languages of Africa belong to the *Niger-Congo* family, a huge family comprising more than one-fifth of the world's languages (about fifteen hundred). This family encompasses the Bantu languages, a group which contains more than 500 members, including Swahili and Zulu.

Nearly as numerous, the *Austronesian* family contains about thirteen hundred languages, spoken over a wide expanse of the globe from Madagascar, off the coast of Africa, to Hawaii. Hawaiian is an Austronesian language, as are: Maori, spoken in New Zealand; Tagalog, spoken in the Philippine Islands; and Malay, spoken in Malaysia and Singapore.

Surprisingly, the third most numerous family, called *Trans-New Guinea,* is crowded into the relatively small geographic area of New Guinea and neighboring islands, and contains nearly five hundred languages.

Dozens of families and hundreds of languages are, or were, spoken in North and South America. Knowledge of the genetic relationships among these families is often tenuous, and because so many of the languages are approaching extinction, there may be little hope for a thorough understanding of their language families.

For those readers interested in more information regarding endangered languages, please examine the website *http://www.endangeredlanguages.com*.

Types of Languages

All the Oriental nations jam tongue and words together in the throat, like the Hebrews and Syrians. All the Mediterranean peoples push their enunciation forward to the palate, like the Greeks and the Asians. All the Occidentals break their words on the teeth, like the Italians and Spaniards. . . .

ISIDORE OF SEVILLE, 7th century CE

There are many ways to classify languages. One way already discussed in this chapter is according to the language family—the genetic classification. This method is like classifying people according to whether they are related by blood. Another way of classifying languages is by certain linguistic traits, regardless of family. With people, this method would be like classifying them according to eye color, political preference, religion, degree of wealth, and so on.

So far in this book we have hinted at the different ways that languages might be classified. From a phonological point of view, we have tone languages versus non-tone languages—Thai versus English. Languages vary in the number of vowel phonemes, from as few as three to as many as a dozen or more. Languages may also be classified according to the number and kinds of consonants they have and also in terms of what combinations of consonants and vowels may form syllables. Japanese and Hawaiian allow few syllable types (CV and V, mostly), whereas English and most Indo-European languages allow a much wider variety. Languages may use stress to distinguish words like *cóntent* and *contént* (English), or not (French).

From a morphological standpoint, languages may be classified according to the richness of verb and noun morphology. For example, Vietnamese has little if any word morphology, so its words are monomorphemic; there are no plural affixes on nouns or agreement affixes on verbs. Such languages are referred to as **isolating** or **analytic**.

Languages like English have a middling amount of morphology, much less than Old English or Latin once had, or than Russian has today. Languages that average more than one morpheme per word are called **synthetic**.

Yet other languages—termed **polysynthetic** by linguists—have extraordinarily rich morphologies in which a single word may have ten or more affixes and carry the semantic load of an entire English sentence. Many native languages of North America are polysynthetic, including Mohawk, Cherokee, and Menominee. For example, the Menominee word *paehtāwāēwesew* means "He is heard by higher powers."

Some synthetic languages are **agglutinative**: words may be formed by a root and multiple affixes where the affixes are easily separated and always retain the same meaning. Swahili is such a language (see Exercise 9, Chapter 2). The word *ninafika* is *ni* + *na* + *fika*, meaning "I-present tense-arrive"; *ni* + *ta* + *fika* means "I-will-arrive"; *wa* + *li* + *fika* means "we-past tense-arrive"; and so on. Each morpheme is unchanging in form and meaning from one word to the next. Turkish is also an agglutinative language, as illustrated in Exercise 17 in Chapter 2.

In a **fusional** synthetic language, the morphemes are, well, fused together, so it is hard to identify their basic shape. Many Indo-European languages are of this type, such as Spanish. In *hablo, hablan, hablé*, meaning "I speak", "they speak", "I spoke," the affixes carry a fusion of the meanings "person" and "number" and "tense" so that *-o* means "first person, singular, present," *-an* means "third person, plural, present" and *-é* means "first person, singular, past." The affixes themselves cannot be decomposed into the individual meanings that they bear.

From a lexical standpoint, languages are classifiable as to whether they have articles like *the* and *a* in English; as to their system of pronouns and what distinctions are made regarding person, number, and gender; as to their vocabulary for describing family members; as to whether they have noun classes such as the masculine, feminine, and neuter nouns of German, or the multiple noun classes present in Swahili that we observed in Chapter 2, and so on.

Every language has sentences that include a subject (S), an object (O), and a verb (V), although individual sentences may not contain all three elements. From the point of view of syntax, languages have been classified according to the dominant order in which these elements occur in sentences. There are six possible orders—SVO (subject, verb, object), SOV, VSO, VOS, OVS, and OSV—permitting, in theory, six possible language types. Of these, SVO and SOV languages make up nearly 90 percent of investigated languages in roughly equal proportions. English, Spanish, and Thai are SVO; German, Dutch, and Japanese illustrate SOV languages.

In SVO languages, auxiliary verbs precede main verbs, adverbs follow main verbs, and prepositions precede the noun in PPs. Here are English examples:

They are eating. (Aux-V)
They sing beautifully. (V-Adv) (Cf. *They beautifully sing.)
They are from Tokyo. (Prep-N)

In SOV languages, the opposite tendencies are true. Auxiliary verbs follow the main verb, adverbs precede main verbs, and "prepositions," now called *postpositions*, follow the noun in PPs. Here are Japanese examples:

Akiko	wa	sakana	o	tabete	iru. (V-Aux)
Akiko	*topic marker*	fish	*object marker*	eating	is

"Akiko is eating fish."

Akiko	wa	hayaku	tabemasu.	(Adv-V)
Akiko	*topic marker*	quickly	eats	Akiko

"Akiko eats quickly."

Akiko	wa	Tokyo	kara	desu.	(N-PostP)
Akiko	*topic marker*	Tokyo	from	is	Akiko

"Akiko is from Tokyo."

These differences, and many more like them, stem from a single underlying parameter choice: the placement of the head of phrase. SVO languages are head-initial; SOV languages are head-final.

The question of why SVO and SOV languages are dominant is not completely understood, but linguists have observed that two principles or constraints are favored:

1. Subjects precede objects.
2. The verb V is adjacent to the object O.

SVO and SOV are the only two types that obey both principles. The next most common type in appearance is VSO, here illustrated by Tagalog, which is widely spoken in the Philippine Islands:

Sumagot   siya   sa   propesor.
answered   he   the   professor
"He answered the professor."

VSO languages account for nearly 10 percent of languages investigated—the lion's share of what's left over after SVO and SOV languages. It is possible, however, that the VSO order is derived from an underlying order in which the verb and object are adjacent, so there is no violation of principle (2).

Malagasy, spoken on the island of Madagascar, has sentences that on the surface translate literally as the VOS sentence *put—the book on the table—the woman,* meaning "The woman put the book on the table." This would violate principle (1). However, linguists have shown that such sentences are derived from a deeper SVO order that is then transformed by rules that move constituents. Apparent OVS and OSV languages may also be derived from underlying orders that are either SVO or SOV and conform to the two principles, though this remains a subject for linguistic research.

That a language is SVO does not mean that SVO is the only possible word order in surface structure. The correlations between language type and the word order of syntactic categories in sentences are *preferred* word orders, and for the most part are violable tendencies. Different languages follow them to a greater or lesser degree. Thus, when a famous comedian said "Believe you me" on network TV, he was understood and imitated despite the VSO word order. Yoda, the Jedi Master of *Star Wars* fame, speaks a strange but perfectly understandable style of English that achieves its eccentricity by being OSV. (Objects may be categories other than Noun Phrases.) Some of Yoda's utterances are:

Sick I've become.
Around the survivors a perimeter create.
Strong with The Force you are.
Impossible to see the future is.
When nine hundred years you reach, look as good you will not.

For linguists, the many languages and language families provide essential data for the study of Universal Grammar. Although these languages are diverse in many ways, they are also remarkably similar in many ways. We find that languages from northern Greenland to southern New Zealand, from the Far East to the Far West, all have similar sounds, similar phonological and syntactic rules, and similar semantic systems.

Why Do Languages Change?

Some method should be thought on for ascertaining and fixing our language forever. . . .
I see no absolute necessity why any language should be perpetually changing.

JONATHAN SWIFT (1667–1745)

Stability in language is synonymous with rigor mortis.

ERNEST WEEKLEY (1865–1954)

No one knows exactly how or why languages change. As we have shown, linguistic changes do not happen suddenly. Speakers of English did not wake up one morning and decide to use the word *beef* for "ox meat," nor do all the children of one particular generation grow up to adopt a new word. Changes are more gradual, particularly changes in the phonological and syntactic system.

For any one speaker, certain changes may occur instantaneously. When someone acquires a new word, it is not acquired gradually, although full appreciation for all of its possible uses may come slowly. When a new rule enters a speaker's grammar, it is either in or not in the grammar. It may at first be an optional rule, so that sometimes it is used and sometimes it is not, possibly determined by social context or other external factors (see previous chapter), but the rule is either there and available for use or not. What is gradual about language change is the spread of certain changes through an entire speech community.

A basic cause of change is the way children acquire the language. No one teaches a child the rules of the grammar. Children construct the grammar of their language alone, generalizing rules from the linguistic input they receive. As we shall see in the following chapter, the child's language develops in stages until it approximates the adult grammar. The child's grammar is never exactly like that of the adult community because children receive diverse linguistic input. Certain rules may be simplified or overgeneralized, and vocabularies may show small differences that accumulate over several generations.

The older generation may be using certain rules optionally. For example, at certain times they may say "It's I" and at other times "It's me." The less formal style is usually used with children, who may use only the "me" form of the pronoun as they become adults. In such cases, the grammar will have changed.

The reasons for some changes are relatively easy to understand. Before Facebook there was no such word as *facebook*. Today it's a common lexical item. Borrowed words, too, generally serve a useful purpose, and their entry into the language is not mysterious. Other changes are more difficult to explain, such as the Great Vowel Shift in English.

One plausible source of sound change is *assimilation*, an *ease of articulation* process in which one sound influences the pronunciation of an adjacent or nearby sound. For example, vowels are frequently nasalized before nasal consonants as we saw in Chapter 5. Once the vowel is nasalized, the contrast that the nasal consonant provided can be equally well provided by the nasalized vowel alone, and the redundant consonant may no longer be pronounced. The contrast between oral and nasal vowels that exists in many languages of the world today (such as French) resulted from just such a historical sound change.

In reconstructing older versions of French, it has been hypothesized that *bol,* "basin," *botte,* "high boot," *bog,* "a card game," *bock,* "Bock beer," and *bon,* "good," were pronounced [bɔl], [bɔt], [bɔg], [bɔk], and [bɔ̃n], respectively. The nasalized vowel in *bon* resulted from the final nasal consonant. Because of a conditioned sound change that deleted nasal consonants in word-final position, *bon* is pronounced [bɔ̃] in modern French. The nasal vowel alone maintains the contrast with the other words.

Another example from English illustrates how such assimilative processes can change a language. In Old English, word initial [kʲ] (like the initial sound of *cute*), when followed by /i/, was further palatalized to become our modern palatal affricate /tʃ/, as illustrated by the following words:

Old English (c = [kʲ])	Modern English (ch = [tʃ])
ciese	"cheese"
cinn	"chin"
cild	"child"

Ease of articulation processes, which make sounds more alike, are countered by the need to maintain distinctness. Thus, sound change also occurs when two sounds are so acoustically similar that there is a risk of confusion. We saw a sound change of /f/ to /h/ in an earlier example that can be explained by the acoustic similarity of [f] to other sounds.

Analogic change is a generalization of rules that reduces the number of exceptional or irregular morphemes. It was by analogy to *plow/plows* and *vow/vows* that speakers started saying *cows* as the plural of *cow* instead of the earlier plural *kine*. In effect, the plural rule became more general.

The generalization of the plural rule continues today with forms such as *yous* (plural of you) used by many speakers in place of the homophonous *you* for singular and plural.

Plural marking continues to undergo analogic change, as exemplified by the regularization of exceptional plural forms. The plural forms of borrowed words such as *datum/data, agendum/agenda, curriculum/curricula, memorandum/memoranda, medium/media, criterion/criteria,* and *virtuoso/virtuosi* are being replaced by regular plurals by many speakers: *agendas, curriculums, memorandums, criterias,* and *virtuosos.* In some cases, the borrowed original plural forms were considered to be the singular (as in *agenda* and *criteria*), and the new plural (e.g., *agendas*) is therefore a "plural-plural." In addition, many speakers now regard *data* and *media* as nouns that do not have plural forms, such as *information.* All these changes are "economy of memory" changes and lessen the number of irregular forms that must be remembered.

The past-tense rule is also undergoing generalization. By analogy to *bake/baked* and *ignite/ignited,* many children and adults now say *I waked last night* (instead of *woke*) and *She lighted the bonfire* (instead of *lit*). These regular past-tense forms are found in today's dictionaries next to the irregular forms, with which they currently coexist.

Assimilation and analogic change account for some linguistic changes, but they cannot account for others. Simplification and regularization of grammars occur, but so does elaboration or complication. Old English rules of syntax became more complex, imposing a stricter word order on the language, at the same time that case endings were being simplified. A tendency toward simplification is counteracted by the need to limit potential ambiguity. Much of language change is a balance between the two.

Language contact is also a vehicle of language change, particularly with respect to lexical changes due to borrowing, and also phonological changes such as the introduction of new phonemes. As we saw earlier, /v/ came into English owing to its intimate contact with French following the Norman invasion.

Many factors contribute to linguistic change: simplification of grammars, elaboration to maintain intelligibility, borrowing, and so on. Changes are actualized by children learning the language, who incorporate them into their grammar. The exact reasons for linguistic change are still elusive, although it is clear that the imperfect learning of the adult languages by children is a contributing factor. Perhaps language changes for the same reason all things change: it is the nature of things to change. As Heraclitus pointed out centuries ago, "All is flux, nothing stays still. Nothing endures but change."

The History of Writing

An Egyptian legend relates that when the god Thoth revealed his discovery of the art of writing to King Thamos, the good King denounced it as an enemy of civilization. "Children and young people," protested the monarch, "who had hitherto been forced to apply themselves diligently to learn and retain whatever was taught them, would cease to apply themselves, and would neglect to exercise their memories."

WILL DURANT, *The Story of Civilization*, vol. 1, 1935

The creation and development of writing systems is one of humanity's greatest achievements. Unlike spoken/sign languages, which are biologically innate and need not be purposefully learned, writing is a result of human ingenuity, more like the wheel than the ability to walk upright on two legs.

There are many stories about the invention of writing. Greek legend has it that Cadmus, Prince of Phoenicia and founder of the city of Thebes, invented the alphabet and brought it with him to Greece. In one Chinese fable, the four-eyed dragon-god Cang Jie invented writing, but in another, writing first appeared as markings on the back of the chi-lin, a white unicorn of Chinese legend. In other myths, the Babylonian god Nebo and the Egyptian god Thoth gave writing as well as speech to humans. The Talmudic scholar Rabbi Akiba believed that the alphabet existed before humans were created, and according to Hindu tradition the Goddess Saraswati, wife of Brahma, invented writing.

Although these are delightful stories it is evident that uncountable billions of words were spoken before a single word was written. The invention of writing comes relatively late in human history and its development was gradual. It is doubtful that a gifted ancestor bounded naked from his bath one fine morning shouting "Eureka, I have invented writing."

Pictograms and Ideograms

One picture is worth a thousand words.

CHINESE PROVERB

The roots of writing were the early drawings made by ancient humans. Cave art, called **petroglyphs**, have been found in such places as the Chauvet-Pont-d'Arc cave in southern France, the so-called "Cave of Forgotten Dreams." These can be "read" today although they were created by humans living 30,000 or more years ago. They are literal portrayals of life at that time. We don't know why they were produced; they may be esthetic expressions rather than pictorial communications.

Later drawings, however, are clearly "picture writings," or **pictograms**. Unlike modern writing systems each pictogram is an image of the object it represents. There is an explicit relationship between the shape of the symbol and its meaning. Comic strips, minus captions, are pictographic—literal representations of the ideas to be conveyed. This early form of writing represented objects in the world directly rather than through their linguistic names. Thus, they did not represent the words and sounds of spoken language.

Pictographic writing has been found throughout the ancient and modern world, from Africa to Oceania to the contemporary world of Internet communications. Email, Instant Messaging, Twittering, texting and other forms of electronic communication make copious use of **emoticons** and **emoji** (a Japanese loanword), which are pictographic symbols such as :-) and ☹, which convey specific meanings independent of any language. Pictograms are also found today in international road signs, where the native language of a region might not be understood by all travelers. You do not need to know English to understand the signs used by the U.S. National Park Service (Figure 8.6).

Once a pictogram was accepted as the representation of an object, its meaning was extended to attributes of that object, or concepts associated with it. A picture of the sun could represent warmth, heat, light, daytime, and so on. Pictograms began to represent ideas rather than objects. Such generalized pictograms are called **ideograms** ("idea pictures" or "idea writing").

FIGURE 8.6 | Six of seventy-seven symbols developed by the National Park Service for use as signs indicating activities and facilities in parks and recreation areas. These symbols denote, from left to right: "environmental study area," "grocery store," "men's restroom," "women's restroom," "fishing," and "amphitheater." Certain symbols are available with a prohibiting slash—a diagonal red bar across the symbol that means that the activity is forbidden.

National Park Service, U.S. Department of the Interior

The difference between pictograms and ideograms is not always clear. Ideograms tend to be less direct representations, and one may have to learn what a particular ideogram means. Pictograms tend to be more literal. For example, the no parking symbol Ⓟ is an ideogram. It represents the idea of no parking abstractly. A sign like ⊘ meaning "no bicycles" is more like a pictogram.

Inevitably, pictograms and ideograms became highly stylized and difficult to interpret without learning the words of the language that the ideograms represented. Thus, the ideograms became linguistic symbols. They stood for the words, both the meanings and sounds that represented the ideas. This stage was a revolutionary step in the development of writing systems.

Cuneiform Writing

Much of what we know about writing stems from the records left by the Sumerians, an ancient people of unknown origin who built a civilization in southern Mesopotamia (modern Iraq) more than six thousand years ago. They left tens of thousands of inscribed clay tablets containing business documents, epics, prayers, poems, proverbs, and so on, written in an elaborate pictography. Some examples are shown here:

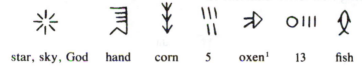

star, sky, God	hand	corn	5	oxen[1]	13	fish

Over the centuries the Sumerians simplified their pictographs and began to write them by pressing a wedge-shaped stylus into soft clay tablets, which the desert sun baked hard to produce enduring records. This form of writing is called **cuneiform**—literally, "wedge-shaped" (from Latin *cuneus*, "wedge"). Here is an illustration of the evolution of Sumerian pictograms to cuneiform:

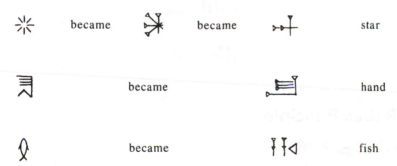

The cuneiform symbols in the third column do little to remind us (or the Sumerians) of the meaning represented. As cuneiform evolved its users began to think of the symbols more in terms of the name of the objects represented than of the object itself. Eventually cuneiform script came to represent words of the language directly, and through them the meaning. Such a system is called **logographic**, or **word writing**, and the symbols themselves are called **logograms**.

---

[1]The pictograph for 'ox' evolved, much later, into the letter *A*.

Cuneiform writing spread throughout the Middle East and Asia Minor. The Babylonians, Assyrians, and Persians made use of it by adapting the cuneiform characters to represent the sounds of the syllables in their own languages. In this way, cuneiform evolved into a **syllabic writing** system or **syllabary**.

In a syllabic writing system, each syllable in the language is represented by its own symbol, and words are written syllable by syllable. Cuneiform was never purely syllabic as many symbols remained that stood for whole words. The Assyrians retained many word symbols even though every word in their language could be written out syllabically. Thus, they could write ⩗ *mātu* "country" as:

The Persians (ca. 600–400 BCE) devised a greatly simplified syllabic alphabet for their language, which was in wide use by the reign of Darius I (521–486 BCE). The following characters illustrate it:

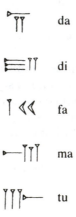

The Rebus Principle

two bee, oar knot two bee

WILLIAM SHAKESPEARE, *Hamlet*, c. 1600

When a graphic sign no longer has a visual relationship to the word it represents, it becomes a **phonographic symbol**, standing for the sounds that represent the word. A single sign can then be used to represent all words that sound alike. If, for example, the symbol ⊙ stood for *sun* in English, it could then be used in a sentence like *My ⊙ is a doctor*. This sentence is an example of the **rebus principle**.

A rebus is a representation of words by pictures of objects whose names sound like the word. Thus, 👁 might represent *eye* or the pronoun *I*. The sounds of the two words are identical, even though the meanings are not. Similarly, 🐝🍃 could represent *belief* (*be* + *lief* = *bee* + *leaf*), and 🐝🍃🍃 could be *believes*.

This system has drawbacks because words cannot always be divided into sequences of sounds that have meaning by themselves. It would be difficult, for example, to represent the word *English* (/ɪŋ/ + /glɪʃ/) in English according to the rebus principle. *Eng* by itself does not mean anything, nor does *glish*.

From Hieroglyphics to the Alphabet

At the time that Sumerian pictography was flourishing (around 4000 BCE), the Egyptians were using a similar system called **hieroglyphics** from Greek *hiero*, "sacred," + *glyphikos*, "carvings". These sacred carvings originated as pictography as shown by the following:

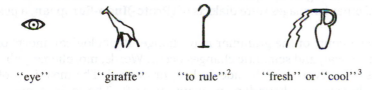

"eye"   "giraffe"   "to rule"[2]   "fresh" or "cool"[3]

Eventually, these pictograms came to represent both the concept and the word for the concept. Once this happened hieroglyphics became a bona fide logographic writing system. Through the rebus principle, hieroglyphics also became a syllabic writing system.

The Phoenicians, a Semitic people who lived in what is today Lebanon, were aware of hieroglyphics as well as the offshoots of Sumerian writing. By 1500 BCE they had developed a writing system of twenty-two characters, the West Semitic Syllabary. Mostly, the characters stood for consonants alone. The reader provided the vowels, and hence the rest of the syllable, through knowledge of the language. (Cn y rd ths?) Thus the West Semitic Syllabary was both a syllabary and a **consonantal alphabet** (also called **abjad**).

The ancient Greeks tried to borrow the Phoenician writing system, but it was unsatisfactory as a syllabary because Greek has too complex a syllable structure. In Greek, unlike in Phoenician, vowels cannot be determined by context so they had to be specifically written. Fortuitously, Phoenician had more consonants than Greek, so when the Greeks borrowed the system they used the leftover consonant symbols to represent vowel sounds. The result was **alphabetic writing**, a system in which both consonants and vowels are symbolized. (The word *alphabet* is derived from *alpha* and *beta*, the first two letters of the Greek alphabet.)

Most alphabetic systems are based on the Greek system. The Etruscans knew the Greek alphabet and through them it became known to the Romans, who used it for Latin. The alphabet spread with Western civilization, and today most nations of the world are able to use alphabetic writing.

---

[2]The symbol portrays the Pharaoh's staff.

[3]Water trickling out of a vase.

Readers of this book will understand that if language did not consist of discrete individual sounds, no one could have invented alphabetic letters to represent them. When humans started to use one symbol for one phoneme, they were revealing their intuitive knowledge of the phonological system of their language.

Summary

All living languages change. Linguistic change such as **sound shift** is found in the history of all languages, as evidenced by the **regular sound correspondences** that exist between different stages of the same language, different dialects of the same language, and different languages. Languages that evolve from a common source are **genetically related**. Genetically related languages were once dialects of the same language. For example, English, German, and Swedish were dialects of a postulated earlier form of Germanic called **Proto-Germanic**, whereas earlier forms of Romance languages, such as Spanish, French, and Italian, were dialects of Latin. Going back even further in time, earlier forms of Proto-Germanic, Latin, and other languages were dialects of **(Proto-)Indo-European**, a postulated ancestor.

All components of the grammar may change. Phonological, morphological, syntactic, lexical, and semantic changes occur. Words, morphemes, phonemes, and rules of all types may be added, lost, or altered. The meanings of words and morphemes may **broaden, narrow**, or shift. The lexicon may expand by **borrowing**, which results in **loan words** in the vocabulary. This is very common in **language contact** situations. It also grows through word coinage, blends, compounding, acronyms, and other processes of word formation. On the other hand, the contemporary lexicon may shrink as the frequency of usage of words like *typewriter, blackboard, record player,* and *phone booth* fall below a threshold level.

The study of linguistic change is called **historical and comparative linguistics**. Linguists use the **comparative method** to identify regular sound correspondences among the **cognates** of related languages and systematically reconstruct an earlier **protolanguage**. This **comparative reconstruction** allows linguists to peer backward in time and determine the linguistic history of a language family, which may then be represented in a tree diagram similar to Figure 8.5. **Internal reconstruction** uses the same methods applied to different stages of the same language. Where available, written texts are also used to inform linguists about language change.

Recent estimates place the number of languages in the world today at approximately 7,000 plus a hundred or more sign languages. These languages are grouped into families, subfamilies, and so on, based on their genetic relationships. A vast number of these languages are dying out because in each generation fewer children learn them. However, attempts are being made to preserve dying languages and dialects for the knowledge they bring to the study of Universal Grammar and the cultures in which they are spoken.

Languages may also be classified according to certain characteristics such as a rich versus an impoverished morphology (**synthetic** versus **analytic**), or according to whether their basic word order is Subject–Verb–Object (SVO) like English, or Subject–Object–Verb (SOV) like Japanese, or possibly some other order.

No one knows all the causes of linguistic change. Some sound changes result from assimilation, a fundamentally physiological process of ease of articulation. Others, like the **Great Vowel Shift**, are more difficult to explain. Some grammatical changes are **analogic changes**, generalizations that lead to more regularity, such as *cows* instead of *kine* and *waked* instead of *woke*.

Writing is a basic tool of civilization. Without it, the world as we know it could not exist. The precursor of writing was "picture writing," which used **pictograms** to represent objects directly and literally. Pictograms are called **ideograms** when the drawings become less literal, and the meanings extend to concepts associated with the objects originally pictured. When ideograms become associated with the words for the concepts they signify they are called **logograms**. Logographic systems are true writing systems in the sense that the symbols stand for words of a language.

The Sumerians first developed a pictographic writing system to keep track of commercial transactions. It was later expanded for other uses and eventually evolved into the highly stylized (and stylus-ized) **cuneiform** writing. Cuneiform was generalized to other writing systems by application of the **rebus principle**, which uses the symbol of one word or syllable to represent another word or syllable pronounced the same.

A different pictographic system known as **hieroglyphics** arose in ancient Egypt. Under its influence the Phoenicians developed the West Semitic Syllabary which was borrowed by the Greeks who used the symbols to represent both consonants and vowels, thus inventing the first alphabet.

References for Further Reading

Algeo, J. 2010. *The origins and development of the English language, 6th ed.* Boston: Wadsworth/Cengage.

Bybee, J. L. 2015. *Language change.* New York: Cambridge University Press.

Campbell, L. 2004. *Historical linguistics: An introduction, 2nd ed.* Cambridge, MA: MIT Press.

Comrie, B. (ed.). 1990. *The world's major languages.* New York: Oxford University Press.

Fischer, R. S., 2004. *A history of writing.* London: Reaktion Books.

Lewis, M. Paul (ed.), 2009. *Ethnologue: Languages of the world, 16th ed.* Dallas, TX.: SIL International. (http://www.ethnologue.com/)

Michel, J-B, et al. "Quantitative analysis of culture using millions of digitized books." *Science,* v. 331, pp 176–182, Jan 14, 2011.

Normile, D. "Experiments probe language's origins and development." *Science,* v. 336, pp 408–411, Apr 27, 2012.

Wolfram, W. 2001. Language death and dying. In Chambers, J. K., Trudgill, P., and Schilling-Estes, N. (eds.), *The handbook on language variation and change.* Oxford, UK: Basil Blackwell.

Exercises

1. Many changes in the phonological system have occurred in English since 449 CE. Below are some Old English words (given in their spelling and phonetic forms) and the same words as we pronounce them today. They are typical of regular sound changes that took place in English. What sound change or changes have occurred in each case?

   Example: OE hlud [xlu:d] → Mod. Eng. loud

   Changes: (1) The [x] was lost.

   (2) The long vowel [u:] became [aʊ].

OE		Mod E
a. crabba [kraba]	→	crab
Changes:		
b. fisc [fɪsk]	→	fish
Changes:		
c. fūl [fu:l]	→	foul
Changes:		
d. gāt [ga:t]	→	goat
Changes:		
e. lǣfan [læ:van]	→	leave
Changes:		
f. tēþ [te:θ]	→	teeth
Changes:		

2. The Great Vowel Shift left its traces in Modern English in such meaning-related pairs as:

   (1) serene/serenity [i]/[ɛ]
   (2) divine/divinity [aɪ]/[ɪ]
   (3) sane/sanity [e]/[æ]

   List five such meaning-related pairs that relate [i] and [ɛ] as in example (1), five that relate [aɪ] and [ɪ] as in example (2), and five that relate [e] and [æ] as in example (3).

	[i]/[ɛ]	[aɪ]/[ɪ]	[e]/[æ]
a.			
b.			
c.			
d.			
e.			

3. Sentences a–g, taken from Old English, Middle English, and early Modern English texts, illustrate some changes that have occurred in the syntactic rules of English grammar. (Note: In the sentences, the earlier spelling forms and words have been changed to conform to the spelling of Modern English. That is, the OE sentence *His suna twegen mon brohte to þæm cynige* would be written as *His sons two one brought to that king,*

which in Modern English would be *His two sons were brought to the king.*)
Underline the parts of each sentence that differ from Modern English.
Rewrite the sentence in Modern English. State what changes must have
occurred.

> *Example*: It <u>not</u> belongs to you. (Shakespeare, *Henry IV*)
>
> Mod. Eng.: It does not belong to you.

Change: At one time a negative sentence simply had a *not* before the
verb. Today, the word *do,* in its proper morphological form, must
appear before the *not.*

a. It nothing pleased his master.
b. He hath said that we would lift them whom that him please.
c. I have a brother is condemned to die.
d. I bade them take away you.
e. I wish you was still more a Tartar.
f. Christ slept and his apostles.
g. Me was told.

4. Yearbooks and almanacs (including ones online) often publish new-
    words lists. In 2016, several new words, such as *crowdfunding, koozie,
    photobomb* and *vaping* were said to have entered the English language,
    leastwise officially. Before that, new words such as *byte* and *modem*
    arrived together with the computer age. Other words have been
    expanded in meaning, such as *memory* to refer to the storage part of
    a computer and *crack* meaning a form of cocaine. Sports-related new
    words include *threepeat* and *skybox;* Harry Potter's world has donated
    apparate and *muggle,* among others. Some fairly recent arrivals came
    with the new millennium and include *Viagra, Sudoku,* and *fracking*
    (from "hydraulic fracturing" meaning "to free oil and gas from
    rock").

    a. Find five other words or compound words that have entered the
    language in the last ten years. Describe briefly the source of each
    word.

    b. Think of three words that might be on the way out. (Hint: Consider
    flapper, groovy, and *slay/slew.* Dictionary entries that say "archaic"
    are a good source.)

    c. Think of three words whose dictionary entries do not say they are
    verbs, but which you've heard or seen used as verbs. Example: "He
    went to piano over at the club," meaning (we guess) "He went to play
    the piano at the club."

    d. Think of three words that have become, or are becoming, obsolete as
    a result of changes in technology. Example: *Mimeograph,* a method of
    reproduction, is on the way out because of advances in xerography.

    e. One of the trendy words of the current millennium is *power* as used
    prolifically, if not productively, in new compounds such as *power walk*
    and *power lunch.* Find five or ten such usages and document a refer-
    ence where you observed each usage, such as a magazine article or a
    news report on the radio, Internet, or television.

f. Now that *blog* is a full-fledged word both as a noun and a verb it may become the root for many more words through the attachment of prefixes and suffixes. Some of these stem (pardon the pun) from productive affixes: *reblog,* "to blog again"; *blogify,* "to write a blog about something"; *nonblog,* "writing that isn't a blog, such as this exercise"; *blogness,* "the quality of being a blog." Using affixes, make up some "words" and "definitions" with *blog,* say five or ten. Use your imagination. Go bananas! For example, *blogaroo,* "a blogger who writes about rodeos," or *blogorama,* "a blog with a wide vista."

5. Here is a table showing, in phonemic form, the Latin ancestors of ten words in modern French (given in phonetic form):

Latin	French	Gloss
kor	kœr[4]	heart
kantāre	ʃãte	to sing
klārus	klɛr	clear
kervus	sɛr	deer
karbō	ʃarbɔ̃	coal
kwandō	kã	when
kentum	sã	hundred
kawsa	ʃoz	thing
kinis	sãdrə	ashes
kawda/koda[5]	kø[4]	tail

Are the following statements true or false? Justify your answers.

	True	False
a. The modern French word for "thing" shows that a /k/, which occurred before the vowel /o/ in Latin, became [ʃ] in French.	____	____
b. The French word for "tail" probably derived from the Latin word /koda/ rather than from /kawda/.	____	____
c. One historical change illustrated by these data is that [s] became an allophone of the phoneme /k/ in French.	____	____
d. If there were a Latin word *kertus,* the modern French word would probably be [sɛr]. (Consider only the initial consonant.)	____	____

6. Here is how to count to five in a dozen languages, using standard Roman alphabet transcriptions. Six of these languages are Indo-European and six are not. Which are Indo-European?

---

[4]œ and ø are front, rounded vowels.

[5]/kawda/ and /koda/ are the words for "tail" in two Latin dialects.

	L1	L2	L3	L4	L5	L6
a.	en	jedyn	yi	eka	ichi	echad
b.	twene	dwaj	er	dvau	ni	shnayim
c.	thria	tři	san	trayas	san	shlosha
d.	fiuwar	štyri	ssu	catur	shi	arba?a
e.	fif	pjeć	wu	pañca	go	chamishsha

	L7	L8	L9	L10	L11	L12
a.	mot	ün	hana	yaw	uno	nigen
b.	hai	duos	tul	daw	dos	khoyar
c.	ba	trais	set	dree	tres	ghorban
d.	bon	quatter	net	tsaloor	cuatro	durben
e.	nam	tschinch	tasŏt	pindze	cinco	tabon

7. The vocabulary of English consists of native words as well as thousands of loan words. Look up the following words in a dictionary that provides etymologies. Speculate how each word came to be borrowed from the particular language.

   Example: *Skunk* was a Native American term for an animal unfamiliar to the European colonists, so they borrowed that word into their vocabulary so they could refer to the creature.

a. size	h. robot	o. coyote	v. pagoda
b. royal	i. check	p. chocolate	w. khaki
c. aquatic	j. banana	q. hoodlum	x. shampoo
d. heavenly	k. keel	r. filibuster	y. kangaroo
e. skill	l. fact	s. astronaut	z. tomato
f. ranch	m. potato	t. emerald	
g. blouse	n. muskrat	u. sugar	

8. Analogic change refers to a tendency to generalize the rules of language, a major cause of language change. We mentioned two instances, the generalization of the plural rule (*cow/kine* becoming *cow/cows*) and the generalization of the past-tense formation rule (*light/lit* becoming *light/lighted*). Think of at least three other instances of nonstandard usage that are analogic; they are indicators of possible future changes in the language. (Hint: Consider fairly general rules and see whether you know of dialects or styles that overgeneralize them, for example, comparative formation by adding -er.)

9. Linguists have noted the "paradox" that *sound change is regular, but produces irregularity,* and *analogic change is irregular, but produces regularity.* Explain what this means, and illustrate your explanation with specific examples. (Hint: Revisit Exercises 2 and 8.)

10. Study the following passage from Shakespeare's *Hamlet*, Act IV, Scene iii, and identify every difference in expression between Elizabethan and current Modern English that is evident (e.g., in line 3, *thou* is now *you*).

    HAMLET: A man may fish with the worm that hath eat of a king, and eat of the fish that hath fed of that worm.

    KING: What dost thou mean by this?

HAMLET: Nothing but to show you how a king may go a progress
          through the guts of a beggar.
KING: Where is Polonius?
HAMLET: In heaven. Send thither to see. If your messenger find him
          not there, seek him i' the other place yourself. But indeed, if
          you find him not within this month, you shall nose him as
          you go up the stairs into the lobby.

11. Travelers to Spain who know a little Latin American Spanish are often
     surprised to encounter speakers who appear to have a lisp. That is, they
     pronounce an expected [s] as [θ], and moreover they pronounce an
     expected [j] as a palatal lateral whose IPA symbol is [ʎ]. Of course, if
     you've read this chapter you know that this is a dialectal variation. Con-
     sider the following data from two dialects of Spanish:

Dialect 1	Dialect 2	Gloss	Earlier Form (to be completed)
[kasa]	[kaθa]	hunt (noun)	*
[si]	[si]	yes	*
[gajo]	[gaʎo]	rooster	*
[dies]	[dieθ]	ten	*
[pojo]	[pojo]	kind of bench	*
[kaje]	[kaʎe]	street	*
[majo]	[majo]	May	*
[kasa]	[kasa]	house	*
[siŋko]	[θiŋko]	five	*
[dos]	[dos]	two	*
[pojo]	[poʎo]	chicken	*

   a. Find the correspondence sets—there are fourteen of them, for exam-
      ple p-p.
   b. Reconstruct each of the fourteen protosounds: for example, *p.
   c. What, if any, are the sound changes that took place in the two
      dialects?
   d. Complete the table by filling in the reconstructed earlier form.

12. Here are some data from four Polynesian languages:

Maori	Hawaiian	Samoan	Fijian	Gloss	Proto-Polynesian (to be completed)
pou	pou	pou	bou	post	*
tapu	kapu	tapu	tabu	forbidden	*
taŋi	kani	taŋi	taŋi	cry	*
takere	kaʔele	taʔele	takele	keel	*
hono	hono	fono	vono	stay, sit	*
marama	malama	malama	malama	light, moon	*
kaho	ʔaho	ʔaso	kaso	thatch	*

   a. Find the correspondence sets. (Hint: There are 14: for example, o-o-o-o,
      p-p-p-b.)

b. For each correspondence set, reconstruct a protosound. Mention any sound changes that you observe. For example:

o-o-o-o *o
p-p-p-b *p   p → b in Fijian.

c. Complete the table by filling in the reconstructed words in Proto-Polynesian.

13. Consider these data from two American Indian languages:

Yerington Paviotso = YP	Northfork Monachi = NM	Gloss
mupi	mupi	nose
tama	tawa	tooth
piwɨ	piwɨ	heart
sawa?pono	sawa?pono	(a feminine name)
nɨmɨ	nɨwɨ	liver
tamano	tawano	springtime
pahwa	pahwa	aunt
kuma	kuwa	husband
wowa?a	wowa?a	Indians living to the west
mɨhɨ	mɨhɨ	porcupine
noto	noto	throat
tapa	tape	sun
?atapɨ	?atapɨ	jaw
papi?i	papi?i	older brother
patɨ	petɨ	daughter
nana	nana	man
?atɨ	?etɨ	bow, gun

a. Identify each sound correspondence. (Hint: There are ten correspondence sets of consonants and six correspondence sets of vowels: for example, p-p, m-w, a-a, and a-e.)

b. (1) For each correspondence you identified in (a) not containing an m or w, reconstruct a protosound (e.g., for h-h, *h; o-o, *o).

(2) If the protosound underwent a change, indicate what the change is and in which language it took place.

c. (1) Whenever a *w* appears in YP, what appears in the corresponding position in NM?

(2) Whenever an *m* occurs in YP, what two sounds may correspond to it in NM?

(3) On the basis of the position of *m* in YP words, can you predict which sound it will correspond to in NM words? How?

d. (1) For the three correspondences that you discovered in (a) involving *m* and *w*, should you reconstruct two or three protosounds?

(2) If you chose three protosounds, what are they and what did they become in the two daughter languages, YP and NM?

(3) If you chose two protosounds, what are they and what did they become in the daughter languages? What further statement do you need to make about the sound changes? (Hint: One protosound

will become two different pairs, depending on its phonetic environment. It is an example of a conditioned sound change.)

e. Based on the above, reconstruct all the words given in the common ancestor from which both YP and NM descended (e.g., "porcupine" is reconstructed as *mihi).

14. The people of the Isle of Eggland once lived in harmony on a diet of soft-boiled eggs. They spoke proto-Egglish. Contention arose over which end of the egg should be opened first for eating, the big end or the little end. Each side retreated to its end of the island, and spoke no more to the other. Today, Big-End Egglish and Little-End Egglish are spoken in Eggland. Below are data from these languages.

a. Find the correspondence sets for each pair of cognates, and reconstruct the proto-Egglish word from which the cognates descended.

b. Identify the sound changes that have affected each language. Use *classes* of sounds to express the change when possible. (Hint: There are three conditioned sound changes.)

Big-End Egglish	Little-End Egglish	Gloss	Proto-Egglish (to be completed)
ʃur	kul	omelet	*
ve	vet	yolk	*
rɔ	rɔk	egg	*
ver	vel	eggshell	*
ʒu	gup	soufflé	*
vel	vel	egg white	*
pe	pe	hard-boiled (obscene)	*

15. Consider the following Latin and Greek words. Each of them has provided a root for many English words. Give three examples of English words derived from each of the Latin and Greek roots below (the roots are in boldface). (Note: The English word need not begin with the root: e.g., *depose* is derived from the Latin *positus*.)

Example: Latin *pater* "father": English *paternal, patricide, expatriate*. Note that *paternalistic, paternalistically,* and other morphological derivations of *paternal* <u>do not count</u>.

Greek		Latin	
pente	"five"	**acer**	"sharp"
anthropos	"man"	**mater**	"mother
arche	"beginning"	**bell**um	"war"
pathos	"feeling"	**arbor**	"tree"
morphe	"shape"	**pos**itus	"put, place"
exo	"outside"	**par**	"equal"
sophos	"wise"	**nepos**	"grandson"
gamos	"marriage"	**tac**ere	"to be silent"
logy	"word"	**scrib**ere	"to write"
gigas	"huge, enormous"	**lingua**	"tongue, language"

16. There are some exceptions to the Adj-Noun order in Modern English, as
the examples in column A and B illustrate:

A	B	C
A man alone	*an alone man	a lone man
No man alive	*no alive man	no living man
A lion asleep	*an asleep lion	a sleeping lion

  a. Can you identify a common feature of the adjectives that are grammatical in post-noun position?

  b. Provide some other examples like those in column A.

  c. The expressions in column C have the normal Adj-N order. Do they
have the same meaning as their respective items in column A? If not,
say how they are different.

17. Part One: "Write" the following words and phrases, using pictograms
that you invent:

  a. eye
  b. a boy
  c. two boys
  d. library
  e. tree
  f. forest
  g. war
  h. honesty
  i. ugly
  j. run
  k. Scotch tape
  l. smoke

Part Two: Which words are most difficult to symbolize in this way?
Why?

Part Three: How does the following statement reveal the problems in
pictographic writing? "A grammar represents the unconscious, internalized linguistic competence of a native speaker."

18. A *rebus* is a written representation of words or syllables that uses
pictures of objects whose names resemble the sounds of the intended
words or syllables. For example, might be the symbol for "eye" or
"I" or the first syllable in "idea."

Part One: Using the rebus principle, "write" the following words:

  a. tearing
  b. icicle
  c. bareback
  d. cookies

Part Two: Why would such a system be a difficult system in which to
represent all words in English? Illustrate with an example.

19. **A.** Construct non-Roman alphabetic letters to replace the letters used to represent the following sounds in English:

    [t r s k w tʃ i æ f n]

    B. Use the letters you created plus the regular alphabet symbols for the other sounds to write the following words in your "new" orthography.
    a. character
    b. guest
    c. cough
    d. photo
    e. cheat
    f. rang
    g. psychotic
    h. tree

20. Suppose the English writing system was a *syllabic* system instead of an *alphabetic* system. Use capital letters to symbolize the necessary syllabic units for the following words, and list your "syllabary". Example: Given the words *mate, inmate, intake,* and *elfin,* you might use A = mate, B = in, C = take, and D = elf. In addition, write the words using your syllabary. Example: *inmate*—BA; *elfin*—DB; *intake*—BC; *mate*—A. (Do not use more syllable symbols than you absolutely need.)

    a. childishness
    b. childlike
    c. Jesuit
    d. lifelessness
    e. likely
    f. zoo
    g. witness
    h. lethal
    i. jealous
    j. witless
    k. lesson

9

Language Acquisition

The capacity to learn language is deeply ingrained in us as a species, just as the capacity to walk, to grasp objects, to recognize faces. We don't find any serious differences in children growing up in congested urban slums, in isolated mountain villages, or in privileged suburban villas.

DAN SLOBIN, *The Human Language Series program 2*, 1994

As we have seen in preceding chapters, language is extremely complex. Yet very young children—before the age of five—already know most of the intricate system that is the grammar of their language. Before they can add small numbers or tie their shoes, children are inflecting verbs and nouns, forming questions, negating sentences, using pronouns appropriately, embedding clauses and effortlessly producing and understanding a limitless number of sentences they never heard before. How children accomplish this prodigious task is the subject of this chapter.

The Linguistic Capacity of Children

We are designed to walk. . . . That we are taught to walk is impossible. And pretty much the same is true of language. Nobody is taught language. In fact you can't prevent the child from learning it.

NOAM CHOMSKY, *The Human Language Series* program 2, 1994

Clearly, children do not learn a language simply by memorizing sentences. Rather, they acquire a system of grammatical rules of the sort we have discussed in previous chapters. They are not taught these rules explicitly, but must extract the rules from the language they hear around them, in effect "reinventing" the grammar of mature speakers. No specific kind of environment is required for them to do this. Children exposed to different languages under different cultural and social circumstances all develop their native language during a narrow window of time, going through similar, possibly universal, developmental stages. Even deaf children of deaf signing parents acquire signed languages in stages that parallel those of children acquiring spoken languages.

The uniformity of language development in the face of varying environments and (as we will see) impoverished input leads many linguists to believe that children are equipped with an innate template or blueprint for language—which we have referred to as Universal Grammar (UG)—and that this blueprint aids the child in the task of constructing a grammar for her language.

What's Learned, What's Not?

"WHAT'S THE BIG SURPRISE? ALL THE LATEST THEORIES OF LINGUISTICS SAY WE'RE BORN WITH THE INNATE CAPACITY FOR GENERATING SENTENCES."

ScienceCartoonsPlus.com

The **innateness** hypothesis receives its strongest support from the observation that the grammars people ultimately end up with contain many abstract rules and structures that are not directly represented in the linguistic input they receive. In this sense, the input to the child is said to be **impoverished** and this argument for the innateness of UG is called the **poverty of the stimulus**.

The principle of structure dependency illustrates one way in which the linguistic input is impoverished. Structure dependency, discussed in Chapter 3, refers to the fact that grammatical rules are dependent on hierarchical structure and not on serial order. For example, the rule that moves the auxiliary in English questions, illustrated in (1), must refer to the *main* auxiliary of the sentence and not merely to the *first* auxiliary.

1. The boy is sleeping. → Is the boy sleeping?

This is clearly shown by introducing a more complex sentence containing a relative clause. We see that moving the main auxiliary, as in (2), produces a grammatical output, while moving the first auxiliary, as in (3), leads to ungrammaticality:

The boy who is sleeping was dreaming.

2. Was the boy who is sleeping _____ dreaming?
3. *Is the boy who _____ sleeping was dreaming?

Naturalistic and experimental studies show that young children do not produce sentences such as (3). Presented with simple declarative-question pairs such as (1), children infer the structure-dependent rule, and when tested on the more complex cases, they correctly invert the *main* auxiliary and not the *first* auxiliary. The fact that children come up with a structure-dependent rule means that they know that sentences are organized hierarchically, and this is not information that is provided in the input.

Many grammatical rules rely on the structural difference between main and subordinate clauses. For example, a pronoun can sometimes refer to a following NP as in (1) where *he* can refer to *Billie*. But sometimes pronouns cannot co-refer in this way, as in (2).

1. When *he* lost the race *Billie* was sad.
2. *He* was sad when *Billie* lost the race. (ungrammatical with *he* = *Billie*)

The linear relationship between the pronoun and the NP is the same in both sentences, so this cannot be the reason for the difference in grammaticality. Rather, the rule that permits co-reference in (1) but not (2) is structure-dependent (and it is also universal): it states (roughly) that a pronoun in hierarchically higher position (e.g. root subject) cannot refer to a name in lower position (e.g. embedded subject). As in the case of the question formation rule, when tested on sentences such as (1) and (2) children allow co-reference in (1), but not in (2), showing that they are sensitive to the structural difference between the two sentences and to the structure-dependent pronoun rule.

Children are not provided with information about structure dependency, constituent structure or indeed about any other abstract property of grammar. Their language input consists of sequences of sounds (or signs), not sets of phrase structure trees. Yet, children formulate rules that are sensitive to structure. According to the innateness hypothesis, the child does not need to learn structure dependency or the pronoun rule or any other universal principle of sentence formation, such as the rule that heads of categories can take complements. These aspects of grammar are part of the innate blueprint for language.

At the same time, it is clear that some aspects of language are learned. Children exposed to English acquire English, not some other language, and similarly for all other languages. The specific sounds and words of a language, as well as the language-specific ordering and movement rules, must be learned by the child based on the linguistic input. For example, children acquiring English must learn that it is an SVO language while Japanese children learn that their language is SOV. These orderings are clearly demonstrated in the language they hear spoken around them.

English-speaking children must also learn that yes–no questions are formed by moving the auxiliary while Japanese children learn that to form a yes–no question, the morpheme *-ka* is suffixed to a verb stem.

Tanaka ga sushi o tabete iru.	"Tanaka is eating sushi."
Tanaka ga sushi o tabete iru**ka?**	"Is Tanaka eating sushi?"

As in the case of word order, this information is provided in the linguistic input. The process of acquiring language is rooted in human biology and supported by linguistic input from the environment.

One of the central goals of linguistic theory is to solve *the logical problem of language acquisition*:

What accounts for the ease, rapidity, and uniformity of language acquisition in the face of impoverished data?

A partial answer is that children are able to acquire a complex grammar quickly and easily without any particular help beyond exposure to the language because they do not start from scratch. Innate principles of UG such as structure dependency and X-bar theory, among many others, provide them with a significant head start. UG constrains the kinds of grammatical rules children formulate. It predisposes them to follow a restricted course of development that avoids many grammatical errors and that gives rise to uniform developmental stages, as we will discuss in the next section.

The innateness hypothesis also predicts that all languages will conform to UG principles. While we are still far from understanding the full structure of UG, research on different languages provides a way to test any principles that linguists propose. Hypotheses may be revised based on new evidence, as is the case in any science. But there is little doubt that human languages conform to abstract universal principles and that the human brain is specially equipped for acquisition of human language grammars, as we will discuss in the following chapter.

Stages in Language Acquisition

... for I was no longer a speechless infant; but a speaking boy. This I remember; and have since observed how I learned to speak. It was not that my elders taught me words ... in any set method; but I ... did myself ... practice the sounds in my memory.... And thus by constantly hearing words, as they occurred in various sentences ... I thereby gave utterance to my will.

ST. AUGUSTINE, *Confessions*, 398 CE

Children do not wake up one morning with a fully formed grammar in their heads. In moving from first words to adult competence children pass through linguistic stages. They begin by babbling, they then acquire their first words, and in just a few months they begin to put words together into sentences.

Studies of language acquisition are based on various sources including tape recordings and videotapes of children's spontaneous language, usually in interactions with adults, as well as controlled experiments that test both their productive abilities and their comprehension of language. Researchers have also invented ingenious experimental techniques for studying the linguistic abilities of infants, who are not yet speaking.

Children's early utterances may not look exactly like adult sentences, but child language is not just a degenerate form of adult language. The words and sentences that the children produce at each stage of development reflect the set of grammatical rules they have developed to that point. Children's "errors" can therefore provide researchers with a window into their grammars.

Although child grammars and adult grammars differ in certain respects, they also share many formal properties. Like adults, children have grammatical categories such as NP and VP, rules for building phrase structures and for moving constituents, as well as phonological, morphological, and semantic rules, and they adhere to universal principles such as structure dependency.

Children are biologically equipped to acquire all aspects of grammar. In the following sections, we will look at development in each of the components of language, and we will illustrate the role that Universal Grammar and other factors play in this development.

The Perception and Production of Speech Sounds

An infant crying in the night:

An infant crying for the light:

And with no language but a cry.

ALFRED LORD TENNYSON, *In Memoriam A.H.H.*, 1849

Any notion that a person is born with a mind like a blank slate is belied by a wealth of evidence showing that newborns react to some subtle distinctions in their environment and not to others. Infants will respond to visual depth and distance distinctions, to differences between rigid and flexible physical properties of objects, and to human faces rather than to other visual stimuli. Infants also show a very early response to different properties of language. Experiments demonstrate that infants will increase their sucking rate—as measured by ingeniously designed pacifiers—when the stimuli (visual or auditory) presented to them are varied, but will decrease the sucking rate when the same stimuli are presented repeatedly. When tested with a preferential listening technique, slightly older infants will turn their heads toward and listen longer to sounds, stress patterns, and words that are familiar to them. On the other hand, they will also respond to novel patterns, showing that they can distinguish the different linguistic elements being tested. These instinctive responses can be used to measure a baby's ability to discriminate and recognize different linguistic stimuli.

A newborn will respond to phonetic contrasts found in human languages even when these differences are not phonemic in the language spoken in the baby's home. A baby hearing a human voice over a loudspeaker saying [pa] [pa] [pa] will slowly decrease her rate of sucking. If the sound changes to [ba] or even [pʰa], the sucking rate increases dramatically. Adults find it difficult to differentiate between the allophones of a phoneme, but for infants it comes naturally. Japanese infants can distinguish between [r] and [l] whereas their parents cannot; babies can hear the difference between aspirated and unaspirated stops even if students in an introductory linguistics course cannot. Babies can discriminate between sounds that are phonemic in other languages and nonexistent in the language of their parents. For example, in Hindi, there is a phonemic contrast between a retroflex *t* [ʈ] (made with the tongue curled back) and the alveolar [t]. To English-speaking adults, these may sound the same; to their infants, they do not. However, babies will not react to distinctions that do not correspond to phonemic contrasts in any human language, such as sounds spoken more or less loudly or by speakers of different ages and genders.

Because infants are born with the ability to perceive just those sounds that are phonemic in some language, it is possible for them to learn any human language they are exposed to. During the first year of life, the infant's job is to uncover the sounds of the ambient language. From around six months, he begins to lose the ability to discriminate between sounds that are not phonemic in his own language as his linguistic environment begins to shape his initial perceptions. Japanese infants can no longer hear the difference between [r] and [l], which do not contrast in Japanese, whereas babies in English-speaking homes retain this perception. They have begun to learn the sounds of the language of their parents. Before that, they appear to know the sounds of human language in general.

Babbling

"Hi & Lois"/King Features Syndicate

The child's linguistic environment shapes not only the child's perceptions of speech sounds but also his productions. Babbling illustrates the readiness of the human mind to respond to linguistic input from a very early stage.

At around six months, the infant begins to babble. The sounds produced in this period include many sounds that do not occur in the language of the household, but belong to the set of possible human speech sounds. By the end of the first year the babbles come to include only those sounds and sound combinations that occur in the target language, and also conform to the specific intonation pattern of the language. At around nine months old children's babbles consist mainly of repeated consonant-vowel sequences, like *mama, gaga,* and *dada.* Later babbles are more varied and begin to sound like words, although they may not have any specific meaning attached to them. At this point English-speaking adults can distinguish the babbles of an English-babbling infant from those of an infant babbling in Cantonese or Arabic. Deaf children exposed to sign language also babble–on their hands. They produce repetitive hand motions consisting of elements of the sign languages used in deaf communities around the world. During the first year of life, the infant's perceptions and productions are being fine-tuned to the surrounding language(s).

First Words

> From this golden egg a man, Prajapati, was born. A year having passed, he wanted to speak. He said "bhur" and the earth was created. He said "bhuvar" and the space of the air was created. He said "suvar" and the sky was created. That is why a child wants to speak after a year. . . . When Prajapati spoke for the first time, he uttered one or two syllables. That is why a child utters one or two syllables when he speaks for the first time.
>
> HINDU MYTH

Some time after the age of one, children begin to use the same string of sounds repeatedly to mean the same thing, thereby producing their first words. The age at which first words appear can vary and has nothing to do with the child's intelligence.

The child's first words may not sound exactly like the adult versions. The following words of one child, J. P., at the age of sixteen months, illustrate the point:

[ʔaʊ]	"not," "no," "don't"	[s:]	"aerosol spray"
[bʌʔ]/[mʌʔ]	"up"	[sʲuː]	"shoe"
[da]	"dog"	[haɪ]	"hi"
[iʔo]/[siʔo]	"Cheerios"	[sr]	"shirt," "sweater"
[sa]	"sock"	[sæː]/[əsæː]	"what's that?"/"hey, look!"
[aɪ]/[ʌɪ]	"light"	[ma]	"mommy"
[baʊ]/[daʊ]	"down"	[dæ]	"daddy"

What is important is not that these words differ from the adult's, but that they represent a fixed sound-meaning pairing.

Most children go through a stage in which they utters only single words. It is interesting to note that even though a child may only be producing one word at a time, he can understand utterances of greater complexity. Controlled experiments show that children in the one-word stage understand simple sentences such as "Ernie washed Bert", distinguishing this from "Bert washed Ernie".

Similarly, a child's one-word utterance may convey more meaning than just the single word. When J. P. says "down" he may be making a request to be put down, or he may be commenting on a toy that has fallen down from the shelf. When he says "cheerios" he may simply be naming the box of cereal in front of him, or he may be asking for some Cheerios. For this reason, the one-word stage is sometimes referred to as the **holophrastic** (whole phrase) stage because these one-word utterances seem to convey the meaning of an entire sentence. This suggests that children have a more complex mental representation of their language than they are able to express and that their productive abilities do not fully reflect their underlying grammatical competence.

It has been claimed that deaf babies develop their first signs earlier than hearing children speak their first words. This has led to the development of Baby

Sign, a technique in which hearing parents learn and model for their babies various "signs," such as signs for "milk," "hurt," and "mother." The idea is that the baby can communicate his needs manually even before he is able to articulate spoken words. Promoters of Baby Sign (and many parents) say that this leads to less frustration and less crying. The claim that signs appear earlier than words is controversial. Some linguists argue that what occurs earlier in both deaf and hearing babies are pre-linguistic gestures that lack the systematic meaning of true signs. Baby Sign may be exploiting this earlier manual dexterity, and not indicative of a precocious linguistic development.

Segmenting the Speech Stream

I scream, you scream, we all scream for ice cream.

TRANSCRIBED FROM VOCALS BY TOM STACKS, performing with Harry Reser's Six Jumping Jacks, January 14, 1928

Speech is a continuous stream broken only by breath pauses. The intonation breaks that do exist do not always correspond to word, phrase, or sentence boundaries. The adult speaker can use his knowledge of the lexicon and grammar of a language to impose structure on the speech he hears. But how do babies, who have not yet acquired a lexicon or the grammar rules, extract the words from the speech they hear around them? Children are in the same fix that you might be in if you tuned in a foreign-language radio station. You wouldn't have the foggiest idea of what was being said or what the words were. The ability to segment the continuous speech stream into discrete units—words—is one of the remarkable feats of language acquisition.

Studies show that infants are remarkably good at extracting information from continuous speech. They seem to know what kind of cues to look for in the input that will help them to isolate words. One of the cues that English-speaking children use to figure out word boundaries is stress.

As noted in Chapter 5 every content word in English has a stressed syllable. (Function words such as the, *a, am, can,* etc. are ordinarily unstressed.) If the content word is monosyllabic, then that syllable is stressed as in *dóg* and *hám.* Bisyllabic content words can be **trochaic**, which means that stress is on the first syllable, as in *páper* and *dóctor,* or **iambic**, which means stress is on the second syllable, as in *giráffe* and *devíce.* The vast majority of English words have trochaic stress. In controlled experiments adult speakers are quicker to recognize words with trochaic stress than words with iambic stress. This can be explained if English-speaking adults follow a strategy of taking a stressed syllable to mark the onset of a new word.

Can children avail themselves of the same strategy? Stress is very salient to infants, and they are quick to acquire the rhythmic structure of their language. Researchers have shown that at just a few weeks or months old infants are able to discriminate native and non-native stress patterns. This is shown in production as well. Before the end of the first year, their babbling takes on the intonation pattern of the ambient language. At about nine months old, English-speaking children prefer to listen to bisyllabic words with initial rather than final stress. And most notably, studies show that infants acquiring English can indeed use stress cues to segment words in fluent speech.

In a series of experiments, seven-and-a-half-month-old infants listened to passages with repeated instances of trochaic words such as *púppy*, and passages with iambic words such as *guitár*. They were then played lists of words, some of which had occurred in the previous passage and others that had not. Experimenters measured the length of time that they listened to the familiar versus unfamiliar words. The results showed that children listened significantly longer (indicated by turning their head in the direction of the loudspeaker) to words that they had heard in the passage, but only when the words had the trochaic pattern *(púppy)*. For words with the iambic pattern *(guitár)*, the children responded only to the stressed syllable *(tár)*, though the monosyllabic word *tár* had not appeared in the passage. These results suggest that the infants—like adults—are taking the stressed syllable to mark the onset of a new word. Following such a strategy will sometimes lead to errors (for iambic words and unstressed function words), but it provides the child with a way of getting started. This is referred to as **prosodic bootstrapping**. Infants can use the stress pattern of the language as a start to word learning.

Infants are also sensitive to phonotactic constraints and to the distribution of allophones in the target language. In English, aspiration of voiceless stops typically occurs at the beginning of a stressed syllable—[pʰɛ̃n] *(pen)* versus [opə̃n] (open). This provides the infant with a phonetic cue. Another cue is that certain combinations of sounds occur only at the end of a syllable rather than at the beginning– [rt], [mp], [nk], and so on. Studies of English and other languages show that nine-month-olds can use this information to help segment speech into words.

Languages differ in their stress patterns as well as in their allophonic variation and phonotactics. This means the infant would first need to figure out what stress pattern he is dealing with, or what the allophones and possible sound combinations are, before he could use this information to extract the words of his language from fluent speech. This seems to be a classic chicken and egg problem—he has to know the language to learn the language. A way out of this conundrum is provided by the finding that infants may also rely on statistical properties of the input to segment words such as the frequency with which particular sequences of sounds occur.

In one study, eight-month-old infants listened to two minutes of speech formed from four nonsense words, *pabiku, tutibu, golabu, babupu*. The words were produced by a speech synthesizer and strung together in three different orders, analogous to three different sentences, without any pauses or other phonetic cues to the word boundaries. Here is an example of what the children heard:

golabupabikututibubabupugolabubabupututibu . . .

After listening to the strings the infants were tested to see whether they could distinguish "words" of the language like *pabiku* (which, recall, they had never heard in isolation before), from sequences of syllables that spanned word boundaries, such as *bubabu* (which the authors refer to as "partwords"). Despite the very brief exposure and the lack of boundary cues, the infants were able to distinguish the words from the partwords. The authors of the study conclude that the children do this by tracking the frequency with which the different sequences of syllables occur: The sequences inside the words (e.g., *pa-bi-ku*) remain the same whatever order the words are presented in, but the sequences of syllables that cross word boundaries will change in the different presentations and hence will occur much less frequently.

Though it is still unclear how far such statistical procedures can get the child in segmenting real language input, which is vastly larger and more varied, this experiment and others like it show that babies can use statistical information as well as linguistic structure to extract words from the input. Children may first rely on statistical properties to isolate some words, and then, based on these words, learn the rhythmic, allophonic, and phonotactic properties of the language, which they then use for further segmentation.

Studies that measure infants' reliance on statistics versus stress for segmenting words support this two stage model: younger infants (seven-and-a-half months old) respond to frequency while older infants (nine-month-olds) attend to stress.

The Acquisition of Phonology

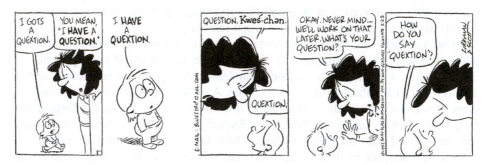

"Baby Blues", Baby Blues Partnership. Reprinted with permission of King Features Syndicate

In terms of his phonology, J. P. is like most children at the one-word stage. The first words are generally monosyllabic with a CV (consonant-vowel) form and the child's phonemic inventory is much smaller than is found in the adult language. It appears that children first acquire the small set of sounds common to all languages regardless of the ambient language(s), and in later stages acquire the less common sounds of their own language. J. P.'s sound system followed this pattern. His phonological inventory at an early stage included the consonants [b], [m], [d], and [k], which are frequently occurring sounds in the world's languages.

The distribution and frequency of sounds in a language can also influence the acquisition of certain segments. Sounds that are expected to be acquired late may appear earlier in children's language when they are frequently occurring. The fricative [v] is a very late acquisition in English but it is an early phoneme in Estonian, Bulgarian, and Swedish, languages that have several [v]-initial words that are common in the vocabularies of young children.

If the first year is devoted to figuring out the sounds of the target language, the second year involves learning how these sounds are used in the phonology of the language, especially which contrasts are phonemic. When children first begin to contrast one pair of a set (e.g., when they learn that /p/ and /b/ are distinct phonemes due to a voicing difference), they also begin to distinguish between other similar pairs (e.g., /t/ and /d/, /s/, and /z/, and all the other voiceless/ voiced phonemic pairs). As we would expect, the generalizations refer to natural classes of speech sounds.

Children may produce certain sounds in a way that makes them indiscernible to adult observers. A child's pronunciation of *wing* and *ring* may seem the same to the adult ear, but acoustic analyses of his utterances can show that they are physically different sounds. And in a picture identification experiment the child will correctly identity both a ring and a wing. As a further example, a spectrographic analysis (see Chapter 10) of *ephant*, "elephant," produced by a three-year-old child, clearly showed an [l] in the representation of the word, even though the adult experimenter could not hear it.

Anecdotal reports also show the disparity between the child's production and his phonological representation. An example is the exchange between a linguist and his two-year-old son (linguists love to experiment on their own children). At this age the child's pronunciation of "mouth" is [maʊs].

FATHER:	What does [maʊs] mean?
CHILD:	Like a cat.
FATHER:	Yes, what else?
CHILD:	Nothing else.
FATHER:	It's part of your head.
CHILD:	(*fascinated*)
FATHER:	(*touching child's mouth*) What's this?
CHILD:	[maʊs]

It took the child a few seconds to realize that he was pronouncing "mouse" and "mouth" the same. This is probably because his lexical representations of the two words were closer to the adult forms than were his actual pronunciations. Children seem to accurately perceive the adult form, and represent it as such (approximately) in their lexicon, but they are unable in these early years to produce it correctly. Therefore, even at this early stage, it is not possible to determine the extent of the grammar of the child—in this case, the phonology—simply by observing speech production. It is often necessary to use various experimental and instrumental techniques to reveal the child's underlying competence.

A child's first words show many substitutions of one feature for another or one phoneme for another. In the preceding examples, *mouth* [maʊθ] is pronounced *mouse* [maʊs], with the alveolar fricative [s] replacing the less common interdental fricative [θ]; and *ring* is pronounced *wing*, with the glide [w] replacing the liquid [r]. In general glides are acquired earlier than liquids, and hence substitute for them. Similarly, alveolars are acquired earlier than interdentals and replace them in production. These substitutions are simplifications of the adult pronunciation. They make articulation easier until the child achieves greater articulatory control.

Children's early (mis-)pronunciations are not haphazard. The phonological substitutions are rule-governed. The following is an abridged lexicon for another child, Michael, between the ages of eighteen and twenty-one months:

[pun]	"spoon"	[maɪtl]	"Michael"
[pem]	"plane"	[daɪtər]	"diaper"
[tɪs]	"kiss"	[pati]	"Papi"
[taʊ]	"cow"	[mani]	"Mommy"
[tin]	"clean"	[bərt]	"Bert"
[polər]	"stroller"	[bərt]	"(Big) Bird"

Michael systematically substituted the alveolar stop [t] for the velar stop [k] as in his words for "cow," "clean," "kiss," and his own name. He also replaced labial [p] with [t] when it occurred in the middle of a word, as in his words for "Papi" and "diaper." He reduced consonant clusters in "spoon," "plane," and "stroller," and he devoiced final stops as in "Big Bird." In devoicing the final [d] in "bird," he created an ambiguous form [bərt] referring both to Bert and Big Bird. Little wonder that only parents understand their children's first words!

Michael's substitutions are typical of the phonological rules that operate in the very early stages of acquisition. Other common rules are reduplication—"bottle" becomes [baba], "water" becomes [wawa]; and the dropping of final consonants—"bed" becomes [be], "cake" becomes [ke]. These two rules show that the children prefer simple CV syllables. Of the many phonological rules that children create, no child will necessarily use all rules.

Early phonological rules generally reflect natural phonological processes that also occur in adult languages. For example, various adult languages have a rule of syllable-final consonant devoicing (for example, in German hʊnd/ 'dog' is pronounced [hʊnt]. Children do not create bizarre or whimsical rules. Their rules conform to the possibilities made available by Universal Grammar.

The Acquisition of Word Meaning

> Suddenly I felt a misty consciousness as of something forgotten—a thrill of returning thought; and somehow the mystery of language was revealed to me . . . Everything had a name, and each name gave birth to a new thought.
>
> HELEN KELLER, *The Story of My Life*, 1903

How do children figure out the meaning of a word? Most people do not see this aspect of acquisition as posing a great problem. The intuitive view is that children look at an object, the mother says a word, and the child connects the sounds with the object. However, this is not as easy as it seems. As the linguist Lila Gleitman points out:

> A child who observes a cat sitting on a mat also observes . . . a mat supporting a cat, a mat under a cat, a floor supporting a mat and a cat, and so on. If the adult now says "The cat is on the mat" even while pointing to the cat on the mat, how is the child to choose among these interpretations of the situation?[1]

Even if the child succeeds in associating the word *cat* with the animal on the mat he may mistakenly interpret "cat" as "Cat," the name of that particular animal, instead of a type of animal. Upon hearing the word *dog* in the presence of a dog, say, a poodle, how does the child know that "dog" can also refer to

[1]Gleitman, L.R., and E. Wanner. 1982. *Language acquisition: The state of the art.* Cambridge, UK: Cambridge University

huge mastiffs, tiny terriers, bulldogs, and greyhounds, all of which look rather different from one another? What about cows, lambs, and other four-legged mammals? Why are they not "dogs"? The child has to figure out that certain words refer to classes of objects and not just to the object in a particular situation. To do this, he must determine what relevant features (four legs, fur, tail, bark, etc.) define that class of objects, and he must do this largely on his own. Nobody provides the child with explicit information on how to extend the use of a word to other entities that the word refers to. In learning the meanings of words, as in other aspects of language acquisition, children are confronted with impoverished data.

The child's early vocabulary provides insight into how children use words and how they construct word meaning. J. P. originally used his word for *sock* not only for socks but for other undergarments that are put on over the feet such as undershorts. Similarly, a child may use the word *doggie* to refer to any four-legged animal or *daddy* to refer to any adult male. This is referred to as **overextension**: The child's word seems to encompass a broader class than the adult's. This might be because he has a different meaning for the word, or, that he lacks familiarity with the more specific terms and actually knows the adult meaning.

Controlled experiments reveal that overextensions are usually based on physical attributes such as size, shape, and texture. *Ball* may refer to all round things, *bunny* to all furry things, and so on. But children will not make overextensions based on color. In experiments, they will group objects by shape and give them a name, but they will not assign a name to a group of red objects. Children are predisposed to attach and extend labels to objects in particular ways. In this instance, they show a *form over color* learning principle.

Similarly, if an experimenter points to an unfamiliar object and uses a non-sense word like *zav*, saying "that's a zav," the child will interpret the word to refer to the whole object, not to one of its parts or attributes, the *whole object* principle. On the other hand, if the experimenter utters "that's a zav" in the presence of an object whose name is already known to the child such as a boat, the child will take *zav* to refer to a part of the boat like the sail. Children initially assume that if an object has one name it cannot have another: a *boat* can't also be a *zav*. This "one name one thing" principle ensures that children are able to learn words that refer to things other than whole objects such as parts and attributes of objects.

Given the poverty of stimulus, principles like "form over color," "whole object" and "one name one thing" facilitate word learning. Without such principles, it is doubtful that children could learn words as quickly as they do. Children learn approximately fourteen words a day for the first six years of their lives. That averages to about 5,000 words per year. How many students know 10,000 words of a foreign language after two years of study?

There is also experimental evidence that children can learn the meaning of one class of words—verbs—based on the syntactic environment in which they occur. If you were to hear a sentence such as *John blipped Mary the gloon*, you would not know exactly what John did, but you would likely understand that the sentence is describing a transfer of something from John to Mary. Similarly, if you heard *John gonked that Mary . . .* , you would conclude that the verb *gonk* was a verb of communication like *say* or a mental verb like *think*. The complement types that a verb selects can provide clues to its meaning and thereby help the child. This learning of word meaning based on syntax is referred to as **syntactic bootstrapping**.

The Acquisition of Morphology

"Baby Blues", Baby Blues Partnership. Reprinted with permission of King Features Syndicate

Children's acquisition of morphology provides some of the clearest evidence of rule learning. Their errors in inflectional morphology reveal that children acquire the regular rules of the grammar and then overapply them. This **overgeneralization** occurs when children treat irregular verbs and nouns as if they were regular. We have probably all heard children say *bringed, goed, drawed,* and *runned,* or *foots, mouses,* and *sheeps.*

These mistakes tell us much about how children learn language because such forms could not arise through imitation. They tell us that children are acquiring rules and that they apply these rules broadly before learning that there are exceptions such as *mice, ran,* and so on. Some studies of the acquisition of morphology are based on children's spontaneous use of language. Other studies rely on experiments that elicit particular forms from children. A classic experimental study of English-speaking children was based on the "wug test" (Berko, 1958). Children were shown a drawing of a nonsense animal like the funny creature shown in the following picture. Each "animal" was given a nonsense name. The experimenter would then say to the child, pointing to the picture, "This is a wug."

Then, the experimenter would show the child a picture of two of the animals and say, "Now here is another one. There are two of them. There are two _____."

The child's task was to give the plural form, "wugs" [wʌgz]. Another little make-believe animal was called a "bik," and when the child was shown two biks, he or she again was to say the plural form [bɪks]. The children applied regular plural formation to words they had never heard, showing that they had acquired the plural rule. Their ability to add [z] when the animal's name ended with a voiced sound, and [s] when there was a final voiceless consonant, showed that the children were also using allomorphy rules based on an understanding of natural classes of phonological segments, and not simply imitating words they had previously heard. Similar elicitations were done for past tense -*ed* and present tense -*s*, among other forms.

Studies of children acquiring languages with richer inflectional morphology than English reveal that they learn agreement rules at a very early age. For example, Italian verbs must be inflected for number and person to agree with the subject. This is similar to the English agreement rule "add *s* to the verb" for third-person, singular subjects—*He giggles a lot* but *We giggle a lot*—except that in Italian more verb forms must be acquired. Italian-speaking children between the ages of 1;10 (one year, ten months) and 2;4 correctly inflect the verb, as the following utterances of Italian children show:

Tu leg**gi** il libro.	"You (second person singular) read the book."
Io va**do** fuori.	"I go (first person singular) outside."
Dorme miao dorme.	"Sleeps (third person singular) cat sleeps."
Leg**giamo** il libro.	"(We) read (first person plural) the book."

Similar results have been shown for children acquiring other richly inflected languages such as Spanish, German, Catalan, and Swahili. It is rare for them to make agreement errors, just as it is rare for an English-speaking child to say "I goes."

Many languages, including the ones just noted, also have gender and number agreement between the head noun and the article and adjectives inside the noun phrase. Children as young as two years old respect these agreement requirements when producing NPs, as shown by the following Italian examples:

E mi**a** gonn**a**.	"(It) is my (feminine singular) skirt."
Questo mio bimb**o**.	"This my (masculine singular) baby."
Guarda **la** mel**a** piccolin**a**.	"Look at the little (feminine singular) apple."
Guarda **il** top**o** piccolin**o**.	"Look at the little (masculine singular) mouse."

Experimental studies with two-year-old French-speaking children show that they use gender information on determiners to help identify the subsequent noun: *le ballon* (the-masc. balloon) versus *la banane* (the-fem. banana).

Children also show knowledge of the derivational rules of their language and use these rules to create novel words, as illustrated in English where we can derive verbs from nouns. From the noun *Google* we now have a verb *to google*; from the noun *friend* Facebook users derived the verb *to friend*. Children acquire the noun to verb rule early and use it often because there are lots of gaps in their verb vocabulary.

Child Utterance	**Adult Translation**
You have to scale it first.	"You have to weigh it first."
Don't broom my mess!	"Don't sweep up my mess!."
Mommy nippled Anna.	"Mommy breastfed Anna."
Will you chocolate my milk?	"Will you put chocolate in my milk?"

Children also overgeneralize some derivational morphemes such as the -*er* suffix used to mark agents and instruments:

cooker   cook
brakers   car brakes
storier   story teller
mistaker   mistake maker

And they create their own compounds:

crow-bird   crow
firetruck-man   firefighter
mower-blower   gardener
sky-car   airplane

These novel forms provide further evidence that language acquisition is a creative process and that children's utterances reflect their internal grammars, which include both derivational and inflectional rules.

The Acquisition of Syntax

"Doonesbury" 1984 G.B. Trudeau. Reprinted with permission of Universal Press Syndicate

When a child is still in the holophrastic stage, adults listening to the one-word utterances often feel that the child is trying to convey a more complex message. Experimental techniques show that at that stage (and even earlier), children have knowledge of some syntactic rules. In these experiments, the infant sits on his mother's lap and hears a sentence over a speaker while seeing two video displays depicting different actions, one of which corresponds to the sentence. Infants tend to look longer at the video that matches the sentence they hear. This methodology allows researchers to tap the linguistic knowledge of children who are using only single words or who are not talking at all. Results show that children as young as seventeen months can understand the difference between sentences such as "Ernie is tickling Bert" and "Bert is tickling Ernie."

Because these sentences have all the same words, the child cannot be relying on the words alone to understand the meanings. He must also understand the word-order rules and how they determine the grammatical relations of subject and object. This same preferential looking technique has shown that eighteen-month-olds can distinguish between subject and object in *wh* questions such as *What did the apple hit?* and *What hit the apple?* These results and many others strongly suggest that children's syntactic competence is ahead of their productive abilities, as we have also seen in children's lexical acquisition and the development of other components of grammar.

Around the time of their second birthday children begin to put words together into utterances such as the following:[2]

Cat stand up table.	Mommy sock.
What that?	Ride truck.
He play little tune.	Milk in there.
Want that.	Doggie big.
Cathy build house.	Bib off.
No sit there.	Ride truck.
Show Mommy that.	Bye bye boat.

These early utterances express a variety of semantic and syntactic relations. For example, noun + noun sentences such as *Mommy sock* can be a subject + object relation when the mother is putting the sock on the child, or a possessive relation when the child is pointing to Mommy's sock. When children first produce multi-word utterances, they are inconsistent in their use of function words (grammatical morphemes) such as *a* and *the,* subject pronouns like *I* and *we,* auxiliary verbs such as *can* and *is,* and in some languages, verbal inflection. Many (though not all) of their utterances consist only of open-class or content words. During this stage, children often sound as if they are sending a text message or reading an old-fashioned telegram (which contains only the required words for basic understanding). For this reason, such utterances are sometimes called "telegraphic speech," and we call this period of development, the **telegraphic stage**.

Unlike the adult sending a text, however, the child does not deliberately leave out function words. Telegraphic sentences reflect her linguistic capacity at that particular stage of language development. It can take many months before a child uses all the grammatical morphemes consistently.

There is a great deal of debate among linguists about how to explain telegraphic speech: Do children omit function morphemes because of limitations in their ability to plan and produce longer, more complex sentences? Or do they omit these morphemes because their grammar permits such elements to be unexpressed? On the first account telegraphic speech is due to performance limitations. Since there is an upper limit on the length of utterances a child can produce, and function morphemes are less important to comprehension, they are omitted. On the second view telegraphic speech is an early grammatical stage

---

[2]Many of the examples of child language in this chapter are taken from CHILDES (Child Language Data Exchange System), a computerized database of the spontaneous speech of children acquiring English and many other languages. MacWhinney, B., and C. Snow. 1985. The child language data exchange system. *Journal of Child Language* 12: 271–96.

similar to adult languages like Italian or Spanish that allow subject pronouns to be dropped, as in *Hablo ingles* "(I) speak English."

Some features of telegraphic speech are universal. All children have a tendency to drop the subject of the sentence, as in *Want that* meaning "*I* want that," whether their language permits it or not (English does not, Spanish does). On the other hand, certain features of a child's telegraphic speech occur in some languages and not others, such as the omission of verb inflection in *Cathy build house*. Children acquiring inflectional languages like Italian or Russian do not drop verb endings.

Although children's sentences during the telegraphic stage may lack certain function morphemes, they nevertheless obey syntactic rules similar to those in the adult grammar. Children almost never violate the word-order rules of their language. In languages with relatively fixed word order, such as English and Japanese, children use the required order (SVO in English, SOV in Japanese) from the earliest stage. In languages with freer word order, such as Turkish and Russian, where grammatical relations are indicated by case markers, children quickly learn this morphology, marking subjects with nominative case and objects with accusative case with few errors.

The correct use of word order, case marking, and agreement rules shows that even though children may often omit function morphemes, they are aware of constituent structure, which, as in adult grammar, may be represented with these (simplified, non X-bar) phrase structure trees:

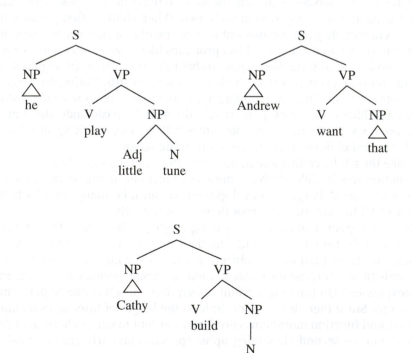

In order to apply the morphological and syntactic rules, she must know what syntactic categories the words in his language belong to. But how exactly does the child come to know that *want* and *dance* are verbs and *song* and *house* are nouns? One suggestion is that children first rely on the meaning of a word to figure out its category. This is called **semantic bootstrapping**. The child may have rules such as "if a word refers to a physical object, it's a noun" or "if a word refers to an action, it's a verb," and so on. However, the rules that link certain meanings to specific categories are not foolproof. The word *action* denotes an action, but it is not a verb; *know* is not an action, but is a verb; and *justice* is a noun though it is not a physical object. But the rules that drive semantic bootstrapping might be helpful for the kind of words children learn early on, which tend to refer to objects and actions.

Word frames may also help the child determine when words belong to the same category. Studies of the language that adults use to children show that there are certain frames that occur frequently enough to be reliable for categorization, for example, "you ___ it" and "the ___ one." Most typically, verbs such as *see, do, did, win, fix, turned,* and *get* occur in the first frame while adjectives like *red, big, wrong,* and *light* occur in the second. If a child knows that *see* is a verb, then he could also deduce that all the other words appearing in the same frame are also verbs. This *distributional evidence* is not foolproof, however. "It___ the" can frame a verb, as in *It hit the car*, but it can also frame a preposition, as in *I hit it **across** the street*. Nevertheless, like semantic bootstrapping, this evidence may be reliable enough to give the child a head start into the complex task of learning the syntactic categories of words.

The most frequent frames typically consist of function words, determiners such as *the* and *a*, and pronouns like *it* and *one*. This suggests that children recognize and learn from function morphemes in the input even though they omit these elements in their own speech. Indeed, comprehension studies show two-year-olds respond more appropriately to grammatical commands such as *Find the bird* than to commands with an ungrammatically positioned function word as in *Find was bird*. This means that children pay attention to the particular function morphemes and not just to the prosody of the sentence, which is the same in the two commands. Other studies show that function morphemes such as determiners and verb inflections help children in word segmentation and categorization.

Sometime between the ages of 2;6 and 3;6, a virtual language explosion occurs. At this point it is difficult to identify distinct stages because the child is undergoing so much development so rapidly. By the age of 3;0, most children are consistent in their use of function morphemes. Moreover, they have begun to produce and understand a variety of complex structures. Following is a sample of Michael's utterances between the ages of 2;1 and 3;2 which illustrate the speed with which children's language development progresses during this period.

2;1   Monsters eating turkey.
        Cow tired.
        Derz (there's) Mommy Rabbit sleeping.
        Use potty.
        Bringing toys.
        Take it out.

2;5   I bang it down like this.
        What's that one over there?
        I'm gonna dump [jump] in the swimming pool.
        I went in the potty last night.
        I trying to reach a carrot.
        I gotta get those cookies over der [there].
        He have a belly ache.
        We not strong enough.

2;7   Her baby is like this.
        I didn't like those friends
        Why they would be hard?
        No, 'cause there's a monster and the monster can [s]care you.
        I thought it was a ladder
        I see a man who plays football.
        He putting the fire in the dragon's mouth.

2;11   Do you give me a big piece, mom?
        We didn't save it 'cause somebody throwed it in the grass.
        Mommy, is it ok to take a walk?
        I bumped into people I went past and I bumped into those things.
        Why does he have colors on his arm?
        Now you need to hold the basket.
        I like it when it's Christmas.
        I can't find a block that's big.
        I just want to do it by myself.

3;2   Watch what I'm doing.
        I want her to be the doctor.
        Ok, but first I need to stand on here.
        I said when I start all these machines you can do it.
        Now give it back to me and we put it where all the other things are
        I forgot to press the buddons [buttons].
        I have it in someplace nobody can see it.
        I need to show you what I can sing.
        You know what we can hang up here
        Mom, can you put sand on this?

In less than a year, Michael has gone from telegraphic utterances to fully formed, grammatical adultlike sentences. His use of coordinated sentences, relative clauses and other kinds of embedded clauses illustrate his knowledge of recursive rules and his potential to produce an infinite range of sentences. By the age of four, Michael, like all children everywhere, will have acquired much of the complexity of the adult grammar.

The Acquisition of Pragmatics

"Baby Blues", Baby Blues Partnership. Reprinted with permission of King Features Syndicate

In addition to acquiring the rules of grammar, children must learn the appropriate use of language in context, or pragmatics. The cartoon is funny because of the inappropriateness of the interaction, showing that Zoe hasn't completely acquired the pragmatic "maxims of conversation" discussed in Chapter 4.

Context is needed to determine the reference of pronouns. A sentence such as "Surely he loves her anyway" is uninterpretable unless both speaker and hearer understand who the pronouns *he* and *her* refer to. If the sentence were preceded by "I saw John and Mary arguing in the park," then the referents of the pronouns would be clear. Children are not always sensitive to the needs of other speakers and they may fail to establish the referents for pronouns. It is not unusual for a three- or four-year-old (or even older children) to use pronouns out of the blue, like the child who cries to her mother "He hit me" when mom has no idea who did the deed.

The speaker and listener form part of the context of an utterance. The meaning of *I* and *you* depends on who is talking and who is listening, which changes from situation to situation. Younger children (around age two) have difficulty with the "shifting reference" of these pronouns. A typical error that children make at this age is to refer to themselves as "you," saying "You want to take a walk" when they mean "I want to take a walk."

Children also show a lack of pragmatic awareness in the way they sometimes use articles. Like pronouns, the interpretation of articles depends on context. The definite article *the*, as in "the boy," can be used felicitously only when it is clear to speaker and hearer what boy is being discussed. In a discourse, the indefinite article *a/an* must be used for the first mention of a new referent, but the definite article (or pronoun) may be used in subsequent mentions, as illustrated following:

A boy walked into the class.
He was in the wrong room.
The teacher directed the boy to the right classroom.

Children do not always respect the pragmatic rules for articles. In experimental studies, three-year-olds may use the definite article for introducing a new referent. In other words, the child tends to assume that his listener knows who he is talking about without having established this in a linguistically appropriate way.

Implicatures are another part of pragmatics that young children have difficulty with. (Implicatures are discussed in Chapter 4.) An adult hearing the sentence *Some of the children are playing ball* would infer that not all the children are playing ball. This is because adults follow Grice's conversational maxims, among which is the principle that speakers are maximally informative. If all the children were playing ball, a cooperative speaker would say so even though if *all* the children are playing ball then it is logically true that *some* of the children are playing ball. Interestingly, children under the age of seven or often fail to get such implicatures. Various experimental studies have shown that when presented with a description of a scenario in which a stronger, more informative term such as *all* would be appropriate, children readily accept a weaker, less informative *some*. For example, in one experiment the child is shown an animated video in which a mouse, who likes vegetables, picks up all the carrots in the display. A puppet who is watching the animation with the child then says "The mouse picked up some of the carrots." When the child is then asked by the experimenter if the puppet said the right thing, he responds "yes," while adults in this situation would say" No, he picked up *all* of the carrots." In one sense, the child is not wrong in his response—the mouse did pick up some of the carrots—in fact he picked them all up. But, adults use pragmatic principles in such cases while children seem to rely more heavily on the literal or logical meaning.

It may take a child months or years to master those aspects of pragmatics that involve the felicitous use of determiners and pronouns, or the conversational maxims which when flouted result in implicatures. Other aspects of pragmatics are acquired very early. Even in the holophrastic stage children use their one-word utterances with different illocutionary force (see Chapter 4). The utterance "up" spoken by J. P. at sixteen months might be a simple statement such as "The teddy is up on the shelf," or a request: "Pick me up." By age three, Michael was producing grammatically well-formed, and pragmatically appropriate, declaratives, interrogatives and imperatives. And as we will discuss below, bilingual children—even very young ones—understand which of their languages to use in different conversational contexts.

The Development of Auxiliaries: A Case Study

We have seen in this chapter that language acquisition involves development in various components—the lexicon, phonology, morphology, and syntax, as well as pragmatics. These different modules interact in complex ways to chart an overall course of language development.

As an example, let us take the case of English auxiliaries. As noted earlier, children in the telegraphic stage do not typically use auxiliaries such as *can, will,* or *do,* and they often omit *be* and *have* from their utterances. Several syntactic constructions in English depend on the presence of an auxiliary, the most central of which are questions and negative sentences. To negate a main verb requires an auxiliary verb (or *do* if there isn't one) as in the following examples:

I don't like this book.
I won't read this book.

An adult does not say "I not like this book."

Similarly, as discussed in Chapter 3, English yes–no and *wh* questions are formed by moving an auxiliary to precede the subject, as in the following examples:

Can I leave now?
Do you love me?
Where should John put the book?

Although the two-year-old does not produce auxiliaries and therefore cannot use Aux movement to form questions, she can produce a question using the rising intonation typical of yes–no questions in English, as in the following examples:

Yes–No Questions	Wh Questions
I ride train?	What he eat?
Mommy eggnog?	Where Daddy go?
Have some?	What dat train doing?

The *wh* questions also lack auxiliaries, but they show that the child knows the grammatical rule that requires *wh* phrases to move to a fronted position. She also has the pragmatic knowledge to make a request or ask for information, and she has the appropriate prosody, which depends on knowledge of phonology and the syntactic structure of the question. Many components of language must be in place to form an adultlike question.

In languages that do not require auxiliaries to form questions, children appear more advanced. For example, in Dutch and Italian the main verb moves. Because many main verbs are acquired before auxiliaries, Dutch and Italian children produce questions in the telegraphic stage that follow the adult rule (the moved verb is underlined):

Dutch

En wat <u>doen</u> ze daar?	and what do they there	"And what are they doing there?"
<u>Wordt</u> mama boos?	becomes mama angry	"Is mommy angry?"
<u>Weet</u> je n kerk?	know you a church	"Do you know a church?"

Italian

Cosa <u>fanno</u> questi bambini?	what do these children	"What are these babies doing?"
Chando <u>vene</u> a mama?	when comes the mommy	"When is Mommy coming?"
<u>Vola</u> cici?	flies birdie	"Is the birdie flying?"

The Dutch and Italian children demonstrate that there is nothing intrinsically difficult about syntactic movement rules. The delay that English-speaking children show in producing adultlike questions may simply be because auxiliaries are acquired later than main verbs and because English is idiosyncratic in forming questions by moving only auxiliaries.

The lack of auxiliaries during the telegraphic stage also affects the formation of negative sentences. During this stage the English-speaking child's negative sentences do not look very adultlike:

He no bite you.
Wayne not eating it.
Kathryn not go over there.
That no fish school.

However, the negative marker is appropriately positioned before the verb. Children never produce errors such as "Mommy dances not." Children at this stage also understand the pragmatic force of negation. The child who says "No!" when asked to take a nap knows exactly what he means.

As children acquire the auxiliaries, they generally use them correctly; that is, the auxiliary usually appears before the subject in yes–no questions, but not always in *wh* questions.

Yes–No Questions
Does the kitty stand up?
Can I have a piece of paper?
Will you help me?
We can go now?

Wh Questions
Which way they should go?
What can we ride in?
What will we eat?

Once auxiliaries are introduced into the child's grammar they are correctly negated, although *be* is still missing in many cases.

Paul can't have one.
Donna won't let go.
I don't want cover on it.
I am not a doctor.
It's not cold.
Paul not tired.
I not crying.

In languages such as French and German, which are like Italian and Dutch in having a rule that moves inflected main verbs, the verb appears before the negative marker. French and German children respect this rule, as shown below (the moved verb is underlined). (In the German examples *nich* is the baby form of *nicht*.)

French
<u>Veux</u> pas lolo.	want not water	"I don't want water."
<u>Marche</u> pas.	walks not	"She doesn't walk."
Ça <u>tourne</u> pas.	that turns not	"That doesn't turn."

German

<u>Macht</u> nich aua.	makes not ouch	"It doesn't hurt."
<u>Brauche</u> nich lala.	need not pacifier	"I don't need a pacifier."
<u>Schmeckt</u> auch nich.	tastes also not	"It doesn't taste good either."

Though the stages of language development are universal, they are shaped by the grammar of the particular adult language the child is acquiring. During the telegraphic stage, German, French, Italian, and English-speaking children all omit auxiliaries, but they form negative sentences and questions in different ways because the rules of question and negative formation are different in the respective adult languages. This tells us something essential about language acquisition: Children are sensitive to the syntactic rules of the adult target language at the earliest stages of development. Just as their phonology is quickly fine-tuned to the ambient language(s), so is their syntax.

Setting Parameters

Nowhere is the interplay of universal and language-specific properties within acquisition better illustrated than in children's setting of UG parameters.

Children acquire some aspects of syntax very early, even while they are still in the telegraphic stage. Many of these early developments correspond to what we have referred to as the parameters of UG. One such parameter determines whether the head of a phrase comes before or after its complements—that is, whether the order of the VP is verb–object (VO) as in English or OV as in Japanese. Children produce the correct word order of their language from their earliest multiword utterances, and they understand word order even when they are in the one-word stage of production. According to the parameter model of UG, the child does not actually have to formulate a word-order rule. Rather, he must choose between two already specified values: *head first* or *head last,* based on the language he hears around him. The English-speaking child can quickly figure out that the head comes before its complements; a Japanese-speaking child can equally well determine that his language is head-final.

Other parameters of UG involve the verb movement rules. In some languages, the verb can move out of the VP to higher positions in the phrase structure tree, as illustrated in the Dutch and Italian questions just discussed. In other languages, such as English, verbs do not move (only auxiliaries do). The verb movement parameters provide the child with an option: "my language does/ does not allow verb movement." As we saw, Dutch- and Italian-speaking children quickly set the verb movement parameters to the "does allow" value, and so they form questions by moving the verb. English-speaking children never make the mistake of moving the verb, even when they don't yet have auxiliaries. In both cases, the children have set the parameter at the correct value for their language. Even after English-speaking children acquire auxiliaries and the Aux movement rule, they never overgeneralize this movement to include verbs. This supports the hypothesis that the parameter is set early in development and cannot be undone. As with word order, the child does not have to formulate a rule of verb movement; he does not have to learn when the verb moves and where it moves to. This is all given by UG. He simply has to decide based on the sentences he hears around him whether verb movement is possible in his language.

The parameters of UG limit the grammatical options to a small well-defined set—is my language head-first or head-last, does my language have verb movement or not, and so on. Parameters greatly reduce the acquisition burden on the child and contribute to explaining the ease and rapidity of language acquisition.

The Acquisition of Signed Languages

Deaf children who are born to deaf signing parents are naturally exposed to sign language just as hearing children are naturally exposed to spoken language. Given the universal aspects of sign and spoken languages, it is not surprising that language development in these deaf children parallels the stages of spoken language acquisition. Deaf children babble, they then progress to single signs similar to the single words in the holophrastic stage, and finally they begin to combine signs. There is also a telegraphic stage in which the function signs may be omitted. Use of function signs becomes consistent at around the same age for deaf children as function words in spoken languages. The ages at which signing children go through each of these stages are comparable to the ages of children acquiring a spoken language.

We saw earlier that question formation in various spoken languages is a complex phenomenon with many interacting components, some of which are acquired early and others of which show up later in development. In *wh* questions in ASL, the *wh* phrase can move or it can be left in its original position. Both of the following sentences are grammatical:

_____whq
WHO BILL SEE YESTERDAY?
_____whq
BILL SAW WHO YESTERDAY?

(Note: We follow the convention of writing the glosses for signs in uppercase letters.)

There is no Aux movement in ASL, but a question is accompanied by a facial expression with tilted head and furrowed brows. This is represented by the *whq* above the ASL glosses. Such *non-manual markers* are part of the grammar of ASL. It is like the rising intonation of questions in English and other spoken languages.

Signing children easily learn the rules associated with the *wh* questions in ASL. The children sometimes move the *wh* phrase and sometimes leave it in place, as adult signers do. But they often omit the nonmanual marker, an omission that is not grammatical in the adult language.

Sometimes the parallels between the acquisition of signed and spoken languages are striking. For example, some of the grammatical morphemes in ASL are semantically transparent or **iconic**, that is, they look like what they mean. Not surprisingly, the sign for the pronoun "I" is the speaker pointing to his chest whereas the sign for the pronoun "you" is a point to the chest of the addressee.

As noted earlier, at around age two, children acquiring spoken languages often reverse the pronouns *I* and *you*. Interestingly, at this same age signing children make this same error. They will point to themselves when they mean "you" and point to the addressee when they mean "I." Children acquiring ASL make this error despite the transparency or iconicity of these particular signs, because signing children (like signing adults) treat these pronouns as linguistic symbols and not simply as pointing gestures. As part of the language, the shifting reference of these pronouns presents the same problem for signing children that it does for speaking children.

Deaf children of hearing parents who are not exposed to sign language from birth suffer a severe handicap in acquiring language. They have great difficulty learning a spoken language because normal speech depends largely on auditory feedback. To learn to speak, a deaf child requires extensive training in special schools or programs designed especially for deaf people and they rarely achieve the proficiency that hearing children do.

Late learners of sign language do not achieve the same level of competence as children who are exposed early in life, similar to late learners of spoken language. Yet, the instinct to acquire language is so strong in humans that deaf children often begin to develop their own manual gestures. A study of six such children revealed that they not only developed individual signs but also joined pairs and formed sentences with definite syntactic order and systematic constraints. Although these "home signs," as they are called, are not fully developed languages like ASL, they have a linguistic complexity and systematicity that could not have come from the input, because there was no input. Cases such as these demonstrate not only the strong drive that humans have to communicate through language, but also the innate basis of language structure.

The Role of the Linguistic Environment: Adult Input

[The acquisition of language] is doubtless the greatest intellectual feat any one of us is ever required to perform.

LEONARD BLOOMFIELD, *Language*, 1933

Children deprived of linguistic input show a clear drive to acquire language and may even create a rudimentary linguistic system, as illustrated by deaf children who create home signs. But there is little doubt that children require a language environment to develop a mature linguistic system. But what exactly is the function of the linguistic input that children receive? Parameter-setting models of acquisition suggest that children use the linguistic data to extract the underlying rules and parameter settings of their language.

Other approaches to understanding language acquisition afford a much more pronounced and formative role to the input provided by adults. Early behaviorist views as well as some more recent theories that stress the role of general learning mechanisms, hold that the adult input and feedback to the child is paramount. However, most linguists and psychologists now recognize that language is a complex cognitive system that cannot be fully acquired by behaviorist or general learning principles. In the next section, we discuss some of the mechanisms once proposed by behaviorists to account for language acquisition.

The Role of Imitation, Reinforcement, and Analogy

CHILD: My teacher holded the baby rabbits and we patted them.
ADULT: Did you say your teacher held the baby rabbits?
CHILD: Yes.
ADULT: What did you say she did?
CHILD: She holded the baby rabbits and we patted them.
ADULT: Did you say she held them tightly?
CHILD: No, she holded them loosely.

ANONYMOUS ADULT AND CHILD

A common misconception about language acquisition is that children simply listen to what is said around them and imitate the speech they hear. Imitation is involved to some extent, of course. An American child hears *milk* and a Mexican child *leche* and each child attempts to reproduce what he hears. But children's early words and sentences show that they are not simply imitating adult speech. Children use inflectional and derivational processes to produce novel words, and their early sentences diverge from the language of their environment in systematic and interesting ways.

Moreover, even when children are trying to imitate what they hear, they are unable to produce sentences outside of the rules of their developing grammar. The following are a child's attempts to imitate something the adult has said:

Adult	Child
He's going out.	He go out.
That's an old-time train.	Old-time train.
Adam, say what I say:	Where I can put them?
Where can I put them?	

Imitation also fails to account for the fact that children who are unable to speak for neurological or physiological reasons are able to learn the language spoken to them and understand it. When they overcome their speech impairment, they immediately use the language for speaking.

Another proposal in the behaviorist tradition is that children learn to produce correct (grammatical) sentences because adults positively reinforce them when they say something grammatical and negatively reinforce them by correction when they say something ungrammatical. But studies show that parents seldom correct their children, and when they do it is usually for mispronunciations or incorrect reporting of facts and not for "bad grammar." When uttered, the ungrammatical sentence "Her curl my hair" was not corrected because it was true: the child's mother was in fact curling her hair. However, when the child uttered the grammatical sentence "Walt Disney comes on Tuesday," she was corrected because the television program was shown on Wednesday. One researcher concluded somewhat wryly that it is "truth value rather than syntactic well-formedness that chiefly governs explicit verbal reinforcement by parents—which renders mildly paradoxical the fact that the usual product of such a training schedule is an adult whose speech is highly grammatical but not notably truthful."

Adults will sometimes **recast** children's utterances into an adultlike form, as in the following examples:

Child	Mother
It fall.	It fell?
Where is them?	They're at home.
It doing dancing.	It's dancing, yes.

In these examples, the mother provides the correct model without actually correcting the child. Although recasts are potentially helpful to the child, they are not used in a consistent way. One study of forty mothers of children two to four years old showed that only about 25 percent of children's ungrammatical sentences are recast and that overall, parents recast grammatical sentences as often as bad ones. Because parents focus more on the content than on the form of their children's utterances, and allow many ungrammatical utterances to "slip by" while correcting grammatical ones, a child that relies on recasts to learn grammar would be mightily confused.

Even if adults did correct children's syntax it would still not explain how or what children learn from such adult responses, or how children discover and construct the correct rules. Children do not know what they are doing wrong and are unable to make corrections even when "errors" are pointed out, as shown by the following exchange:

CHILD:	Nobody don't like me.
MOTHER:	No, say "Nobody likes me."
CHILD:	Nobody don't like me.
	(dialogue repeated eight times)
MOTHER:	Now, listen carefully; say "Nobody likes me."
CHILD:	Oh, nobody don't <u>likes</u> me.

It has also been suggested that children put words together to form phrases and sentences by **analogy**, by hearing a sentence and using it as a model to form other sentences. In some sense, this must be true. Children must generalize from particular instances to form a general rule. The problem with analogy is that the child must also know when the general rule does not work, as one developmental psycholinguist explains:

[S]uppose the child has heard the sentence "I painted a red barn." So now, by analogy, the child can say "I painted a blue barn." That's exactly the kind of theory that we want. You hear a sample and you extend it to all of the new cases by similarity. . . . In addition to "I painted a red barn" you might also hear the sentence "I painted a barn red." So it looks as if you take those last two words and switch their order. . . . So now you want to extend this to the case of seeing, because you want to look at barns instead of paint them. So you have heard, "I saw a red barn." Now you try (by analogy) a . . . new sentence—"I saw a barn red." Something's gone wrong. This is an analogy, but the analogy didn't work. It's not a sentence of English.[3]

Similarly, based on the sentence "John eats tomatoes" we can say "John eats" with the meaning "John eats *something*." But we cannot analogously say, based on the sentence "John grows tomatoes" that "John grows" to mean "John grows *something*."

Children do not make syntactic errors of this sort. They may overgeneralize a morphological rule or omit function morphemes. But they seem to know enough about syntactic structure not to assign a uniform analysis to sentences with *eat* and *grow* or *paint and see,* each of which has different syntactic properties. Analogy—to the extent it is used by children—must be constrained by the child's knowledge of the general structural principles provided by UG.

The Role of Structured Input

Yet, another suggestion is that children are able to learn language because adults speak to them in a special "simplified" language sometimes called **motherese**, or **child-directed speech (CDS)** (or more informally, **baby talk**). This hypothesis also places a lot of emphasis on the role of the environment in facilitating language acquisition.

In most cultures, adults talk to young children in a special way. They tend to speak more slowly and more clearly; they may speak in a higher pitch and exaggerate their intonation; and sentences directed to children are generally grammatical. Infants prefer to listen to motherese over normal adult speech. Researchers believe that the exaggerated intonation and other properties may be useful for getting a child's attention and making salient certain features of language.

However, motherese is not syntactically simple. It includes a range of complex sentences such as questions *(Do you want your juice now?);* embedded sentences *(Mommy thinks you should sleep now);* imperatives *(Pat the dog gently!);* and negatives with tag questions *(We don't want to hurt him,* do we?). Moreover, adults do not simplify their language by dropping inflections from verbs and nouns or by omitting function words such as determiners and auxiliaries, though children do this all the time.

Studies show that children's overall language development is not significantly affected by the use of motherese. The child whose mother uses more features of motherese will not develop language any faster than another child whose mother uses fewer features of this mode of speech. Adults seem to be the followers rather than the leaders in this enterprise. The child does not develop linguistically because he is exposed to ever more adultlike language. Rather, the adult adjusts his language to the child's increasing linguistic sophistication.

---

[3]Gleitman, L., in Searchinger, G. 1994. *The Human Language Series, program 2. Acquiring the Human Language.* Video New York: Equinox Film/Ways of Knowing Inc.

Imitation, reinforcement, and analogy cannot account for language development because they are based on the (implicit or explicit) assumption that what the child acquires is a set of sentences or forms rather than a set of grammatical rules and linguistic structures. Theories that assume that acquisition depends on a specially structured input also place too much emphasis on the environment rather than on the grammar-making abilities of the child. These proposals do not explain the creativity that children show in acquiring language, why they go through the stages they do, or why they make some kinds of "errors" but not others. A child may or may not say, "It doing dancing," but never "Was the boy who sleeping is dreaming?" None of those proposals address the question of how the child comes to know as much as he does about his language based on varying and impoverished input.

Knowing More Than One Language

He that understands grammar in one language, understands it in another as far as the essential properties of Grammar are concerned. The fact that he can't speak, nor comprehend, another language is due to the diversity of words and their various forms, but these are the accidental properties of grammar.

ROGER BACON (1214–1294)

People can acquire a second language under many different circumstances. You may have learned a second language when you began middle school, or high school, or college. Moving to a new country often means acquiring a new language. Other people live in communities or homes in which more than one language is spoken and may acquire two (or more) languages simultaneously. The term **second language acquisition**, or **L2 acquisition**, generally refers to the acquisition of a second language by someone (adult or child) who has already acquired a first language. This is also referred to as **sequential bilingualism**. **Bilingual language acquisition** refers to the (more or less) simultaneous acquisition of two languages beginning in infancy (or before the age of three years), also referred to as **simultaneous bilingualism**.

Childhood Bilingualism

Frank and Ernest

Bob Thaves Tom Thaves/Frank and Ernest/THE CARTOONIST GROUP

Approximately, half of the people in the world are native speakers of more than one language. This means that as children they had regular and continued exposure to those languages. In many parts of the world, especially in Africa and Asia, bilingualism (even multilingualism) is the norm. In contrast, many Western countries (though by no means all of them) view themselves as monolingual, even though they may be home to speakers of many languages. In the United States and many European countries, bilingualism is often viewed as a transitory phenomenon associated with immigration.

Bilingualism is an intriguing topic. People wonder how it's possible for a child to acquire two (or more) languages at the same time. There are many questions, such as: Doesn't the child confuse the two languages? Does bilingual language acquisition take longer than monolingual acquisition? Does bilingualism help or hinder children in their cognitive and academic development? How much exposure to each language is necessary for a child to become bilingual?

Much of the early research into bilingualism focused on the fact that bilingual children sometimes mix the two languages in the same sentences, as the following examples from French-English bilingual children illustrate. In the first example, a French word appears in an otherwise English sentence. In the other two examples, all of the words are English but the syntax is French.

His nose is perdu.	"His nose is lost."
A house pink	"A pink house"
That's to me.	"That's mine."

In early studies of bilingualism, this kind of language mixing was viewed negatively. It was taken as an indication that the child was confused or having difficulty with the two languages. In fact, many parents, sometimes on the advice of educators or psychologists, would stop raising their children bilingually when faced with this issue. However, it now seems clear that some amount of language mixing is a normal part of the early bilingual acquisition—and not an indication of any language problem.

Indeed, various researchers have claimed that language mixing in bilingual children is similar to **codeswitching** used by many adult bilinguals (discussed in Chapter 7). In specific social situations, bilingual adults may switch back and forth between their two languages in the same sentence, saying things like "I put the forks en las mesas" ("I put the forks on the tables"). Codeswitching reflects the grammars of both languages working simultaneously; it is not "bad grammar" or "broken English." Adult bilinguals codeswitch only when speaking to other bilingual speakers and various studies have shown that bilingual children as young as two make contextually appropriate language choices: In speaking to monolinguals the children use one language, and in speaking to bilinguals they mix the two languages.

Theories of Bilingual Development

There is no reason to believe that the underlying principles and mechanisms of language education [in bilinguals] are qualitatively differed from those used by monolinguals.

JURGEN MEISEL, *Linguistics* 24, 1986

These mixed utterances raise an interesting question about the grammars of bilingual children. Does the bilingual child start out with only one grammar that is eventually differentiated, or does she construct a separate grammar for each language right from the start? The **separate systems hypothesis** says that the bilingual child builds a distinct lexicon and grammar for each language.

Evidence for separate systems comes from the observation that bilingual children acquire the different rules for each of the languages in areas of grammar where the two languages diverge. Spanish-English and French-German bilingual children have been shown to use the word orders appropriate to each language, as well as the correct agreement morphemes for each language. Other studies have found that children set up two distinct lexicons and that their pronunciation reflects the phonemes and phonological rules for each language. And bilingual children—even very young ones—understand which language to use in different conversational contexts.

The separate systems hypothesis also receives support from the study of hearing children of deaf parents who are acquiring both sign and spoken languages. Canadian bilingual children who acquire Langues des Signes Quebecoise (LSQ), or Quebec Sign Language, develop the two languages exactly like bilingual children acquiring two spoken languages. The LSQ/French bilinguals reached linguistic milestones in each of their languages in parallel with Canadian children acquiring French and English. They produced their first words, as well as their first word combinations, at the same time in each language. In reaching these milestones, neither group showed any delay compared to monolingual children.

The LSQ-French bilinguals have semantically equivalent words in the two languages, just as bilinguals acquiring two spoken languages do. In addition, these children, like all bilingual children, were able to adjust their language choice to the language of their addressees. Like most bilingual children, the LSQ-French bilinguals produced mixed utterances containing words from both languages. What is especially interesting is that these children showed simultaneous language mixing. They would produce an LSQ sign and a French word at the same time, something that is only possible if one language is spoken and the other signed. However, this finding has implications for bilingual language acquisition in general. It shows that the language mixing of bilingual children is not caused by confusion, but is rather the result of two grammars operating simultaneously.

Bilingual children develop their two grammars along the same lines as monolingual children. They go through a babbling stage, a holophrastic stage, a telegraphic stage, and so on. During the telegraphic stage they show the same characteristics in each of their languages as monolingual children, further evidence of separate systems. We find that monolingual English-speaking children omit verb endings in sentences such as "Eve play there" and "Andrew want that," while German-speaking children use infinitives as in "S[ch]okolade holen" ("chocolate get-infinitive"). Spanish- and Italian-speaking monolinguals never omit verbal inflection or use infinitives in this way. Remarkably, two-year-old German-Italian bilinguals use infinitives when speaking German but not when they speak Italian. Young Spanish-English bilingual children drop the English verb endings but not the Spanish ones, and German-English bilinguals omit verbal inflection in English and use the infinitive in German. Results such as these have led some researchers to suggest that from a grammar-making point of view, the bilingual child is like "two monolinguals in one head."

The Role of Input

One issue that concerns researchers studying bilingualism, as well as parents of bilingual children, is the relationship between language input and proficiency. What role does input play in helping the child to "separate" the two languages? One input condition that has traditionally been thought to promote bilingual development is *une personne-une langue* (one person, one language)—as in, Mom speaks only language A to the child and Dad speaks only language B. The idea is that keeping the two languages separate in the input will make it easier for the child to acquire each without influence from the other. Whether this method influences bilingual development in some important way has not been established. In practice this "ideal" input situation may be difficult to attain. It may also be unnecessary. We saw earlier that babies are attuned to various phonological properties of the input language such as prosody and phonotactics. Various studies suggest that this sensitivity provides a sufficient basis for the bilingual child to keep the two languages separate.

Another question is how much input does a child need in each language to become "native" in both? It seems intuitively clear that if a child hears twelve hours of English a day and only two hours of Spanish, he will probably develop English more quickly and completely than Spanish. Even with unequal exposure there may still be sufficient input for dual fluency though one language may dominate to a lesser or greater degree. What is not known definitively is how much exposure is necessary in each language to produce a balanced bilingual. For now, the assumption is that the child should receive roughly equal amounts of input to achieve native proficiency in both.

Second Language Acquisition

Those who know nothing of foreign languages know nothing of their own.

JOHANN WOLFGANG VON GOETHE, *Maxims and Reflections*

In contrast to the bilinguals just discussed, many people are introduced to a second language (L2) after they have achieved native competence in a first language (L1). If you have had the experience of trying to master a second language as an adult, no doubt you found it to be a challenge quite unlike your first language experience.

Is Adult L2 Acquisition the Same as L1 Acquisition?

With some exceptions, adults do not readily become proficient in a second language. It usually requires conscious attention, studying, and memorization. Again, with the exception of some remarkable individuals, adult second-language learners (L2ers) do not often achieve native-like competence in the L2, especially with respect to pronunciation. They generally have an accent, and they may make syntactic or morphological errors that are unlike the errors of children acquiring their first language (L1ers). L2ers often make word order errors, especially early in their development, as well as morphological errors in verb agreement, grammatical gender and case marking. L2 errors may **fossilize** so that no amount of teaching or correction can undo them.

Unlike L1 acquisition, which is uniformly successful across children and languages, adults vary considerably in their ability to acquire an L2 completely. Some are very talented language learners; others are hopeless. Most people fall somewhere in the middle. Success may depend on a range of factors, including age, talent, motivation, and whether the learner is in a country where the language is spoken or in a classroom a few days a week without further contact with native speakers. For all these reasons, it appears that adult second language acquisition is different from first language acquisition, which expresses the **fundamental difference hypothesis** of L2 acquisition. Proponents of this hypothesis believe that adult L2ers construct grammars using general problem solving abilities such as chess-playing, and lack access to the specifically linguistic principles of UG that L1ers have to help them.

In certain important respects, however, L2 acquisition is like L1 acquisition. Like L1ers, L2ers do not acquire their second language overnight; they go through stages like L1ers, L2ers construct grammars. These grammars reflect their competence in the L2 at each stage, and so their language at any particular point, though not native-like, is rule-governed and not haphazard. The intermediate grammars that L2ers create on their way to the target have been called **interlanguage grammars.**

Consider word order in the interlanguage grammars of Romance language native speakers learning German as a second language. The word order of the Romance languages is Subject–(Auxiliary)–Verb–Object (like English). German has two basic word orders depending on the presence of an auxiliary. Sentences with auxiliaries have Subject–Auxiliary–*Object–Verb*, as in (1). Sentences without auxiliaries have Subject–*Verb–Object*, as in (2). (Note that as with the child data above, these L2 sentences may contain various "errors" in addition to the word order facts we are considering.)

1. Hans hat ein Buch gekauft.   "Hans has a book bought."
2. Hans kauft ein Buch.   "Hans buys a book."

Studies have shown that Romance speakers acquire German word order in pieces. During the first stage they use German words but the S–Aux–V–O word order of their native language, as follows:

Stage 1:   Mein Vater hat gekauft ein Buch.
          "My father has bought a book."

At the second stage, they acquire the VP word order Object–Verb.

Stage 2:   Vor Personalrat auch meine helfen.
          in the personnel office [a colleague] me helped
          "A colleague in the personnel office helped me."

At the third stage, they acquire the rule that places the verb or (auxiliary) in second position.

Stage 3:   Jetzt kann sie mir eine Frage machen.
          now can she me a question ask
          "Now she can ask me a question."

          Ich kenne nich die Welt.
          I know not the world.
          "I don't know the world."

These stages differ from those of children acquiring German, who more quickly acquire the SOV word order.

Many L2 acquisition researchers reject the idea that L2 acquisition is fundamentally different from L1 acquisition. They point to various studies that show that interlanguage grammars do not generally violate principles of UG, which makes the process seem more similar to L1 acquisition. In the German L2 examples above, the interlanguage rules may be wrong for German, or wrong for Romance, but they are not impossible rules. These researchers also note that although L2ers may fall short of L1ers in terms of their final grammar, they appear to acquire rules in the same way as L1ers.

Native Language Influence in Adult L2 Acquisition

One respect in which L1 acquisition and L2 acquisition are clearly different is that adult L2ers already have a fully developed grammar of their first language. As discussed in Chapter 1, linguistic competence is unconscious knowledge. We cannot suppress our ability to use the rules of our language. We cannot decide not to understand English.

Similarly, L2ers—especially at the beginning stages of acquiring their L2—seem to rely on their L1 grammar to some extent. This is shown by the kinds of errors L2ers make, which often involve the **transfer** of grammatical rules from their L1. This is most obvious in phonology. L2ers generally speak with an accent because they transfer the phonemes, phonological rules, syllable structures, stress placement or intonational patterns of their first language to their second language. We see this in the Japanese speaker, who does not distinguish between *write* [raɪt] and *light* [laɪt] because the r/l distinction is not phonemic in Japanese; in the French speaker, who says "ze cat in ze hat" because French does not have [ð]; in the German speaker, who devoices final consonants, saying [hæf] for *have;* and in the Spanish speaker, who inserts a schwa before initial consonant clusters, as in [əskul] for *school* and [əsnab] for *snob.*

Similarly, English speakers may have difficulty with unfamiliar sounds in other languages. For example, in Italian long (or double) consonants are phonemic. Italian has minimal pairs such as the following:

fato	"fate"	fatto	"fact"
pala	"shovel"	palla	"ball"
dita	"fingers"	ditta	"company"

English-speaking L2 learners of Italian have difficulty in hearing and producing the contrast between long and short consonants.

We also find native language influence in the syntax and morphology. Sometimes this shows up as a wholesale transfer of a particular piece of grammar. A Spanish speaker acquiring English might drop subjects in nonimperative sentences because this is possible in Spanish, as illustrated by the following examples:

Hey, is not funny.
In here have the mouth.
Live in Colombia.

Or speakers may, in the early stages of learning, use the word order of their native language, as we saw in the Romance-German interlanguage examples.

Native language influence may show up in more subtle ways. It is common for L1 German speakers to acquire English yes–no questions faster than Japanese speakers do. This is because German has a verb movement rule for forming yes–no questions that is similar to the English Aux movement rule, while in Japanese there is no syntactic movement in question formation.

The Creative Component of L2 Acquisition

It would be an oversimplification to think that L2 acquisition involves only the transfer of L1 properties to the L2 interlanguage. There is a strong creative component to L2 acquisition. Many language-specific parts of the L1 grammar do not transfer. Items that a speaker considers irregular, infrequent, or semantically difficult are not likely to transfer to the L2. Speakers will not typically transfer L1 idioms such as *He hit the roof* meaning "He got angry." They are more likely to transfer structures in which the semantic relations are transparent. For example, a structure such as (1) will transfer more readily than (2).

1. It is awkward to carry this suitcase.
2. This suitcase is awkward to carry.

In (1) the NP "this suitcase" is in its logical direct object position, while in (2) it has been moved to the subject position away from the verb that selects it.

Many of the "errors" that L2ers do make are not derived from their L1. Turkish speakers at a particular stage in their development of German often use S–V–Adv (Subject–Verb–Adverb) word order in embedded clauses (the *wenn* clause in the following example) in their German interlanguage, even though both their native language and the target language have S–Adv–V order:

| Wenn | ich | geh | zuruck | ich | arbeit | elektriker | in der Turkei. |
| if | I | go | back, | I | work (as an) | electrician | in Turkey |

(Cf. *Wenn ich **zuruck geh** ich arbeit elektriker*, which is grammatically correct German.)

The embedded S–V–Adv order is most likely an overgeneralization of the verb-second requirement in German main clauses. As in L1 acquisition overgeneralization is a clear indication that a rule has been acquired.

Why certain L1 rules transfer to the interlanguage grammar and others don't is not well understood. It is clear, however, that although construction of the L2 grammar is influenced by the L1 grammar, developmental principles— possibly universal—also operate in L2 acquisition. This is best illustrated by the fact that speakers with different L1s go through similar L2 stages. Turkish, Serbo-Croatian, Italian, Greek, and Spanish L1ers acquiring German as an L2 all drop articles to some extent. Because some of these L1s have articles and some do not, this cannot be caused by transfer, but must involve some more general property of L2 acquisition.

Heritage Language Learners

A **heritage language** learner is one who was raised with a strong cultural connection to a language spoken in his family as a result of immigration and who decides at some point to study that language more formally. The heritage language learner may have no prior linguistic knowledge of the language, or he may be bilingual to some degree in the heritage language (his weaker language). Often heritage language learners are exposed to the heritage language in childhood and then switch to another dominant language later in life, perhaps when they enter school. At this point, they may begin to lose the heritage language—a process known as **language attrition**. On the other hand, the heritage language may be maintained if the speaker continues to use it alongside the dominant language in his home or community. Sometimes a heritage language learner may speak the language, but be unable to either read or write it because he was educated only in the dominant language.

There has been growing interest in the language abilities of heritage language learners. Preliminary results suggest that the length and manner of exposure to the heritage language in childhood are important determinants of later proficiency. Learners who have consistent exposure to the language until the end of the critical period (roughly puberty) have an advantage over other L2 learners of that language, especially in the areas of phonology and lexicon. Also, studies show that parents' attitude towards the home language and culture influence children's later ability in the heritage language.

Is There a Critical Period for L2 Acquisition?

I don't know how you manage, Sir, amongst all the foreigners; you never know what they are saying. When the poor things first come here they gabble away like geese, although the children can soon speak well enough.

MARGARET ATWOOD, *Alias Grace*, 1996

Age is a significant factor in L2 acquisition. The younger a person is when exposed to a second language, the more likely she is to achieve native-like competence.

In a classic study of the effects of age on ultimate attainment in L2 acquisition, researchers tested several groups of Chinese and Korean speakers who had acquired English as a second language. The subjects, all of whom had been in the United States for at least five years, were tested on their knowledge of specific aspects of English morphology and syntax. They were asked to judge the grammaticality of sentences such as:

The little boy is speak to a policeman.
The farmer bought two pig.
A bat flewed into our attic last night.

The test results depended heavily on the age at which the person had arrived in the United States. The people who arrived as children (between the ages of three and eight) did as well as American native speakers. Those who arrived between the ages of eight and fifteen did not perform like native speakers. Moreover, every year seemed to make a difference for this group. The person who arrived at age nine did better than the one who arrived at age ten; those who arrived at age eleven did better than those who arrived at age twelve, and so on. The group that arrived between the ages of seventeen and thirty-one had the lowest scores.

Children introduced to a second language after their first language is fairly well established, at the age of 4 or so (called **child L2ers**), also show transfer of their L1 onto their L2, like adult L2ers. However, they recover more quickly. They also produce "errors" similar to monolingual learners of the language. The earliest sentences of a Turkish child acquiring English will often contain English words in the SOV word order of Turkish as in the following examples:

Would you like to outside ball playing.

I something eating.

Television watching.

At the same time, however, he will use the -*ing* form of the verb (without the auxiliary *be*), something that is typical of an L1 English learner but not a feature of Turkish early language development.

Does this mean that there is a critical period for L2 acquisition, an age beyond which it is *impossible* to acquire the grammar of a new language? Most researchers would hesitate to make such a strong claim. Although age is an important factor in achieving native-like L2 competence, it is certainly possible to acquire a second language as an adult. Many teenage and adult L2 learners become proficient, and a few highly talented ones even manage to pass for native speakers. The *ultimate attainment* of adult L2ers may fall short of native competence, but that does not necessarily mean that the *process* of L2 acquisition is fundamentally different from L1 acquisition.

It is more appropriate to say that L2 acquisition abilities gradually decline with age and that there are "sensitive periods" for native-like mastery of different aspects of the L2. The sensitive period for phonology is the shortest. To achieve native-like pronunciation of an L2 generally requires exposure during childhood. Other aspects of language, such as syntax, may have a larger window.

Some interesting research with heritage language learners provides additional support for the notion of sensitive periods in L2 acquisition. This finding is based on studies into the acquisition of Spanish by college students who had overheard the language as children (and sometimes knew a few words), but who did not otherwise speak or understand Spanish. The *overhearers* were compared to people who had no exposure to Spanish before the age of fourteen. All of the students were native speakers of English studying their heritage language as a second language. The results showed that the overhearers acquired a more native-like accent than the other students did. However, the overhearers did not show any advantage in acquiring the grammatical morphemes of Spanish. Early exposure may leave an imprint that facilitates the later acquisition of certain aspects of language.

Recent research on the neurological effects of acquiring a second language shows that left hemisphere cortical density is increased in bilinguals relative to monolinguals and that this increase is more pronounced in early versus late second-language learners. The study also shows a positive relationship between brain density and second-language proficiency. The researchers conclude that the structure of the human brain is altered by the experience of acquiring a second language. Additionally, a recent Canadian study of elderly adults showed a protective effect of lifelong bilingualism against Alzheimer's disease. Among hundreds of people with probable Alzheimer's the bilinguals showed their first symptoms of the disease five years later than monolinguals.

Summary

When children acquire a language, they acquire the grammar of that language—the phonological, morphological, syntactic, and semantic rules. They also acquire the pragmatic rules of the language as well as a lexicon. Children are not taught language. Rather, they extract the rules (and much of the lexicon) from the language(s) spoken around them.

The ease and rapidity of children's language acquisition and the uniformity development for all children and all languages, despite the **poverty of the stimulus** they receive, suggest that the language faculty is innate and that the infant comes to the complex task already endowed with a Universal Grammar. UG is not a grammar like the grammar of English or Arabic, but represents the principles and parameters to which all human languages conform. Children create grammars based on the linguistic input and are guided in this process by UG. Language acquisition is a creative process.

Language development proceeds in stages. During the first year of life children develop the sounds of their language. This begins in the **babbling stage**. They first produce and perceive many sounds that do not exist in their linguistic environment. Gradually their productions and perceptions are fine-tuned to their surroundings. Children's late babbling has all the phonological characteristics of the input language. Deaf children who are exposed at birth to sign languages also produce manual babbling, showing that babbling is a universal, biologically-triggered first stage in language acquisition that is shaped by the linguistic input received.

At the end of the first year, children utter their first words. During the second year, they learn many more words and they develop much of the phonological system of the language. Children's first utterances are one-word "sentences" (the **holophrastic** stage).

Many experimental studies show that children are sensitive to various linguistic properties such as stress and phonotactic constraints, and to statistical regularities of the input that enable them to segment the fluent speech that they hear into words. One method of segmenting speech **is prosodic bootstrapping**. Other bootstrapping methods can help the child to learn verb meaning based on syntactic context **(syntactic bootstrapping)**, or syntactic categories based on word meaning **(semantic bootstrapping)**. Distributional evidence such as **word frames** contributes both to syntactic and semantic knowledge.

After a few months, the child puts two or more words together. These early sentences are not random combinations of words—the words have definite patterns and express both syntactic and semantic relationships. During the **telegraphic stage,** the child produces longer sentences that often lack function or grammatical morphemes. The child's early grammar still lacks many of the rules of the adult grammar, but is not qualitatively different from it. Children at this stage have correct word order and rules for agreement and case, which show their knowledge of structure.

Children make specific kinds of errors while acquiring their language. For example, they will **overgeneralize** morphology by saying *bringed* or *mans*. This shows that they are acquiring rules of their particular language. Children do not seem to make errors that violate principles of Universal Grammar.

In acquiring the lexicon of the language, children may **overextend** word meaning by using *dog* to mean any four-legged creature. Despite these categorization "errors," children's word learning, like their grammatical development, is guided by general principles.

Deaf children exposed to **sign language** show the same stages of language acquisition as hearing children exposed to spoken languages. That all children go through similar stages regardless of language shows that they are equipped with special abilities to know what generalizations to look for and what to ignore, and how to discover the regularities of language, irrespective of the modality in which their language is expressed.

Several learning mechanisms have been suggested to explain the acquisition process. **Imitation** of adult speech, **reinforcement**, and **analogy** have all been proposed. None of these learning mechanisms account for the fact that children create novel (and non-adultlike) sentences according to the rules of their language, that they make certain kinds of errors but not others, and that they display knowledge of structures for which there is no evidence in the input. Empirical studies of the **motherese** hypothesis show that grammar development does not depend on the grammaticality of the linguistic input.

Children may acquire more than one language at a time. **Bilingual** children seem to go through the same stages as monolingual children except that they develop two grammars and two lexicons simultaneously. This is true for children acquiring two spoken languages as well as for children acquiring a spoken language and a sign language. Whether the child will be equally proficient in the two languages depends on the input he or she receives and the social conditions under which the languages are acquired.

In **second language acquisition, L2** learners construct grammars of the target language—called **interlanguage grammars**—that go through stages, like the grammars of first-language learners. Influence from the speaker's first language makes L2 acquisition appear different from L1 acquisition. Adults often do not achieve native-like competence in their L2, especially in pronunciation, though child L2 learners typically do. The difficulties encountered in attempting to learn languages after puberty may be because there are sensitive periods for L2 acquisition. Some theories of second language acquisition suggest that the same principles operate that account for first language acquisition. A second view suggests that the acquisition of a second language in adulthood involves general learning or cognitive mechanisms rather than the specifically linguistic principles used by children.

The universality of the language acquisition process, the stages of development, and the relatively short period in which the child constructs a complex grammatical system without overt teaching suggest that the human species is innately endowed with special language acquisition abilities and that language is based in human biology.

All normal children learn whatever language or languages they are exposed to, from Afrikaans to Zuni. This ability is not dependent on race, social class, geography, or even intelligence (within a normal range). This ability is uniquely human.

References for Further Reading

Bloom, P. 1993. *Language Acquisition: Core Readings*. Cambridge: MIT Press.

Gass, S. and L. Selinker. 2008. *Second language acquisition: An introductory course, 3rd ed.* NJ: Lawrence Erlbaum.

Guasti, M. T. 2016. *Language acquisition: The growth of grammar.* 2nd edition. Cambridge, MA: MIT Press.

Hakuta, K. 1986. *Mirror of language: The debate on bilingualism.* New York: Basic Books.

Ingram, D. 1989. *First language acquisition: method, description and explanation.* New York: Cambridge University Press.

Jakobson, R. 1971. *Studies on child language and aphasia.* The Hague: Mouton.

Lust, B. and Foley, 2004. *First Language Acquisition: The Essential Readings.* Oxford, UK: Blackwell Publishing.

O'Grady, W. 2005. *How children learn language.* Cambridge, UK: Cambridge University Press.

Ortega, L. 2009. *Understanding second language acquisition.* London: Hodder Education.

White, L. 2003. *Second language acquisition and Universal Grammar.* Cambridge, UK: Cambridge University Press.

Exercises

1. *Baby talk* is a term used to label the word forms that many adults use when speaking to children. Examples in English are *choo-choo* for "train" and *bow-wow* for "dog." Baby talk seems to exist in every language and culture. At least two things seem to be universal about baby talk: The words that have baby-talk forms fall into certain semantic categories (e.g., food and animals), and the words are phonetically simpler than the adult forms (e.g., *tummy* /tʌmi/ for "stomach" /stʌmik/). List all the baby-talk words you can think of in your native language; then (1) separate them into semantic categories, and (2) try to state general rules for the kinds of phonological reductions or simplifications that occur.

2. In this chapter, we discussed the way children acquire rules of question formation. The following examples of children's early questions are from a stage that is later than those discussed in the chapter. Formulate a generalization to describe this stage.

Can I go?	Can I can't go?
Why do you have one tooth?	Why you don't have a tongue?
What do frogs eat?	What do you don't like?
Do you like chips?	Do you don't like bananas?

3. Find a child between two and four years old. Note the age in years; months, and play with the child for about thirty minutes. Keep a list of all words and/or "sentences" that are not adult-like. Describe what you think the child means by these words and sentences. Describe the syntactic or morphological errors (including omissions). If the child is producing multiword sentences, write a grammar that could account for the data you have collected.

4. Roger Brown and his coworkers at Harvard University studied the language development of three children, referred to in the literature as Adam, Eve, and Sarah. The following is a sample of their two-word utterances.

a coat	my stool	poor man
a celery	that knee	little top
a Becky	more coffee	dirty knee
a hands	more nut	that Adam
my mummy	two tinker-toy	big boot

One observation made by Brown was that many of the sentences and phrases produced by the children were ungrammatical from the point of view of the adult grammar. Mark with an asterisk any of the above NPs that are ungrammatical in the adult grammar of English and state the "violation" for each starred item. For example, if one of the utterances were *Lotsa book,* you might say: "The modifier *lotsa* must be followed by a plural noun."

5. In the holophrastic (one-word) stage of child language acquisition, the child's phonological system differs in systematic ways from that in the adult grammar. The inventory of sounds and the phonemic contrasts are smaller, and there are greater constraints on phonotactic rules. (See Chapter 6 for a discussion of these aspects of phonology.)

   a. For each of the following words produced by a child, state what the substitution is, and any other differences that result.

      Example:

      spook   [pʰuk] Substitution: initial cluster [sp] reduced to single consonant; /p/ becomes aspirated, showing that child has acquired the aspiration rule.

      (1) don't   [dot]
      (2) skip   [kʰip]
      (3) shoe   [su]
      (4) that   [dæt]
      (5) play   [pʰe]
      (6) thump   [dʌp]
      (7) bath   [bæt]
      (8) chop   [tʰap]
      (9) kitty   [kɪdi]
      (10) light   [waɪt]
      (11) dolly   [daʊi]
      (12) grow   [go]

   b. State general rules that account for the children's deviations from the adult pronunciations.

6. Children learn demonstrative words such as *this, that, these,* and *those*; temporal terms such as *now, then,* and *tomorrow*; and spatial terms such as *here, there, right,* and *behind* relatively late. What do all these words have in common? (Hint: See the pragmatics section of Chapter 4.) Why might that factor delay their acquisition?

7. We saw in this chapter how children overgeneralize rules such as the plural rule, producing forms such as *mans* and *mouses*. What might a child learning English use instead of the adult words given?

   a. children
   b. went
   c. better
   d. best
   e. brought
   f. sang
   g. geese
   h. worst
   i. knives
   j. worse

8. The following words are from the lexicons of two children ages one year six months (1;6) and two (2;0) years old. Compare the pronunciation of the words to adult pronunciation.

   Child 1 (1;6)

soap	[doup]	bib	[bɛ]
feet	[bit]	slide	[daɪ]
sock	[kak]	dog	[da]
goos	[gos]	cheese	[tʃis]
dish	[dɪtʃ]	shoes	[dus]

   Child 2 (2;0)

light	[waɪt]	bead	[biː]
sock	[sʌk]	pig	[pɛk]
geese	[gis]	cheese	[tis]
fish	[fɪs]	bees	[bis]
sheep	[ʃip]	bib	[bɪp]

   a. What happens to final consonants in the language of these two children? Formulate the rule(s) in words. Do all final consonants behave the same way? If not, which consonants undergo the rule(s)? Is this a natural class?
   b. On the basis of these data, do any pairs of words allow you to identify any of the phonemes in the grammars of these children? What are they? Explain how you were able to determine your answer.

9. Make up a "wug test" to test a child's knowledge of the following morphemes:

comparative	-er	(as in *bigger*)
superlative	-est	(as in *biggest*)
progressive	-ing	(as in *I am dancing*)
agentive	-er	(as in *writer*)

10. Children frequently produce sentences such as the following:

    Don't giggle me.
    I danced the clown.
    Yawny Baby—you can push her mouth open to drink her.
    Who deaded my kitty cat?
    Are you gonna nice yourself?

    a. How would you characterize the difference between the grammar or lexicon of children who produce such sentences and that of adult English?
    b. Can you think of similar, but well-formed, examples in adult English?

11. Many Arabic speakers tend to insert a vowel in their pronunciation of English words. The first column has examples from L2ers whose L1 is Egyptian Arabic; the second column has examples from L2ers whose L1 is Iraqi Arabic (consider [tʃ] to be a single consonant):

L1 = Egyptian Arabic		L1 = Iraqi Arabic	
[bilastik]	plastic	[ifloːr]	floor
[θiriː]	three	[ibleːn]	plane
[tiransilet]	translate	[tʃilidren]	children
[silaid]	slide	[iθriː]	three
[firɛd]	Fred	[istadi]	study
[tʃildiren]	children	[ifrɛd]	Fred

a. What vowel do the Egyptian Arabic speakers insert and where?
b. What vowel do the Iraqi Arabic speakers insert and where?
c. Based on the position of the italicized epenthetic vowel in "I wrote to him," can you guess which list, A or B, belongs to Egyptian Arabic and which belongs to Iraqi Arabic?

Arabic A		Arabic B	
kitabta	"I wrote him"	katabtu	"I wrote him"
kitabla	"He wrote to him"	katablu	"He wrote to him"
kitabitla	"I wrote to him"	katabtilu	"I wrote to him"

12. Following is a list of utterances recorded from Sammy at age two-and-a-half:

a. Mikey not see him.
b. Where ball go?
c. Look Mommy, doggie.
d. Big doggie.
e. He no bite ya.
f. He eats mud.
g. Kitty hiding.
h. Grampie wear glasses.
i. He funny.
j. He loves hamburgers.
k. Daddy ride bike.
l. That's mines.
m. That my toy.
n. Him sleeping.
o. Want more milk.
p. Read moon book.
q. Me want that.
r. Teddy up.
s. Daddy 'puter.
t. 'Puter broke.
u. Cookies and milk!!!
v. Me Superman.

w. Mommy's angry.

x. Allgone kitty.

y. Here my batball.

What stage of language development is Sammy in? Explain your answer.

13. Children mature at different rates and the age at which children start to put words together varies and, so chronological age is not a good measure of a child's language development. Instead, researchers use the child's **mean length of utterances (MLU)** to measure progress. MLU is the average length of the utterances the child is producing at a particular point. MLU is usually measured in terms of morphemes, so words like *boys*, *danced*, and *crying* each have a value of two (morphemes). The researcher calculates the length of each of the child's utterances (usually around 100 utterances) and then divides the total by the number of utterances to obtain MLU.

   a. Calculate the number of morphemes in each of Sammy's utterances in Exercise 12.

   b. What is Sammy's MLU in morphemes? In words?

   Challenge question: Deciding the morpheme count for several of Sammy's words requires some thought. For each of the following, determine whether it should count as one or two morphemes and why.

   allgone

   batball

   glasses

   cookies

14. Challenge exercise: The following sentences were uttered by children in the telegraphic stage (the second column contains a word-by-word gloss, and the last column is a translation of each sentence that includes elements that the child omitted):

	Child's utterance	Gloss	Translation
Swedish	Se, blomster har	look flowers have	"Look, (I) have flowers."
English	Tickles me		"It tickles me."
French	Mange du pain	eat some bread	"S/he eats some bread."
German	S[ch]okolade holen	chocolate get	"I/we get chocolate."
Dutch	Earst kleine boekje lezen	first little book read	"First, I/we read a little book."

In each of the children's sentences, the subject is missing, although this is not grammatical in the respective adult languages (in contrast to languages such as Spanish and Italian in which it is grammatical to omit the subject).

We noted two hypotheses as to why the child might omit sentence subjects during this stage. Hypothesis 1 was that "children are limited in the length of sentences they can produce, so they drop subjects." The other was that children have a different grammar from the adult, more like Italian, for example, in which it is grammatical to omit subjects.

Evaluate the different hypotheses, citing some pros and cons. For example, an objection to the hypothesis given in (a) might be "If length is the relevant factor, why do children consistently drop subjects but not objects?"

15. Following is a list of overextensions that various children have made. In each case say what the basis is for the overextension. For example, the basis for the overextension of *ball* in example (a) is shape. All the objects in column B are round.

	A	B
a.	*ball*	balls, balloon, marble, grapefruits, oranges, pompoms
b.	*cookie*	cookies, Cheerios, cucumbers
c.	*birdie*	birds, airplanes, flies, bees, kites
d.	*bowwow*	dogs, cows, guinea pigs, cats, hamsters
e.	*truck*	firetruck, garbage truck, bus, van
f.	*dada*	father, policeman, mailman, doctor, men's tie, baseball cap
g.	*moon*	moon, half-moon shaped lemon slice, circular chrome dial on dishwasher, half a Cheerio, hangnail

16. Review Michael's utterances on page 402. Provide two examples of each the following sentence types and the age at which Michael first produced each type of sentence:

a. coordinations (sentences conjoined by *and*)
b. embedded clauses
c. relative clauses

10

Language Processing and the Human Brain

No doubt a reasonable model of language use will incorporate, as a basic component, the generative grammar that expresses the speaker-hearer's knowledge of the language; but this generative grammar does not, in itself, prescribe the character or functioning of a perceptual model or a model of speech production.

NOAM CHOMSKY, *Aspects of the Theory of Syntax*, 1965

The Human Mind at Work

Psycholinguistics is an area of experimental linguistics that is concerned with linguistic performance—how we use our linguistic competence—in speech (or sign) production and comprehension. The human brain not only acquires and stores the mental lexicon and grammar, but also accesses that linguistic storehouse to speak and understand language in real time.

When we speak, we access our lexicon to find the words, and we use the rules of grammar to construct novel sentences and to produce the sounds that express them. When we listen to speech we also access the lexicon and grammar to assign a structure and meaning to the sequence of words we hear. We also connect the sentences we hear into a mental model of the discourse relying on both our linguistic and real-world knowledge.

The grammar relates sounds and meanings, and contains the units and rules of the language that make speech production and comprehension possible. However, other psychological processes are also involved in the production and comprehension of language. Various mechanisms enable us to break the continuous stream of speech sounds into linguistic units such as phonemes, syllables, and words in order to comprehend a message and to compose sounds into words in order to produce meaningful speech. Other cognitive mechanisms determine how we pull words from the mental lexicon, and still others explain how we assemble these words into a structural representation.

Ordinarily we have no difficulty understanding or producing sentences. We do it without effort or conscious awareness of the processes involved. However, we have all had the experience of making a speech error, or having a word on the "tip of our tongue," or failing to understand a perfectly grammatical sentence such as (1):

1. The horse raced past the barn fell.

On hearing this sentence many individuals will judge it to be ungrammatical; yet they will judge as grammatical a sentence with the same syntactic structure, such as (2):

2. The bus driven past the school stopped.

Similarly, people will have no problem with sentence (3), which has the same meaning as (1).

3. The horse that was raced past the barn fell.

Conversely, some ungrammatical sentences are easily understandable, such as sentence (4). This mismatch between grammaticality and interpretability tells us that language processing involves more than grammar.

4. *The baby seems sleeping.

A theory of linguistic performance tries to detail the psychological mechanisms that work with the grammar to facilitate language production and comprehension.

Comprehension

"I quite agree with you," said the Duchess; "and the moral of that is—'Be what you would seem to be'—or, if you'd like it put more simply—'Never imagine yourself not to be otherwise than what it might appear to others . . . to be otherwise.'"

"I think I should understand that better," Alice said very politely, "if I had it written down: but I can't quite follow it as you say it."

LEWIS CARROLL, *Alice's Adventures in Wonderland*, 1865

The sentence uttered by the Duchess is another example of a grammatical sentence that is difficult to understand. The sentence is very long and difficult to process because of the double negation and the multiple use of *otherwise*. Alice notes that if she had a pen and paper she could "unpack" this sentence more easily. The different kinds of breakdowns in performance, such as tip of the tongue phenomena, speech errors, and failure to comprehend tricky sentences, can tell us a great deal about the processes people normally use in speaking and understanding language, just as children's acquisition errors tell us a lot about the mechanisms involved in language development.

The Speech Signal

Understanding a sentence involves analysis at many levels. One of the first questions of linguistic performance concerns segmentation of the acoustic signal. How do we understand the individual speech sounds we hear? To understand this process, some knowledge of the signal can be helpful.

In Chapter 5, we described speech sounds according to the ways in which they are produced. These involve the position of the tongue, the lips, and the velum; the state of the vocal cords; whether the articulators obstruct the free flow of air; and so on. All of these articulatory characteristics are reflected in the sound wave itself and so speech sounds can also be described in physical or **acoustic** terms.

Physically, a sound is produced whenever there is a disturbance of air molecules. The ancient philosophers asked whether a sound is produced if a tree falls in the forest with no one to hear it. This question has been answered by the science of acoustics. Objectively, a sound is produced; subjectively, no sound is heard. In fact, there are sounds we cannot hear because our ears are not sensitive to the full range of frequencies. Many animals, such as dogs, hear a wider range of sounds than humans. *Acoustic phonetics* is concerned only with speech sounds, all of which can be heard by the normal human ear.

When we push air out of the lungs through the glottis, it causes the vocal cords to vibrate; this vibration in turn produces pulses of air that escape through the mouth (and sometimes the nose). These pulses are actually small variations in air pressure caused by the wavelike motion of the air molecules.

The sounds we produce can be described in terms of how fast the variations of the air pressure occur. This determines the **fundamental frequency** of the sounds and is perceived by the hearer as *pitch*. Along with fundamental frequency, when the vocal cords vibrate, they also produce a series of harmonics. A harmonic is a special frequency that is a multiple (2, 3, etc.) of the fundamental frequency. We can also describe the magnitude, or **intensity**, of the variations, which determines the loudness of the sound. The quality of the speech sound—whether it's an [i] or an [a] or whatever—is determined by the shape of the vocal tract when air is flowing through it. This shape modulates the strength of the harmonics into a spectrum of frequencies of greater or lesser intensity, and the particular combination of "greater or lesser" is heard as a particular sound. (Imagine smooth ocean waves with regular peaks and troughs approaching a rocky coastline. As they crash upon the rocks, they are "modulated" or broken up into dozens of "sub waves" with varying peaks and troughs. That is similar to what is happening to the glottal pulses as they "crash" through the vocal tract.)

Computer programs can be used to decompose the speech signal into its frequency components. When speech is fed into a computer (from a microphone or a recording), an image of the speech signal is displayed. The patterns produced are called **spectrograms** or more vividly, **voiceprints**.

A spectrogram of the words *heed, head, had,* and *who'd* is shown in Figure 10.1 (on the next page). Time in milliseconds is represented on the *x*-axis; frequency (pitch) is represented on the *y*-axis. The intensity of each frequency component is indicated by the degree of darkness: the more intense, the darker. Each vowel is characterized by dark bands, called **formants**, which differ in their placement

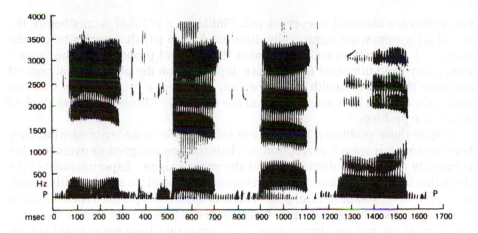

FIGURE 10.1 | A spectrogram of the words *heed*, *head*, *had*, and *who'd*, spoken with a British accent (speaker: Peter Ladefoged, February 16, 1973).

From LADEFOGED/JOHNSON. *A Course in Phonetics (with CD-ROM)*, 6E. © 2011 Cengage Learning. Reproduced by permission.

according to the particular vowel. They represent the strongest harmonics (or sub waves) produced by the shape of the vocal tract. Each vowel has its own formant frequencies, which account for the different vowel qualities you hear. The spectrogram also shows the pitch of the entire utterance (intonation contour) on the line marked P. The striations, or thin vertical lines, indicate a single opening and closing of the vocal cords. When the striations are far apart, the vocal cords are vibrating slowly and the pitch is low; when the striations are close together, the vocal cords are vibrating rapidly and the pitch is high.

By studying spectrograms of many different speech sounds, we can learn a great deal about the basic acoustic components produced by the various shapes of the vocal tract.

Speech Perception

The mice think they are right, but my cat eats them anyways (sic) . . . perception is everything.

TERRY GOODKIND (B. 1948)

Speech is a continuous signal. In natural speech, sounds overlap and influence each other, and yet listeners have the impression that they are hearing discrete units such as words, morphemes, syllables, and phonemes. A central problem of speech perception is to explain how listeners carve up the continuous speech signal into meaningful units. This is referred to as the "segmentation problem."

Another challenge is to understand how the listener manages to recognize particular speech sounds when they are spoken by different people and when they occur in different contexts. For example, how can a speaker tell that a [d] spoken by a man with a deep voice is the same unit of sound as the [d] spoken in the high-pitched voice of a child? Acoustically, they are distinct. Indeed, no two voices are identical in every detail. Similarly, a [d] that occurs before the vowel [i] is somewhat acoustically different from a [d] that occurs before the vowel [u]. Even within a single speaker the physical properties of the "same" sound vary from utterance to utterance depending on the phonological context and even the state of health of the speaker. How does a listener know that two physically distinct instances of a sound are the same? This is called the "lack of invariance problem."

Despite these problems, listeners are usually able to understand what they hear because our speech perception mechanisms are designed to overcome the variability and lack of discreteness in the speech signal. Experimental results show that listeners calibrate their perceptions to control for speaker differences, and can quickly adapt to foreign-accented or distorted speech. When listening to distorted speech, for example, listeners need to hear only two to four sentences to adjust, and can then generalize to words they have never heard before. It takes about a minute to adapt to non-native accents. Similarly, listeners adjust how they interpret timing information in the speech signal as a function of how quickly the speaker is talking. These *normalization* procedures enable the listener to understand a [d] as a [d] regardless of the speaker or speech rate. Listeners can exploit various acoustic cues in the signal, as well as relationships among different acoustic elements, to get around the lack of invariance problem. For example, the frequency of the first or lowest formant for /a/ is high relative to /i/ and /u/, though the precise values may differ among speakers. Additionally, certain types of speech sounds have characteristic properties that can be relied upon for identification. Stops have a brief period of silence followed by a burst; fricatives produce high-frequency noise; and vowels are associated with particular formant structures. These acoustic cues help listeners identify phonological units in the signal regardless of the speaker.

As we might expect, the units we perceive depend on the language we know, especially its phonemic inventory. For example, the initial consonant in [di], [da], and [du] are physically distinct from one another because of the formant transitions from the consonant to the different vowels—a coarticulation effect. Nevertheless, speakers perceive the [d]s as instances of the same phonological unit, namely the phoneme /d/. This phenomenon is known generally as **categorical perception**: Speakers perceive physically distinct stimuli as belonging to the same category because their perceptions are assisted by knowledge of the underlying classificatory system. In the case of language, varying sounds are ascribed to phonemes based on a speaker's knowledge of the phonology of his language. Categorical perception is one of the mechanisms that the speech perception system uses to deal with variability in the signal.

Similarly, speakers of English can perceive the difference between [l] and [r] despite their acoustic similarity because these phones represent distinct phonemes in the language. Speakers of Japanese have great difficulty in differentiating the two because in that language they are allophones of one phoneme. As we saw in our discussion of language development in Chapter 9, infants develop these different perceptual biases during the first year of life.

Returning to the segmentation problem, words and syntactic units such as phrases and sentences are seldom surrounded by boundaries such as pauses. Nevertheless, words are obviously units of perception. The spaces we put between them in writing supports this view. How do we find the words and syntactic constituents in the speech stream?

Stress and intonation provide some cues to these units. For example, in English 90% of the words used in conversation begin with a stressed syllable. Experiments have shown that when English listeners hear a stressed syllable, they are likely to treat it as the onset of a new word. Stress and intonation can also cue syntactic constituents. We know that the different meanings of the sentences *He lives in the white house* and *He lives in the White House* can be signaled by differences in their stress patterns. It is also true that syllables at the end of a phrase are longer in duration than at the beginning, and intonation contours mark clause boundaries. In addition, listeners use their lexical knowledge to identify words in the signal. This process is called **lexical access**, or word recognition, discussed in detail later.

Bottom-Up and Top-Down Models

I have experimented and experimented until now I know that [water] never does run uphill, except in the dark. I know it does in the dark, because the pool never goes dry; which it would, of course, if the water didn't come back in the night. It is best to prove things by experiment; then you know; whereas if you depend on guessing and supposing and conjecturing, you will never get educated.

MARK TWAIN, *Eve's Diary*, 1906

Language comprehension is very fast and automatic. We understand an utterance as fast as we hear it or read it. Ordinarily, we can process spoken language at a rate of around twenty phonemes per second. A visually impaired person who relies on a sped-up synthetic voice to read written material can comprehend speech at rates near one hundred phonemes per second. To a sighted person, this rate of speech would sound like chipmunks chattering.

Successful language comprehension requires that a lot of operations take place at once—what is called "parallel processing"—including the following: segmenting the continuous speech signal into phonemes, morphemes, words, and phrases; looking up the words and morphemes in the mental lexicon; finding the appropriate meanings of ambiguous words; placing them in a constituent structure; choosing among different possible structures when syntactic ambiguities arise; interpreting the phrases and sentences; making a mental model of the discourse and updating it to reflect the meaning of the new sentence; and factoring in the pragmatic context to assist with the other tasks.

To account for this vast amount of mental computation, and owing to the sequential nature of language, psycholinguists believe that listeners make guesses as to what and what not to expect next, thus eliminating unneeded processing. They suggest that perception and comprehension must involve both **top-down processing** and **bottom-up processing**.

Bottom-up processing moves step-by-step from the incoming acoustic signal, to phonemes, morphemes, words and phrases, and ultimately to semantic interpretation. The listener uses acoustic information to build a phonological representation of words that he can then look up in the lexicon. According to this model, the speaker waits until hearing an article followed by a noun and then constructs a noun phrase while awaiting the next word, and so on.

In top-down processing, the listener relies on higher-level semantic, syntactic, and contextual information to analyze the acoustic signal. For example, upon hearing the determiner *the,* the speaker expects the next word to be a noun or adjective rather than a verb or preposition. In this instance, the listener's knowledge of phrase structure would be the source of information.

Psycholinguists try to determine the extent to which comprehension is based solely on the acoustic signal (bottom up) and how much help comes from contextual (sentence or discourse) information (top down). When the acoustic signal is inadequate to understand a word or phrase, top-down information can enable the hearer to choose from among a range of possibilities. Evidence for top-down processing is found in experiments that require subjects to identify spoken words in noisy conditions. Listeners make more errors when the words occur in isolation than when they occur in sentences. Moreover, they make more errors if the words occur in nonsense sentences, and they make the most errors if the words occur in ungrammatical sentences.

Another source of evidence for top-down processing comes from **shadowing tasks** in which subjects are asked to repeat what they hear as promptly as possible. Subjects often produce words in anticipation of the input. They can guess what's coming next by having processed the sentence to that point. Fast shadowers often correct speech errors or mispronunciations unconsciously and add inflectional endings if they are absent, showing rapid processing of the structural relations of immediately preceding words. Corrections are more likely to occur when the target word can be predicted from what has been said previously.

Top-down processing is also supported by a different kind of experiment. Subjects hear recorded sentences in "noisy conditions" in which some part of the signal is removed and a cough or buzz is substituted, such as the boldfaced "s" in the sentence *The state governors met with their respective legislature**s** convening in the capital city.* They "hear" the sentence without any phonemes missing, and have difficulty saying where in the word the noise occurred. This effect is called *phoneme restoration.* It appears that subjects can guess that the word containing the cough was *legislatures* and moreover, they truly believe they are hearing the [s] even when they're told it's not there. In this case, top-down information apparently overrides bottom-up information.

There is also a role for top-down information in segmentation. Sometimes an utterance can be divided in more than one way. For example, the phonetic sequence [grede] in a discussion of meat or eggs is likely to be heard as *Grade A,* but in a discussion of the weather as *grey day.*

In other cases, both bottom-up and top-down information may bear on the ultimate decision of what was spoken. Consider the sequence of phonemes /naɪtret/. It is compatible with two segmentations: [naɪtʰret] with an aspirated [tʰ] meaning "nitrate"; and [naɪtret] with an unaspirated [t] meaning "night rate." Bottom-up information such as the phonetic details of pronunciation can signal where the word boundary is. If the first /t/ is heard as aspirated, it must belong to the onset of the second syllable, so the decision is *nitrate.* If it is unaspirated, it must be part of the coda of the first syllable, so the decision is *night rate.*

But top-down information may also weigh in, so that [naɪtʰret] is favored following the word *sodium* or in the context of chemistry whereas [naɪtret] would be more plausible in the context of hotels. If the bottom-up cue is insufficient because of signal noise, or the top-down cue is vague because of an inconclusive context, then the other cue may weigh more heavily in the final decision.

None of this decision-making is conscious reasoning; it is all done for us by the grammatical engine that operates on the subconscious level.

Lexical Access and Word Recognition

Oh, are you from Wales?

Do you know a fella named Jonah?

He used to live in whales for a while.

GROUCHO MARX (1890–1977)

Psycholinguists have conducted a great deal of research on *lexical access* or *word recognition,* the process by which listeners obtain information about the meaning and syntactic properties of a word from their mental lexicon. Several different experimental techniques have been used in studies of lexical access.

One technique is to ask whether a string of letters or sounds is or is not a word. Subjects must respond by pressing one button if the stimulus is an actual word, and a different button if it is not, so they are making a **lexical decision**. During these and similar experiments, measurements of *response time* (RT) is taken. The assumption is that the longer it takes to respond to a particular task, the more processing is involved. RT measurements show that lexical access depends to some extent on the word's frequency of usage: More commonly used words such as *car* are responded to more quickly than words that are rarely encounter such as *cad.*

Lexical decision tasks can also provide information about how we use our phonological knowledge in lexical access. Studies show that listeners respond more slowly to "possible" non-words such as *floop* and *plim* than to "impossible" non-words such as *tlat* and *mrock.* The listener can quickly reject the impossible words based on phonotactic knowledge so that a lexical search is unnecessary. That possible and impossible non-words are processed differently is supported by brain imaging studies showing that the same areas of the brain are involved in accessing real words and possible non-words, while different areas respond to impossible non-words.

The speed with which a listener can retrieve a particular word also depends on the size of the word's phonological "neighborhood." A neighborhood is comprised of all the words that are phonologically similar to the target word. A word like *pat* has a dense neighborhood because there are many similar words—*bat, pad, pot, pit,* and so on, while a word like *crib* has far fewer neighbors. Words with larger neighborhoods take longer to retrieve than words from smaller ones because more phonological information is required to single out a word in a denser neighborhood.

Psycholinguists believe that each word in the mental lexicon is associated with a "resting level of activation," with some words more active than others. Each time the listener accesses a word its level rises a little bit. Thus, more frequently used words have a higher resting level of activation, and listeners show faster RTs to these words in decision tasks. Indeed, in reading tasks, subjects appear to "skip over" the short, high frequency function words, so quickly are they accessed. Top-down information may also play a role, allowing us quicker access to less frequent words when they are highly predictable from context.

Words can also be activated by hearing semantically related words. This effect is known as **semantic priming**. A listener will be faster at making a lexical decision on the word *doctor* if he has just heard *nurse* than if he just heard a semantically unrelated word such as *flower*. The word *nurse* is said to "prime" the word *doctor*. When we hear a priming word, related words are "awakened" and become more readily accessible for a few moments. This priming effect might arise because semantically related words are near each other or linked to each other in the mental lexicon. In bilinguals, a word may be primed in one language by a semantically related word in the other language. For example, in French-English bilinguals access to *cat* is facilitated by both *dog* and *chien*.

Morphological priming is a kind of semantic priming in which a morpheme of a multimorphemic sword primes a related word. For example, *sheepdog* primes *wool* as a result of *sheep*. Even when one morpheme is free and the other bound as in *runner*, the free morpheme *run* primes words like *race*. Stranger yet, even in pseudo-multimorphemic words such as *summer*, which does not mean "one who sums," the word "sum" is primed much as *paint* is primed by the word *painter*. These examples suggest that morphological decomposition is taking place automatically based on the phonetics of the word irrespective of the semantics.

Lexical decision techniques can be evaluated alongside results from brain studies to provide a more detailed understanding of the process of lexical access. In some cases, electrical brain activity in experimental subjects indicates that lexical access is occurring even though RT measurements do not. For example, *teach* may prime the related *taught* according to brain activity but not according to RT measurements. This result suggests that lexical decision occurs in stages, and that RT measurements are insensitive to earlier stages, whereas the brain measurements are taken continuously and reflect both earlier and later stages. (We discuss brain studies in more detail later in this chapter.)

Lexical ambiguities also provide important insights into how listeners access the mental lexicon. In certain experimental tasks, RTs are longer with ambiguous words than unambiguous ones, suggesting that ambiguous words require more processing resources. Indeed, studies show that listeners retrieve all meanings of an ambiguous word even when the sentence containing the word is biased toward one of the meanings. For example, when the word *palm* is heard in *The gypsy read the young man's palm* it primes both the word *hand* and the word *tree* according to RT measurements. The other meaning of *palm* (as in *palm tree*) is apparently activated even though that meaning is not a part of the meaning of the priming sentence. At a subsequent stage of processing—after about 250 milliseconds—the listener makes a decision about which meaning is the intended one based on the information in the rest of the sentence. This suggests that the initial accessing of a word is strictly bottom-up—every lexical entry that matches the phonological representation is activated—while the subsequent selection of the contextually appropriate meaning is a top-down process. Interestingly, young children do not show priming of all meanings of an ambiguous word, but only the most frequently used meaning. This is most likely because children have more limited processing resources than adults.

Syntactic Processing

Teacher Strikes Idle Kids

Enraged Cow Injures Farmer with Ax

Two Sisters Reunited after 18 Years in Checkout Counter

Stolen Painting Found by Tree

AMBIGUOUS HEADLINES

Understanding a sentence involves more than merely recognizing its individual words. The listener must also determine the syntactic relations among the words and phrases. This mental process, referred to as **parsing**, is largely governed by the rules of the grammar and strongly influenced by the sequential nature of language.

Listeners actively build a structural representation of a sentence as they hear it. They must therefore decide for each incoming word what its grammatical category is and how it fits into the structure that is being built. Often sentences present "temporary ambiguities" such as a word or words that belong to more than one syntactic category. For example, the string *The warehouse fires* . . . could continue in one of two ways:

1. . . . were set by an arsonist.
2. . . . employees over sixty.

Fires is a noun in sentence (1) and a verb in sentence (2). Experimental studies of such sentences show that both meanings and categories are activated when a subject encounters the ambiguous word. The ambiguity is quickly resolved based on syntactic and semantic context. Disambiguation is usually so fast and seamless that unintentionally ambiguous newspaper headlines such as those at the head of this section are scarcely noticeable except to the linguists who collect them.

Another important type of temporary ambiguity arises in cases in which the grammar permits a constituent to fit into a sentence in two different ways, as illustrated by the following example:

After the child visited the doctor prescribed a course of injections.

When readers encounter the phrase *the doctor* they immediately perceive it as the direct object of the verb *visit*. When they later come to the verb *prescribed*, they must "change their minds" or backtrack, and reanalyze *the doctor* as subject of a main clause instead. Sophisticated laboratory procedures that track the reader's eye movements can pinpoint difficult regions of the sentence and can see when the reader regresses to an earlier part of the sentence. Sentences that induce this backtracking effect are called **garden path sentences**. The sentence presented at the beginning of this chapter, *The horse raced past the barn fell*, is also a garden path sentence. People naturally interpret *raced* as the main verb, when in fact the main verb is *fell*.

The initial structural choices that lead people astray may reflect general principles that are used by the mental parser to deal with syntactic ambiguity. Two such principles are known as **minimal attachment** and **late closure**.

Minimal attachment says, "Build the simplest structure consistent with the grammar of the language." In the string *The horse raced* . . . , the simpler structure is the one in which *the horse* is the subject and *raced* the main verb; the less simple structure is similar to *The horse that was raced* . . . with *fell* as the main verb.

Late closure says "Attach incoming material to the phrase that is currently being processed," as the following sentence illustrates:

The doctor said the patient will die yesterday.

Readers often experience a garden path effect at the end of this sentence. The reader encounters *yesterday* nearest to the embedded clause *the patient will die*, which is closest to *yesterday*, and immediately tries to work it into the meaning. This fails because *yesterday* conflicts with the future marker *will* so the reader backtracks to attach *yesterday* to the main clause where it modifies *said*.

The syntactic parsing of sentences depends on different sources of information. The parser depends on the grammar to inform it as to how the incoming words can be grouped together into well-formed constituents. In cases of ambiguity, there are various structural possibilities to choose from. Principles such as "minimal attachment" and "late closure" guide the parser to choose the computationally simplest structure among the different grammatical possibilities. Garden path effects arise when listeners make a strong commitment to the simpler structure and are then "jarred" out of it by some kind of incongruity.

In some cases, frequency factors cause the reader to garden path, as illustrated by the following sentence:

The faithful people our church every Sunday.

People occurs much more frequently as a noun than a verb, leading the reader to initially analyze *the faithful people* as an NP, but this does not jibe with the rest of the sentence, which lacks a verb. The reader must backtrack and reanalyze *people* as the main verb meaning "to populate."

Other factors such as prosody, lexical biases, and even visual context can also influence the parser in its structural choices, and may even weaken the effects of the parsing principles. For example, the following sentence is ambiguous: Either the actress or the maid can be understood as the one on the balcony:

Someone photographed the maid of the actress who was on the balcony.

"Late closure" would place the actress on the balcony as the preferred interpretation. Studies show that placing an intonation pause after *the maid* greatly increases the chances of the listener assigning this meaning. On the other hand, a pause after *the actress* increases the likelihood of the interpretation where the maid is on the balcony.

Studies of other languages may call into question the universality of "late closure". Given the Spanish equivalent of the *actress-maid* type sentences, Spanish listeners prefer the interpretation in which the maid is on the balcony. Spanish speakers still obey late closure with other constructions, however.

Verb choice may also influence the parser's structural decisions. In a sentence such as (1) the processor is led to parse *the problem* as the direct object of the verb *understood* (minimal attachment) and will have to backtrack when *had no solution* is encountered, while in (2) such a garden path effect is less likely:

1. Tom understood the problem had no solution.
2. Tom thought the problem had no solution.

This is because the verb *understand* can be followed by both an NP and a sentence *(Tom understood the story, Tom understood the story was false)*, while the verb *think* can be followed by a sentence but not an NP. *(Tom thinks the story is crazy, *Tom thinks the story)*. The sentence processor is sensitive to subcategorization information in the lexical entries of verbs and also the frequency of occurrence of different contexts for particular verbs. (Subcategorization is discussed in Chapter 3.)

Surprisingly, the parser does not seem to make use of nonlinguistic information to make structural decisions. For example, you might think that a garden path is less likely in sentence (1) than sentence (2) because real-world knowledge tells us that performers are routinely sent flowers and florists routinely *send* them.

1. The performer sent the flowers was very pleased.
2. The florist sent the flowers was very pleased.

But this is not the case. Eye-tracking studies have shown that readers garden path equally on these two sentences despite the difference in plausibility.

However, in a different task, when readers are asked to paraphrase the two sentences, they do better with the more plausible *performer sent the flowers* sentence, indicating that nonlinguistic context facilitates comprehension at some point, though not at the parsing stage. Sentences that create problems for the parser, such as garden path sentences, tell us a great deal about how the sentence processor operates.

Another striking example of processing difficulty is illustrated by a rewording of a Mother Goose poem. In its original form we have:

> This is the dog that worried the cat that killed the rat that ate the malt that lay in the house that Jack built.

No problem understanding that. Now try this equivalent description:

> Jack built the house that the malt that the rat that the cat that the dog worried killed ate lay in.

No way, right?

Although the confusing sentence follows the rules of relative clause formation—you have little difficulty with *the cat that the dog worried*—it seems that once is enough; when you apply the same process twice, getting *the rat that the cat that the dog worried killed*, it becomes quite difficult to comprehend but perhaps possible. If we apply the process three times, as in *the malt that the rat that the cat that the dog worried killed ate*, all hope is lost.

The difficulty in parsing this kind of sentence is related to memory constraints. In processing the sentence, you have to keep *the malt* in mind all the way until *ate*, but while doing that you have to keep *the rat* in mind all the way until *killed*, and while doing that . . . It's a form of structure juggling that is difficult to perform; we evidently don't have enough of the right kind of memory capacity to keep track of all the necessary items. Though we have the competence to create such sentences, performance limitations prevent the creation and comprehension of such monstrosities.

The ability to comprehend what is said to us is a complex psychological process involving the internal grammar, parsing principles such as "minimal attachment" and "late closure", linguistic context, lexical information such as the subcategorization of verbs, prosody, frequency factors, and memory limitations.

Speech Production

> Speech was given to the ordinary sort of men, whereby to communicate their mind; but to wise men, whereby to conceal it.
>
> ROBERT SOUTH, sermon at Westminster Abbey, April 30, 1676

As we saw in the previous sections, the listener's job is to decode the intended meaning of a message from the speech signal produced by a speaker. The speaker's job is the reverse. He must encode an idea into an utterance using speech sounds and words (or signs) organized according to the grammatical structures of the language. It is more difficult to devise experiments that provide information about how the speaker proceeds than to do so for the listener's side of the process. Much of the best information about speech production has come from observing and analyzing spontaneous speech, especially speech errors.

Lexical Selection

> Humpty Dumpty's theory, of two meanings packed into one word like a portmanteau, seems to me the right explanation for all. For instance, take the two words "fuming" and "furious." Make up your mind that you will say both words but leave it unsettled which you will say first. Now open your mouth and speak. If . . . you have that rarest of gifts, a perfectly balanced mind, you will say "frumious."
>
> LEWIS CARROLL, Preface to *The Hunting of the Snark*, 1876

In our previous discussion of comprehension, we saw that semantically related words are activated or primed during lexical retrieval. In production, we see a similar effect with slips of the tongue or speech errors (see Chapter 6), especially word substitution errors. Word substitutions are seldom random; they show that in our attempt to express our thoughts, we may make an incorrect lexical selection based on partial similarity or relatedness of meanings. This is illustrated in the following examples:

Bring me a **pen.**	→ Bring me a **pencil**.
It stays **light** out late here.	→ It stays **dark** out late here.
Please set the **table**.	→ Please set the **chair**.
Are my **tires** touching the curb?	→ Are my **legs** touching the curb?

Blends (see Chapter 8), in which we produce part of one word and part of another, illustrate how we may select two or more words to express our thoughts and instead of deciding between them, we produce them as "portmanteaus," as Humpty Dumpty calls them. Such blends are illustrated in the following errors:

1. splinters/blisters   → splisters
2. edited/annotated   → editated
3. a swinging/hip chick   → a swip chick
4. frown/scowl   → frowl

These blend errors are typical in that the segments stay in the same position within the syllable as they were in the target words.

In comprehension, lexical retrieval is affected by the number of words that are phonologically related to the target: what we earlier referred to as "phonological neighborhoods." In production, speakers often make speech errors involving the substitution of a word that is phonologically related to the target but unrelated in meaning, as the following examples show:

Did you feed the **bunny?**	→ Did you feed the **banana?**
We need a few laughs to break up the **monotony.**	→ We need a few laughs to break up the **mahogany.**
The flood damage was so bad they had to **evacuate** the city.	→ The flood damage was so bad they had to **evaporate** the city.

Just as more common words are accessed faster in comprehension than less common, so are they retrieved more easily in production. Speakers come up with *knife* more quickly than *bayonet*, for example. This is shown in studies of speaker hesitations or pauses, which are more common before low frequency words.

It is not surprising that many of the same factors that influence the listener in comprehension also affect the speaker in production–semantic and phonological relatedness of words, and word frequency. Whether you are speaking or listening you are accessing the same mental lexicon.

Application and Misapplication of Rules

I thought . . . four rules would be enough, provided that I made a firm and constant resolution not to fail even once in the observance of them.

RENÉ DESCARTES, *Discourse on Method*, 1637

Spontaneous errors show that the rules of morphology and syntax are also applied (or misapplied) when we speak. It is difficult to see this process in normal error-free speech, but when someone says *groupment* instead of *grouping, ambigual* instead of *ambiguous*, or *bloodent* instead of *bloody*, it shows that regular rules are applied to combine morphemes and form possible but nonexistent words.

Errors may also involve inflectional rules. The UCLA professor who said **We swimmed in the pool* knows that the past tense of *swim* is *swam*, but he mistakenly applied the regular rule to an irregular form. We also see evidence of the order of application of morphophonemic rules in production. Consider the *a/an* alternation rule in English. Errors such as *a burly bird* for the intended *an early bird* show that the rule applies after the stage at which *early* has slipped to *burly*.

Similarly, an error such as *bin beg*, pronounced [bĭn bɛg] for the intended *Big Ben* [bɪg bẽn] (made by an announcer during the 2012 Olympic Games in London) shows that allophonic rules apply after phonemes are misordered. If the allophonic nasalization rule applied before the reordering, the result would have been [bĭn bẽg].

Planning Units

We might suppose that speakers' thoughts are simply translated into words one after the other via a semantic mapping process. Grammatical morphemes would be added as demanded by the syntactic rules of the language. The phonetic representation of each word in turn would then be mapped onto the neuromuscular commands to the articulators to produce the acoustic signal representing it.

We know, however, that this is not a true picture of speech production. Although sounds within words and words within sentences are linearly ordered, speech errors or slips of the tongue show that the prearticulation or planning stages involve units larger than the single phonemic segment or even the word, as illustrated by the "U.S. Acres" cartoon. That error is an example of a **spoonerism**, named after William Archibald Spooner, a distinguished dean of an Oxford college in the early 1900s who is reported to have referred to Queen Victoria as "That queer old dean" instead of "That dear old queen," and berated his class of students by saying, "You have hissed my mystery lecture. You have tasted the whole worm," instead of the intended "You have missed my history lecture. You have wasted the whole term."

Indeed, speech errors show that features, segments, words, and phrases may be conceptualized well before they are uttered. This point is illustrated in the following examples of speech errors (the intended utterance is to the left of the arrow; the actual utterance, including the error, is to the right of the arrow):

1. The *h*iring of minority faculty. → The *f*iring of minority faculty.
   (The intended *f* is replaced by the *f* of *faculty*, which occurs later in the intended utterance.)
2. *a*d h*o*c → *o*dd h*a*ck (The vowels /æ/ of the first word and /a/ of the second are exchanged or reversed.)
3. *b*ig and *f*at → *p*ig and *v*at (The values of a single feature are switched: in *big* [+ voiced] becomes [–voiced] and in *fat* [–voiced] becomes [+ voiced].)
4. There are many ministers in our church. → There are many churches in our minister. (The root morphemes *minister* and *church* are exchanged; the grammatical plural morpheme remains in its intended place in the phrase structure.)
5. salute smartly → smart salutely (heard on *All Things Considered*, National Public Radio (NPR), May 17, 2007) (The root morphemes are exchanged, but the *-ly* affix remains in place.)
6. Seymour sliced the salami with a knife. → Seymour sliced a knife with the salami. (The entire noun phrases—article + noun—were exchanged.)

In these errors, the intonation contour (primary stressed syllables and variations in pitch) remained the same as in the intended utterances, even when the words were rearranged. In the intended utterance of (6), the highest pitch would be on *knife*. In the misordered sentence, the highest pitch occurred on the second syllable of *salami*. The pitch rise and increased loudness do not therefore depend on the individual words but are determined by the syntactic structure of the sentence.

These errors show us that syntactic structures exist independently of the words that occupy them, and intonation contours can be mapped onto those structures without being associated with particular words.

Errors like those just cited are constrained in interesting ways. Phonological errors involving segments or features, as in (1), (2), and (3), primarily occur in content words, and not in grammatical morphemes, showing the distinction between these lexical classes. In addition, free morphemes may be interchanged, bound morphemes may not be. We do not find errors like *The boying are sings* for *The boys are singing*. Typically, as example (4) illustrates, the affixes are left behind when root morphemes switch, and then attach to the moved morpheme. Errors like those in (1)–(6) show that speech production operates in real time using the features, segments, morphemes, words, and phrases that exist in the grammar. They also show that when we speak, words are chosen and sequenced ahead of when they are articulated. Planning also goes on at the sentence level. In experimentally controlled settings, speakers take longer to initiate (begin uttering) passive sentences like (1a) than active sentences like (1b). They also take longer to begin uttering subject–object relative clauses (underlined once) like (2a) than object–subject relative clauses (doubly underlined) like (2b).

(1) a. The ball was chased by Nellie.
    b. Nellie chased the ball.

(2) a. The cat that scratched the dog climbed the tree.
    b. The cat that the dog chased climbed the tree.

These findings suggest that more planning goes into sentences that have a less common word order than into sentences with subject–verb–object word order. Interestingly, however, speakers are more likely to produce a passive sentence after hearing a passive, despite its non-typical word order. In syntactic priming experiments, speakers are asked to describe a scene after hearing an unrelated active or passive sentence. Results show that they are more likely to describe the scene using a passive if that is what they have just heard. Researchers believe that once a particular structure has been built, it remains "active" in memory and facilitates the subsequent building of a similar structure.

Speakers must also combine simple sentences into complex structures containing embedded clauses, relative clauses, and so on. Studies of speakers' hesitations show that planning for complex structures happens at the beginning of clauses. For example, the initiation time is shorter for producing a simple NP subject such as (1):

1. The large and raging river . . .

than for a subject NP like (2):

2. The river that stopped flooding . . . ,

which contains a relative clause, even though both NPs are the same length (in terms of number of syllables).

Pauses occur more often at the beginning of clauses than within them, and speech errors involving exchanges of linguistic units, such as those in (4)–(6) above, happen within clauses and not across clause boundaries. These findings among others support the hypothesis that the clause boundary is the locus of planning in complex sentences, and that sentences are bundled into clause-size units before they are produced.

The comprehension and production of language is an enormously complex process that depends on many aspects of our linguistic knowledge, as well as dedicated processing principles and other cognitive capacities such as memory. Both normal conversational data and experimental data provide the psycholinguist with information about the different units, mechanisms, and stages speakers use to encode an idea into speech and listeners use to decode the speech signal into a linguistic message.

Brain and Language

How can you talk if you don't have a brain?

DOROTHY: FROM THE MOTION PICTURE *The Wizard of Oz*, 1939.

Attempts to understand the complexities of human cognitive abilities, especially language, are as old and as continuous as history itself. What is the nature of the brain? What is the nature of human language? And what is the relationship between the two? Philosophers and scientists have grappled with these kinds of questions over the centuries. But modern advances in brain technology have enabled researchers to study the brain-language connection in ways scarcely imagined in earlier times. The study of the biological and neural foundations of language is called **neurolinguistics**. Like psycholinguistics, neurolinguistics is largely an experimental science. Neurolinguistic research is often based on data from atypical or impaired language and uses such data to understand properties of human language in general.

The Human Brain

The human brain is unique in that it is the only container of which it can be said that the more you put into it, the more it will hold.

GLENN DOMAN

The brain is the most complex organ of the body. The surface of the brain is the **cortex**, often called "gray matter," consisting of 100 billion neurons (nerve cells) and even more glial cells (which support and protect the neurons and have as yet unknown other functions). The cortex is the decision-making organ of the body. It receives messages from all of the sensory organs, initiates all voluntary and involuntary actions, and is the storehouse of our memories and the seat of our consciousness. It is the organ that most distinguishes humans from other animals. It's where human language resides.

The brain is composed of a right and a left **cerebral hemisphere**, joined by the **corpus callosum**, a network of more than 200 million fibers (see Figure 10.2 below). The corpus callosum allows the two hemispheres of the brain to communicate with each other. Without this system of connections, the hemispheres would operate independently. In general, the left hemisphere controls the right side of the body, and the right hemisphere controls the left side. If you point with your right hand, the left hemisphere is responsible for your action. Similarly, sensory information from the right side of the body (e.g., right hand, right visual field) is received by the left hemisphere of the brain, and sensory input to the left side of the body is received by the right hemisphere. This is referred to as **contralateral** brain function. The following quote from the Bible suggests that the connection between control of the right side of the body and speech has been suspected for a long time.

If I forget thee, O Jerusalem, let my right hand forget her cunning.

If I do not remember thee, let my tongue cleave to the roof of my mouth;

Psalm 137, King James Version

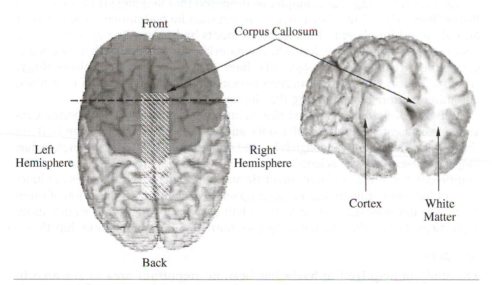

FIGURE 10.2 | Three-dimensional reconstruction of the normal living human brain. The images were obtained from magnetic resonance data using the Brainvox technique. *Left panel* = view from top. *Right panel* = view from the front following virtual coronal section at the level of the dashed line.

Courtesy of Hanna Damásio.

The Localization of Language in the Brain

An issue of central concern has been to determine which areas of the brain are responsible for human linguistic abilities. In the early nineteenth century, Franz Joseph Gall proposed the theory of **localization**, which is the idea that different human cognitive abilities and behaviors are localized in specific parts of the brain. In light of our current knowledge about the brain, some of Gall's particular views are amusing. For example, he proposed that language is located in the frontal lobes of the brain because as a young man he had noticed that the most articulate and intelligent of his fellow students had protruding eyes, which he believed reflected overdeveloped brain material. He also put forth a pseudoscientific theory called "organology" that later came to be known as **phrenology**, which is the practice of determining personality traits, intellectual capacities, and other matters by examining the "bumps" on the skull.

A disciple of Gall's, Johann Spurzheim, introduced phrenology to America, constructing elaborate maps and skull models such as the one shown in Figure 10.3 (on the next page) in which language is located directly under the eye. Phrenology has long been discarded as a scientific theory, but Gall's view that the brain is not an undifferentiated mass, and that linguistic and other cognitive capacities are functions of localized brain areas, has been upheld by scientific investigation of brain disorders, and, over the past three-and-a-half decades, by numerous studies using sophisticated technologies examining both normal and impaired brain function.

Aphasia

The study of **acquired aphasia** has been an important area of research in understanding the relationship between the brain and language. Aphasia is the neurological term for any language disorder that results from brain damage caused by disease or trauma.

In the second half of the nineteenth century, significant scientific advances were made in localizing language in the brain based on the study of people with aphasia. In the 1860s, the French surgeon Paul Broca proposed that language is

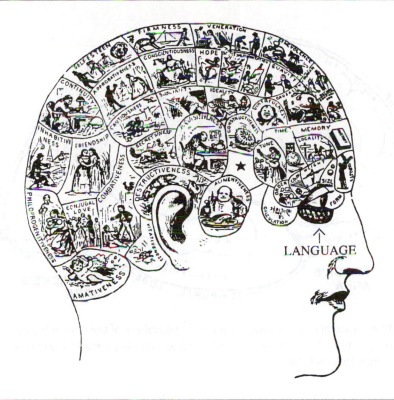

LANGUAGE

FIGURE 10.3 | Phrenology skull model.

localized in the left hemisphere of the brain, and more specifically in the front part of the left hemisphere (now called **Broca's area**). At a scientific meeting in Paris, he claimed that we speak with the left hemisphere. Broca's claim was based on a study of his patients who suffered language deficits after brain injury to the left frontal lobe.

A decade later, Carl Wernicke, a German neurologist, described another variety of aphasia that occurred in patients with lesions in areas of the left temporal lobe, now known as **Wernicke's area**. **Lateralization** is the term used to refer to the localization of function to one hemisphere of the brain. Language is lateralized to the left hemisphere, and the left hemisphere appears to be the language hemisphere from infancy on. Figure 10.4 (on the next page) is a view of the left side of the brain that shows Broca's and Wernicke's areas.

The Linguistic Characterization of Aphasic Syndromes

Most aphasics do not show total language loss. Rather, different aspects of language are selectively impaired, and the kind of impairment is generally related to the location of the brain damage. Because of this damage-deficit correlation, research on patients with aphasia has provided a great deal of information about how language is organized in the brain.

Patients with injuries to Broca's area may have **Broca's aphasia**, as it is often called today. Broca's aphasia is characterized by labored speech and certain kinds of word-finding difficulties, but it is primarily a disorder that

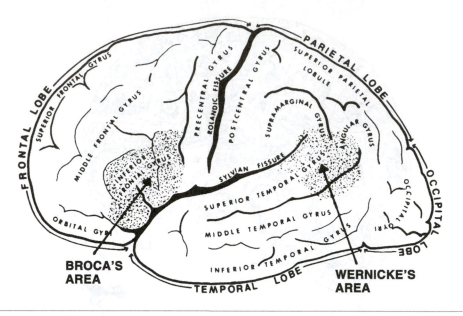

FIGURE 10.4 | Lateral *(external)* view of the left hemisphere of the human brain, showing the position of Broca's and Wernicke's areas—two key areas of the cortex related to language processing.

affects a person's ability to form sentences with the rules of syntax. One of the most notable characteristics of Broca's aphasia is that the language produced is often **agrammatic**, meaning that it frequently lacks articles, prepositions, pronouns, auxiliary verbs, and other function words. Broca's aphasics also typically omit inflections such as the past tense suffix *-ed* or the third person singular verb ending *-s*. Here is an excerpt of a conversation between a patient with Broca's aphasia and a doctor:

DOCTOR: Could you tell me what you have been doing in the hospital?
PATIENT: Yes, sure. Me go, er, uh, P.T. [physical therapy] none o'cot, speech . . . two times . . . read . . . r . . . ripe . . . rike . . . uh write . . . practice . . . get . . . ting . . . better.
DOCTOR: And have you been going home on weekends?
PATIENT: Why, yes . . . Thursday uh . . . uh . . . uh . . . no . . . Friday . . . Bar . . . ba . . . ra . . . wife . . . and oh car . . . drive . . . purpike . . . you know . . . rest . . . and TV.

Broca's aphasics (also often called **agrammatic aphasics**) may also have difficulty understanding sentences that have non-canonical word order due to the application of movement rules. They are far better at understanding a subject *wh* question like:

Which girl kissed the boy?

which adheres to S–V–O (girl-kiss-boy) word order, than an object *wh* question such as:

Which girl did the boy kiss?

which disrupts canonical word order (girl-boy-kiss). Similarly, they will understand sentences with a subject relative clause (in brackets) such as:

The girl [who is drawing the boy] is wearing a hat.

where S–V–O (girl-draw-boy) order is preserved more reliably than sentences with an object relative clause such as:

The girl [who the boy is drawing] is wearing a hat.

where the object (*the girl*) is displaced resulting in non-canonical order. They have trouble with passives sentences for the same reason. In a passive sentence such as:

The cat was chased by the dog.

the subject (*the cat*) is the logical object of the verb (*chase*) and the NP in the *by*-phrase (*the dog*) is the logical subject.

Agrammatic aphasics will have less difficulty understanding "transformed" sentences:

Which book did the boy read?

or

The car was chased by the dog.

where they can figure out who did what to whom based on nonlinguistic knowledge.

It's implausible for books to read boys or for cars to chase dogs, and aphasic people can use that knowledge to interpret the sentence. Unlike Broca's patients, people with **Wernicke's aphasia** produce fluent speech with good intonation, and they may largely adhere to the rules of syntax. However, their language is often semantically incoherent. For example, one patient replied to a question about his health with:

I felt worse because I can no longer keep in mind from the mind of the minds to keep me from mind and up to the ear which can be to find among ourselves.

Another patient described a fork as "a need for a schedule" and another, when asked about his poor vision, replied, "My wires don't hire right."

People with damage to Wernicke's area have difficulty naming objects presented to them and in choosing words in spontaneous speech. They may make numerous lexical errors (word substitutions), often producing **jargon** and **nonsense words**, as in the following example:

The only thing that I can say again is madder or modder fish sudden fishing sewed into the accident to miss in the purdles.

Another example is from a patient who was a physician before his aphasia. When asked whether he was a doctor, he replied:

Me? Yes sir. I'm a male demaploze on my own. I still know my tubaboys what for I have that's gone hell and some of them go.

The linguistic deficits exhibited by people with Broca's and Wernicke's aphasias point to a **modular** organization of language in the brain. Damage to different parts of the brain results in different kinds of linguistic impairment (e.g., syntactic versus semantic). This supports the hypothesis that the mental grammar, like the brain itself, is not an undifferentiated system, but rather consists of distinct components or modules. The kind of word substitutions that aphasic patients produce also tell us about how words are organized in the mental lexicon. Sometimes the substituted words are similar to the intended words in their sounds. For example, *pool* might be substituted for *tool*, *sable* for *table*, or *crucial* for *crucible*. Sometimes they are similar in meaning (e.g., *table* for *chair* or *boy* for *girl*). These errors resemble the speech errors that unimpaired speakers might make, but they occur far more frequently in people with aphasia. The substitution of semantically or phonetically related words tells us that neural connections exist among semantically related words and among words that sound alike. Words are not mentally represented in a simple list but rather in an organized network of connections, comprising lexical neighborhoods.

Most of us have experienced word-finding difficulties in speaking if not in reading, as Alice did in "Wonderland" when she said:

"And now, who am I? I will remember, if I can. I'm determined to do it!" But being determined didn't help her much, and all she could say, after a great deal of puzzling, was "L, I know it begins with L."

This **tip-of-the-tongue phenomenon** is not uncommon. Aphasics who suffer from **anomia (anomic aphasia)** have constant word-finding difficulties.

Deaf signers with damage to the left hemisphere show aphasia for sign language similar to the language breakdown in hearing aphasics, even though sign language is a visual-spatial language, and the right hemisphere is the one specialized for most aspects of visual and spatial cognition. Moreover, in tests measuring hemispheric activation (some of which we discuss below), one finds that it is the *auditory* cortex in the left hemisphere of deaf individuals attempting to process signs that is activated—the very area we might expect to be the *least* responsive to language in the deaf.

Deaf patients with lesions in Broca's area show language deficits like those found in hearing patients, namely, severely dysfluent, agrammatic sign production. Likewise, those with damage to Wernicke's area have fluent but often semantically incoherent sign language, filled with made-up signs. Although deaf aphasic patients show marked sign language deficits, they have no difficulty producing nonlinguistic gestures or sequences of nonlinguistic gestures, even though both nonlinguistic gestures and linguistic signs are produced by the same "articulators"—the hands and arms. Deaf aphasics also have no difficulty in processing nonlinguistic visual-spatial relationships, just as hearing aphasics have no problem with processing nonlinguistic auditory stimuli.

The language difficulties suffered by aphasics are not caused by any general cognitive or intellectual impairment or loss of motor or sensory control. of the speech organs or hearing apparatus. Aphasics can produce and hear sounds and their other cognitive abilities may be intact. Whatever loss they suffer has to do only with the language faculty (or specific parts of it).

In addition to the evidence provided by deaf aphasics there is also considerable experimental evidence showing that sign language grammar—like spoken language grammar—resides in the left hemisphere. These findings are important because they show that the left hemisphere is lateralized for language—an abstract system of symbols and rules—and not simply for hearing or speech. Language can be realized in different modalities, spoken or signed, but is organized in the brain in the same way regardless of modality.

The kind of selective impairments that we find in people with aphasia has provided important information about the organization of language and other cognitive abilities in the brain, especially grammar and the lexicon. It tells us that language is a separate cognitive module—so aphasics can be otherwise cognitively normal—and that within language, separate components can be differentially affected by damage to different regions of the brain.

Acquired Dyslexia

Evidence concerning the organization of the lexicon and how we access it is also provided by people with **acquired dyslexia**, a disorder in which reading ability is disrupted due to brain damage to the left hemisphere. Two types of acquired dyslexia have been identified, each with different effects.

People with *deep dyslexia* make many word substitutions such as the following:

Stimulus	Response 1	Response 2
act	*play*	*play*
applaud	*laugh*	*cheers*
example	*answer*	*sum*
heal	*pain*	*medicine*
south	*west*	*east*

The patient was unable to read the stimulus word presented on a card, though his responses were semantically related to the target, indicating that he was able to get to the correct lexical neighborhood but retrieved the wrong item.

People with deep dyslexia also have particular difficulty reading function words such as prepositions, conjunctions, and auxiliaries. The patient who produced the semantic substitutions cited previously was not able to read function words at all. When presented with words such as *which* or *would*, he just said, "No" or "I hate those little words." However, he could read phonetically identical nouns and verbs, though with many semantic mistakes, as shown in the following:

Stimulus	Response	Stimulus	Response
witch	*witch*	which	*no!*
hour	*time*	our	*no!*
eye	*eyes*	I	*no!*
hymn	*bible*	him	*no!*
wood	*wood*	would	*no!*

These errors, like those of people with agrammatic aphasia, provide evidence that content words and function words are processed in different brain areas or by different neural mechanisms, further supporting the view that both the brain and language are structured in a complex, modular fashion.

Fluent readers can access a familiar word in the mental lexicon just by seeing it, without sounding it out. People with *surface dyslexia* cannot do this. They must "sound out" every word, just like a beginning reader or an adult encountering a new word. This makes reading difficult and laborious and makes many words unreadable in a language like English with a very opaque spelling system. Like aphasia, deep dyslexia and surface dyslexia provide information about the lateralization of the mental lexicon to the left hemisphere and about its nature, organization, and access routes.

Japanese readers provide additional evidence regarding hemispheric specialization. The Japanese language has two main writing systems. One system, *kana*, is based on the sound system of the language; each symbol corresponds to a syllable. The other system, *kanji*, is ideographic; each symbol corresponds to a word. (Writing systems are discussed in Chapter 8.) *Kanji* is not based on the sounds of the language. Japanese speakers with left-hemisphere damage are impaired in their ability to read the phonetically based *kana*, whereas ones with right-hemisphere damage are impaired in their ability to read the ideographic *kanji* symbols. In addition, experiments with unimpaired Japanese readers show that the right hemisphere is better and faster than the left hemisphere at reading *kanji*, and conversely, the left hemisphere does better with *kana*, though the left hemisphere can read both systems.

Brain Imaging in Aphasic Patients

Today we no longer need to rely on surgery or autopsy to locate brain lesions. Noninvasive neuroimaging technologies such as computer tomography (CT) scans and **magnetic resonance imaging (MRI)** can reveal lesions in the living brain shortly after the damage occurs. In addition, **functional positron emission tomography (fPET)** scans and **functional MRI (fMRI)** scans can reveal the brain in action by measuring blood flow and oxygen utilization in different areas of the brain during the performance of various linguistic and other cognitive tasks. It is now possible to detect changes in brain activity and to relate these changes to localized brain damage and specific linguistic and nonlinguistic cognitive tasks.

Figures 10.5 and 10.6 show MRI scans of the brains of a Broca's aphasic patient and a Wernicke's aphasic patient. The black areas show the sites of the lesions. Each diagram represents a slice of the left side of the brain.

Dramatic evidence for a differentiated and structured brain is also provided by studies of patients with lesions in regions of the brain other than Broca's and Wernicke's areas. Some patients have difficulty speaking a person's name; others have problems naming animals; and still others cannot name tools. fMRI studies have revealed the shape and location of the brain lesions in each of these types of patients. The patients in each group had brain lesions in distinct, nonoverlapping regions of the left temporal lobe. In an associated PET scan study, normal subjects were asked to name persons, animals, or tools. Experimenters found

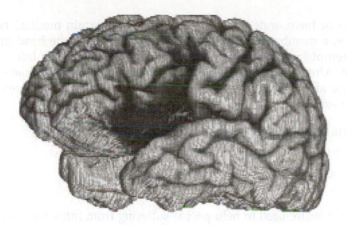

FIGURE 10.5 | Three-dimensional reconstruction of the brain of a living patient with Broca's aphasia. Note area of damage in left frontal region (*dark gray*), which was caused by a stroke.
Courtesy of Hanna Damásio.

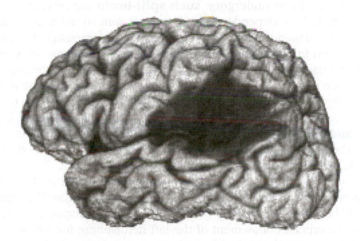

FIGURE 10.6 | Three-dimensional reconstruction of the brain of a living patient with Wernicke's aphasia. Note area of damage in left posterior temporal and lower parietal region (*dark gray*), which was caused by a stroke.
Courtesy of Hanna Damásio.

that in the normal brains there was differential activation in just those sites that were damaged in the aphasics Similarly, some brain-damaged patients lose the ability to recognize sounds or colors or familiar faces while retaining all other functions. A patient may not be able to recognize his wife when she walks into the room until she starts to talk. This suggests the separability of many aspects of visual and auditory processing.

Other sources of evidence concerning the functional differences between the left and right hemispheres is provided by individuals who have suffered trauma to the brain or have undergone brain surgery for certain medical conditions. For example, a member of the U.S. Congress was shot in the head in an assassination attempt in 2011, with the bullet passing through the left hemisphere of the brain. After a year of courageous recovery, news reports made clear that her linguistic ability was still severely compromised and TV images distinctly revealed an asymmetric weakness to the right side of the body.

Split Brains

It takes only one hemisphere to have a mind.

A. L. WIGAN, *The Duality of the Mind*, 1844

An extreme measure used to help people suffering from intractable epilepsy is a procedure in which a surgeon severs the corpus callosum (see Figure 10.2), the fibrous network that connects the two halves. When this pathway is severed, there is no communication between the "two brains," making it possible to test the functions of each (now isolated) hemisphere without interference from the other.

In people who have undergone **such split-brain** surgery, the two hemispheres appear to be independent, and messages sent to the brain result in different responses, depending on which side receives the message. For example, if a pencil is placed in the left hand of a split-brain person whose eyes are closed, the person can use the pencil appropriately but cannot name it because only the left hemisphere can speak. The right brain senses the pencil but the information cannot be relayed to the left brain for linguistic naming because the connections between the two halves have been severed. By contrast, if the pencil is placed in the right hand, the subject is immediately able to name it as well as to describe it because the sensory information from the right hand goes directly to the left hemisphere, where the language areas are located.

Studies of split-brain patients have also shown that when the interhemispheric visual connections are severed, visual information from the right and left visual fields becomes confined to the left and right hemispheres, respectively. Because of the crucial endowment of the left hemisphere for language, written material delivered to the right hemisphere cannot be read aloud if the brain is split, because the information cannot be transferred to the left hemisphere. Thus, an image or picture that is flashed to the right visual field of a split-brain patient (and therefore processed by the left hemisphere) can be named. However, when the picture is flashed in the left visual field and therefore "lands" in the right hemisphere, it cannot be named. It is only under special, experimental circumstances that independent functions of the hemispheres are revealed. Under normal living circumstances both hemispheres have access to whatever a person sees or hears.

Experiments of this sort have provided information on the different capabilities of the two hemispheres. The right brain does better than the left in pattern-matching tasks, in recognizing faces, and in spatial tasks. The left hemisphere is superior for language, rhythmic perception, temporal-order judgments, and arithmetic calculations. According to the psychologist Michael Gazzaniga, "the right hemisphere as well as the left hemisphere can emote and while the left can tell you why, the right cannot."

Neural Evidence of Grammatical Phenomena

The human brain is a most unusual instrument of elegant and as yet unknown capacity.

STUART SEATON

Thanks to the invention of imaging and other technologies, much can be learned about the lateralization of language and other cognitive functions from looking at healthy brains. Experimental tests of unimpaired people are used to map the brain and to investigate the independence of different aspects of language as well as the independence of language from other cognitive systems.

In addition to fMRI and fPET discussed earlier, other widely used techniques include *Event-related potentials (ERPs* and *Magnetoencephalography (MEG)*. **Event-related potentials (ERPs)** are the electrical signals emitted from the brain in response to different linguistic stimuli and can be monitored through electrodes taped to different areas of the skull. This technique, based upon EEG (electroencephalogram) readings, exploits the fact that the brain is electrically active and that this electrical activity can be measured both for its strength (amplitude) and for its pattern of responses over time.

Magnetoencephalography (MEG) records small changes in the brain's magnetic fields and provides information on which parts of the brain are involved in particular language-related tasks. Like ERPs, MEG provides information about how the brain reacts over time.

These noninvasive methods can also reveal how the healthy brain reacts to particular linguistic stimuli. For example, how the normal brain responds in deciding whether two or more sounds are the same or different, whether a sequence of sounds constitutes a real or possible word, or whether a sequence of words forms a grammatical or ungrammatical sentence. The results of these studies reaffirm earlier findings that language resides in specific areas of the left hemisphere, and demonstrate the neurological reflexes of many of the linguistic categories and constraints posited by linguists.

Neurolinguistic Studies of Speech Sounds

These new techniques have provided many insights into how the human brain responds to sounds. A first important finding is that the brain reacts differently to speech versus non-speech sounds. ERP responses are greater from the left hemisphere when the subject hears speech sounds.

Many studies also provide neurolinguistic evidence for the categories and concepts that linguists postulate in their descriptions of sound systems. Experiments using ERPs and MEGs have shown a neural reflex of categorical perception: The brain reacts differently to sounds that are phonemically different (e.g., [t] and [k]) than to sounds that are acoustically distinct (e.g., [p] and [pʰ]) but non-phonemic. The overall patterns of response to phonemes versus allophones differ in intensity, speed, and location in the brain. An fMRI experiment involving French and Japanese speakers has demonstrated distinct response patterns for phonotactically permissible versus impermissible sequences of sounds in their language as well as faster reaction times to the phonotactically correct sequences. Similar results have been found in studies of deaf signers who show different neurological responses to phonotactically permissible and impermissible hand configurations in sign language.

Neurolinguistic Studies of Sentence and Word Structure

Modern technologies have also been used to examine the brain's response to the syntactic patterns of language. ERP experiments show variations in timing, pattern, amplitude, and hemisphere of response when subjects hear sentences that are meaningless, such as:

The man admired Don's headache of the landscape.

as opposed to meaningful sentences such as:

The man admired Don's sketch of the landscape.

Even Jabberwocky sentences—sentences that are grammatical but contain nonsense words, such as Lewis Carroll's *'Twas brillig, and the slithy toves* elicit an asymmetrical left-hemisphere ERP response, demonstrating that the left hemisphere is sensitive to grammatical structure even in the absence of meaning. Such findings provide neurological evidence for the separation between syntax and semantics posited by linguists. Moreover, because ERPs also show the timing of neuronal activity as the brain processes language, they provide insight into the mechanisms that allow the brain to process language quickly and efficiently, on the scale of milliseconds.

Another set of studies has examined brain responses to syntactic dependencies of the sort shown in *wh* questions (see Chapter 2). Subjects hear sentences in which the underlying subject or object has been moved to the beginning of the sentence. In the case of a moved subject in example (1), the movement is shorter and the basic word order is kept:

(1) Who . . ___ left the room?

On the other hand, movement from object position as in example (2) involves a longer distance between the moved element *(which bagel)* which psycholinguists call the "filler," and the position from which it moves, referred to as the "gap".

(2) Which bagel did Seymour slice ___?

Various studies show that sentences with moved objects elicit longer response times than sentences with moved subjects, providing neural correlates of different *wh* movements (as discussed in Chapter 2).

Many neurolinguistic studies have examined the brain's response to ungrammatical sentences, manifested by a type of ERP pattern called a MisMatch Negativity (MMN). These experiments find that different types of ungrammatical sentences evoke distinct waveforms. Thus, violations of phrase structure, C-selection, agreement rules, among others produce a specific neural "signature."

Interestingly, the brain responds at once to morphosyntactic violations (e.g., *a boys is running*) and does so outside the scope of attention. In one study, subjects were divided into three groups: One group simply listened to grammatical and ungrammatical phrases; another watched a video while listening to the same phrases; and a third performed a complex auditory task while listening to the phrases. An MMN response to the syntactic violations was almost immediate, within the first 100–200 milliseconds after hearing the phrase, and the response was equally rapid and strong whether or not the listeners had to perform another task. Particularly striking was the response of those subjects who had to do the auditory task. They had the same strong MMN response, showing that even a complex task requiring considerable attention *in the same auditory modality* did not compete with syntactic processing. The results of this study demonstrate that syntactic processing is like a reflex, in being both automatic and attention-free.

Recent studies have also used fMRI to examine brain activation for past tense, present tense and agreement morphology. The results showed different neural signatures for the different inflectional morphemes, and was also distinct from the neural reflex of processing bare verb stems.

Experimental evidence from these various neurolinguistic experiments has provided considerable insight into how the brain processes language, and has also lent empirical support to many of the abstract categories, rules, concepts, and components of grammar.

Language and Brain Development

If the brain were so simple we could understand it, we would be so simple we couldn't.

LYALL WATSON

Numerous neurolinguistic studies have found that the way the brain is organized for language and grammar in the adult is already reflected in the brains of newborns and young infants. Lateralization of language to the left hemisphere is a process that begins very early in life, even before language actively develops. For example, Wernicke's area is visibly distinctive in the left hemisphere of the fetus by the twenty-sixth gestational week. Moreover, infants show evidence of many of the neural correlates of linguistic categories that we observe in adults.

Left Hemisphere Lateralization for Language in Young Children

JUMP START © Robb Armstrong. Reprinted with permission of ANDREWS MCMEEL SYNDICATION. All rights reserved.

Everyone loves a smiling baby, but babies' smiles do more than light up a room. They reveal something very important about how the developing brain is organized for language.

In a very intriguing study, researchers videotaped smiling babies and babbling babies (producing syllabic sequences like *mamama* or *gugugu*) between the ages of five and twelve months. The videotapes showed that when the babies were smiling their mouths were opened wider on the left side (the side controlled by the right hemisphere) whereas when they babbled the *right* side of their mouths (controlled by the left hemisphere) were opened wider, indicating greater left hemisphere involvement for language even during the babbling period (see Chapter 9).

Many other studies of infants and young children support this conclusion. For example, infants as young as one week old show a greater electrical response in the left hemisphere to language and in the right hemisphere to music, similar to adults. A study measuring brain activation in awake and sleeping three-month-old infants when hearing forward and backward speech showed that different areas of the cortex responded in the two cases.

We noted in previous chapters, that behavioral tests show that infants—like adults—perceive speech sounds categorically. ERP studies have found neurological correlates of categorical perception in infants, just as for adults. These studies show that the infant brain responds differently, and with the same pattern and speed as found in adults, to *phonemic* categories than to non-phonemic acoustic distinctions. This neural pattern occurs even in sleeping babies, showing that the response is automatic and does not require the attention of the infant.

These and similar experiments show that from birth onward, the left hemisphere differentiates between nonlinguistic acoustic processing and the linguistic processing of sounds, and uses the same neural pathways as adults. Other studies indicate the same holds true for syntax. Very young children seem to process syntactic structures in the same area of the brain and with the same neurological indices as adults, albeit slightly more slowly. In one study, two-year-olds listened to grammatical and ungrammatical sentences. Some of the ungrammatical sentences had nouns where verbs should be, and some had verbs in noun positions. The toddlers showed a clear left-lateralized response to the ungrammatical sentences and even different patterns for the noun versus verb substitutions.

Brain Plasticity

While the left hemisphere is innately predisposed to specialize for language, there is also evidence of considerable *plasticity* (i.e., flexibility) in the system during the early stages of language development. This means that under certain circumstances, the right hemisphere can take over many of the language functions that would normally reside in the left hemisphere.

An impressive illustration of plasticity is provided by children who have undergone a procedure known as **hemispherectomy**, in which one hemisphere of the brain is surgically removed. This procedure is used to treat otherwise intractable cases of epilepsy. In cases of left hemispherectomy after language acquisition has begun, children experience an initial period of aphasia. However, in certain cases, depending on the underlying disease that led to the epilepsy, the child may reacquire a linguistic system that is virtually indistinguishable from that of normal children. They also show many of the developmental patterns of normal language acquisition. UCLA researchers who have studied many of these children hypothesize that the latent linguistic ability of the right hemisphere is "freed" by the removal of the diseased left hemisphere, which may have had a strong inhibitory effect before the surgery.

In adults, however, surgical removal of the left hemisphere inevitably results in severe loss of language function (and so is done only in life-threatening circumstances), whereas adults (and children who have already acquired language) who have had their right hemispheres removed generally retain their language abilities. Other cognitive losses may result, such as those typically lateralized to the right hemisphere. The plasticity of the brain decreases with age and with the increasing specialization of the different hemispheres and regions of the brain.

Despite strong evidence that the left hemisphere is predetermined to be the language hemisphere in most humans, some studies suggest that the right hemisphere also plays a role, especially in the earliest stages of language acquisition. Children with prenatal, perinatal, or childhood brain lesions in the right hemisphere can show delays and impairments in babbling and vocabulary learning, whereas children with early left hemisphere lesions demonstrate impairments in their ability to form phrases and sentences. In addition, many children who undergo right hemispherectomy before two years of age do not develop language, even though they still have a left hemisphere.

Various findings converge to show that the human brain is essentially designed to specialize for language in the left hemisphere but that the right hemisphere is involved in early language development. They also show that the brain is remarkably resilient and that if left brain trauma occurs early in life, its normal functions can be taken over by the right hemisphere.

The Critical Period

Under ordinary circumstances a child is introduced to language virtually at the moment of birth. Adults talk to him and to each other in his presence. Children do not require explicit language instruction, but they do need exposure to language to develop normally. Children who do not receive linguistic input during their formative years do not achieve native-like grammatical competence. Moreover, behavioral tests and brain imaging studies show that late exposure to language alters the fundamental organization of the brain for language.

The **critical-age hypothesis** asserts that language is biologically based and that the ability to learn a native language develops within a fixed period, from birth to middle childhood. During this **critical period**, language acquisition proceeds easily, swiftly, and without external intervention. After this period, the acquisition of grammar is difficult and, for most individuals, never fully achieved. Children deprived of language during this critical period show atypical patterns of brain lateralization.

Many species have a critical period for specific, biologically triggered behaviors. For example, during the period from nine to twenty-one hours after hatching, ducklings will follow the first moving object they see, whether or not it looks, quacks, and waddles like a duck. Such behavior is not the result of a conscious decision, external teaching, or intensive practice. It unfolds according to what appears to be a maturationally determined schedule that is universal across the species. Similarly, as discussed in Chapter 1, certain species of birds develop their bird song within a biologically determined window of time.

Instances of children reared in environments of extreme social isolation constitute "experiments in nature" for testing the critical-age hypothesis. The most dramatic cases are those described as "wild" or "feral" children. A celebrated case, documented in Francois Truffaut's film *The Wild Child*, is that of Victor, "the wild boy of Aveyron," who was found in 1798. It was ascertained that he had been left in the woods when very young and had somehow survived. In 1920, two children, Amala and Kamala, were found in India, supposedly having been reared by wolves.

Other children have been deliberately isolated from normal social interaction and language. In 1970, a child called Genie in the scientific reports was discovered. She had been confined to a small room under conditions of physical restraint and had received only minimal human contact from the age of eighteen months until nearly fourteen years.

Regardless of the cause of the isolation, none of these children was able to speak or knew any language at the time they were reintroduced into society. This linguistic inability could be simply explained by the fact that these children received no linguistic input, showing that language acquisition, though an innate, neurologically-based ability, must be triggered by input from the environment. In the documented cases of Victor and Genie, however, these children were unable to acquire grammar even after years of exposure, and despite the ability to learn many words.

Genie was able to learn a large vocabulary, including words for colors, shapes, objects, natural categories, and abstract as well as concrete terms, but her grammatical skills never fully developed. The UCLA linguist Susan Curtiss, who worked with Genie for several years, reported that Genie's utterances were, for the most part, "the stringing together of content words, often with rich and clear meaning, but with little grammatical structure." Many utterances produced by Genie at the age of fifteen and later are like those of two-year-old children, and not unlike utterances of Broca's aphasia patients, or people with Specific Language Impairment (SLI, discussed below). Some such utterances are:

Man motorcycle have.
Genie full stomach.
Genie bad cold live father house.
Want Curtiss play piano.
Open door key.

Genie's utterances lacked articles, auxiliary verbs like *will* or *can*, the third-person singular agreement marker -*s*, the past-tense marker -*ed*, question words like *who, what,* and *where,* and pronouns. She had no ability to form more complex types of sentences such as questions (e.g., *Are you feeling hungry?).* Genie started learning language after the critical period and was therefore never able to fully acquire the grammatical rules of English.

Tests of lateralization (ERP experiments and others) showed that Genie's language was lateralized to the *right* hemisphere. Her test performance was similar to that found in split-brain and left hemispherectomy patients, yet Genie was not brain damaged. Curtiss speculates that after the critical period, the usual language areas functionally atrophy because of inadequate linguistic stimulation. Genie's case also demonstrates that language is not the same as communication, because Genie was a powerful nonverbal communicator, despite her limited ability to acquire grammar.

Chelsea, another case of linguistic isolation, is a woman whose situation also reflects the critical-age hypothesis. She was born deaf but was wrongly diagnosed as intellectually disabled. When she was thirty-one, her deafness was finally diagnosed and she was fitted with hearing aids. She has received extensive language training and therapy for years and has acquired a large vocabulary. She can even invent new words when she doesn't have a word for something in her lexicon (e.g. *doctor tie* for *stethoscope*).

Like Genie, Chelsea readily learned new words, but she was even more impaired than Genie in the ability to develop grammar. While Genie developed some grammatical knowledge, such as the ability to distinguish transitive and intransitive verbs, Chelsea developed no knowledge of grammar at all. ERP studies of Chelsea's brain have revealed an equal response to language in both hemispheres. In other words, like Genie, Chelsea also fails to show the normal asymmetric brain organization for language.

More than 90 percent of children who are born deaf or become deaf before they have acquired language are born to hearing parents. These children also provide information about the critical age for language acquisition. Most parents of deaf children do not know sign language at the time their children are born, and hence most deaf children receive delayed language exposure. Several studies have investigated the acquisition of American Sign Language (ASL) among deaf signers exposed to the language at different ages. Early learners who received ASL input from birth and up to six years of age did much better in the production and comprehension of complex signs and sign sentences than late learners who were not exposed to ASL until after the age of twelve, even though all of the subjects at the time of these studies had used sign for more than twenty years. There was little difference; however, in vocabulary or knowledge of word order.

In a study comparing lateralization patterns in adult native speakers of English, adult native signers, and deaf adults who had not been exposed to sign language, the nonsigning deaf adults did not show the same cerebral asymmetries as either the hearing adults or the deaf signers. In recent years, there have been numerous studies of late learners of sign language, all with similar results.

A recent study reports that only deaf children whose hearing was successfully remediated (either by cochlear implants or hearing aids) by the age of eight months went on to develop rich grammars. This finding suggests the developmental "window of opportunity" for acquiring complex syntax may be far smaller than previously thought.

The cases of Genie and other isolated individuals, as well as deaf learners of ASL show that children cannot fully acquire language unless they are exposed to it within a biologically determined window of opportunity. This critical period is linked to brain lateralization. The human brain is primed to develop language in specific areas of the left hemisphere, but the normal process of brain specialization depends on early and systematic experience with language. Language acquisition plays a critical role in, and may even be *the* trigger for, the realization of normal cerebral lateralization for higher cognitive functions in general, not just for language.

Beyond the critical period, the human brain seems markedly impaired in the ability to acquire the grammatical aspects of language, even with substantial linguistic training or many years of exposure. However, it is possible to acquire words and various conversational skills after this point. This evidence suggests that the critical period for first language holds for the acquisition of grammatical abilities, but not necessarily for all aspects of language. The selectivity in acquisition that occurs beyond the critical period, like the selective impairment that occurs in various language disorders, points to a strongly compartmentalized language faculty. Language is separate from other cognitive systems and is itself a complex system with various components.

The Modular Mind: Dissociations of Language and Cognition

[T]he human mind is not an unstructured entity but consists of components which can be distinguished by their functional properties.

NEIL SMITH AND IANTHI-MARIA TSIMPLI, *The Mind of a Savant: Language, Learning, and Modularity*, 1995

The modular view of cognition is also supported by various case studies of extraordinary individuals who show deficits in certain cognitive domains alongside normal or superior abilities in other areas. The individuals we discuss below show *dissociations* between their linguistic abilities and other nonlinguistic cognitive abilities. In some cases, their language abilities far outpace the other areas, and in other cases, the reverse is true.

Linguistic Savants

There are numerous cases of intellectually handicapped individuals who, despite their disabilities in certain spheres, show remarkable talents in others. Such people are referred to as **savants**. Some of the most famous savants are human calculators, who can perform arithmetic computations at phenomenal speed, or calendrical calculators, who can tell you without pause on which day of the week any date in the last or next century falls.

Until recently, most such savants have been reported to be linguistically handicapped. They may be good mimics who can parrot speech, but they show meager creative language ability. But there are also cases of language savants, people who have acquired the highly complex grammar of their language (as well as other languages in some cases) but who lack nonlinguistic abilities of equal complexity. Laura and Christopher are two such cases.

Laura was a severely cognitively impaired young woman with a nonverbal IQ of 41 to 44. She lacked almost all number concepts, including basic counting principles, and could draw only at a preschool level. She had an auditory memory span limited to three units. Yet, when at the age of sixteen she was asked to name some fruits, she responded with *pears, apples,* and *pomegranates.* In this same period, she produced syntactically complex sentences such as *He was saying that I lost my battery-powered watch that I loved,* and *She does paintings, this really good friend of the kids who I went to school with and really loved,* and *I was like 15 or 19 when I started moving out of home. . . .*

Laura could not add 2 + 2. She didn't know how old she was or whether 15 is before or after 19. Nevertheless, Laura produced complex sentences with multiple phrases and embedded sentences. She used and understood passive sentences, and she was able to inflect verbs for number and person to agree with the subject of a sentence. She formed past tenses in accord with adverbs that referred to past time. She could do all this and more, but she could neither read nor write nor tell time. She did not know who the president of the United States was or what country she lived in. Her drawings of humans resembled potatoes with stick arms and legs. Yet, in a sentence imitation task, she both detected and corrected grammatical errors.

Laura is but one of the many examples of children who display well-developed grammatical abilities, less-developed abilities to associate linguistic expressions with the objects they refer to, and severe deficits in nonlinguistic cognition.

Another linguistic savant, Christopher, has a nonverbal IQ between 60 and 70. He lives in an institution because he is unable to take care of himself. The tasks of buttoning a shirt, cutting his fingernails, or vacuuming the carpet are too difficult for him. However, his linguistic competence is as rich and as sophisticated as that of any native speaker. Furthermore, when given written texts in some fifteen to twenty languages, he translates them quickly, with few errors, into English. The languages include Germanic languages such as Danish, Dutch, and German; Romance languages such as French, Italian, Portuguese, and Spanish; as well as Polish, Finnish, Greek, Hindi, Turkish, and Welsh. He learned these languages from speakers who used them in his presence, or from grammar books. Christopher loves to study and learn languages. Little else is of interest to him. His situation strongly suggests that his linguistic ability is independent of his general intellectual ability.

The question as to whether the language faculty is a separate cognitive system or whether it is derivative of more general cognitive mechanisms is controversial and has received much attention and debate among linguists, psychologists, neuropsychologists, and cognitive scientists. Cases such as Laura and Christopher argue against the view that linguistic ability derives from general intelligence because these two individuals (and others like them) developed language despite pervasive intellectual deficits. A growing body of evidence supports the view that the biologically determined human language faculty is highly specific and does not derive from general human intellectual ability.

Specific Language Impairment

People like Laura and Christopher have normal or superior linguistic skills though their abilities in other areas are very limited. There are also individuals who show the opposite profile: Among these are children with **Specific Language Impairment (SLI)**.

Children with SLI have do not have brain lesions, but they nevertheless have difficulties acquiring language or are much slower the average child. They show no other cognitive deficits, they are not autistic or intellectually impaired, and they have no perceptual problems. Only their linguistic ability is affected, and often only very specific aspects of grammar are impaired.

Children with SLI have problems with the use of function words such as articles, prepositions, and auxiliary verbs. They also have difficulties with inflectional suffixes on nouns and verbs such as markers of plurality or tense. The following examples from a four-year-old boy with SLI illustrate this:

Meowmeow chase mice.
Show me knife.
It not long one.

An experimental study of several children with SLI showed that they produced the past tense marker on the verb (as in *danced*) about 27 percent of the time, compared with 95 percent by the normal control group. Similarly, the children with SLI produced the plural marker -*s* (as in *boys*) only 9 percent of the time, compared with 95 percent by the normal children.

Other studies reveal broader grammatical impairments, involving difficulties with sentences in which phrases have moved, such as *Mother is hard to please*, a rearrangement of *It is hard to please Mother*, and also with sentences involving *wh* movement. In many respects, these difficulties resemble the impairments demonstrated by agrammatic aphasics. This may suggest that certain grammatical structures or operations are particularly vulnerable to language impairment both in development and breakdown. In addition, ERP studies of certain children with SLI have shown that they do not exhibit the expected response levels for syntactic processing, which jibed with their inability to process many syntactic structures normally.

As is the case with aphasia, these studies of individuals with SLI provide important information about the nature of language and help linguists develop theories about the underlying properties of language and its development in children. Children with SLI, like the other cases of dissociation discussed above, show that language may be impaired while general intelligence remains intact, supporting the view of a grammatical faculty that is separate from other cognitive systems.

Genetic Basis of Language

Studies of genetic disorders also reveal that one cognitive domain can develop normally along with abnormal development in other domains, and they also underscore the strong biological basis of language.

Children with Turner syndrome (a chromosomal anomaly) have normal language and advanced reading skills even though they have serious nonlinguistic (visual and spatial) cognitive deficits. Similarly, studies of the language of children and adolescents with Williams syndrome reveal a unique behavioral profile in which certain linguistic functions seem to be relatively preserved in the face of visual and spatial cognitive deficits and moderate intellectual impairment. Recent studies of men with Klinefelter syndrome (another chromosomal anomaly) show quite selective syntactic and semantic deficits alongside intact intelligence.

SLI also appears to have a genetic basis. Epidemiological and familial aggregation studies show that SLI runs in families. One such study is of a large multigenerational family, half of whom are language impaired. The impaired members of this family have a very specific grammatical problem: They do not reliably use verb inflections or "irregular" verbs correctly. They routinely produce sentences such as the following:

She remembered when she hurts herself the other day.
He did it then he fall.
The boy climb up the tree and frightened the bird away.

Studies of twins show that monozygotic (identical) twins are more likely to both suffer from SLI than dizygotic (fraternal) twins, also pointing to a genetic basis to SLI.

Summary

Psycholinguistics is concerned with **linguistic performance** or processing, which is the use of linguistic knowledge (competence) in speech production and comprehension.

Comprehension, the process of understanding an utterance, requires the ability to access the mental lexicon to match the words in the utterance to their meanings. Comprehension begins with the perception of the **acoustic speech signal.** The speech signal can be described in terms of the **fundamental frequency**, perceived as pitch; the intensity, perceived as loudness; and the quality, perceived as differences in speech sounds, such as between an [i] and an [a]. The speech wave can be displayed visually as a **spectrogram**, sometimes called a **voiceprint.** In a spectrogram, vowels exhibit dark bands where frequency intensity is greatest. These are called **formants** and result from the emphasis of certain harmonics of the fundamental frequency, as determined by the shape of the vocal tract. Each vowel has a unique formant pattern.

The speech signal is a continuous stream of sounds. Listeners who know the language have the ability to segment the stream into linguistic units and to recognize acoustically distinct sounds as the same linguistic unit.

Psycholinguistic studies are aimed at uncovering the units, stages, and processes involved in linguistic performance. Several experimental techniques, including **lexical decision tasks**, have proved helpful in understanding **lexical access.** The measurement of response times, RTs, shows that it takes longer to retrieve less common words than more common words; longer to retrieve possible non-words than impossible non-words; longer to retrieve words with larger **phonological neighborhoods** than ones with smaller neighborhoods; and longer to retrieve lexically ambiguous words than unambiguous ones.

A word may **prime** another word if the words are semantically, morphologically, or phonologically related. The priming effect is shown by faster RTs to related words than to unrelated words. In addition to using behavioral data such as RT, researchers can now use various measures of electrical brain activity such as event related potentials (**ERPs**) to learn about language processing.

Perception of the speech signal and retrieval of words are necessary but not sufficient for the comprehension of speech. To get the full meaning of an utterance, the listener must **parse** the string into syntactic constituents, because meaning depends on word order and constituent structure in addition to the meaning of individual words. This is done according to the rules of the grammar of the language and also following structural parsing principles that favor simpler structures. Two such principles are **minimal attachment** and **late closure**. Other factors such as prosody, frequency of occurrence, and lexical biases can also influence the parser in its structural choices.

It is likely that we use both **top-down processing** and **bottom-up processing** during comprehension. Top-down processing uses semantic and syntactic information in addition to the lexical and phonological information drawn from the sensory input; bottom-up processing gives primacy to the information contained in the sensory input.

Language is filled with **temporary ambiguities**, points at which the sentence can continue in more than one way because of word category ambiguity or different structural possibilities. Usually these ambiguities are quickly resolved and may not be noticed except under experimental conditions.

Occasionally, the reader goes down a **garden path**, a structural misanalysis in which he must backtrack and redo the parse. **Eye tracking** techniques can determine the points of a sentence at which readers have such difficulties. These experiments provide strong evidence that the parser has preferences in how it constructs trees. Other sentences, such as multiple center embeddings, are difficult to parse because of memory constraints.

Another technique is **shadowing**, in which subjects repeat as fast as possible what is being said to them. Subjects often correct errors in the stimulus sentence, suggesting that they use linguistic knowledge rather than simply echoing sounds they hear. Shadowing experiments provide strong evidence of the use of top-down information in sentence processing.

Much of the best information about the units and stages of speech production comes from observing and analyzing spontaneous speech, especially speech errors. Many of the same factors that influence the listener in comprehension also affect the speaker in production. Lexical access is influenced in both cases by semantic and phonological relatedness of words and word frequency.

Speech errors such as **spoonerisms** show that features, segments, words, and phrases may be conceptualized or planned well before they are uttered. Anticipation errors, in which a sound is produced earlier than in the intended utterance, show that we do not produce one sound or one word or even one phrase at a time. Rather, we construct and store larger units with their syntactic structures specified.

The attempt to understand what makes the acquisition and use of language possible has led to research on the brain-mind-language relationship.

Neurolinguistics is the study of the brain mechanisms and anatomical structures that underlie linguistic competence and performance.

The brain is the most complex organ of the body, controlling motor and sensory activities, and thought processes. Research conducted for more than a century has shown that different parts of the brain control different body functions. The nerve cells that form the surface of the brain are called the **cortex**, which serves as the intellectual decision maker, receiving messages from the sensory organs and initiating all voluntary actions. The brain of all higher animals is divided into two **cerebral hemispheres**, which are connected by the **corpus callosum**, a network that permits the left and right hemispheres to communicate.

Each hemisphere exhibits **contralateral** control of functions. The left hemisphere controls the right side of the body, and the right hemisphere controls the left side. Despite the general symmetry of the human body, much evidence suggests that the brain is asymmetric, with the left and right hemispheres specialized for different functions. **Lateralization** is the term used to refer to the localization of function to one hemisphere of the brain.

Language is lateralized to the left hemisphere. Much of the early evidence for language lateralization comes from the study of **aphasia**, which is the neurological term for any language disorder that results from acquired brain damage caused by disease or trauma. Lesions in the part of the left hemisphere called **Broca's area** may suffer from **Broca's aphasia**, which results in impaired syntax and **agrammatism**. Damage to **Wernicke's area**, also in the left hemisphere, may result in **Wernicke's aphasia**, in which fluent speakers produce semantically anomalous utterances. Damage to yet different areas can produce **anomia**, a form of aphasia in which the patient has word-finding difficulties.

Deaf signers with damage to the left hemisphere show aphasia for sign language similar to the language breakdown in hearing aphasics, even though sign languages are visual-spatial languages.

Evidence for language lateralization as well as the contralateral control of function is also provided by **split-brain** patients and by neurolinguistic studies of grammatical phenomena. By studying people with aphasia and other neurological conditions such as **acquired dyslexia** localized areas of the brain can be associated with particular language functions.

Advances in technology have provided a variety of non-invasive methods for studying the living brain as it processes language. By measuring electromagnetic activities (ERPs and MEGs), and through imaging techniques such as CT, MRI, fMRI, and fPET scans, both damaged and healthy brains can be observed and evaluated. These studies confirm earlier results concerning the lateralization of language to the left hemisphere, and provide evidence of neural reflexes of various linguistic categories and constraints, such as categorical perception, phonotactic constraints, and *wh* movement. These studies also demonstrate that grammatical processing is automatic and attention-free, like a reflex.

Lateralization of language to the left hemisphere is a process that begins very early in life. Numerous neurolinguistic studies have found that brain organization for language and grammar found in adults is already reflected in the brains of newborns and young infants. Infants also show evidence of the many of the neural correlates of linguistic categories that we observe in adults.

While the left hemisphere is innately predisposed to specialize for language, there is also evidence of considerable **plasticity** in the system during the early stages of language development. Children who undergo a left **hemispherectomy** experience an initial period of aphasia, but in certain cases may reacquire a linguistic system like that of normal children. The plasticity of the brain decreases with age and with the increasing specialization of the different hemispheres and regions of the brain.

The **critical-age hypothesis** states that there is a window of opportunity for learning a first language. The imperfect learning of grammatical rules in people exposed to language after this period supports the hypothesis.

The language faculty is **modular**. It is independent of other cognitive systems with which it interacts. Evidence for modularity is found in the selective impairment of language in aphasia, in children with **specific language impairment (SLI)**, in linguistic **savants**, and in children who learn language past the critical period. The genetic basis for an independent language module is supported by studies of SLI in families and twins and by studies of genetic anomalies associated with language disorders.

References for Further Reading

Ahlsén, E. 2006. *Introduction to neurolinguistics*. Amsterdam: John Benjamins.

Caplan, D. 2001. *Neurolinguistics: The handbook of linguistics*, M. Aronoff and J. Rees-Miller (eds.). London: Blackwell Publishers.

Carroll, D. W. 2007. *Psychology of language, 5th ed.* Belmont, CA: Wadsworth.

Curtiss, S. 1977. *Genie: A linguistic study of a modern-day "wild child."* New York: Academic Press.

Curtiss, S. 2013. Revisiting modularity: Using language as a window to the mind. In M. Piatelli-Palmarini and R.C. Berwick (Eds.) *Rich Languages from Poor Inputs*. Oxford: Oxford University Press, 68–90.

Damásio, H. 1981. Cerebral localization of the aphasias. *Acquired aphasia*, M. Taylor Sarno (ed.). New York: Academic Press, 27–65.

Fernandez, E.M. and Cairns, H.S. 2010. *Fundamentals of psycholinguistics*. Oxford, UK: Wiley-Blackwell.

Fromkin, V. A. (ed.). 1980. *Errors in linguistic performance*. New York: Academic Press.

Gazzaniga, M. S. 1970. *The bisected brain*. New York: Appleton-Century-Crofts.

Geschwind, N. 1979. Specializations of the human brain. *Scientific American* 206 (September): 180–199.

Ingram, J. 2007. *Neurolinguistics: An introduction to spoken language processing and its disorders*. Cambridge, U.K.: Cambridge University Press.

Johnson, K. 2003. *Acoustic and Auditory Phonetics, 2nd ed.* Oxford, UK: Blackwell.

Ladefoged, P. 1996. *Elements of acoustic phonetics*, 2nd ed. Chicago: University of Chicago Press.

Lenneberg, E. H. 1967. *Biological foundations of language*. New York: Wiley.

Obler, L. K., and K. Gjerlow. 1999. *Language and brain*. Cambridge, UK: Cambridge University Press.

Patterson, K. E., J. C. Marshall, and M. Coltheart (eds.). 1986. *Surface dyslexia*. Hillsdale, NJ: Lawrence Erlbaum.

Pinker, S. 1994. *The language instinct*. New York: William Morrow.

Poizner, H., E. S. Klima, and U. Bellugi. 1987. *What the hands reveal about the brain*. Cambridge, MA: MIT Press.

Searchinger, G. 1994. The human language series: 1, 2, 3. Videos. New York: Equinox Film/Ways of Knowing, Inc.

Smith, N. V., and I-M. Tsimpli. 1995. *The mind of a savant: Language learning and modularity*. Oxford, UK: Blackwell.

Springer, S. P., and G. Deutsch. 1997. *Left brain, right brain, 5th ed.* New York: W. H. Freeman and Company.

Stromswold, K. 2001. The heritability of language. *Language* 77(4): 647–721.

Traxler, Mathew J. 2012. *Introduction to psycholinguistics*. Oxford, UK: Wiley-Blackwell.

Yamada, J. 1990. *Laura: A case for the modularity of language*. Cambridge, MA: MIT Press.

Exercises

1. Speech errors ("slips of the tongue" or "bloopers") illustrate a difference between linguistic competence and performance, because our recognition of them as errors shows that we have knowledge of well-formed sentences. Furthermore, errors provide information about the grammar. The following utterances are part of the UCLA corpus of more than five thousand English speech errors. Most of them were actually observed. One is attributed to Dr. Spooner.

   a. For each speech error, state what kind of linguistic unit or rule is involved (i.e., phonological, morphological, syntactic, lexical, or semantic). In items (16)–(18), also state the nonlinguistic influences.
   b. State, to the best of your ability, the nature of each error, or the mechanisms that produced it.

   (Note: The intended utterance is to the left of the arrow; the actual utterance to the right.)

   Example: ad hoc → odd hack

   a. phonological vowel segment   b. reversal or exchange of segments

   Example: she gave it away → she gived it away

   a. inflectional morphology   b. incorrect application of regular past-tense rule to exceptional verb

   Example: When will you leave? → When you will leave?

   a. syntactic rule   b. failure to move the auxiliary to form a question

   (1) brake fluid → blake fruid
   (2) drink is the curse of the working classes → work is the curse of the drinking classes (Spooner)
   (3) I have to smoke a cigarette with my coffee → . . . smoke my coffee with a cigarette
   (4) untactful → distactful
   (5) an eating marathon → a meeting arathon
   (6) executive committee → executor committee

    (7) lady with the dachshund → lady with the Volkswagen
    (8) are we taking the bus back → are we taking the buck bass
    (9) he broke the crystal on my watch → he broke the whistle on my crotch
  (10) a phonological rule → a phonological fool
  (11) pitch and stress → piss and stretch
  (12) Lebanon → Lemadon
  (13) speech production → preach seduction
  (14) he's a New Yorker → he's a New Yorkan
  (15) I'd forgotten about that → I'd forgot abouten that
  (16) It can deliver a large payload → It can deliver a large payroll (spoken by a congressional representative)
  (17) He made headlines → He made hairlines (referring to a barber)
  (18) I never heard of classes on Good Friday → I never heard of classes on April 9 (spoken by a student when Good Friday fell on April 9 that year)

2. Consider the following ambiguous sentences. Explain each ambiguity, give the most likely interpretation, and state what a computer would have to have in its knowledge base to achieve that interpretation.

Example: A cheesecake was on the table. It was delicious and was soon eaten.

    a. Ambiguity: "It" can refer to the cheesecake or the table.
    b. Likely: "It" refers to the cheesecake.
    c. Knowledge: Tables are not usually eaten.

    (1) For those of you who have children and don't know it, we have a nursery downstairs. (Sign in a church)
    (2) The police were asked to stop drinking in public places.
    (3) Our bikinis are exciting; they are simply the tops. (Bathing suit ad in newspaper)
    (4) It's time we made smoking history. (Anti-smoking campaign slogan)
    (5) Do you know the time? (Hint: This is a pragmatic ambiguity.)
    (6) Concerned with spreading violence, the president called a press conference.
    (7) The ladies of the church have cast off clothing of every kind and they may be seen in the church basement Friday. (Announcement in a church bulletin)
    (8) She earned little as a whiskey maker but he loved her still.
    (9) The butcher backed into the meat grinder and got a little behind in his work.
  (10) A dog gave birth to puppies near the road and was cited for littering.
  (11) A hole was found in the nudist camp wall. The police are looking into it.
  (12) A sign on the lawn at a drug rehab center said, "Keep off the Grass."

The following three items are newspaper headlines:
(13) Red Tape Holds Up New Bridge
(14) Kids Make Nutritious Snacks

(15) Sex Education Delayed, Teachers Request Training

3. Create five sentences containing temporary ambiguities. For example, *Mary believed the boy was lying.* For each, explain how and when the ambiguity is resolved.

4. Consider the following two headlines:

    Physicists Thrilled to Explain What They Are Doing to People

    Two Sisters Reunited after 18 Years in Checkout Line

    a. What principle explains the unintended, funny interpretations of these headlines?
    b. How might you reorganize the words in the headlines to get rid of the unintended meanings?
    c. Check your local newspapers (or other sources) and see whether you can find similar examples.

5. Some sentences are more likely than others to give rise to a garden path effect even though they have the same structures. This is true of the sentence pairs below. Psycholinguistic experiments show that people misparse the (a) sentences less than the (b) sentences. Explain why.

    (1) a. The frustrated tourists understood the snow would mean a late start.
         b. The frustrated tourists understood the message would mean they couldn't go.

    (2) a. The ticket agent admitted the airplane had been late taking off.
         b. The ticket agent admitted the mistake had been careless and stupid.

    (3) a. Mary Ann's mother feared the dress would get torn and dirty.
         b. Mary Ann's mother feared the large wolf would escape from its cage.

6. Priming can be used not only by psycholinguists to study how language is organized in the brain, but also to tell jokes and annoy your friends. Here are two jokes. Try them out on a number of people and report on what percentage "fall for it." In addition, explain why priming is signifi-cant in the effectiveness of these jokes and what is primed. It's different in the two cases.

    (1) Begin my asking your friend to respond quickly without thinking as you rapidly say:

        If a soft drink is a coke,

        And a funny story is a joke,

        What do you call the white of an egg?

You'll be amazed at how many people will answer "yolk," whereas the answer is something like "albumin."

(2) Begin by telling your friend: "An airliner crashes, killing all aboard and comes to rest perfectly straddling the international border between the United States and Canada. Where do they bury the survivors?" Record the amount of time spent pondering this question before coming up with an answer. The answer doesn't matter; it may be one country or the other, or both, or simply "I don't know." In addition, record the percentage of subjects who realize that survivors are not (generally) buried.

7. The Nobel Prize laureate Roger Sperry has argued that split-brain patients have two minds:

> Everything we have seen so far indicates that the surgery has left these people with two separate minds, that is, two separate spheres of consciousness. What is experienced in the right hemisphere seems to lie entirely outside the realm of experience of the left hemisphere. (Sperry, R. W. [1966]. Brain bisection and mechanisms of consciousness. In J. C. Eccles [ed.] *Brain and consciousness experience.* Heidleberg: Springer-Verlag.)

Another Nobel Prize winner in physiology, Sir John Eccles, disagrees. He does not think the right hemisphere can think; he distinguishes between "mere consciousness," which animals possess as well as humans, and language, thought, and other purely human cognitive abilities. In fact, according to him, human nature is all in the left hemisphere.

Write a short essay discussing these two opposing points of view, stating your opinion on how to define "the mind."

8. a. Some aphasic patients, when asked to read a list of words, substitute other words for those printed. In many cases, the printed words and the substituted words are similar. The following data are from actual aphasic patients. In each case, state what the two words have in common and how they differ:

	Printed Word	Word Spoken by Aphasic
i.	liberty	freedom
	canary	parrot
	abroad	overseas
	large	long
	short	small
	tall	long
ii.	decide	decision
	conceal	concealment
	portray	portrait
	bathe	bath
	speak	discussion
	remember	memory

    b. What do the words in groups **(i)** and **(ii)** reveal about how words are likely to be stored in the brain?

9. The following sentences spoken by aphasic patients were collected and analyzed by Dr. Harry Whitaker. In each case, state how the sentence deviates from normal nonaphasic language.

    a. There is under a horse a new sidesaddle.
    b. In girls we see many happy days.
    c. I'll challenge a new bike.
    d. I surprise no new glamour.
    e. Is there three chairs in this room?
    f. Mike and Peter is happy.
    g. Bill and John likes hot dogs.
    h. Proliferate is a complete time about a word that is correct.
    i. Went came in better than it did before.

10. The investigation of individuals with brain damage has been a major source of information regarding the neural basis of language and other cognitive systems. One might suggest that this is like trying to understand how an automobile engine works by looking at damaged engines. Is this a good analogy? If so, why? If not, why not? In your answer, discuss how a damaged system can or cannot provide information about the normal system.

11. What are the arguments and evidence that have been put forth to support the notion that there are two separate parts of the brain?

12. Discuss the statement: It only takes one hemisphere to have a mind.

13. In early neurolinguistic research, listening tests in which subjects hear different kinds of stimuli in each ear were studied. These tests showed that there were fewer errors made in reporting linguistic stimuli such as the syllables *pa, ta,* and *ka* when heard through an earphone on the right ear; other nonlinguistic sounds such as a police car siren were processed with fewer mistakes if heard by the left ear. This is a result of the contralateral control of the brain. There is also a technique that permits visual stimuli to be received either by the right visual field, that is, the right eye alone (going directly to the left hemisphere), or by the left visual field (going directly to the right hemisphere). What are some visual stimuli that could be used in an experiment to further test the lateralization of language?

14. The following utterances were made either by Broca's aphasics or Wernicke's aphasics. Indicate which is which by writing a "B" or "W" next to the utterance.

    a. Goodnight and in the pansy I can't say but into a flipdoor you can see it.
    b. Well . . . sunset . . . uh . . . horses nine, no, uh, two, tails want swish.

    c. Oh, ... if I could I would, and a sick old man disflined a sinter, minter.

    d. Words . . . words . . . words . . . two, four, six, eight, . . . blaze am he.

15. Shakespeare's Hamlet surely had problems. Some say he was obsessed with being overweight because the first lines he speaks in the play when alone on the stage in Act II, Scene 2, are:

    O! that this too too solid flesh would melt,
    Thaw, and resolve itself into a dew;

Others argue that he may have had Wernicke's aphasia, as evidenced by the following passage from Act II, Scene 2:

    Slanders, sir: for the satirical rogue says here
    that old men have grey beards, that their faces are
    wrinkled, their eyes purging thick amber and
    plum-tree gum and that they have a plentiful lack of
    wit, together with most weak hams: all which, sir,
    though I most powerfully and potently believe, yet
    I hold it not honesty to have it thus set down, for you
    yourself, sir, should be old as I am, if like a crab
    you could go backward.

Take up the argument. Is Hamlet aphasic? Argue either case.

16. **Research projects:**

    a. Recently, it's been said that persons born with "perfect pitch" nonetheless need to exercise that ability at a young age or it goes away by adulthood. Find out what you can about this topic and write a one-page (or longer) paper describing your investigation. Begin with defining "perfect pitch." Relate your discoveries to the critical-age hypothesis discussed in this chapter.

    b. Consider some of the high-tech methodologies used to investigate the brain discussed in this chapter, such as PET scans, fMRIs, and MEGs. What are the upsides and downsides of the use of these technologies on healthy patients? Consider the cost, the intrusiveness, and the ethics of exploring a person's brain weighed against the knowledge obtained from such studies.

    c. Investigate claims that PET scans show that reading silently and reading aloud involve different parts of the left hemisphere.

17. **Article review project:** Read, summarize, and critically review the article that appeared in *Science*, Volume 298, November 22, 2002, by Marc D. Hauser, Noam Chomsky, and W. Tecumseh Fitch, entitled "The Faculty of Language: What Is It, Who Has It, and How Did It Evolve?"

18. As discussed in the chapter, agrammatic aphasics may have difficulty reading function words, which are words that have little descriptive content, but they can read content words such as nouns, verbs, and adjectives.

a. Which of the following words would you predict to be difficult for such a person?

ore	bee	can (be able to)	but
not	knot	may	be
may	can (metal container)	butt	or
will (future)	might (possibility)	will (willingness)	might (strength)

b. Discuss three sources of evidence that function words and content words are stored or processed differently in the brain.

19. The traditional writing system of the Chinese languages (e.g., Mandarin, Cantonese) is ideographic (each concept or word is represented by a distinct character). More recently, the Chinese government has adopted a spelling system called *pinyin*, which is based on the Roman alphabet, and in which each symbol represents a sound. Following are several Chinese words in their character and *pinyin* forms. (The digit following the Roman letters in *pinyin* is a tone indicator and may be ignored.)

木	mu4	tree
花	hua1	flower
人	ren2	man
家	jia1	home
狗	gou3	dog

Based on the information provided in this chapter, would the location of neural activity be the same or different when Chinese speakers read in these two systems? Explain.

20. **Research project:** Dame Margaret Thatcher, a former prime minister of the United Kingdom, has been (famously) quoted as saying: "If you want something said, ask a man . . . if you want something done, ask a woman." (She is also the subject of a major motion picture entitled *The Iron Lady* that won many awards in 2012.) Her remark suggests, perhaps, that men and women process information differently. This exercise asks you to take up the controversial question: *Are there gender differences in the brain having to do with how men and women process and use language?* You might begin your research by seeking answers (try the Internet) to questions about the incidence of SLI, dyslexia, and language development differences in boys and girls.

21. **Research project:** Discuss the concept of *emergence*, namely, that "A major step in the development of language most probably relates to evolutionary changes in the brain," and its relevance to the quoted material

below, contrasting the views of Chomsky and Gould as opposed to Pinker. The linguist Noam Chomsky expresses this view:

> It could be that when the brain reached a certain level of complexity it simply automatically had certain properties because that's what happens when you pack 10^{11} neurons into something the size of a basketball.[1]

The biologist Stephen Jay Gould expresses a similar view:

> The Darwinist model would say that language, like other complex organic systems, evolved step by step, each step being an adaptive solution. Yet language is such an integrated "all or none" system, it is hard to imagine it evolving that way. Perhaps the brain grew in size and became capable of all kinds of things which were not part of the original properties.[2]

Other linguists such as Stephen Pinker, however, support a more Darwinian natural selection development of what is sometimes called "the language instinct":

> All the evidence suggests that it is the precise wiring of the brain's microcircuitry that makes language happen, not gross size, shape, or neuron packing.[3]

---

[1]Chomsky, N., in Searchinger, G. 1994. The human language series 3. Video. New York: Equinox Film/Ways of Knowing, Inc.

[2]Gould, S. J., in Searchinger, G. 1994. The human language series 3. Video. New York: Equinox Film/Ways of Knowing, Inc.

[3]Pinker, S. 1995. *The language instinct.* New York: William Morrow.

Glossary

AAE Abbreviates **African American English.**[1] *See* **Ebonics, AAVE.**

AAVE Abbreviates **African American Vernacular English.** *See* **Ebonics, AAE.**

abjad Consonantal alphabet writing system; the **consonantal alphabet** of such a system.

accent Prominence. *See* **stressed syllable;** the phonology or pronunciation of a specific **regional dialect:** for example, Southern accent; the pronunciation of a language by a nonnative speaker: for example, French accent.

accidental gap Phonological or morphological form that constitutes possible but non-occurring lexical items: for example, *blick* and *unsad.* Also called **lexical gap.**

acoustic phonetics The study of the physical characteristics of speech sounds.

acquired dyslexia Loss of ability to read correctly following brain damage in persons who were previously literate.

acronym Word composed of the initials of several words and pronounced as such: for example, PET scan from *positron-emission tomography* scan. *See* **alphabetic abbreviation.**

active sentence A sentence in which the noun phrase **subject** in d-structure is also the noun phrase subject in s-structure: for example, *The dog chased the car. See* **passive sentence.**

adjective (Adj) The syntactic category, also lexical category, of words that function as the head of an **adjective phrase,** and that have the semantic effect of qualifying or describing the referents of nouns: for example, *tall, bright,* and *intelligent. See* **adjective phrase.**

adjective phrase (AP) A syntactic category, also phrasal category, whose head is an adjective possibly accompanied by premodifiers, that occurs inside noun phrases and as complements of the verb to be: for example, *worthy of praise, several miles high, green,* and *more difficult.*

adjunct A phrasal category that is sister to X-bar.

adverb (Adv) The syntactic category, also lexical category, of words that qualify the verb such as manner adverbs like *quickly* and time adverbs like *soon.* The position of the adverb in the sentence depends on its semantic type: for example, *John will soon eat lunch, John eats lunch quickly.*

affix A **bound morpheme** attached to a stem or root. *See* **prefix, suffix, infix, circumfix, stem, and root.**

affricate A sound produced by a stop closure followed immediately by a slow release characteristic of a **fricative;** phonetically a sequence of stop + fricative: for example, the *ch* in *chip,* which is [tʃ] and like [t] + [ʃ].

African American (Vernacular) English (AA(V)E) Dialects of English spoken by some Americans of African descent, or by any person raised from infancy in a place where AAE is spoken. *See* **Ebonics.**

agent The **thematic role** of the noun phrase whose referent does the action described by the verb: for example, *George* in *George hugged Martha.*

---

[1]Bold words in definitions have a separate entry in this glossary, regardless of whether the bold word or term is preceded by the expression *See.*

agglutinative language A type of **synthetic language** in which a word may be formed by a root and multiple affixes where the affixes are easily separated and always retain the same meaning.

agrammatic aphasics Persons suffering from **agrammatism**.

agrammatism (agrammatic) Language disorder usually resulting from damage to Broca's region in which the patient has difficulty with certain aspects of syntax, especially functional categories. *See* **Broca's area**.

agreement The process by which one word in a sentence is altered depending on a property of another word in that sentence, such as gender or number: for example, the addition of *s* to a regular verb when the subject is third-person singular (in English).

allomorph Alternative phonetic form of a **morpheme:** for example, the [-s], [-z], and [-əz] forms of the plural morpheme in *cats, dogs,* and *kisses*.

allophone A predictable phonetic realization of a **phoneme:** for example, [p] and [pʰ] are allophones of the phoneme /p/ in English.

alphabetic abbreviation A word composed of the initials of several words and pronounced letter-by-letter: for example, *MRI* from magnetic resonance imaging. *See* **acronym**.

alphabetic writing A writing system in which each symbol typically represents one sound segment.

alveolar A sound produced by raising the tongue to the **alveolar ridge:** for example, [s], [t], and [n].

alveolar ridge The part of the hard palate directly behind the upper front teeth.

ambiguous, ambiguity The terms used to describe a word, phrase, or sentence with multiple meanings.

American Sign Language (ASL) The sign language used by the deaf community in the United States. *See* **sign languages**.

analogic change A language change in which a rule spreads to previously unaffected forms: for example, the plural of *cow* changed from the earlier *kine* to *cows* by the generalization of the plural formation rule or by **analogy** to regular plural forms. Also called **internal borrowing**.

analogy The use of one form as an exemplar by which other forms can be similarly constructed: for example, based on *bow/bows* and *sow/sows,* English speakers began to say *cows* instead of the older *kine.* Analogy also leads speakers to say **brang* as a past tense of *bring* based on *sing/sang/sung, ring/rang/rung,* and so on.

analytic Describes a sentence that is true by virtue of its meaning alone, irrespective of context: for example, *Kings are male. See* **contradiction**.

analytic (language) A language in which most words contain a single morpheme, and there is little if any word morphology: for example, there are no plural affixes on nouns or agreement affixes on verbs. Also called **an isolating language.** Vietnamese is an example of an analytic language.

anomalous Semantically ill-formed: for example, *Colorless green ideas sleep furiously*.

anomaly A violation of semantic rules resulting in expressions that seem nonsensical: for example, *The verb crumpled the milk*.

anomia A form of **aphasia** in which patients have word-finding difficulties. *See* **tip of the tongue phenomenon**.

antecedent A noun phrase with which a pronoun is **coreferential:** for example, *the man* is the antecedent of the pronoun *himself* in the sentence *The man shaved himself*.

anterior A phonetic feature of consonants whose place of articulation is in front of the palato-alveolar area, including **labials, interdentals,** and **alveolars**.

antonyms Words that are opposite with respect to one of their semantic properties: for example, *tall/short* are both alike in that they describe height, but opposite in regard to the extent of the height. *See* **gradable pair, complementary pair, and relational opposites**.

aphasia Language loss or disorder following brain damage.

approximants Sounds in which the articulators have a near frictional closeness, but no actual friction occurs: for example, [w], [j], [r], and [l] in English, where the first three are central approximants, and [l] is a lateral approximant.

arbitrary Describes the property of language, including sign language, whereby there is no natural or intrinsic relationship between the way a word is pronounced (or signed) and its meaning.

argot The specialized words used by a particular group, such as pilots or linguists: for example, *morphophonemics* in linguistics.

arguments The various NPs that occur with a verb: for example, *Jack* and *Jill* are arguments of *loves* in *Jack loves Jill*.

argument structure The various NPs that occur with particular verbs, called its arguments: for example, **intransitive verbs** take a subject NP only; **transitive verbs** take both a subject and direct object NP.

article (Art) One of several subclasses of determiners: for example, *the* and *a*.

articulatory phonetics The study of how the vocal tract produces speech sounds; the physiological characteristics of speech sounds.

aspirated Describes a voiceless stop produced with a puff of air that results when the vocal cords remain open for a brief period after the release of the stop: for example, the [pʰ] in *pit*. *See* **unaspirated**.

assimilation rules/assimilation A phonological process that changes feature values of segments to make them more similar: for example, a vowel becomes [+nasal] when followed by [+nasal] consonant. Also called **feature-spreading rules.**

auditory phonetics The study of the perception of speech sounds.

Aux A syntactic category containing **auxiliary verbs** and abstract tense morphemes that function as the **heads** of **sentences (S** or **TP).**

Aux inversion A transformational (movement) rule of English that relocates tense or an auxiliary to the beginning of the sentence to form a question.

auxiliary verb A verbal element, traditionally called a "helping verb," that co-occurs with, and qualifies, the **main verb** in a verb phrase with regard to such properties as tense: for example, *have, be,* and *will*.

babbling Speech sounds produced in the first few months after birth that gradually come to include only sounds that occur in the language of the linguistic environment of the child. Deaf children babble with hand gestures.

baby talk A certain **style** of speech that many adults use when speaking to children that includes among other things exaggerated intonation. *See* **motherese and child-directed speech (CDS).**

back-formation Creation of a new word by removing an affix from an old word: for example, *donate* from *donation;* or by removing what is mistakenly considered an affix: for example, *edit* from *editor*.

backtracking The process of undoing an analysis—usually a top-down analysis—when sensory data indicates it has gone awry, and beginning again at a point where the analysis is consistent with the data: for example, in the syntactic analysis of *The little orange car sped,* analyzing *orange* as a noun, and later reanalyzing it as an adjective. *See* **top-down processing.**

base Any **root** or **stem** to which an affix is attached.

bidialectal Persons who know two or more **dialects** and speak the one most appropriate to the sociolinguistic context, often mixing the several dialects. *See* **codeswitching.**

bilabial A sound articulated by bringing both lips together.

bilingualism The ability to speak two (or more) languages with native or near native proficiency, either by an individual speaker **(individual bilingualism)** or within a society **(societal bilingualism).**

bilingual language acquisition The (more or less) simultaneous acquisition of two or more languages before the age of three years such that each language is acquired with native competency.

bilingual maintenance (BM) Education programs that aim to maintain competence in both languages for the entire educational experience.

birdcall One or more short notes that convey messages associated with the immediate environment, such as danger, feeding, nesting, and flocking.

bird song A complex pattern of notes used to mark territory and to attract mates.

blend A word composed of the parts of more than one word: for example, *smog* from *smoke + fog.*

blocked A derivation that is prevented by a prior application of other morphological rules: for example, when *Commun + ist* entered the language, words such as *Commun + ite* (as in *Trotsky + ite)* or *commun + ian* (as in *grammar + ian)* were not needed and were not formed.

borrowing The incorporating of a loan word from one language into another: for example, English borrowed *buoy* from Dutch. *See* **loan word**.

bottom-up processing Data-driven analysis of linguistic input that begins with the small units like phones and proceeds stepwise to increasingly larger units like words and phrases until the entire input is processed, often ending in a complete sentence and semantic interpretation. *See* **top-down processing**.

bound morpheme A **morpheme** that must be attached to other morphemes: for example, *-ly, -ed, non-.* Bound morphemes are **prefixes, suffixes, infixes, circumfixes,** and some **roots** such as *cran* in *cranberry. See* **free morpheme**.

broadening A semantic change in which the meaning of a word changes over time to become more encompassing: for example, *dog* once meant a particular breed of *dog.*

Broca, Paul A French neurologist of the nineteenth century who identified a particular area of the left side of the brain as a language center.

Broca's aphasia *See* **agrammatism**.

Broca's area A front part of the left hemisphere of the brain, damage to which causes **agrammatism** or **Broca's aphasia.** Also called Broca's region.

case A characteristic of nouns and pronouns, and in some languages articles and adjectives, determined by their function in the sentence, and generally indicated by the morphological form of the word: for example, *I* is in the nominative case of the first-person singular pronoun in English and functions as a subject; *me* is in the accusative case and functions as an object.

case endings Suffixes on a noun based on its grammatical function, such as s of the English genitive case indicating possession: for example, Robert's sheepdog. *See* **case morphology.**

case morphology The process of **inflectional morphemes** combining with nouns to indicate the grammatical relation of the noun in its sentence: for example, in Russian, the inflectional suffix *-a* added to a noun indicates that the noun is an object.

case theory The study of thematic roles or grammatical case in languages of the world.

cerebral hemispheres The left and right halves of the brain, joined by the **corpus callosum.**

Chicano English (ChE) A **dialect** of English spoken by some bilingual Mexican Americans in the western and southwestern United States.

child-directed speech (CDS) The special intonationally exaggerated speech that some adults sometimes use to speak with small children, sometimes called **baby talk.** *See* **motherese**.

circumfix A **bound morpheme,** parts of which occur in a word both before and after the root: for example, *ge—t* in German *geliebt,* "loved," from the root *lieb.*

classifier A **grammatical morpheme** that marks the semantic class of a noun: for example, in Swahili, nouns that refer to human artifacts such as beds and chairs are prefixed with the classifiers *ki* if singular and *vi* if plural; *kiti,* "chair" and *viti,* "chairs."

click A speech sound produced by sucking air into the mouth and forcing it between articulators to produce a sharp sound: for example, the sound often spelled *tsk.*

clipping The deletion of some part of a longer word to give a shorter word with the same meaning: for example, *phone* from *telephone.*

closed class A category, generally a **functional category,** that rarely has new words added to it: for example, prepositions and conjunctions. *See* **open class.**

coarticulation The transfer of **phonetic features** to adjoining segments to make them more alike: for example, vowels become [+nasal] when followed by consonants that are [+nasal].

coda One or more phonological segments that follow the **nucleus** of a syllable: for example, the /st/ in /prist/ *priest.*

codeswitching A bilingual person's movement back and forth between two languages or dialects within the same sentence or discourse.

cognates Words in related languages that developed from the same ancestral root, such as English *man* and German *Mann.*

coinage The construction and/or invention of new words that then become part of the lexicon: for example, *podcast.*

comp (C) A grammatical category, also functional category, that is the head of CP. *See* **complementizer, grammatical category, functional category.**

comparative linguistics The branch of historical linguistics that explores language change by comparing related languages.

comparative method The technique linguists use to deduce forms in an ancestral language by examining corresponding forms in several of its descendant languages.

comparative reconstruction The deducing of forms in an ancestral language of genetically related languages by application of the **comparative method.**

competence, linguistic The knowledge of a language represented by the mental grammar that accounts for speakers' linguistic ability and creativity. For the most part, linguistic competence is unconscious knowledge.

complement Constituent(s) in a phrase other than the head that complete(s) the meaning of the phrase and which is **C-selected** by the verb. The right sister to the head in the X-bar schema. In the verb phrase *found a puppy,* the noun phrase *a puppy* is a complement of the verb *found.*

complementary distribution The situation in which phones never occur in the same phonetic environment: for example, [p] and [pʰ] in English. *See* **allophone.**

complementary pair Two **antonyms** related in such a way that the negation of one is the meaning of the other: for example, *alive* means *not dead. See* **gradable pair and relational opposites.**

complementizer A category of words, including *that, if, whether,* that introduce an **embedded sentence:** for example, *his belief that sheepdogs can swim,* or, *I wonder whether sheepdogs can swim.* The head of a complementizer phrase (CP) in the X-bar schema. The complementizer has the effect of turning a sentence into a complement. *See* **comp.**

complementizer phrase (CP) An X-bar phrase whose whose head, C, may be a complementizer or possibly a preposed auxiliary, whose complement is S or TP and whose specifier may be a preposed *wh* word.

compositional semantics A theory of meaning that calculates the truth values or meanings of larger units by the application of semantic rules to the truth values or meanings of smaller units.

compound A word composed of two or more words, which may be written as a single word or as words separated by spaces or hyphens: for example, *dogcatcher, dog biscuit,* and *dog-tired*.

conditioned sound change Historical phonological change that occurs in specific phonetic contexts: for example, the voicing of /f/ to [v] when it occurs between vowels.

connotative meaning/connotation The evocative or affective meaning associated with a word. Two words or expressions may have the same **denotative meaning** but different connotations: for example, *president* and *commander-in-chief*.

consonant A speech sound produced with some constriction of the air stream. *See* **vowel**.

consonantal The phonetic feature that distinguishes the class of obstruents, liquids, and nasals, which are [+consonantal], from other sounds (vowels and glides), which are [−consonantal].

consonantal alphabet The symbols of a **consonantal writing** system.

consonantal writing A writing system of symbols that represent only **consonants;** vowels are inferred from context: for example, Arabic.

constituent A syntactic unit in a **phrase structure tree:** for example, *the girl* is a noun phrase constituent in the sentence *The boy loves the girl*.

constituent structure The hierarchically arranged syntactic units such as noun phrase and verb phrase that underlie every sentence. Also **constituent structure tree, phrase structure tree**.

constituent structure tree *See* **phrase structure tree**.

content words The nouns, verbs, adjectives, and adverbs that constitute the major part of the vocabulary. *See* **open class**.

context The discourse preceding an utterance together with the real-world knowledge of speakers and listeners. *See* **linguistic context and situational context**.

continuant A speech sound in which the air stream flows continually through the mouth; all speech sounds except stops and affricates.

contour tones In tone language, tones in which the **pitch** glides from one level to another: for example, from low to high as in a rising tone.

contradiction Describes a sentence that is false by virtue of its meaning alone, irrespective of context: for example, *Kings are female*. *See* **analytic and tautology**.

contradictory Mutual negative entailment: the truth of one sentence necessarily implies the falseness of another sentence, and vice versa: for example, *The door is open* and *The door is closed* are contradictory sentences. *See* **entailment**.

contralateral Refers to neural signals that travel between one side of the body (left/right) and the opposite **cerebral hemisphere** (right/left).

contrast Different sounds contrast when their presence alone distinguishes between otherwise identical forms: for example, [f] and [v] in *fine* and *vine,* but not [p] and [pʰ] in [spik] and [spʰik] (two variant ways of saying *speak*). *See* **minimal pair**.

contrasting tones In tone languages, different tones that make different words: for example, in Nupe, *bá* with a high tone and *bà* with a low tone mean "be sour" and "count," respectively.

contrastive stress Additional stress placed on a word to highlight it, sometimes to clarify the referent of a pronoun: for example, in *Joe hired Bill and he hired Sam,* with contrastive stress on *he,* it is usually understood that Bill rather than Joe hired Sam.

convention, conventional The agreed-on, although generally arbitrary, relationship between the form and meaning of words.

cooperative principle A broad principle within whose scope fall the various **maxims of conversation**. It states that in order to communicate effectively, speakers should agree to be informative and relevant.

coreference The relation between two noun phrases that refer to the same entity: for example, In the sentence *John said he was happy* he can refer to John.

coreferential Describes noun phrases (including pronouns) that refer to the same entity.

coronals The class of consonants articulated by raising the tip or blade of the tongue, including **alveolars** and **palatals**: for example, [t] and [ʃ].

corpus callosum The nerve fibers connecting the right and left **cerebral hemispheres**.

cortex The approximately ten billion neurons that form the outside surface of the brain; also referred to as gray matter.

count nouns Nouns that can be enumerated: for example, *one potato* and *two potatoes*. *See* **mass nouns**.

cover symbol A symbol that represents a class of sounds: for example, C for consonants and V for vowels.

creativity of language, creative aspect of linguistic knowledge Speakers' ability to combine the finite number of linguistic units of their language to produce and understand an infinite range of novel sentences.

creole A language that begins as a **pidgin** and eventually becomes the native language of a speech community.

creolization The linguistic *expansion* in the lexicon and grammar, and an increase in the contexts of use, of an existing **pidgin**. *See* **pidginization**.

critical-age hypothesis The theory that there is a window of time between early childhood and puberty for learning a first language, and beyond which first language acquisition is almost always incomplete.

critical period The time between early childhood and puberty during which a child can acquire a native language easily, swiftly, and without external intervention. After this period, the acquisition of the grammar is difficult and, for some individuals, never fully achieved.

C-selection The classifying of verbs and other lexical items in terms of the syntactic category of the complements that they accept (C stands for categorial), sometimes called **subcategorization**: for example, the verb *find* C-selects, or is subcategorized for, a noun phrase complement. *See* **transitive verb**.

cuneiform A form of writing in which the characters are produced using a wedge-shaped stylus, and most notably utilized by ancient civilizations of the Middle East such as the Sumerians.

declarative (sentence) A sentence that asserts that a particular situation exists. *See* **interrogative**.

declension A list of the inflections or **cases** of nouns, pronouns, adjectives, and determiners in categories such as grammatical relationship, number, and gender.

deep structure *See* **d-structure**.

definite Describes a noun phrase that refers to a particular object known to the speaker and listener.

deictic/deixis Refers to words or expressions whose reference relies on context and the orientation of the speaker in space and time: for example, *I, yesterday, there, this cat*.

demonstrative articles, demonstratives Words such as *this, that, those,* and *these* that function syntactically as articles but are semantically dependent on the situational context, which is needed to determine the referents of the noun phrases in which they occur.

denotative meaning The referential meaning of a word or expression. *See* **connotative meaning**.

dental A place-of-articulation term for consonants articulated with the tongue against, or nearly against, the front teeth. *See* **interdental**.

derivation The steps in the application of rules to an underlying form that results in a surface representation: for example, in deriving a syntactic s-structure from a d-structure, or in deriving a phonetic form from a phonemic form.

derivational affix *See* **derivational morpheme**.

derivational morpheme A **morpheme** added to a stem or root to form a new stem or word, possibly, but not necessarily, resulting in a change in syntactic category: for example, *-er* added to a verb like *kick* to give the noun *kicker*.

derived structure Any structure resulting from the application of transformational rules.

derived word The form that results from the addition of a **derivational morpheme:** for example, *firmly* from *firm* + *ly*.

descriptive grammar A linguist's description or model of the mental grammar, including the units, structures, and rules. An explicit statement of what speakers know about their language. *See* **prescriptive grammar, teaching grammar**.

determiner(Det) The syntactic category, also functional category, of words and expressions, which when combined with a noun form a noun phrase. Includes the articles *the* and *a,* **demonstratives** such as *this* and *that* and quantifiers such as *each* and *every*.

diacritics, diacritic marks Additional markings on written symbols to specify various phonetic properties such as **length, tone, stress, and nasalization;** extra marks on a written character that change its usual value: for example, the tilde ~ drawn over the letter ñ in Spanish to represent a palatalized nasal rather than an alveolar nasal.

dialect A variety of a language whose grammar differs in systematic ways from other varieties. Differences may be lexical, phonological, syntactic, and semantic. *See* **regional dialect, social dialect, and prestige dialect**.

dialect area A geographic area defined by the predominant use of a particular language variety, or a particular characteristic of a language variety: for example, an area where *bucket* is used rather than *pail*. *See* **dialect, dialect atlas, and isogloss**.

dialect atlas A book of **dialect maps** showing the areas where specific dialectal characteristics occur in the speech of the region.

dialect continuum A geographic range of slightly varying **dialects** occurring between two distinct different dialects spoken in different regions of a language area.

dialect leveling Movement toward greater uniformity or decrease in variations among dialects.

dialect map A map showing the areas where specific dialectal characteristics occur in the speech of the region.

diphthong A sequence of two vowels run together as a single phonological unit: for example, [aɪ], [aʊ], and [ɔɪ] as in *bite, bout,* and *boy*. *See* **monophthong**.

direct object The grammatical relation of a noun phrase when it appears immediately below the verb phrase (VP) and next to the verb in deep structure; the noun phrase complement of a transitive verb: for example, *the puppy* in *The boy found the puppy*.

discontinuous morpheme A **morpheme** with multiple parts that occur in more than one place in a word or sentence: for example, *ge* and *t* in German *geliebt,* "loved." *See* **circumfix**.

discourse A linguistic unit that comprises more than one sentence.

discreteness A fundamental property of human language in which larger linguistic units are perceived to be composed of smaller linguistic units: for example, *cat* is perceived as the phonemes /k/, /æ/, and /t/; *the cat* is perceived as *the* and *cat*.

dissimilation rules Phonological rules that change feature values of segments to make them less similar: for example, a fricative dissimilation rule: /θ/ is pronounced [t] following another fricative. In English dialects with this rule, *sixth* /sɪks + θ/ is pronounced [sɪkst].

distinctive Describes linguistic elements that contrast: for example, [f] and [v] are distinctive segments: for example, *feel* and *veal*. Voice is a distinctive phonetic feature of consonants.

distinctive features Phonetic properties of phonemes that account for their ability to contrast meanings of words: for example, *voice, tense.* Also called **phonemic features**.

ditransitive verb A verb whose complement contains a noun phrase and a prepositional phrase: for example, *give* in *He gave a cat to Sally.* Some ditransitive verb phrases have an alternative form with two noun phrases in the complement as in *He gave Sally a cat.*

dominate In a **phrase structure tree,** when a continuous downward path can be traced from a node labeled A to a node labeled B, then A dominates B.

downdrift The gradual lowering of the absolute **pitch** of tones during an utterance in a tone language. During downdrift, tones retain their *relative* values to one another.

d-structure Any **phrase structure tree** generated by the phrase structure rules (i.e., by the X-bar schema) of a transformational grammar; the basic syntactic structures of the grammar. Also called **deep structure.** *See* **transformational rule.**

Dual Language Immersion An education program that enrolls English-speaking children and minority-language students in roughly equal numbers, with the intention of making all students bilingual.

dyslexia A cover term for the various types of reading impairment.

Early Middle English Vowel Shortening A sound change that shortened vowels such as the first *i* in *criminal.* As a result, *criminal* was unaffected by the **Great Vowel Shift,** leading to word pairs such as *crime/criminal.*

ease of articulation The tendency of speakers to adjust their pronunciation to make it easier, or more efficient, to move the articulators. Phonetic and phonological rules are often the result of ease of articulation: for example, the rule of English that nasalizes vowels when they precede nasal consonants.

Ebonics An alternative term, first used in 1997, for the various dialects of **African American English**.

embedded sentence A sentence that occurs within a sentence in a **phrase structure tree**: for example, *sheepdogs cannot read* in *Everyone knows that sheepdogs cannot read.*

emoji A Japanese loan word for emoticon.

emoticon A string of text characters that, when viewed sideways, forms a face or figure expressing a particular emotion: for example, [8,<\ to express "dismay." Frequently used in electronic communications such as Twitter.

entail One sentence entails another if the truth of the first necessarily implies the truth of the second: for example, *The sun melted the ice* entails *The ice melted* because if the first is true, the second must be true.

entailment The relationship between two sentences, where the truth of one necessitates the truth of the other: for example, *Corday assassinated Marat* and *Marat is dead;* if the first is true, the second must be true.

epenthesis The insertion of one or more **phones** in a word: for example, the insertion of [ə] in *children* to produce [tʃɪlədrẽn] instead of [tʃɪldrẽn].

eponym A word taken from a proper name, such as *Hertz* for "unit of frequency."

etymology The history of words; the study of the history of words.

euphemism A word or phrase that replaces a **taboo** word or is used to avoid reference to certain acts or subjects: for example, *powder room* for *toilet.*

euphemism treadmill The process whereby a euphemism takes on the taboo characteristics of the word it replaced, thereby requiring another euphemism: for example, *cripple—handicapped—disabled—challenged.*

event/eventive A type of sentence that describes activities such as *John kissed Mary* as opposed to describing states such as *John knows Mary. See* **state/stative.**

event-related brain potentials (ERP) The electrical signals emitted from different areas of the brain in response to different kinds of stimuli.

experiencer The thematic role of the noun phrase whose referent perceives something: for example, *Helen* in *Helen heard Robert playing the piano.*

feature-changing rules Phonological rules that change feature values of segments, either to make them more similar (*see* **assimilation rules**) or less similar (*see* **dissimilation rules**).

feature matrix A representation of phonological segments in which the columns represent segments and the rows represent features, each cell being marked with a + or − to designate the presence or absence of the feature for that segment.

feature-spreading rules *See* **assimilation rules**.

finger spelling In **signing,** hand gestures that represent letters of the alphabet used to spell words for which there is no sign.

flap A speech sound in which the tongue touches the alveolar ridge and withdraws. It is often an allophone of /t/ and /d/ in words such as *writer* and *rider.* Also called **tap**.

fMRI Functional Magnetic Resonance Imaging: scans that can reveal the brain in action by measuring blood flow and oxygen utilization in different locations in the brain during the performance of various linguistic and other cognitive tasks.

formant In the frequency analysis of speech, a band of frequencies of higher intensity than surrounding frequencies, which appears as a dark line on a **spectrogram.** Individual vowels display different formant patterns.

free morpheme A single **morpheme** that constitutes a word: for example, *dog.*

free variation Alternative pronunciations of a word in which one sound is substituted for another without changing the word's meaning: for example, pronunciation of *bottle* as [batəl] or [baʔəl].

fricative A consonant sound produced with so narrow a constriction in the vocal tract as to create sound through friction: for example, [s] and [f].

front vowels Vowel sounds in which the tongue is positioned forward in the mouth: for example, [i] and [æ].

function word A word that does not always have a clear lexical meaning but has a grammatical function; function words include conjunctions, some **prepositions, articles,** auxiliaries, **complementizers,** and pronouns. *See* **closed class**.

functional category The syntactic categories of **Determiner, T(ense), Comp**. These categories are not lexical or phrasal categories. *See* **lexical category and phrasal category**.

fundamental difference hypothesis The idea that adult second language acquisition (L2) differs fundamentally from first language acquisition (L1).

fundamental frequency In speech, the rate at which the vocal cords vibrate, symbolized as F0, called F-zero, perceived by the listener as **pitch**.

fusional languages Synthetic languages in which several meanings are packed into what appears to be a single affix, such as *-amos* in Spanish *hablamos* meaning "first person, plural, present tense."

garden path sentences Sentences that appear at first blush to be ungrammatical, but with further syntactic processing turn out to be grammatical: for example, *The horse raced past the barn fell.*

geminate A sequence of two identical sounds; a long vowel or long consonant denoted either by writing the phonetic symbol twice as in [biiru] and [sakki] or by use of a colon-like symbol [biːru] and [sakːi].

generate To specify precisely, concisely, and in all particulars: for example, syntactic rules generate the different kinds of sentence structures of a language.

generative grammar A grammar that accounts for linguistic knowledge by means of rules that generate all and only the grammatical sentences of the language.

genetically related Describes two or more languages that developed from a common, earlier language: for example, French, Italian, and Spanish, which all developed from Latin.

glide A speech sound produced with little or no obstruction of the air stream that is always preceded or followed by a vowel: for example, [w] in *we* and [j] in *you*.

gloss A word in one language given to express the meaning of a word in another language: for example, "house" is the English gloss for the French word *maison*.

glottal/glottal stop A speech sound produced with constriction at the **glottis**; when the air is stopped completely at the glottis by tightly closed vocal cords, a glottal stop is produced.

glottis The vocal cords themselves and/or the opening between the vocal cords.

goal The thematic role of the noun phrase toward whose referent the action of the verb is directed: for example, *the theater* in *The kids went to the theater.*

gradable pair Two **antonyms** related in such a way that more of one is less of the other: for example, *warm* and *cool*; more warm is less cool, and vice versa. See **complementary pair and relational opposites**.

grammar The mental representation of a speaker's linguistic competence; what a speaker knows about a language, including its phonology, morphology, syntax, semantics, and lexicon. A linguistic description of a speaker's mental grammar.

grammar translation A method of second-language learning in which the student memorizes words and syntactic rules and translates them between the native language and target language.

grammatical, grammaticality Describes a well-formed sequence of words, one conforming to rules of **syntax**.

grammatical categories Traditionally called "parts of speech"; also called **syntactic categories**; expressions of the same grammatical category can generally substitute for one another without loss of grammaticality: for example, **noun phrase, verb phrase, adjective, and auxiliary verb**.

grammatical morpheme A **function word** or **bound morpheme** required by the syntactic rules: for example, *to* and *s* in *He wants to go. See* **inflectional morpheme**.

grammatical relation Any of several structural positions that a noun phrase may assume in a sentence. *See* **subject and direct object**.

Great Vowel Shift A sound change that took place in English some time between 1400 and 1600 CE in which seven long vowel phonemes were changed.

Grimm's Law The description of a phonological change in the sound system of an early ancestor of the Germanic languages formulated by Jakob Grimm.

head (of a compound) In English, the rightmost word in a compound: for example, *house* in *doghouse*. It generally indicates the category and general meaning of the compound.

head (of a phrase) The central word of a phrase whose lexical category defines the type of phrase: for example, the noun *men* is the head of the noun phrase *three fat men;* the verb *wrote* is the head of the verb phrase *wrote a letter to his mother;* the adjective *red* is the head of the adjective phrase *very bright red* or *red with rage.*

hemiplegic An individual (child or adult) with acquired unilateral lesions of the brain who retains both hemispheres (one normal and one diseased).

hemispherectomy The surgical removal of a hemisphere of the brain.

heritage language A language with which a person has a strong cultural connection through family interaction, but that isn't learned natively: for example, Yiddish in a Jewish household.

heteronyms Different words spelled the same (i.e., **homographs**) but pronounced differently: for example, *bass,* meaning either "low tone" [bes] or "a kind of fish" [bæs].

hierarchical structure The groupings and subgroupings of the parts of a sentence into syntactic categories: for example, *the bird sang* [[[the] [bird]] [[sang]]]; the groupings and subgroupings of morphemes in a word: for example, *unlockable* [[un] [[lock] [able]]]. Hierarchical structure is generally depicted in a **tree diagram**.

hieroglyphics A writing system used by the Egyptians around 4000 BCE that began as a **pictographic writing** system and evolved over time into a **logographic writing** and **syllabic writing** system.

historical and comparative linguistics The branch of linguistics that deals with how languages change, what kinds of changes occur, and why they occur.

holophrastic The stage of child language acquisition in which one word conveys a complex message similar to that of a phrase or sentence.

homographs Words spelled identically, and possibly pronounced the same: for example, *bear* meaning "to tolerate," and *bear* the animal; or *lead* the metal and *lead,* what leaders do.

homonyms/homophones Words pronounced, and possibly spelled, the same: for example, *to, too,* and *two;* or *bat* the animal, *bat* the stick, and *bat* meaning "to flutter" as in "bat the eyelashes."

homorganic consonants Two sounds produced at the same place of articulation: for example, [m] and [p]; [t], [d], and [n]. *See* **assimilation rules.**

homorganic nasal rule A phonological assimilation rule that changes the place of articulation feature of a nasal consonant to agree with that of a following consonant: for example, /n/ becomes [m] when preceding /p/ as in *impossible.*

hypercorrection Deviations from the "norm" thought by speakers to be "more correct," such as saying *between he and she* instead of *between him and her.*

hyponyms Words whose meanings are specific instances of a more general word: for example, *red, white,* and *blue* are hyponyms of the word *color; triangle* is a hyponym of *polygon.*

iambic Stress on the second syllable of a two-syllable word: for example, *giráffe.*

iconic, iconicity A nonarbitrary relationship between form and meaning in which the form bears a resemblance to its meaning: for example, the male and female symbols on (some) restroom doors.

ideogram, ideograph A character of a word-writing system, often highly stylized, that represents a concept, or the pronunciation of the word representing that concept.

idiolect An individual's way of speaking, reflecting that person's grammar.

idiom/idiomatic phrase An expression whose meaning does not conform to the **principle of compositionality,** that is, may be unrelated to the meaning of its parts: for example, *kick the bucket* meaning "to die."

illocutionary force The intended effect of a speech act, such as a warning, a promise, a threat, or a bet: for example, the illocutionary force of *I resign!* is the act of resignation.

immediately dominate If a node labeled A is directly above a node labeled B in a phrase structure tree, then A immediately dominates B.

implicature An inference based not only on an utterance, but also on assumptions about what the speaker is trying to achieve: for example, *Are you using the ketchup?* to mean "Please pass the ketchup" while dining in a café.

impoverished data Refers to the incomplete, noisy, and unstructured utterances that children hear, including slips of the tongue, false starts, and ungrammatical and incomplete sentences, together with a lack of concrete evidence about abstract grammatical rules and structure.

individual bilingualism The ability of an individual speaker to speak two (or more) languages with native or near native proficiency. *See* **bilingualism and societal bilingualism.**

Indo-European The descriptive name given to the ancestor language of many modern language families, including Germanic, Slavic, and Romance. Also called **Proto-Indo-European**.

infinitive A form of a verb without tense or agreement marking: for example, (to) *swim*.

infinitival sentence An **embedded sentence** that does not have a tense and therefore is a "to" form (in English): for example, *sheepdogs to be fast readers* in the sentence *He believes sheepdogs to be fast readers*.

infix A **bound morpheme** that is inserted in the middle of another morpheme: for example, Tagalog *sulat* "writing" but *sumulat* "to write" after insertion of the infix *um*.

inflectional affix *See* **inflectional morpheme**.

inflectional morpheme A bound **grammatical morpheme** that is affixed to a word according to rules of syntax: for example, third-person singular verbal suffix -*s*.

innateness hypothesis The theory that the human species is genetically equipped with a **Universal Grammar**, which provides the basic design for all human languages.

instrument The thematic role of the noun phrase whose referent is the means by which an action is performed: for example, *a paper clip* in *Houdini picked the lock with a paper clip*.

intensity The magnitude of an **acoustic signal**, which is perceived as loudness.

interdental A sound produced by inserting the tip of the tongue between the upper and lower teeth: for example, the initial sounds of *thought* and *those*.

interlanguage grammars The intermediate grammars that second-language learners create on their way to acquiring the (more or less) complete grammar of the target language.

internal borrowing *See* **analogic change**.

internal reconstruction The application of the **comparative method** to earlier and later forms of the same language.

International Phonetic Alphabet (IPA) The **phonetic alphabet** designed by the International Phonetic Association to be used to represent the sounds found in all human languages.

International Phonetics Association (IPA) The organization founded in 1888 to further phonetic research and to develop the International Phonetic Alphabet.

interrogative (sentence) A sentence that questions whether a particular situation exists. *See* **declarative**.

intonation The variation of **pitch** while speaking, which is not used to distinguish words, though it may affect meaning.

intransitive verb A verb that must not have (does not **C-select** for) a direct object NP complement: for example, *sleep* and *rise*.

ipsilateral Refers to neural signals that travel between one side of the body (left/right) and the same cerebral hemisphere (left/right). *See* **contralateral**.

isogloss A geographic boundary that separates areas with **dialect** differences: for example, a line on a map on one side of which most people say *faucet* and on the other side of which most people say *spigot*.

isolating language A language in which most words contain a single morpheme, and there is little if any word morphology: for example, no plural affixes on nouns or agreement affixes on verbs. Also called an analytic language: for example, Vietnamese.

jargon Special words peculiar to the members of a profession or group: for example, *glottis* for phoneticians. *See* **argot**. Also, the nonsense words sometimes used by Wernicke's aphasics.

L2 acquisition *See* **second language acquisition**.

labial A sound articulated at the lips: for example, [b] and [f].

labiodental A sound produced by touching the bottom lip to the upper teeth: for example, [v].

labio-velar A sound articulated by simultaneously raising the back of the tongue toward the velum and rounding the lips. The [w] of English is a labio-velar glide.

language attrition The gradual loss of heritage language competence owing to lack of use. *See* **heritage language**.

language contact The situation in which speakers of different languages regularly interact with one another, and especially in which there are many bilingual or multilingual speakers.

language isolate A natural language with no demonstrable genealogical relationship with other living languages.

larynx The structure of muscles and cartilage in the throat that contains the vocal cords and **glottis;** often called the "voice box. "

late closure principle A psycholinguistic principle of language comprehension that states: Attach incoming material to the phrase that was most recently processed. For example, *He said that he slept yesterday* associates *yesterday* with *he slept* rather than with *he said.*

lateral A sound produced with air flowing past one or both sides of the tongue: for example, [l].

lateralization, lateralized Terms used to refer to cognitive functions localized to one or the other hemisphere of the brain.

lax vowel A vowel produced with relatively less tension in the vocal cords and little tendency to diphthongize: for example, [ʊ] in *put,* [pʊt]. Most lax vowels do not occur at the ends of syllables, that is, [bʊ] is not a possible English word. *See* **tense**.

length A prosodic feature referring to the duration of a segment. Two sounds may contrast in length: for example, in Japanese the first vowel is [+long] in /biːru/ "beer" but [−long], therefore short, in /biru/ "building."

level tones Relatively stable (nongliding) **pitch** on syllables of tone languages. Also called **register tones**.

lexical access The process of searching the mental **lexicon** for a phonological string to determine whether it is an actual word.

lexical ambiguity Multiple meanings of sentences due to words that have multiple meanings: for example, *He blew up the pictures of his ex-girlfriend.*

lexical category A general term for the word-level syntactic categories of noun, verb, preposition, adjective, and adverb. These are the categories of words like *man, run, large,* and *rapidly,* as opposed to functional category words such as *the* and *and. See* **functional category, phrasal category, and open class**.

lexical decision A task performed by subjects in psycholinguistic experiments who on presentation of a spoken or printed stimulus must decide whether it is a word or not.

lexical gap A possible but nonoccurring word; a form that obeys the **phonotactic constraints** of a language yet has no meaning: for example, *blick* in English. Also called **accidental gap**.

lexical paraphrases Sentences that have the same meaning due to synonyms: for example, *She lost her purse* and *She lost her handbag.*

lexical semantics The subfield of semantics concerned with the meanings of words and the meaning relationships among words.

lexicon The component of the grammar containing speakers' knowledge about morphemes and words; a speaker's mental dictionary.

lexifier language The dominant language of a **pidgin** (or **creole**) that provides the basis for the majority of the lexical items in the language.

lingua franca A language common to speakers of diverse languages that can be used for communication and commerce: for example, English is the lingua franca of international airline pilots.

linguistic competence *See* **competence and linguistic**.

linguistic context The discourse that precedes a phrase or sentence that helps clarify meaning.

linguistic determinism The strongest form of the **Sapir–Whorf hypothesis**, which holds that the language we speak establishes how we perceive and think about the world.

linguistic performance *See* **performance and linguistic**.

linguistic relativism A weaker form of the **Sapir–Whorf hypothesis**, which holds that different languages encode different categories, and that speakers of different languages therefore have different conceptual categories. For example, speakers of languages that have fewer color words will be less sensitive to gradations of color.

linguistic sign A sound or gesture, typically a morpheme in a spoken language and a sign in a sign language, that has a form bound to a meaning in a single unit: for example, *dog* is a linguistic sign whose form is its pronunciation [dag] and whose meaning is *Canis familiaris* (or however we define "dog").

linguistic theory A theory of the principles that characterize all human languages. *See* **Universal Grammar**.

liquids A class of consonants including /l/ and /r/ and their variants that share vowel-like acoustic properties and may function as syllabic nuclei.

loan translations Compound words or expressions whose parts are translated literally into the borrowing language: for example, *marriage of convenience* from French *mariage de convenance*.

loan word Word in one language whose origins are in another language: for example, in Japanese, *besiboru*, "baseball," is a loan word from English. *See* **borrowing**.

localization The hypothesis that different areas of the brain are responsible for distinct cognitive functions. *See* **lateralization**.

location The thematic role of the noun phrase whose referent is the place where the action of the verb occurs: for example, *Oslo* in *It snows in Oslo*.

logograms The symbols of a **word-writing** or **logographic writing** system.

logographic writing *See* **word writing**.

magnetic resonance imaging (MRI) A technique to investigate the molecular structures in human organs including the brain, which may be used to identify sites of brain lesions.

magnetoencephalogram (MEG) A record of the magnetic field of the brain.

main verb The verb that functions as the head in the highest verb phrase of a sentence: for example, *save* in *They save money to travel*. *See* **head of a phrase**.

manner of articulation The way the air stream is obstructed as it travels through the vocal tract. **Stop, nasal, affricate,** and **fricative** are some manners of articulation. *See* **place of articulation**.

marked In a masculine/feminine pair, the word that contains a derivational morpheme, usually the feminine word: for example, *princess* is marked, whereas *prince* is unmarked. *See* **unmarked**.

mass nouns Nouns that cannot ordinarily be enumerated: for example, *milk, water; *two milks* is ungrammatical except when interpreted to mean "two kinds of milk," "two containers of milk," and so on. *See* **count nouns**.

maxim of manner A conversational convention that a speaker's discourse should be brief and orderly, and should avoid ambiguity and obscurity.

maxim of quality A conversational convention that a speaker should not lie or make unsupported claims.

maxim of quantity A conversational convention that a speaker's contribution to the discourse should be as informative as is required, neither more nor less.

maxim of relation A conversational convention that a speaker's contribution to a discourse should always have a bearing on, and a connection with, the matter under discussion.

maxims of discourse Conversational conventions such as the **maxim of quantity** that people appear to obey to give coherence and sincerity to discourse.

mean length of utterances (MLU) The average number of words or morphemes in a child's utterance. It is a more accurate measure of the acquisition stage of language than chronological age.

meaning The conceptual or semantic aspect of a sign or utterance that permits us to comprehend the message being conveyed. Expressions in language generally have both form—pronunciation or gesture—and meaning. *See* **extension, intension, sense, and reference**.

metaphor Nonliteral, suggestive meaning in which an expression that designates one thing is used implicitly to mean something else: for example, *The night has a thousand eyes,* to mean "One may be unknowingly observed at night."

metathesis The phonological process that reorders segments, often by transposing two the sounds: for example, the pronunciation of *ask* /æsk/ in some English dialects as [æks].

minimal attachment principle The principle that in comprehending language, listeners create the simplest structure consistent with the grammar: for example, *The horse raced past the barn* is interpreted as a complete sentence rather than a noun phrase containing a relative clause, as if it were *the horse* (that was) *raced past the barn*.

minimal pair (or set) Two (or more) words that are identical except for one phoneme that occurs in the same position in each word: for example, *pain* /pen/, *bane* /ben/, and *main* /men/.

modal An **auxiliary verb** other than *be, have,* and *do,* such as *can, could, will, would,* or *must*.

modularity hypothesis The hypothesis that the brain and mind have distinct, independent, and autonomous parts that interact with each other.

monogenetic theory of language origin The belief that all languages originated from a single language. *See* **Nostratic**.

monomorphemic word A word that consists of one morpheme. For example, *sing* but not *singer, finger* but not *fing,* and *misogynist* but not *ogynist*.

monophthong A single vowel that functions as a single phonological unit: for example, [ɪ], [ʊ], and [ɔ] as in *bit, but,* and *bought. See* **monophthong**.

monosyllabic Having one syllable: for example, *boy* and *through*.

morpheme Smallest unit of linguistic meaning or function: for example, *sheepdogs* contains three morphemes, *sheep, dog,* and the plural morpheme, *-s*.

morphological rules Rules for combining morphemes to form stems and words.

morphology The study of the internal structure of words; the component of the grammar that includes the rules of word formation.

morphophonemic rules Rules that specify the pronunciation of morphemes; a morpheme may have more than one pronunciation determined by such rules: for example, the plural morpheme /z/ in English is regularly pronounced [s], [z], or [əz].

motherese *See* **child-directed speech (CDS)**.

movement rules Transformational rules that relocate elements generated by the phrase structure rules to different parts of the structure. Movement rules help account for sentence relatedness such as a declarative sentence and the corresponding yes–no question: for example, *John will arrive late* and *Will John arrive late?*

naming task An experimental technique that measures the response time between seeing a printed word and saying that word aloud.

narrowing A semantic change in which the meaning of a word changes in time to become less encompassing: for example, *deer* once meant "animal."

nasal (nasalized) sound Speech sound produced with an open nasal passage (lowered velum), permitting air to pass through the nose as well as the mouth: for example, /m/. *See* **oral sound**.

nasal cavity The passageways between the throat and the nose through which air passes during speech if the velum is open (lowered). *See* **oral cavity**.

natural class A class of sounds characterized by a phonetic property or feature that pertains to all members of the set: for example, the class of stops. A natural class may be defined with a smaller feature set than that of any individual member of the class.

negative polarity item (NPI) An expression that is grammatical in the presence of negation, but ungrammatical in simple affirmative sentences: for example, *any* in *James does not have any money* but **James has any money.*

Neo-Grammarians A group of nineteenth-century linguists who claimed that sound shifts (i.e., changes in phonological systems) took place without exceptions.

Neo-Grammarian hypothesis The claim that sound shifts (i.e., changes in phonological systems) take place without exceptions.

neurolinguistics The branch of linguistics concerned with the brain mechanisms that underlie the acquisition and use of human language; the study of the neurobiology of language.

neutralization Phonological processes or rules that obliterate the contrast between two phonemes in certain environments: for example, in some dialects of English /t/ and /d/ are both pronounced as voiced flaps between vowels, as in *writer* and *rider,* thus neutralizing the voicing distinction so that the two words sound alike.

node A labeled branch point in a phrase structure tree; part of the graphical depiction of a transition network represented as a circle, pairs of which are connected by arcs. See **arc, phrase structure tree, and transition network**.

noncontinuant A sound in which air is blocked momentarily in the oral cavity as it passes through the vocal tract. *See* **stops and affricate**.

nondistinctive features Phonetic features of phones that are predictable by rule: for example, aspiration in English.

nonsense word A permissible phonological form without meaning: for example, *slithy.*

noun (N) The syntactic category, also lexical category, of words that can function as heads of noun phrases, such as *book, Jean,* and *sincerity.* In many languages, nouns have grammatical alternations for number, case, and gender and occur with determiners.

noun phrase (NP) The syntactic category, also phrasal category, of expressions containing some form of a noun or pronoun as its head, and which functions as the subject or as various objects in a sentence.

nucleus That part of a syllable that has the greatest acoustic energy; the vowel portion of a syllable: for example, /i/ in /mit/ *meet.*

obstruents The class of sounds consisting of nonnasal stops, fricatives, and affricates. *See* **sonorants**.

onomatopoeia/onomatopoeic Words whose pronunciations suggest their meanings: for example, *meow* and *buzz.*

onset One or more phonemes that precede the syllable **nucleus:** for example, /pr/ in /prist/ *priest.*

open class A category of words that commonly adds new words: for example, nouns and verbs.

oral cavity The mouth area through which air passes during the production of speech. *See* **nasal cavity**.

oral sound A non-nasal speech sound produced by raising the velum to close the nasal passage so that air can escape only through the mouth. *See* **nasal sound**.

orthography The written form of a language; spelling.

overextension The broadening of a word's meaning in language acquisition to encompass a more general meaning: for example, using *dog* for any four-legged animals including cats or horses.

overgeneralization Children's treatment of irregular verbs and nouns as if they were regular: for example, *bringed, goed, foots,* and *mouses,* for *brought, went, feet,* and *mice.* This shows that the child has acquired the regular rules but has not yet learned that there are exceptions.

palatal A sound produced by raising the front part of the tongue to the palate.

palate The bony section of the roof of the mouth behind the **alveolar ridge**.

paradox A declarative sentence to which it is impossible to ascribe a truth value: for example, *This sentence is false.*

parameters The small set of alternatives for a particular phenomenon made available by Universal Grammar. For example, Universal Grammar specifies that a phrase must have a head and possibly complements; a parameter (the Head Parameter) states whether the complement(s) precedes or follows the head.

paraphrases Sentences with the same truth conditions; sentences with the same meaning, except possibly for minor differences in emphasis: for example, *He typed up the report* and *He typed the report up. See* **synonymy**.

passive sentence A sentence in which the verbal complex contains a form of *to be* followed by a verb in its participle form: for example, *The girl was kissed by the boy; The robbers must not have been seen.* In a passive sentence, the direct object of a transitive verb in d-structure functions as the subject in s-structure. *See* **active sentence.**

performance, linguistic The *use* of linguistic competence in the real-time production and comprehension of language, as distinguished from linguistic knowledge or competence: for example, linguistic competence permits one-million-word sentences, but performance limitations prevents this from happening.

performative sentence A sentence containing a performative verb used to accomplish some act. Performative sentences are affirmative and declarative, and are in first- person, present tense: for example, *I now pronounce you husband and wife,* when spoken by a justice of the peace in the appropriate situation, is an act of marrying.

performative verb A verb, certain usages of which result in a **speech act:** for example, *resign* when the sentence *I resign!* is interpreted as an act of resignation.

petroglyph A drawing on rock made by prehistoric people.

pharynx The tube or cavity in the vocal tract above the glottis through which the air passes during speech production.

phone A phonetic realization of a **phoneme.**

phoneme A contrastive phonological **segment** whose phonetic realizations are predictable by rule.

phonemic features Phonetic properties of phonemes that account for their ability to contrast meanings of words: for example, *voice* and *tense.* Also called **distinctive features**.

phonemic principle The principle that underlies alphabetic writing systems in which one symbol typically represents one phoneme.

phonemic representation The phonological representation of words and sentences prior to the application of phonological rules.

phonetic alphabet Alphabetic symbols used to represent the phonetic segments of speech in which there is a one-to-one relationship between each symbol and each speech sound.

phonetic features Phonetic properties of segments (for example, voice, nasal, and alveolar) that distinguish one segment from another.

phonetic representation The representation of words and sentences after the application of phonological rules; symbolic transcription of the pronunciation of words and sentences.

phonetic similarity Refers to sounds that share most phonetic features.

phonetics The study of linguistic speech sounds, how they are produced (**articulatory phonetics**), how they are perceived (**auditory** or perceptual **phonetics**), and their physical aspects (**acoustic phonetics**).

phonetic transcription The "spelling" of a word in terms of the individual phones it contains with a **phonetic alphabet** as opposed to ordinary orthography: for example, [fə̃nɛɪɪk] for *phonetic*.

phonological rules Rules that apply to phonemic representations to derive phonetic representations or pronunciation.

phonology The sound system of a language; the component of a grammar that includes the inventory of sounds (phonetic and phonemic units) and rules for their combination and pronunciation; the study of the sound systems of all languages.

phonotactics/phonotactic constraints Rules stating permissible strings of phonemes within a syllable: for example, a word-initial nasal consonant may be followed only by a vowel (in English). *See* **possible word, nonsense word, and accidental gap**.

phrasal category The class of syntactic categories that contain heads in an X-bar structure including NP, VP, AP, PP, AdvP, CP and TP. *See* **lexical category and functional category**.

phrase structure rules Principles of grammar that specify the hierarchical organization of syntactic categories and which is expressed in phrase structure trees: for example, NP → Det N, or VP → V NP.

phrase structure tree A tree diagram with syntactic categories at each node that reveals both the linear and hierarchical structure of phrases and sentences.

phrenology A pseudoscience of examining bumps on the skull to determine personality traits and intellectual ability. Its contribution to neurolinguistics is that its methods were highly suggestive of the modular theory of brain structure.

pictogram A symbol in a writing system that resembles the object represented in a direct way; a nonarbitrary form of writing.

pictographic writing A method of writing that utilizes **pictograms**, or literal representations of words.

pidgin A simple but rule-governed language developed for communication among speakers of mutually unintelligible languages, often based on one of those languages called the **lexifier language**. *See* **substrate languages**.

pidginization The process of creating a pidgin that involves the simplification of the grammars of the impinging languages and a reduction of the number of situations in which the language is used. *See* **creolization and pidgin**.

Pinyin An alphabetic writing system for Mandarin Chinese using a Western-style alphabet to represent individual sounds.

pitch The **fundamental frequency** of sound perceived by the listener.

pitch contour The intonation of a sentence.

place of articulation The part of the vocal tract at which constriction occurs during the production of consonants. *See* **manner of articulation**.

plosives Oral, or non-nasal, stop consonants, so-called because the air that is stopped explodes with the release of the closure.

polyglot A person who speaks several languages.

polymorphemic word A word that consists of more than one **morpheme**.

polysemous/polysemy Describes a single word with several closely related but slightly different meanings: for example, *face,* meaning "face of a person," "face of a clock," "face of a building."

polysynthetic language Language with an extraordinarily rich morphology, in which a single word may carry the semantic content of an entire sentence.

positron emission tomography (PET) Method to detect changes in brain activities and relate these changes to localized brain damage and cognitive tasks.

possessor The thematic role of the noun phrase to whose referent something belongs: for example, *the dog* in *The dog's tail wagged furiously.*

possible word A string of sounds that obeys the **phonotactic constraints** of the language but has no meaning: for example, *gimble.* Also called a **nonsense word**.

poverty of the stimulus *See* **impoverished data**.

pragmatics The study of how context and situation affect meaning; the study of extra-truth-conditional meaning.

predicate A cover term for verbs, adjectives, and common nouns.

predictable feature A nondistinctive, noncontrastive, redundant phonetic feature: for example, aspiration in English voiceless stops, or nasalization in English vowels.

prefix An **affix** that is attached to the beginning of a morpheme or stem: for example, *in-* in *inoperable.*

preposition(P) The syntactic category that heads a prepositional phrase: for example, *at, in, on,* and *up.*

prepositional object The grammatical relation of the noun phrase complement that occurs immediately following the prepositional head in a **prepositional phrase(PP)** in d-structure: for example, *skis* in *on skis.*

prepositional phrase (PP) The syntactic category, also phrasal category, consisting of a prepositional head and a noun phrase complement: for example, *with a key, into the battle,* and *over the top.*

prescriptive grammar Rules of grammar brought about by grammarians' attempts to legislate what speakers' grammatical rules should be, rather than what they are. *See* **descriptive grammar and teaching grammar**.

prestige dialect The dialect usually spoken by people in positions of power, and the one deemed correct by prescriptive grammarians: for example, RP (received pronunciation) (British) English, the dialect spoken by the English royal family.

presupposition An implicit assumption about the world required to make an utterance meaningful or relevant: for example, "John used to smoke" is a presupposition of *John finally stopped smoking.*

priming An implicit memory effect in which exposure to a word or sentence influences response to a later word or sentence.

priming experiment An experimental procedure that measures the response to hearing a word or sentence, as a function of whether the participant has heard a related word or sentence type previously. *See* **semantic priming**.

principle of compositionality A principle of semantic interpretation that states that the meaning of a word, phrase, or sentence depends on both the meaning of its components (morphemes, words, and phrases) and how they are combined structurally.

productive Refers to **morphological rules** that can be used freely and apply to all forms to create new words: for example, the addition to an adjective of *-ish* meaning "having somewhat of the quality," such as *newish, tallish,* and *incredible-ish.*

proper name A word or words that refer to a person, place, or other entity with a unique reference known to the speaker and listener. Usually capitalized in writing: for example, Nina Hyams, New York, and Atlantic Ocean.

prosodic bootstrapping The learning of word or phrase segmentation by infants inferred from the stress pattern of a language.

prosodic feature The duration **(length)**, **pitch,** or loudness of speech sounds.

Proto-Germanic The name given by linguists to the language that was an ancestor of English, German, and other Germanic languages.

Proto-Indo-European (PIE) *See* **Indo-European**.

protolanguage The earliest identifiable language from which genetically related languages developed.

psycholinguistics The branch of linguistics concerned with **linguistic performance,** and speech production and comprehension.

rebus principle In writing, the use of a **pictogram** for its phonetic value: for example, using a picture of a bee to represent the verb *be* or the sound [bi].

recast The repetition with "corrections" of a child's utterance by an adult. For example, the child says *I holded the rabbit,* and the adult corrects by saying *You mean you held the rabbit.*

recursive rules (recursive set) Rules with symbols like S and VP that occur on both the left and right side of some of the rules. *See* **linguistic competence**.

reduced vowel A vowel that is unstressed and generally pronounced as schwa [ə] in English.

redundant Describes a nondistinctive, nonphonemic feature that is predictable from other feature values of the segment: for example, [+voice] is redundant for any [+nasal] phoneme in English because all nasals are voiced.

reduplication A morphological process that repeats or copies all or part of a word to produce a new word: for example, *wishy-washy, teensy-weensy, hurly-burly.* Also used in some languages as an inflectional process: for example, Samoan *manao/mananao,* "he wishes/they wish."

reference That part of the meaning of a noun phrase that associates it with some entity. That part of the meaning of a declarative sentence that associates it with a **truth value,** either true or false. Also called **extension**. *See* **referent and sense**.

referent The entity designated by an expression: for example, the referent of *John* in *John knows Sue* is the actual person named John; the referent of *Raleigh is the capital of California* is the truth value *false*. Also called **extension**.

reflexive pronoun In English and many other languages, a pronoun ending with *-self* or its equivalent that generally requires a noun-phrase antecedent within the same minimal S: for example, *myself, herself, ourselves,* and *itself*.

regional dialect A dialect spoken in a specific geographic area that may arise from, and is reinforced by, that area's integrity. For example, a Boston dialect is maintained because large numbers of Bostonians and their descendants remain in the Boston area. *See* **social dialect**.

register A stylistic variant of a language appropriate to a particular social setting. Also called **style**.

register tones In tone languages, level tones; high, mid, or low tones.

regular sound correspondence The occurrence of different sounds in the same position of the same word in different languages or dialects, with this parallel holding for a significant number of words: for example, [aɪ] in non-Southern American English corresponds to [a:] in Southern American English. Also found between newer and older forms of the same language.

relational opposites A pair of **antonyms** in which one describes a relationship between two objects and the other describes the same relationship when the two objects are reversed: for example, *parent/child, teacher/pupil; John is the parent of Susie* describes the same relationship as *Susie is the child of John*. *See* **gradable pair and complementary pair**.

retroflex sound A sound produced by curling the tip of the tongue back behind the alveolar ridge: for example, the pronunciation of /r/ by many speakers of English.

rime The **nucleus** + **coda** of a syllable: for example, the /en/ of /ren/ *rain*.

root The **morpheme** that remains when all affixes are stripped from a complex word: for example, *system* from *un + system + atic + ally*.

rounded vowel A vowel sound produced with pursed lips: for example, [o].

rules of syntax Grammar rules that account for the grammaticality of sentences, their hierarchical structure, their word order, whether there is structural ambiguity, etc. *See* **phrase structure rules and transformational rules**.

SAE *See* **Standard American English**.

Sapir–Whorf hypothesis The proposition that the structure of a language influences how its speakers perceive the world around them. It is often presented in its weak form, **linguistic relativism,** and its strong form, **linguistic determinism**.

savant An individual who shows special abilities in one cognitive area while being deficient in others. Linguistic savants have extraordinary language abilities but are deficient in general intelligence.

second language acquisition The acquisition of another language or languages after first language acquisition is under way or completed. Also called **L2 acquisition**.

segment An individual sound that occurs in a language; the act of dividing utterances into sounds, morphemes, words, and phrases.

semantic bootstrapping The learning of the grammatical category of a word inferred from the meaning of the word: for example, a word whose meaning is a person, place, or thing would be considered a noun.

semantic features Conceptual elements by which a person understands the meanings of words and sentences: for example, "female" is a semantic feature of the nouns *girl* and *filly;* "cause" is a semantic feature of the verbs *darken* and *kill*.

semantic priming The effect of being able to recognize a word (for example, *doctor)* more rapidly after exposure to a semantically similar word (for example, *nurse)* than after exposure to a semantically more distant word. The word *nurse* primes the word *doctor*.

semantic properties *See* **semantic features**.

semantic rules Principles for determining the meanings of larger units like sentences from the meanings of smaller units like noun phrases and verb phrases.

semantics The study of the linguistic meanings of morphemes, words, phrases, and sentences.

sense The inherent part of an expression's meaning that, together with context, determines its referent. Also called **intension.** For example, knowing the sense or intension of a noun phrase such as *the president of the United States in the year 2010* allows one to determine that Barack Obama is the referent. *See* **intension and reference**.

sentence(S) A syntactic category of expressions consisting minimally of a **subject noun phrase (NP)** and a **verb phrase (VP).** Also called a **TP (tense phrase),** the head of which is the category **T** which may be empty except for tense.

sequential bilingualism The acquisition of a second language by someone (adult or child) who has already acquired a first language. More commonly referred to as child or adult **second language (L2) acquisition**.

shadowing task An experiment in which subjects are asked to repeat what they hear as rapidly as possible as it is being spoken. During the task, subjects often unconsciously correct "errors" in the input.

sibilants The class of sounds that includes alveolar and palatal **fricatives** and **affricates,** characterized acoustically by an abundance of high frequencies perceived as "hissing," for example, [s] and [tʃ]

sign languages The languages used by people whose hearing is compromised in which linguistic units such as morphemes and words as well as grammatical relations are formed by manual and other body movements.

simultaneous bilingualism Refers to the (more or less) simultaneous acquisition of two languages beginning in infancy (or before the age of three years).

sisters In a phrase structure tree, two categories that are directly under the same node: for example, V and the direct object NP are sisters inside the verb phrase.

situational context Knowledge of who is speaking, who is listening, what objects are being discussed, and general facts about the world we live in, used to aid in the interpretation of meaning.

slang Words and phrases used in casual speech, often invented and spread by close-knit social or age groups, and fast-changing.

slip of the tongue An involuntary deviation of an intended utterance. *See* **spoonerism**. Also called **speech error**.

social dialect A dialect spoken by members of a group delineated by socioeconomic class, racial background, place of origin, or gender, and perpetuated by the integrity of the social class. *See* **regional dialect**.

societal bilingualism The mutual abilities of a community to speak two (or more) languages with native or near native proficiency. *See* **bilingualism and individual bilingualism**.

sociolinguistic variable A linguistic phenomenon, such as double negation in English, whose occurrence varies according to the social context of the speaker.

sonorants The class of sounds that includes **vowels, glides, liquids,** and **nasals;** non-obstruents. *See* **obstruents**.

sound change *See* **sound shift**.

sound shift Historical phonological change. Also called **sound change**.

sound symbolism The notion that certain sound combinations occur in semantically similar words: for example, *gl* in *gleam, glisten,* and *glitter,* which all relate to vision.

source The thematic role of the noun phrase whose referent is the place from which an action originates: for example, *Mars* in *Mr. Wells just arrived from Mars.*

specific language impairment (SLI) Difficulty in acquiring language by certain children with no other cognitive deficits.

specifier The sister of $\overline{X}$ in the X-bar schema: for example, a **determiner** in an NP. It is a modifier of the head+complement and is often optional.

spectrogram A visual representation of speech decomposed into component frequencies, with time on the horizontal axis, frequency on the vertical axis, and intensity portrayed on a gray scale—the darker, the more intense. Also called **voiceprint**.

speech act The action or intent that a speaker accomplishes when using language in context, the meaning of which is inferred by hearers: for example, *There is a bear behind you* may be intended as a warning in certain contexts, or may in other contexts merely be a statement of fact. *See* **illocutionary force**.

speech error An inadvertent deviation from an intended utterance that often results in ungrammaticality, nonsense words, anomaly, and so on. *See* **slip of the tongue, spoonerism**.

spelling reform The attempt by governments or academic institutions to change the spellings of words to more accurately reflect their current pronunciations.

spell-out rules Rules that convert abstract inflectional morphemes such as tense, agreement, and possessive into phonetically realized affixes: for example, [+pst] into *-ed.*

split brain The result of an operation for epilepsy in which the **corpus callosum** is severed; thus, separating the brain into its two hemispheres; split-brain patients have been studied to determine the role of each hemisphere in cognitive and language processing.

spoonerism A **speech error** in which phonemic segments are reversed or exchanged: for example, *you have hissed my mystery lecture* for the intended *you have missed my history lecture;* named after the Reverend William Archibald Spooner, a nineteenth-century Oxford don.

s-selection The classifying of verbs and other lexical items in terms of the semantic category of the head and complements that they accept, for example, the verb *assassinate* S-selects for a human subject and a prestigious, human NP complement.

s-structure The structure that results from applying transformational rules to a **d-structure.** It is syntactically closest to actual utterances. Also called **surface structure.** *See* **transformational rule.**

standard The **dialect** (regional or social) considered to be the norm.

Standard American English (SAE) An idealized dialect of English that some prescriptive grammarians consider the proper form of English.

state/stative A type of sentence that describes states of being such as *Mary likes oysters,* as opposed to describing events such as *Mary ate oysters. See* **event/eventive.**

stem The base to which an affix is attached to create a more complex form that may be another stem or a word. *See* **root and affix.**

stops [–continuant] sounds in which the airflow is briefly but completely stopped in the oral cavity: for example, [p], [n], and [g].

stress describes a syllable with relatively greater length, loudness, and/or higher pitch than other syllables in a word, and therefore perceived as prominent. Also called **accent.**

stress-timed language A language in which some syllables are longer and some shorter and the intervals between stressed syllables are roughly equal in length.

structural ambiguity The phenomenon in which the same sequence of words has two or more meanings accounted for by different phrase structure analyses: for example, *He saw a boy with a telescope.*

structure dependent A principle of Universal Grammar that states that the application of **transformational rules** is determined by phrase structure properties, as opposed to unstructured sequences of words or specific sentences; the way children construct rules using their knowledge of syntactic structure irrespective of the specific words in the structure or their meaning.

style A situation dialect: for example, formal speech and casual speech; also called **register.**

subcategorization *See* **C-selection.**

subject The grammatical relation of a noun phrase to a S(entence) when it appears immediately below that S (TP) in a phrase structure tree: for example, *the zebra* in *The zebra has stripes.*

subject–verb agreement The addition of an **inflectional morpheme** to the main verb depending on a property of the noun phrase subject, such as number or gender. In English, it is the addition of *-s* to a verb when the subject is third-person singular present tense: for example, *A greyhound runs fast* versus *Greyhounds run fast.*

substrate languages The language(s) of the indigenous people in a language contact situation that contribute(s) to the lexicon and grammar of a pidgin or creole but in a less obvious way than the **superstrate language.**

suffix An **affix** that is attached to the end of a morpheme or stem: for example, *-er* in *Lew is taller than Bill.*

superstrate language The language that provides most of the lexical items of a pidgin or creole, typically the language of the socially or economically dominant group. Also called **lexifier language.** *See* **substrate languages.**

suppletive forms A term used to refer to **inflected morphemes** in which the regular rules do not apply: for example, *went* as the past tense of *go.*

suprasegmentals Prosodic features: for example, length and tone.

surface structures: See **s-structure.**

syllabary The symbols of a syllabic writing system.

syllabic A phonetic feature of those sounds that may constitute the nucleus of syllables; all vowels are syllabic, and liquids and nasals may be syllabic in such words as *towel, button,* and *bottom.*

syllabic writing A writing system in which each syllable in the language is represented by its own symbol: for example, Cherokee and Japanese.

syllable A phonological unit composed of an **onset, nucleus,** and **coda:** for example, *elevator* has four syllables: *el e va tor; man* has one syllable.

syllable-timed language A language in which the syllables have approximately the same loudness, length, and pitch, as opposed to a **stress-timed language.** French, for example, is such a language.

synonyms Words with the same or nearly the same meaning: for example, *pail* and *bucket.*

synonymy (synonymous) Having the same meaning in all contexts. More technically, in the semantic component of the grammar, two sentences are synonymous if they **entail** each other: for example, *the cat ate the rat; the rat was eaten by the cat. See* **paraphrases**.

syntactic bootstrapping The learning of word meaning inferred from syntax: for example, when a child hears *John glouted Mary a clibe* he realizes that *glout* is a verb and likely means the transferring of something from one person to another.

syntactic category/class *See* **grammatical categories**.

syntax The rules of sentence formation; the component of the mental grammar that represents speakers' knowledge of the structure of phrases and sentences.

synthetic language A language in which words often contain multiple morphemes: for example, English and Indo-European languages in general.

T(tense) The syntactic category that is the head of **TP (tense phrase)** or **sentence (S).** Also, the time frame of a sentence, for example, past or present.

taboo Words or activities that are considered inappropriate for "polite society," for example, *cunt, prick,* and *fuck* for vagina, penis, and sexual intercourse, respectively.

tap A speech sound in which the tongue quickly touches the alveolar ridge, as in some British pronunciations of /r/. Also called **flap**.

tautology A sentence that is true in all situations; a sentence true from the meaning of its words alone: for example, *Kings are not female.* Also called **analytic**.

teaching grammar A set of language rules written to help speakers learn a foreign language or a different dialect of their language. *See* **descriptive grammar and prescriptive grammar**.

telegraphic speech Utterances of children that may omit **grammatical morphemes** and/or **function words:** for example, *He go out* instead of *He is going out.*

telegraphic stage The period of child language acquisition when children begin producing multi word utterances and often omit function words and morphemes. *See* **telegraphic speech**.

tense A **phonetic feature** that distinguishes similar pairs of vowels. Vowels that are [+tense] are somewhat longer in duration and higher in tongue position and pitch than the corresponding [–tense] (lax) vowel: for example, in English [i] is a high front tense vowel whereas [ɪ] is a high front lax vowel. *See* **lax vowel.** Also a term referring to the syntactic category that heads **T(ense)P** or **S(entence),** and usually abbreviated **T**.

thematic role The semantic relationship between the verb and the noun phrases of a sentence, such as **agent, theme, location, instrument, goal, and source**.

theme The thematic role of the noun phrase whose referent undergoes the action of the verb: for example, *Martha* in *George hugged Martha.*

theta assignment The ascribing of thematic roles to the syntactic elements in a sentence.

tip of the tongue phenomenon The difficulty encountered from time to time in retrieving a particular word or expression from the mental lexicon. Anomic aphasics suffer from an extreme form of this problem. *See* **anomia**.

tone The contrastive **pitch** of syllables in **tone languages.** Two words may be identical except for such differences in pitch: for example, in Thai *naa* [naː] with falling pitch means "face," but with a rising pitch means "thick." *See* **register tones and contour tones**.

tone language A language in which the **tone** or **pitch** on a syllable is phonemic, so that words with identical segments but different tones are different words: for example, Mandarin Chinese and Thai.

topicalization A transformation that moves a syntactic element to the front of a sentence: for example, deriving *Greyhounds I love very much* from *I love greyhounds very much.*

TP (tense phrase) A term sometimes used in place of **sentence (S),** especially in the X-bar schema, where it is a phrasal category whose head is **T.**

transcription, phonemic The phonemic representation of speech sounds using phonetic symbols, ignoring phonetic details that are predictable by rule, usually given between slashes: for example, /pæn/ and /spæn/ for *pan* and *span* as opposed to the phonetic representation [pʰæn] and [spæn].

transcription, phonetic The representation of speech sounds using phonetic symbols between square brackets. It may reflect nondistinctive predictable features such as aspiration and nasality: for example, [pʰat] for *pot* or [bõn] for *bone.*

transfer (of grammatical rules) The application of rules from one's first language to a second language that one is attempting to acquire. The "accent" that second-language learners have is a result of the transfer of first language phonetic and phonological rules.

transformational rule, transformation A syntactic rule that applies to an underlying phrase structure tree of a sentence (either **d-structure** or an intermediate structure already affected by a transformation) and derives a new structure by moving, deleting or inserting elements: for example, the transformational rules of wh movement and *do* insertion relate the deep structure sentence *John saw who* to the surface structure *Who(m) did John see.*

transitional bilingual education (TBE) Educational programs in which students receive instruction in both English and their native language, for example, Spanish, and the native language support is gradually phased out over two or three years.

transitive verb A verb that C-selects (subcategorizes) an obligatory noun-phrase complement: for example, *find.*

tree diagram A graphical representation of the linear and hierarchical structure of a phrase or sentence. *See* **phrase structure tree.**

trill A speech sound in which part of the tongue vibrates against part of the roof of the mouth: for example, the /r/ in Spanish *perro,* "dog," is articulated by vibrating the tongue tip behind the alveolar ridge; the /r/ in French *rouge,* "red," may be articulated by vibrations at the uvula.

trochaic Stress on the first syllable of a two-syllable word: for example, *páper.*

truth conditions The circumstances that must be known to determine whether a sentence is true, which are therefore part of the meaning, or **sense,** of declarative sentences.

truth-conditional semantics A theory of meaning that takes the semantic knowledge of when sentences are true and false as basic.

truth value TRUE or FALSE; used to describe the truth of declarative sentences in context; the **reference** of a declarative sentence in **truth-conditional semantics.**

unaspirated Phonetically voiceless stops in which the vocal cords begin vibrating immediately upon release of the closure: for example, [p] in *spot. See* **aspirated.**

unconditioned sound change Historical phonological change that occurs in all phonetic contexts: for example, the **Great Vowel Shift** of English in which long vowels were modified wherever they occurred in a word.

Universal Grammar (UG) The innate principles and properties that pertain to the grammars of all human languages; the basic blueprint that all languages follow.

unmarked In a masculine/feminine pair, the word that does not contain a derivational morpheme, usually the masculine word: for example, *prince* is unmarked, whereas *princess* is marked. *See* **marked**.

uvula The fleshy appendage hanging down from the end of the **velum** (soft palate).

uvular A sound produced by raising the back of the tongue to the **uvula**.

velar A sound produced by raising the back of the tongue to the soft palate, or **velum**.

velum The soft palate; the part of the roof of the mouth behind the hard palate.

verb (V) The syntactic category, also lexical category, of words that can be the head of a verb phrase. Verbs denote actions, sensations, and states: for example, *climb, hear,* and *understand.*

verb phrase (VP) The syntactic category of expressions that contain a verb as its head along with its complements such as noun phrases and prepositional phrases: for example, *gave the book to the child.*)

verbal particle A word identical in form to a preposition which, when paired with a verb, has a particular meaning. A particle, as opposed to a preposition, is characterized syntactically by its ability to occur next to the verb, or transposed to the right: for example, *out,* in *spit out* as in *He spit out his words,* or *He spit his words out.* Compare with *He ran out the door* versus **he ran the door out,* where *out* is a preposition.

Verner's law The description of a conditioned phonological change in the sound system of certain Indo-European languages wherein voiceless fricatives were changed when the preceding vowel was unstressed. It was formulated by Karl Verner as an explanation to some of the exceptions to **Grimm's law.**

vocal tract The oral and nasal cavities, together with the vocal cords, glottis, and pharynx, all of which may be involved in the production of speech sounds.

vocalic A phonetic feature that distinguishes vowels and liquids, which are [+vocalic], from other sounds (obstruents, glides, and nasals), which are [–vocalic]. The feature is little used in contemporary linguistic literature.

voiced sound A speech sound produced with vibrating vocal cords.

voiceless sound A speech sound produced with open, nonvibrating vocal cords.

voiceprint A common term for a **spectrogram**.

vowel A sound produced without significant constriction of the air flowing through the **oral cavity**.

Wernicke, Carl Neurologist who showed that damage to specific parts of the left cerebral hemisphere causes specific types of language disorders.

Wernicke's aphasia The type of aphasia resulting from damage to **Wernicke's area**.

Wernicke's area The back (posterior) part of the left brain that if damaged causes a specific type of aphasia. Also called Wernicke's region.

***wh* questions** Interrogative sentences beginning with one or more of the words *who(m), what, where, when,* and *how,* and their equivalents in languages that whose question words do not begin with *wh,* such as *quién* in Spanish: *A quién le gusta?* "Who(m) do you like?"

word frames Lexical contexts often used by adults such as *the _ one* that assist a child learning language to categorize words, in this case adjectives.

word writing A system of writing in which each character represents a word or morpheme of the language: for example, Chinese. *See* **ideograph and logographic writing**.

X-bar theory A universal schema specifying that the internal organization of all phrasal categories (i.e., NP, PP, VP, TP(S), AP, AdvP, and CP) can be broken down into three levels: for example, NP, N̄, and N.

yes–no question An interrogative sentence that asks for confirmation of a situation: for example, *Is the boy asleep?*

Index